THE DCI JACK LOGAN COLLECTION

BOOKS 1-3

JD KIRK

ZERTEX CRIME

THE DCI JACK LOGAN COLLECTION
ISBN: 978-1-912767-27-4

Published worldwide by Zertex Media Ltd.
This edition published in 2020.

www.jdkirk.com
www.zertexmedia.com

A LITTER OF BONES

DCI JACK LOGAN BOOK ONE

CHAPTER ONE

THE TOTAL COLLAPSE OF DUNCAN REID'S LIFE BEGAN WITH A GATE IN the arse-end of nowhere.

There was a trick to opening this particular gate, Duncan knew. The arm of the metal slider had been buckled for years, and if you tried hauling it in the direction the bend suggested it should go you were doomed to failure. The trick was to twist and jiggle, creaking the slider loose of its mooring, allowing the whole thing to eventually swing free.

Or, if you were a seven-year-old with more energy than sense, you could clamber up the metal spars, jump down, and stand triumphantly on the other side waiting for your dad to get a move on.

"I win," cheered Connor. He broke into a little dance. *The Floss*, he called it. All the rage, apparently.

Down at Duncan's feet, their Golden Retriever wriggled impatiently, the entirety of her copper-coloured backend wagging, her front feet pawing at the ground with barely contained excitement.

"Alright, Meg. Give us a minute," Duncan told the animal.

The slider *clunked* free. The gate had barely swung six inches towards him when Meg nosed it open and squeezed through. Connor dodged aside as the dog went haring past him. She bulleted ahead, running for no other reason than the sheer unbridled joy of being out of the car and off the lead.

"Someone's in a hurry," Duncan remarked.

They watched as she detoured off into the trees that lined the track on the right, quickly vanishing from sight beneath the moss-covered trunks.

"Meg!" Connor called after her. "Come back."

"She'll be fine," Duncan said. He pulled the gate closed behind them, wiggling the slider just enough to jam it shut, but not so far that he'd have to go through the whole process again when they left. "She's been exploring round here since before you were born."

Connor didn't look convinced but fell into step beside his dad as they set off along the track.

Living up here, they were spoiled for choice when it came to dog-walking routes. Granted, it was pretty much the only thing they were spoiled for choice for, but it was something. But, of all the routes available to them, this one stood out as a favourite.

The only downside was getting to it. The drive along the main Fort William to Spean Bridge road could be a nightmare in the summer. At this time of year, though, before the campervans piloted by overly cautious tourists had started to clog everything up, it flew by.

After that, it was just a turn up the Leanachan Forest road, a mile or so along a single-track lane with the fingers crossed that no-one was coming the other way, and then the usual wrestling match with the gate.

And then... bliss. Miles of forestry track, cracking views, and rarely another living soul in sight. In all the years that Duncan had been making the same walk, he'd met maybe twenty walkers, half a dozen cyclists, and one guy on stilts.

That one had caught him off guard and had sent Meg into a frenzy of panicked barking. It was a sponsored hike for charity, it turned out. Cancer, or something. Duncan had been too busy trying to get ahold of the dog and quieten her down to really pay too much attention.

Once he'd got her by the collar, he'd chucked a couple of quid into the collection tin and kept hold of Meg until the guy had teetered off around the corner, out of sight.

Today was looking like it'd be free of interruptions, and Duncan felt physically lighter as he let himself relax. Meg was a good dog, for the most part, but didn't handle strangers well, so the lack of life signs always came as a relief.

Sure, someone might come around one of the bends further down the track and set her off, but that was a problem for later. For now, the coast was clear.

Far off on the left, across a graveyard of tree stumps, the A82 curved ahead to the Commando Memorial, and onwards to Inverness. An irregular stream of traffic meandered up it, paintwork glinting in the uncharacteristically bright April sunshine.

At this distance, the traffic was whisper quiet. The only sounds to be heard were the *chirping* of the birds, and the faint crunch of the stony ground beneath Duncan's boots.

Up ahead, Meg exploded from within a crop of trees, ploughed through a mud puddle that painted her brown from halfway down her legs, then stopped in the middle of the path. She watched them for a while, tongue hanging out and chest heaving as she checked that they were still headed in the same direction.

When she was sure they weren't about to turn around and head for the car, she returned to the trees, getting back to whatever business she'd left unattended in there.

"See, told you she'd be fine," Duncan said, giving his son a playful nudge. "Filthy, I'll give you, but fine."

"Did you see how much mud is on her?"

"I did."

"She's *covered*!"

"She is. And guess who's cleaning her up when we get home," Duncan said.

Connor grinned up at him. "You!"

"Me? No way! You!" Duncan said.

"Nuh-uh!"

"Yuh-huh! I'll give you a scrubbing brush and a bucket," Duncan said. He gave a little gasp as an idea hit him. "You can do the car when you're at it. Two birds with one stone."

Connor shook his head emphatically.

"Fine. You can hold her while I hose her down."

Connor had no real objection to that, but it had become a game now, and so he continued to resist.

"Nope!"

Duncan stroked his chin, his finger and thumb rasping against his stubble. "OK, she can hold you, and I'll hose *you* down." He made a sound like skooshing water, and mimed blasting the boy with it. "How about that?"

Connor giggled. "I had a bath this morning."

"You did? God, is it April already?" Duncan teased.

Connor didn't quite get the dig but giggled again, regardless.

They walked on for several minutes, rounding the gentle curve of the track, passing the little quarry on the left-hand side, where two diggers had sat mostly motionless for the past year or so. Rarely, when Duncan came up this way, they'd have moved a few feet, or the angle of the buckets would have shifted. He'd never seen any sign of anyone sat behind the controls, though, much less doing any actual digging.

It had been a while since Connor had said anything, and although Duncan was enjoying the peace and quiet, it wasn't normal. Friday was swimming day at school, and the boy would normally be full of stories about who was proving to be the best at backstroke, and which of his classmates had come closest to drowning.

Today, though, he'd barely spoken a word that Duncan hadn't teased out of him first.

"You alright, Con?"

"Yeah, fine," Connor said, not looking up. He had found a stick that was almost the height of himself, and was walking with it like a wizard with a staff.

"If Meg sees you with that, she'll be away with it," Duncan warned.

Connor nodded, but said nothing.

"How was swimming?"

"Good."

"Everyone survive?"

Connor nodded. "Yep."

They continued on in silence for a while longer. A bird of prey circled in the air above them. A buzzard, Duncan guessed, although he had no idea. It might've been an eagle. It could've been a big pigeon. He'd lived his life in the Highlands, but the particulars of its wildlife were lost on him.

Similarly, the trees lining the tracks beside them. He had no idea what those were, either. Pine? Maybe. Beech? Very possibly. Oak? He didn't think so, but he had no idea what he was basing that on. They were trees. That was about as specific as he could get.

"Dad?" Connor said, after a few more steps. His eyes were still fixed on the ground, his voice quiet. "You know Ed?"

Duncan ran through his mental checklist of the kids in Connor's class. He couldn't place an Ed.

"Which one is he? The one with the orange mum?"

Connor glanced up at him, brow furrowed in confusion. "Next door Ed."

"Oh, *next door* Ed. Yes. Sorry. I thought you meant someone in your class."

"There's no-one in my class called Ed," Connor replied.

"No, I know. I was..." Duncan gave his head a little shake. "Next door Ed. Aye. What about him?"

Connor seemed to wrestle briefly with his next question. "Do you like him?"

Duncan puffed out his cheeks. "Do I like him? Next door Ed?" He shrugged. "Suppose. I mean, I don't really know him. He seems nice enough. I think he's settling in alright. Why?"

Connor tapped the ground with the bottom of his stick as they walked, drumming out a little beat.

"Does Mum like him?"

Duncan stopped. "I don't know. Why, what makes you ask that?"

Connor walked on a few paces, then he stopped, too. He stood there, chewing his lip, twisting the staff in his hand. "Nothing. I was just wondering."

Duncan cocked his head a little, regarding his son quizzically. "That's a weird thing to just start wondering."

Connor's cheeks blushed red.

"Con?"

"Where's Meg?" the boy suddenly asked, his eyes darting to the tree line.

"She's in there. She'll be fine," Duncan said, shooting the forest the most fleeting of glances. "She'll come back when we call her. Why were you asking about—?"

"Meg!" Connor shouted. "Meg, where are you?"

He put his fingers in his mouth and attempted a whistle. All he managed was a blast of damp-sounding air.

Duncan sighed, then formed a C-shape with thumb and forefinger and jammed them in his mouth. His whistle was shrill and loud. It cut off the birdsong, instantly reducing it to an indignant sort of silence.

"Where is she?" Connor asked, scanning the trees. "Why isn't she coming back?"

"She'll be fine," Duncan assured him, but he gave another whistle and followed with a shout. "Meg! Come on, Meg!"

Nothing moved in the trees. The canopy of leaves and branches cast the undergrowth into a gloomy darkness. There was still an hour or so until sunset, but the shadows were growing longer, and the breeze had gained a chillier edge.

"Stupid bloody dog," Duncan muttered.

"What if she's hurt?" Connor fretted. "What if something's happened to her?"

"Nothing will have happened to her. She's probably just rolling in something. You know what she's like."

Duncan cupped his hands around his mouth and called the dog's name again.

"Me-eg!" he shouted, stretching it across two syllables.

They waited. The trees creaked. The wind whispered through the grass.

But beyond that, nothing.

"Bugger it," Duncan muttered.

"Dad?" said Connor, his eyes wide with alarm. "Why's she not coming?"

"She'll be fine. She's always fine," Duncan said. "But I'll go in and look for her, if it makes you feel better. You stay here and shout me when she comes back."

Connor glanced both ways along the empty track, then nodded. "But what if she doesn't?"

"She'll be back," Duncan promised.

"But what if she's not?"

"She will."

"But—"

"I won't stop looking. Alright?" said Duncan, a little irritably. He forced a smile. "She'll be fine. She's just being a pain. You wait here."

Connor nodded again. "OK. I'll wait here."

"Good lad. And shout when she comes out. Nice and loud, alright?"

"I will, Dad."

Duncan clapped a hand on the boy's shoulder. "And don't worry. We'll get her. She won't have gone far."

"BASTARD," Duncan hissed, clutching his cheek where a thin branch had whipped at him. There was no blood, but he could feel a welt forming, raising a thin red line across his skin.

The ground was moist and spongy beneath his feet, and a dampness crept up the legs of his jeans, sticking them, cold and clammy, to the tops of his ankles.

"Any sign, Con?" he called over his shoulder.

"Not yet!" his son shouted back, his voice muffled by the surrounding woodland.

Duncan cursed the dog a few times, then just cursed in general as he trudged onwards, his boots snagging in the undergrowth, the branches determined to have one of his eyes out.

Half a dozen shambling steps later, something moved suddenly on his right, rustling through the tangle of grasses. He turned, startled, almost losing his balance as he searched for the source of the sound.

A rabbit appeared briefly from a knot of weeds, realised its mistake, then vanished again just as quickly. Duncan didn't see it again, but heard it scamper off to some hiding place deeper into the forest.

"Bloody thing," he grumbled, listening to the fading *swish* of the rabbit through the grass.

He was only a couple of minutes' walk into the trees, but light was already in short supply. Everything was painted in a gloominess that turned the shadows to pools of black and tinted everything else in shades of grey and blue.

"You got her, Connor?" Duncan shouted.

He waited for a response from his son.

"Connor?" he called again, when no answer came. "You got Meg yet?"

Nothing.

"Con?"

The trees groaned around him. The breeze murmured through the undergrowth. Everything else had fallen silent.

Looking back, Duncan wouldn't be able to say for sure why he ran. Not really. There was nothing to suggest anything had happened. No one thing he could pinpoint as the reason for his sudden panic. Realistically, Connor simply hadn't heard him. That was all. It wasn't unusual for the boy to get distracted. His selective deafness was an ongoing family joke.

And yet, Duncan ran. He ran, fuelled by fear, pushing his way through the grasping undergrowth and the whipping branches, splashing through the soggy dips, and stumbling over the moss-covered rocks, something hot and urgent gnawing away at his insides.

"Connor!"

He hurtled out of the trees, slipped on an unexpected embankment, and slid down it on his arse. The puddle of mud at the bottom cushioned his fall, then *schlopped* forlornly as it lost its grip on him when he pulled himself free.

"Con? Connor?"

He'd emerged from the forest thirty feet or so from where he'd first entered it. He had a clear view of the spot where he'd told Connor to wait, but hurried over to it, anyway, in case he was somehow overlooking something.

In case he was somehow overlooking his son.

Where the boy had been was a long, crooked stick, lying on the ground. A staff, abandoned by its wizard.

"Connor?" Duncan bellowed. His voice echoed in both directions along the empty track, up into the forest, off across the graveyard of stumps, and on towards the distant road. "Connor! Where are you? Con?"

And then, from behind him, came the sound of movement.

He sobbed, relief flooding him, lightening his head, slackening muscles he hadn't felt go tight.

"Connor, I thought I told you to—?"

He stopped when a muddy Golden Retriever padded out of the trees, tail wagging, tongue lolling happily.

Something deep in Duncan's gut twisted into a knot. He spiralled around, searching for his son. "Connor!" he bellowed. "Con, where are you?"

No answer came. Meg crept to Duncan's side, her head low, sensing his distress.

"This is your fault! Stupid bloody dog!" Duncan snapped.

Meg lowered her head, her eyes gazing uncomprehendingly up at him.

Duncan's voice softened. It took on a pleading edge. "Go find him. Go find Connor," he said. His fingers fumbled for the phone in his pocket as he stared at the dog, willing her to listen, willing her to understand.

He thumbed the phone awake. No signal. *No fucking signal.*

Duncan shot the dog a desperate, hopeless look. His voice cracked.

"Go find our boy."

CHAPTER TWO

Detective Chief Inspector Jack Logan waited for the door to buzz open, then continued through it and along another of the stark, unwelcoming corridors of Carstairs State Hospital.

He turned left at the bottom, through another set of doors, then up the wide staircase to the next floor. He could've taken the lift, but the stairs were usually quicker. Besides, you never knew who you might end up sharing the lift with, and what they might try to get up to in the confined space.

His feet led him through the hospital on auto-pilot, having made this journey too many times to count. There were plenty of places Logan wished he knew like the back of his hand. Venice. The South of France. The Bahamas, maybe.

But no. Instead, the place on Earth he was probably most familiar with was a maximum-security psychiatric hospital in South Lanarkshire hoaching with rapists, murderers, and all manner of worse.

Once-upon-a-time, he would have struggled to believe the 'and worse' part, but twenty years on the job had soon leathered any such doubts out of him.

The beat days had been bad enough, giving him a wee taster menu of the sort of horrors he'd eventually be forced to gorge himself on.

It had gone from bad to worse when he'd moved up to CID, and since transferring to the Major Investigations Team he'd seen things that would make the average murdering rapist shake their heads in disgust.

Another door blocked his path, its two double-glazed square windows each encasing a mesh of thick wire. He stopped and fixed the camera mounted above it with an impatient look.

Logan caught sight of himself in the camera's wide lens and made a half-hearted attempt at smoothing down his hair. He ran a hand across his chin, as if he could wipe away the stubble that had been shading-in his jawline for the past few days.

He had the look of someone who had been destined to find himself involved with the law, although not necessarily on the side he'd ended up on. He was tall and broad, but generally held himself a little stooped as if trying to keep his size a secret.

The door buzzed. Logan pulled it open, gave a nod to the camera, then continued through, grateful the delay had been a minor one.

They knew his face well here. Hardly surprising. He was more regular a fixture than some of the doctors.

There was a reception-style desk along the corridor behind the next door, a plexiglass shield protecting the staff member behind it. Logan stopped at the counter, set down the dog-eared folder he carried under his arm, then signed himself in.

"You're later today," said the woman behind the shield. She was relatively new. He'd first seen her four, maybe five visits ago, so she was only a couple of months into the job. She was plump and soft-looking, and Logan doubted she'd last much longer. A quick glance at the newspaper open at the job section on the desk beside her confirmed his suspicions.

He didn't blame her.

"Crazy morning," he replied, then briefly winced at his choice of words. "Busy, I mean."

His eyes flicked to the clock mounted on the wall behind reception. There was a little round cage over it, securing it in place. Logan knew it was there to stop any of the residents hauling the thing off the wall and quite literally clocking some poor bastard with it, but he liked to imagine that it was an inmate here, locked away like the rest of them.

He signed his name with a blip and a squiggle, then picked up his folder. "Is he ready?"

The receptionist nodded. "He's ready. Well, as he ever is. I wouldn't expect much."

Logan grunted in response, then stepped away from the counter.

"Oh, but Chief Inspector?"

"Yes?"

The receptionist mustered a worried-looking smile. "Dr Ramesh wants to see you before you go in."

Logan stopped, turned. "Who?"

"Mr Logan?"

A bearded Asian man in his mid-forties leaned out of a door a little way along the corridor and made a beckoning motion that Logan very much did not approve of.

"My office, please. I'd like a word."

RAMESH WAS NEW, too. Newer than the receptionist, even. Unlike her, he had an efficient, by-the-book air to him that came across as rude, but ensured he had a better chance of sticking the job than she had. He took a seat behind his desk as Logan closed the office door, then motioned to the chair opposite for the DCI to do the same.

"I'll stand, thanks."

Ramesh tutted softly, took a moment to conclude that he didn't like having such a dramatic height disadvantage, and got to his feet.

The office was small, but fastidiously neat to the point it didn't look like a functioning workplace at all. Rather, it was like something IKEA might use as a showpiece for its new office range designed for the deeply unimaginative.

The desk was irritatingly uncluttered, aside from a vertical stack of six hefty-looking medical tomes all angled so their barely decipherable titles could be read by anyone sitting across from the doctor. Each spine was smooth and crease-free, and the carefully presented showpiece told Logan pretty much everything he needed to know about the office's current occupier.

"I'm not happy about this," Ramesh said. He prodded the desktop with his index finger. "I'm not happy about this at all."

There was an accent there, but it had been smoothed over and filled in around the edges with Received Pronunciation. No doubt at some private boarding school down south somewhere, Logan guessed. This did not do his opinion of the man any favours.

"Not happy about what?"

"You. Him. This whole thing. You shouldn't be coming in like this. It's not fair."

Logan shifted his weight, eliciting a groan from the carpeted floorboards beneath him.

"*Fair?*"

"Mr Petrie is a patient here," said Ramesh. He was a few inches shorter than Logan but was doing an admirable job of pretending not to notice. He was also doing a better job of holding the DCI's gaze than most polis ever managed.

"Mr Petrie is a convicted killer who murdered three children," Logan replied. "He's also a key witness in an ongoing investigation."

"Yes, but it isn't an ongoing investigation, is it, Inspector?" Ramesh asked, his accent bubbling up. "You caught him. He stood trial."

"*Detective Chief* Inspector," Logan corrected. He raised his head and straightened his shoulders, forcing the doctor to lean back a fraction to maintain eye contact. "And I'm well aware that we caught him, but he has continued to withhold vital information that will allow us to fully mark the case closed. Hence why I'm here."

"Again," said Ramesh. He pushed his high-backed leather chair in below his desk and rested his hands on it. "I've looked back at the records. It seems you come here often."

"Frequently," said Logan.

"Some would call that harassment."

"They can call it whatever they like," Logan responded. "Until he gives us the information we need, it's an ongoing investigation. After that, I will happily never give the bastard another thought." He raised an index finger and leaned in a little closer. "Although, I might spare a few minutes to dance on his grave."

He turned his mouth into something that was designed to resemble a smile but wasn't quite there. "How's that sound?"

Ramesh's fingers kneaded the back of his chair, as if massaging it. He inhaled slowly through his nose, either stalling for time or building up to saying something he thought might escalate the situation further.

The latter, it turned out.

"I know your Superintendent," the doctor said. He left a pregnant pause there, giving that new nugget of information a moment to sink in. "We're in the same golf club."

Logan sniffed, shrugged, gave a shake of his head. "I wouldn't know. Always struck me as an arsehole's game. I'm more of a darts man, myself."

He tilted his head forward, giving the doctor the briefest of nods. "No offence."

From the look on Ramesh's face, offence had clearly been taken. Logan wouldn't lose any sleep over it. God knew, he got little enough already.

"Well, I'm going to talk to him. To Gordon. About..." Ramesh gestured vaguely in Logan's direction. "...all this. It's not fair. It's not on. My predecessor may have tolerated it, but... It's not on. I'm not having it."

"Aye, well, tell Gordie I said hello," Logan replied. He held up the battered cardboard folder as if in salute. "And I'll be out of your hair just as soon as Mr Petrie answers my questions. Alright?"

The doctor's fingers tightened their grip on the chair as Logan turned and opened the door.

"And how is he supposed to do that, exactly?" Ramesh demanded. "Hmm? How is he supposed to do that?"

Logan paused in the doorway, filling it. He narrowed his eyes, considering this, then clicked his tongue against the roof of his mouth.

"I'm sure we'll figure something out," he said, then he slipped out into the corridor and closed the door behind him.

CHAPTER THREE

LOGAN SAT IN A MOULDED PLASTIC CHAIR AND GAZED UPON THE FACE of evil. For its part, the face of evil smiled vaguely back at him, its eyes shimmering in confusion, never quite focusing all the way on the visitor.

Logan wasn't buying it. He had never bought it. No matter what the doctors said.

Owen Petrie. *Mister Whisper,* the papers had called him back in the day. Back when he'd abducted and murdered three wee boys and done his damnedest to snatch away two more.

It was statements from the two close-calls that had led to the nickname. They'd both mentioned his voice as he'd tried to talk them into his van—a soft, whispering rasp—and the tabloids had lapped it up.

He sat in an old-fashioned high-backed armchair now, cowed and shrunken by the size of it. Back when he'd been on the outside, he'd been a right Dapper Dan, suiting and booting it whenever he was out and about. Shirt. Tie. The works.

Now, he sat slouched in an old pair of grey joggies and an off-white t-shirt that was threatening to drown him. Food stains dotted the front of it, varying shades of orange blemishes suggesting curry was a regular staple on the hospital menu.

He hadn't shaved in days. Or been shaved, Logan supposed. His stubble was a salt and pepper lavvy brush, heavy on the salt. His hair had been trimmed on the left side of his head. The right side was mostly bald, the hair there never having grown back around the site of the injury that had put him in his current condition.

Supposedly put him in his current condition.

The room was a private one, and as drab as any of the others in the hospital. Aside from the chairs, there was a narrow bed, a narrower wardrobe, and a desk that never got used. The edges of all the furniture had been smoothed off, the corners chunky and rounded.

There was a good-sized window, divided into much smaller chunks by a crisscross of sturdy spars. The bleakness of the view—the window looked directly onto another even grimmer section of the hospital—pleased Logan immensely. Good enough for the bastard.

Too good.

The little rolling hospital table that was usually positioned by the bed had been set up like a barrier between both men. A plastic jug of room temperature water sat on it, untouched. Logan lifted the jug and placed it on the desk which, like everything else in the room, was within easy arm's reach.

"Owen," Logan began, opening his folder. "I'm told you've been bright these last few weeks. I'm hoping that means you're ready to help me."

Petrie's brow knotted. Speaking was a struggle, like he was wrestling the words from his mouth one at a time, and they were putting up a bloody good fight. The voice still had the low throaty hiss that had earned him his nickname, and the sound of it made Logan's skin crawl.

"Help you? H-how?"

Logan held his gaze. "You know how, Owen. We've been through this."

He produced an A4 photograph from his folder and sat it on the table between them. It was a blown-up image, full colour but grainy, showing a smiling boy dressed as the Red Ranger from *Power Rangers*. The outfit was too big for him, the sleeves folded back to make it fit, but he didn't care. He looked proud as punch, his face upturned to the camera, his hands raised in a mock-karate pose.

Logan didn't need to see the picture to know any of this. It was long-since burned in.

"Dylan Muir. Aged three."

Petrie didn't look at the photograph. Not at first. It was only when Logan rapped his knuckles on the plastic table top that Petrie's eyes went to it. He smiled, not unkindly, and made a little, 'Aw,' noise that forced Logan to grip his chair to stop himself lunging for the bastard.

"He l-looks like a nice boy." The words were slow, laborious.

Logan counted to five in his head, before continuing.

"Aye. He was nice, Owen. He was a good lad. Much loved by everyone. His pals. His sister. His parents. A great wee lad," Logan said. "And then, he died."

A flicker of a frown crossed Petrie's face. He tapped the edge of the photograph with the tip of a finger, prodding at it as if to check if it were real.

"Oh," he said, dragging his gaze up to meet Logan's. He continued to tap the bottom of the photograph as he battled with the next few words. "What hap-p-pened to him?"

Logan leaned in, closing the gap between them. His voice became lower, his tone more menacing. "That's why I'm here, Owen. I was hoping that maybe you could tell me."

Petrie didn't flinch or make any attempt to draw back. Nothing flickered behind his eyes. He was good, Logan would give him that.

"I d-don't know."

"See, I think you do," Logan told him. He shook his head. "No. I *know* you do, Owen."

He placed another three photographs down. Dylan Muir on the swings. Dylan Muir in at his mum's make-up, a line of lipstick smeared across his forehead. Dylan Muir with his hand buried up to the wrist in a bag of *Monster Munch*. Petrie watched them being set out with the concentration of a punter at a magic show, trying to figure out the trick and second-guess how it was done.

Logan gave him a few moments to take those images in before setting down the final photograph. This one was smaller than the rest, and the only one that wasn't in colour. It went on top of the others, slap bang in the middle.

Dylan Muir, tied to a chair, tears cutting tracks down his dirty cheeks. Logan could see the boy's expression without looking. Every line. Every crease. Every moment of suffering etched across his features. He knew it all.

Petrie lowered his head and peered at the final image, as if looking over the top of a pair of glasses. He studied it like this for a few seconds, then drew back suddenly, like he'd finally figured out what he was looking at.

"I d-don't like that one," he said, his voice a slurred staccato.

"No, I don't like that one either," Logan agreed. He fished in the folder and produced two more images. He set them down, one at a time. "And I don't like that one of Lewis Briggs. Or this one of Matthew Dennison."

Petrie's gaze was aimed squarely over Logan's shoulder now, out through the window at the grey building beyond. The DCI leaned to the right, interrupting the view.

"Look at them, Owen."

Petrie shook his head.

"Look at the photos."

"I d-don't w-want to."

Logan snatched the photographs up, one in each hand, holding them in front of Petrie. "We found Lewis. We found Matthew. Too late, aye. Far too late, but we found them. At least we could give their families that."

He set the pictures down and picked up the black and white image of Dylan Muir, holding it with almost reverential care as he gazed into the boy's wide, trusting eyes.

For a while, Logan had imagined that they might find the boy alive. Somewhere. Somehow. Someday.

But then, in a rare moment of lucidity, Petrie had finally confessed to his murder, and shattered that dream.

Just like he'd shattered so many others.

"But we never found Dylan. You never let us give him back so we could give his family some sort of peace."

Petrie's mouth flapped open and closed. His eyes were glazed, and he had a look of a goldfish about him, staring out at the world from behind a wall of glass.

"Cut that shite out," Logan hissed. He clicked his fingers up close in the other man's face. Petrie's eyelids fluttered, but he was looking through Logan now, staring at empty space.

"Where is he, Petrie?" Logan demanded. "Tell me what you did with him. Tell me where you left him. Tell me where to find him."

Across the table, Petrie's frown deepened, the wrinkles on his forehead furrowing into shadowy grooves. He remained like that for a good ten seconds, then he blinked. Once. Twice. A hypnotist's patient coming out of a trance.

His face relaxed. He looked at Logan and smiled vaguely, as if seeing him for the first time but finding something familiar about him. Petrie's hand came up and idly traced the dent that had forever altered the shape of his skull, his fingertips following the line of his scar.

Finally, he looked down at the spread of photographs of the smiling three-year-old set out before him. "H-he looks nice," he mumbled. He ran his fingers across one of the photographs and raised his eyes to meet Logan's. "Is he yours?"

Logan couldn't stop himself. He lunged across the table and caught Petrie by the food-stained t-shirt. Petrie's vacant, not-quite-there smile remained fixed on his face. He didn't flinch, not even when the DCI's other arm drew back, his fingers balling into a fist.

"Mr Logan!"

The voice snapped Logan out of it, brought him back to his senses. He released his grip but wasn't gentle about it. Petrie *thudded* back into the padding of the chair.

Turning, Logan saw Dr Ramesh holding the door open. "I think you've outstayed your welcome for one day," Ramesh said. "Mr Petrie needs his rest."

The door *squeaked* as he opened it wider.

"Don't make me ask you again."

Petrie's vague smile twitched as he watched Logan gather up his photographs and replace them in the folder.

"I'll see you again soon, Owen," the DCI said. A threat and a promise. "Maybe we'll jog your memory next time."

"I'm sure we can arrange something through the proper channels," Ramesh said. "But for now, I'm afraid I must ask you to leave."

Tucking the folder under his arm, Logan made for the door. He stopped when he was level with the doctor, drawing himself up to his full height for maximum looming potential.

"I'll be reporting this," Ramesh said.

"Good luck with that."

He was about to leave when Petrie called to him. "Sir? Excuse me, s-sir?"

Logan stopped, turned.

The smile crept higher on Petrie's face. His voice was a whisper, the words tumbling freely from his mouth. "Say hello to that little boy for me."

CHAPTER FOUR

LOGAN WAS HALFWAY ACROSS THE CARPARK WHEN HIS PHONE RANG. He cursed out loud when he saw the name flash up.

Gordon Mackenzie.

Detective Superintendent Gordon Mackenzie.

The Gozer.

As nicknames went, it went around the houses a bit. From what Logan understood of it, 'Gordon the Gopher' had been an early draft, but it had been widely agreed by everyone at the time that it was far too obvious, and that should he overhear anyone referring to 'The Gopher' in conversation, the then-going-places DS wouldn't need to draw on much of his polis training to put two and two together.

And so, an alternative had been sought. Something that summed up his personality, maybe gave a wee nod to the Gopher thing, but wasn't as blatantly on-the-nose. One of the DCs in the department at the time had been a big fan of *Ghostbusters*. And, what with Mackenzie being a boggle-eyed bastard with a flat-top, he'd been named after the film's villain, an equally boggle-eyed bastard with a flat-top.

If you wanted to get technical about it, the handle didn't actually stand up to scrutiny. The boggle-eyed, flat-topped bastard in *Ghostbusters* was Zuul. Gozer was the unseen evil entity who eventually manifested as the *Stay Puft Marshmallow Man*, but any attempt by anyone to raise this as an objection was quickly shouted down. *Gordon the Gozer* just worked, and the Strathclyde polis never let semantics get in the way of a solid nickname.

Logan's thumb hovered over the green phone icon on the screen, shifted to the red, then back again. That wee rat bastard of a doctor must've got straight onto the Gozer before Logan was even out of the building. It was barely after eleven on a Sunday morning. The DSup wouldn't be happy.

He decided to answer. Better to face his wrath now, than give it a chance to snowball into something worse.

"Sir?" he said. "To what do I owe the pleasure?"

"Where are you?" the Gozer asked. His voice was clipped, efficient. Either Logan was in more trouble than he thought, or something else was going down.

"Just about at my car. Why?"

"We need you in at the office, ay-sap."

Logan grimaced. *Ay-sap.* The first time he'd heard the Gozer say that, he'd assumed it was a wind-up. Surely no-one actually spoke like that? But, aye. Some folk did, it turned out, and the DSup was one of them.

What was wrong with 'now'? Or even just the standard one-letter-at-a-time pronunciation of ASAP?

Fucking *ay-sap.*

"Logan?"

"Sorry. Aye. Here, sir," Logan replied. "What's the score?"

"Best if I explain in person."

In person? So, the Gozer was in the office on a Sunday morning? Jesus, it must be serious.

"I can be there in an hour."

"An hour? What are you going to do, the Moonwalk?" the Gozer asked. "Wait. Sunday. End of the month. You've been in seeing him again, haven't you?"

Logan made a non-committal *hmm* noise. At least Ramesh hadn't phoned his old golfing buddy to report him yet. That was something.

"We'll talk about this at a later date, Detective Chief Inspector," said the Gozer, his tone suggesting it would not be an enjoyable chat for at least one of them. "For now, just get yourself in here."

"Will do, sir."

"Oh, and if you're passing your house, you might want to grab some clothes and a toothbrush. Quickly, though."

"How come?"

"You're being seconded. Up north. They've asked for you personally."

Logan stopped walking in the middle of the car park. "What? Why?"

"You wouldn't believe me if I told you," said the Gozer. "Just get in here. And don't spare the horses."

CHAPTER FIVE

UNDER NORMAL CIRCUMSTANCES, LOGAN WOULD'VE APPRECIATED THE view.

He wasn't that sort of guy, generally—a view sort of guy—but there was something about the landscape of the route between Glasgow and Fort William that could grab even the most ardent non-view guys by the collar and force them to sit up straight.

Most people thought it started at Rannoch Moor, and continued to improve during the twenty-mile build-up to Glencoe. To Logan, though, it started before that. The meandering road up Loch Lomond-side held its own charms, he'd always thought.

Granted, you didn't want to get caught behind a campervan. And the old stone bridges were so narrow they regularly brought traffic to a standstill as two buses jostled for position, their wing mirrors kissing as they inched past. But despite all that, there were few places on Earth quite like it.

It had been a while since Logan had been up this way, and the Crian-larich bypass was new to him. It shaved, by his reckoning, about nine seconds off the previous route, and he failed to see the point. Considering everything else that needed doing on the A82, it seemed like an odd choice.

From the new roundabout, it was a few minutes to Tyndrum, a quick stop at the Green Welly for a slash, then on up the hill into the great beyond.

It was round about that stage of the journey that he'd normally be forced to admit that actually, on reflection, Loch Lomond-side couldn't hold a candle to this. A couple of turns up the hill presented you with a view that almost went on forever, only interrupted by the conical snow-covered peak of Beinn Dorain, and its neighbour, Beinn an Dothaidh.

That was how his thought process usually went. Not today, though. Today, was different.

The Gozer had been even more ashen-faced than usual when Logan had turned up at the office. The flat-top that had once helped crown him in both a literal and metaphorical sense was now a distant memory, along with eighty-percent of his hair in general. The boggly eyes were still a thing, though. Thyroid-related, apparently. Logan didn't like to ask.

The DSup had sat him down and offered him coffee. That was when the alarm bells had really started to ring. Logan had turned down the offer, keen by this point to crack on and find out what the hell was going on.

"A boy's gone missing up north, near Fort William. Connor Reid. Aged seven," the Gozer had said, rattling off the details as if reading from a list. "Last seen two days ago ten miles north of the town at..."

He consulted a notebook. "Leanachan Forest."

"So?" Logan had asked, then he'd immediately winced at how it sounded. "I mean, aye, I saw something about it in the papers. Out with his old man, wasn't he?"

The DSup nodded the affirmative.

"That's CID though, surely?" Logan had asked. "What's it got to do with MIT? Or with me, for that matter?"

Behind the wheel of his Ford Focus, Logan flexed his fingers, exhaled slowly, then tightened his grip as he replayed what had happened next. He didn't want to be replaying it. Not again. But it had been on loop inside his head for the past hour and a half, and it didn't look like he was getting a lot of choice in the matter.

Time had wound itself into slow motion as the Gozer had produced an A5 print. The thick photo paper had made a definitive *click* when the DSup placed it on the desk in front of Logan.

The image was new, yet familiar.

Achingly, gut-wrenchingly familiar.

A boy. A chair. A rope.

Tears carving trenches down filthy cheeks.

"It arrived this morning."

"Jesus. Where? Here?"

"At the house. That's a copy the local boys emailed down. We printed it off."

"Delivered on a Sunday? Courier?"

"Couriers don't run weekends up there," the Gozer had said.

"Hand-delivered, then," Logan reasoned, still studying the picture. "Anyone see anything?"

"Not that we know of."

"How was it delivered? Through the letterbox?"

"Left on the step."

The way the DSup said it had made Logan look up.

"On its own?"

The Gozer had shaken his head, just once. "In an envelope. Attached to a soft toy." He gave that a moment to sink in. "Like before."

Recalling the conversation again now made Logan's pulse quicken and his breath go short. He swung the car out into the right-hand lane and hammered the accelerator, sweeping past an old Clio that had been crawling along at under forty, the driver probably admiring the scenery.

It flashed its lights at him as he pulled back in. For a second, he considered hitting the blues and pulling the slow bastard over, but while he most definitely had the inclination, he was tight for time. He settled for raising a middle finger to the back windscreen, then continued on down the straight, widening the gap between them.

Even as he raced ahead, though, his mind went wandering back to Glasgow.

"A copycat," he'd said. It hadn't been a question. Not really. A question implied doubt, of which he'd had none. Not then.

He'd been surprised when the Gozer had given another shake of his head. "We don't know."

"What do you mean, we don't know? We do know. Petrie's in Carstairs. I spoke to him myself this morning, so I reckon we can safely score him off the list of suspects. No' unless he's got a jetpack and a time machine."

The Gozer hadn't looked amused.

"The envelope had the same message on the front. 'Surprise Inside. Open me.' Same typewritten text. Same spacing. Same three exclamation marks after both statements." The DSup puffed out his cheeks. "Same everything."

Logan had fallen silent at that. The details of the other envelopes had been kept secret. They'd never been given to the press, or even shared outside those closest to the original investigation.

"Then it leaked," he'd said. "Someone leaked it."

"Maybe."

"*Maybe?*"

"Probably. I mean, aye. That must be it," the Gozer had said. He'd sucked in his bottom lip, making his mouth go thin. "The only alternative—"

"The only alternative is that we got the wrong man. That Petrie didn't do it. And we know he did."

The Gozer had perched on the edge of the desk then. "Do we?"

"What's that supposed to mean?" Logan had demanded, momentarily forgetting who he was speaking to. "Aye. We know he did it. We got a solid conviction."

The Detective Superintendent sighed wearily, but nodded. "Aye. I suppose so."

"It's a copycat, boss. That's all. The envelope stuff leaked, and some sick bastard is out there playing at being Petrie."

Gozer said nothing at first. He picked up a stapler from the desk and fiddled with it, not making eye contact.

"And if it isn't?"

Logan stood. The face of the boy gazed imploringly up at him from the photograph.

"Then it'll be down to God to judge us, Sir."

CHAPTER SIX

LOGAN FOUND THE STATION AFTER TWO FALSE STARTS. IT WAS situated across from a very loud, very active building site, and it was only as Logan pulled up that he spotted the BBC van tucked in behind a digger.

He muttered something uncomplimentary as he pulled the Focus into one of the many empty parking spaces. Then, he got out, blanked the five-strong pack of journalists who turned to study him as he approached, and pushed on through the station doors.

The building had been constructed recently, and still had that new smell to it. Logan had been to the old station a few times over the years, and while it had been in need of a lick of paint and a bit of tarting up, he'd have taken it over this one any day.

It was the remoteness he didn't like. The old station had been right in the middle of the town. Right in the heart of the action. The new one was out on an industrial estate three miles from Fort William town centre. How were you supposed to keep on top of things way out here?

It wasn't just that, though. The old station had felt like a proper nick. It had character and history baked into every one of its unappealing concrete blocks. This place was all plexiglass and curves, better suited to a call centre than a cop shop.

"You alright there?" asked a woman behind the screened-off front desk. She wasn't in uniform, but was instead dressed in a navy trouser-suit and frumpy hairstyle that made her look ten years older than she probably was.

"DCI Jack Logan. Major Investigations Team," said Logan, producing his ID.

The woman opened a little hatch in the bottom of the plexiglass screen and motioned for him to slide the warrant card through. Fishing a pair of reading glasses from her pocket, she scrutinized the identification document.

"What did you say your name was?" she asked after a moment, as if to catch him out.

"Logan. I've been sent up from the Central Belt."

"No one told me," the woman said, still holding onto the card.

Logan gave her due consideration, then shrugged. "I don't care." He pointed to a heavy door off to the right of the desk. "Can you buzz me in?"

"No one said anything about you coming," the woman reiterated.

Logan sighed, ran his hand down his face, then tried to readjust his features into something more friendly.

"Look... sorry, what's your name?"

She peered at him over the top of her angular glasses. Like the rest of her get-up, they looked designed for someone in their sixties. "Moira."

"Moira? Moira what?"

"Corson."

"Right. Nice to meet you," Logan said. He leaned on the edge of the desk, his face close enough to the screen that his breath fogged the plexiglass. "Listen, I'm sorry you weren't forewarned, but I've had a long day, Moira. And I suspect it's just getting started. So, how about you do us both a favour and buzz me through, eh? Can you do that for me?"

Moira held his gaze for a few seconds, then very slowly and deliberately placed his warrant card face down on the photocopier. She held his gaze as the machine *whirred* into life, scanning the document.

"You'll have to sign in," she said, indicating two ledgers on the desk on Logan's right.

Wearily, Logan picked up a pen and began to write.

"Not that one."

Logan drew her a fierce look, then tutted and signed himself in on the other book.

By the time he'd finished writing, Moira had slid his ID back through the hatch.

"Thank you," he said, slipping it back into the inside pocket of his coat. He pointed to the door. "Now, can—"

The door buzzed, and Logan hurried to push it open. The buzzing continued a while longer until Moira eventually removed her finger from the button and silence returned.

"Where did you say you'd come from, again?" she asked him.

"Glasgow."

Moira looked him up and down, taking him all in and not approving of what she saw.

"Aye," she said, smiling thinly. "I should've guessed."

"You FOUND IT ALRIGHT, THEN?" asked DI Ben Forde, handing Logan half a cup of tea.

Technically, it was a full cup, but there wasn't a lot of cup to fill. Logan wasted a couple of seconds trying to fit a finger through the handle, then gave up and wrapped his hand around the cup, instead.

"Eventually," he said, taking a sip. He'd given up milk a few weeks back, and the tea tasted thin and disappointing. "The sign at the roundabout said 'superstore.'"

"Oh, aye. That's the sign for the new Tesco," said Forde.

He was older than Logan, although Logan had never figured out by how much. He'd been, "No' a kick in the arse off retirement," for at least a decade now, but showed no signs of making the leap.

For the most part, DI Forde was genial and soft-spoken. 'Gentle Ben' they called him, although Logan had once had the pleasure of seeing him take down a wee ned who'd been waggling a broken bottle around, and there had been hee-haw gentle about it.

He was a good few inches shorter than Logan, and lacked the girth that helped make the DCI so imposing. Still, he was a vicious wee bastard when he had to be, and while the arm of this particular lawman might not be all that long, you were in trouble if it got a hold of you.

Logan took another sip of tea. "New Tesco? Is that what they're building across the road?"

"Hmm? Oh, no. That's the hospital."

"So..." Logan glanced out through the window at the waste ground beyond. "Where's the Tesco?"

"It's not happening?"

"It's what?"

"They're not building it. They changed their mind. They're building a hospital, instead."

Logan blinked. "Who is? Tesco?"

DI Forde gave a little chuckle. "No. Tesco sold the land."

"But..."

"But they'd already put up the 'superstore' sign, so they just left it."

Logan's eyebrows raised, then lowered. Forde beamed a big broad grin, then patted the DCI on the shoulder. "Welcome to the Highlands, Jack," he said, then he jabbed a thumb in the direction of the Incident Room. "Shall we?"

CHAPTER SEVEN

WHILE LOGAN AND DI FORDE WENT BACK A FAIR FEW YEARS, THE other faces were completely new to him. No doubt he'd have seen one or two in passing at various events, but none of them were familiar to him now. Forde wasted no time getting stuck into the introductions.

"We'll start at the top and work our way down to the riff-raff," Ben announced, shooting a look of mock contempt at a young Detective Constable who was perched with half an arse-cheek on an otherwise uncluttered desk.

Very few of the desks in the Incident Room were cluttered, in fact, which made Logan uneasy. He was used to rooms stacked high with documents—reports, witness statements, CCTV printouts, and all the other paperwork that piled up during an investigation. The fact that this one looked practically unused did not bode well for how things had been going thus far.

"You mean save the best for last, sir," said the DC. He was late-twenties, Logan thought. Hair gelled, or waxed, or puttied, or whatever the hell they did with it these days, stubble carefully cultivated to make it look like he just hadn't got around to shaving for a while. Logan got the measure of him right away.

DI Forde gave a derisory snort. "Aye, you tell yourself that if it helps, son," he said, then he turned his attention to the only woman in the room.

"Detective Sergeant Caitlyn McQuarrie," Ben said. "Originally from

Orkney, transferred to Northern MIT in... what? Two-thousand-and-sixteen?"

"Twenty-seventeen," the DS said, and Logan detected just a bit of an island twang. Not the lilting teuchter of the Western Isles, but even in just those two words there was something that was unmistakably not of the mainland.

Her hair was flame-red, but cut short and tied back out of the way. She'd probably endured a lifetime of 'ginger' comments, and the hairstyle was a hundred-percent about functionality, zero percent about style.

She was closer to Logan's age than to DI Forde's. Eight or nine years younger than himself, Logan thought, which put her mid-to-late-thirties. She was short and slight—five-four, five-five—but had a presence about her that would doubtless add a few inches when required.

"Much as it pains me to say so, Caitlyn's one of the best detectives I've ever worked with," continued Ben.

"Arguably *the* best," the DS added, although the way she said it—light on the ego, heavy on the sarcasm—told Logan they were going to get along just fine.

"I suppose you could technically argue any old shite, if you put your mind to it," Ben conceded.

He moved onto the only person in the room who hadn't opened his mouth yet—a well-presented, mid-thirties Asian man standing stiffly just a half-step removed from the rest of the group. He wore a new suit and a worried expression, and Logan would put money on him having recently transferred.

"DC Hamza Khaled. Recently joined us from CID," said Ben, confirming Logan's suspicions. "We haven't really got to know each other that well yet, but I've heard only good things," Ben continued.

"We've obviously been talking to some very different people," volunteered the as-yet-unnamed officer with the landscaped stubble. Khaled shot him an anxious look, then saw the guy's grin and clicked that he was joking.

"Where were you based before?" Logan asked, still trying to get the measure of the man.

"Aberdeen, sir," Hamza replied, and Logan found himself surprised by the heavy Doric accent. *Aiberdeen.*

"Wait. Khaled," said Logan, something stirring at the back of his mind. He clicked his fingers a couple of times, egging it on. "Weren't you involved in that people trafficking thing with the fishing boats?"

"No' in the actual trafficking part, sir, but aye, I was one of the arresting officers," DC Khaled said. He smiled, but warily, like he thought his jokey remark might land him in trouble.

"From what I heard you pretty much cracked the whole thing wide open."

Hamza was quick to shake his head. "Team effort, sir."

"Aye, well, it was good work," Logan told him. The DC seemed to relax a little then, the validation helping push away any thoughts of impostor syndrome.

"Last, and by every means least, Detective Constable Tyler Neish."

The DC flashed his superior a grin, showing off his well maintained teeth. "You love me really, boss."

Ben made a weighing motion with both hands. "Meh."

DC Neish held a hand out to Logan, but remained half-seated on the desk. Logan considered the younger man's offer, then extended his own hand, keeping his feet planted in a way that suggested he had no intention whatsoever of moving any closer. Ben smirked as he watched the power struggle unfold, knowing full well who was going to emerge victor.

After a half-second or so of internal struggle, Tyler stood, took the necessary step closer to Logan, then shook his hand just a little sheepishly. "Nice to meet you, sir."

"Aye," Logan said. "I know."

Ben had to briefly turn away, his shoulders shaking with barely contained laughter.

Logan waited until DC Neish had returned to his perch, then addressed the lot of them. "Thank you for the introductions, DI Forde. It's good to meet you all. Just a pity about the circumstances, but then I'm sure we're all used to that by now."

Logan realised he was still wearing his coat, and began the process of shrugging it off as he continued.

"I'm sure Ben's already filled you in, but in case you need a refresher, I'm DCI Jack Logan. I was the arresting officer in the Mister Whisper case a few years back. I've been brought in to lead the charge on this one because of the similarities between both cases."

He looked around for somewhere to put his coat, then tossed it over a chair, simultaneously disposing of the garment and staking his claim to that seat.

"Let me make one thing clear before we go any further," Logan said, meeting everyone's eye in turn. "Regardless of how similar aspects of these cases may be, Owen Petrie—Mister Whisper—is not behind them. We caught him. We put him away."

Tyler raised a hand, but didn't wait to be asked. "Didn't he fall or something during the arrest?"

Logan nodded. "Off a car-park roof. Fell three floors, but lived to tell the tale. More or less."

"How did that happen, sir?" asked Hamza.

There was a long, pregnant pause as Logan considered his answer. "I cornered him. I guess the old 'fight or flight' response kicked in. He elected to fly, which went about as well for him as you might imagine."

"Sounds like an unfortunate business, sir," said DS McQuarrie. There was an edge to her tone that wasn't accusing, exactly, but was certainly making an insinuation or two.

"Very much so," Logan agreed. "Although, on the bright side, it couldn't have happened to a nicer man. Regardless, we're a hundred percent that we have the right man locked up, and we know he can't have been behind this latest abduction. So, we need to figure out who is, find out where they are, and get that boy home."

He let that settle for a moment. Then, when he was sure they were all on the same page, he looked to Ben. "What's the latest?"

DI Forde cleared his throat. This seemed to be the trigger that switched him into polis mode, and his previously avuncular tone changed to a much more business-like one.

"We had the handover from CID this morning. I thought DCs Neish and Khaled could go over the report and look through the statements. Not that there's much in there. I've got uniform out doing door-to-doors around the abduction scene, but it's going to take a while."

Logan raised an eyebrow. "Lot of doors to knock?"

"No, opposite problem. Very few, but they're all a long way down dirt tracks. Almost certainly a waste of time, but you never know."

"Has anyone spoken to the parents again this morning?" asked Caitlyn.

Ben shook his head. "We've got a liaison there with them, and a couple of bigger lads to keep the press from making a nuisance of themselves, but no, we've still to get around there."

"I'll do that," Logan said. "Unless any of you already have a relationship?"

The others confirmed that none of them had spoken to the family.

"Right. I'll speak to them, then. Be good to get a look at them. I want a look at the crime scene first, though," Logan said. "What about the stuff that arrived this morning?"

Ben gave a nod to DC Khaled. "Hamza, could you...?"

Hamza sprang into life, crossing quickly to a desk in the corner, where a number of exhibits sat wrapped in plastic evidence bags. He retrieved three, placed them in a small cardboard box, and carried them back to the group.

Logan peered in as the box was placed on the desk beside him. "This is the hand-delivered stuff," Hamza said. He motioned back to the desk. "CID took the cards and letters that arrived over the past couple of days, too. Nothing interesting, as far as we can tell."

"Right. Good," said Logan, absent-mindedly. He was staring down at the contents of the box, fighting the rising urge to vomit.

The bear was bad enough, with its faded grey fur and glassy eyes. It had been the first thing he'd seen, and the sight of it had stoked those initial fires of nausea.

The photo was several magnitudes worse, of course. Connor Reid looked nothing like the previous victims, and yet exactly like them. He shared the same look of raw terror that the other boys had, and the staging of the photograph was similar enough to be more than coincidence.

It was the envelope that tightened Logan's chest and set his guts churning, though. The Gozer hadn't been lying. It was identical—*identical*—to those that Petrie had sent. The second he'd clapped eyes on it through the plastic, Logan had been transported back almost fifteen years. Back to when he'd first joined the ongoing investigation. Back to when that bastard had been out there hunting wee boys.

Back to Dylan Muir. Back to Lewis Briggs. Back to Matthew Dennison, and to three families whose lives had been chewed up and spat out.

"You alright, boss?"

Logan blinked at the sound of Ben Forde's voice, whooshing back to the present. "Aye. Fine. Have forensics looked at these?"

"Not yet," Ben said. "We need to get them up the road to Inverness for that."

"Right. Aye, of course," Logan said, irritating as news of the potential delay was. "I'll take a look at them first, then one of the uniforms can horse them up there."

He stole another look into the box. "Do the press know about this yet?"

"Not that we know of," said Ben.

"Thank Christ. We keep this to ourselves, alright? This does not get out into the wild until we say so. DS McQuarrie—"

"Caitlyn's fine, sir."

Logan gave a brief nod. "Get onto the liaison over at the house. Make sure the family understands the importance of keeping schtum about this. The vultures are circling out there, already. If this gets out, it'll be a bloody zoo."

"Sir," Caitlyn said, before reaching for her phone and heading for an empty desk in the corner.

He looked very deliberately to DC Neish. "Where do I get a coffee around here?"

Tyler responded with a downturned mouth and a little shrug. "Dunno, sir. First time here."

"Right, then," said Logan, picking up the box. He nodded to the door. "In that case, let's make that your first line of enquiry. Black. Two sugars. Oh!"

Tyler hesitated halfway out of his seat.

"And make it to go."

CHAPTER EIGHT

LOGAN STOOD IN A FINE HIGHLAND DRIZZLE, SIPPING LUKEWARM coffee through the narrow slot in a plastic lid and watching the SOC officers pack up their equipment. There had been a fresh surge of searching after the photo had arrived and the missing child case had been confirmed as an abduction, and Logan was hoping some new nugget of information might turn up.

No such luck. The second search hadn't turned up anything that wasn't already picked up first time round. And that wasn't much.

"We got a footprint," said Ben, gesturing off the path and into the woods. "Headed that way. Size nine or ten."

"Male, then," Logan mused.

"Or a real brute of a lassie, aye," Ben agreed.

Logan sucked some more coffee through the plastic lid and cast his eye across their surroundings. There was a cordon of tape blocking the path ahead, and then another back where the path started, just on the other side of an open gate.

The little parking area beyond the gate was probably busier than it had ever been, thanks to the platoon of polis vehicles currently crammed into it. Logan hadn't been able to squeeze the Focus in, so had abandoned it with two wheels on a grassy verge, the other half clogging up the already too-narrow road.

A few uniforms were scattered around, heads tucked into the shoulders of their high-vis vests, feet stamping to drive out the cold. DS McQuarrie was over talking to some of the SOC lot. She had a notebook open, but didn't seem to have heard anything worth writing down as of yet.

The path—a gravel track probably wide enough for a forestry vehicle, provided the driver had his wits about him—stretched out for a third of a mile or more in both directions, before reaching the gate on one side and a bend at the other. That was almost a mile of visibility.

Off to one side of the path was a couple of acres of scrub, tree stumps, and not a whole lot else. Not a lot of hiding places, and none within easy reach.

Logan walked through it in his head. "So, the dad goes into the trees after the dog. Our man is presumably waiting in the trees, grabs the boy, and heads back into the forest before the dad gets back."

"That's about the size of it," Ben confirmed.

"Dogs been in?"

Ben nodded. "Tracked him headed northwest through the forest. There's a little carpark—well, a bit of waste ground, really, but it gets used as a carpark. Trail goes dead there."

"Anyone see anything parked there?"

Ben shook his head. "Sadly not. But an old boy at one of the cottages reckons he heard a motorbike roughly around the timeframe we're looking at."

Logan tried to visualize this. "Struggling kid on a motorbike. How would that work?"

"With difficulty," said Ben. "We're checking it out, but it's worth noting that the fella who told us about it is ninety-three, has two hearing aids, and reckons he invented Roger the Dodger, so we're not putting a lot of stock in it."

"Sounds sensible, but worth checking."

"I'm sure it won't come as a surprise, but we have no CCTV."

"CCTV?" Logan looked around at the rugged Highland landscape. "I'd imagine *colour* TV is stretching it. What else do we have?"

Ben consulted his notebook, flipped a page, then flipped back. "Right now? That's about your lot. The Scene of Crime lot took a cast of the print, so we're trying to find out what kind of shoe it is. Walking boot of some kind, they reckon, but then that's pretty much par for the course up here."

"What about the trees?" Logan asked. "Have the forensics guys searched the route the dogs followed?"

"To an extent, aye."

"What do you mean 'to an extent'?"

Ben shrugged. "It's a big forest. And CID organised a search the day the boy went missing. Public got involved and trampled right through it."

"Jesus Christ," Logan sighed. "So, for all we know the footprint belongs to one of them?"

"No. That was spotted before the search. Dogs went through before anyone else went in," Ben said. "We don't know much, but we're pretty sure on what we have."

Logan grunted begrudgingly. "That's something."

A movement along the road leading to the gate caught his attention. A *Sky News* van drew to a halt behind Logan's car, unable to get past. The driver gave a couple of short blasts on the horn.

"Did he...?" Logan shifted his gaze from the van to Ben and back again. "Did he just *toot* at me?"

"He did," Ben confirmed. "Twice."

Logan jabbed a finger in the direction of the van. "Do me a favour. Get over there and get rid. I'd do it, but I'll only end up strangling someone."

Ben was well aware of the DCI's feelings on the media, and touched a finger to his forehead in salute. "No bother, boss," he said. "Although..."

"What?"

"We should maybe think about giving them something. Throwing them a scrap to fight over while we crack on. A quote, maybe."

"A quote?" Logan ran his tongue across the front of his teeth, considering this. "How about, 'Crawl in a hole and die, you parasitic bastards?'" he suggested. "What do you think? Reckon that'll suffice?"

Ben half-smiled. "I'll maybe leave it for now."

"Aye, maybe do that," Logan told him, then he teased another sip of coffee from the slot on the coffee cup lid as Ben hurried off to intercept the news van.

The rain had abated slightly, the drizzle becoming something more akin to a damp mist that hung as tiny droplets in the air. If anything, it only served to make everything wetter, and Logan resigned himself to the fact that the chances of getting any new forensic evidence from the area were now practically non-existent.

A footprint. That was it. A footprint, and *maybe* the sound of a motorbike. Not a lot to go on. Hopefully, the teddy bear and photograph would give them something useful. Otherwise, they were in trouble.

Two days. That was how long Lewis Briggs and Matthew Dennison had been kept alive after their parents had received similar packages. Forty-eight hours. That was it.

And the clock was already ticking.

BAAAAAAA.

Logan blinked and looked around. A long black face with bulging, mournful-looking eyes glared back at him from twenty feet away.

"You've got to be kidding," he muttered.

Clicking his fingers, Logan beckoned to one of the uniformed officers standing nearby.

"You. What the hell is this?"

The PC pushed back his cap a little. "It's a sheep, sir."

"No, I know it's a fu—" Logan pinched the bridge of his nose. "I can see it's a sheep. I know what a sheep is. What's it doing on my crime scene?"

The constable regarded the sheep. "Just standing there, sir."

"Jesus Christ. How did you get into the polis, son? Was there a raffle?" Logan snapped. He gestured angrily with a thumb. "Get rid of it."

For a moment, the uniformed officer just stood staring, his head tick-tocking between the DCI and the offending animal. Then, with a determined nod, he squatted down beside the sheep and tried to wrap his arms around it. It shrugged him off, *baaa'd* in protest, then scuttled a few feet along the path.

"Go on. Shoo. Piss off," ordered a female uniformed officer, clapping her hands and stamping her feet. The sheep shot her a dirty look, then obligingly pissed off, picking its way through the scrub and tree stumps, headed for the rest of the flock standing gathered in the distance.

"Thank you," Logan said. "Good to see someone's got some sense around here." He glared at the male constable. "I mean, *picking it up.* Jesus."

"Happy to help, sir," said the female officer.

She was young—early twenties, barely out of the cellophane—but carried herself like someone with ten years more experience. Aye, she was bluffing it, Logan could tell, but then weren't they all on some level?

"What's your name?"

"Sinead." She shook her head, admonishing herself. "PC Bell, sir."

"You down from Inverness?"

"No, sir. Local."

Logan drained the final dregs of his coffee. "Know the family?"

Sinead nodded. "My brother's in school with Connor. Year above, but it's not a big school so they all hang out."

"You've met his mum and dad?"

"A few times, aye. Don't know them well, but know them to see."

"Good. I'm heading over to speak to them. You can come with me."

"I can't, sir."

Logan's brow furrowed. "What? How not?"

"I'm finishing in twenty minutes."

Logan felt himself bristle. His face must've shown it.

"I'd stay on if I could, but it's my brother, sir. He's at the babysitter, and I need to pick him up."

"Well, can't one of your parents do it?"

Something flashed across Sinead's face—there one minute, gone the next.

"No, sir."

"Why not?"

"They're not available, sir," the PC explained. "But... I could maybe ask the babysitter to hang onto him for a couple of hours."

"Right. Good. Do that, then. I'd appreciate it."

Sinead fished her phone from inside a vest pocket and turned away to make the call.

Logan clicked his fingers and pointed to the male officer again. "You. Captain Obvious. Think you can manage to keep the wildlife off the scene?"

"I'll do my best, sir."

"Good man," said Logan. He started to head for the car, then stopped a couple of paces in. "Oh, and try to resist molesting anything next time, if you can. It doesn't reflect well on any of us."

CHAPTER NINE

THE REIDS LIVED IN A MID-TERRACE HOUSE WITH A FRONT GARDEN that was roughly the size of a postage stamp, but immaculately cared for. A multi-coloured monoblock path led up to a rustic-looking front door that was completely out of character with the house, and different to the other three doors in the block.

The number eighteen was embossed on the frame above the door, but an ornate wooden sign announced the house name as 'The Willows'. It was, from what Logan could see, the only house with a name on the block, and probably in the whole of the estate.

The street leading up to the house was dense with polis and news vans. A couple of uniforms out front were keeping the scrum of journalists from getting too close. One of them shifted a traffic cone as the Focus arrived, making room for the car directly in front of the house.

The excitement levels of the journo crowd picked up. Microphones were produced. Cameras were trained. Throats were cleared.

"You ready for this?" Logan asked.

In the passenger seat, PC Sinead Bell nodded. "Ready."

"OK. Keep your mouth shut. Don't swear. Try not to punch anyone."

Sinead gave a thin smile. "Will do."

"Hmm? Oh, no. I wasn't talking to you. That was for me," Logan said, then he opened the car door and stepped out into the rabble of press. The questions came thick and fast.

"Any update?"

"What are you doing to find Connor?"

"What do you think happened?"

Logan ignored them, letting the uniforms keep them at bay. He opened the garden gate and indicated for Sinead to go ahead of him. He was about to close it behind him when a familiar voice rang out over the general hubbub.

"Is it happening again, DCI Logan?"

Logan stopped momentarily. His eyes met a silver-haired journalist with all the plastic insincerity of a used-car salesman. He held an iPhone in one hand, extended like a microphone. One eyebrow was raised, and there was the beginning of a smirk tugging at one side of the man's mouth.

Ken Henderson, freelance journalist and thoroughly horrible bastard. Granted, those two things usually went hand-in-hand, but Henderson seemed to take it to another level. Annoyingly, he was also a good reporter with an eye for a story and a brass neck that could deflect bullets. He'd covered a lot of the 'Mister Whisper' stuff back in the day, and had asked a lot of difficult questions about the accident that had left Petrie in his current condition.

Logan groaned inwardly at the sight of him but did his best not to let it show on the outside.

Is it happening again? Why the hell was he asking that? What did he know?

He looked across the faces of the gathered press. There were only nine of them for now, but that would only be the beginning.

"The only thing happening again is you lot getting on my tits," Logan told them. "I'll answer one question, and one question only."

The mob erupted, firing questions at him. He ignored them, and pointed to a young, hapless-looking lad who practically screamed *local press*.

"You."

The young lad's eyes widened in shock. "What, me?"

"Aye. And that was your question. Threw that opportunity away, didn't you?" Logan said. He briefly met Henderson's eye, then shot the rest of the group a contemptuous glare. "Now, how about you all try pretending to be human beings for once and give the family some peace, eh?"

With that off his chest, and feeling marginally better about the world, Logan *clacked* the gate firmly closed, and stalked up to the front door with Sinead hurrying along in his wake.

After the handshakes and the introductions, Logan sat on a big, solid-looking brute of a couch that immediately tried to swallow him into its cushions. He perched himself near the front, sitting upright, and smiled gratefully as Catriona Reid handed him a cup and saucer.

Connor's mother was awkwardly tall, with a short, feathered haircut that gave her a vaguely elf-like appearance. Her eyes were like dartboard bullseyes—red in the middle, a ring of black running around them. She had tried to disguise her grief with make-up, but it hadn't held up well.

Given the circumstances, Logan wasn't going to hold it against her.

She was doubtlessly exhausted, but her movements were alive with nervous energy, her face twitching, her fingers knotting together, her gaze darting to the window at every sign of movement.

"Thank you," Logan told her.

Catriona's eyes blurred with tears, like this simple expression of gratitude was the thing that might finally break her. She sniffed and pulled herself together, though, and turned to PC Bell who stood off to the side of the couch.

"You sure I can't get you anything, Sinead? Tea? Coffee?"

"I'm fine, thanks," Sinead replied, smiling kindly.

"Juice? There's apple juice." Catriona's lips went thin. Her throat tightened, the thought of the unused carton of apple juice in the fridge almost cutting through her defences again.

"Honestly, I'm fine. Thanks, Catriona," Sinead assured her. "You should take a seat."

"How can I take a seat?" Catriona snapped. The venom in her voice caught her by surprise and her eyes went wide. "I'm sorry."

Sinead shook her head. "Don't be."

Catriona bent, brushed some fluff off the arm of a big round armchair, then perched on it next to her husband. If Catriona Reid was a bundle of anxious energy, Duncan was the polar opposite.

He sat slouched in the armchair, one elbow leaning against the armrest, his hand jammed against the side of his head like his skull was too heavy to stay up without support. There was something haunted about his expression. A step removed from the world, or a step behind it, maybe. Logan had seen similar looks before. Too many times before.

His clothes looked slept in. Or, more likely, not-slept in. They were a stark contrast to the figure-hugging jeans and neatly-pressed purple shirt his wife wore.

"That's a good cup of tea," the DCI said, setting the cup back in the saucer. He looked around for somewhere to sit it, then settled on the polished wooden floor at his feet. "Now, I hope you don't mind, but I'd like to ask you both a few more questions."

Catriona was quick with an, "Of course," but Duncan gave a vague wave of a hand, as if half-heartedly batting away a fly.

"We've already gone over it. There's nothing more to say. Why aren't you out there finding him? Why haven't you found Connor?"

"Rest assured, Mr Reid, we're working on it," Logan replied. "I promise you, we're doing everything we can to get Connor home safely, and as quickly as possible."

Duncan's hand dropped into his lap. He exhaled. "Sorry. Aye. I know. I know you are. It's just..." He sighed again.

"It's frustrating having to go over it all again. I understand it's a difficult thing to have to relive," Logan told him. "But we all want Connor home, and you can help make that happen."

Duncan nodded, and drew himself upright in the chair. His wife's hand slipped into his and he squeezed it.

"You're right. You're absolutely right, detective..."

"Jack. Please."

"Jack." Duncan took another steadying breath. "Go for it. What do you want to know?"

Logan caught Sinead's eye, then pointed to the couch beside him. She hurried over and sat down, producing her notebook without having to be prompted.

Promising, Logan thought.

"The package that arrived last night. The teddy bear," he began, eyes flitting between husband and wife. "Who found it?"

"It was the policewoman," said Catriona. "The... what do you call it?"

"Liaison?"

"Yes. Her. Jess, was it?"

Logan shot Sinead a look. She nodded to confirm. "Jess French."

"There were a few things left on the step. Flowers, mostly. Someone left chocolates," Duncan continued.

"Roses," Catriona added.

Sinead paused, mid-scribble. "Which?"

The other three occupants of the room looked at her, and she wilted slightly. "You said 'roses.' Did you mean the flowers or the chocolates?" She deliberately avoided meeting the DCI's gaze. "Because it... it can be both."

"The chocolates," said Catriona.

"Does that matter?" asked Duncan.

"Well, I mean..." Sinead began, then she finally relented and caught the look from Logan. She quietly cleared her throat. "Sorry, no. Go on."

"You sure?" Logan asked.

Sinead blushed and nodded, fixing her gaze firmly on her pad as she jotted down the now-clarified information. Logan offered a smile by way of apology to the Reids.

"So, the liaison officer arrived in the morning, picked up everything on the step and then brought it in?"

"Right," Duncan confirmed.

"She's lovely," Catriona added. "She's been very kind."

"I'm glad to hear that," said Logan. "And, when did you notice the teddy?"

Duncan and Catriona exchanged glances. "Must've been... what? Just after seven?" Duncan ventured.

"About quarter past," Catriona clarified. "The Yoga alarm had just gone off."

Sinead looked up from her pad, began to open her mouth, then thought better of it. Luckily, Logan asked the question for her.

"Yoga alarm?"

"I do Yoga every morning," Catriona explained. "Seven-fifteen."

"She sets an alarm," said Duncan.

"I set an alarm," his wife confirmed. "Keeps me from forgetting."

Logan set out the timeline in his head. "So, Yoga alarm, liaison turns up, find the teddy. That right?"

"No. The liaison turned up around seven," Catriona corrected. "We were looking through everything that had been left—well, I was. Duncan wasn't really in the mood, but I think if people are going to go out of their way to show support, it's the least we can do to look at it."

She shot her husband a sideways look. Clearly, this had been a bone of contention between them.

"The cards looked nice up on the mantelpiece," Catriona continued. Her eyes went to the bare mantle and she deflated a little. "Of course, the other policemen took them away."

"We'll try to get them back to you as soon as we can, Mrs Reid," Logan told her. "Now, you were saying about the alarm?"

"Right. Yes. The alarm rang, I turned it off, and it was around then that I spotted the teddy."

She gave a little shudder and seemed to shrink into herself. Duncan gave another squeeze of her hand, but if she noticed, she didn't let on.

"There was something about it. Something... I don't know. Do you believe in energy?"

Logan tried to keep his face relatively impassive. "Energy?"

"Spiritual energy. Positive, negative. *Energy*," Catriona continued. "I just got a bad feeling from it, that was all. A bad vibe. It was dirty. Like it had been in a puddle," Catriona continued. Her eyes were glassy, as if she could see the soft toy in the air in front of her.

"Was it one of Connor's?" Logan asked.

Catriona and Duncan both looked surprised by the question.

"I don't know," Duncan admitted. "Maybe. He has one similar, I think. I mean, not all manky, but... Maybe."

"If you could try to find out for us, that would be useful," Logan said, then he turned his attention back to Catriona. "So, sorry. You got a bad feeling from the teddy bear. And then...?"

"And then we saw the envelope."

Her voice went higher, her throat tightening. The sentence ended in a breathless sob, and Duncan gave her another hand-squeeze before taking over.

"We thought it was another card," he said, his own voice not much better. "And then... And then..."

He looked away. His jaw tensed, the effort of holding everything back making him shake. "We opened it."

"Who did?" Logan enquired, as gently as possible.

Duncan gestured wordlessly to his wife. If she'd looked upset when recalling the soft toy, the thought of the image in the envelope was positively haunting her. Her face seemed to grow thinner before Logan's eyes, the features drawing together as if finding comfort and safety in numbers.

"I didn't realise what it was. Not at first," Catriona said. She was whispering, but not through choice. It was as if her throat had constricted to the point that only the faintest suggestion of words could escape. "It was just... It was just..."

She pressed the fingers of her right hand against her skull, as if trying to push down something bubbling up inside it. "It was just a shape. That was all. I wouldn't... I couldn't..."

The tears came then, big silent sobs that contorted her face into something ugly and raw. If she was hiding something, she was bloody good. Whatever else might have happened, the grief was real.

Not that Logan had any reason to suspect her of being involved. Neither of them. Not officially, anyway. And yet, he couldn't help himself. It was right that the courts worked on the 'innocent until proven guilty' principle, but Logan tended to approach investigations from the opposite end.

Still, if Catriona Reid was involved in the abduction of her son, two decades of polis instincts had let him down.

He gave the couple a moment to console each other, then offered an apologetic smile. "I know it's difficult. You're doing really well. Maybe we can go back to Friday?"

Catriona nodded hastily, relieved to be able to switch out this recent nightmare for one that was less vivid and fresh.

"Mr Reid, you were with Connor?"

"Aye. We went for a walk after school," Duncan confirmed. "With the dog."

Logan glanced around the room.

"Meg. She's out back," Duncan explained. "She goes mental at new people."

"She doesn't bite. She's not like that," Catriona quickly added. "Just barks."

"She's a biddable big thing when you get to know her," Sinead confirmed. "Just... noisy."

"Meg is certainly that!" Catriona said. She half-laughed, then everything about the situation came rushing back in, shattering her moment of respite.

"Can you talk me through what happened?" Logan asked, keen to get past the dog chat. "You went for a walk after school..."

Duncan sat up straighter in the chair. "We drove up to Leanachan. It's a good walk. You don't see anyone. We were just doing that, just walking and then..."

He took a breath, centring himself.

"Meg ran into the trees. We shouted, but she wasn't coming back. And, so..."

He ran his tongue across his lips, his eyes locked on Logan. There was a hopelessness there. A desperation. A cry for help.

"So, you went after her," said Logan. "It's OK. I'd have done the same."

Duncan nodded wordlessly.

"And then what?"

"I... I shouted. I kept shouting to him. To make sure he was OK," Duncan continued. "I didn't want him to get scared. He... he gets scared. We have to leave the light on for him."

This time, it was Catriona's turn to do the supporting hand-squeeze.

Duncan's nostrils flared and his mouth turned downward. His eyes filled with fear, self-loathing, and everything in between. His tears, when they fell, were like the waters of purification, cleansing everything away and allowing him to struggle on.

"So, I shouted, and he shouted back. And then, one time, he didn't."

He stared past the DCI to the wall beyond, as if watching everything play out there. "I knew something was wrong. I don't know how, but I *knew* it. I ran back, and he was... He was gone."

Duncan raised his eyes to his wife, like a penitent man before God. "I only left him for a couple of minutes. Just a couple of minutes, that was all. I swear."

"I know," Catriona told him. She slid down onto the seat beside him, and he sagged against her. "I know."

"And you didn't see or hear anything?" Logan asked. "There was no sign of anyone else in the area?"

Duncan shook his head. "No."

"They said he was probably hiding in the trees," Catriona said. "Is that true?"

"We're looking into it. But aye, that's our theory at the moment," Logan told her. He shifted his attention back to Duncan. "How was Connor during the walk? Anything seem different?"

"He was quiet."

"Doesn't sound like him," said Sinead, glancing up from her pad.

"No," Duncan agreed. He frowned. "He was talking and everything. Just... Not the same. Not his usual self. He normally doesn't shut up. And they had swimming at school that day."

"He never stops talking about swimming," Catriona added. The words seemed to take a physical toll on her, and she sagged further into the armchair.

"Did you ask him about it?" Logan pressed.

"Aye. He said he was fine. But, he just... I don't know. There was something."

Logan glanced down at Sinead's notebook to make sure she was writing this down.

"Did he say anything else? Had he fallen out with anyone at school, maybe?"

"At school?" said Catriona, incredulous. "You think someone from school did this? They're eight!"

"Just pursuing all avenues, Mrs Reid," Logan told her.

"You already know who it is!" she replied, her voice rising. "We looked on the internet. We know all about him."

Logan bristled. "About who?"

"Mister Whisper. He's done this before, hasn't he?" Catriona continued. Duncan tried to quieten her, but she pulled her hand free from his and batted his protests away. "It's him, isn't it? It's the same thing. The teddy. The photo. It's the same!"

"We caught him, Mrs Reid. I can assure you, whoever took Connor, it wasn't..." He rolled the words around in his mouth, as if unable to spit them out. "*Mister Whisper*. Owen Petrie, the man responsible for those children's..."

He caught himself just in time. "The man who took those children, he's in Carstairs. We believe the individual who took Connor is trying to emulate Petrie's abductions."

"He killed them. Didn't he?" Catriona asked, her tone harsh and accusing, daring him to say no. Or praying he would, perhaps. "He killed those boys."

Logan hesitated, then gave a nod. "He did, aye. But we're not dealing with the same man. There's no saying that's his intention with Connor."

"*There's no saying?*" Duncan yelped. He jumped to his feet, his eyes blazing. "That's the best you've got? Our boy's out there, and that's all you can tell us? *There's no saying?*"

"Like I say, I understand it's frustrating, Mr Reid, but—"

"It's not fucking frustrating!" Duncan bellowed, looming over the DCI. "A Rubik's Cube's frustrating. A jar you can't get the lid off. Not this. Not *this!*"

Sinead stood up and took Duncan gently by the arm. "We know. We understand, Duncan. We do. And we're going to do everything we can to get him back home, alright?"

At the back of the room, the kitchen door opened, and Jess, the family liaison officer looked in. Logan dismissed her with a shake of his head and she slipped out of sight again.

The fury that had propelled Duncan to his feet was already burning itself out. He locked eyes with Sinead, and the hand on his arm became the only thing holding him up.

"I'm sorry," he whispered. "I just... I just..."

"You're fine. We get it," Sinead told him. "I understand."

"Of course you do, sweetheart," Catriona said. She reached up and took one of Sinead's hands for a moment. "After what happened with your mum and dad."

Sinead smiled awkwardly, and very deliberately did not meet Logan's inquisitive gaze. Instead, she helped Duncan back down into the chair beside his wife. Duncan kept his eyes on the floor, embarrassed by his outburst.

"He didn't mean that," Catriona said, putting a hand on her husband's shoulder.

"He did," said Logan. "And he's absolutely right. Cards on the table? I can't begin to imagine what you're going through. None of us can. And I don't have a lot of information I can give you right now, but what I can give you is my word. I—we—will not stop until we find who's responsible for this, and get your son back. Whatever it takes, whatever we have to do, we will bring Connor home. That's a promise."

The Reids said nothing, but both seemed to grow in stature a little, buoyed by the speech. Duncan wiped his nose on the sleeve of his creased shirt, screwed the heels of his hands into his eye sockets for a few seconds, then gave a nod.

"What else do you want to know?"

Logan caught Sinead's gaze, then flicked his eyes to the couch beside him. She sat again, pencil poised.

"You said he seemed out of sorts, but was there anything else? Anything specific he said that seemed unusual?"

"No, he was just worried about the dog getting lost. It was only because he was panicking that I..."

His forehead creased. He blinked, caught off guard by something.

"Wait. Ed."

Catriona shifted in the chair so she could look at him. "What?"

"Ed. He asked about Ed."

"Ed who?" Logan probed.

"Next Door Ed?" Catriona asked. "Why was he asking about Next Door Ed?"

"I don't know. He just... He asked if I liked him."

"If you liked *Ed*?"

Logan cleared his throat, drawing their attention back to him. "Sorry, who is this we're talking about?"

"Sorry. Ed, uh, Walker, I think," Duncan said. He looked to his wife for confirmation. "Walker?"

"Ed Walker, yes," Catriona said. "He lives next door."

"Only bought the place a few months back," Duncan said.

"Renting," his wife corrected. She dialled back the certainty a touch. "I think he's renting, anyway."

Duncan shook his head. "He must've bought. He was working on converting the loft just before he moved in, I think. Lot of racket, anyway."

"Which direction?" Logan asked, steering the conversation back on track.

Catriona drew a look to the wall on her left, but said nothing.

"That way," Duncan said, gesturing in the same direction. He sat forward, his frown deepening. "He asked if I liked him, and then he asked if *you* liked him."

Catriona gave a little snort. "What, me?"

Duncan nodded. "Aye. He said, 'Does Mum like Ed?'"

"Why would he ask if I liked Ed?"

"I don't know. I asked him, but that's when he got panicky about Meg."

"I'm sure it was nothing," Catriona said. The abruptness of it made Logan's Polis-sense tingle, but he let it slide for the moment.

"Almost certainly," Logan agreed. "But we'll arrange to have a chat with him."

He stood up. Sinead hurriedly finished scribbling a note, then got to her feet.

"Thank you for your time. You've been very helpful," Logan told them. "If you need anything—anything at all—please just ask..."

He clicked his fingers softly a couple of times.

"Jess," said Sinead.

"Jess. She'll keep you up to date and get you anything you need. And, if the press lot start to get too annoying, you have my full permission to set the dog on them."

Duncan and Catriona moved to get up, but Logan motioned for them to stay seated. "It's fine. We'll see ourselves out. Thank you again."

He turned, caught sight of the pack of vultures loitering out front, and then turned back. "The back garden. Can I get next door from there?"

"Aye, but the dog'll go mental," Duncan said.

"I'm sure we'll cope," Logan told him.

"Are you going to see Ed?" Catriona asked. She shot the briefest of glances at her husband. "Next Door Ed, I mean?"

"Aye," said Logan. He looked over at the dividing wall, then down at the couple in the chair. "We'll at least pop our heads round the door."

CHAPTER TEN

TRUE TO FORM, THE DOG WENT BANANAS WHEN LOGAN STEPPED OUT
through the back door and into the garden. Meg raced for him, barking furiously, fur rising on the back of her neck.

Logan ignored her and plodded down the steps onto the path. The back garden was a little larger than the front, but less neatly turned out.

There were no raised flowerbeds here, no manicured lawn. Just a shed, some stacks of planks, and a whisky cask the size of a caravan. It had roofing felt on top, and Logan had a vague recollection of seeing something similar before.

"Is that a sauna?" he asked, as Sinead stepped out of the house behind him. The dog redoubled its efforts to be an annoying wee bastard.

"Yes, sir."

"A sauna. In Fort William?" the DCI continued. He gestured at the smirr of fine rain falling from the dark grey clouds overhead. "Isn't this, like, the wettest place in Europe?"

"Three years running, sir," Sinead replied, almost proudly. "We got a certificate."

"Well, I hope to Christ it was laminated," Logan replied, pulling his coat closed. He sized the sauna up. "Is that normal?"

"Well, I've not got one myself, sir. But it's got a roof, so I don't imagine the rain's a big problem," Sinead said. "Anyway, I think he makes them, or sells them, or something. He's always advertising them on Facebook."

Down at their feet the dog upped its barking game from 'bananas' to 'batshit'.

"Hello! Yes, I see you. I see you!" Sinead said, baby-voicing the bloody thing. She squatted down, making the dog skitter back away from her, all its weight on its hind legs. "What's all the noise about? Hmm? What's all that noise for?"

"Ignore it," Logan told her.

"Sorry, sir?"

"If you ignore them, they eventually shut up," he explained. "It'll just keep going if you make a fuss."

Sinead held the back of her hand out to the dog. Meg sniffed it, then gave a tentative lick. Her tail wagged as Sinead stroked the top of her head.

"There you go. That's better. See? No need for all the noise."

She stood up, looking just a tiny bit smug.

Logan raised an index finger. "Wait for it."

Meg erupted into barking again, and it was Logan's turn to look pleased with himself. "See?" he said. "Told you. Ignore them. They get bored eventually."

The dog ushered them down the back path and continued to announce their departure as they pushed through the gate and into the alleyway that ran behind the block.

"I'd never endorse cruelty to animals," Logan said, heading for the next gate along. "But I'd happily strangle that bugger if it kept that up."

"Sounds *quite* cruel, sir," Sinead pointed out.

"I'd make it quick," Logan told her. "Big hands."

He held up his hands to demonstrate that they were indeed big.

Sinead smirked. "Should I be writing this down?"

"Probably best not," Logan told her.

They stopped at the back gate of the neighbouring house. Unlike the Reids' gate, this one and the surrounding fence were double-height, making it difficult to see much of the garden or the lower half of the building.

The curtains upstairs were closed in one bedroom, but there were no lights in any of the windows.

"Right. Next Door Ed, then," Logan announced. "Thoughts?"

Sinead's eyes widened a little, caught off guard. "Uh... he's got a big gate."

"He *has* got a big gate," Logan confirmed. "I was hoping for something a bit more insightful and that wasn't currently staring me in the face, but that's a start."

He put a hand on the handle. It had a thumb-operated latch that *clacked* metallically when Logan pushed it down. The gate was a little too wide for the gap, and he had to give it a shove to budge it.

Logan stopped then, the gate ajar. "What happened to your parents? If you don't mind me asking?"

"Road Traffic Accident, sir," Sinead replied. The answer snapped out of her in an instant, like it had been pre-programmed. "Eighteen months ago."

She coughed gently. "Well, nineteen," she corrected, and something about the way she said it told Logan she could've given it to him in hours and minutes.

"Christ. I'm sorry. You should've said," Logan told her. "So now it's..."

"Me and my wee brother, sir, aye," Sinead confirmed.

Logan exhaled through his nose, looked up at the house, then pulled the gate closed. "Let's get you home. I'll come back later."

Sinead frowned. "Are you joking, sir?"

"What?"

"Well... You think he might be in there, don't you? Connor, I mean." Sinead asked. "You jumped up off the couch as soon as they told us he'd asked about Ed. "

"Not necessarily..." Logan began, but it was clear from the way she looked at him that she wasn't buying it.

"That's why you wanted to come in the back way, so the press didn't see."

Logan chuckled drily. "Maybe I'm the one who should be taking notes."

He glanced up at the house again. "Do you know him? Ed, I mean."

Sinead shook her head. "No. Never met him."

"Right." Logan pushed the gate open. "Stay close, follow my lead, and don't do anything stupid."

"Should I radio it in?"

"Remember that 'don't do anything stupid' bit? That would qualify," Logan told her. "We don't want to put the wind up him. Not yet. It's just a routine door to door at this stage."

"Won't us going to the back door make him suspicious?"

"Trust me, if he's kidnapped the boy, we'll soon be the last of his back door's worries."

It took Sinead a moment to understand what the DCI meant. "Oh. Prison?"

"They've been known to be somewhat unwelcoming to certain categories of prisoner," Logan confirmed. "Or overly welcoming, depending on your point of view."

He dropped his voice down low. "Now, mouth shut, ears open. Ready?"

"Ready, sir."

"Well, you fell at the first hurdle on the whole 'mouth shut' thing, but we'll let it slide this time."

Raising a hand, he knocked on the door. It was a classic policeman's knock—loud, no-nonsense, and clearly announcing its intention not to go away until someone answered.

When no-one did, Logan knocked again, even louder this time.

He stepped back and looked up at the windows. The smirr of rain had been promoted to a drizzle, and he had to squint in order to see the top half of the house.

There was a set of chrome-coloured blinds on the kitchen window, slanted at an angle that only let Logan see the ceiling when he tried to peer through.

"Mr Walker? Can you come to the door, please?" he called.

"Maybe he's not in," Sinead ventured, then she immediately realised this was the most obvious thing she could've said, and cursed herself inside her head.

"We'll make a detective of you yet," Logan told her, absent-mindedly. The living room curtains were open, but the window itself was too high to see through.

Logan found a cracked terracotta plantpot and turned it upside down below the window. It creaked ominously when he stood on it, but somehow managed to take his weight.

"See anything?" Sinead asked.

Logan wiped a layer of grime off the window with the sleeve of his coat. The room was dark inside, and barely resembled a room at all. It was more like a campsite, with the only furniture a folding camping chair, a little plastic table, and a pyramid of Tennent's Lager cans, presumably all empty. He wasn't sure that last one technically qualified as 'furniture' but it wasn't the time to split hairs.

A *Pot Noodle* sat on the table, a fork sticking up through the peeled-back foil lid. From his angle, Logan couldn't tell if it was empty, full, or somewhere inbetween.

"Not a lot," he said, stepping down. "But it doesn't fill me with confidence."

He put a hand on Sinead's shoulder. "You should go."

"What? Why?"

"Because I'm telling you to, constable," Logan said, his tone becoming officious. "You've done well. You show a lot of promise, but you should get home. Call it a night."

Sinead looked past him at the living room window, then up at the closed curtains above.

"But... I want to help."

"And that's to your credit." He jabbed a thumb back over his shoulder. "But, in a minute, I'm going to hear a cry for help from within this house, giving me no choice but to break this door down and investigate. It wouldn't be wise for you to be here when that happens."

Sinead chewed her bottom lip. Her eyes searched the house again. "What if we both heard it, sir?" she asked. "I just don't think you should be going in there by yourself."

"I'm a big boy. And I've been in a lot worse places, believe me," Logan told her. He smiled, not unkindly. "Go home, Sinead. That's an order."

Sinead hesitated, then nodded. "Yes, sir," she said. "But... can I make a suggestion?"

Logan nodded. He watched as Sinead leaned past him, turned the handle, and pushed the door open. "It's the Highlands," she told him. "We don't always lock our doors."

"Daft bastard," Logan muttered, although it wasn't clear if he was referring to himself or to Next Door Ed. "Thank you, Sinead," he said, pulling on a thin smile.

Reaching into his pocket, he produced a pair of thin blue rubber gloves, and began the laborious process of wrestling his oversized hands into them.

"Now, piss off before you get us both into trouble."

CHAPTER ELEVEN

THE AIR IN THE KITCHEN WAS OLD AND STALE, FLAVOURED WITH something damp that clawed up inside the nostrils and down the back of the throat.

Logan eased the door closed behind him and listened for any sign of movement from elsewhere in the house.

Nothing.

There were no appliances in the kitchen, just the open voids and trailing wires where a washing machine and oven should've been. Water pooled from the end of a hose in one of the cavities, forming a puddle on the scuffed lino floor.

Outside, the evening was drawing in, and the last of the sunlight had a fight on its hands to get through the blanket of cloud. The kitchen was washed in a gloomy half-darkness, but Logan could see just enough to know that there wasn't a lot worth looking at.

He quietened his breath and moved to the door leading out of the kitchen, the bottom of his coat brushing against his knees.

The living room looked much like it had from the window. Camping chair. Plastic table. Stack of lager cans. They were empty, as he'd guessed, but there were a few unopened tins in a *Spar* bag under the table.

The *Pot Noodle* was two-thirds eaten. Logan touched the side of the pot. Cold, he thought, although the gloves made it difficult to be sure.

There was another window at the far end of the room that looked out onto the street at the front. Logan could see a couple of press vans out there, but the journos themselves were still assembled outside the Reids' house, waiting in the rain for him to come striding down the path.

They'd be disappointed.

Keeping as far from the window as possible, Logan made for the room's second door. It rubbed against the carpet as he eased it open, and he stopped a couple of times to listen for the sound of anyone moving around upstairs that would suggest someone had heard him.

Silence.

On the other side of the door was a small hall, barely larger than the inside of a hotel lift. The house's front door was on Logan's right, an internal door on his left, and then a staircase led up to the floor above.

There was no furniture in the hall, either, just a worn-out old mat, a stack of letters on the floor that mostly looked like junk, and a little mirror fixed to the wall around Logan's chest height.

The door on the left led to a cupboard. A disposable waterproof jacket hung from a hook, and a couple of pairs of trainers had been left on the floor. Logan squatted and picked a couple of the shoes up. There were no size markings inside one of the pairs, but the other had a tag sewn into the inside of the tongue.

Size ten.

Setting the trainers down again, Logan returned to the hallway, and crept to the bottom of the narrow stairs. A bathroom door stood open at the top, the light through the dimpled window mottling the shadows on the staircase walls.

Logan held his breath. Listened.

A couple of cars passed outside. One of the uniforms ordered some over-eager press bastard to, 'Keep back from the gate.'

But, from inside the house, there was nothing.

There were thirteen steps. Every single one of them creaked and groaned beneath the carpet as Logan made his way up, sounding out a fanfare to anyone lurking above.

By the fourth step, Logan decided to abandon his attempts at stealth and just charge up the stairs as quickly as he could. He braced himself as he reached the top, fists clenching, ready for someone to come swinging at him from behind the bannister.

No-one did. The cramped upstairs landing was as empty as the floor below.

There were four doors, including the bathroom. Logan spent a second giving that room a cursory once-over. A similar damp smell to the one in the kitchen loitered around in there, too, thick and claggy in the DCI's throat.

Two of the other doors were open. The other had been pulled fully closed. Judging by position, it was the room with the closed curtains he'd seen from outside.

He checked the other two first. Both bedrooms, he supposed, although they both lacked anything in the way of beds. They both lacked anything in the way of very much, in fact.

One had a threadbare carpet, while the other had bare floorboards that had been badly painted in an ill-judged shade of lilac at some point in the dim and distant past. The décor in both was shabby and long past its best, and Logan got the sense that neither room had been in use for some time.

More importantly than any of that, neither room was occupied, so no big bastards were likely to come rushing up behind him when he entered the other room.

He stole a glance down the stairs, listened for a moment, then turned his attention to the fourth and final door.

The floorboards upstairs were more solid than those on the staircase, and he was able to approach the door in relative silence. He waited outside it, breath held, ear pointed to the wood, ready for anything but prepared for nothing.

There was no point doing all the announcement stuff. He wasn't officially here. Instead, he pushed down the handle and simultaneously put his shoulder to the wood, throwing the door wide.

The smell hit him almost immediately—the sour tang of sweat mixed with the sweeter notes of cannabis. The heavy curtains and lack of light from elsewhere made it hard to make out the details of anything, but there was a single mattress in the corner of the room, a dark lump curled up on top of it.

Child-sized.

Motionless.

No. God, no.

Not again.

Logan flicked the light switch and a bare bulb sparked into life, pushing back the darkness. Logan saw the mattress properly, and the knot in his stomach slackened a little.

A sleeping bag. Just a sleeping bag. That was all.

He gave it a nudge with his foot.

Empty.

The rest of the room was a graveyard of crisp bags, pizza boxes, *Irn Bru* bottles, and other junk-food detritus. Logan carefully opened the lid of one of the cardboard pizza containers. There was half a slice left. Ham and pineapple.

"Bloody savage," he muttered, nostrils flaring in distaste.

Closing the lid, he took out his phone and snapped a photo of the logo and phone number printed on the box.

That done, he patted down the sleeping bag. Tucked in at the bottom was a little wooden box containing half a packet of green Rizla, some torn-up strips of what looked like a cereal box, and a few crumbs of hash that'd struggle to choke a mouse.

He replaced the box, then turned, still crouched, and took another look at the room. It was grim, no doubt about that, but there was nothing to suggest that Connor had been here. Which meant that Logan was officially breaking and entering without anything even vaguely resembling an excuse.

Time to go.

He began to stand, then hesitated. On a hunch, he slipped a hand beneath the mattress. Almost immediately, the side of his pinkie finger bumped against something solid.

Raising the edge of the mattress, Logan found himself staring down at an old battered laptop.

"Shite," Logan spat, torn by the discovery.

Two very different 'next steps' presented themselves to him. He spent a few moments considering the implications of each. Then, reluctantly, he lowered the edge of the mattress again, covering the laptop.

He made for the door, took another look around the room, then switched the light off before stepping out onto the upstairs landing and pulling the door closed.

Logan was at the top of the stairs when a thought that had been niggling at him for the past few minutes pushed its way forward.

His eyes crept up to the ceiling, and to the hatch built into it.

He was working on converting the loft.

A tingling crept up the back of Logan's neck. The thin rubber of his gloves *creaked* as he flexed his fingers in and out.

And then, he stretched up and slid the snib aside. An exhalation of stale air hit him as the hatch swung down, revealing a yawning chasm of blackness.

There was a ladder attached to the hatch. Logan fiddled with the hook until the bottom half slid down to the floor at his feet.

Reaching up, he took hold of one of the rungs and shook it, testing its sturdiness.

And then, with his heart thudding in his chest, he began to climb.

CHAPTER TWELVE

If Next Door Ed was converting the loft, it wasn't immediately apparent what he was converting it into. Logan swept his phone's torch across it, taking it all in.

A few planks had been nailed across the exposed ceiling beams, forming a haphazard pathway leading to the wall that divided this attic space from the one next door.

Or, what was left of the wall, at least. A hole had been knocked through it, the crumbling bricks stacked up on another clumsily floored area. The planks used for the flooring looked like the same ones in the Reids' back garden. Presumably they had been nicked at some point.

The rafters creaked ominously as Logan made his way across the makeshift floorboards. The hole in the wall wasn't particularly big, but large enough for an adult to clamber through, provided dignity wasn't high on their list of priorities.

The loft on the other side of the wall was empty, aside from some thick rolls of insulation between the ceiling joists, and another couple of the same planks Logan was standing on. They had been laid across the insulation but weren't nailed down.

Logan snapped a couple of pictures of the hole, a few of the loft beyond, then did another sweep of the space around him. The wind whistled through gaps in the sloping roof. A percussion of rain played on the tiles overhead.

The oval of torchlight tracked across the exposed beams, and probed the corners where the floor met the roof. Just like downstairs, there was nothing to actively suggest that Connor had been there.

Still, even before venturing into the attic space, Logan had been keen to talk to Ed Walker as a matter of urgency. Now, after this, he was suspect number one.

Technically, suspect number *only*, but Logan didn't really want to dwell on that right now.

After taking another few pictures, he clambered down the ladder, the rungs groaning in protest as he picked his way to the bottom.

Once down, he manhandled the bottom part of the ladder back up into position, then closed the hatch and fastened the snib.

He was halfway down the stairs when he stopped.

Logan stood in the mottled darkness, chewing his bottom lip.

"Bollocks," he muttered.

His eyes flitted upwards in the direction of the closed door.

THE JOURNOS HADN'T EXPECTED him to approach around the side of the house, and Logan was almost back at his car before they spotted him. They moved through the rain like a single organism—one that was generously endowed with limbs and heads, but distinctly lacking in moral integrity.

"Detective Chief Inspector!"

"What is the family saying?"

"Do you know where Connor is?"

Their voices were raised, shouting to be heard over the growing wind. Logan muttered something deeply uncomplimentary and fished his car keys from his pocket. The Focus *chirped* as he thumbed the button, its wing mirrors unfolding as if giving him a welcoming wave.

"Is the boy alive?"

"When will you be making an official statement?"

"Do you have any leads yet?"

Logan shot the approaching throng a glare. If looks could kill, this one would've taken out the whole front row, and probably left the rest of them fighting for their lives in the ICU.

He had just hauled the driver's door open when one voice in particular rose up above the others. One familiar, fork-scraping-on-a-plate voice that stirred some primal response deep in Logan's gut.

Ken Bloody Henderson.

"Is it true there was a teddy and a photo, Jack?"

Logan tried to rein in the look of shock he could feel spreading across his face, but only managed to temper it a little. He stood there, frozen, the car door held open.

The rest of the journalists had fallen quiet. For a moment, it was just Logan and Henderson, eye to eye, the reporter holding his phone out, the microphone aimed at the DCI.

"What?" Logan asked. His mind raced. "Where did you hear that?"

Henderson shrugged nonchalantly. He said nothing, but there was a little smirk on his face that Logan would've dearly loved to wipe off. Ideally, with the sole of his shoe.

"No comment," Logan told him. He jumped into the car and slammed the door shut.

He sat swearing below his breath for a moment, then glanced in the wing mirror and caught sight of Henderson and his gaggle of bastards hanging around behind the car. Grimacing, he fired up the engine and slipped a gloved hand inside his coat.

He took out the *Spar* bag containing the laptop, placed it carefully on the passenger seat, and spent a few seconds considering the ramifications of it.

The car's automatic windscreen wipers kicked in, swishing a slick of rain from the glass and drawing Logan's gaze away from the bag with the battered computer inside.

With a final glance back at the houses, Logan crunched the car into first, pulled away from the kerb, and set off into the strengthening storm.

CHAPTER THIRTEEN

DI BEN FORDE AND THE REST OF THE MAJOR INVESTIGATIONS TEAM eyed Logan warily as he stormed into the Incident Room with a face like thunder.

"It's out," Logan barked. "They know. About the bear. They know."

"Shite," Ben groaned.

"Aye. Shite. You can say that again."

Logan paced back and forth, exorcising the tension that had been steadily building during the drive over.

"Who knows?" asked DC Neish. He had been pinning photographs of the abduction scene to a board on the wall that was already heavily decorated with other pictures and notes. A school photograph of Connor Reid smiled out at Logan, jarring disturbingly with a blown-up version of the image that had been delivered to the parents earlier that day.

"The press. Who do you think?" Logan snapped. "Someone told them. Someone blabbed."

He pointed to the only female detective in the room and clicked his fingers. "DS... sorry."

"McQuarrie, sir," Caitlyn replied.

"Ken Henderson. He's a journalist. Freelance, but writes for the Herald, I think. Bring him in. Put him in cuffs, if necessary. Hogtie the bastard, if you have to."

Caitlyn glanced at DI Forde, then back to Logan. "On what pretext, sir?"

Logan stopped pacing. "On the pretext that I said so," he snapped.

"Jack," Ben soothed. "Wherever it came from, it didn't come from in here."

For a moment, it looked like Logan might dispute that, but then he sighed and shook his head. "Aye. No. I know," he admitted, his tone losing some of its edge. "But there's a leak, so let's find out where."

"On it, boss," said Caitlyn. "Ken Henderson, did you say?"

Logan nodded. "Aye. He might refer to himself as 'Kenderson,' though, on account on him being a massive arsehole. Get him in, and let me know when he's here."

Caitlyn confirmed, unhooked her jacket from a hook by the door, then hurried out, already drawing her phone from her pocket as she left.

With the immediate drama over, Tyler went back to pinning up the crime scene photos. DC Khaled sat at a desk, rifling through a depressingly small bundle of paperwork, and dividing it into different piles.

"Hamza, wasn't it?" Logan asked.

"Aye, sir," Hamza said, looking up. He had a hopeful look on his face, like he might be about to be reassigned to do something more interesting.

"Know anything about computers?"

"A bit, aye. Why?"

Logan fished the *Spar* bag from inside his coat and deposited it on top of the paperwork piles. "See what you can get from that laptop, will you?"

Hamza reached for the bag.

"Wear gloves," Logan instructed. "It could be evidence."

"Shouldn't it go to forensics?" Hamza asked.

"Eventually, aye. But take a wee look first, eh? See if anything jumps out."

"Right, sir."

While DC Khaled went to fetch himself a pair of gloves, Logan rounded on Tyler. "Come back to that later. We need to put out a shout. Ed Walker. Lives next door to the Reids, right-hand side looking from the front. Don't know the number. I think he might be our man. I went round, but there was no-one home."

"Why? What did you find out?" asked Ben.

"The father says Connor was acting strangely when they were out walking. Quieter than usual."

"Aye, that's in his original statement," said Hamza, snapping on a pair of thin blue gloves as he returned to his desk.

"Connor also asked about Walker. 'Next Door Ed,' they call him. He asked if his dad liked him, then he asked his dad if he thought his mum liked him."

"Liked Ed?" said Ben.

"Aye. Connor asked his dad if his dad thought his mum liked Ed," Logan explained, trying to clarify but not making a particularly good job of it.

"And does she?" Tyler asked.

"That's not really the point, is it, son?" Ben said, shooting the younger officer a dismissive look.

"Maybe not, no," Logan agreed. "But I did get the impression that she knew him better than the husband did. Nothing concrete, but I wouldn't be surprised."

"An affair, you think?"

Logan tilted his head from side to side in a sort of weighing gesture. "Doubt it. Maybe, though. But I reckon she's a woman who likes the finer things. Or would like the chance to like them, anyway. Not sure Next Door Ed would fit that description. The house is a shithole."

"Maybe she just likes a bit of rough, boss," suggested Tyler. He waggled his eyebrows suggestively and grinned at both superior officers.

"Is it my imagination, or is he still here?" Logan asked Ben.

"Unfortunately," Ben said. He clapped his hands twice. "What are you standing around here for? Go put out the shout."

"Sorry, Boss," Tyler said, then he turned and hurried out of the room.

Ben waited until he was gone, looked over to where Hamza was hunched over the laptop, then sidled closer to Logan.

"House is a shithole? I thought he wasn't home?"

Logan nodded, not looking at him. Instead, his eyes were fixed on 'the Big Board,' as he'd always referred to it, and the all-too-sparse collection of leads currently pinned to it.

"Door wasn't locked."

"Jesus, Jack," Ben whispered. He pointed to the computer Hamza was working at. "And did you get that...?"

Logan nodded.

"Christ. That's a big bloody risk," Ben warned. "And not just for you, for all of us."

"Aye," Logan admitted. He finally turned in the DI's direction, and there was something dark and hollow behind his eyes. "But you didn't see them, Ben. Last time, I mean. Those kids. You didn't see them."

Ben said nothing. What was there to say?

"I know it's not him doing this. It can't be him," Logan said. "But someone has done a bang-up job of copying him this far, and if they stick to the script and see this thing through, then we have less than two days to find that boy."

He cleared his throat, inhaled through his nose, pulled together his fraying edges. "So, I'll be the one to take the risks. It won't reflect on anyone else. Buck stops with me. You're all just following orders."

"You know that's not how it works, Jack. They won't buy that."

Ben sighed and rubbed a finger and thumb against his forehead, kneading away the beginnings of a migraine.

"What are you saying?" Logan asked.

Ben dragged his top teeth over his bottom lip, scraping at the smoothly shaved skin.

He stopped rubbing his head and nodded, a decision reached.

"I'm saying that the buck stops with both of us," Ben said, keeping his voice low. "We're both responsible. The rest of them aren't."

"Ben..."

"That's the deal on offer, Jack."

Logan briefly considered protesting, but he knew the DI well enough not to waste his breath. Instead, they shook hands and patted shoulders.

"I'll take it, then," Logan said. "And thank you."

"He's a wee boy, Jack," Ben said. "Fuck the risks. Let's just get him home."

"No arguments from me," Logan said, shrugging off his coat.

"Oh, but before you get too comfy, the Chief Inspector wants to see you," Ben said.

"The Chief Inspector? Of what? This place?"

Ben gave a nod. Something mischievous sparkled behind his eyes.

"Shite. Who is it?" Logan asked, recognising that expression. He quickly flicked through his mental Rolodex but came up blank.

DI Forde's mouth curved up into the beginnings of a smirk.

"Jinkies."

A groan burst unbidden from Logan's lips. He finished taking off his coat and let it flop down onto his desk. "Of course," he said with a grimace. "I should've bloody guessed."

CHAPTER FOURTEEN

Chief Inspector Hugh Pickering was sitting behind a large, well-organised desk when Logan entered the office. He was writing studiously in a large notebook, the shiny top of his head pointed to the door, a fountain pen scratching across the paper.

Without looking up, he gestured to the chair across from him. Logan closed the door, stood behind the chair, and waited.

The pen continued to scratch across the page.

"You're making the place look untidy, Jack."

Logan recognised the power play, but had no interest in competing. He pulled out the chair, sat in it, then leaned forward with his hands clasped, so his forearms were resting on the edge of the desk.

"You wanted to see—"

Pickering raised a hand, still not looking up.

Once Logan fell silent, the Chief Inspector lowered his hand and returned to writing.

"I won't keep you."

Logan resisted the urge to point out that he was already keeping him, aware that it would only drag things out further. He sat back and waited.

Pickering had earned the nickname 'Jinkies' on his very first day of training at Tulliallan. It had been coined due to the then constable's striking resemblance to Velma, one of the characters from the cartoon series, *Scooby-Doo*.

At first glance, there had been a passing resemblance, mostly down to Pickering's reddish-brown hair and thick-rimmed glasses. Weirdly, though, the longer you looked at him, the more he resembled the canine-accompanied ghost-hunter.

He had a round face—'Bawchops,' had been another popular designation for a while—and a scattering of freckles across each cheek. Someone had got him drunk one night and talked him into putting on an orange roll-neck jumper, thus cementing his status as, 'What, that guy who looks like Velma out of *Scooby-Doo?*' for the rest of his career. And, if Logan had anything to do with it, far beyond.

Poor Velma had let herself go in recent years, though. Jinkies' distinctive hair had been vacating the premises for a while now, and only a few stragglers were hanging around the edges like the last revellers at a school disco.

His already round face was now substantially rounder and was carrying some extra baggage under its chin. He still wore the glasses, though, and if Logan didn't know better, he'd have sworn they were the same pair.

Jinkies had never been cut out for front line policing. Not really. In some ways, it wasn't his fault. It couldn't have been easy to walk through Sauchiehall Street after closing on a Saturday with some mouthy wee bam shouting, "Fuck me, is that no' her out of Scooby-Doo?" at you at the top of his lungs.

He'd taken a desk job as quickly as humanly possible, and hadn't stepped out from behind one since. At least, not to do anything useful.

From the looks of him, he'd been golfing today. He wore a V-neck Pringle jumper with no sleeves and an eyeball melting diamond pattern knitted into the front. Beneath it, he wore a short-sleeved polo-neck with the top button done up, presumably in some token nod to formality.

Logan couldn't see Jinkies' legs, but he was picturing some truly horrifying checked trousers. Or worse—shorts.

He pushed the image away and was giving serious consideration to grabbing the Chief Inspector's pen and ramming it up his arse when the scratching stopped. Logan watched impatiently as Jinkies scanned over what he'd written, lips moving silently.

Then, with a nod, the Chief Inspector slid the page aside, interlocked his fingers on the desk in front of him, and finally raised his head.

"Jack! Good to see you," he said.

"Hugh," replied Logan, non-committal. "Ben said you wanted to see me."

Jinkies frowned, as if this was news to him. Then, his eyes widened behind his glasses and he bumped his hands against the desktop.

"Ah, yes. I did. That's right."

Logan waited.

But not for long.

"Well? What for?" he asked. "Not sure if you've noticed, Hugh, but we've got a live abduction going on."

Jinkies smiled magnanimously. "That was why I wanted to see you, Jack. I just wanted to let you know that whatever you need, it's yours. "Mi casa, su casa. My house is your house."

"I know what it means," Logan grunted. He checked himself and managed something that was within spitting distance of being a smile. "Thanks, Hugh. I appreciate that."

Jinkies leaned forward a fraction. "But, so we're clear, it is *mi casa*, Jack." He tapped a pudgy finger against the desk. "My house. My rules. You have your team, I have mine. We will offer any and all assistance we can, but they answer to me. Is that clear? To me. Not you. I'm not interested in a *who's got the biggest willy* contest."

This was understandable. Logan had seen Jinkies in the shower. It was a contest the Chief Inspector couldn't hope to win.

"Got it? Mi casa, mi..." The Chief Inspector realised, too late, that he had exhausted his Spanish. "...rulios. Capiche?"

"I'm not here to get in anyone's way, Hugh," Logan said. The words were designed to be reassuring, but the tone of his voice didn't back them up. "But this is a major investigation, and I'm heading the Major Investigations Team. In about..."

He checked his watch.

"...six hours the whole world is going to be watching this case, scrutinising every bloody thing we do. And that's going to be on me, Hugh. Not you. So, I'm going to do whatever I have to do to get that boy home, so if I tell your lads to jump, I want to hear, 'How high?' and not, 'I'll have to run it by the boss.' While that boy is missing, I'm the boss, alright?"

He tapped a finger against the desk, just as Jinkies had done.

"*Mi* casa."

Across the table, the Chief Inspector leaned back, his face searching for an expression but not quite finding one. "We both know that's not how it works, Jack. There's an order of—"

"Today, that's how it works," Jack said, standing up. "And tomorrow."

Two days.

"After that... We'll see where we are."

Logan looked the Chief Inspector up and down, scarcely bothering to hide his distaste. "But don't you worry about it. You enjoy your golf."

He made it to the door without Jinkies saying a word, but stopped when he got there and turned.

"What's the story with PC Bell?"

"Which one's she?"

"Sinead. Young lassie. Parents died in an RTA."

"Oh, her. Yes. She's promising," Jinkies said. He puffed out his ample cheeks. "Nasty business with the accident, though. It was down the lochside. They were headed back up the road from Glasgow, or somewhere, if I recall. Sinead was first on the scene."

"Jesus."

"Don't think it was pretty, by all accounts."

"I can't imagine it would be, no," Logan said. "I want her assigned to my team for this."

Jinkies looked the DCI up and down, then raised a salacious eyebrow. "Bit young for you, isn't she, Jack?"

"Don't judge us all by your own standards, Jinkies," Logan told him. He enjoyed the little flinch the Chief Inspector gave upon hearing his old nickname. "She's a well-known face. Local knowledge. Seems bright. She'll be an asset."

"Plain clothes?"

Logan shook his head. "We'll keep her in uniform. For now, anyway. Could be handy."

Jinkies clicked his tongue against the back of his teeth, then nodded. "Fine. You can have her on your team."

Logan smiled grimly. "Thanks," he said, pulling open the door. "But I wasn't really asking."

IF THE SIGHT OF JINKIES' face had wound him up, the next one Logan saw almost tipped him over the edge.

"Alright, Jack? You going to give me an exclusive?"

"Henderson," said Logan, practically spitting the word out.

The journalist was being led along the corridor by DS McQuarrie. She hadn't cuffed him or, to Logan's immense disappointment, set about him with a baton.

Logan intercepted them outside a closed door. He caught Henderson by the arm, shot Caitlyn a look, and jerked his head in the direction of the door.

"This an interview room?"

"Uh, no. Cleaning cupboard, I think," Caitlyn replied.

"It'll do."

Shoving the door open, Logan bundled Henderson inside. The smug wee bastard went *clattering* into a shelf of polishes and sprays as a single light automatically blinked on above them.

"Watch it, Jack," Henderson smarmed, his weasel smile showing off the gap in his two front teeth. "Don't want to get yourself in trouble again."

"Uh, boss?" asked Caitlyn, peering into the cupboard from out in the corridor. "I'm not sure we should be..."

"It's fine. We go way back," Logan told her, just as the door *squeaked* closed between them.

Henderson straightened and brushed himself down. "No need to be so rough, Jack. You know I'm always happy to help a fine establishment such as yours."

"Who told you?" Logan demanded.

"Who told me what?"

"You know what. Stop wasting my time."

"People tell me a lot of things, Jack. You'll have to remind me what—"

Logan's hand caught him by the front of the jacket. Henderson's smile only broadened as he was pinned against the shelves.

"Police brutality is still a hot topic, Jack. I could get a centre spread out of this."

"Centre spread? Is that still a thing? I thought you'd all been replaced by blogs and Twitter."

"Not quite yet," Henderson said.

Logan sneered. "Are you no' tired of trailing the country looking for dirt to dig up?" he asked. "Aren't you a bit old for all this shite?"

Henderson held the detective's gaze, his smile fixed in place. "Aren't you?"

For a second, maybe two, Logan and Henderson just stared at each other, combatants sizing each other up before a duel.

Then, with a grunt, Logan released his grip.

"Aye. Maybe," he admitted. "The teddy. Who told you about the teddy?"

Henderson smoothed himself down for the second time in as many minutes. "A good reporter never reveals his sources, Jack. You know that."

Logan's jaw tensed. He eyeballed Henderson, but turned his head a fraction towards the door.

"DS McQuarrie?"

"Yes, boss?" Caitlyn's voice was muffled through the door.

"Go get yourself a cup of tea, will you?"

There was a pregnant pause. A moment of hesitation.

"Shouldn't I maybe hang on in case..."

"Caitlyn. Go get yourself a cup of tea."

Another pause, shorter than the last one.

"Yes, boss."

Logan listened until he heard the DS's footsteps fading along the corridor. Then, he unbuttoned the cuff of one shirt sleeve, and began to roll it up.

"Come on now, Jack. There's no need to go acting the Big Man," Henderson told him.

Logan said nothing. He finished rolling up the first sleeve, then set to work on the second.

"I'm sure we can figure something out," Henderson said, his eyes darting briefly down to follow the sleeve's progress. "I'm sure I could be persuaded to help if you were to, say, offer me something I could use. You tell me something, I'll tell you something."

Logan finished rolling up the second sleeve, then opened and closed his fingers a few times, flexing the tendons. He cracked his knuckles. He cricked his neck.

"Nothing major, just a nugget or two. A crumb, that's all," Henderson said. "A fair swap."

"We're talking about a boy's life," Logan reminded him.

"And a man's career. Namely, mine. Maybe that's not as important to you, but it's all relative, isn't it?" Henderson said. He eyed the DCI's hulking great hands, then smiled. "You said yourself, those arseholes online are cannibalising us. Come on, Jack. Scratch my back. What have you got?"

Logan balled his fingers into fists, and the smug look slid from Henderson's face, swept aside by various flavours of panic. Logan allowed himself a moment to savour it, before throwing the journo a bone.

"Ed Walker."

Henderson's eyelids fluttered as if Logan had thrown a punch at him but stopped short of landing it.

"What?"

"Ed Walker," Logan said again. "The neighbour. We're interested in speaking to him."

"You think he did it?" Henderson asked.

"We're interested in speaking to him," Logan said again. "That's all. We're going to announce it in the morning if we haven't found him, so I'm giving you the jump on it. Ed Walker. Write it down."

Henderson tapped the chest pocket of his jacket and smiled. "Don't worry. I'm recording every word."

"Aye. No, you're not," said Logan. He produced a phone from one of his own pockets and passed it back to the journalist. "You need to be more careful with that thing, Ken. They're no' cheap."

Henderson gave his jacket a more thorough pat down.

"How the fu—" he muttered, then he snatched the phone back.

"Now," Logan began. "I've scratched your back. Who told you about the teddy?"

Henderson sniffed and shrugged. "One of the local press boys. Works for one of the weeklies. Tom something. The guy who threw the question away outside the Reids. Him."

"And where did he hear about it?"

"Well, I don't know, do I?" Henderson said. His eyes blazed as he scrutinised Logan's face. "True then, is it?"

Logan sighed. "Aye. Aye, it's true. Looks like we've got a copycat."

"And you think it's this Walker fella?"

"He's a person of interest," Logan said. "That's all at this stage."

"How much interest? Scale of one to ten."

Logan pulled the door open. "Get out, Henderson. We're done," he instructed. "And leave the parents alone, eh? They've already suffered enough."

"Suffering sells papers, Jack. Not nice, but it's how it is," Henderson told him. He followed the DCI out of the cupboard and into the corridor. "Thanks for the information. Very interesting. I'll see myself out."

"Aye, nice try," Logan told him. He beckoned over to where DS McQuarrie was hovering by the canteen door. "Escort Mr Henderson off the premises, would you? And keep an eye on him to make sure he doesn't try to sneak back in."

Henderson grinned, showing off his crooked teeth again. "You know me too well, Jack."

"Well, we've all got our crosses to bear," Logan replied.

Along the corridor, Caitlyn scanned her pass and opened the door that led out to the reception area. Henderson shuffled towards it, head down, already tapping out a number on his phone.

"Oh, Jack?" he said, stopping a pace or two before he reached the door.

"What now?"

"The boy. I hope you find him."

A flash of surprise registered on Logan's face.

"Aye," he said, once it had passed. "You and me both."

CHAPTER FIFTEEN

DI FORDE WAS TALKING TO A COUPLE OF SHIRT-AND-TIES WHEN Logan returned to the Incident Room. One of them, who had been perched on the edge of the DCI's desk, jumped up as if an electrical charge had just shot up his arse.

"DCI Jack Logan, this is DS Boyle and DC Innes," Ben said, hand-signalling his way through the introductions. "They're CID. Offered to clue our lot up with the local gen."

"Good. That's good. Thanks," said Logan, shaking both offered hands in turn. "Don't suppose you know anywhere to get something decent to eat nearby?"

DS Boyle sucked air in through his teeth. "Sunday."

"There's J.J.'s along the road," suggested DC Innes, gesturing off in the direction of the town centre. "They do a good breakfast."

Logan's eyes went to his watch.

"Aye, an All-Day Breakfast, I mean. Sausage, egg, nice bit of black pudding. *Mushrooms*, if you like that sort of thing."

From the way he said it, and the expression on his face, it was evident that DC Innes very much did not like that sort of thing one little bit.

"Sounds good," said Logan.

"J.J.'s is shut."

All eyes went to DS Boyle.

"Shut?" said Innes. "J.J.'s?"

"Aye."

"What, like *shut* shut? Or just shut?"

"Well, no' *shut* shut, but no' just shut. *Shut*," said Boyle, with varying degrees of emphasis. "They're on holiday."

"Oh, so *shut*. Right." Innes nodded, then turned to Logan. "J.J.'s is shut."

"Aye, I picked up on that," Logan said. "Anywhere else?"

Both CID detectives gave this some thought.

"Pizza place in the village," suggested Innes.

"Aye! What time is it?" asked Boyle. He checked his watch. "Aye. That'll be open."

Pizza place. Logan remembered the photo on his phone.

"Want me to ring you something in?" Ben asked.

"Actually, no. Leave it," said Logan. "I might go round in a bit. What time does it shut?"

"Same time Sean Connery gets to Wimbledon, sir," said Innes.

Logan and the others all looked at the DC blankly. Their expression remained unchanged when he continued in an utterly dire Sean Connery impression.

"*Tennish.*"

From the look on their faces, it was obvious that nobody was impressed. Innes wilted, his cheeks burning. Logan decided to gloss right over it and pretend it had never happened. He turned his attention to DS Boyle, instead.

"Ed Walker. Next door to the Reids. Anyone talk to him?"

"Not sure. I'll check. Probably, if he was in," Boyle said. "I'll find out."

"Thanks. And Tom... something. He's been blabbing about the teddy bear. I want to know how he knew about it. He's a reporter for one of the local papers."

"There's just the one," said Boyle.

"Reporter?"

"Paper. Don't know him, though. We'll see what we can find out."

Boyle put a hand on DC Innes's shoulder and guided him towards the door. "If there's anything else, just shout. We all want to see the wee lad home safe."

Logan nodded. "Thanks."

"And try the pizza place. It's good. Well, not *good*, but... good."

"Will do," said Logan.

He watched the DS manhandle the junior officer out into the corridor, and caught a hissed, "Fucking '*tennish*,'" before the door clunked closed behind them.

"They're a good bunch," Ben said. "You'd think they've probably got it a bit easy up here, but they know their stuff. Made some big drugs collars. Like, major."

"Good to know," Logan said.

He looked across to Hamza's desk, where the DC was still hunched over the laptop, his blue-gloved fingers tapping away at the keys.

"Getting anywhere?"

"Well, I'm in, so aye. Getting somewhere. Nowhere exciting, mind. There's not a lot on it."

"Shite." Logan groaned. "Still, good job on getting in. That was quick."

Hamza shrugged. "His password was '12345.' It wasn't exactly rocket science, sir."

"Keep looking. See if anything turns up."

The door to the Incident Room flew open, and Tyler came rushing in clutching a bundle of printouts.

"What have you got?" Logan asked.

"Ed Walker, sir. He's got previous," Tyler announced, waving the bundle. "Just out of a stretch at the Big Hoose."

"Barlinnie? What for?"

"Possession of a Class A, and assaulting a police officer," Tyler replied. He thrust the folder of paperwork into the DCI's waiting hands. "Shocking beard, an' all, although I suppose that's not technically a crime."

Logan flipped open the folder, then whistled quietly through his teeth when he saw the mugshot within. Walker glared sheer contempt back up at him.

"Jesus," Logan muttered. "That is a shocker, isn't it?"

He skimmed through the first couple of pages, then handed the folder to Ben. "We should put it up on the board."

DI Forde opened the folder. "God. You're right. That is a shite beard."

"Any word on his whereabouts?" Logan asked.

Tyler shook his head. "Not yet, boss."

"Keep an eye on the house and start knocking doors," Logan instructed. "Find out if anyone's seen him coming and going since Friday."

"It's getting late," Tyler pointed out, glancing at the clock.

"Good, then we might actually catch some of them at home," Logan replied. "Check if there's any family or known associates in the area. And get his photo and description out in circulation. We need to find him and find him fast. CID said they'll help. Hold them to that."

"Yes, boss."

Logan glowered at him.

"Oh, you want me to... Now? Right."

Tyler scuttled off. Logan pulled the swivel chair out from beneath the desk he had claimed as his own and flopped into it.

He sagged for a moment, tiredness slackening his muscles and dragging him down into the cracked leather of the seat.

A headache had been making itself at home in his skull for the past couple of hours, and felt like it was settling in for the long haul. Hunger wasn't yet gnawing at him, exactly, but it was certainly making its presence felt.

It had been hours since Tyler had brought him that biscuit. Even then, it had only been a Rich Tea, and man could not get by on mere Rich Teas alone.

Well, he probably could, but it'd be a fucking miserable existence.

"You alright?" Ben asked him.

Logan sat up and nodded. "Aye. Aye. Just a long day."

"Looks like your hunch might be right," Ben said. "Ed Walker, I mean."

"Hm."

Ben rolled another chair over and took a seat. "What's 'Hm'?" he asked. "You don't think it's him?"

"I think we need to talk to him," Logan said. He waved a hand. "It probably is. I mean, it's looking like it."

"But...?"

"But how would he know about the envelope? The writing on the front? That's the bit I don't get."

Ben flipped idly through the paperwork. "He'd have to have come into contact with someone who knew. Someone from the original case?"

"Aye. Who, though?"

"Petrie?" Ben hazarded.

"Petrie's a cabbage. Or, so he wants us to believe. He's got a cushy wee number in Carstairs. Compared to where he should be, I mean. He wouldn't risk giving the game away by blabbing to some scrote he didn't know," Logan reasoned.

"Unless he did know him," said Ben.

Logan's eyes narrowed, but he looked unconvinced. "What is Walker? Fifties?"

Ben flicked back a few pages. "Forty-three," he said. He studied the photo again. "Bloody Hell. The years have not been kind."

"We could look for a link between him and Petrie, but I doubt we'll find one. Still, worth a try. Get DS McQuarrie on it," Logan said. "And check for any connection with the original families, too. But discreetly."

Logan's headache stabbed at him. The families. Shite. The arrival of the teddy was going to catapult the story to the front page of every newspaper in the country. It had been twenty years since Mister Whisper had taken Dylan Muir. His parents—not to mention the parents of Lewis Briggs and Matthew Dennison—were about to have it raked up all over again.

He'd have to phone the Gozer, ask him to send officers round to help prepare them for the media shitestorm. Probably too late tonight, but first thing in the morning. The last thing they needed was the polis hammering on their doors in the wee small hours. Not again.

"We need to get forensics into Walker's house," Logan said.

"Going to take time to get a warrant."

"Not necessarily. I'm pretty sure he's squatting there. Find out who owns it, then we can go in."

Ben nodded and reached for the phone.

"Hamza? Get anything yet?"

"A lot of porn, sir. Aye, I mean a *lot* of porn," Hamza said. He tilted his head a little, frowned like an art critic trying to work out the meaning of a masterpiece, then his eyes widened and he quickly clicked the trackpad. "Didn't need to see that," he muttered.

"Anything dodgy?"

"Pretty standard stuff, sir. It's more the quantity rather than the content that's worth noting."

"Anything else?"

"Actually, aye. This is interesting. He did a couple of searches on DNA markers and how DNA evidence gets processed on..."

Hamza tapped at the trackpad.

"Wednesday. Well, no, early hours of Thursday."

Logan and Ben exchanged glances.

"Still have your doubts?" Ben asked.

Logan stood up. "We need to find this bastard, Ben," he said. He flicked his eyes from the DI to Hamza. "We all know what we're doing?"

Ben nodded and punched a series of numbers on the phone. DC Khaled looked up from the laptop.

"Just got a few more folders to go through, sir," he said. "Then, if it's alright with you, there's a couple of things I want to check out on the map."

"We need all hands on deck."

"It won't take long, sir. Just a hunch, but... It might be something."

"Fine. Do it. Then, get yourself a coffee," Logan told him. "I can't see any of us getting any sleep tonight."

CHAPTER SIXTEEN

DARKNESS.

It surrounded him. Smothered him. Claimed him for its own.

He'd always hated the darkness, hated the feelings it conjured up inside him, feelings that burned bright and clear, but which he didn't yet have the vocabulary to put a name to. 'Fear,' yes, but it was something more than that, something deeper, more pure.

The ties were cutting into his wrists. The gag tasted bad in his mouth. Oily. Sour. Foul. A shiny film of snot coated the outside of it, glistening like the trail of a slug.

He snorted in some air. Gulped it down. Tried to breathe. The gag made it difficult. Impossible, sometimes, and his chest held more panic than breath.

He wanted to sob, to scream, to make himself heard. To make the whole world know where he was.

But that would bring the man back. He didn't like it when the man came back. Hated it, in fact. Hated the way he looked at him, hated the way he smiled, hated the way his voice came as a breathless whisper in the half-dark.

He couldn't scream anyway, even if he tried. There was another gag somewhere deep down in his throat—a slab of solid fear preventing everything but the occasional whimper from escaping.

During his more rational moments—those times when he calmed down enough to think straight—he thought he was in a cupboard. The walls felt close and oppressive, his cheeps and whimpers rebounding inside the narrow space. It stank of stale and damp. Foosty, his mum would've said.

He thought of his mum, and sobbed silently in the darkness.

The stench of his own urine had permeated everything in the confined space, but the warmth of it had long since become a cloying coldness around his thighs. His cheeks burned with shame when he thought about it.

The man had seemed annoyed when it had happened. The boy with him had laughed and laughed and laughed until the man had closed the door.

He didn't like the man.

But, he liked the boy even less.

CHAPTER SEVENTEEN

DS McQuarrie stepped back from the Big Board and admired her handiwork. Walker's mugshot had been stuck up, shocking beard and all, and she'd added a few key details about what they knew so far. She'd connected some of it together with lengths of red wool. There weren't many strands, but those there were all led back to Walker.

DCI Logan had handed her another folder full of paperwork to add to the board but had then decided against it and taken it back. It sat on his desk now, open slightly, teasing her with its contents.

It had been over an hour since the shout had gone out about Walker. The forensic team were on their way down the road from Inverness, and extra uniforms had been drafted in from the surrounding areas to help with the search. Fort William was in the process of being turned upside down, but so far there was no sign of the bastard.

"Done, boss," Caitlyn announced. "Anything I've missed?"

Ben Forde twisted in his chair and looked back at the board over his shoulder. "Nothing jumping out. Good work. Jack?"

Logan looked up from a typed-up copy of the notes Sinead had made back at the Reids'. She'd dropped them in at the station on the way home, surmising that Logan probably hadn't had her write everything down for a laugh.

She was going to go far, that one.

He scanned the board. "Shoes."

Caitlyn frowned. "Sir?"

"Shoes. Trainers. He had size tens in the cupboard under the stairs," Logan told her. "And he's knocked a hole through the loft wall into the Reids' loft next door."

"When did he do that?" Ben wondered. "Wouldn't they have heard?"

"They did. The husband, what's his name? Duncan. He thought Walker was doing a loft conversion."

Logan stood up. "Is the liaison still round there? Ask her to find out when they heard it. And has anyone told them about Walker yet?"

"Not that I know of. We were waiting until you gave the word."

"Good. I want to tell them myself," Logan said. He pulled on his coat. "But first, is anyone else hungry?"

"I could eat, sir, aye," said Caitlyn.

"Hamza?"

Across at his desk, DS Khaled looked up from the laptop. What he'd thought were just a few more folders to check had led to dozens more, and he was still clicking through, hunting for anything that might help them figure out Walker's motive, whereabouts, current state of mind, or anything else that might prove useful.

"Sir?"

"Hungry?"

"Eh, aye. Pretty famished, actually. Want me to get something?"

"I'll get it. It's fine. Ben? Pizza?"

DI Forde shook his head. "I've got a packed lunch in the fridge."

Logan hesitated, his coat halfway on. "Packed lunch?"

Ben patted his ample stomach. "Wife's orders."

"Wife's no' here."

Ben looked torn, but it only lasted for a moment. "Go on then. Something meaty. And maybe some of them cheese bite things."

Satisfied, Logan pulled his coat on the rest of the way. "Right."

"And double chips."

"Jesus. I'm no' the Sultan of Brunei."

Ben reached for his wallet.

"Shut up, I'm kidding," Logan told him.

He crossed to the Big Board, took out his phone, and snapped a close-up of Walker's mugshot.

"Anyone else got any particular preference, or will I just get a mix of meat and veggie?"

"Not fussy," said Caitlyn.

"Hamza? Do you need, like... halal, or...?"

DC Khaled's face split into a grin. "Nah, you're alright, sir."

Logan nodded a little awkwardly. "Right. Grand. Won't be long. Phone me if anything comes up."

He marched out of the Incident Room.

A moment later, the door opened again and his head popped around the doorframe.

"By the way, anyone have any idea where the shop is?"

"Oh, and double chips. In fact, double chips twice."

The lad behind the counter glanced up from the till. "Quadruple chips?"

"Aye. If you like," Logan replied. He fished his wallet from his coat pocket. "How much is all that?"

The till *bleeped* a few times. Logan shifted impatiently from foot to foot, watching the lad pick a path through the buttons. "That's..."

Logan sucked air in through his teeth. "That's...?"

"Thirty-eight forty—Wait. No."

More bleeps.

"Forgot the chips."

Logan stood, wallet poised.

"Forty-four forty-five."

Logan muttered something about 'double chips,' then produced his debit card.

"Sorry, we don't take cards."

"What?"

"We don't take cards."

Logan looked down at his card, then up at the kid behind the counter. His face was contorted in confusion, like none of this made any sense.

"You don't take cards?"

"No."

"How can you not take cards? What are we in, the roaring twenties?"

The lad shrugged.

"You seriously don't take cards? In this day and age?"

"There's a cash machine up the street," the kid offered. "But you'll have to be quick, we shut in forty-five minutes."

"I thought you shut at ten?" Logan said.

"We do."

Logan glanced at his watch. "Jesus. Right, fine. How far up the street?"

"About... a mile and a half."

"Fuck off!" Logan retorted, the words tumbling out of him before he could stop them. "*A mile and a half?* It's pissing down."

The kid glanced at the big windows like he hadn't previously noticed the onslaught of water hammering against the outside.

"You could order online," he suggested. "We take cards online."

Logan's mind, which had already been struggling to deal with the fact that this place didn't accept card payments, practically exploded.

"I can pay by card *online*, but not in person?"

"Cash only in person," the employee confirmed. From the expression on his face, it was clear that he'd had this same conversation on several occasions before, and very probably had to go through it on a daily basis.

"Jesus." Logan slotted the card back into his wallet. "Fine. Where's this cashline, then?"

The lad rattled off a concise but detailed explanation without very much thought, reaffirming Logan's suspicions that he was an old hand at this particular conversation. Logan made a mental note of the directions, then opened the door. A gust of wind and a blast of icy rain swirled in, scattering a bundle of menus piled up on the counter.

"Stick it all on now, I won't be long," he said.

"We don't usually start making the food until people come back," the employee explained. "Because a lot of the time they don't bother."

"I'll be back," Logan told him, a touch more *Terminator*-like than he'd intended.

The kid wavered, unsure. Logan let the door close, crossed to the counter, and flashed his warrant card.

"I'll come back. Alright? Pinkie swear."

"Right. OK. Good," the lad said, snapping to a sort of panicky attention. "I'll get it all put on for you now."

"Thank you," said Logan, trying not to sound sarcastic, but failing. As he turned, his eyes fell on the logo on the pizza box. He took out his phone and opened the photo app. "Quick question. Does this guy look familiar?"

He showed the kid the snap he'd taken of Walker's mugshot, and watched as the boy looked at it, his eyes lifeless and disinterested.

"No. Don't know him."

"He's not a customer?"

"Not that I've seen. Why?"

Logan returned the phone to his pocket. "Nothing. Doesn't matter. I'll go get that cash."

He was halfway to the door again when the phone rang. He paused, listening to the kid rattle off a robotic salutation and take an order.

Once the lad had hung up, Logan approached the counter. "Do people phone in orders a lot?"

"Huh? What?" The kid's eyes went to the phone, like the answer might be written there. "Yes?" he said, more like a question than an answer.

"For delivery?"

"Um, yeah. Why?"

"What about Cowie Avenue?"

"What about it?"

"Number sixteen. Ever get orders phoned in from there?"

The kid looked blank.

"Ham and Pineapple."

"You mean a Hawaiian?"

Logan's eye twitched. "I don't want to debate the semantics. Does he ever phone an order in?"

"What?"

Logan rapped his knuckles on the stainless steel counter.

"Wake up. The guy at Sixteen Cowie Avenue. Ham and Pineapple. Does he ever phone in?"

"I think so. Yeah. Yeah, a few times. Why? Is that the guy in the picture?"

"When was the last time he ordered anything?"

"I don't know. I don't work every night."

Logan's nostrils flared. "Well, when's the last time you remember?"

He watched the kid thinking, could practically see the steam coming out of his ears as he ploughed through his memories.

"Thursday, maybe?" he decided. "I think it was Thursday."

Logan sighed, unable to hide his disappointment. "Thursday. Right." He turned to the door. "Get the food on. I won't be long."

"OK," the kid said. Then: "Actually, wait."

Logan stopped.

Turned.

"I *think* he might've phoned in last night, too," the lad said. "But he didn't get it delivered to the usual place."

Something lit-up inside Logan's head. Something fluttered in his chest. "Do you remember where?"

"It'll be written down," said the kid, jabbing a thumb over his shoulder in the direction of nowhere in particular.

Logan's hand slipped into his pocket, reaching for his phone again. "Good. Then hold the food, son," he instructed. "And get me that address."

CHAPTER EIGHTEEN

THE CALEDONIAN CANAL WAS A WORLD-RENOWNED TOURIST attraction, apparently. Logan couldn't really figure out why. It was, as far as he could tell, just a canal like any other. Water. Lock gates. Boats. The usual. Nothing startling about any of it.

Sure, if you were into that sort of thing it was probably nice enough, but it didn't do a lot for him. Maybe it was because it was getting dark.

Or, more likely, because he had more pressing issues to think about.

He sat behind the wheel of the Focus, peering ahead through the gloom at a long wooden houseboat moored a few hundred yards along the canal path, just off a little wooden jetty. It sat low in the water, rocking gently as the wind shoved it around.

The curtains were drawn over the boat's windows. Behind them was mostly darkness, but occasionally an oblong of light would sweep across the curtains from the inside, as if someone was moving a torch around.

"How long until armed response gets here?" Logan asked. He clicked the windscreen wipers on for a moment, clearing the rain away.

"Forty-five minutes, maybe," said Ben from the passenger seat.

Logan drummed his fingers on the steering wheel.

"We can't wait that long."

"Aye, we can," Ben argued.

"No saying what's going on in there," Logan said, his gaze boring into the side of the boat as if some previously latent X-Ray vision might suddenly kick in.

"Well, no, but..."

Ben sighed.

"You couldn't have got me the bloody chips first?" he muttered, then he sighed a second time for effect. "Fine. What's the plan?"

"It's no' really a 'plan' as such. 'Plan' would be stretching it," Logan said. "Is everyone in position? Path blocked further up?"

"Tyler's got a couple of cars and a van up around the corner," Ben replied, motioning ahead to where the towpath curved around to the right. The area on the right of the path was fenced off and thick with trees that nicely hid the vehicles stopped round the bend. "Caitlyn has a crew covering the exits behind."

"Good," said Logan. The door *clunked* as he pulled the handle and shouldered it open. "Right, then. You stay here. Eyes peeled."

As Logan exited the car, Ben clambered clumsily across into the driver's seat. "For Christ's sake, be careful," he warned.

Logan gave him a curt nod, then gently pushed the door just far enough for the mechanism to click into place. He didn't want to risk fully closing it, in case the sound of it alerted Walker.

Pulling his collar up against the rain, then thrusting his hands deep into his pockets, Logan set off walking up the path. He kept to the right, away from the boat, eyes fixed on the path ahead like he had a very specific destination planned, and it wasn't anywhere around here.

His boots made a series of soft crunching sounds on the limestone surface of the path, but he reckoned the sound of the wind and rain against the boat's windows should mask that, with a bit of luck.

The torchlight licked the inside of the curtains. Logan picked up the pace.

He was twenty feet away when the door at the back of the houseboat opened and a wild-haired man in a leather jacket launched himself onto the path.

"Shite!" Logan spat. "Walker, stay where you are!"

Walker clearly wasn't great at following instructions. He set off at a clip, racing away from the DCI, headed in the direction of the bend. He glanced back, and the sight of Logan kicked his legs into higher gear.

"Get him, I'll check the boat." Ben's voice came in snatches from behind Logan, sliced and diced by the storm.

Logan didn't need telling twice. He knew the coat would only slow him down, so he shrugged it off. Then, head down, arms pumping, he set off after the bastard.

His old P.E. teacher had always told him that, 'You might be a big lad, but you can fair move.' Logan demonstrated that again now, his size twelves slamming against the limestone path, propelling him on through the rain like pistons.

Walker was almost at the bend, and was about to run straight into Tyler's team, but Logan very much wanted to be there to see him getting collared.

With a final glance back at the pursuing detective, Walker lumbered around the curve and out of sight. Being unable to see him spurred Logan on. Digging deep, he found some extra reserves of speed, and was soon clattering around the corner himself, chest heaving beneath his now almost-transparent shirt.

The curve went on for a couple of dozen yards. Logan was halfway around it when the worry kicked in. There was no shouting. No raised voices. No barked commands.

He stumbled onto the straight, then hissed when a set of car headlights illuminated, blinding him.

"Stay where you are!" barked a voice from beyond the lights.

Tyler.

"It's me, you daft bastard," Logan spat. "Where is he?"

"We haven't seen him, boss. We thought you were—"

"Bastard! He's gone into the trees."

Logan vaulted over the wire fence that ran alongside the path, misjudged the landing, and went staggering down the grassy incline on the other side, branches whipping at him.

"Well, don't just fucking stand there!" he bellowed back over his shoulder as he plunged on into the woods, gravity and momentum pulling him down the steepening hill.

A van door slid open. Two car doors slammed. Logan heard the fence shake and feet come *thudding* onto the wet grass as he pushed through the trees.

"On the right!" called someone from behind. Logan's eyes shot in that direction and caught a glimpse of a burly figure haring away from him.

The route in front of Logan was uneven and choked with scrub and branches, but it was a dream compared to what Walker had to go through. The beardy-bastard alternated between cursing and sobbing as he struggled through a tangle of jaggy bushes, the thorns ripping at his legs through his faded jeans.

There was a path or road ahead through the trees, maybe fifty feet away. Walker was desperately making his way towards it, but Logan was going to make bloody sure he never got there.

Thundering down the hill, the detective skirted the jaggies, used the trunk of a tree as an anchor point, and swung himself sideways into Walker, hammering him with a shoulder-barge that sent him crashing into the undergrowth.

"Right, then—" Logan wheezed, making a grab for Walker's arm. Walker twisted, swung. Logan caught a fleeting glimpse of something metallic, and then pain exploded across the side of his skull and his legs turned to jelly.

He sensed Walker's movement more than saw it, and grabbed for him. His fingers found the leather jacket, but Walker shrugged him off.

The forest spun. The rain, which had been falling from above now came at Logan from all directions at once, a cyclone of icy droplets that twirled him around and sent waves of nausea flooding through him.

"You alright, boss?"

"Get after him!" Logan hissed. He shook his head and Tyler's face blurred into focus.

Tyler set off again. Logan started to run, but his legs objected, and his head voiced its own concerns with a series of stabbing pains that almost dropped him to his knees.

An uneven line of uniforms in high-vis vests came scrambling past him. Blinking against the rain, Logan was just able to make out Walker stumbling the final few feet towards the edge of the tree-line.

He was going to make it. The bastard was going to make it.

A blue light illuminated directly ahead of Walker as he launched himself onto the road. Logan heard a shout, a grunt, a *clatter*.

"Get off me! Get the fuck off me!" Walker howled.

"Edward Walker? I am arresting you on the suspicion of the abduction of Connor Reid."

That was DS McQuarrie's voice. Logan let out a little groan of satisfaction and slumped against the trunk of the nearest tree, his semi-transparent shirt pinkening down the front with his blood.

"You are not obliged to say anything, but anything you do say will be noted and may be used in evidence."

Logan raised his eyes to the sky, letting the rain wash over him.

"Got the bastard," he said, and then he pushed himself away from the tree, dabbed at his wound with his sleeve, and set off down the hill.

By the time Logan reached the bottom, Walker was already cuffed and in the process of being bundled into the back of one of the cars with the lights flashing. He had been putting up a bit of a struggle, but the sight of the blood-soaked Logan striding closer made him practically throw himself into the back seat.

"I didn't do nothing, alright?" he protested. "I didn't do it."

DS McQuarrie, who had been standing back while a couple of uniforms manhandled Walker into the car, pulled her phone from her pocket and glanced at the screen.

"Boss," she said, showing Logan the message she had received.

Boat empty. No sign of boy.

Logan's face darkened. He tore his eyes from the screen and marched to the car.

"Where is he? Where's Connor?"

"I told you, I don't know!" Walker protested. He was vibrating, tears streaming down his cheeks. "I knew this would happen. I fackin' knew it. I didn't have nothing to do with it, alright? I ain't seen him."

Logan's fists clenched. His teeth ground together.

He slammed the door before he could do anything stupid.

"Get him to the station. Log him in, then get him in an interview room," he instructed anyone and everyone within ear shot. "Do not let him talk to anyone. Do not let him eat or drink. Don't even let him go for a slash. Get him booked in, get him sat down, and get him warned that he had better start talking."

Logan raised his voice to ensure Walker heard the next part. "Or I may not be responsible for my actions."

"You need your head looked at," Tyler said.

Logan turned on him, eyebrows furrowed. "Sorry?"

"I mean, no. I'm not saying you're mental, or anything, sir. I mean..." Tyler pointed to the side of Logan's head, just above the temple. "That might need stitching."

Logan dabbed at the wound with the back of a hand. It came away bloody. Very bloody, in fact.

"Bollocks. Fine. DS McQuarrie, can you...?"

"Hop in, boss," Caitlyn said, indicating her car. "We'll swing by the hospital."

"Right. Thanks," Logan said. He eyeballed Tyler while stabbing a finger in Walker's direction. "Not a bite to eat, not a drop to drink, not a moment to piss. Alright?"

"Got it."

"But try to get him talking before you get him in. If he knows where Connor is, we need to find out pronto."

"Will do, boss."

Bending, Logan brought his face close to the back window of the police car. Walker slid a little further along the seat away from him as Logan glowered at him through the tinted glass.

"I'll see you soon, Eddie."

CHAPTER NINETEEN

Half an hour later, Logan sat in the front seat of Caitlyn's car, gingerly brushing his fingers across three neat sutures on the line of his head where skin met scalp. The car's wipers were *thunking* away, working overtime to push back against the rain.

"I'll tell you, for a wee hospital, they're good," Logan said. "What was that? In and out in twenty minutes? You wouldn't get that down the road."

"Aye, pretty good," DS McQuarrie agreed. "I mean, you did go in flashing your ID and declaring it a police emergency, but still…"

"Never hurts to light a fire under them," Logan said. He gazed out through the windscreen at the police station looming ahead of them. "Does it ever stop raining around here?"

"Occasionally, aye. Nice when it does."

"Shite when it doesn't, though, I'd imagine."

"Oh God, aye," Caitlyn confirmed.

She pulled into a parking space at the side of the station, then flipped the little lever that activated the automatic handbrake. The fact you had to flip a lever seemed to negate the 'automatic' bit, she'd always thought, but it was still better than wrestling with the pull-up handle she'd had in her previous cars.

"Right then," said Logan, unclipping his belt. "Let's go see what Mr Walker has to say for himself."

He caught the door handle, but didn't pull it yet. "I want you sitting in on the interview."

"Me? What about DI Forde?"

"He's tired. He needs a break," Logan told her. "Besides, Ben'll let me get away with murder. I want you keeping things by the book. Alright?"

Caitlyn nodded. "Sure. Aye. No bother."

"Right. Good," Logan said. He pulled the handle and opened the door. "Let's go find that boy."

"You might want to get changed first, sir," Caitlyn suggested.

Logan looked down at his shirt. It was in a hell of a state, quite frankly—soaked through, smeared with dirt, and stained down one side with blood. Between that and the stitches, he reckoned he must've made for a truly horrifying sight.

"Nah," he said, stepping out into the downpour. "Adds to the effect."

LOGAN AND CAITLYN sat across the table from Ed Walker in one of the station's two interview rooms, audio and video recorders listening in and watching on.

Someone suitably junior from one of the local legal firms had been dragged out of his warm house and was scanning through a bundle of documents DI Forde had presented him with when he'd arrived. Lawrence, someone had said his name was, although Logan didn't know if this was his first name or his last name. Nor did he care.

"Sorry. Sorry, won't be..."

Lawrence licked a finger and flipped on a page. His lips moved silently as he quickly read.

Logan's chair creaked as he leaned back and sighed, very deliberately.

"Sorry!"

Walker's head was down, his eyes fixed on the table in front of him. Like Logan, he was still wet, although nowhere near to the extent the detective was, his leather jacket having protected him from the worst that the weather had thrown at them.

"Right. Aaaaand done. Sorry," said Lawrence, dragging his eyes up from the page and setting the document back on the table. "Now, what did you—?"

"Where is he?" Logan asked, brushing the young solicitor's question aside before he could finish it. "What did you do with the boy?"

"I told you, I ain't seen him," Walker said, raising his gaze to meet the DCI's.

"Then why hide? Eh? Why run? Why clout me with a bloody torch?" Logan asked, indicating the sutures on his head. "If you had nothing to do with Connor's abduction, why do all that?"

"Because I've been inside, ain't I?" Walker spat. "I know what you lot are like. Ex-con living next door. Kid goes missing? I know what you'll be thinking."

Logan leaned forward, interlocking his fingers on the desk before him. "Trust me, Eddie, you have *no idea* what I'm thinking. If you did—if you had even the *faintest notion* of what's going on in my head right now—you'd be much more forthcoming with information, I can assure you."

Lawrence shot a look across the table at DS McQuarrie, but she ignored it.

"Where is he?" Logan asked again.

"I told you, I don't know. I only heard about him going missing on Friday night. I haven't seen him since... I don't know, Wednesday, maybe."

"Where did you see him on Wednesday?"

"Coming home from school."

"Did you follow him?"

Walker tutted. "Out the window."

"Right. Out the window. Got you," said Logan. "So, not through the holes you made in his bedroom ceiling, then?"

Walker snorted. "What holes? What are you on about?"

"We'll come back to that," Logan told him. "We're circling around the big issue here a bit, don't you think?"

He slowed his voice down, speaking each word very deliberately in turn. "Where. Is. Connor?"

Walker ran his tongue across the front of his bottom teeth. He ran his fingers through his beard, which was even worse in real life than it had been in the photograph.

"Neverland."

"What?"

"Through the Looking Glass. Outer space." Walker leaned in closer, his voice rising. "I keep telling you, I don't fackin' know where he is! I'd never hurt any kid, never mind him. If I did know where he was, I'd say, but I don't. Alright? I don't."

Logan's eyes became narrow slits. He squeezed his hands together. As long as they were together, they weren't around Walker's throat.

He was annoyed at himself for bringing DS McQuarrie in. And yet, at the same time, relieved she was there.

"What do you mean 'never mind him'?" Logan asked. "What's so special about him?"

"What? Nothing," said Walker. He settled back in his chair, his eyes darting away from Logan.

"Aye there is. You singled him out. You wouldn't hurt any kid, *never mind him.* Why wouldn't you hurt him in particular?" Logan pressed.

"Because he's my neighbours' kid, ain't he?"

Logan laughed. "Neighbours? It's no' Ramsay Street. You're squatting, Eddie. Illegally. Which, in case your crack legal team here hasn't already informed you, is a clear violation of your parole."

Lawrence half-smiled and frowned at the same time, like he'd just heard a joke he didn't quite get, but which he suspected he was the punchline of.

"Isn't that right, DS McQuarrie?"

"Blatant breach, sir," Caitlyn confirmed.

"Shocking violation," Logan reiterated. "Although, would you say it's currently Mr Walker's biggest problem?"

"Far from it. I'd say it's the least of his worries, sir."

"Hear that? The least of your worries." Logan jabbed a thumb in Caitlyn's direction. "And she knows her stuff. Believe me."

He started to count on his fingers. "Let's look at those worries, shall we? Breaking and entering. Squatting. Criminal damage. Possession of a Class B drug. Resisting arrest. Clouting a police officer with a dirty great torch, and... Oh, aye. Lest we forget. Kidnapping."

He shot Caitlyn a sideways look. "Anything I missed?"

"Did you count B&E twice, sir?" DS McQuarrie asked. "The boat."

"The *boat.* God, aye. I forgot the boat." He beamed a broad grin across the table at Walker. "Told you she's good. That's potentially a long stretch. A *long* stretch. I mean, I've been doing this a while, I could probably get you six months for just the state of this shirt alone, never mind what you'd get sent down for for the rest of it."

Sucking in his bottom lip, he shook his head. "No. It is *not* looking good, Eddie. It's not looking good at all."

Logan stopped there for a while, letting the silence worm its way into Walker's head and do his talking for him.

It was important to give it all a bit of time to sink in. Bed down. If you knew what you were looking for during an interview, you could actually see the moment the full gravity of the situation hit them, and watch as the idea of a lengthy sentence and all its horrible repercussions took root in their heads.

Walker was no different. His breathing became short, his eyes shimmered, and somewhere in that badger's arse of a beard, his bottom lip gave a wobble.

Bingo.

"Of course, we could make a lot of that stuff go away," Logan said, dropping his voice to a conspiratorial whisper. "Breaking in. The drugs." He indicated the wound on his forehead. "I'm even prepared to overlook this, Eddie, and I do not say that lightly. Do I, Detective Sergeant McQuarrie?"

"No, boss. You do not say that lightly."

"I do *not* say that lightly," Logan reiterated. "We can do it, too. Me and her. We can make all that other stuff go away. We're nice like that. But you have to tell us where Connor is, Eddie."

"I don't know."

"Come on, Eddie! This is your future we're talking about."

"I don't *know!*"

"I'm running out of patience fast here, so I'm going to ask you one more time," Logan said. He leaned forward, his face twisting into an involuntary snarl. "Where's Connor? What have you done with him?"

"Nothing! I don't fackin' know where he is! I keep telling you!" Walker blurted, tears rolling down his cheeks. "If I knew, I'd tell you, but I don't! I swear, I don't!"

"I think you're lying to me, Eddie."

Walker's face was a scrunched up mess of tears and snot now. His shoulders shook as he sobbed silently, eyes closed.

"Maybe we could take a break," Lawrence volunteered.

"He'll get a break when he tells us where the boy is," Logan said.

"He says he doesn't know," the solicitor said, his tone bordering on apologetic.

"I know what he said. I don't believe him," Logan countered. "What about the teddy? The envelope? How did you know about that?"

Walker sniffed and wiped his eyes on his sleeve. "What teddy? What are you on about?"

"Don't give me your shite!" Logan snapped. His fist thumped the table. Lawrence jumped in his chair. "The teddy you left on the doorstep. With the photo. How did you know about the writing?"

"What teddy? What photo?" Walker asked. He looked to his brief for support. "I don't know what he's talking about."

There was a knock at the door. Logan tutted. "What?"

The door opened a crack, revealing a narrow strip of DC Khaled. "Boss. You got a minute?"

"Kind of busy right now."

"It's important. You're going to want to see."

Logan eyeballed Walker. "I'll be right back. You use this time wisely, Eddie. Think about your options. It shouldn't take you long."

He stood up so he towered above the other man. "You've no' got all that many left."

CHAPTER TWENTY

"THIS HAD BETTER BE BLOODY IMPORTANT."

"It's major, sir," Hamza told him, leading the DCI back into the Incident Room. Tyler Neish stood a good eight or nine feet from DS Khaled's desk, where the laptop was sitting open. Hamza gestured to it wordlessly, then hung back with Tyler while Logan approached.

"What am I meant to be looking...?" Logan began, then his voice trailed off as he got closer and saw what was currently displayed on the screen. "Hang on. Is that...?"

"Aye. Looks like it, sir," Hamza said. "Didn't notice at first, but I spotted it when going back through."

A jumble of thoughts spun around inside Logan's head, none of them quite falling into place. The photo was a gamechanger, no question about it. He just had no idea what the game was going to change into, that was the problem.

"Can you run me off a couple of copies of this?" he asked, pointing to the screen.

Hamza nodded. "It'll take about fifteen minutes. I'll have to get a USB to take—"

"Do whatever you need to do."

Logan turned his attention to Tyler. He noticed that the younger officer had got himself tidied up after the chase through the trees. He looked immaculate, with only a few hairs out of place, and even those had been styled that way deliberately.

"Is the liaison still with the Reids?" Logan asked him.

"Not sure, sir."

"Check and find out. Then, send someone to get Catriona Reid. In fact, you go. Tell her we need to ask her a few questions. Nothing major, tell her, just some background stuff. Keep the husband at home in case anyone tries to get in contact."

"Got it."

Logan looked around the Incident Room. "DI Forde around?"

"He's getting his head down for an hour, sir," Hamza explained. "Thought it was a good time. Plans doing the nightshift, if we need to."

"Right. Fine."

"What do you want me to do with Catriona Reid when I bring her in?" Tyler asked.

"There's another interview room, right? Stick her in that, then come get me."

"It's occupied, sir," Hamza said.

Logan frowned. "What? Who by?"

"Your journalist," Tyler volunteered.

"Henderson?"

Tyler shook his head. "Nah. The other one. The local guy. Fisher, is it?"

"Thomas Fisher," said Hamza.

"Alright, you fucking swot," Tyler teased. "We didn't have to go far to find him, he was out front with the rest of them."

"Right, aye. I'd forgotten about him. Anyone spoken to him yet?"

"Not really, boss, no," said Tyler. "He's sitting in there looking fit for tears, though."

Logan sighed. "Fine. Tyler, go get Catriona Reid. Hamza, I don't hear that printer going."

Hamza practically snapped to attention. Tyler took out his car keys and spun them on a finger, like a Wild West Sheriff with a six-shooter.

Logan turned to the door. "Right, Mr Fisher. Let's get you out of the road."

Tom Fisher gave a throaty little sob at the sight of Logan when the DCI threw the Interview Room door wide open. He stood there in the doorway, one hand on the handle, a shoulder resting against the frame.

The young journalist's eyes widened in horror as he took in the blood on Logan's shirt, and the cakes of dried crimson on the side of his neck.

"I d-didn't do anything!"

Logan smiled, good-naturedly. "Relax, Mr Fisher. You're not under arrest. I just need you to help clarify something for us."

He entered the room but didn't close the door all the way. Tyler had said that Fisher had been close to tears, but by the looks of him now he'd fully succumbed to those at some point, and was now all red-ringed eyes and dried snot.

"Don't worry, Mr Fisher. We're going to have you out of here in just a couple of minutes," Logan soothed. "I just have a question about Ken Henderson."

Fisher frowned. He was younger than most journalists Logan had dealt with, although a lot of the local reporters tended to be that bit less experienced. Not all, of course—Logan had come across some right terriers in the local press over the years—but for some it was the first rung on a career ladder that would ultimately take them all the way to the bottom.

"Who's Ken Henderson?"

"Another journalist. Freelance. Grey hair. Smarmy bastard."

"Oh. Yes. Him. From Glasgow?" Fisher asked. He nodded even before Logan had volunteered an answer. "Yes. I was talking to him this morning. He seemed nice enough."

"Oh, aye. He does seem nice. He seems *lovely*, in fact, when he wants to," Logan agreed. "He isn't, though. You'll want to watch yourself there."

Fisher said nothing. He'd had acne in his younger years, and the scars of it dotted his cheeks. Logan vaguely recalled seeing him in the scrum outside the Reids' house earlier in the day. He couldn't place exactly where he'd been, but he seemed familiar enough.

"Ferguson said you told him about a teddy bear that was delivered to the home of Connor Reid. Is that true?"

Fisher was quick to nod. "Yes."

Logan closed the door. Fisher's eyes darted from the DCI to the door and back again. He shifted anxiously in his seat.

"And how did you come to know about this teddy bear?"

"The Spar. You know, down the road from the house? Not the one up the hill."

Logan had no idea where either of the shops were, but didn't say as much.

"Go on."

"Someone in there was talking about it," Fisher continued. "Well, I mean, everyone was, really. Two women were chatting about it. And an old fella. They said something about it having a ransom note?"

Fisher sucked in a steadying breath, then swallowed. "Is that... Is that true?" he asked.

"I think we'll stick to me interviewing you, son, if you don't mind?" Logan told him.

Fisher blushed and immediately looked away. "I wasn't..." he began to protest, but then clearly thought better of it. "Sorry."

"We're all just doing our jobs. I get it," Logan told him. "So, it was general chatter, was it? About the bear, I mean. You didn't see anything yourself?"

"No. I mean, yes. I mean... People talking. That was all. I just... I passed it on. Ken, was it? He said we should keep each other in the loop with stuff, so I told him about it."

"Aye. That sounds like him," Logan said. "I'm guessing he hasn't been quick to keep you 'in the loop' at his side?"

Fisher blushed again and shook his head.

"No, thought not."

"There was..."

The young journo's voice fell away.

"What?"

"Nothing. I mean. No. I mean... It was just that he didn't seem surprised or anything," Fisher said. "About the teddy and the ransom note, or whatever it was. He didn't seem surprised."

"You think he already knew?"

"I'm not saying that, no. I'm not..." Fisher shook his head. "He probably was surprised, just didn't show it."

"Aye," said Logan. "Probably."

He opened the door.

"Right, thanks for your time."

Fisher's face almost collapsed in on itself with relief. "That's it? I can go?"

"You can go," Logan told him.

The legs of the young journalist's chair scraped on the floor as he rushed to his feet. He was at the door when Logan stopped him.

"One thing, just quickly," the DCI said. "Could you tell me where you were on Friday around one-thirty in the afternoon?"

The boy looked flustered. For a moment, Logan thought he might burst into tears again right there in the doorway.

"It's just for our records, that's all. Nothing to worry about."

Fisher's brow furrowed. His eyes flitted left to right, desperately searching. "I don't... Friday? I'm not..."

Something slotted into place and he let out something that was part-sob, part-cheer. "Friday. Lunchtime? Yes, I was doing an interview!" he said, sounding like he'd never been more happy about anything in his life. "Mary Grigor. Her cats keep going missing."

It was Logan's turn to frown. "What?"

"Her cats. They keep going missing. She's had four disappear in the last three months."

Fisher squirmed a hand down into the pocket of his too-tight jeans. "Hang on, I've got a picture."

Producing his phone, he tapped the screen a couple of times, then swiped with his thumb. "No, no, no, not that... There."

He turned the phone so Logan could see the photograph displayed on screen. A woman in her eighties, or thereabouts, sat in a worn old armchair, keeping a firm grip on an unhappy-looking cat.

"She had five," Fisher explained. "Well, no, she had three, then she lost two, so she got another—"

"It's fine. I don't need her life story," Logan said, gesturing for him to put the phone away. "And there's been no sign of them? The cats."

Fisher shook his head and slipped his phone back into his pocket.

"Has she reported it?"

"I think so, yes. She said she had, but she's a bit... dottled."

"Aye, I can imagine. Someone at the paper can verify you were at her house around lunchtime?"

"No, probably not," Fisher admitted. "They know I covered the story, but... Wait. No. They can! I sent the photos across right after. Probably about... ten to two? I'm sure if you check with Mary, she'll be able to tell you I was there, too."

Logan flashed him the thinnest of smiles. "That won't be necessary, Mr Fisher. Like I say, just for our records. Thank you again for your time, and sorry for the inconvenience."

He held the door open and motioned for the journalist to go through. "I'll have someone see you out."

DS Khaled was lurking out in the corridor when Logan and Fisher emerged from the room. He immediately offered the DCI an unmarked cardboard folder. "Those printouts you wanted, sir."

"Grand. Swap," said Logan, taking the folder. "Can you see Mr Fisher out. Get someone to give him a run home."

"It's OK. I've got my bike," Fisher said. "I only live around the corner."

Logan looked past him to the window. The rain was no longer sideways, but was still coming down. "You sure? You'll get soaked."

For the first time since arriving, Fisher smiled. "It's the Highlands. We're used to it."

"Ha. Aye. Fair enough," Logan said. "Thanks again for your time."

He gestured for Hamza to lead the journalist out to reception, then turned and flipped open the folder. Two faces gazed up at him, both smiling.

"Right then," he muttered, when the door through to reception clunked closed behind him. "Let's see what this is all about."

CHAPTER TWENTY-ONE

How long had it been quiet, out there beyond the door? An hour? A day? He couldn't tell. All he knew was it was dark, and he was cold, and he was scared, and that he wanted, more than anything, to go home.

His wrists hurt where they were tied. His legs were numb. His throat was raw from keeping his sobs inside. He risked letting one out now. It was muffled by the gag across his mouth, but the sound was enough to startle him, to send electric shocks of panic coursing through his veins.

What if they heard? What if they got angry? What if they hurt him?

Tears came at the thought of them hurting him. He didn't want them to hurt him.

Not again.

He'd seen what they had done to the cat. What was left of it. It had looked like roadkill when the boy had brought it to him on the tray, all bright red flesh and exposed white bone. The smell had been horrible. It had forced its way up his nostrils, turning his stomach and making him feel sick.

He had almost been sick when the cat had moved. Its head had twitched. A wet, mournful sort of sound had emerged from its mouth, and the boy had erupted into delighted laughter before skipping off with the tray held high like some sort of trophy.

The man had appeared a moment later. The man had stared in around the edge of the door as he inched it shut, sealing him back inside the cupboard.

That had been a while ago. He hoped, for the cat's sake, that it was dead by now.

Alone in the darkness, he prayed that he wouldn't be next.

CHAPTER TWENTY-TWO

"HAVE ANY CHANGES OF HEART WHILE I WAS AWAY, EDDIE?" LOGAN asked, settling back into his seat. "You ready to tell us where Connor is yet?"

"I already told you. I don't—"

"You don't know, aye. You did mention that," Logan said.

"For the benefit of the recording, DCI Logan has now re-entered the room," Caitlyn announced.

"Sorry, aye. Always forget that bit," Logan said.

He placed the folder on the desk in front of him, one hand on top of it to keep it closed.

"How do you know the Reids, Eddie?"

Walker's eyes went to the folder, then back to the DCI. "How do you think? I live next door to them."

"And that's it, is it? That's the extent of it."

"What do you mean?" Walker asked.

"It's not a hard question, Eddie. I think it's pretty clear. Before you illegally moved in next door to them, had you ever met either Mr or Mrs Reid?"

The eyes flicked to the folder again. This time, they lingered for a moment before Walker dragged them back up.

"No."

"No? You've never met them?"

The solicitor, Lawrence, cleared his throat. "Detective Chief Inspector, I think—"

"Shh," Logan told him. He tapped a finger on top of the folder, beating out a slow, steady rhythm. "I'm going to ask you again, Eddie. And I want you to *really think* about the answer this time, alright? Really try for me. OK?"

He leaned forward in his chair. "Did you know either Mr or Mrs Reid prior to the day you moved into the house next door to theirs?"

Walker opened his mouth to respond. Logan raised a hand to stop him.

"At-at-at. Think before you answer, Eddie. Take your time to consider your response before you say anything."

Logan tapped his finger against the folder again. Slow. Steady.

Tik. Tik. Tik.

"No," said Walker, although he sounded even less convincing now than he had been. "I didn't know either of them."

"Uh-huh," Logan mused.

Then, without a word, he opened the folder and slid one of the photographs across the table so it was directly in front of Walker. He handed the other copy to Caitlyn, who looked significantly more surprised by it than Walker did.

"That's you in that picture, Eddie. Right?"

Walker's gaze was fixed on the image. He nodded once, but said nothing.

"And can you tell us, for the benefit of the tape, who that is you're pictured with?"

Walker's eyes met Logan's across the table, wide and defiant. "Fuck you."

"Language, Eddie!" Logan scolded. He shrugged. "Fair enough, I'll say it."

Reaching across the table, Logan tapped the smiling face of the woman next to Walker in the photograph. His arm was around her shoulder, pulling her in close. "That's Catriona Reid."

Walker's brief, Lawrence, leaned over and peered down at the photo. His eyes flitted to Walker, then back again. He hadn't come into the interview room particularly confident, but now he looked positively crestfallen.

"So, what happened there then, Eddie? Slip your mind, did it?" Logan pressed. "Because you look pretty close in that photo."

He turned the picture around so it was facing him on the desk. "You look better without the beard, if you don't mind me saying. How long ago was this taken? Ten years?"

Walker ground his teeth together, as if chewing over his answer. "Eight."

"Eight? Right, so..."

Logan groaned.

"Jesus."

"Boss?" asked Caitlyn.

"Eight years. That was *eight years* ago," Logan said. He glowered at Walker, speaking more quickly as things slotted into place. "DNA. You were looking up DNA."

"So?" Walker grunted, shifting in his chair.

"You think he's yours, don't you? Connor. You think you're his dad."

"What? No! No, nothing like that."

"That's it, isn't it? You think he's your son," Logan said. "Is that why you took him, Eddie? Is that why you grabbed him?"

"I didn't! It wasn't me! You've got it all wrong."

"Have I? Then explain it to me, Eddie. Because right now, the story I've got up here..." He tapped the side of his head. "...it all makes sense. It's no' pleasant, but it makes sense. You think he's your son, so you took him, and tried to throw us off with the teddy bear and the envelope."

"What fackin' teddy bear? I don't know what you're on about!" Walker yelled.

And then, like a switch had been flicked, something changed. His breathing and movements, which had both been growing wilder, became slower, more controlled. He clasped his hands on the table top in front of him, a sort of resigned tranquillity falling over him.

"I want a lawyer."

"You've got one," Logan told him.

"A proper one. Not this useless prick."

Lawrence looked briefly put-out but didn't voice any objections. If anything, he looked relieved.

"Stop wasting time, Eddie. Where's the boy? Where's Connor?"

Walker leaned forward. "I don't know. I mean it. I've got no idea," he said, his voice measured. "Which means that someone's still got him. He's out there now somewhere, and you ain't doing nothing about it. You ain't even trying."

He sat back. "Now, I ain't saying anything else until I get a proper lawyer."

He glanced briefly in Lawrence's direction. "No offence."

"None taken," said Lawrence. He already had his briefcase on the table, and was shoving his notepad and pen inside.

Logan stood, his face a storm cloud of contempt. "DS McQuarrie. Put Mr Walker in a cell."

He shot her a sideways look. "We do have cells in this place, right?"

"We do," Caitlyn confirmed.

"Good. Right. Pick the worst one and chuck him in it," Logan instructed. "We'll continue this after I've spoken to Mrs Reid." He picked up the photo from the table and tucked it back into the folder. "Maybe she'll have something more to tell us."

CHAPTER TWENTY-THREE

CATRIONA REID LOOKED DRAWN AND TIRED, ALL HER PREVIOUS nervous energy having long-since burned itself out. There was a greyness about her, a flatness to her hair, a lack of flesh-tones to her skin. Logan had seen it before. He'd watched grief and fear sepia-tone too many other parents just like her.

Catriona looked up as Logan and Caitlyn entered the interview room. Her face was in turmoil, wrestling with itself, part resigned acceptance, part refusal to believe what her head was telling her.

"You found him, didn't you?" she blurted, tripping, stumbling, and almost choking on the words. "You found him."

Logan closed the door. "Who?"

Catriona visibly flinched. "What do you mean, 'who?' Connor. You found him. He's dead, isn't he? You found him and he's dead."

"No. It's nothing like that," Logan assured her. "To the best of our knowledge, Mrs Reid, Connor is still alive and unharmed. We have nothing to suggest otherwise, and getting him home safely is still the focus of our investigation."

"He's... He's alive?"

"We believe so, yes."

Catriona broke. That was the only way to describe it. Whatever last vestiges of resolve had been holding her together collapsed, and she buried her face in her hands, sobbing with what most people would assume was relief.

And it *was* relief.

Partly.

Logan had never had to go through what Catriona was going through, but he'd seen it often enough, and had been involved in some frank and forthright discussions with other parents at similar moments.

Relief was a big chunk of it. The majority of it, probably.

And yet, as much of a relief as it was to be told their son or daughter was still alive, it only fuelled the little nagging voice that told them that their child might well be suffering somewhere right now, and reminded them there was nothing they could do to stop it.

At this very moment, Catriona was probably picturing unspeakable tortures being inflicted upon her son. She'd be watching him cry, hearing him calling out for her, hopelessly, desperately.

Sure, he's alive, the voice would be telling her. *But at what cost, Catriona? At what cost?*

"Caitlyn, go get Mrs Reid a cup of tea, would you? I'll have one, too, if you don't mind?"

DS McQuarrie glanced sympathetically at Catriona Reid, then nodded. "Of course. Will do."

Logan's stomach growled like a hungry animal. This did not go unnoticed.

"And I'll bring the biscuits, sir."

Once Caitlyn had left, Logan sat across the table from Catriona Reid. He'd had the forethought to bring a box of tissues in with him, and she gratefully plucked a few from the opening on top to wipe her eyes and blow her nose. He set the box and the folder containing the photographs down on the table, the tissues much closer to her than to him.

"Thank you," Catriona said, her voice taking on a flat, expressionless tone.

Logan had seen this before, too—the battening down of the hatches, hammering any and all emotion into submission before it could bubble over and become unmanageable.

"You're welcome. How are you holding up?" Logan asked. It was a stupid question, and one he already knew the answer to. It was written all over her face.

Catriona sniffed. "About what you'd think."

"And how's your husband doing?"

"He still thinks it's his fault," Catriona said. She looked away. "I'm trying not to."

"It isn't. You can't watch your kids twenty-four-seven, much as we'd all like to," Logan told her. "The only person to blame for this is the person who took Connor. Your husband shouldn't hold himself responsible. And neither should you."

Catriona nodded, but it was disinterested, like she was humouring him. "I'll try," she said, then her head twitched a little, like something had just flicked her. "Oh. I almost forgot to say. The teddy. The one that was delivered?"

"What about it?"

"We checked. It isn't Connor's."

Logan's chair creaked beneath him as he shifted his weight. "It isn't?"

"He has one a bit like it, but we found that in his..." Her chest tightened as it all hit home again. "It was in his bed."

Catriona cleared her throat a few times, trying to free it up. "But the one that was delivered, it's not his."

"Right. OK," Logan muttered, his mind racing as it tried to figure out what, if anything, this new piece of information meant. He filed it away to come back to later. "Thanks for that. Really useful."

The door opened behind him, and Caitlyn entered carrying a tray of mugs, a scattering of sugar sachets, and a little carton with a dribble of milk in the bottom.

"Here we go," she said, setting the tray down. Logan nudged the folder aside to make room, and Caitlyn began distributing the mugs. They were all colourful and mismatched. Logan's had the *Maltesers* logo emblazoned across the side and had originally probably come with an Easter Egg inside.

Catriona Reid wrapped both hands around her mug as if warming them. She stared into the dark depths and breathed in the steam.

"Thank you."

"No bother at all," Caitlyn said, relocating the milk, sugar, and a plate of biscuits from the tray to the table.

She placed the tray on the floor, propped up against the table leg, then moved to take a seat beside Logan. He motioned with his eyes for her to sit next to Catriona, instead. It was an interview of sorts, yes, but the last thing the poor woman needed was to feel like they were ganging up on her.

Logan's stomach grumbled. There were three biscuits on the plate—a digestive, a hobnob, and a Tunnocks Caramel Wafer. He knew which one he had his sights on, but a nagging sense of decency made him wait.

"Biscuit?" DS McQuarrie asked Catriona, indicating the plate.

Catriona peered at the plate, blinking slowly, as if seeing some sort of weird alien specimen for the first time.

"Oh. No. Thank you."

Logan had the Caramel Wafer in his hands before Catriona had finished talking. "Sorry," he said, taking a chomp out of the end. "Starving."

"DCI Logan has been working around the clock to bring Connor home," said Caitlyn, filling in while Logan munched his way through the chocolate biscuit. "We all have."

"But you haven't found him," Catriona said, just a touch accusingly.

"Not yet, no. But we think we're close. We have some really strong leads."

Logan swallowed, spent a few seconds, running his tongue across his teeth, then took a glug of tea. There was no sugar in it, but the lingering sweetness of the Tunnocks did the job.

Clearing his throat, Logan picked up the folder. "Mrs Reid, you're probably wondering why I asked you to come in and see us. First up, let me assure you, you're not in any kind of trouble at the moment."

"Trouble?" Catriona echoed. She frowned. "What do you mean *trouble?*"

The tail-end of the sentence hit home.

"What do you mean *at the moment?*"

"What can you tell us about Edward Walker?" Logan asked.

Across the table, Catriona sat up straight, practically squaring her shoulders. "What? What do you...?"

The effort became too much. She sagged, and as she did all the fight went out of her.

"It wasn't him," she said. "I should've told you. But it wasn't him."

Logan opened the folder and placed the photograph between them. It had been taken in what looked like some kind of American Diner, judging by the food on the table, and what could be made out of the background.

Catriona and Ed Walker were sitting on the same side of the table, close together, him with his arm around her. They were both smiling, although Walker looked a touch more relaxed about it than Catriona did.

The photograph seemed to come almost as a relief to her now. Her face attempted something that wasn't quite a smile but was headed in that general direction.

"I never actually saw that picture before," she said. "It was in Inverness. We'd arranged to meet up."

"This was taken around eight years ago. Does that sound about right?"

A jerk of Catriona's head confirmed it. "A few months before Connor was born. I'd been seeing him occasionally. We were just sort of... getting to know each other, I suppose."

Catriona took another tissue and blew her nose. "I never told him. I was going to, but then Ed just disappeared. Prison, I eventually found out, but..." She shook her head. "No, I never told him."

"This is going to be a difficult question, Mrs Reid, but it's important you answer truthfully," Logan said. He watched for something in her eyes that told him she understood, and continued once he'd seen it. "Is Ed Walker Connor's father?"

Catriona's eyes widened. Her voice, once she found it, was incredulous with disgust. "What? No! Of course not! Is that what you think? That I'd...? No! *No!*"

"Could he believe he's Connor's father?"

"No! Of course he couldn't," Catriona insisted.

"So—and, again, apologies for the bluntness of this question, Mrs Reid —you're saying you never slept with him?"

"Slept with him? What are you talking about? Of course I didn't sleep with him!"

Catriona's voice was becoming higher, her emotions betraying her and making a mockery of her attempts to rein them in. "He's not Connor's father. *Of course* he isn't Connor's father," she said.

"He's *mine.*"

CHAPTER TWENTY-FOUR

LOGAN STOOD IN THE FOYER OF THE STATION, WATCHING DC NEISH'S car pull out of the car park. He caught a glimpse of Catriona Reid in the front passenger seat as the car turned onto the road, but then a streetlight reflected off the glass, hiding her, and the car rolled off into the night.

"Didn't see that coming," said DS McQuarrie.

"No. Nor me," Logan admitted. "Should've, though."

Catriona Reid's story had seemed legitimate enough, once she'd explained it.

Growing up, she'd never known much about her father, other than the constant reminders from her mother that he was a no-good waster who'd had his wicked way, then cleared out at the first sign of a belly bump.

She'd been trained to hate him by rote, and had always insisted to her then fiancé, Duncan, that she had no interest in ever finding out where he was, what he was doing, or why he had turned his back on her all those years ago.

And then, he'd found her through Facebook, and all that had gone out the window.

She hadn't told anyone about their meetings. It would've killed her mother, and after her claiming complete disinterest in the man for years, Duncan wouldn't have understood.

But she'd met him. She felt she should hear him out. And, more importantly, that he should hear her out. She had a lot of questions, and the opportunity to get some answers had been something she couldn't bring herself to pass up.

To her surprise, he'd answered them all honestly. He'd messed up. He wasn't ready. He let her down. He'd thought about her every night for years, wondered where she was, what she was doing. All that stuff.

To her amazement, she'd found herself warming to him. They'd arranged to meet again. And again. And again. Each time they did, she found herself enjoying his company more. He was funny. Smart. Kind. So far removed from everything her mother had told her.

And then, out of nowhere, he'd stopped contacting her. All efforts to get in touch with him had failed. He'd vanished. He'd left her, all over again. And, she hadn't even got a chance to tell him he was going to be a grandfather.

Eight years later, he turned up. He contacted her online, explained he'd been in prison. She'd resisted at first, but it had been her who had eventually suggested the house next door. Although, to be fair, she'd expected him to rent it, not just move himself in.

"But he didn't take Connor," Catriona had insisted when Logan had suggested it. "I went round there on Friday night. I asked him. I even searched the place. He didn't know anything. I could tell. He didn't know anything about it."

Logan turned from the window, yawning. His eyes went to the clock on the wall. After one. Jesus, when did that happen?

"Still think Walker took him, sir?" Caitlyn asked.

Logan grunted. "I wish I did. Be easy, then."

"Where are we if it wasn't him?"

"Back to square one," Logan admitted.

Caitlyn clicked her tongue against the back of her teeth. "Aye. I was afraid you might say that."

"We'll have to talk to Walker again, but it can wait until the morning. My instinct is that he's not a kidnapper, just a bloody idiot," Logan told her. "Mind you, have the forensic boys been over the house and the boat yet?"

"They have, sir. Still waiting on the report."

She looked at the clock, then double-checked on her watch. "Probably be the morning now."

"Aye. Probably. You should get some sleep in the meantime. Not a lot we can do right now," Logan said. "Did you get a hotel sorted?"

"I did, sir. Premier Inn. You?"

Logan shook his head. "No. I'm fine."

"There's an empty office upstairs. The CID guys sometimes use it if they're pulling an all-nighter. You should try to sleep."

"Hmm? Oh. No."

"You said yourself, sir. Not a lot we can do right now," Caitlyn reminded him.

"Thanks for your concern, Detective Sergeant. But I'm alright. Honest."

"Bollocks you are."

The voice crackled from a speaker above the reception desk. Officially, the station was shut down for the night, and there was nobody manning the counter.

Even with the echo and slight hiss of static, Logan recognised the voice as that of Detective Inspector Ben Forde. He searched the corners of the room for a camera, then gazed up into its single eye.

"I'm up and about, Jack," Ben said. "I'll keep a watch on things. You go get some rest. And, for God's sake, get yourself cleaned up, man."

Logan looked down at himself, and the dirt and blood that stained his clothes. Jesus, what must Catriona Reid have been thinking?

It wouldn't hurt to get an hour or two, Logan supposed. It had been a long day, and it was going to happen all over again tomorrow, but with the potential to be much, *much* worse. There was certainly an argument to be made for getting some kip.

"Right, well just make sure—"

"Aye. Don't worry. I'll wake you if anything happens," Ben told him. "Now go. You're no use to anyone if you're dead on your feet."

Logan nodded reluctantly, then turned to DS McQuarrie. "Back here at eight, alright?"

"Yes, sir," Caitlyn said. "See you then."

"Aye, see you then," Logan told her. "Oh, and Caitlyn," he added, as she headed for the door.

"Yes, sir?"

"Bring some more of them Caramel Wafers when you're coming back in."

Caitlyn smiled grimly. "Yes, sir," she said. "I'll see what I can do."

CHAPTER TWENTY-FIVE

THERE WAS A BATON IN HIS HAND. COOL. RIGID. LOGAN COULDN'T SEE it, exactly, but he could sense it. He knew it was there. Poised. Ready.

Useless.

The door to the flat was locked, like always. No time for formalities. Never any time to waste. It flew open with a kick—flew away, maybe—and a rush of warm, putrid air rushed past him like the breath of a dragon.

Or the contents of Pandora's Box.

He was inside the flat now. The smell wrapped around him, its flickering fingers of green the only visible thing in the otherwise empty void. He could feel it, hear it, *taste it* all around him. The mulchy stink of rot, and decay, and of things long dead.

His grip tightened on the baton.

From the darkness, he heard a voice. Two voices. Three.

Boys. Children.

Victims.

They clawed at him, tearing at his skin with their scratchy sobs, exposing the flesh beneath.

"Why didn't you save us?"

"Why didn't you come?"

"Why? Why? *Why?*"

The scene shifted. Elsewhere in the flat now. Lights on. Stench stronger than ever.

A cupboard. A door. A hand, reaching for a handle. His hand, he thought, although he wasn't in control of it. He was a passenger. An observer. A bystander, nothing more.

The handle turned. The door opened. Three dead boys cried somewhere behind him.

And from the cupboard came the nightmares. From the cupboard came the sorrow.

From the cupboard came the bones.

CHAPTER TWENTY-SIX

THERE WAS A FACE HANGING OVER HIM, LOOKING DOWN. LOGAN HAD it by the throat before he was fully awake, forcing it back from him, keeping it at bay.

His brain caught up a moment later, and quickly persuaded his hand to release its grip.

"Shite, sorry. Sorry," he said, wincing and raising his hands in a gesture of surrender. "You alright?"

"My fault," said Sinead, rubbing her throat just above the collar of her uniform. "I shouldn't have startled you. You weren't waking up."

"No. Wasn't your fault, it was absolutely..."

He blinked in the glow of the sunlight streaming through the blinds. "Wait, what time is it?"

"Just after eight, sir."

"*Eight?*" Logan gasped. "In the morning? Jesus. Why did no one wake me?"

"Maybe worried about being throttled, sir," Sinead ventured.

Logan gave a little snort. "Aye. Aye, that might be it. Sorry again. But, Jesus Christ. Eight."

"Chief Inspector Pickering said you wanted to see me. I reported in, and DI Forde told me to come wake you," Sinead explained.

"Right. Good. What else did Jinkies tell you?"

"Not a lot, sir," Sinead replied. "Just that you wanted to see me."

It pleased Logan immensely to know that the rank-and-file were fully up to speed on Pickering's nickname. There hadn't been so much as a flicker of confusion on Sinead's face, either, suggesting the name was old news to her.

Excellent.

"Did I do something wrong?" Sinead asked.

"No. Nothing like that. The opposite, actually," said Logan. He started to stretch, but then caught a whiff of his armpit and hastily aborted. "You did good. I want you working with the MIT on this. You've got local knowledge, and you seem to know your stuff."

Sinead looked flabbergasted, but it only lasted a moment. She'd processed the shock quickly, and was now moving on. Always a good sign.

"Thank you, sir. I don't know what to say. I won't let you down."

"I'm sure you won't, Constable," Logan said. He yawned into his hand, then gave himself a shake. "Now, let's go talk to DI Forde and find out the latest."

Sinead looked him up and down in one swift flick of the eyes. "You think you should maybe...?" she began, then she pointed over her shoulder. "I think there's some spare shirts next door."

Logan regarded his own shirt. It had been in a pretty shocking state the night before, and a few hours spent tossing and turning in an office chair hadn't done it any favours.

"Aye, good call," Logan said. "And, if you happen to stumble upon a can of deodorant anywhere, I wouldn't say no."

———

"SLEEPING BEAUTY AWAKES," said Ben, grinning at Logan as he and PC Bell entered the Incident Room. "I was starting to think you'd died up there."

"Aye, you wish," Logan replied, fastening his tie and adjusting it as best he could by touch alone.

Ben gave a tut, then stepped in and fixed it properly, before straightening the DCI's collar. "I'll be wiping your arse for you next."

"Again, you wish," Logan said.

Ben's nostrils flared, his face becoming a mask of revulsion as he looked Logan up and down.

"No, I don't actually know why I said that," Logan admitted. "Sorry. Probably best we don't ever speak of it again."

"Aye," said Ben. "You wish. That'll be going in the staff newsletter."

He motioned vaguely in the direction of the reception.

"Tyler's bringing bacon rolls in for us. He should be back in a few—"

The door opened and DC Neish almost walked straight into the back of Sinead.

"Oh, sorry. Didn't see you there," he said.

"You're alright," Sinead said.

"Tyler," said the DC, repositioning his stash of white paper bags until he had a hand free. He offered it to Sinead. "I mean, Detective Constable Tyler Neish."

"Sinead. Bell. Sinead Bell."

"Nice to meet you."

Sinead smiled back at him, then stepped aside when Logan thrust a hand out in the DC's direction, palm open. "Hurry up. I'm famished here."

"What are you on for, boss? Bacon, square sausage—?"

"I don't care," Logan said.

Tyler selected a bag at random and deposited it in the DCI's hand like an offering to the gods.

"Thank you."

"Any time, boss."

While Logan stalked off to his desk, Tyler flashed Sinead an apologetic smile. "Sorry, I didn't know anyone else would be here. You can have mine, if you like."

"I'm fine, ta. I ate this morning."

"Oh, thank Christ," said Tyler, visibly relieved.

He continued past her, opening one of the bags and peering inside. "Hamza. Cheese salad roll, you freak."

Hamza, who had been staring intently at the monitor of his PC, Meerkatted up from behind it at the mention of his name.

"Shut it, ya dick," he said, placing his hands together and opening them for a pass. He caught the bag, winked theatrically to celebrate his catching prowess, then diverted his attention back to the screen.

"Detective Sergeant McQuarrie, bacon, link, or square sausage?"

Caitlyn seemed to wrestle with her conscience for a few seconds, then held a hand out. "I'll take the link, then, if no-one else wants it."

"I'm not fussed," said Tyler, passing over another bag.

"Whatever's going for me," said Ben.

"Right you are, sir," said Tyler, holding out a bag.

"Just not the square sausage," Ben added.

Tyler hesitated for a moment, then swapped bags. "Sorted. Bacon it is."

Sinead shifted awkwardly, watching the others settle down to eat. "Should I make tea, or something?" she asked.

Logan forced down a lump of his dry roll. The bacon was so crispy it could cut glass, and he was pretty sure it lacerated his throat on the way down.

"You're not here to make tea, Constable. You're a valued and respected part of this team, no' a skivvy," the DCI told her. He gestured with the half-eaten roll. "Tyler can make the tea."

"What? I got the rolls!"

Sinead backed towards the door. "It's not a problem. You're all eating. I don't mind. Might as well make myself useful."

"I can think of a few ways she could make herself useful," Tyler muttered, once Sinead had left.

A lump of diamond-hard bacon *pinged* off the side of his head.

"Ow!"

"DC Neish, if I ever hear you speaking like that again about one of my officers, or anyone else for that matter, then we're going to have a big problem," Logan warned. "Is that clear?"

"No, I didn't mean..." Tyler began to protest, but there wasn't really anywhere for him to go with it. "She seems nice, is all I was saying."

"That wasn't what you were saying. But you're right. She is. Hence why you're not going to be allowed anywhere near her," Logan told him.

He addressed the rest of the group.

"If anyone hears DC Neish making similar comments again, or witnesses him attempting to ingratiate himself with Constable Bell, you all have my permission to kick the living shite out of him. Everyone clear?"

The responses were all far too enthusiastic for Tyler's liking. "It's not what I meant," he mumbled, then he filled his mouth with a big bite of roll to stop himself getting into any more trouble.

The rolls were polished off. The tea arrived. Introductions were made. And then began the process of getting everyone—Sinead in particular—up to speed.

As all this was taking place, DS McQuarrie worked her magic with the Big Board, scribbling notes on Post-Its and sticking them in place, connecting Walker and Catriona Reid with another length of red wool, and generally reorganising things based on what they now knew.

"You're good at that," said DC Khaled, watching her over the top of his computer.

"We sent her on a course," said Ben. "Two days of sticking things to a wall. Taxpayers money well spent."

"It wasn't *just* sticking things to a wall, sir," Caitlyn protested. "I mean, aye, it was *mostly* that, but they gave us lunch, too."

Once the Big Board had been fully updated, Logan and the others took a few moments to study it. There was more information on it this morning than there had been the night before—no question about that. It was just that Logan had his doubts as to whether any of the information was useful, or if the board was essentially just a collage of meaningless bullshit that told them very little.

"Preliminary forensics on Walker's house and the boat came in around half-seven," Ben said.

"Anything?" Logan asked.

"Not a sausage. Nothing to suggest Connor was anywhere near the place."

"What about the loft?" Logan asked. "Walker was pretty insistent that he hadn't been up there."

"Nothing back on that yet," Ben said. "I'll get them chased up."

"They'll give us it when they have it," Logan said, taking a sip of his tea. He considered Walker's mugshot over the rim of his cup. "I hate to say it, but I don't think it was him."

"The loft?"

"Any of it," said Logan. "Duncan Reid said the work in the loft was done before Walker moved in. Could've been someone else."

"Walker's our best lead at the minute," Ben pointed out.

"Best? He's our only bloody lead," Logan replied. "But I still don't think it was him. It doesn't make sense. I don't think he knew about the teddy bear, and I can't figure out how he'd know about what was written on the envelope in the original case."

"He had been inside," DS McQuarrie reminded everyone. "Some of the lags talking, maybe?"

"Unless he was locked up with Owen Petrie in Carstairs, nobody should've known about that envelope," Logan said. His eyes glazed over a little, a memory taking over. "And the way it was laid out. The spacing, or whatever. It was spot on. I mean, like, *spot on*. He couldn't have heard about it, he'd have to have seen it. And how could he have seen it?"

The others had to admit that they had no idea.

"We'll keep him in for now, we've got a few hours left before we have to decide if we're going to charge him," Logan reasoned.

"We'll be charging him for the head injury, I assume?" Ben said. "If nothing else."

Logan appeared momentarily surprised, then brushed his fingertips across the neat stitches. "No. Aye. Maybe. We'll see if we need an excuse to hold onto him."

A silence fell over the Incident Room as they all went back to studying the Big Board. Sinead stood at the rear of the group, her arms wrapped across her middle. She wasn't quite sure what she was meant to be looking at, exactly, but she was looking damn hard at it, regardless.

It was Tyler who eventually asked the question most of them were thinking.

"So, if Walker doesn't have the kid, who does?"

"Not important," said Logan. He finished his tea and set the mug down on his desk with a *thunk*.

"Sir?"

"The *who* can wait. It's the *where* we need to worry about," the DCI continued. "If the kidnapper is determined to replicate the Petrie case—and he's been doing a bang-up job of it so far—then Connor has less than twenty-four hours left."

Logan looked across their faces. "I'll say that again. Connor Reid has less than twenty-four hours left to live, unless we get our fingers out and find him."

He gave that some time to sink in. But not much. They couldn't spare much.

"So, does anyone have anything? Anything at all?"

"Email in from the forensics guys," said Hamza, as his computer gave a *ping*. "They're loading everything they've got so far onto HOLMES. We should start seeing it in ten minutes."

"That's something," Logan said.

"I might have something else, too, sir," Hamza continued. "But it's a stretch."

"I'd rather be stretching than sitting here scratching my arse. What is it?" Logan said. He gave Hamza a quick once-over, noting the slightly rumpled appearance, and the fact he was wearing the same clothes as yesterday. "Have you been at it all night?"

"Aye, sir. Fell down a bit of a rabbit hole with a lead."

Hamza took a Sharpie from the pen pot on his desk and approached the Big Board. "You know I said I had a long shot I wanted to look into?" the DC began. "It might be something."

He studied the map for a moment, then drew a circle around a spot about three miles north of where Connor Reid went missing.

At first glance, there was nothing in the circle but trees and a section of track. It was only as Logan looked closer that he saw a tiny black rectangle there, slap-bang in the middle.

"What's that? A house?"

"Aye. Well, kind of, sir. It was a croft. *Ravenwood*, it's called. Derelict now, from what I can tell on Google Maps. Been no one living there for decades. There's a few places like this dotted all over the area, so I thought I'd have a check through the Land Registry and see if any of them were interesting."

"And this one was?" asked Ben.

"It was, sir. Aye. It changed hands about twenty-two years ago. Current owner's some Indian company who probably just bought it for the land, but never did anything with it," Hamza said.

"You and me have a very different definition of 'interesting,' mate," said Tyler. He grinned at Sinead, started to wink, then caught the daggers Logan was shooting in his direction and turned his attention back to Hamza.

"That's not the interesting bit," Hamza concluded. "It's the previous owners. Limited company. Shell company, basically, but one of the directors of that company was *another* limited company."

Something tickled down the length of Logan's neck. Somehow, he knew. Even before Hamza said the words, he knew.

"Petrie Construction."

DC Khaled tapped his pen against the little black rectangle. "Owen Petrie used to own that house."

CHAPTER TWENTY-SEVEN

He hadn't known. How could he not have known?

Years back, Logan had combed through every file, every document, every damn scrap of paper connected to Owen Petrie, building the case that would keep him inside for the rest of his life.

He'd had access to bank accounts, tax returns, bloody *Primary School reports*. He'd turned the man's whole life inside out and upside down, and compiled a report on everything he'd found.

For a while, he could recite Petrie's assets from memory, including those of his construction company. There was a point when he could've told the court how many teaspoons the bastard owned, and fairly accurately described their condition.

But he had a house. Another house, tucked away in the Highlands.

And Logan had known nothing about it.

"When was he there?" Logan demanded.

Hamza puffed out his cheeks. "Hard to say, sir. Not sure he was ever actually there. Looks like it was bought by the company with a view to developing, but it never happened. But the company owned it between..."

He consulted a Post-It note he'd left stuck to his computer monitor.

"1992 and 2001," Hamza concluded.

Logan reeled. "Jesus Christ."

He stepped in closer to the map and stared intently at the black rectangle, like he could somehow see through the roof and into the building below. "Dylan Muir," he murmured.

"What's that, Jack?" asked Ben.

Logan tore his eyes from the map and turned. "Dylan Muir went missing in 1999. The bodies of Petrie's other victims were found in or around properties he owned. We never found Dylan. We found his clothes, and Petrie admitted to killing him, but he's never told us where to find the body."

"Isn't he brain damaged now though, sir?" Tyler asked.

"Allegedly, aye," said Logan.

"You think Connor could be being held there now?" asked DS McQuarrie.

"Connor? No. That wouldn't make any sense," Logan said. He looked across their faces. "Petrie didn't do this. You do understand that, yes? Petrie's not involved."

"Is it possible that Petrie wasn't responsible for—" Sinead began, then an urgent shake of DI Forde's head cut her off before she could finish.

The warning came too late, however. Logan's face darkened. "No, Constable, it's not possible that he wasn't responsible for killing those boys. I know, because I was there. I saw what he'd done. Alright? Owen Petrie is guilty. And Owen Petrie is safely under lock and key a hundred-and-fifty miles away."

"Right, sir. Sorry, sir," Sinead said, her cheeks burning. DS McQuarrie caught her eye, and offered a reassuring smile. Or possibly one of condolences.

"Do I think we'll find Connor Reid at that house?" asked Logan, addressing the room as a whole. "No. No, I don't. Of course not. Do I think we'll find Dylan Muir?"

He glanced back over his shoulder at the map. "Aye. Maybe."

"I'd like to go check it out, sir," Hamza volunteered.

"You need to get to your bed," Logan told him. "You've done enough. That was good polis work, Hamza, but this has waited twenty years. It can wait another few days."

Hamza gave a grateful nod. "Thanks. But, I'd really like to see it through, sir. I could take a quick drive up that way on the way to the hotel. It'll only take twenty minutes."

"Fine. Swing by and take a look. But don't go trampling around the place. We'll have to arrange a full search. Is there a ground radar team locally?"

Logan shook his head.

"What am I saying? Of course not. We'll have to get one brought in. Forensic archaeologists, too."

"You want to take Tyler with you?" DI Forde asked Hamza.

"No. We need him here," said Logan. "We can't spare the resources."

"Could be dangerous, Jack," Ben said.

Logan shook his head. "You're at it, too. Owen Petrie does not have Connor. He can't. Hamza, if you want to take a look, feel free, just be careful. Phone in when you're done, then go get some rest."

"Will do, sir. Thank you."

"You might want to go out the side door, mate," Tyler told him.

"Eh? How come?" Hamza asked.

"You mean, you don't know?"

"Know what?" Logan asked.

Tyler looked from Hamza to the DCI and back again. "You haven't been outside?"

The penny dropped for DCI Logan. "Aw, bollocks. Press?"

"Aye, sir," confirmed Tyler. "You can say that again."

LOGAN AND BEN FORDE stood at an upstairs window, gazing down at the scrum below. Four uniforms were in the process of trying to corral twenty-two parasitic bastards into a makeshift holding pen they'd put together using a couple of plastic barriers they'd borrowed from the building site across the road.

The journos were firing out questions. Logan couldn't hear them, but he could guess the sort of thing—wildly insensitive, massively speculative, and occasionally stomach-turning. The officers down there almost certainly hadn't had to deal with this sort of thing before, but from what Logan could tell, they were handling it admirably, with just the right balance of politeness and utter contempt.

Ben eyed the crowd of reporters. He didn't despise them to the extent that Logan did, but then he didn't have as many reasons to.

They all pushed forward behind the barriers, arms stretching, mouths moving. A zombie horde.

"You'll have to give them something," he said.

"A bloody good hiding would be my preferred option," Logan grunted.

He scanned the crowd, expecting to see Ken Henderson somewhere near the front. But no. For once, Henderson wasn't in amongst it.

Small mercies, Logan thought.

Although, if Henderson wasn't making an arsehole of himself here that just meant he would be making an arsehole of himself somewhere else.

"We should get onto the liaison. Check the Reids are alright. If this lot are here, it'll be worse over there."

Ben nodded his agreement. "I'll get someone on that."

He took a breath, then shot the DCI a sideways look. "You seen the headlines yet?"

"No. But I can guess. 'Mister Whisper Returns!' is it?"

"Pretty much, aye. Just the Scottish papers for now, but a couple of the UK-wides have put it on their websites. The Gozer's coming up the road to handle the press conference later today. Caitlyn's preparing a report for him now."

"The Gozer? How come he's coming up? I thought someone from up north would handle it?"

"Assistant Chief Constable's request, apparently," Ben replied. "She's very keen he should do it. Can't imagine he's thrilled at the prospect."

"You can say that again. Suits me, though. Means I don't have to talk to this lot," Logan said. He cast a look to the mostly clear blue sky and sighed. "The one day you want it to be raining."

"Aye. Where's a bloody great downpour when you really need one?" Ben agreed.

There was a knock at the door. It opened without waiting to be told, and DC Neish appeared in the doorway. "Boss?" he said, although it wasn't clear which of them he was directly addressing. "Update on HOLMES."

Tyler gave a backwards tilt of his head, indicating for the other two men to follow. "I think we've got something."

CHAPTER TWENTY-EIGHT

LOGAN STOOD BY TYLER'S DESK, FACE TO FACE WITH A MUGSHOT ON the computer screen.

He was an ugly bugger, whoever he was. Scrawny, dirty, and with all the hallmarks of a long standing heroin habit. One side of his face drooped like he'd had a stroke, and his mouth was a graveyard of worn brown stumps.

"Who am I looking at?" Logan asked.

"He's..." Tyler began, but then he stepped aside and motioned to PC Bell like a compere welcoming a new act to the stage.

"Forbes Bamber, sir," Sinead said. "Local scrote. Harmless enough, but got a string of shoplifting charges, and various drugs-related stuff. He's a pain in the arse, but I wouldn't peg him for something like this."

"Then why have we?" Logan asked. "What's come up?"

"Fingerprint," said Tyler. "From the envelope that was delivered with the teddy to the Reids."

Logan perked up. "Now you're talking. Delivery man, maybe. He might be able to ID whoever gave it to him."

"I wouldn't hold my breath, sir," Sinead said. "He's usually pretty wasted."

"Well, here's hoping," Logan said. He turned back to DC Neish. "Anything else come through?"

Tyler Alt-Tabbed to another window on his desktop. "Nothing yet, sir. Shouldn't be long."

"OK. Fine. Go back to the junkie."

Tyler clicked the mouse. Bamber's face flashed up like a prop in a Ghost Train.

"You've dealt with him before?" Logan asked Sinead.

"God, aye. We all have. No saying he'll remember me, though."

"Well, let's go see if we can jog his memory," Logan said, grabbing his coat. "Tyler, keep an eye on HOLMES. If anything new comes in, text me."

"Gotcha, boss."

Pulling on his coat, Logan took a look around the Incident Room. DS McQuarrie was typing up the report for the Gozer, her fingers darting impressively across the keys in stark contrast to Logan's usual single-digit prodding.

"Hamza left?"

"Aye. He's going to swing by that croft, then go get some kip. We've to phone him if we need him," said Ben.

"He'll check in though, aye?"

"Aye. Once he's had a look he's going to give us a ring and let us know he's clear."

"Good. Right. Then, I'll leave everything in your capable hands," Logan said. He turned to Sinead. "My car's out front, and I don't fancy walking past that shower of bastards. Am I right in thinking all the polis vehicles are out back?"

"Yes, sir," Sinead confirmed.

"Good. We'll take one of those. You can drive."

Logan stood in front of DI Forde and held his hands out at his sides. "Tidy enough?"

Ben flicked a crumb from the DCI's lapel. "I suppose you'll do."

"Right, then," Logan said. His coat swished behind him as he turned and stalked towards the door. "Let's go pay Mr Bamber a visit."

———

"Bloody hell," Hamza muttered as a front tyre hit another pothole, bouncing his car violently around on the narrow track.

He was crawling along, but the holes were too frequent to avoid, and deep enough that there wasn't much he could do when he hit one except grit his teeth, grip the wheel, and try not to bite off his tongue.

His phone was mounted in its holder on the dashboard, Google Maps open and tracking him. Or trying to track him, at least. It was currently accusing him of being several hundred yards away from the closest road, and seemed to be under the impression that he was driving through a stream.

Occasionally, the little triangle representing his car would randomly teleport to another location nearby, spin in clueless circles for a few seconds, then snap back to its original position.

The phone signal was patchy, and the upcoming section of map hadn't downloaded. As a result, Hamza was about to drive into a perfectly square beige-coloured void, with no idea what awaited him.

So much for bloody technology.

He was reaching into the glove box for the map when a sheep launched a Kamikaze run. It bounded out onto the track directly ahead of him, bleating furiously and stamping its feet like some self-appointed Guardian of Sweet-Fuck-All.

Hamza hammered the brake, churning up the shale beneath the car's wheels. He cursed as the back end spun into a skid, all his police driving training going completely out the window as he wrestled frantically with the wheel.

The car *thumped* into another pothole. The sudden stop threw Hamza forward in the seat and sent his phone clattering into the passenger footwell.

Hamza took a moment to check nothing was broken, then looked out over the dash. The sheep glowered in at him with its big boggly eyes. It gave an accusing *baa*, then trotted across the track, up the banking, and into the trees that lined the left-hand side.

"Thanks for that," Hamza called after it.

Then, with a tut, he unfolded the map, glanced around him, and tried to figure out where he was supposed to be going.

FORBES BAMBER SWAYED in the doorway of his house, scowling out at the morning sunshine, and the two police officers standing on his step. His eyes were taking it in turn to blink, like they'd fallen out of sync at some point, and had never been able to get their timing right since.

If you were being generous, you might describe Bamber's house as a 'detached two-bedroom'. That was, on a strictly technical level, correct. In reality, it was a hideous concrete cube not much bigger than a shoebox, with barely an ant's pube-width gap between it and the two identikit hovels on either side.

A good Estate Agent could also argue that it had a garden, although they'd gloss over the fact it was eight feet long, made of broken bricks and rubble, and covered in dogshit.

Bamber stood in what might generously be described as a porch. There had presumably been an internal door hanging in the frame behind him once—the holes in the wood suggested the presence of hinges at some point —but it had been removed.

The sound of a child screaming came through the opening. It wasn't a scream of pain or fear, but rather one of those high-pitched screeches some kids liked to do for the sole purpose of being annoying. Judging by the hollered, "Fucking shut up!" the screams earned from a female voice further back in the house, it was proving to be a successful strategy.

"Ye can't come in," Bamber said. His voice was a slur that dribbled through his rotten teeth and down onto the front of a filthy t-shirt that was big enough to drown him. A faded print on the front of the t-shirt showed a grinning blue cartoon character with a white hat and glasses.

Irony, thought Logan, *thy name is Brainy Smurf.*

Other than the t-shirt, Bamber was dressed in mismatched socks and faded grey boxer shorts that Logan didn't even want to think about.

"We don't want to come in," The DCI said. This was true. The last thing Logan wanted was to set foot inside this house.

"Ye need a what-do-you-call-it to come in. The paper 'hing."

"A warrant," said Sinead. "Well, we do, and we don't."

"Again, though, we don't want to come in," Logan reiterated.

"Warrant, aye," mumbled Bamber, his brain slowly catching up. "Have ye got wan o' them?"

"No. We don't have a warrant," PC Bell admitted.

"Cos, if ye don't, ye're no' getting in."

Bamber pointed to the ground.

"'At's my garden."

Logan twitched, irritated. "What?"

"'S my garden," Bamber said. "'S my property, an' that. Ye're no' allowed on my property."

"Well, we are..." Sinead said.

"Naw, yer no'. I'll call the polis."

Sinead shot Logan a glance. "We are the polis, Forby. That's why I'm dressed like this."

Bamber leaned back and peered down his nose at her, as if just noticing her outfit for the first time. "Seriously? You're the polis?"

"Aye."

He wiped his nose on his bare arm, leaving a silvery trail along it and briefly revealing the crook of his elbow that was a pincushion of red dots and bruising.

"If you're the polis, ye need wan o' them 'hings before ye can get in. What's it called?" Bamber slurred. "Ye shouldnae even be in my garden."

Logan had had enough. Bamber yelped as one of the DCI's hands clamped down on top of his head and tore him out of the house. Logan marched along the path, dragging Bamber by the hair.

"Hoi! Fuck off! Ye can't do this!"

Logan opened the gate, pulled the struggling scrote through it, and slammed him hard against the outside of his fence.

"There, now we're not on your property," the DCI hissed. Ignoring the potential health risks, he was right up in Bamber's face, a hand still clamped on his head. "Now, Forby. I've got some questions for you. Are you going to help me out by answering them?"

Logan tightened his grip on Bamber's hair, drawing a sob through those rotten tooth-stumps.

"Or am I going to get to do this the hard way?"

CHAPTER TWENTY-NINE

HAMZA SAT IN HIS CAR, HIS EYES FLITTING FROM THE MAP SPRAWLED open across the steering wheel to the ramshackle house that slouched in the trees ahead of him.

It was bigger than he'd been expecting, more of a manor house than a croft. The forest had been working to claim the ground back for a while now, and a tree was growing out through one of the building's downstairs windows.

Like the rest of them, this window had been boarded over, but the tree had made short work of that, and the square of plyboard now lay rotten on the ground in front of the house.

"Is this it?" Hamza wondered aloud. He fished around in the footwell until he found his phone, and checked Google Maps. He had one bar of phone signal, but no data connection. According to Google, he was right in the middle of a desert, with nothing of note for miles in any direction.

It wasn't too far off the mark, he supposed.

With nothing to tell him from this distance if he was in the right place, Hamza refolded the map, tossed it onto the passenger seat, then got out of the car.

Birds chirped and tweeted and hoo-hoo'ed from the treetops, singing to him as he turned towards the house. He locked the car, more out of habit than any worry that someone might try to nick it out here. Unless the squirrels were crafty bastards, he was pretty sure he didn't have to worry about that.

The forest had closed in around the back of the house, making it almost completely inaccessible. The front was mostly mud, stones, and weeds, with the track Hamza had followed, leading off past the building to the left. If the map was right, it came to a stop half a mile or so further on, becoming just a footpath that eventually led in a wide loop around to the main road half a day's walk away.

Picking his way through the mud, and avoiding the gloopy brown puddles as best he could, Hamza approached the house.

A nagging voice still told him that this couldn't be the place, although the only thing he had to base that on was the mental picture he had of traditional croft houses. He had no idea where that mental picture had originally come from, though. For all he knew, all croft houses were two storey mini-mansions.

It was only when he saw the sign above the front door that he concluded he was in the right place. A smooth piece of wood had been fixed above the lintel, a single word carved studiously but inexpertly into its well-sanded surface. Moss and time had stained the edges of the letters, but Hamza was able to make the word out.

Ravenwood.

This was the place, alright.

The door, unlike the windows, wasn't boarded up. Hamza tried the handle. Locked. The wood had seen better days, though. One good shoulder would open it.

But, what would be the point? There was no-one here. Or, if they were, they'd been dead a long, long time.

With a final glance up at the house, Hamza headed back towards the car. He was barely halfway when he saw the imprint in the mud. It led from a little further down the track from where he'd left his car, curving towards the front of the house.

Tyre tracks.

Motorbike.

Recent.

Hamza tapped the screen of his phone. The solitary bar had become an empty right-angle triangle in the top right corner.

"Magic," he muttered.

He stood rooted to the spot, halfway between the house and his car, tapping his phone against the side of his leg.

"Bugger it. I've come this far," he decided.

And then, slipping his phone in his pocket and adopting his best police-man's walk, DC Khaled approached the building's front door.

CHAPTER THIRTY

"It was just a guy! Just a guy!"

Logan gave Bamber a shake. Beside the men, Sinead glanced along the street at the twitching curtains and parted blinds.

"What *guy*?" Logan demanded. "What did he look like?"

"I don't know! Just a guy! He just looked like a guy!"

Logan produced his phone, opened the photo app, and swiped until he found the mugshot of Ed Walker. "Was this him?" he asked, holding the phone up in front of Bamber's face.

"I don't know, I cannae see it. It's too close," Bamber said, his eyes blinking in turn as he tried unsuccessfully to focus.

Muttering, Logan released his grip on the scrote's hair and brought the phone back a foot.

"Naw. Naw, that's no' the guy. He looked different."

"Different in what way?" Logan asked.

"Just different. Like... different," Bamber slurred.

Logan sighed. "Jesus Christ. Older? Younger? Fatter? Thinner? Different how?"

"His face was like..."

Bamber gestured vaguely to his own face.

"...different. Aye, like, it wisnae the same. Know?"

"I know what 'different,' means, aye."

"He didnae have a beard for wan thing," Bamber said. "Aye, like no' like a *beard*."

"Right. OK. Now we're getting somewhere."

Bamber's pock-marked brow furrowed. "Or maybe he did. I cannae mind."

Logan clenched his jaw, swallowed back his rage.

Behind him, Sinead's radio squawked into life on her shoulder. "Control to PC Bell. You there, Sinead?"

Sinead looked to Logan for his approval, then retreated when he gave her the nod. "It's Sinead, Moira. What's up?" she asked.

Bamber watched her, his face fogged with confusion. "That's a shite phone," he remarked. "I've got a better phone than that."

Logan caught Bamber's chin and turned his head so the junkie's glassy eyes were focused vaguely in the DCI's direction.

"You're wasting my time here, Forby. Right now, we've got evidence that connects you to the abduction of a child. I could haul you into the station now and keep you there for *days*," Logan told him. "When did you have your last fix, Forby? How do you fancy a week of cold turkey in a wee grey box?"

His eyes went to Bamber's house.

"A different wee grey box, I mean."

The expression on Bamber's face made his thoughts on the matter very clear.

"No, thought not," Logan said. "So, you need to give me something useful. Something more than 'just some guy.'"

A few yards along the street, PC Bell swore urgently.

"Shit, shit, shit," she said, scrabbling for her phone.

"What's the matter?" Logan asked.

"It's my brother, sir," Sinead said, hurriedly thumbing through her contacts. "School's been on the phone to the station. He hasn't turned up."

Logan checked his watch. "Ten past nine. Could he no' just be late?"

Sinead shook her head. "He goes to Breakfast Club at eight. I walked him to the end of the road before I came in. He wasn't there, either, so I don't—"

A car trundled past. Sinead put her finger in one ear, pressing the phone more firmly against the other. "Hello? Hello, Anna? It's Sinead. Harris's sis—Aye. No. No, he definitely left. He should've been at Breakfast Club."

She listened for a moment, her face telling the story of what the person on the other end was saying. "Well, where is he?" she asked, her voice rising. "Where is he?"

Logan jabbed a finger in Bamber's face. "Don't leave town. I'm not finished with you," he said, then he placed a hand on Sinead's back and guided her towards the car.

"Get in," he told her. He held his hands out for the keys. "I'll drive."

CHAPTER THIRTY-ONE

"ROUNDABOUT! *ROUNDABOUT!*"

Logan held steady, siren screaming as he flew across the junction in a near-perfect straight line.

"It's painted on. It doesn't count," he said, shooting a glance back in the car's rear view mirror.

A bus chugged along ahead of them. Jerking the wheel, Logan swung out onto the other side of the road, then immediately swung back in again to avoid a head-on collision with a delivery van coming the other way.

"Jesus, is everyone deaf around here?" he asked. "Sirens, people, sirens."

He made a non-specific but almost certainly rude gesture to the driver of the van, then eased out enough to see past the bus. It had indicated to the left and was slowing down to let him by, but the road ahead was clear now, so he gunned the engine and roared on past it, blue lights licking across the *Shiel Buses* logo painted along the vehicle's side.

"Where now?"

"Left past the traffic lights. Across the bridge, then left again."

Traffic lights. Traffic lights.

There.

The lights were on red. He ignored that fact and sped through, hanging a left at another roundabout—a proper one, this time—just beyond them.

Sinead gasped and grabbed for the solid plastic handle of the door as the car swung around the corner, rear tyres smoking.

"Been ages since I've done this," Logan said.

"I couldn't tell," Sinead hissed, bracing herself against the seat. "Left up here past *Farmfoods*."

More lights, but the filter arrow was green this time. The tyres howled in protest as Logan skidded the car around the bend. Sinead caught a glimpse of a terrified looking older driver in the opposite lane, but then they were past it, leaving the junction behind them in a cloud of burning rubber.

"And there's nowhere else he'd go?" Logan asked, crunching up into third and kangarooing past a couple of cars whose drivers had had the foresight to pull into a bus stop.

"No. Nowhere. He must've gone back home. He has to be there," Sinead said. "If he's not..."

Logan shot her the briefest of sideways glances, before returning his eyes to the road. "He'll be there. Don't worry. He'll be fine."

He added the '*Please, God*' silently in his head so Sinead couldn't hear it, then he jammed his foot down on the accelerator and powered the car along the narrow, winding road towards whatever awaited them ahead.

DC NEISH LOOKED up from his computer screen. "Email in from up the road, boss. There was a hold-up with the DNA stuff. We'll have it in the next twenty minutes."

"Good. About time," said Ben. He was perched on the edge of his desk, studying the Big Board. "Any word back from Hamza yet?"

"Nah. Want me to give him a ring?"

"Please."

Standing, Ben followed the strands of wool around the board, pausing to take in the contents of the Post-It notes dotted all over it. He'd read them so often now that he knew most of them off by heart but he read them again, anyway, in case this time they triggered some new idea, or potential line of enquiry.

"Dead, boss," said Tyler.

Ben turned. "What?"

"His phone. It's dead. Probably no signal."

"Oh. Right. Aye."

DI Forde turned back to the board. He sucked in his bottom lip, his gaze falling on the little black rectangle circled on the map. He scratched his chin, his fingernails rasping across a day or two's worth of stubble.

"You fancy checking on him?"

Tyler looked down at the phone. "Already tried, boss. Told you, no signal."

"No, I get that. I was asking if you fancied taking a drive up there and checking on him," Ben said. He looked back over his shoulder. "And, to be clear, I wasn't *actually* asking."

SINEAD RATTLED the handle of her front door, finding it locked.

"He's not in. He's not here," she said, panic rising like a bubble in her throat. She pushed back a jolly-looking garden gnome that stood at the edge of a small lawn that hadn't seen a mower in a while. Something metallic shone from the dirt below.

"The key's still there. He can't get in without the key."

Cupping his hands around his eyes, Logan peered in the downstairs window into the living room. A pair of blue pyjamas was spread across a couch, one leg turned inside-out. A mug and a plate sat on a little coffee table, half a slice of toast left on top.

"Can't see him in there," Logan remarked. "Is there a back door?"

"Aye, but it's locked. The key's in it on the inside. There's no way in," Sinead said. "Shit. Where can he be?"

"We'll call it in, get folk out looking for him," Logan told her. "We'll find him."

Sinead chewed her thumbnail, her eyes shimmering with worry. "Right. Aye," she mumbled. She reached for the walkie talkie on her shoulder and was about to thumb the button when Logan caught her by the arm, stopping her.

"Wait. Hang on," he said, lowering his voice. "Listen."

Sinead listened, as instructed, but the thumping of her own heart and the traffic passing out beyond the end of the garden path made it difficult for her to hear anything.

"What? What is it?"

"Round the back," Logan said.

Sinead moved to hurry past him, but he blocked the way. "Wait. Let me go first."

"Why?" Sinead demanded. She searched his face. "What is it?"

"I don't know. But stay behind me."

Constable Bell shook her head. "No. Sorry, sir, but no."

She ran up the path and out of the front garden, then sprinted off towards the house at the end of the block.

"Bugger it," Logan grunted, hurrying to keep up. Sinead was twenty years younger, though, and Logan had never been built for running.

He caught up with her at the back gate. She stood there at the end of the house's back path, watching a boy in school uniform digging with a rusty spade. The spade thacked when it hit the grass—the sound Logan had heard from out front.

Halfway between the gate and the boy, the shed door stood open. A badly weathered padlock hung from its broken latch.

The boy had his back to the gate and hadn't noticed Sinead and Logan's presence yet. He grunted with effort as he plunged the blade of the spade into the grass, and prised a little mound of dirt free.

"Harris? Harris, what are you doing?" Sinead asked.

Her little brother jumped with fright. He turned the spade clutched before him like a weapon.

It was then that they saw the blood. It plastered the front of his jacket and smeared up his chin. It pooled between his fingers and ran down the handle of the shovel in long, weaving strands.

Harris swallowed when he saw his sister and Logan standing there.

"Sinead," he said, his voice an anxious squeak. "Am I in trouble?"

CHAPTER THIRTY-TWO

WHAT HAMZA HAD ASSUMED WAS THE FRONT DOOR HAD IN FACT opened into a good-sized kitchen and dining area at the back of the house.

The size was the only good thing about it.

It had been tiled once, but damp had cancered the walls behind them, and most of the tile-work now lay smashed on the floor.

Cabinets had fallen from their mountings, smashing through the rotten wood of the lower storage units below. An old-style porcelain sink had cracked in two, spewing a greenish-black gunge through the gap.

The lino flooring was curling up in places, the edges pitted and gnawed away by rats. Alternate layers of mulch and moss and dust clung to most surfaces, and as Hamza creaked into the room, a carpet of woodlice hurried to clear a path.

"Shit," he ejected, burying his face in the crook of his elbow. He coughed, his eyes watering, his gag reflex demanding to know what the hell he thought he was playing at.

His eyes travelled to the corners of the room, saw things there that they wished they hadn't, then shot a longing look back at the fresh air of outside.

The place wasn't just giving him the boak, it was gift-wrapping it for him and presenting it on a silver platter. Every instinct told him to get out of there before he caught something. Every thought was of turning around and walking away.

Logan was right, he'd had a long night. He needed to be in bed, not poking around in a decaying old death trap filled with beasties. He forced himself to look at the squirming mound of woodlice, then shuddered at the sight of them, and at the thought of the millions of others no doubt roaming around in the house like they owned the place.

Something *clacked* onto the floor beside him, making him jump. Another of the fat, wriggling bugs lay on its back, legs bicycling frantically in the air. Hamza looked up, then jumped back into the doorway when he saw the ceiling was heavy with more insects. Not just woodlice but spiders, beetles, centipedes, and a variety of other bugs he didn't know the names of but despised on sight.

Part of the ceiling had collapsed, the plasterboard buckled to reveal part of a wooden beam and the underside of some floorboards above. Hamza retreated until he was standing under the doorframe. He'd heard somewhere that it was the safest place in an earthquake, as the house was less likely to fall on your head.

He wasn't expecting the ground to start trembling, but the house spontaneously collapsing on him felt like a very real possibility.

Taking out his phone, Hamza snapped off a few photos. The light from the door didn't stretch far into the room, so he took a few more with the flash on. The brightened images revealed more detail about the place but fell well short of conveying the horror of it.

There were a couple of doors leading off from the kitchen area. Both doors were open, and by leaning forward a little, Hamza could see what looked like a small utility room through one of them.

The angle of the second door blocked his view in that direction, but he guessed it must lead into the rest of the house. A living room or hallway, maybe. The window with the tree sprouting through it was in that direction somewhere, and while he was quite interested in getting a look at that, he was even more interested in getting back into the fresh air of outside, and away from this shitehole of a place.

Besides, if Dylan Muir's body was here somewhere, he didn't want to contaminate the place.

He cast a final glance around at the filth and debris.

Contaminate it any more than it already was, anyway.

Hamza was turning to leave when he heard the sound. Short. Sudden.

Thump.

He stopped, tensed, breath held, head cocked. His eyes moved left to right, seeing nothing as he listened.

A few seconds passed.

A minute.

Hamza's heart rate slowed. He allowed himself to breathe again.

Nothing. Probably just his imagination going into over—

Thump.

There was no mistaking it, that time. No denying it. A sound. But not *just* a sound.

A movement.

Upstairs.

Slowly—ever so slowly—Detective Constable Khaled leaned back, his eyes creeping to the ceiling above him.

CHAPTER THIRTY-THREE

"HARRIS? WHAT HAVE YOU DONE? WHAT DID YOU DO?" SINEAD whispered, edging along the path towards her brother.

Harris shook his head. "It wasn't me."

"What wasn't you, son?" Logan asked, eyeing the boy's blood-soaked clothes and the spade in his hands.

"I just found it."

"Found *what*?" Sinead demanded.

The sharpness of her voice made the boy jump, and brought tears bubbling to the surface. He tried to speak, but the words wouldn't come, so he stepped aside and pointed, instead.

A cat lay on the grass beside the hole Harris had been digging. Most of a cat, anyway.

An oblong of fur and flesh had been torn from its side, exposing part of its ribcage and a purple jelly of intestines. Its back legs hadn't been broken so much as mangled, bones jutting through meat at a range of stomach-churning angles.

"Jesus," Sinead hissed.

"It was... It was on the pavement," Harris said.

"And what? You picked it up?" Sinead yelped. "What were you thinking?"

Harris sniffed. His blood-spattered face burned with shame.

"You can't just pick up dead cats, Harris! That's *mental*!" Sinead continued. "You should be in school. Do you have any idea how worried I was? Do you?"

Harris shook his head, keeping his gaze fixed on the ground between them.

"It's not just me, is it?" Sinead asked, turning to Logan. "It's mental?"

"Well, I mean..." was all Logan could really add.

"It had been in an accident," he croaked. His shoulders shook. "Like... Like Mum and Dad were. I couldn't just leave it. I couldn't just... I couldn't just..."

Sinead was at him in three big steps, her arms around him, pulling him in. He dropped the spade and buried his face against her high-vis vest, his body wracked by big breathless sobs.

Logan watched Sinead's bottom lip start to wobble, then had the good grace to look away. Bending, he retrieved the spade.

"Why don't you two go inside?" he suggested. "I'll take care of this."

"You've got to bury it," Harris told him, turning his face but not releasing his grip on his sister. His words were wobbly, carried on unsteady breaths. "When things die, we bury them. That's just what we do."

Logan nodded. "You're right, son. We do. And, I will. I promise."

Sinead shot him an apologetic look, but he dismissed it with a shake of his head. "Away inside. Get him calmed down and cleaned up. It's fine."

"Thank you," she mouthed, then she turned with her brother and steered him out of the garden and around the block.

Logan waited until they were out of sight before squatting down, leaning on the spade for balance as he examined the cat.

It could've been an accident, he supposed, but the hole in the animal's side was neater than he'd have expected to see, the size and placement making it a near-perfect window into the poor thing's insides.

Similarly, the leg breakages were messy, but calculated. It was *possible* that a car could've done damage like that, but unlikely. The bones had splintered in opposite directions, so each leg was a mirror image of the other. Unless the animal had been lying with its legs spread in an open invitation to an oncoming tyre, Logan couldn't imagine how they had broken the way they had.

The front of the cat was in perfect condition, other than the redness matting its black and white fur. Its eyes were closed, its mouth open. It was missing a few teeth, Logan noted, although nothing out of the ordinary.

He wanted to believe it was an accident. He wanted to believe that nobody would do something like this on purpose. But, the unfortunate truth of it was, he'd seen similar to this before.

Too similar.

Once, in particular.

Fishing a pen from his pocket, he carefully prodded around at the edges of the wound, trying to figure out if the flesh had been torn off or cut away. The smell from the cat's insides snagged at the back of his throat and filled his mouth with saliva. He swallowed it down, still leaning on the spade as he continued his inspection.

He was looking closely at the injury when the cat twitched, its eyes opening, its face contorting in pain. It *mewed* desperately, piteously, its front paws kicking at nothing, its tail sticking straight out behind it.

Logan jerked back and jumped to his feet, the cat's pained cries carrying across the garden and up towards the house. Its head twisted. Its eyes met Logan's. Frightened. Desperate.

"Poor wee bugger," Logan muttered.

And, with that, he raised the spade.

CHAPTER THIRTY-FOUR

Hamza stood halfway up the stairs, darkness hanging heavy and oppressive overhead.

The lack of signal had rendered his phone mostly useless, but at least the shite *Vodafone* service didn't affect the torch function. He clutched the phone in his rubber-gloved hands, directing the torchlight upwards. It pushed back against the gloom, sending shadows scurrying across the peeling wallpaper and the blooms of black mould.

Each step groaned beneath his weight, a chorus of suffering singing him up the stairs.

There had been no more sounds since he'd left the kitchen beyond those he made himself. Creaking floorboards. Rustling clothes. The odd panicky gasp whenever something scurried out of a hole in the plasterboard or scuttled across the floor.

From the rest of the house, though, came only silence.

The upstairs landing was L-shaped, with six doors that Hamza could see, and probably at least one that he couldn't because of the corner. None of the doors looked particularly inviting. One had a little brass plate fixed to it that announced it as the 'Little Boys Room'.

Bathroom. Almost certainly. And yet, that particular choice of words meant Hamza had no choice but to check.

The door opened with a nudge. Hamza shone the torchlight inside, then stepped back, burying his face in his arm again. An overflowing toilet stood in the corner, a jagged hole in front of it where the floor had collapsed down into the room below. He flashed the torch across the rest of the room, finding nothing but a wash basin, an empty bath with a mildew-stained curtain hanging limply from a rail above it, and a generous amount of decay.

Hamza closed the door again, and turned his attention to the rest of the landing. The five other doors were unmarked. One stood ajar, giving him a glimpse of a carpet so damp it was literally sprouting mushrooms.

He decided to leave that one for now, and considered the others, instead. He thought about calling out, but a tightness in his throat prevented him. He told himself it was his body's way of resisting the urge to vomit. That was all.

Not fear.

His feet scuffed on the bare floorboards of the landing as he turned to the next door. An army of ants swarmed across the edges of the frame and up the wall between that door and the next.

Hamza had just decided to give this door a miss for now, too, when he saw the blood.

He didn't realise it was blood. Not right away. It was a dried puddle, a stain, a congealed pool of blackish red that had seeped out under the door and glossed the floorboards.

The truth of what he was looking at hit him with a sudden jolt that forced him back a step and brought a hissed expletive to his lips.

He should go, get out, drive until he found a signal and call for back-up. That was what he *should* do. No question.

He reached for the handle. Turned. Pushed.

The door remained closed. It took him another couple of attempts before he discovered it opened outwards.

The smell hit him first. It was unlike anything he'd ever smelled before —richer, blacker, more pungent.

The bones came next. They rattled and clunked out of the cupboard and onto the floorboards as an avalanche of yellows and browns. Long. Thin.

Child-sized.

"Fuck, fuck, fuck!" Hamza croaked, the phone shaking in his hand, the trembling torchlight making the bones' shadows dance.

Dylan Muir. Had to be.

THUD.

Everything but Hamza's eyes froze. They darted instinctively in the direction the sound had come from.

Around the corner. The other leg of the L.

He held his breath. Stood his ground. A voice in his head screamed at him to run. Another voice—Logan's, he thought—warned him not to fucking dare.

Do your job, that one told him. *Just do your bloody job.*

He checked his phone screen again, just in case. Still no signal.

The floorboards shifted noisily as he crept towards the corner and peeked around it into a shorter branch of the upstairs hallway. A single door stood at the far end. Mounted to the wall above it, the antlers of a deer's skull stabbed up at the decaying ceiling.

He heard the *thump* of movement from beyond the door again. There was more though, this time. A squeak. A sob. The whimper of a wounded animal.

Or a frightened child.

The uncertainty that had been crippling Hamza evaporated and he knew, with crystal-clarity, what he had to do.

He reached the door in three big *creaks*, and threw it open.

Hamza didn't notice the room. Not at first. All he saw was the chair, and the ropes, and the wide, staring eyes of a boy whose face he had previously only seen in photographs.

"Connor," Hamza exhaled. "Connor? It's OK, I'm with the police. I'm with the police, OK? I'm here to rescue you."

Bound to the chair, Connor Reid wheezed desperately into his gag. He kicked his bare feet, thudding his heels against the rotten carpet, squirming and thrashing in panic.

"Shh, it's OK, it's OK," Hamza promised. "I'm going to get you out. I'm going to get you home."

He took a step closer. The floorboards squeaked.

Twice.

A voice came from right behind him.

No, not a voice.

A *whisper*.

"Naughty, naughty," it said.

And then, before Hamza could turn, something cold and sharp was buried low down in his back, and his world fragmented into shards of pain.

CHAPTER THIRTY-FIVE

LOGAN STOOD BY THE KITCHEN WINDOW DRINKING TEA FROM A chipped mug and admiring the view. The house looked directly onto Ben Nevis, and the mid-morning sun was dappling the mountain's snow-covered peak.

He'd never been much into climbing himself, but looking up at the mountain now—The Ben, as the locals referred to it—he could almost see the appeal.

Almost.

A train rattled past just up the road from the house. There was a steam train that ran along this route, he knew. Part of the track up towards Glenfinnan had featured in the *Harry Potter* movies, and fans flooded the area during the summer, trying to get a glimpse of the train, or paying through the nose to ride on it.

It was a bog-standard old diesel that came thundering past now, though, vibrating the breakfast dishes in the sink. Probably headed to Glasgow, Logan thought, and part of him wished he was sitting on it.

Although, he noted with interest, maybe not as big a part of him as he'd have thought.

He turned away from the window. Sitting at the kitchen table, Harris immediately turned his head, trying not to let on that he'd been scoping the DCI out. Logan could hear Sinead through in the living room, explaining the situation to the school. By the sounds of things, she was glossing over the 'he'd picked up a dead cat,' thing. He couldn't really blame her.

"How you doing, son?" Logan asked the boy.

Harris looked young for his age. Physically, at least. Not behind the eyes, though. Behind the eyes, where it counted, he was old. Older than his sister. Older, perhaps, than Logan himself.

Harris shrugged.

"Aye. Get used to that. When you get to my age, that's pretty much the default," Logan said. "In fact..."

He shrugged.

"...is a good day once you're past forty. Enjoy your..."

He shrugged again.

"...while it lasts."

Harris smiled. Logan rewarded himself with another sip of tea.

"Do you think I'm mental?" Harris asked.

Logan did him the courtesy of not answering right away.

"I think we're all mental, son," he told the boy. "Some of us more than others. If it's any consolation, you're way down near the bottom of the list."

Harris's brow furrowed.

"No. I don't think you're mental," Logan clarified. "I think you tried to do a good thing, even though you knew it'd get you into trouble. There's hee-haw mental about that."

Harris relaxed a little, the lines of confusion lifting from his forehead.

"I mean, did you *look* mental plastered in blood and waving a spade around? God, aye," Logan told him. "You did. But looks can be deceiving. Take me, for example."

Harris looked him up and down, not understanding.

"Ballet dancer," said Logan over the top of his mug.

Harris exploded into laughter.

"What?" Logan demanded. "What's so funny?"

"No, you're not!" the boy giggled. "You're not a ballet dancer."

"Aye, I am! What are you saying, like?" Logan retorted, mock-offended.

Sinead came in from the hallway, thumbing the hang-up button on the phone. She looked from the DCI to Harris and back again. "What's going on?"

"Your brother is casting aspersions on my dancing skills," Logan told her. "Can you believe the bloody cheek?"

"Ballet dancer!" Harris exclaimed.

Sinead smiled weakly. "Right. I'm really sorry about this, sir."

Logan waved the apology away. "I helped myself to a cup of tea."

"No, it's not fair, sir. We're up against the clock with..."

She shot Harris a look and stopped herself before she finished the sentence.

"...everything. This is slowing us down."

"It's fine. I can multi-task. I texted DI Forde. He's getting your man... what's his name? Bamber, brought in. CID are going to give him a going over, see if they can figure out who 'just some guy' is. Asked him to have Social Services pop their heads in, too, to check on the wean."

Sinead nodded. "OK. I'm really sorry, though." She began jabbing digits on the phone. "I'll see if I can get Maureen down the road to watch him. I've told the school he's not coming in."

She looked between them both. "You OK here for a minute?"

"Aye. As long as he doesn't start having a go at my singing voice next, I'm sure we'll get on just fine."

"OK, that's..." Sinead turned and marched out into the hall. "Hello? Alan? Is Maureen...? Aye. Aye, that's right. Thanks."

Logan tipped the rest of his tea down the sink, swirled out the mug, then sat it on the draining board. Harris was watching him when he turned and leaned against the kitchen worktop.

"So. This cat, then," Logan said.

"Did you bury it?" Harris asked. The question came out of him in a flash, like he'd been holding it back until now.

"I did," Logan said.

A lie, but a necessary one. The boy never needed to know the animal's remains were currently stashed in a Bag for Life in the boot of the polis car.

Harris nodded, satisfied. "Good. That's what you're meant to do."

"It is," Logan agreed.

He took a seat across the table from the boy. "You remember where you found it?"

Harris shifted uncomfortably, like he was resisting the memory.

Then, just when Logan was about to tell him not to worry about it, he nodded.

"Can you tell me where it was?"

Harris nodded again. "You know where the Co-op is?"

"No."

The fact that someone didn't know where the Co-op was appeared to momentarily blow the boy's mind. He sat in silence for a while, his eyes fixed on Logan, an expectant expression on his face like he was waiting for a punchline.

"I'm not from around here," Logan explained. He brought out his phone and tapped the Maps icon. "Can you show me on this?"

He handed the phone over. "You can move the map around by…"

Logan opted to shut his face when Harris took the phone, pinch-zoomed in, and swiped a finger across the screen.

"Aye, like that," the DCI said, when the boy handed him the phone back. He'd marked the spot with a little red flag.

How the bloody hell had he done that? Was that a thing you could do? Logan hadn't had a clue.

"Right. And it was there, was it?"

Harris nodded. "It was beside the road. Just lying there. A car must've hit it."

"Aye. Aye, it must've," said Logan.

Another lie, probably. Forensics would have to confirm.

"Did you see anyone around?" Logan asked.

Harris frowned. "What do you mean?"

"Just, like, anyone watching. Or acting strange."

"There was an old woman," Harris said. "She shouted at me."

"Did she? What did she say?"

Harris shot a look in the direction of the hallway. "I'm not allowed to swear."

"I won't tell anyone," Logan promised.

The boy chewed his lip for a moment, then spat it out. "Put that f'ing thing down. You don't know where it's f'ing been," he said. He glanced furtively in the direction of the hall. "Except she didn't say f'ing."

"Right.

"She said 'fucking.'"

"Gotcha. And what did you say?"

"Nothing. I just ran past her. I was nearly home by then."

Logan nodded. "Ah, OK. No-one around where you found the cat, though?"

"No. Not that I saw," said Harris. He wrung his hands and looked up at the DCI. "Are you going to find who killed it?"

"I'm going to do my best," Logan told him, then they both turned as Sinead entered from the hallway, a child's jacket held open before her like a Matador's cape. It was not the same jacket he'd been wearing earlier.

Considering that one now resembled a butcher's apron, Logan reckoned this was probably for the best.

"Right, you. Jacket on. Maureen's going to watch you for the day."

Harris hopped up from his chair and inserted an arm into a sleeve.

"And for God's sake," Sinead told him. "Don't mention the cat."

CHAPTER THIRTY-SIX

Tyler bent and peered in through the driver's side window of DC Khaled's car, then up at the ramshackle house a few dozen yards ahead.

The journey up here had taken longer than he'd expected, largely on account of him getting completely lost twice. Quite how he'd managed to get lost on what was, essentially, a single road with no junctions, he wasn't sure. One thing he did know, though—he'd never mention it to anyone, and especially not to Hamza. The bastard would never let him live it down.

"Ham?" Tyler bellowed in the direction of the house. A flock of birds rose from the trees at the sound of his voice, cawing and squawking their displeasure. "Helloooo?"

He checked his phone. One bar. Just. He tried calling Hamza, but was met by a lengthy silence, then—eventually—the dulcet tones of the voice-mail greeting.

"Bollocks."

The door to the house stood open. Even from that distance, it wasn't exactly inviting.

Tyler looked across the boarded windows and moss-coated stone of the building's frontage. "Hamza, you in there, mate?"

He waited for an answer that didn't come.

"I swear to God, if I come in there and you jump out at me, I'll kill you," Tyler warned.

Silence.

Tyler reiterated the "Bollocks," and then set off in the direction of the door.

Something stopped him a few paces in. A doubt. A niggle. A creeping sensation down his spine that told him something wasn't right.

Returning to his car, he popped the boot, grabbed the torch and extendable baton that were in there, then closed it again with a *clunk*.

He flicked the torch's switch, checking the battery. All good.

Flicking his wrist, Tyler extended the baton to its full length.

"Right, then, Detective Constable Khaled," he muttered. "Good luck to you if you come jumping out at me now."

"THANKS, Maureen, I really appreciate this. I owe you one."

Logan stood back at the car, watching Sinead express her gratitude to the white-haired woman in the doorway for about the third time since Harris had disappeared inside. Maureen, for her part, looked thrilled to have the boy, and had beamed from ear to ear when he'd hugged her briefly on his way into the house.

Still, time was getting on. Logan cleared his throat just loudly enough to catch PC Bell's attention. She shot a look back over her shoulder, smiled apologetically, then beat a hasty retreat up the path.

"If there's anything, just call the station. You've got the number."

"He'll be fine. He's always fine. Off you go. We'll give him his dinner."

"Thank you!"

"Christ, are you rehearsing for your Oscars speech?" Logan asked, holding the gate open. "You're grateful. She gets it."

Sinead gave the old woman a wave, and mouthed another silent, 'Thanks!'

"It's short notice. I don't like dumping him on her at short notice."

"Dumping him on her? Did you see her face? I think you just made her day."

He held out the car keys. "Not sure your nerves'll handle me driving."

"Aye, they've had enough for one day, I think," Sinead agreed. She took the keys. "Sorry again, sir."

"Not at all. It was... enlightening," Logan said, pulling open the passenger door.

"You're good with him. Harris, I mean. Have you got kids?"

Logan hesitated, the door open. "Aye. A daughter. Older, though. Not a kick in the arse off your age."

"Oh? What does she do?"

"Eh... I don't know. Not too sure, actually."

Sinead swore at herself inside her head.

"Oh. Right," she said, then she pulled open her door and got into the driver's seat. She spent a few moments adjusting the position of it, then pulled on her belt.

"By the way, thanks," she said, as Logan clambered in beside her. "You know, for burying the cat. You didn't need to do that."

"The cat. Aye," Logan said. He clipped in his own belt, then shot her a sideways look. "About that..."

MOIRA CORSON TURNED from the reception desk as Logan and Sinead came in through one of the front office's side doors. There was a soft *thud* as the DCI deposited a *Marks & Spencer* Bag for Life on the desk beside her.

"For me?" she asked, peering down at it. "What is it?"

"It's a cat," Logan told her.

Moira's face remained largely impassive. "I don't want a cat."

"Well, you certainly won't want this one," Logan said.

Moira leaned forward to look into the bag. Logan motioned for her not to. "I wouldn't. I need a postmortem done on it ASAP."

"A postmortem?" said Moira. "On a cat?"

"Aye. On a cat. On this particular cat."

Sighing, Moira reached for her notepad. "What do you need to know? Cause of death?"

Logan shook his head. There was a bag of Mint Imperials open on Moira's desk. He helped himself to one, drawing a furious glare from the receptionist.

"I already know how it died. It was whanged on the head with a spade."

Moira flicked her gaze down into the opening at the top of the bag. "How do you know that?"

"Because I'm the one who whanged it," Logan told her. "I need to know if the other injuries were accidental or deliberately inflicted. Can you get that processed for me?"

Moira's face said 'no,' but her words said otherwise. "Fine. Yes. I'll see what I can do."

"Thanks," said Logan. He took another mint, then held it back over his shoulder for Sinead. "Sweetie?"

"I'm alright, thanks," said Sinead. It was one thing for Logan to get on Moira's bad side. He could clear off back to Glasgow when the case was over and done with. Sinead, on the other hand, was stuck with the old bat.

"Suit yourself," said Logan, popping the mint in his mouth. He gave the receptionist a nod. "Give us a shout when they come back with something."

Moira's response was ejected through gritted teeth. "Will do, Detective Chief Inspector."

Logan led Sinead through the back into the corridor that led to the Incident Room. As they walked, he prodded experimentally at the stitches on his forehead. Pain stabbed through him, making him hiss.

"You shouldn't fiddle with it, sir."

"I'm not fiddling with it. I'm assessing the damage."

"You're fiddling with it. You'll start it bleeding," Sinead told him.

"Fine. There. I'm not touching it," Logan told her, pushing open the door to the Incident Room. "Happy now?"

He strode in, ready to start barking orders, then stopped when he saw DI Forde hurriedly pulling on his coat.

"Ben? Everything alright?" Logan asked, but he knew the answer to that already. If the urgency of Ben's movements hadn't told him, then the look of shock on DS McQuarrie's face certainly had. "What's happened?"

"Tyler's just been on the phone. He's in a panic. Hasn't had a signal until now."

"And?"

"It's Hamza," Ben said. "Tyler's got him in the car. Didn't trust the ambulance to be able to find the place."

"Ambulance? What are you talking about?" Logan asked. "What ambulance?"

DI Forde glowered at Logan. And, although the DCI had a substantial height and weight advantage, in that moment he was sure that Ben could've leathered seven bells out of him.

"Hamza's been attacked, Jack," Ben said. He shook his head, his face ash-grey. "And it's not looking good."

CHAPTER THIRTY-SEVEN

The silence in the Incident Room was palpable. It hung in the air, casting a cloud over everyone and everything.

Logan stood facing the Big Board. Or, more accurately, *not* facing the rest of the team. The CID guys had been brought in, and even Jinkies was hanging around near the back of the room, back straight, buttons polished.

The others—Ben, Caitlyn, and Tyler—stood in a huddle near Hamza's desk, as if drawing comfort from it. Sinead hung back from the others, trying not to look as awkward and self-conscious as she felt.

It was DI Forde who eventually spoke. The words came slowly and tentatively, like he was taking his time to choose just the right ones.

"It wasn't your fault, Jack," he said. "You weren't to know."

"Bollocks it wasn't," Tyler spat. His pale blue shirt had been purpled by blood, and all the nooks and crannies of his hands were caked with the stuff.

"DC Neish!" Ben snapped.

"Well, you said it yourself. Ham shouldn't have been up there on his own," Tyler continued. "He should never have gone up there without support."

"That's enough, Tyler," Ben warned. "I won't tell you again."

Up front, Logan turned to face them all. "He's right. Leave him, Ben. He's right. This should never have happened. I didn't think it could be connected to the live case. I thought it was historic. Not..."

He sighed and looked up at the ceiling tiles, gathering his thoughts.

"I made a bad call. Hamza never should've been up there on his own." He looked across their faces. "I'm sorry."

At the back of the room, Jinkies cleared his throat. "Can I ask? What's DC Khaled's condition?"

"They're airlifting him to Glasgow Royal, sir," DI Forde explained. "Haven't got the facilities here. His condition's critical, but they've got him stable enough to move to ICU down the road."

"Family?" Jinkies asked.

"Wife and a little one, sir," Tyler said. The words were meant for Logan as much as for the Chief Inspector.

"Bugger." Pickering stood up. "I'll arrange transport for them. Blue light them down there, if needs be."

"Thank you, Hugh," said Logan.

"Least we can do," said Jinkies, more than a little reproachfully. He gave a nod to the room. "Good luck."

The door *squeaked* as he left to get the transportation sorted.

"There are two ways we can play this," said Logan. "We can all, myself included, stand around here blaming me for this. Or, we can catch this bastard, get Connor home, and make him pay for what he did to Hamza. What's it to be?"

"There's not even a question there, Jack," said DI Forde. He looked to the rest of the team. "Is there?"

Everyone was in agreement, although some more enthusiastically than others. Logan gave a clap of his hands. The *bang* they made was a starting pistol designed to propel everyone into motion.

Caitlyn and Ben returned to their desks. The CID boys sat up straighter. Constable Bell, who wasn't entirely sure what she was supposed to be doing, took out her notebook. She wasn't sure why she took out her notebook, exactly—it was a brand new one, with only a few scribbled remarks from the discussion with Bamber earlier on the first page—but it was better that than just standing there doing nothing at all.

"I think the boy was there."

Tyler's words stopped everyone in their tracks.

"What?" Logan asked.

"I'm not sure. Hamza was going in and out," Tyler said. His eyes were glassy as he replayed the memory in his head. "I think he said he saw Connor. In the house."

Logan leaned against the edge of the desk. "Connor? He saw Connor? Alive?"

"Alive, I think. Pretty sure he was trying to save him when he... You know."

"Jesus," Logan muttered. He turned to Ben. "Have we organised—"

"Tyler called it in on the way down the road," said Ben, interrupting. "Got uniforms sealing the place off. Crime scene boys are already there, combing over everything."

"And?"

"Nothing. If Connor was there, he's not now."

"Right. Aye. Suppose it was too much to hope for," Logan said. He nodded at Tyler. "Good work, son."

DC Neish flashed a sarcastic smile. "Gee. Thanks, boss."

"Tyler..." Ben warned.

"It's fine," Logan told him. He beckoned the young DC closer. "Come here."

Tyler hesitated.

"Hurry up. Come here," Logan said.

All eyes watched as Tyler approached the DCI. He stopped a couple of feet away, eyeing the bigger man warily.

"You want to hit me?" Logan asked.

Tyler said nothing.

"Do you? Because you can. I'll give you one free shot. One-time offer. No consequences, no repercussions. One free smack in the mouth, punch in the guts, or whatever you prefer," Logan said. "Ideally, not the balls, but whatever you think'll help."

Tyler's gaze flicked to DI Forde. Ben offered him nothing in response.

"Come on, son. Get it over with," Logan told him. "The sooner you get it out of your system, the sooner we can get back to work."

He jutted his jaw out, offering it as a target. "So, hurry up. Hit me."

"I don't want to hit you," Tyler said.

"No? Last chance."

Tyler shook his head. One of Logan's meat slab hands fell on his shoulder.

"I made the wrong call, son. That's on me," the DCI told him. "We can talk about it later. But for now, how about we stop with the squabbling and catch this prick?"

There was a nod from Tyler, a straightening of his back, a firming-up of the lines of his face.

"Yes, boss," he said. "I'm all for that."

"Alright, then," Logan said. "Go grab a fresh shirt, take a minute to get yourself cleaned up, then get back here."

Tyler didn't argue. As he headed for the door, Logan called over to DS Boyle and DC Innes from CID. "Get anywhere with Mr Bamber?"

"Not really," said Boyle. "The most he's been able to tell us about the person who gave him the teddy was that it was, 'some guy,' which doesn't really narrow it down."

"Narrows it to half the population," DS McQuarrie pointed out.

"Well, aye, there's that," agreed Boyle. "We're bringing in a sketch artist to see if we can get some sort of picture."

"How long will that take? Do they have to come down the road from Inverness, too?"

"Normally, sir, aye. But, we've asked one of the art teachers from the high school to come in and have a bash while we wait. He used to be Bamber's teacher for a while. Reckons he might be able to get something out of him."

"Good. OK. Keep on that, give me a shout when you have something more," Logan told them. "Can you also coordinate with the Scene of Crime team up at the house? Anything that comes in, no matter what it is, I want to see it. Even if it's their lunch order, I want to see it."

"Got it, sir," said Boyle. He and DC Innes got to their feet. "We'll be in the office next door. We're already set up, no sense moving."

"Aye. Time is against us, lads," Logan reminded them. "Best case scenario, Connor has maybe twelve hours left. Worst case...? Well, let's not dwell on the worst case. Twelve hours. Keep that in mind. And, let's not forget, that this is no longer just about Connor Reid. We're also investigating the attempted murder of one of our colleagues. One of us."

"Yes, sir."

"We're on it, sir."

Even before the CID boys had reached the door, Logan had wheeled around to address DI Forde and DS McQuarrie. "Right. What else? Anything on HOLMES yet?"

"Shit. Forgot to check, sir," said Caitlyn. "Sorry, just... with Hamza, and everything."

"Don't apologise, Detective Sergeant, just look," Logan instructed. "Constable Bell, get onto the local paper, will you? They're running a story about a woman who keeps losing her cats. Try to find out where she lives, then get a description of the cats, see if any of them match ours?"

"You think the cat's connected, sir?" Sinead asked.

"Maybe. Petrie had a habit of torturing them. Dogs, too. Can't hurt to look into it."

"Right," said Sinead, just happy to finally have a purpose. She reached for her mobile, but Logan stopped her.

"Take a desk. Get set-up."

Sinead looked from the DCI to the vacant desks, then back again. "Uh, right. OK, sir. Thanks."

"Don't thank me, just get it done," Logan told her.

As she hurried off, Logan turned on his heels to face DI Forde.

"Why was Connor there, Ben?" he said, voicing his thoughts aloud. "We didn't even know about the Petrie connection to the place until today. How did someone else? And why use there to hide him?"

"It's out of the way. No-one to see you coming and going," said Ben.

"But there are loads of places like that," Logan said, gesturing to the map on the Big Board. "Why *that* house? It has to be the Petrie connection, but... I don't get it. The bear, the envelope, and now the house. It has to be someone close to the case. Someone who's been involved from early on."

"And someone savvy enough to be able to figure out the house thing before we did," Ben added.

"No answer at the paper, sir," Sinead called over from the desk she had installed herself at.

"Damn. There's a journalist." Logan clicked his fingers a few times, searching for the name. "Fisher. Tom Fisher. He might be out front. See if you can dredge him up."

"Aw, shite," Ben said, jumping to his feet.

"What now?"

"He's not out front. None of them are. They're at the hotel for the press conference. The Gozer wants you sitting in."

"Bollocks. What time?" Logan asked, checking his watch.

"Twelve."

"Twenty minutes. How far away is it?"

"Maybe five," said Ben. He looked the DCI up and down. "You going to smarten yourself up a bit?"

"For the press? What do *you* think?"

Ben managed a grim smile. "Good man."

"Right, fifteen minutes," Logan boomed. He nodded an acknowledgement at Tyler as he returned to the room, fastening the top button of a fresh shirt. "How far can we get in the next quarter of an hour? What else have we got?"

"Something I forgot to mention, boss," Tyler began, pulling his tie over his head. "There were bones in the house. In a cupboard at the top of the stairs."

Logan stopped, turned on his heels. "Bones?"

"Yeah. And not like a cat or a dog, or whatever. Bigger. Bloodstains on the floor, too. Old. Way back."

Logan felt the room undulate around him. He leaned on the desk, steadying himself for a moment.

Dylan Muir.

Finally.

"We'll let the crime scene lot worry about that for now," Logan said, dragging his thoughts back to the present. "Let's concern ourselves with the living for the moment."

"Update in, sir," said Caitlyn, looking up from her screen. "DNA results back from the teddy bear. As suspected, nothing connecting it with Ed Walker. They've got a match for Forbes Bamber, but we already knew he made the delivery."

"Anyone else?" Logan asked.

Caitlyn's gaze returned to the screen. She stared at it for a while, her mouth moving silently, like she was trying to figure out how to describe what she was seeing.

"Detective Sergeant?" Logan prompted.

"Aye, sir. Sorry. Three other samples. One of them hasn't yet been identified."

"And the other two?"

"Owen Petrie, sir," Caitlyn replied. "And Matthew Dennison."

She raised her gaze until it met Logan's. He stared back at her, too stunned to speak.

"Petrie's third victim."

CHAPTER THIRTY-EIGHT

HE COULD HEAR THEM. MOVING. TALKING. LAUGHING. OUT THERE, beyond the door, beyond his little cube of darkness and fear.

Beyond his prison.

He was hungry and thirsty, his stomach cramping, his lips cracked and dry. They felt raw against the rough material of the gag, like it was sandpapering them down, whittling them out of existence.

The boy had put the cat in with him a few hours ago, set it on his lap, watched and laughed as he'd sobbed into the mouth covering.

When the door had closed, he'd tried to shake the cat off him, but the ropes were too tight, and his legs were asleep. There was nothing he could do but sit there with it on him, feeling what was left of its life soak into his trouser-legs, whimpering whenever it twitched and spasmed.

Once, it had mewed angrily, its front claws scratching at his legs. He'd screamed and screamed and screamed, but nobody had come. Nobody had heard.

Or nobody had cared.

After a while, the cat stopped fighting. It stopped breathing shortly after. He'd heard the life leave it in a throaty gasp, and had cried for a while. Tears of relief, and of helplessness, and of hot, burning shame.

And of fear, of course. The ever-growing sense of dread that told him no one was coming. No one was going to save him.

He would die here, alone and afraid, like the cat on his lap.

The voices became louder. Closer. His breath wheezed through his nose, adrenaline flooding him, preparing him for what might come next. For what they might do.

There was a knock on the cupboard door. Sharp, but jolly.

"Everything alright in there?"

The man's voice. That hoarse, scratchy rasp.

"You decent?"

The door opened. Two faces looked in at him. Both were smiling. Happy. Excited.

Eager.

Tears came then. He thought he'd run out of them hours ago, but they flowed freely, caressing the lines of his cheeks before soaking into the gag.

"Look who I found," said the boy. He held up a threadbare grey teddy bear, then moved its head as if making it speak.

"Hello, Matthew," the boy said in a high-pitched baby-voice. "Haven't you been naughty, naughty?"

And there, with the man and the boy leering in at him, Matthew Dennison knew that the end was near.

CHAPTER THIRTY-NINE

"THANK YOU FOR COMING. WE'RE GOING TO KEEP THIS BRIEF. I HAVE a short update to provide you with, then I'll take one or two questions along-side DCI Logan, who is heading up the investigation."

Logan nodded, just briefly, at the sound of his name. Instinct, nothing more.

Physically, he was present. Physically, he was sitting beside the Gozer at a long table in a hotel not far from where he'd nabbed Ed Walker, gazing out at a sea of faces, microphones, and cameras.

Physically, he was right there in the room.

Mentally, though, Logan was elsewhere. His mind had been a whirl-wind since Caitlyn had dropped the DNA bombshell, thoughts crashing together as he struggled to come up with an explanation.

It didn't make sense. None of it made sense.

The teddy bear that had been left at the Reids' house carried the DNA of Owen Petrie, a man who had been in near solitary confinement for the best part of a decade.

Worse, it carried the DNA of Matthew Dennison, a boy who had been murdered all the way back in 2005, and whose remains had been buried four years later in a small private ceremony that Logan had been invited to but had the good grace not to attend.

DS McQuarrie was getting in touch with Matthew's parents to see if the teddy bear looked familiar. Logan suspected that it would turn out to have belonged to the boy.

Which meant... what? How had someone come into possession of it? Why here? Why now?

What did any of it mean?

He kept an ear open, listening as the Gozer rattled off the usual stuff. *Family devastated. Support of the community. A number of promising leads.*

Logan sat up straighter at the mention of DC Khaled's name, watched the vultures scrambling to write down all the lurid details.

He recognised a few of the faces, but most were new. The old print guard had been getting gradually pushed out for a while now, their ranks thinning year-on-year. Logan had no sympathy for them, but if there was one thing he hated more than old school print journalists was new school digital ones. At least a handful of the journos in the room were from online-only outlets.

Fucking *bloggers*.

"And now, we'll take a few questions," said the Gozer. "Although, you'll appreciate we don't have a lot of time."

A dozen or more hands raised. Detective Superintendent Mackenzie looked around for a friendly face, then settled on a woman near the front. "Yes."

"Can you confirm if the abduction is related to the Owen Petrie 'Mister Whisper' investigation from a decade ago?" she asked. "And, if so, what's the connection?"

Logan waited for the Gozer to respond, then realised that the Detective Superintendent was looking to him for answers.

"Oh." Logan sat forward. "We don't believe there's a direct connection at the moment, as such."

"But there are similarities?" the female journalist pressed.

Logan nodded. "We think we're looking at a copycat situation. It's ten years since Petrie's arrest. Twenty since he abducted his first victim. Fourteen since he killed Matthew Dennison, his last victim. Or the last one that we know of. We think someone is trying to capitalize on Petrie's—and I hesitate to use this word—'fame.'"

"Why would they do that?"

Logan scratched his chin. "Why do any of them do any of it? Notoriety? To get their kicks?"

"We wouldn't like to speculate at this time," said the Gozer, shooting Logan a warning look. "Next question."

The hands went back up again. The Gozer considered the alternatives, but it was Logan who singled one out. Tom Fisher, the local boy. Might as well give him a second chance to shine.

"Yes?"

Fisher looked taken aback at having been picked. "Um..."

His eyes went to his notes.

"Did you have a question?" Logan pressed, sensing the impatience and growing resentment from the other journalists.

"Uh, yes. Yes. I did. I just... Yes."

Fisher cleared his throat. His cheeks were reddening before Logan's eyes, like someone had just slapped him on both sides of his face.

"It was... I was just going to ask, is it possible that you got the wrong man? Owen Petrie, I mean? Is it possible that he wasn't guilty of what he was guilty of?" Fisher shook his head, annoyed at himself. "At what he was accused of, I mean? Could it have been someone else?"

"No," said Logan, dismissing the question with a shake of the head and a scowl.

"Right. It's just... With the..." Fisher swallowed, wilting under Logan's gaze. "How can you be sure?"

"Because the court found him guilty," said the Gozer, spotting the warning signs in Logan's body language and interrupting before the situation could escalate. "Because he confessed to all three murders, and because we were able to gather overwhelming evidence that proved his guilt beyond any measure of reasonable doubt."

"Right. Right. Cool," said Fisher. His blush deepened. "I mean, not 'cool,' but... Thank you. Thanks. That was my only question. Thanks."

More hands shot up. Logan watched Tom Fisher scribbling down the answer the Gozer had given in his notepad. Or, attempting to, anyway. He was having problems getting his pen to write by the looks of things, and kept shaking it every few seconds to get the ink flowing.

Fair play to the kid, though. The question had taken Logan by surprise. He'd have expected that sort of thing from Ken Henderson, but not from a snottery-nosed wee...

Logan's eyes flicked across the faces of the reporters, searching for Henderson but failing to find him. He wasn't there. Henderson wasn't at the conference.

Arguably the one man on Earth who had invested as much of his career into the Petrie case as Logan had, *wasn't there.*

"DCI Logan?"

Logan became aware of everyone in the room watching him, waiting for an answer to a question he hadn't heard.

"Huh?"

"Do you want to field that one?" the Gozer pressed.

Logan blinked. The legs of his chair scraped across the vinyl flooring as he pushed it back. He stood up, leaned on the table, and glowered out at the media.

"Henderson," he said. "Has anyone seen Ken Henderson?"

CHAPTER FORTY

LOGAN RAPPED HIS KNUCKLES AGAINST THE BIG BOARD.

"Where's my picture of Henderson? Come on, come on, people."

"Coming, sir," said DS McQuarrie, grabbing a sheet of A4 from the printer the moment the machine spat it out. "It's a blow-up from the web, so not great but—"

"It'll do," said Logan, glancing at it then motioning for her to put it on the board. He shot looks at Ben, Tyler, and Sinead, making sure they were paying attention.

"Kenneth Henderson, fifty-eight, freelance journalist and all-round pain in the arse. Made his name reporting on the Petrie case, and dined out on it for years after. Knows almost as much about the investigation as I do. I've now been told that he's even interviewed Petrie a couple of times in the past few years for follow-up stories, although they never saw the light of day."

"Petrie could've told him about the house," suggested Ben.

"And the envelopes," added Tyler from his desk.

"Aye, it's a theory," Logan agreed. "We said it had to be someone involved in the original investigation. Someone close. They didn't get much closer than Henderson. Our priority now is finding him. Tyler, find out what car he's driving, get everyone on the look-out for it. Circulate a digital copy of his picture, too. And get word down the road to Glasgow. Check out his old haunts. I want the bastard sweating in an interview room within the hour."

"On it, boss."

Ben ran a hand through his thinning hair, teasing what was left of it around his fingers. "You really think he'd do something like this? Henderson?" the DI asked. "I mean, he's an arsehole, no doubt about that, but this... And with Hamza...? That's way beyond arsehole territory."

"I don't know. I honestly don't," Logan admitted. "By all accounts, he's had it rough, lately. Job's not as safe as it once was. He needs a scoop, and what better than the Ghost of Mister Whisper? He's built a career on Petrie's story. Maybe he thought another chapter would help put him back on top."

"Seems a stretch," said Ben.

"It is. I'm not saying he did it, I'm saying we need to talk to him. Any time anything happens with the Petrie case, Henderson is right there, front and centre," Logan said. "But not today. Today, right after one of our officers was attacked, he's nowhere to be seen. I want to know why."

Caitlyn's phone rang. She hurried back to her desk and picked up the receiver.

"Detective Sergeant McQuarrie," she said, then she tucked the handset between her ear and her shoulder, and started making notes.

Tyler popped up from behind his screen. "Henderson's driving a red Vauxhall Mokka, boss. 2014 plate. Putting a shout out for it now."

"Good," Logan said, then, "*Shite.*"

"Boss?" Tyler asked.

"No, not you. I forgot I meant to talk to Tom Fisher and ask him about the cat story. Sinead, can you chase up the paper again? Find out where that woman lives."

Sinead nodded and picked up her phone.

"We have anything back on the cat I brought in?" Logan asked.

"Aye, didn't you get the note?" Ben answered. "Moira got the local vet to take a look. Injuries were inflicted deliberately, he reckons."

Logan had been expecting that answer, but hoping for a different one. He groaned, rubbing his temples to nurse the headache that was building behind his eyes.

"God. OK. Right."

"What's with the cat anyway, boss?" asked Tyler.

"Petrie used to... I don't know. Torture them, I suppose," Logan explained. "Cut them open, break their bones. The usual mental bastard script."

He leaned on his desk, taking some of the weight off his feet. His eyes went to the battered cardboard folder he'd left there earlier, and his mind went back a decade or more.

"When we initially tracked Petrie down, we... There was a cupboard in his flat, and it was..."

Logan sucked in his bottom lip, then spat it out again. "I opened it, and there was just... death. Just all this death, that came tumbling out onto the carpet at my feet."

"Death?" Tyler looked around at the others. "I don't follow."

"There was an old poem I heard once. Or, I don't know, a song, maybe. It had this line in it. '*A litter of bones strewed the mighty bestiarium.*' That's what popped into my head when I opened the door. Can't even remember where I heard it."

He stared blankly at the folder on the table, as if seeing through it.

"A *litter of bones*. Cats. Dogs."

He swallowed.

"Children."

Logan gave himself a shake and straightened. "We thought they were all in there. The boys, I mean. I thought we'd found them all. If I'd known we hadn't, I wouldn't..."

He course-corrected.

"I would have made more of an effort to catch Petrie. Before he fell."

He contemplated the folder for a while longer, then snatched it up with both hands. "Let's get this stuff up on the board," he said, flicking the folder open. "Henderson's our first priority, but let's see if we can make some connections. If it was him, how did he get that teddy bear? How did he find out about the house and the text on the envelope? Was it Petrie? If so, we need to know when they spoke, what was said, and what else Henderson knows."

There was a *clack* as DS McQuarrie put down the phone. "Report from the crime scene, sir. The bones in the cupboard at the house?"

"Yes?" said Logan, then he held his breath.

"Not Dylan Muir's. Not even human, sir. Sheep."

Logan's heart plunged down into his stomach. "Sheep?"

"Aye, sir. A lot of the bones had been broken. Deliberately, they think."

"Damn it!" Logan kicked his chair, sending it clattering across the floor. "I thought we'd found him. I thought we'd got him."

"It's unfortunate, Jack, but not our priority," Ben reminded him. "This isn't that case, you said so yourself. Dylan might still be there, but for now we need to focus on Connor."

"Aye. Aye, you're right," Logan agreed. "What about the sketch artist? Any luck with the junkie, do we know?"

"Not that I know of, but I can check," said Ben, heading for the door.

"Show Bamber a picture of Henderson. See if that jogs his memory."

"Good idea," said Ben. "You're no' just a pretty face."

Caitlyn cleared her throat. "There's something else, sir. Update on HOLMES. The DNA on the teddy? The one they couldn't identify? They've got a match."

"Henderson?" Logan guessed.

"No, sir," Caitlyn replied. She looked at her screen again, checking the information for the fourth or fifth time.

"It's Dylan's, sir. It's Dylan Muir's."

Logan staggered, like he'd been physically struck. The room spun. First one way, then the other, the walls blurring as his brain tried to process this new revelation.

Tried, but failed.

How could Dylan Muir's genetic material be on Matthew Dennison's teddy bear? The boys had been taken six years apart. There had been traces of Dylan's DNA in Petrie's flat, but not in the cupboard. Not on Matthew Dennison's remains.

He steadied himself against the Big Board, pulling himself together.

There were dozens of ways the bear could've been cross-contaminated, he told himself. Hundreds. Maybe Petrie had stored it alongside something of Dylan's. Kept it in his schoolbag, perhaps, which had never been recovered. Stuffed it in one of the boy's shoes.

There were explanations. Lots of explanations. *Plausible* explanations.

And yet, the room was still spinning, Logan's heart was still racing, and nausea was churning through his insides.

He'd had a suspicion before. No, not a suspicion, a concern. A *dread*. A nagging fear that ate away at him some nights when he lay awake, and wormed its way into his nightmares while he slept. He had always dismissed it, pushed it away, beaten it down. It didn't make sense. He *refused to let it* make sense.

And yet, it did. Here, now, it was perhaps the only thing that did, and the realisation of that fact knocked the air from Logan's lungs and threatened to bring him to his knees.

Someone connected to the original case.

Someone close *to it.*

Closer, even, than himself.

"The sketch artist," Logan said, closing his eyes to block out the whirling, twirling walls. "Tell him to forget Bamber."

"Oh. Right. Want me to send him home?" Ben asked. He was standing over by the door, the update from Caitlyn having stopped him in his tracks.

Logan shook his head. "Get him in here. I need him to try draw someone else."

"Who?" asked Ben.

Reaching into the folder, Logan took out a photo of smiling, three-year-old Dylan Muir, his hand buried in a bag of *Monster Munch*. "Him. I want him to draw him," he said.

"But twenty years older."

CHAPTER FORTY-ONE

The clock ticked, the hands simultaneously counting forwards and counting down. Logan tried not to look at it, to focus instead on the scratching of the pencil on the paper, the look of concentration on the artist's face as he carried out his task.

How long did Connor have left now? A few hours, at best. At worst, he'd been dead from the moment Hamza had discovered him in that house. Teams were sweeping the forest surrounding the building. Nothing, so far, but there was a lot of ground to cover.

"How's it going now?" Logan asked for the third or fourth time.

The artist was an older guy. Thin, prissy, face like a bulldog licking piss off a nettle. He sat with his legs crossed, his pad resting on a knee, half a dozen pencils tucked into the top pocket of his shirt.

"Getting there," he said.

He'd been *getting there* for the past twenty minutes now. Logan had taken a look over his shoulder a couple of times, but *there* hadn't looked like it was going to be anywhere useful.

Ben had warned him he was expecting too much. The guy wasn't a trained sketch artist, he was a high school art teacher. Sure, he could probably pull together something half-decent from a detailed description, but asking him to accurately predict what a three-year-old would look like as an adult was a big leap from there.

Logan looked around the Incident Room at the others. Aside from Ben, who was reading the Petrie case file at his desk, the others were all on phone calls. There had still been no sign of Ken Henderson or his car. Tyler was talking to the CCTV boys to see if it had been picked up heading back down the road to Glasgow, but cameras were few and far between along the route, and the line of enquiry was looking increasingly like another dead end.

Sinead was still trying to get through to the newspaper. She'd found a couple of numbers for the publisher who owned the paper, and was working her way down from there until she reached the local editor.

Caitlyn, meanwhile, was back onto the lab. Logan wanted to know if they could tell how recent the sample of Dylan Muir's DNA had been, or take a stab at how old he'd been when he'd come into contact with the teddy bear.

She was looking pretty animated, and her voice was stern, so Logan guessed he wasn't going to get the information anytime soon.

"Getting there. Almost done," said the artist, correctly predicting Logan's question before he could ask it.

Across the room, Sinead stood up, the phone still cradled to her ear. "Thank you. No... That's... Yes, thank you. You've been very helpful," she said into the receiver, her eyes meeting Logan's.

"Well?" he asked, before she'd even had a chance to hang up. "You find out where the cat lady lives?"

"No, sir," Sinead said. "I spoke to the editor. Got her mobile from her boss. They're not running any cat story this week."

"I don't care when they're going to run it, I just need to know where the woman lives."

"No, I mean, there is no cat story, sir. She knew nothing about it," Sinead said. "And she doesn't know anything about a Tom Fisher, either. He doesn't work there. Never has."

"Ta-daa!"

The artist turned the pad. Logan knew what was going to be on it before he saw it.

"Shite!" Logan spat. He raced out of the room, skidded along the corridor, then launched himself through the reception area and out to the front of the station.

Cameras flashed. Microphones were switched on. A sea of faces turned his way.

"Where is he? Where's Tom Fisher?" he demanded, suddenly wishing he'd brought the pad. "The kid at the press conference. The one who asked if Petrie might not be guilty. Where is he?"

There was some confused murmuring. A few of the journalists glanced around, but most had started to fire questions at him.

"Why do you want to know?"

"Is he involved?"

"Is Connor Reid still alive?"

Logan growled. "Ah, get it up ye," he told them, then he turned and thundered back inside.

Moira buzzed him in without a word, the expression on his face making it very clear that he was not in the mood for a debate.

He was barking orders before he'd even entered the office. "Ben, Caitlyn, coordinate from here. Find me everything you can on Tom Fisher, starting with his address. Tyler, Sinead, you're with me."

Everyone jumped to it. The art teacher got up from his chair, looking uncertain.

"Someone mentioned I'd get forty quid," he said.

Logan's eyebrows practically knotted themselves together. "What?"

"For the..." He gave a little wave of his sketchpad. "For the drawing."

"Oh, for fu—" Logan spat. "Ben, give him forty quid, then get rid of him. Keep that drawing."

Grumbling, DI Forde reached for his wallet. Grabbing his coat, Logan turned and stalked back towards the exit, beckoning Tyler and Sinead with one finger.

"Right. You two, get a shifty on."

"Where we going, boss?" Tyler asked, falling into step behind the DCI.

Logan raised his phone, the map screen open, a red flag standing proud in the centre.

"There," he said. "Wherever the hell that is, we're going there."

CHAPTER FORTY-TWO

LOGAN SAT BEHIND THE WHEEL OF HIS FORD FOCUS, WATCHING TYLER pinch-zoom in on the map screen of the DCI's phone. He had parked up just along the road from a little Co-op supermarket, across from a building that, Sinead had told him, had been one of the small local polis stations until the new soulless monstrosity had been built on the outskirts of town.

"So, if the kid is right, he found the cat up there," Tyler said, pointing ahead to where a row of green wheelie bins stood with their backs to the metal mesh of a fence.

"That seem right?" Logan asked, glancing in his rear-view mirror.

"That's the way he'd walk to school, aye," Sinead agreed. "I drop him at the road end here, and he walks the rest of the way himself."

"Right. Tyler, you're with me. Sinead, wait here, up front. I'll leave you the keys. If Fisher's around, I don't want him seeing the uniform and getting spooked."

"You mean Dylan, boss," said Tyler.

"I mean Fisher. He might not even know that he ever was Dylan Muir," Logan said. "What do you remember from when you were three?"

Tyler nodded. "Aye. Suppose you're right."

"I'm always right, son," Logan told him. He caught the look on the younger officer's face, and thought of DC Khaled lying in the ICU at Glasgow Royal. "Well, most of the time. Now, come on. Let's see what we can see. Sinead, up front, but don't get out of the car in case he spots you."

"What am I meant to do, clamber through?"

"Bingo," Logan told her. "I'll leave the keys in the ignition. We've got radios. If he shows face, call us. Don't engage unless you absolutely have to."

He and DC Neish both opened their doors and stepped out onto the pavement. The sun had tucked in behind a growing bank of grey cloud, and Tyler shivered in the cool March breeze.

"Chilly, innit?"

Logan glanced both ways along the street, then stalked across it. "Hadn't noticed."

THERE WAS nothing on the ground that corresponded with the flag Harris had placed on the map. Logan had been hoping for... something. A clump of fur and a blood trail, ideally, leading directly to someone's front door, although he knew he wouldn't get that lucky. He never got *that* lucky.

So, he hadn't been expecting to find anything that conclusive, but he'd hoped for something. A suggestion of something, even. A hint that they were on the right lines here, and that this wasn't just a waste of what little time Connor Reid might have left.

Tyler gagged as he poked around in the last of the bins. "Fucking hell," he grimaced. "Why do all bins smell like that? Doesn't matter what they've had in them, they've all got that same smell."

"Aye," Logan agreed, not really listening.

The houses around were all two-storey terraced, with short paths leading to numbered doors. They were not dissimilar to Sinead's house, or the Reids' home. A little older, maybe, the Highland weather having tired the construction out a little more, but more or less the same.

"Should we start knocking on doors, boss?" Tyler asked. "See if anyone's seen him around?"

"Not yet," Logan said. "We'll do another once up and down of the street, see if we can find where the cat was left. Or, if we're lucky, where it crawled to. It hasn't rained this morning, and it was bleeding pretty badly, so there should be... In fact..."

He looked back down the street in the direction of the Focus. "Ask Sinead to give her brother a ring. Try to get him to pinpoint where he found it, or at least narrow it down. If there's still nothing, then we'll start the door knocking."

"Right, boss," Tyler said, setting off in the direction of the car.

He'd only gone half a dozen steps when he stopped and looked down at the vehicle beside him. At first, Logan thought he was checking his reflection in the window, but then he stepped back, frowning.

Logan saw it a moment later.

"Red Vauxhall Mokka," he said.

"2014 plate," Tyler added, checking out the front of the vehicle.

"That's Ken Henderson's car," Logan said. His voice was low. Gruff. "Come on," he said, walking off.

Tyler looked from the car to the house it was parked outside. "What?" he asked, then he hurried after the DCI.

"Stop looking back at the house," Logan warned him. "Once we're around the corner, phone in to the station. Find out who owns that house. There's plenty of parking along this street. Henderson could've parked anywhere, but he's right outside that gate."

They took a right at the end of the block, turning into an alleyway that ran between one end terrace and the next.

"Get us back-up. Tell them to stay out of sight, and no sirens. Last thing we need to do is spook him."

Logan stopped and took the radio from his inside pocket. Beside him, Tyler got dialling on his phone.

"Sinead. You see the red Mokka parked along the street near where we were standing? Keep lookout on that house. Let me know if there's movement, no matter how small."

"Will do, sir," came the reply. "Is that Henderson's car?"

"Aye. It is. So, eyes peeled, constable," he told her. "Shout if there's anything."

Logan and Tyler both finished their conversations at the same time.

"Caitlyn's on it," Tyler said. "DS McQuarrie, I mean."

He leaned out and looked along the front of the row of houses. "So... it's Henderson, then?" he said. "Not Dylan Muir, or Tom Fisher, or whatever we're calling him."

Logan gave a shake of his head. "No, it's Fisher. Dylan."

Saying the name in that context hurt him, made him flinch.

"But I think Henderson might be egging him on. I think that Petrie told him Dylan was alive during one of his visits, and spilled the beans on where to find him. Henderson wouldn't have the balls to kidnap a kid, but he's enough of a weasel to convince some poor mixed-up bastard to do it for him."

Logan took a few steps towards the back of the block and peered over the top of the high fence, counting the gardens until he found the back of the house Henderson's car was parked outside.

"I don't like the man, but I doubt he thought it'd go this far. He's a publicity hungry parasitic bastard, but he's no' a killer."

"So, Fisher attacked Hamza?"

"I reckon so, aye."

"And Fisher's in that house?"

"I think it's a safe bet."

"Then what are we waiting for?" Tyler asked.

"We've got back-up on the way," Logan told him. "We should wait for them to get here."

"And in the meantime what, boss? What happens to the kid, if he's in there with them? You said yourself, we're fighting the clock here."

"I'm not going to let what happened to Hamza happen to anyone else," Logan said.

"Hamza was blindsided. We're going in eyes open."

Logan sucked air in through his teeth, looked the DC up and down, then gave a nod. "Aye. Right. You take the back, I'll go in the front. Wait for my signal."

Tyler bounced from foot to foot, becoming animated. "Alright! Nice one. Let's do it. What will the signal be?"

Logan took a pair of blue gloves from his pocket and slipped them on. The latex *creaked* as he flexed his fingers in and out.

"It'll be a big crash," he told the junior officer. "And quite a lot of shouting."

CHAPTER FORTY-THREE

THE DOOR WAS STURDIER THAN IT LOOKED AND TOOK THREE GOOD kicks before it surrendered. It swung inwards, *banged* against the wall of the hallway, then bounced back again.

Logan shouldered it aside and stormed in, fists raised.

"Fisher? I know you're in here!"

The smell hit him mid-sentence, knocking him back half a step and a whole decade.

Rot.

Decay.

Things long dead.

No. *No.* Not again.

Please God, not again.

Blood spotted the walls in the hallway. A slug trail of the stuff was smeared across the laminate flooring, leading from the living room on the left to what looked to be the kitchen up ahead.

Logan followed the trail, picking his route so as not to contaminate the scene any more than was absolutely necessary.

He didn't know what he'd find at the other end of that streak. Didn't want to know, but had to.

Stopping at the door, he took half a second to compose himself, then leaned through into the kitchen.

Henderson was on the floor. Face down, eyes open but seeing nothing.

His skin was chalk-white, aside from a caved-in area in the side of his forehead. His life was a puddle on the floor beneath him. No point checking for a pulse. A day ago, maybe, but not now.

There was a *thud* against the back door. Then another. Logan heard DC Neish mutter on the other side of it, then turned the key and opened the door just as Tyler let fly at it with another kick.

"Shit!" the DC ejected, stumbling into the kitchen. He slipped on the blood, waved his arms frantically as he tried to find his balance, then caught Logan's offered arm and steadied himself.

"Thanks, boss," he gasped. His eyes went to the floor. "Is that Henderson?"

"What's left of him, aye," Logan confirmed.

"Any sign of Fisher?"

"Not yet. I haven't—"

There was a squeak from beyond another door in the kitchen. A faint cheep, like the wailing of an injured bird. Soft, but unmistakeable.

Motioning for Tyler to open the door, Logan positioned himself in front of it, feet ready to move, hands ready to grab.

With a sideways look to Tyler, he nodded.

The door was pulled open, sharp and suddenly.

A boy was revealed, all sobs and snot, bound and gagged and terrified.

But alive.

Connor.

From out in the hallway there came a *thump*. Footsteps. The front door slamming hard.

"Boss!"

"Stay with the boy!" Logan bellowed.

He dodged past Henderson's body, skidded through the blood, all thoughts of preserving the crime scene now playing second fiddle to catching the bastard responsible.

Logan made it into the garden in time to see the red Mokka roaring away from the end of the gate. He caught a glimpse of Tom Fisher behind the wheel, but then the car was speeding off down the street and hanging a left at the end.

The Focus screeched to a stop in the middle of the road ahead of him. Logan vaulted the gate and hurried around to the passenger side. Sinead had already thrown the door open, and floored the accelerator before Logan could pull it closed again, rendering his shouts of, "Go, go, go!" completely redundant.

Flicking a switch on the dash, Sinead fired up the car's lights and sirens while Logan got on the radio. "All units, all units, we are in pursuit of a red Vauxhall Mokka, registration KT12 XOH, currently headed..."

"South-East."

"South-East, along..."

"Kilmallie Road."

"Kilmallie Road. We're the ones with the flashy blue lights going *nee-naw, nee-naw*. You can't miss us," he said, then he scrabbled for his seatbelt as Sinead skidded off the side-street and onto the main road, drawing a prolonged *honk* from an oncoming Co-op delivery truck.

"Christ, and you said my driving was bad," Logan muttered. "We got Connor."

"You got Connor?"

"I think he's alright."

Sinead's head snapped around, eyes wide. "He's alright?"

"Is there an echo in here?" Logan grunted. He stabbed a finger ahead. "Watch the bloody road!"

Sinead faced front, catching sight of the back of the Mokka just as it powered around a bend.

"What's up ahead?" Logan asked. "Can he get out?"

"They know he's coming," Sinead said. "They'll block the road at the Farmfoods junction. It's his only way out."

Logan punched the roof in triumph. "Yes!" he cheered. "Catch up with him, though. Get right up his arse, I'm not having him slip through our fingers."

Sinead started to respond, then stopped in a gargle of panic. The car decelerated in a sudden lurch, tyres smoking, brakes howling in protest. Logan swore loudly and creatively as he was slammed forward, the seatbelt tightening across his chest.

"What are you doing?" he wheezed.

"He's there. He's there," Sinead cried, unbuckling her belt and scrambling out of the car.

Logan followed her gaze until he found the Mokka. It was halfway through a fence, driver's door open, engine running, abandoned in the small front garden of a house.

No. Not just any house, Logan realised.

Sinead's block.

The neighbour's garden.

Harris.

CHAPTER FORTY-FOUR

SINEAD WAS YOUNGER, FITTER, AND HAD A HEAD START. LOGAN DID his best to catch her, but she was through the hole in the garden fence and up the path before he'd hit top speed. The house's front door stood open. Shouts and screams came from inside the house, all of it escalating when Sinead charged inside, baton extended.

Logan's chest was heaving with the effort when he barrelled inside behind her, almost knocking her off her feet.

Tom Fisher—Dylan Muir—stood in the centre of the living room, a hand clamped down over Harris's head, the retractable blade of a packing knife pressed against his throat.

Maureen, the woman Logan had seen on the doorstep earlier, knelt on the floor next to an old man—her husband, presumably—shielding him with her body. A deep gash ran across the side of his face, splitting his cheek from his ear to his nose.

"Let him go!" Sinead barked. "I swear to God, let him go."

"S-Sinead?" Harris whimpered, then he gasped when Fisher tightened his grip, jerking the boy back by the hair.

"Shut up. All of you, shut the fuck up," Fisher hissed. His eyes were wild, the knife trembling in his grip. He was out of control, or on the brink of becoming so, at least. "Anyone tries anything, and I cut this kid a new mouth!"

Logan raised a hand in a calming gesture and positioned himself between Sinead and her brother. Down on the floor, Maureen quietly comforted her husband and pressed a handkerchief against his wound.

"Alright, alright. Let's all stay calm, OK?" Logan said. "You're fine, Tom. You're fine. Just relax."

"I'm relaxed! *I'm perfectly fucking relaxed!*" Fisher practically screamed. He glared at Logan, eyes blazing. "You want me to kill this kid? I'll kill him. I'll do it. I'll do it. Is that what you want?"

"I don't want that, Tom, no," Logan said. "I don't want anyone to die. Not him, not you, and certainly not me."

Fisher scowled, looking the detective up and down. "You think you're clever, don't you? You think you're so smart. But you didn't see me, did you? None of you saw me. Watching. Listening. That's how I knew when to get the kid. Connor."

He shook Harris. "And this one. He took one of my cats, so I followed him. And I watched."

"I don't think I'm clever, Tom, no. Far from it," Logan said. "If I was clever, I'd be the one holding the knife, not you."

"Exactly. So back off! You hear me? Back off!"

"I'm backing off, Tom. Look? Here's me backing off," Logan said, raising both hands and shuffling back a few paces.

Sinead side-stepped out of the DCI's path, and then took another shuffled sideways step that brought her out of Fisher's immediate line of sight.

"The thing is, it's not me you have to worry about," Logan said. "It's the marksmen."

"What?!"

"Windows, Tom," Logan said, gesturing to the panes of glass at either end of the room. "Direct line of sight, wherever you go. If they think you're going to hurt the boy, then they'll take you out. They have to. They don't have a choice."

Fisher's gaze went first to the window behind Logan, then turned to look at the other window a few feet away at his back.

Sinead shuffled a step closer, staying wide.

"Bullshit. There's no-one there," Fisher spat. "You're lying!"

"I'm not lying, Tom. I wish I was, believe me," Logan told him. "Like I said, the last thing I want is anyone dying today, but I'm afraid that decision is no longer in my hands, son."

Logan indicated the window with a thumb. "It's not even in theirs. It's in yours. You've got the power here, Tom. You're the one making the decisions."

"Fucking right, I am! Fucking right, I've got the power!" Fisher barked.

"I'm glad you understand that, Tom. And I'm sure you appreciate the responsibility that goes along with it."

Fisher's face contorted, his eyes narrowing. "What?"

"Well, decisions have consequences," Logan told him. "And, unless you're careful, one of those consequences is going to involve you getting shot through the head by a polis sniper."

Logan raised his hands again, fingers splayed, palms forward. "And, like I say, I don't want that. I promise you, I will do everything I can to avoid that outcome. But you have to help me, Tom. You've got to give me a hand here."

Down on the floor, Maureen began to cry. "Just let him go. Let him go!"

"Shut up!" Fisher seethed, tightening his grip on Harris's hair. "I told you, everyone *shut up!*"

"This situation isn't as bad as you think it is, Tom," Logan told him. "Connor's unharmed. DC Khaled—the detective you stabbed—he's alive."

"He shouldn't have been there! He shouldn't have come snooping around!"

"Aye, I'm pretty sure he regrets that now," Logan agreed. "But the point is, they're both going to live. They're both going to be OK."

For a second or two, Fisher almost looked like he might buy it, but then his face darkened and his voice took on a desperate, frantic edge.

"What about Henderson? Henderson's not going to be fine, is he?"

"No, but he was probably asking for it," Logan told him. "I've known him for years. It's a miracle I never killed him myself."

Harris squealed as Fisher pressed the knife more firmly against his skin. "You're *joking*. Stop joking! You think this is *funny?*"

"No, Tom, I—"

"You think it'll be funny when I split this kid's throat open? Will you joke about that, too? Eh? Will you?"

"Relax, Tom. Relax. I was just—"

"*Stop telling me to fucking relax!*" Fisher howled. He thrust the knife forward, waving it in Logan's face. "Now fuck off before I—"

The baton caught him on the wrist. Fast. Hard. Sudden.

The room was filled with the sound of breaking bone, although this was almost immediately drowned out by Fisher's screams. The knife landed on the floor at Logan's feet. A sudden shove on the back sent Harris staggering forwards.

Sinead dived and caught him before he could fall, blocking Logan as he tried to grab for Fisher. He missed, tripped, stumbled. Fisher was already racing for the door, his shattered wrist held close to his chest, sobs of agony bursting as bubbles on his lips.

"Stay here. Watch them," Logan instructed.

He was out the door a handful of seconds behind Fisher, along the path in time to see the lad racing along the pavement and tumbling awkwardly over a fence that divided it from a narrow strip of overgrown wasteland.

Fisher wailed with the pain the landing brought, but it drove him on, launching him to his feet and propelling him through the undergrowth.

Logan ducked through the fence like a wrestler entering the ring. He didn't have to catch Fisher, just keep him in sight. He could hear sirens somewhere close by. The place was going to be swarming with uniforms any minute.

There was nowhere left for Fisher to run.

CHAPTER FORTY-FIVE

"The dogs will be coming in a minute, Tom," Logan announced, picking his way through the jaggy bushes and nettles that turned the waste ground into a maze of low-level suffering. "No point running. Not now."

Fisher stumbled up an incline, then stopped at the top. He turned back to Logan, swaying unsteadily, his arm clutched to his chest.

"That *bitch*," Fisher spat. "She broke my wrist. She broke my fucking wrist!"

"You didn't give her a lot of choice in the matter," Logan told him. He stopped halfway up the slope and looked Fisher up and down.

It was there, right enough, around the eyes. The similarity. The resemblance to the boy in those photographs. The boy he'd never found.

The victim he couldn't save.

"Come in quietly, Tom. With me. We can talk," Logan told him. "Given the circumstances... We can talk."

"What *circumstances*?" Fisher said, spitting the word out as if it left a bad taste in his mouth. "I know who you are. I know what you did."

He caught the look on Logan's face and grinned. "Yeah! Didn't know that, did you? I know what you did to my dad. You messed him up. You locked him away."

"Your *dad*?" Logan spluttered. "Who, Petrie? Petrie isn't your dad, son."

"What? Yes, he is!"

"No. No, I'm sorry, Tom. That's not true."

"*Yes, he is!* He's my dad, and you set him up. You threw him off that roof! You took him away!"

"That's what this is about, isn't it?" Logan said, inching closer. "You thought that you could make us doubt the conviction. If Mister Whisper was still out there, then we'd have to let Petrie go."

"Well, you would!" Fisher spat. "You'd have to. Henderson told me!"

"No, son. That's not how it works," Logan said. "Did Henderson put you up to this? Was that it? Did he tell you we'd let Petrie go if you kidnapped Connor and sent the bear?"

A jolt of pain shot through Fisher's arm, making him gasp. He glanced behind him, then danced on the spot, nursing his wrist.

"He was going to turn me in. After I stabbed the policeman. He said it'd gone too far," Fisher said. "I couldn't let him tell you. I couldn't let him tell anyone."

"So, you killed him," Logan said.

"I had to! I didn't have any choice. I just wanted everything to go back to the way it was. I just wanted my dad back!"

"Whatever Owen Petrie made you believe, he is not your dad, son. I've met your dad. He's a good man. He's nothing like Petrie."

"Stop saying that! He's my dad! He's my dad and you took him from me! You took everything from me!"

The way he said it – the twisted snarl, the clenched fists, the shriek of desperation – brought the terrible reality of the situation home for Logan.

"Jesus. You've been alone this whole time," he realised. "Since we caught him. You've been on your own."

Fisher—Dylan—said nothing. He just stood there, staring defiantly as he gulped back tears.

"I'm so sorry, son. I tried to find you. For years. I really did, you have no idea," Logan said, his voice thin and croaky. "But I was looking in all the wrong places."

The ground rumbled faintly. Fisher glanced behind him for a moment, then back to Logan. "You're lying. You locked up my dad, and now you want to lock me up, too."

"You need help, son. Specialist help. You've been lost too long."

Logan held a hand out, bridging the gulf between them. "Come on with me, Dylan. Come on home."

Fisher blinked. Once. Twice. A series of expressions crossed his face. Surprise. Confusion.

"Dylan? Who's...?" he began. "What are you...? What do you...?"

Then his expression became something else. Realisation. Acceptance, maybe.

His eyes went wide. The rest of his face went slack.

He gave a half-hearted snort. The ground rumbled, louder this time.

Logan worked out, too late, what it was.

"Shit, shit, no!" he bellowed, powering up the incline.

"Dylan," Fisher said, rolling the word around inside his mouth.

And then he stepped backwards beyond Logan's reach, fell onto the train tracks on the other side of the incline, directly into the path of the 11:41 to Glasgow.

And was lost to the oncoming thunder.

DCI Jack Logan and DI Ben Forde sat in the front seats of Logan's Ford Focus, watching Duncan and Catriona Reid take their boy home. The family stopped at the gate, as Logan had advised, to let the press photographers fire off a few hundred snaps in the space of three seconds, and to utter a few rehearsed soundbites.

"We're just grateful to have him home."

"We thank the police and the community for all their hard work."

"I'm going to have ice cream!"

That done, Constable Sinead Bell escorted the family up the path, while four other uniformed officers moved in to encourage the press to be on their way.

"You did good, Jack," Ben said.

Logan didn't respond. Not at first. He kept his eyes fixed ahead as a few spots of rain flecked the windscreen. The sky was once more heavy and fat with dark clouds, and they were doing more to chase off the media vultures than the polis.

"Storm's coming," said Logan, looking up.

"There's always a new storm on its way up here," Ben told him. He shrugged. "We get through them. They all pass, sooner or later."

They watched Sinead and the Reids disappear inside the house. The liaison was going to hang around for the rest of the day to offer them any immediate support they might need. Connor had been checked over at the hospital, but he was going to need a lot of help going forward. Professional help.

Logan hadn't been able to stress that to the family enough.

"Christ. We should probably let Ed Walker go," Logan said, his eyes going to the house next door to the Reids.

"God. Aye. I'd forgotten we still had him," Ben said. "What about your head?"

Logan reached up and felt the sharp ends of the sutures with the tips of his fingers. "It's fine."

"He tried to ruin your youthful good looks."

Logan chuckled drily. "Take more than a clout to the head to mess up this mush."

"No charges, then?" Ben asked.

"No charges."

They sat in silence a while longer. The press were all getting into their cars and vans. One by one, they were pulling away, leaving the Reids to get on with their lives.

"So, Henderson, then?" said Ben.

"Aye," Logan confirmed, his contempt evident in just that single word.

"But, I mean... for a *story*? I don't get it. Why would Petrie tell him about Dylan? And, if he did, why didn't Henderson just run with that? He could've found the missing kid. Been a hero."

"Christ knows," Logan sighed. "Maybe Petrie did tell him, or maybe he just figured it out himself, somehow. He's always maintained we didn't do things by the book with the original case. Maybe he thought he could prove he's been right all these years. Get one over on me, or something."

Logan shrugged. "Maybe Petrie put him up to it. Or manipulated him into putting Dylan up to it, anyway. Maybe it was all an attempt to cast more doubt on his conviction. He can be a persuasive bastard when he wants to be."

Ben looked sceptical.

"He's no' the cabbage he makes out he is," Logan insisted.

Ben tactfully steered the conversation in a different direction. "You think Henderson would have let Fisher kill Connor?" Ben asked.

Logan blew out his cheeks. "I don't know. I mean, he was an arsehole to the core, but I'm still not convinced he was a murderer."

"Guess we'll never know," Ben said.

Logan nodded. "Aye. Guess not."

The front door to the house opened. Sinead emerged and stood on the step, chatting to someone inside. She was all smiles and animated gestures, so Logan guessed it was one of the Reids. Catriona, probably.

"She worked out well," Ben said. "You've still got a knack for spotting the good ones."

"Not always," said Logan, shooting Ben a disparaging look.

"Funny," said DI Forde.

Sinead said her farewells and turned away from the house as the door closed.

"Dylan Muir's parents," he said, still facing front. "They never find out."

Ben turned to him. "You're not serious?"

"I am. Dylan helped kill those two boys. And then... all this. With Connor. Henderson. And Hamza."

He met Ben's gaze. "They can't find out. It'd kill them."

"But isn't it better they know? Isn't it better they get some sort of closure?"

"Not this. Not like this," Logan said. "This wouldn't be closure. This would be the end of them."

"Aye. I mean..." Ben began, but words failed him and he stopped there.

"As far as they know, we're still looking for their boy," Logan told him.

He turned the key in the ignition as Sinead closed in on the car.

"And we'll never stop."

CHAPTER FORTY-SIX

THERE WAS A GOING AWAY PARTY FOR LOGAN IN THE STATION canteen. It wasn't a particularly grand affair—DS McQuarrie bought a pack of cakes from the *Farmfoods* up the road, and DC Neish put the kettle on— but it was the thought that counted.

The conversation started slowly, and mostly centred on the case. Gradually, things picked up. They discussed DC Hamza's serious-but-stable condition, the fact that Ben had never got the double chips he'd asked for, and then Sinead had demonstrated, via the medium of mime, what Logan's high-speed driving skills were like.

By the time they were onto Tyler's inability to kick in a door, they were laughing like old friends. But by then, the cherry bakewells had been eaten, and the tea had been drunk, and it was time for the party to come to an end.

Logan wasn't big on goodbyes at the best of times, so he kept things short and sweet. Or sweet by his standards, at least.

"I'll be honest, when I first met you, I wanted to beat the shite out of you," Logan told DC Neish. "Nothing personal, mind. It was just the hair. And a bit the face. Mostly the hair, though."

Tyler grinned and ran his fingers through his immovable locks. He'd reapplied whatever chemical concoction held it in place, and it immediately returned to its original position when he took his hand away.

"You're just jealous, boss," the DC said.

"Aye. Probably," Logan admitted. He shook Tyler's hand. "Good work, son. Pleasure working with you."

"You, too."

"Well, 'pleasure' is maybe stretching it..." Logan added.

Tyler laughed and stepped away as DS McQuarrie approached. Logan spotted Tyler sidling closer to Sinead, considered putting a stop to it, then decided not to bother just this once.

"Sir," said Caitlyn, shaking his hand. "It was good working with you. You have some... interesting methods. I reckon I've learned a thing or two."

"Oh, God. No, forget anything you've learned from me," Logan told her. "Seriously, keep doing it your way. I'm the last person you should be getting inspiration from."

Caitlyn smiled. "Yeah. I was just being polite, sir. I'm not going to do any of that."

Logan wiped a hand across his brow. "Phew. Had me worried for a minute there."

And then, it was DI Forde's turn. Neither man said much. They didn't have to. There was a handshake that became a shoulder-pat, then a hug.

"Tell Alice I said hello," Logan said.

"I will."

"Does she still hate me, by the way?"

"With the fire of a thousand suns."

"Jesus, still?"

Ben shrugged. "You killed Harry."

"By accident," Logan stressed.

"We both know it wasn't an accident, Jack," Ben scolded. "Anyway, even if it had been, it doesn't matter. You still killed him."

Both men realised then that the others were staring at them in confusion.

"Harry Pricklepants," Ben said, as if that explained everything.

"It was this ugly bastard of an ornament," Logan clarified. "Little hedgehog with trousers on. It was a mercy killing, if anything."

The sense of relief from the others was palpable.

"Tell her I said hello, anyway," Logan told Ben.

DI Forde nodded. "I'll pass on your best."

"Mind if I walk you out, sir?" Sinead asked when Logan turned to talk to her.

"Aye, escort this man off the premises, Constable," DI Forde instructed.

He lifted a napkin from the table, revealing the cherry bakewell he'd been keeping hidden, then peeled it out of its little foil case.

"And see that he doesn't come back."

"How's HARRIS?" Logan asked, as they crossed the car park, headed for Logan's car.

"He's alright. Surprisingly," Sinead said. "Our aunt and uncle came down from Nairn. They're going to stay a few days. Jinkies... I mean, Chief Inspector Pickering has said I can take a few days off to get him sorted."

"Take him up on that," Logan advised.

"I will, sir. I just... I wanted to be there this afternoon to get Connor home. I wanted to, I don't know, see it through."

"Aye. I get that," Logan told her.

They reached the car and stopped by Logan's door. The rain had come down in sheets for half an hour, but now the blanket of cloud had become thin and patchy, allowing glimpses of the blue sky beyond.

The storm was over. For now, at least.

"I wanted to say 'thank you,' sir," Sinead said. "For getting me involved. And for everything with Harris. You didn't have to do either."

"Well, I kind of do have to help kids who're being held at knife point," Logan pointed out. "It's pretty much in the job description."

Sinead smiled and nodded. "Oh. Is it? I should probably read that at some point."

Logan wrinkled his nose. "I wouldn't bother. It's a bit dry, and you can see the ending coming a mile off.

"Besides," he added. "You don't need it. Just keep doing what you're doing. You've got this."

"Thanks," Sinead said, blushing slightly. "So, I suppose it's back to directing traffic and stopping the high school kids drinking down the riverbank at lunchtime," she said. She smiled dreamily. "Can't wait."

"Aye. Well, I wouldn't get too used to it," Logan told her.

He offered a hand for her to shake, but she stepped in and hugged him, instead. He patted her back a little awkwardly, then she pulled away and stepped back, making room for him to open his door.

"Safe journey, sir."

"Thanks, Sinead. Tell Harris I'll send him tickets to my next ballet performance. Then we'll see who's laughing."

"I will, sir."

Logan opened the car door, shrugged off his coat, then tossed it onto the passenger seat. He was about to get in when Sinead spoke again.

"You should call her, sir."

Logan paused, one foot in the footwell.

"Your daughter, I mean. You should call her."

For a moment, Logan looked lost in thought.

"Aye," he said, climbing into the car. "Maybe."

And then, he pulled the door closed, fired up the engine, and the Focus swept out of the car park to begin the long journey south.

DC HAMZA KHALED regarded the bag of grapes with an expression that was giving very little away.

"Did you check if they're halal, sir?"

Logan's eyes widened. "What? Shite. No, I thought—"

"I'm kidding," Hamza said. He grimaced as he shuffled himself up the bed a couple of inches. It was the best he could do for now, but it was a start. "Sit down, sit down."

Logan shook his head. "I'm not stopping. I've got an appointment. Just wanted to stop by and say hello. Make sure they were treating you alright."

"It's mental, sir," said Hamza, dropping his voice to a whisper. "They're treating me like a proper hero. I mean, check it out. Private room. Some of the nurses have even been asking for autographs and selfies. Whatever you do, don't tell them all I did was get myself stabbed."

"You did a lot more than that, Hamza," Logan told him. "A lot more."

"Says the man who brought Connor home."

Logan shook his head. "Team effort. All the way."

They chatted for a while. About the case. About the attack. About DC Neish's hair.

Logan apologised. Hamza waved it away.

And then, Hamza's wife popped her head impatiently around the door, and it was time for Logan to go.

"I'll check back in tomorrow," the DCI said. "Assuming I can fight my way through the mob of fans out front."

"Aye, good luck with that," Hamza told him.

He met Logan's eye, and while they said nothing, something passed between them. Some understanding. Some bond.

"So, that's it then, sir? Case closed, all done?"

Logan drew himself up to his full height. "No' yet, son," he intoned. "There's one last thing to take care of."

CHAPTER FORTY-SEVEN

THE CITY HAD FELT MORE CLAUSTROPHOBIC THAN HE REMEMBERED AS he'd made his way through it, the M8 busier and more choked with traffic as he'd crawled along it, heading east.

His conversation with the receptionist had been brief, but friendly enough. She hadn't asked any questions as he'd signed the book. They knew him well here. Well enough.

"Any joy?" he asked, indicating the open newspaper on her desk. A couple of the jobs had been ringed in black pen. She smiled nervously as she flicked the page.

"I was just having a look," she said.

"Don't blame you," Logan replied, finishing his signature with a flourish. He picked up his own newspaper which he'd brought in, then tucked it under his arm. "Good luck."

Petrie was sitting in his usual chair, back to the window, glassy doll-eyes fixed on nothing in particular. Logan approached without a word, then stood looming over him, the two men separated only by the little rolling table where Petrie ate his meals.

Still saying nothing, Logan unfolded the newspaper. It was a copy of that day's *Herald*. He could've picked any one of the Scottish dailies, but had selected this one for the impact its combo of headline and image would make.

He placed the newspaper down, turned to give Petrie the best possible view of the front page. Logan watched him, waiting for the moment when the fog behind Petrie's eyes would briefly clear, revealing the monster that lurked within.

When it happened, Petrie's throat tightened, ejecting an involuntary grunt. His eyes met those of a young man in his early twenties. A pencil drawing, but a damn accurate one. Well worth the forty quid.

KIDNAPPER DIES IN TRAIN SUICIDE was the headline. Logan had liked the simplicity of it. No messing. No wordplay. Just the facts, blunt and raw and brutal.

Logan watched as Petrie tried to stop his shoulders shaking. Almost admired the bastard's attempts to hold himself together.

The door opened at his back. Dr Ramesh's voice was one long sigh of exasperation.

"Detective Chief Inspector Logan. I thought I'd told you not to turn up here? I thought I'd explained you couldn't keep doing this?"

"Don't worry, Doctor," said Logan. "I'm done here."

He allowed himself another moment to enjoy Petrie's suffering.

"I'm done."

And then, he turned to the door, strode out of the hospital, and headed back towards the city he called home.

THICKER THAN WATER

DCI JACK LOGAN BOOK TWO

CHAPTER ONE

THEY WERE GOING TO GET IN TROUBLE. SHE WAS CERTAIN OF IT.

She was sure she could feel her parents' eyes on her as she slid clumsily down the embankment. Sure her dad would shout after her as she sprackled through the heather. Sure she would hear the rustling of the tent being unzipped, and see the beam of a head torch sweeping across the campsite towards her as she stumbled the final few rocky steps to where the water met the land.

But, she didn't. Instead, she stood there shivering at the shore of the loch, listening to the gentle lapping of the waves and the faster crashing of her own heart.

Nathan was a pace or two ahead of her, the moonlight bathing him as he hopped on one leg and wrestled off a shoe.

"We're not actually doing this, are we?" Lolly asked. They were a good hundred yards from the campsite, tucked out of sight, but the fear of getting caught turned the question into a whispered giggle.

She'd only known Nathan for a day and a half, but he'd quickly turned a tedious family camping holiday in Scotland into much less of a soul-crushing ordeal. He was two years older than her—almost in Sixth Form—and she had immediately taken a shine to him.

He was funnier than the boys back home. Smarter, too. He'd been able to tell her all kinds of stuff about the history of the area. Yes, her dad had told her almost exactly the same information during the drive up, but the difference was that Nathan had explained it in a way that didn't make her want to self-harm. He managed to make it *interesting*.

Mind you, she would quite happily listen to him reading the entire GCSE Maths curriculum, she thought.

He was from just outside Oxford, less than a hundred miles away from where she lived. They'd already made plans to meet up back home the night before, arranging the details via Snapchat. Lolly had lain awake in her sleeping bag for hours, listening to her parents snoring through the dividing canvas wall as she and Nathan swapped messages and photos.

His GIF game was top-notch, and when he'd sent a version of the 'distracted boyfriend' meme to her with one of her own photos superimposed over the face of the attractive passing woman, she'd felt her heart skip half a dozen beats.

It had been momentarily concerning, in fact, before she realised that she wasn't about to go into cardiac arrest and that instead this—*this*—was what love must feel like.

"Yes, we are. But it's freezing!" Nathan yelped, placing a bare foot in the water then immediately yanking it back out again. He kicked off his other shoe and tugged on the end of his sock. "Come on, hurry up before I get frostbite!"

"You're not exactly making it sound appealing," Lolly told him, but she pressed the toe of a trainer against the heel of the other shoe and prised it off.

The rocks were smooth and rounded, and she was able to stand on them in her bare feet without too much discomfort. Nathan already had his t-shirt off, and she spent a moment just staring at his exposed top-half, partly in admiration but mostly in shock.

Was this actually happening? She glanced nervously back in the direction of the campsite, still expecting to see that lighthouse-beam of her dad's head torch sweeping out over the water. When she didn't, she wasn't sure if she felt relief or disappointment.

Nathan covered his nipples with two fingers of each hand and fluttered his long eyelashes. Lolly laughed despite her nerves. Or perhaps precisely because of them.

"Don't laugh! You'll make me all self-conscious," he told her.

She stifled the giggles, and he saw the look of uncertainty that moved in to replace the smile on her face.

"You OK?" he asked, dropping his hands to his sides. He reached down for the t-shirt he'd discarded on the rocks. "Want me to put this back on?"

Lolly took a moment, then gave a shake of her head. Her fingers went to the buttons of her shirt and she fumbled with them, her hands shaking through cold and nerves and... something else. Anticipation, maybe. She couldn't give a name to it, but she liked it, she thought.

Mostly.

Her skin goose pimpled along her arms as she folded them across her chest and wished that she'd brought a nicer bra with them on holiday, or that she better filled the one she had on.

Nathan didn't seem to mind, though. She heard his breath catch in his throat and hoped that he wouldn't notice her blushing in the darkness.

"Wow," was all he said, then he set to work unfastening his jeans and wrestling his way out of them.

Once he had struggled his way free, he tossed the jeans down next to his t-shirt and held his arms out, presenting himself like a gameshow prize.

"Ta-daa!"

He grinned at her, showing none of the embarrassment or self-consciousness that Lolly felt. His underwear was tight enough to reveal a bulge that turned Lolly's anticipation into something more apprehensive.

Was she really going to do this?

Nathan noticed where her gaze was pointed and shifted awkwardly. "It's cold out here, alright?" he said, still smiling. "That's my excuse, and I'm sticking to it."

He flicked his gaze to her lower half. "Your turn," he said, indicating her cut-off cargo pants.

She kept her arms folded, hugging herself in an attempt to stop the shaking. Her mouth felt dry. She felt like she should say something, tell him this was a mistake, but the words wouldn't come.

What was wrong with her? She liked him. *Really* liked him. And he liked her. So, it was fine, wasn't it? This was how it was supposed to happen. Better here with him, than back home at some party with someone she had no interest in six months from now.

Right?

He stepped in close, derailing her train of thought. The heat of him warmed her. Melted her.

"Hey, it's OK, it's OK," he soothed, placing his hands on her shoulders. He looked so calm, so serene in the moonlight. Angelic, almost. His skin, unlike her own, was smooth and near-flawless. She felt an urge to run her hand across it, to check if it was real.

"It's just swimming, that's all," he assured her.

Lolly's voice came as a series of unsteady breaths. "Is it?"

"If that's what you want, then yeah," Nathan promised. "I'm not going to do anything that makes you uncomfortable, OK?"

Lolly swallowed. Nodded.

"OK, then. Good." He leaned a little closer until she could feel his breath on her skin. "Trust me, alright?"

She shivered as his fingertips trailed delicately down her arms. Almost spasmed as they tickled down her ribcage, his palms brushing the sides of her covered breasts.

He kissed her. His lips were soft, but the shock of them suddenly pressing against her own hit her like a sledgehammer. She ejected an, "Umf!" of surprise right into his mouth, which made him draw back, a puzzled expression furrowing his brow.

"Sorry," she whispered, flushed with embarrassment. "I was just... You just... I wasn't expecting..."

She tensed and closed her eyes as he kissed her again. This time, to her relief, she was able to avoid making any involuntary sounds of surprise, even when she felt his tongue pushing its way into her mouth.

His tongue. His tongue was in her mouth.

On purpose.

Was this nice? She wasn't sure. Probably. It wasn't *not* nice, exactly. Strange, definitely. It wriggled around like a worm in there, brushing against her own.

She wished she'd brushed her teeth before coming out.

She was so focused on the tongue-waggling, and so worried about her dental hygiene, that she didn't notice him working the buttons of her shorts until they dropped down around her ankles.

He was kissing her neck now, less tenderly than he'd kissed her lips. She felt his hand on her bum, kneading one buttock through the thin cotton of her underwear.

Another hand pushed one side of her bra up, briefly exposing her breast before his fingers clamped over it, concealing it again to everything but his touch. He grunted and pressed himself against her, the bulge in his boxers making its presence felt.

"Wait," Lolly said. "Stop."

He paused just long enough to whisper an, "It's fine," in her ear before he brought his hand around from her bum and moved it between them. She felt it press against her belly, felt the fingers slide down inside her underwear, stalking down through her pubic hair.

"No, I said *stop*," she objected, more forcefully than she'd intended. It got the message across, though.

She pushed back from him and saw a flash of frustration screwing up his face. It lasted only a moment, before he masked it behind something kinder and gentler.

"What's wrong?" he asked. "What's the matter?"

Lolly repositioned her bra and pulled up her shorts.

"What are you doing? Come on," Nathan said. "It's just a bit of fun."

"I don't want to," Lolly said, not meeting his eye. "Sorry."

"What? Why not? I go home tomorrow," Nathan told her, struggling to hide the impatience in his voice. "This is our only chance."

Picking up her shirt, Lolly pushed an arm through the sleeve. "We can meet up back home. Get to know each other a bit before... Before we... You know. Before we do anything."

"For fuck's sake. What are you, *twelve*?" Nathan spat, and the tone of it hit her like a slap to the face. "We live a hundred miles apart. We're not going to meet up. This is it."

"But, I thought we said..."

"Jesus Christ, you actually thought we were going to... what? Become boyfriend and girlfriend? Have a *long-distance relationship*?" Nathan said. The scorn in his voice made Lolly's cheeks sting with shame. "I hate to break it to you, but that's not going to happen. This is it. This is our only chance. It's now or never."

Lolly swallowed down her embarrassment and began buttoning her shirt. To her surprise, her hands didn't shake this time. Not one bit.

"Never, then," she told him.

The firmness in her voice surprised her. From the look on Nathan's face, it surprised him, too.

"Hey, wait. Come on," he said, his voice softening again as he moved to close the gap between them.

"I swear to God, come near me and I'll cave your head in with a rock," Lolly warned.

"OK, OK! Jesus," he said, raising his hands in surrender. "I'm sorry. Honest. I got carried away. I overstepped the mark. It's just..." He motioned to her. "I mean, look at you. You're beautiful."

Lolly said nothing. The breeze coming in across the water toyed with her hair.

"Of course we'll meet up back home. I can get the train over," Nathan told her. "We can get to know each other, like you said. Or you can come to me. I'll introduce you to my mates. They're all dicks, though. I feel I should warn you."

"What, like you?"

"Worse than me," Nathan said. "If you can imagine such a thing."

Lolly sighed. She should be walking away by now, she knew, and yet her feet hadn't found their way back into her trainers.

"Just come swimming. That's all. Just swimming," Nathan pleaded.

"No thanks," she said, although not with the same conviction as just a few moments before.

Nathan backed into the water. He was all smiles again, back on the charm offensive. "But what if Nessie gets me?" he asked. "You're not going to let me face a big scary monster alone, are you?"

Annoyingly, Lolly felt herself smirk as Nathan kicked back through the waves, his eyes and mouth widening into three circles of surprise.

"Shit! It's cold! How can it be this c-cold?"

"It's Scotland."

"But it's July!" Nathan said, slapping at his bare arms.

"But it's *Scotland*," Lolly reiterated.

"I know, but s-still," Nathan continued through chattering teeth. The water sloshed around him as he forced himself back a few more icy-cold steps. "You'd think that it'd at least be a *little bit*—"

He went down suddenly, arms flailing, face twisting in panic. There was a yelp, then a splash.

And then silence.

And then nothing.

"Very funny," Lolly said, watching the spot where he'd gone under.

Ripples expanded lazily across the loch's surface, moonlight dancing across each undulating peak as they steadied back into stillness.

"Nathan?" she said, as loudly as she dared. "Nathan, this isn't funny."

She took a step closer to the water, then cried out in shock when he exploded up from below, eyes wide, breath coming in fast, frantic gasps. He grabbed for her. At first, she thought he was trying to pull her in with him, but then she saw the fear on his face and the panic in his movements.

"What? What's the matter?" Lolly yelped, her voice becoming shriller as Nathan's terror awoke the same response in her. "What is it? What's wrong?"

Slipping and stumbling, Nathan dragged himself clear of the water, clawing his way up onto the rocks on his hands and knees, coughing and wheezing. Lolly saw a dark shape following, sliding out of the water right behind him. He kicked out at it, squealing now like an injured animal, but a long blue tendril was tangled around his foot, attaching him to the shapeless mass.

No, not shapeless. Not exactly.

As the dark water fell away and the moonlight played across the thing, Lolly saw a hand, fingers curling upwards like the legs of a dead spider.

She saw an arm, cold and blue.

She saw a face. Eyeless, yet somehow staring at her from within the folds of a bright green tarpaulin shroud. Begging. Pleading.

Accusing.

With the dark water lapping around her feet, and the cool night air swirling around the rest of her, Lolly screamed and screamed and *screamed*.

CHAPTER TWO

DCI Jack Logan sat in a pokey wee Dumbarton café, nursing a disappointing cup of coffee and briefly glancing up on the rare occasion that the front door opened.

He didn't like waiting. During his time in the polis, and the last few years in the Major Investigations Team in particular, he'd become known for many things. Patience was not one of them.

"You sure I can't get you a menu, son?"

Logan looked up from his two-thirds empty mug and found the café's owner smiling down at him. Standing, she wasn't much taller than he was sitting. Her big square glasses magnified her eyes to bug-like proportions as she watched him expectantly, a laminated piece of A4 held between both hands.

"I'm fine, thanks. I'm just waiting on someone."

"Are ye, aye?" asked the owner. Her voice had the rasp of a lifelong heavy smoker. Her fingers, starkly yellow against the white of the menu, were a giveaway, too.

She looked to the door, then across to the clock on the wall. "It's just it'll be the lunchtime rush soon, son. It gets busy."

Logan cast his gaze across the dozen or so empty tables. Aside from himself, the only other customer in the café was a young woman with a baby.

"You've only got one other customer in here," Logan pointed out.

"Two," she corrected.

"What? The wean?" Logan said. He thumbed in the direction of the baby. It was currently gulping down milk from a bottle. "Hardly going to be ordering up a cheese and ham panini anytime soon, is he?"

"She," said the owner. "That's my granddaughter."

"So, she's not even a real customer, then?"

"We'll need the table, is what I'm saying," the owner said, getting snippy now. "I'm not chucking you out, son, but we'll need the table. For people eating."

Logan sighed. Through the window, he saw a woman in a blue jacket, but she continued on past the door without stopping.

Not her.

"Aye. Fine. I suppose I'd better take a menu, then," he said, holding a hand out.

The owner smiled and nodded, then passed him the laminated sheet. Logan took it and placed it face-down on the table without so much as glancing at it. The old woman's smile faded.

"Are you no' going to look at it?"

"In a minute, aye," Logan told her. "Eventually."

She opened her mouth to reply, then clamped it shut again, the puckering of her wrinkled lips conveying her displeasure before she turned and began noisily clearing some dirty cups from a neighbouring table.

The door opened. Logan's eyes went to it as a couple of workmen entered, newspapers tucked under their arms. Council boys, going by the logo on their high-vis vests. Lunchtime on a Friday. Traditional knocking-off time.

"Alright, hen?" said the older of the two as they both took seats. "Couple of rolls and square sausage when you get a minute."

"No bother, pet," the café owner said, drawing Logan a look that managed to say both, 'I told you so,' and, 'you'd better bloody order something, sharpish,' at the same time. "I'll get that for ye's now."

Logan's gaze followed her to a door at the back of the café, spent a few seconds getting the measure of the council boys, then went back to the door.

Waiting.

He hated waiting.

He especially hated it when he was waiting for something he suspected wasn't going to happen.

He'd first suspected it wasn't going to happen about forty-five minutes ago, when she was a mere twenty minutes late. Now that it was an hour past their arranged meeting time, he was more or less convinced of it.

He'd give her five more minutes.

Ten, maybe. Traffic might be bad. It had been nose to tail across the Erskine Bridge on the way out here, and while she wasn't coming in from the same direction, there was no saying she wouldn't be stuck in a queue somewhere. It was tourist season, after all.

He took a gulp of his coffee, then grimaced. Cold.

He daren't order another without having something to eat, too. It didn't pay to get on the wrong side of a wee Glesga granny, and he reckoned he'd probably pushed his luck far enough as it was.

He turned the menu over and was just considering the Stornoway black pudding with caramelised onions when his phone chirped at him. He knew what it was going to say before he looked at it.

Running late. Cant make it. Sry.

He read the message four or five times before tapping out a reply.

Heading north today. Don't know when I'll be back down. Be good to see you.

He typed it all out properly. He wasn't one for all that '2CU' shite.

Logan re-read the message a couple of times, then deleted the last sentence.

Then, he added it back in again and hit 'Send.'

He waited, his eyes fixed on the screen.

He was still waiting when the owner delivered the rolls to the council boys, then crossed to his table.

"You ready?" she asked.

Logan looked up. "What?"

She pointed to the menu still held between the finger and thumb of his left hand. "You know what you're after yet?"

Logan looked first at the menu, and then at his phone. The screen was dark, the speaker silent.

"Just the bill, please," he said.

The old woman peered at him over the top of her glasses. "What's the matter? Date stand you up?"

"Daughter," Logan corrected, pushing back his chair as he stood. "But aye. Something like that."

LOGAN OPENED the boot of his Ford Focus and tossed his coat in on top of his bags. He'd bought three cases, thinking that would be enough for everything he wanted to take with him. In the end, he'd filled one, half-filled the other, and put the third into the storage unit along with the boxes, bags, and general clutter that he'd emptied out of his flat over the course of a few weekends.

He checked his phone again, just on the off-chance.

Nothing. She'd well and truly dinghied him.

Not that he could blame her, he supposed. God knew, he'd done it to her and her mother often enough over the years.

Sliding the phone into his pocket, he opened the driver's door and stood there for a while, staring at the seat and considering the road ahead. And the one already travelled.

It had been four months since he'd finally been able to close the file on the Owen Petrie case, and put the whole *Mister Whisper* thing behind him.

Or try to, anyway.

The reality of it was, he hadn't got anything like the closure he'd been hoping for. The opposite, if anything. Aye, he finally knew what had happened to Petrie's first victim. He'd got an ending of sorts. It just wasn't the one he'd been expecting.

In hindsight, he'd almost rather not have known.

But still, it was over, and as the weeks passed, Logan had found himself liking Glasgow less and less. He'd grown up in the city, spent most of his adult life there, too, but increasingly it began to feel like a gallery of his greatest failures, filled with reminders of the people he couldn't save, or the cases he'd never been able to crack. Murderers gone unpunished. Victims gone unavenged.

The whole place was filled with everything he'd lost, and crisscrossed by all the lines he'd had to cross to get the job done. A graveyard of bad memories.

Six weeks, almost to the day, since he'd closed his file on Petrie, he'd put in for the transfer up north. The Gozer—or Detective Superintendent Gordon Mackenzie, if you were talking to his face—had objected, of course, and the Assistant Chief Constable was originally having none of it, either. But Logan had too much dirt on both of them, and when he gently reminded them of that fact, their resistance had soon crumbled away.

Besides, DCI Grant had been crying out for a transfer to the Central Belt for years, so it was simple enough to sort out a handover and do a straight swap.

"It'll be quiet up there," the Gozer had said when Logan stood in front of his desk for what would probably be the last time. "You'll crack up."

"Quiet sounds good," Logan had said. "I'll risk it."

They'd shaken hands, then Logan had been on his way, sneaking out through the back to avoid the smiles, well-wishes, and pats on the back from the rest of the team. They were a decent bunch, but that sort of thing had never really been his cup of tea.

Here, now, standing in the ASDA car park, staring at the driver's seat, he gave a single nod.

"Right, then," he said. Then he climbed into the car, closed the door, and fired up the engine.

He was barely five minutes up the road, still on the dual carriageway stretch before the Stirling roundabout, when a call came through from an Inverness number.

"DCI Logan," he said, after tapping the big green icon on the screen.

"Jack. It's Ben. You on the road?"

Logan had known DI Ben Forde for a long time. He knew right away that there was something up.

"Barely, why?"

"You're going to have to make a wee detour on the way to Inverness," Ben said, his voice resonating through the car's speaker system. "Take the back road from Fort Augustus. There's a campsite in Foyers, right down by the loch. We'll meet you there."

Logan shot a glance in his mirror then pulled out into the right-hand lane, powering past a line of slower-moving traffic.

"Something come up?" he asked.

"Aye," said Ben. There was a faint *pop* as he sucked in, then spat out his bottom lip. "You could say that."

CHAPTER THREE

DETECTIVE INSPECTOR BEN FORDE PICKED HIS WAY ACROSS THE rocks, muttering to himself about slipping, and hips, and men of his age. It was a typical summer's day in the Highlands, and so Ben had his jacket zipped right up to the neck.

The loch side had been a hive of activity for the past several hours, and this section of the bank had positively heaved with white paper suits as the crime scene team did their best to gather up what evidence they could. Which, by all accounts, hadn't been much.

"That's where they found her," Ben said, before rounding off the sentence with an, "Ooh, shite," when he almost lost his balance on a wobbly boulder. He took a moment to compose himself before continuing.

"She'd been wrapped in tarp and tied with rope. The lad, Nathan, got it tangled around his legs."

"And what were they doing out here?" asked Logan.

He put a hand on the back of his neck and moved his head around, easing the stiffness that had been building there on the drive up. It had been a long trek, and although he'd turned on the lights and siren to get past a few convoys of camper-vans and meandering sightseers, it had still taken him the best part of four hours to get here.

The last stretch along a winding single-track road had seemed endless, with more time spent manoeuvring past or pulling over for oncoming vehicles than making any sort of onward progress.

His body was not thanking him for the experience, and he suspected that it'd be even less happy with him when he woke up tomorrow morning.

Something to look forward to.

"Swimming, apparently. Well, the boy was. The girl didn't go in the water."

"Ages?"

Ben checked three jacket pockets before finding his notebook. "He's sixteen, she's fourteen."

Logan's eyes narrowed a fraction. "And we're sure it was just swimming?"

"That's what they're both saying," Ben wheezed. "No funny business as far as we... Jesus, it's further than you think."

He stopped, his face pained as he struggled for breath. "This is close enough, isn't it?" he asked, gesturing ahead to a taped-off area down by the water. There were a couple of uniforms standing guard, but the Scene of Crime team had long since departed.

Logan's eyes went to the cordoned-off spot, then traced a route across to the grassy banking that ran down to the rocky section they were standing on. A row of conifers, badly in need of a tidy-up, stood to attention at the top of the slope.

"Campsite's up there?"

"Aye," Ben confirmed. "The boy's family are going home today. We've interviewed him and got everything useful out of him, I think, but we asked them to hang around in case you wanted a chat."

Logan nodded. "Good. And the girl?"

"They're here for another couple of days. At least, that was the plan. A lot of folk are packing up and shipping out. I expect they'll do the same."

Logan shot the DI a questioning look. Ben raised his eyebrows in surprise.

"*Obviously,* we got names and addresses," he said. "Although, one of the bods from SOC reckons the body's been in the water a few days, so if it was someone at the site then chances are they didn't hang around. No saying it was dumped here, though. Could've drifted in from somewhere else. Currents, and what have you."

"Right. Aye."

Logan cast his gaze across the surface of Loch Ness to the shore on the other side. He could see cars meandering up the main road between Fort Augustus and Inverness, but they were too far away for him to hear anything over the lapping of the water and the wheezing of DI Forde.

His mind wandered back to another stretch of water much like this one. Him kneeling by the shore, prodding away at a disposable barbecue, trying to get the bastard to light. Vanessa knee-deep in the water, a squirming Madison in her arms, pudgy hand grabbing for the water well out of reach below. Barely toddling yet, but desperate to get down and investigate the wet stuff swooshing around her mother's legs.

The sun had been beating down that weekend, and half of Glasgow seemed to be camped out along the banks. But Vanessa had known a spot tucked away out of sight, a little bay just thirty feet across, hidden by a curve of trees. They'd had to wade for a few seconds to reach it, but once they had... Bliss.

With the sun shining, Madison giggling, and the water licking the smooth rocks on the shore, you could almost tune out the thunder of traffic winding along the A82 just fifty or sixty feet up the banking behind.

Loch Lomond. Almost... what? Twenty years ago? Christ, had it been that long?

He never had managed to get that barbecue going.

Across the water, a procession of traffic was being led by a couple of caravans and a timber lorry. He pitied the poor bastards stuck behind that lot. They may have been too far away for him to hear the engines, but they were close enough that he could sense their frustration and misery.

Bloody tourists.

The sky was a shade of grey-blue that suggested it hadn't quite made its mind up, weather-wise. The clouds rolling in from the top end of the loch begged to differ.

"I want to talk to the girl first," Logan announced. "What's her name?"

Ben consulted his notebook. "Lolly."

Logan frowned. "Lolly? What's that short for?"

"Nothing," Ben told him. "Just Lolly."

Logan continued to frown as he tried to process this. "What? That's no' her actual name, is it? *Lolly?* Who names their child *Lolly?*"

"That's her actual name," Ben told him.

Logan shook his head. "Well, at least we know that stumbling upon a mutilated corpse isn't the worst thing that's ever happened to the poor lassie. I mean... *Lolly.* Jesus Christ, what were they thinking?"

With a final glance at the cordon tape, he turned and started towards the grassy bank.

"Come on, we'll go talk to her," he said, leading away across the rocks. "Try not to fall on your arse, if you can possibly avoid it."

"No promises," Ben muttered, then he picked his way after Logan, muttering once more about his hips.

Upon meeting them, Logan realised that Lolly's parents were *exactly* the sort of people he'd expect to saddle their child with such a name. If anything, she'd probably gotten off lightly. Under different circumstances, she might've been a Petal Blossom, or a Lily Boo, or some other nonsense. Lolly, on reflection, was a lucky escape.

Mr and Mrs Montague were minted. *Proper* minted. That much was obvious. Sure, they were on a camping holiday in the Scottish Highlands and not, say, swanning in the sunshine of Dubai, but this was clearly a choice, and not something they had done through necessity.

The camping gear was all top of the range stuff and looked brand new. Their car, which was parked right beside their pitch, was a private reg Range Rover. One of the ones with the waiting list, Mr Montague had said, dropping that little titbit into the conversation at the earliest possible opportunity.

Neither of the parents were dressed for camping in Scotland. Not really. They were dressed for what rich people imagined camping in Scotland to be like, all fancy fleeces, tweed bunnets, and three-hundred-quid hiking boots that barely had a mark on them. They could've stepped off the pages of *Horse & Hound*, were it not for the miserable looks on their faces.

Given the circumstances, Logan couldn't really blame them.

They sat either side of their daughter on a PVC couch in the on-site café, which the Major Investigations Team had commandeered for the interviews. The site manager had offered up his office, but as there was barely room to swing a cat in there and the ceiling was black with damp, he'd reluctantly agreed to let them use the café instead, on the understanding that he was reimbursed for any tea and coffee consumed.

Dead woman or not, he wasn't running a bloody charity, and the arrival of a mutilated corpse right on the site's doorstep wasn't exactly going to do wonders for business, so he needed every penny he could get.

"First of all, you've got nothing to worry about," said Logan. He was sitting across from the family on a slightly unsteady wooden chair that wobbled whenever he shifted his centre of gravity. "You're not in any trouble, and I know you've already answered a lot of questions today, but I just have a few more for you, alright?"

"Alright, poppet?" asked Mr Montague, before Lolly had a chance to answer.

"Alright," Lolly said. She was pale, her eyes ringed with concentric circles of red and black from tears and exhaustion.

"Alright," said Mr Montague, looking up from his daughter and beaming at the DCI.

"He heard her, William," said Lolly's mother, practically hissing the words through her teeth. "You're not a bloody translator. She doesn't need you repeating everything parrot-fashion. Do you, darling?"

Lolly shook her head.

"No."

"No," echoed Mrs Montague, shooting her husband a triumphant look. "Precisely."

Logan shot a sideways glance to Ben, who was sitting in an armchair to the side of the family, notebook open, pen poised and ready.

"So, Lolly," Logan began. He felt faintly ridiculous addressing her by that name but tried not to show it. "What time did you leave the tent last night?"

Lolly had pulled her hands into the sleeves of her shirt so only the tips of her fingers were visible. She fiddled with the cuffs, her eyes not quite meeting Logan's own.

"Quarter to one."

"And you met..."

"Nathan Powell," said Ben.

"Nathan. Right. Where did you meet him?"

Lolly's eyes went to the window, then onwards to a row of conifers that marked the edge of the site. "By the trees."

"She had no business being out at that time. We had no idea," said Mr Montague.

"William!" his wife scolded.

"Well, we didn't!"

"It's not about us," Mrs Montague hissed, her face a picture of contempt. "It's about Lolly."

Logan liked her. More than he liked her husband, at any rate, although that wasn't exactly saying much. He was getting the distinct impression, though, that she hadn't been altogether in favour of a camping holiday in the Highlands, even before a mangled corpse had emotionally scarred her daughter for life.

"So, you met Nathan by the trees, then what?" Logan continued.

"We went down to the water," Lolly said.

"Why?"

Lolly shrugged. "To swim."

"And whose idea was that?" Logan asked.

"His, of course," Mr Montague snapped. "He led her astray. She'd never have done anything like this back home."

"William!"

"Well, she wouldn't? Would you, poppet?"

Logan fixed Lolly's father with a look. It wasn't a particularly stern look, but it was one that suggested there was real scope for it to become much sterner at any moment, and implied that this probably would not be an enjoyable experience for anyone who found themselves on the receiving end.

"Mr Montague, this will all be over much quicker if you just let Lolly answer. She's been through quite enough for one day, and I'm sure she just wants to put it all behind her."

He kept the look fixed on Mr Montague for a few moments, then turned to Lolly, his face softening into a smile. "Right?"

Lolly nodded. "Yes."

"OK. I just have a few more questions and you're done, alright?"

Lolly nodded again.

"So, who suggested you go swimming?"

Lolly glanced at her parents, just briefly. "Both of us. We both thought it would be a laugh. We arranged it on Snapchat."

"It's a phone thing," Ben chimed in.

"Aye. I know what Snapchat is," Logan said.

"You're a step ahead of me, then. I had to ask."

Logan leaned in a little and spoke conspiratorially to Lolly. "He's only just figuring out email. He still says, 'all small letters, no spaces,' when he's giving out his address."

"Well, it is all small letters with no spaces," Ben pointed out.

"See?" said Logan.

Lolly smiled at that. Or her mouth did, anyway. Her eyes didn't really get involved. Still, she relaxed a little, and that was the main thing.

"So, you both decided to go swimming. You met up, went down to the water. Then what?"

"Nothing," Lolly said.

"Nothing?" asked Logan.

"I mean..."

Lolly's gaze flitted left and right. It was body language Logan understood all too well. She was about to tell him not the truth, but a version of it. She was carefully selecting a few events from all those that had actually happened to craft a narrative. She wasn't about to lie, exactly, but she wasn't going to be completely honest, either.

"Nothing much. It was cold. I changed my mind about going swimming, but Nathan went in, anyway."

"He didn't... try anything?" Logan pressed.

"I beg your pardon?" blustered Mr Montague. "What are you saying?"

Both parents looked down at their daughter. From their expressions, this thought had not yet occurred to either of them.

"He didn't, did he, poppet?"

"No. No, he didn't try anything," Lolly said. "It was just swimming, that's all."

"Oh, thank God for that," said Mrs Montague. She gave her daughter's shoulder a squeeze.

"Right. OK," said Logan. He didn't believe that, but there was no point dwelling on it. Instead, he shot Ben a glance. The DI's pen scribbled a note on the page.

"So, he got undressed," Logan continued.

"Not all the way," Lolly interjected, her cheeks reddening.

"OK. He got partially undressed, went in the water, and then...?"

The girl's breath caught in her throat. Her eyes glazed over a little as the memory replayed in her mind's eye.

"He fell. He was just... One moment, he was complaining about how cold the water was, and then... He just fell. He went right under," she said, her voice becoming hoarse. "He went right under, and I thought he was joking, but then... But then..."

Mrs Montague's arm tightened around her daughter's shoulders.

"Is this strictly necessary, Detective Chief Inspector?" the girl's mother asked.

"We're almost done, I promise," Logan said. "How long was he under for, Lolly?"

Lolly shrugged. "I don't know. A few seconds, maybe. It felt like a long time, but... A few seconds."

"And then what happened?"

Lolly's expression had become distant again, but her eyes were fixed on a spot somewhere behind Logan, as she recalled—or relived—the memory.

"He... He came back up," she said, hesitantly feeling her way through the words like Ben had picked his path across the rocks. "Just, like, *whoosh*. All of a sudden. He came up, gasping for air. He looked scared. *Really* scared. And then he crawled out. He crawled out of the water and onto the rocks. He was screaming and crying. And then... And then..."

A tear cut a track down her cheek. She was shaking, and if it hadn't been for her parents squashing in on her at either side, she may well have vibrated right off the couch.

"You're doing so well, Lolly," Logan assured her. "And then...?"

"It came out behind him," Lolly whispered. "It was wrapped around his legs. I didn't know what it was to start with, but then I saw..."

Her face crumpled. She wedged both hands between her knees and squeezed them together.

"She was looking at me. It was like she was looking right at me."

The girl's voice was barely audible now, a knot in her throat trying to silence her.

"I think that's quite enough, don't you?" said her father. "Surely you have everything you need? This is the fourth time she's been through all this."

For once, his wife didn't try to shut him up. Instead, she glared at Logan, almost daring him to argue.

"I think you're absolutely right, Mr Montague," Logan said. "Lolly's been through enough."

He stood. After a few false starts as he tried to get himself up out of the low armchair, Ben joined him.

"You've been a big help, Lolly. Thank you. I'm sorry you had to see what you saw."

Lolly sniffed, wiped her eyes on her shirt sleeve, then looked up. "Will you catch him? Whoever did it?"

Logan gave a nod, then reached for his coat, which he'd draped over the back of the chair.

"Aye," he assured her. "We'll do everything we can."

CHAPTER FOUR

THE INTERVIEW WITH NATHAN WENT MUCH THE SAME AS THE conversation with Lolly, with a few minor differences. Only one of the boy's parents were present. He was a little bit mouthier and less helpful. That sort of thing.

The biggest difference came near the end of the interview, when Logan gave the teenager a lengthy explanation of what Statutory Rape was and detailed the dire consequences that might befall a sixteen-year-old who pressured a fourteen-year-old into doing things she wasn't comfortable with.

"And the things they do in prison to kiddie-fiddlers," Logan had said, sucking air in through his teeth. "Isn't that right, DI Forde?"

"Oh God, aye," Ben had agreed, nodding gravely. "Turns the stomach just to think about it."

Funnily enough, a lot of the boy's defiance had deserted him then, and he'd suddenly become much more forthcoming with information.

Essentially, though, the stories were the same. Nathan elected to miss out the part where he was screaming and crying, but otherwise the stories matched.

He went in the water, fell, then got himself tangled in the rope. He'd caught a glimpse of the body when he'd first gone under, the face floating right next to his in the murky darkness. It was a miracle the boy could speak, let alone be a mouthy wee arsehole.

After the interview, Logan had told Nathan's mother that they could go, but that he might be in touch for more information in the next couple of weeks, so not to leave the country.

"Thoughts?" asked Ben, as they watched Nathan and his mother hurry across the rapidly-emptying campsite towards their car. A Mercedes, this time, brand new plate. Was it all bloody toffs who went camping these days?

"The mother's alright. The boy's a thoroughly horrible wee shite. Tried to get his end away, but don't think he got anywhere. Otherwise, he's telling the truth."

"Aye," said Ben, having come to the same conclusion.

His phone rang. Logan continued to look out of the café's window at the campsite while Ben took the call.

"That was Caitlyn," he said, once he'd finished. "DS McQuarrie."

"I remember her."

"We've identified the vic. Mairi Sinclair. Primary school teacher. Aged thirty-one, going on thirty-two. Birthday's on Sunday. Reported missing five days ago."

"By who?"

"Now you're asking," said Ben, his eyes narrowing as he tried to recall. "Sister, I want to say. It's been on the news."

Logan shook his head to indicate that he hadn't seen it.

"There's more. Pathologist wants to see you to go over a few things about the body. Apparently, it's... odd."

"Odd?"

"That's all she's saying. 'Odd.' Make of that what you will."

Logan nodded. "Right, then. Make sure your man here turns over his records. We need details of everyone who was here over the last—"

"Aye, aye. Done," Ben said. He was smiling, but there was a suggestion of reproach colouring the lines of it. "It's no' my first spin around the block, Jack. This is my job, would you believe? They actually *pay me* to do this sort of thing."

"Someone clearly has more money than sense, then," Logan remarked. "I mean, you're no' as young as you used to be."

The DCI didn't rattle off any more instructions, though, which Ben knew was as close to an apology as he was likely to get.

Ben flipped his notebook closed, shoved it into a randomly selected jacket pocket, then drained the final dregs from a mug of coffee. It had been cheap and unpleasant-tasting to start with, and now that it was stone-cold, it had not improved. Still, he'd paid for it, and he was bloody sure he wasn't letting it go to waste.

"Right, then," he said, after a full-body shudder of displeasure. He set the mug down on the café counter, then gestured towards the front door. "Shall we?"

THEY WERE CROSSING the car park when Logan heard the shout. It was loud and piercing, more like a wail of despair that had somehow been formed into words.

"Just tell me! Just bloody tell me what happened!"

"Aw, shite," Ben muttered, as he and Logan both looked in the direction of the sound. A wiry-looking man with salt-and-pepper hair was gesticulating angrily at a uniformed officer. "That's Malcolm Sinclair."

"Who's Malcolm...? Wait. Sinclair? Victim's father?"

Ben nodded. "Aye. He and his wife—Mairi's mother—were informed earlier that her body had been found."

"Did they identify?"

"No. Dental records," Ben said. "We didn't tell him exactly where she'd washed up, but it's not hard to find out. News like this travels fast up here."

"Look, just... get out of the way. I want to see, alright? I want to see where she was found!" Malcolm ranted, the pitch of his voice rising. It was still a couple of octaves below 'fingernails down a blackboard' stage, but it was heading in the right direction.

A woman in her mid-twenties was doing her best to calm him down, but it was clearly a losing battle.

"Dad. Dad. Just... Please. Come home, alright? Come home to Mum," she said. She was smiling, but the effort was visibly taking its toll on her.

"You want to handle this, or will I?" Ben asked. "And, just a reminder, only one of us here is the Senior Investigating Officer. And it's no' me."

Logan sighed. Ben gave him a pat on the back. "Attaboy."

The gravel of the car park surface crunched beneath Logan's feet as he strode over to where the uniform was trying her best to defuse the situation. At the sound of his approach, Malcolm's head snapped towards the DCI, the other officer immediately forgotten.

"You. Are you a detective?" he demanded.

"Mr Sinclair," said Logan, giving the older man a nod. The woman who'd been trying to calm him down shuffled over to join them, but hung back a few paces. "Yes. I'm Detective Chief Inspector Jack Logan. I'm the Senior Investigating Officer. I'm very sorry about your daughter."

"Finally! Someone with a bit of clout," Malcolm said. "I want to see. I want to see where she was found. I want to see where my little girl was found."

"I understand, Mr Sinclair," Logan said.

"No! No, you don't! How can you? *How can you?*"

Logan said nothing. He knew better than to engage. Better to just let the man's anger burn itself out.

"She was my—" Malcolm began, but he choked on the rest of the sentence. Clenching his fists down by his sides, he tried to compose himself.

The woman behind him—another daughter—slipped a hand onto his shoulder and gave it a squeeze. He seemed to deflate, as if the pressure had opened some sort of valve and released whatever had been driving him on.

"I just want to see. I want to see where they found her. That's all. I'm not... I don't..."

He looked down. Logan watched the muscles in his jaw tighten and relax, tighten and relax, over and over.

When he raised his head again, his eyes swam with tears. "I just need to see."

Logan glanced at the uniformed constable, who looked enormously relieved that she no longer had to deal with this situation, then around at DI Forde. Neither one offered anything in the way of suggestions.

"In my experience, Mr Sinclair, it won't help," Logan said. "It'll only make it worse."

"That's what I said, Dad," his daughter said.

"Worse? *Worse?* How can it be worse?" Malcolm demanded. "How can it *possibly* be worse? She's been bloody murdered! It doesn't get any worse!"

Logan knew better. It could always get worse.

Still, the man was grieving. Desperate. And Logan got the impression he wouldn't back down without a fight.

"Very well, Mr Sinclair," he said. "It's against my better judgement, and it's still an active crime scene, so we can't get too close, but if you'd like to follow me I'll show you the spot where Mairi's body was discovered this morning."

He gestured towards the conifer trees that lined the edge of the campsite. The loch stretched out beyond them, deep, and dark, and riddled with secrets.

Malcolm Sinclair didn't move. His gaze went in the direction that Logan had indicated, but his feet remained planted on the ground.

It was the wording that was important. *Mairi's body.* It solidified the idea of it in their minds. Forced them to confront a finality they almost certainly weren't yet ready to accept.

"Mr Sinclair?" Logan asked. "Would you like to see where the body was found?"

Malcolm's bottom lip trembled. His breath whistled in and out through his nose. He shook his head, the sudden movement sending a tear cascading down his cheek. His daughter stepped in closer, sliding an arm around his waist.

"Probably for the best," Logan told him. He put a hand on the older man's shoulder. "We're going to do everything we can to catch the person responsible for this, Mr Sinclair. We're going to make sure whoever did this is brought to justice."

Malcolm nodded, but said nothing.

"Do you have someone to drive you home?" Logan asked.

"I'll take him," the daughter said. She shot Logan a brief smile. "Michelle. Mairi was my sister. Sorry about this. He just... When he heard..."

Her voice failed her. She cleared her throat, then tried again. "We can leave his car here. I'll get it picked up somehow."

"I'm sure we can help with that," Logan told her. He raised his eyes in the direction of the uniformed constable. "Can you take Mr Sinclair's car home for him?"

"Yes, sir. Not a problem."

"Hear that, Dad? They're going to bring your car home. You can come with me," Michelle said.

Logan watched as Malcolm allowed himself to be led away. He moved slowly and unsteadily, but most likely through shock and grief than any ailments or old age.

The gravel crunched as Ben walked up to stand at the DCI's side.

"Nicely done."

"Poor bastard," Logan muttered.

"Aye," Ben agreed, as they watched him be helped into the passenger side of a royal blue BMW hatchback. "You can say that again."

LOGAN WAS first to arrive at Raigmore Hospital, but by the time he'd spent a full twenty minutes circling the car park trying to find a space, Ben had beaten him to the front door.

"Did I no' tell you about the parking?" the DI said, feigning innocence. "They keep a spot for us."

"No, you didn't mention," Logan replied through gritted teeth.

"Shite. Sorry. Must've slipped my mind," Ben said. "Still, you can't blame me. It's no' like I'm as young as I used to be."

With that, he about-turned and led Logan through the sliding doors into the hospital.

"The problem is the free parking, you see?" Ben explained as they passed a little coffee shop. Logan's stomach rumbled, and he realised it had been a long time since he'd almost-but-not-quite eaten lunch.

Still, considering what he was on his way to look at, he thought it maybe best not to go putting anything in his stomach quite yet.

"They run a bus service into town from here," Ben continued. "And, because people are—by and large—a shower of arseholes, anyone working in town uses it as a Park and Ride, hence no bugger can get parked."

"Fascinating," Logan told him.

"It's bloody outrageous, if you ask me," Ben continued, not letting the subject drop.

They took a right at the end of a corridor, then immediately hung a left. Logan hadn't seen any signs for the mortuary yet, but the DI seemed to know where he was going.

"You've got folk coming in for an appointment, or to visit family, or what have you, and they can't get parked. They've to go to Tesco across the road and walk over." He shook his head. "It's not right."

Logan kept quiet, choosing not to get involved. He was relieved when they finally reached an area with 'ZONE 6' plastered across the walls, and saw a sign indicating that the mortuary was nearby.

"I'll wait out here," Ben said, stopping when they reached the doors. "I've a few phone calls to make, and the stomach's no' what it used to be."

Logan patted the older officer on his ample belly. "Aye, you can say that again."

"All bought and paid for," Ben told him. He reached over and pulled open one of the double doors that led through into the morgue. "Enjoy."

CHAPTER FIVE

"I'M LOOKING FOR THE PATHOLOGIST," LOGAN SAID, ADDRESSING A woman who sat behind a desk, hoovering the contents of a *Pot Noodle* into her mouth.

She was dressed in a lab coat, but had fashioned herself something that might have been a napkin, but could equally have been considered a giant bib, out of part of a surgical gown.

"'Mmsec."

Logan took in the room, trying to ignore the hurried *slurping* as the woman wolfed the noodles down.

He'd entered into some sort of office area, with a couple of cheap desks, two chairs that belonged in a skip, and a range of filing cabinets of assorted makes and models. Nothing in the room looked like it was supposed to be there, with the possible exception of the woman herself, who looked right at home as she guzzled her way through the last of her *Bombay Bad Boy*.

She was average height, average build, with hair that was neither one thing nor the other. At first, Logan had thought it was blonde, but there was some auburn in there, too, and maybe a wee touch of ginger when she tilted her head back to drain the sauce dregs from the bottom of the pot.

She was about his age, maybe a year or two either way. The eyes that peered at him over the rim of the pot were a blue that fell a little short of 'brilliant,' but were pretty striking, nonetheless.

"Sorry. Famished," she said, setting the container down on the desk. She pulled the homemade bib off, drew it across her mouth, then wiped her hands on it before scrunching the whole thing up and tossing it into a waste paper basket down behind the desk.

Or, she might've just dumped it on the floor, Logan couldn't really tell from that angle.

He'd been right about the lab coat, although hadn't been expecting the *Batman* t-shirt she wore underneath it. Logan wasn't really up on his superheroes, but that was one of the few whose logos he did recognise.

"Awful bloody things," she said, shooting the *Pot Noodle* tub a dirty look. Her accent had a suggestion of Irish about it. The lilting twang of the republic, rather than the more guttural tones of the north.

"Aye, you can say that again," Logan agreed. It was not unknown for him to partake of the odd *Pot Noodle* himself after a long shift, and he was usually burdened by the same sense of regret that was now painted across the woman's face.

"Shona Maguire," she said. "I'd shake your hand, but I'm all sauce."

She looked him up and down, idly picking at her teeth with the nail of a pinkie finger. "You must be the new fella. DCI Logan, wasn't it?"

"Jack," Logan told her.

She rolled the word around inside her mouth, as if testing it out. "Jack. *Jack.* I knew a Jack once. Another one, I mean. A different one. Not you."

"It's not an uncommon name."

Shona wrinkled her nose. "Wasn't a fan, to be honest. For a number of reasons." She shrugged and stood up. "Still, I'll try not to hold that against you."

Logan had a feeling she expected him to show gratitude for that. He didn't.

There was a little sink in the corner. Shona crossed to it and washed her hands, watching Logan over her shoulder the whole time. "So, you're taking over from DCI Grant, then?"

"As of today, yes."

"Those are some big shoes to fill," Shona said. She shook the water from her hands, then looked around for a towel. "Literally. He was huge."

"Aye. We'd met," Logan said. "Big fella."

"Thick as pigshit, mind," Shona continued. She gave up looking for a towel, and wiped her hands on her coat, instead. She smiled encouragingly in Logan's direction. "Maybe you'll be better."

"You *are* the pathologist, aye?" Logan asked, increasingly doubtful.

The pathologist he'd worked with down the road had been of the classic 'grey-haired-auld-fella' variety, with a plummy Morningside accent and a neat line in tweed waistcoats. He was a million miles away from the woman standing before Logan now.

"I am. I've got a certificate and everything," Shona told him. She glanced briefly around them. "Somewhere."

"I'll take your word for it. DI Forde said you've had a look at the body."

"I have," Shona confirmed.

"And?"

"And, at first I thought it was a bit odd." She raised a finger. "I stress *at first.*"

"So... what, then? You don't now?"

"No." Shona shook her head. "Upon closer inspection, in my professional medical opinion, it's not odd, no."

Her eyes widened, betraying her excitement. "It's *bizarre.*"

Logan glanced in the direction of another set of double doors that presumably led through to the morgue proper.

"Bizarre in what way?"

"Tell me, Detective Chief Inspector," said Shona, adopting a somewhat mysterious tone. "Do you believe in monsters?"

"No," said Logan.

Shona laughed. "No, fair enough. That would be mental," she said. "But, make no mistake, it was a monster who did this."

She gave a little sigh, audibly expressing her disappointment.

"Just a predictably bog-standard human one."

She fished around on one of the desks until she found a cardboard box around the size of a small shoe box. She tossed it to Logan, and when he caught it he turned it over to reveal a hole in the top, and a layer of blue latex inside.

"Stick some gloves on," Shona instructed. "Do you want a mask?"

"Will I need one?" Logan asked, peeling a couple of surgical gloves out of the box.

"I don't know. How strong's your stomach?"

"I've been doing this a while. It's pretty cast iron by this point," Logan told her.

She looked him up and down. "Right," she said. There was a *cluck* sound as she clicked her tongue off the roof of her mouth. "I think I'd best get you a mask."

CHAPTER SIX

LATER, WHEN RECALLING WHAT FOLLOWED, LOGAN WOULD BE grateful for the mask.

Nobody looked their best after being in the water for a few days, and Mairi Sinclair was no exception. Most of her body was covered by a sheet, but the aroma of death lingered around the table she lay on and clung to the very fabric of the room.

The sight of a corpse didn't bother him. God knew, he'd seen enough of them, and often in a rawer, more visceral tableau than the one before him now. He'd been first on the scene at an RTA his first week in uniform, and his life had been an endless parade of horror ever since.

The smell, though? The smell still got him. Dark and bitter, yet somehow cloyingly sweet. It got in about the mucus lining of the nostrils and set up camp there, somewhere near the back where it was best placed to trigger the gag reflex.

It had been years since Logan had last heaved at the smell, but he never ruled out the possibility of it.

He did his best to ignore what he could smell now, and concentrated on what he could see.

The victim's face was a blueish-white, aside from a dark and raw area around her mouth and down over her chin. Having heard the statements made by the teenagers who'd found the body, Logan had been braced for the whole no-eyes thing, but he evidently hadn't been braced enough, as the sight of those sightless black hollows made his breath catch behind the mask.

The skin on her nose and forehead had started to come away in uneven strips. Logan could make out some darker marks around her temples and some relatively fresh scarring on her left cheek.

Logan was so fixated on the body that it took him a while to register the music. Actually, 'music' was a generous description of what he was hearing. It was a strangely rhythmic computerised beat that played through a Bluetooth speaker in the corner of the room. It wasn't dance music, exactly, but shared the same repetitiveness. Just a few seconds after first registering it, Logan could feel it getting right on his tits.

"What's this?" he asked, indicating the speaker.

Shona followed his hand-gesture, frowning like she had no idea what he was talking about.

"Oh, that," she said, once she realised. "It's for concentration."

"Concentration?" asked Logan. The only thing it was helping him concentrate on was the growing headache it was giving him.

"You know binaural beats? Well, this is computer generated *non-*binaural audio," Shona explained. "It's designed to enhance neural synchrony."

"Is it?" asked Logan, as if he had any idea what any of those words meant.

"Yeah. Focuses the old brainwaves," Shona told him, rapping a knuckle on the side of her head. "I find it useful for concentration."

Logan shrugged. "I'm more of a *Come On Eileen* man, myself," he said.

"Want me to stop it?"

"God, aye. Please," the DCI said, rubbing his temples to add a bit of urgency to the request.

Shona depressed a springy button on top of the speaker and it popped up. Blessed, merciful silence fell across the mortuary.

"It's an acquired taste," Shona said, joining him again beside the victim's head. "They do a great one for sleeping, though. It'll help with your insomnia."

"What makes you think I've got insomnia?" Logan asked.

"Because you've all got insomnia," Shona replied. "Must come with the job. You should give the audio a go."

"I'll keep it in mind," Logan said, knowing full well he definitely wouldn't. He looked from the pathologist to the body, then very deliberately back again. "So?"

"Hmm? Oh! Right, yes," said Shona, springing into life. "So, the big headline first. She didn't drown."

"You're sure?"

"Positive. No frothy gunk in the airways, which is a big indicator."

"Could've been washed away."

Shona looked pleasantly surprised. "That's right. It could! Well done. You're doing better than the last one, already!" she told him. "But there are other indicators, too. There's very little in the way of pleural fluid accumulation, and no sign of any sub-pleural haemorrhaging. Investigation of middle-ear and sinuses both back up—"

She burped, then immediately clamped a gloved hand over her mouth, her eyes widening. "I am *so* sorry," she said. "It's that *Pot Noodle.* I knew it was a bad idea."

"It's fine," Logan told her. "Honestly."

He turned his attention back to the body. "I always thought it was difficult to say for certain if someone did or didn't drown."

"It is. Notoriously," Shona agreed.

"So, then how can you be so sure she didn't?"

"Well, all that stuff I mentioned. Those were big pointers," Shona said. "Also, someone force-fed her a caustic substance, gouged her eyes out, knifed her through the heart, and drilled four dirty-great holes in her skull. So, you know, those were all indicators, too."

"Jesus," Logan said.

"It's worse than it sounds," Shona told him. "Hard as that is to believe."

"What? How?"

She began to count on her fingers. "Caustic, eyes, drill, heart," she said. "As best as I can tell, at least. And the stab wound is the one that killed her."

"What are you saying? She was *alive* for the rest of it?"

Shona produced a pen and indicated the bruising on the side of the dead woman's head.

"See this? I think it was some sort of clamp, holding her head in place. One of the drill holes is messy, like she was moving. The other three are neater, like the clamp was applied or possibly just tightened before those were drilled."

"So, you're saying she was *conscious?*"

"Probably just barely at that point. Not that that's much of a consolation," Shona said. "I can't be a hundred-percent, but from what I can tell it all happened quite quickly. She was likely still choking on the caustic substance when her eyes were removed. Blunt instrument jammed in at the bottom of each eyeball. A spoon, possibly. Clumsy, but effective enough."

She gestured with the pen again. "There's some lateral tearing at either side, suggesting a number of violent head movements."

"She was thrashing about," Logan concluded.

"Aye. Poor cow," Shona muttered. She exhaled, her earlier energy deserting her for a moment before she rallied herself again. "Two of the holes failed to puncture all the way through the cranium. The other two went deeper, but not enough to damage the brain itself."

She stepped around to the other side of the victim's head and raised her eyebrows at Logan. "Want a look?"

'Want' wasn't the right word, he thought. There was little he *wanted* less. But he nodded, then joined her in leaning in closer to examine the top of the victim's skull. Sections of her hair had been carefully shaved off, to reveal four holes spaced symmetrically across her scalp.

Two were close to the front, just back from her hairline, several inches apart. These were the shallower of the four, and the one on the left was visibly less precise than its opposite number on the right.

The other two holes were a little back from the top of the skull, and much closer together. They reminded Logan of nostrils, complete with two snot trails of a viscous fluid that seeped out of them.

"Any thoughts of these?" Logan asked.

"What, besides, 'Ooh ya bastard, that looks sore?'" said Shona. She shook her head. "No. Can't say I've seen anything like it before. You?"

"No."

"Well, brace yourself, because it gets weirder," said Shona. "Kind of. I mean... Yeah. Weirder. See for yourself."

She pulled back the sheet. Logan had just half a second to brace himself for the full horror of a post-mortem in progress and was relieved to instead see that the body had been sewn back together. The careful suture work was the first thing he noticed.

The second thing he noticed was the pattern of symbols. They were etched—no, *carved*—into the victim's skin, the wounds slicing deep into the flesh. There were maybe a dozen that he could see on her stomach and breasts, with a couple more on each thigh.

"'Ta-daa," said Shona.

Logan flicked his eyes in her direction, and she cleared her throat. "Sorry, that was inappropriate," she admitted. "Crazy, though, right? There's one on the sole of each foot, too."

"You recognise any of these symbols?" Logan asked.

"Recognise them?" Shona gave a snort. "What do I look like, a witch?"

She held a hand up. "Don't answer that. No, I don't. I can't tell you what they say, but I can tell you that they were carried out both pre and post-mortem. The left side a short time before she died, the right soon after."

She went back to counting on her fingers again. "So, in case you haven't been keeping up, that means we've got, slicey-slicey, caustic mouthwash, eyes out, head drilled, stabby-stabby, and then back to the slicing again," she said. "The only two I'm not certain of are the eyes and the drill. I'm pretty sure that's the order, though, and from her point of view I doubt it made a lot of difference."

"And time of death? Can you tell when she was killed?" Logan asked.

"That's the big question, isn't it? Short answer is 'not with any great degree of accuracy.' Long enough for the water to start taking the skin off her extremities, so... four days? That's rough, though. Could be a day or two before, or a day after."

"She was reported missing five days ago," Logan said.

Shona made a weighing motion, then nodded. "Yeah. That would fit. The water's a bit warmer at this time of year, which is why I said four, but five isn't a stretch. Even six wouldn't be impossible."

"So, she could've been taken on Sunday and kept somewhere for a day or so," Logan said, thinking out loud. "Alive."

"Potentially, yeah. There's some bruising on her wrists and ankles that would back that up."

She took hold of one of the dead woman's hands and held it up enough for Logan to see. A thin purple weal ran across the back of the wrist.

"Cable tie?" Logan guessed.

"I'd say so. But check it out," said Shona. She turned the arm over to show the line didn't continue along the wrist's underside.

"Hands tied together?" Logan guessed.

Shona looked non-committal. "Maybe. But I'd expect the lines to be running diagonally then," she said. She set the victim's arm down, then placed her own hands together with the wrists meeting. Her clenched fists and forearms formed a cross-shape. "Most people are tied like that."

She adjusted her arms so the fists were together. "Not like that. And, if it's behind the back, the angle of the marks on the wrist is even more pronounced. So, I'm thinking—"

"She was tied to something. A chair, maybe," Logan concluded.

"Bingo," said Shona. "Anyone would think you'd done this before, Detective Chief Inspector."

"Once or twice. You got anything else for me?" Logan asked.

He was keen to get out of the room. Now that he had some idea of what the victim had gone through, the smell of death seemed more pungent than ever. It forced its way in through the mask, pushing up his nostrils and snagging at the back of his throat.

"Not yet. Anyway, I reckon that's probably enough to be going on with," Shona told him. "I've got some other tests to run, so I might have more for you later. I took some scrapings from under the fingernails, but it'll be a day or two before I start getting any DNA results back. After a few days in the water, though, I wouldn't go holding my breath for anything overly useful."

"I won't."

Logan gave the body one more quick look over. That's how he'd learned to think of them over the years. This wasn't Mairi Sinclair. She was long gone. This was a clue to who had killed her. A piece of evidence. That was all.

And yet, he had to resist the urge to reach out and squeeze her hand. To tell her he was sorry for what had happened to her. To promise he'd make it right.

"Right, then. Good," he said, pushing the thought away. "Can you put together a report on—"

"Already emailed it over. That's what I was doing when you came in."

"You were eating a Pot Noodle when I came in," Logan reminded her.

"I was multi-tasking. It's a thing women do. You should try it," Shona told him. She checked the clock on the wall. "Now, I'd like to get home at some point tonight, so are we done here, or do you want to hang around for a bit and help me weigh a spleen?"

Logan regarded her curiously for a moment, then jabbed a thumb in the direction of the door. "I'll probably leave you to it."

"Good call. It's not nearly as much fun as it sounds," Shona told him.

Logan backed towards the door. "If anything else does come up..."

She pointed at him, then drew back her thumb and turned the gesture into a finger gun. She mimed firing it in his direction. "You'll be the first to know," she promised.

She smiled. It was not, Logan thought, a wholly unpleasant smile.

"Nice to meet you, Detective Chief Inspector."

"You too," said Logan and he reckoned that, all things considered, he probably meant it. "Enjoy your spleen."

He bumped against the swing doors that led out into the cluttered office, opening them.

"I always do," said Shona. "Oh, and... Jack, was it?"

Logan stopped. "That's right."

"Do me a favour, will you? Catch this sick bastard."

"Funny, you're the second person to suggest that today," he said. He gave her his word with a single nod. "Aye. Will do."

And then, he retreated from the mortuary, bringing the clammy odour of death out into the corridor with him.

"How did it go?" asked DI Forde, folding up a copy of the *Highland News* that he'd procured from somewhere while he was waiting. He grunted audibly as he eased himself up off the moulded plastic chair he'd been trying unsuccessfully to get comfortable on, then pointed to his mouth. "You've still got the mask on, by the way."

Logan glanced down, then removed the paper mask. The gloves *snapped* as he pulled those off, too.

"What did you think of Dr Maguire, then?"

Logan shrugged, non-committal. "Fine. Seems to know what she's doing."

Ben wrinkled his nose. "Bit weird, though, eh?" he said.

"Aye. But, aren't we all?" was all Logan had to say on the matter. "She's emailed over the report. We'll swing into base and—"

"Whoa, whoa. Not so fast there, Jack. Hold your horses," Ben said, raising his rolled-up newspaper like a stop sign. "Alice was expecting us at the house..." He checked his watch. "Eighty-seven minutes ago. And she's no' a woman you keep waiting."

Logan frowned. "Maybe you haven't noticed, but we're investigating a murder here."

"Aye, but we're hardly in the Golden Hour, are we? The liaison's talking to the family, Tyler and Hamza are following up on a few things, and there's hee-haw else we can do at the moment."

"Hamza?"

"Aye. He's back up and about. We're trying to get him to take it easy, but he's no' one for lying down to it."

"Good on him."

Logan wanted to argue about heading into the station. He could think of a dozen things that he could be getting stuck into. Avenues he could be exploring in the hope of dredging up some useful leads.

But, Ben was right. Alice was not the kind of woman you kept waiting.

Besides, he was a guest in their house until he could move into his rented flat on Monday, and Alice hadn't exactly been his biggest fan to begin with.

He made his annoyance felt with a sigh, then nodded. "Right. Aye. Fine. We'll pick up in the morning, then."

Ben tapped the DCI on the chest with his paper. "Good lad. She's doing us a curry," he said, setting off along the corridor. "I mean, technically it's just a sort of stew with some curry powder in it, but it's nice enough, and I don't have the heart to tell her."

"Sounds delicious," said Logan, following along behind.

"Was that sarcasm?"

"Aye."

"Just grin and bear it," Ben told him. "Thankfully, she's no' exactly generous with the portions."

They stepped aside to allow a couple of nurses to pass them in the corridor, then turned the corner that led to the exit.

"She forgiven me yet?" Logan asked.

"For Harry?"

Ben stopped and chewed his bottom lip while he considered this.

"Aye. Aye, she has," he said.

He tilted his head from side to side a couple of times.

"Mostly," he said. "Ish."

"That's a no, then."

"Aye," said Ben. "That's a no."

CHAPTER SEVEN

LOGAN'S FORK *CLINKED* ON HIS PLATE AS HE STABBED AT SOMETHING lumpy, drawing an irritated glare from the woman at the end of the table.

Alice Forde was two years older than her husband, but a regimen of gym sessions, copious amounts of make-up, and some rumoured Botox injections had kept her looking maybe eighteen-months younger than he did.

Given that Ben did very little exercise, regularly drank to excess, and subsisted on a diet predominantly made up of pastry products, Logan was sure that the relatively minimal returns on her efforts must be a constant source of frustration for the poor woman.

She sat at one end of the tile-topped dining table, across from Ben who sat at the other end. Logan was between them, his seat edged closer to Ben so he was just beyond Alice's reach. He wasn't expecting her to take a swing at him, but better safe than sorry.

He'd been in DI Forde's house a few times over the years. He knew the dining room better than he knew most of the other rooms, because this was where it had happened.

This was where Logan had murdered Harry Pricklepants.

He glanced up briefly from his plate, his teeth working their way through a lump of something gristly. His eyes alighted on the spot on the display cabinet where Harry had once stood with his wee hedgehog face beaming as he tipped his colourful little hat at the world.

Alice had left a space where the ornament had been. The rest of the shelves were practically overflowing with a menagerie of similar porcelain monstrosities, but not that space. That was Harry's spot, and Alice wasn't going to let Logan forget it.

He clocked her watching him, her chin resting on the hand that held her fork. She chewed, teeth working their way through a substance Logan was confident was meat, but which he'd need the help of the forensics team to identify further.

"This is lovely, Alice," said Ben, in an attempt to ease the tension. "First class. What do you think, Jack?"

"Aye, it's delicious," said Logan, arranging his expression into something he hoped was convincing enough. "Can't beat a good curry. That's what I always say."

"It's not curry," said Alice, still chewing.

Logan looked down at his dinner. Lumps of the mystery meat lay sprawled in a thin, watery gravy that pooled around an island of mashed potatoes. Of course it wasn't curry. It was nothing bloody like curry, and if Ben hadn't told him that's what it was going to be the thought wouldn't even have crossed his mind.

"That's what I was saying," said Logan, thinking on his feet. "I always say that you can't beat a good curry, but I'm going to have to stop doing that in future."

He motioned to the plate with his fork. Something rubbery went *twang* between his teeth. He grimaced briefly, then pushed right on through. "Because this is better."

Amazingly, that seemed to do the trick. The atmosphere around the table relaxed a fraction, the temperature in the room raised a degree or two above freezing, and over the next few minutes the conversation began to flow just a little more freely.

"How do you think Snecky's going to get on down the road?" Ben asked. He was tackling the mystery meat with a gusto Logan had been unable to summon, and had almost polished off the lot.

"God. Now you're asking," Logan replied, taking a sip of water. He'd been chewing the same piece of meat for the past five minutes, and while it was now a suitably mushy paste, he couldn't swallow it. It was as if his stomach had ordered his throat not to accept any more of *whatever that shite is*, and his mouth was being left to deal with the consequences.

DI Grant had been Christened 'Snecky' years ago, mostly on account of there being little noteworthy enough about him other than his strong Invernesian accent. He was a fairly big fella, and had made his way up the ranks more through dogged perseverance than by demonstrating any natural aptitude for the job, so there had been nickname potential in those. But, the accent—in particular, the way he formed his As somewhere between the top of his nose and the back of his throat—had superseded everything else, so 'Snecky' was what he'd ended up with.

"He's got a good team," Logan said. He was really starting to get the hang of this diplomacy thing, he thought. "If he makes use of them, he'll be fine."

"He won't," Ben said, mashing his mound of potato into the gravy with the back of his fork. "He hasn't the brains. I'm amazed you got the Gozer and the high-heid-yins to agree to the swap. They must've known what they were saddling themselves with."

"I can be pretty persuasive when I want to be," Logan said, and left it there.

"How's Vanessa?" asked Alice, cutting in.

Logan couldn't help but see the warning look Ben shot across the table at his wife, but it bounced off her without her noticing.

"You still keep in touch?"

"Not really," Logan said, trying his best to keep it light and breezy. It was still a sore subject for him. Probably always would be. "Not since the divorce. The odd message here and there."

"Christmas and birthdays?" Alice guessed.

Logan puffed out his cheeks. "House stuff, mostly. And once when her dad was sick. Nothing for a year or two now."

"Oh. That's a shame."

Ben finally managed to catch his wife's eye. A series of looks passed between them that Logan pretended not to notice.

"I'm just making conversation," Alice eventually protested.

"You're being bloody nosy, is what you're doing," Ben told her. "He doesn't want to talk about it."

"How do you know? Have you asked him?"

"Alice..."

Logan knocked together something that resembled a smile. "It's fine. It's fine, honestly," he said.

"See?" Alice said, shooting daggers along the length of the table. "He says it's fine."

Ben muttered something, but was careful to be quiet enough about it that his wife didn't hear.

"Well, next time you're talking to her, tell her I said hello," Alice said. She finished eating, set her fork down, and dabbed at her mouth with a napkin. "And how's your daughter doing these days? What is she now? Twenty?"

There was a loud *clink* as Ben dropped his cutlery onto his plate. Propping his elbows on the table, he turned to Logan.

"So. What did you find out?" he asked. He flicked a look along the table at Alice. "*About the body.*"

"Oh, God, do you have to?" Alice groaned. "I've only just finished my dinner. I don't want to hear about... *dead bodies.*"

She pulled a face and spat out the last two words, like even saying them aloud was turning her stomach.

"Sorry, sweetheart, has to be done," Ben said. "Big case, and all that."

There was a clattering of plates as Alice stood and began to gather up the dishes. "Well, I don't have to listen to it," she decided. "I'll take these to the kitchen, but you can do the dishwasher later."

"You sure you don't want to join us?" Ben asked, knowing full well what the answer would be. "I'm sure it's not all *that* gruesome."

He locked eyes briefly with Logan.

"It's pretty grim, actually," Logan said.

"Ah. Right." Ben said. He smiled apologetically at his wife. "Maybe not, then."

Both men sat in silence while Alice finished collecting the dishes. She paused at the door of the dining room to remind Ben that he was on dishwasher duty, then elbowed the door closed behind her.

"Thanks," Logan said.

"Sorry about that. She can be a right nosy cow when she wants to be."

Ben got up from the table, patted his stomach a few times, then crossed to a little oak cabinet that stood against the back wall. It was an ugly, old-fashioned thing, with Mother of Pearl handles and scuffs in all the wrong places. Ben had picked it up at an auction in Motherwell a decade or so ago. Logan remembered how excited Ben had been about the find, and how misplaced that enthusiasm had seemed at the time.

Now, with the benefit of hindsight, Ben shared Logan's opinion that the thing was a fucking eyesore, but Alice loved it, so it had followed them north when Ben had transferred up the road.

"It's fine," Logan said, waving Ben's apology away. "I broke her wee hedgehog man. She's just getting her own back."

Ben had opened the cabinet and was just producing two glasses and a large bottle of amber-coloured liquid when he stopped.

"Shite. Sorry. Wasn't thinking," he said, wincing. "You still off it?"

"Aye," Logan confirmed. "Mostly. You go ahead, though."

"You sure? I don't mind."

Logan shook his head. "It's your house, Ben. Don't let me stop you."

He rose to his feet, stifling a yawn. "I think I'm going to turn in, though. Long day, and tomorrow's only going to be worse."

"You think?"

"After seeing the state of that body? Aye."

Ben unscrewed the lid of the bottle and poured a glug of whisky into one of the glasses. Logan's eyes followed it.

"Rough one then, is it?" Ben asked.

Logan tore his gaze from the glass. "I'll fill you in tomorrow. Otherwise you'll never get to sleep."

"Shite. That bad?"

"Maybe worse," Logan confirmed.

He stole another glance at the glass. Something stirred deep in the primal parts of his brain, but he wrestled it into submission and turned away.

"But that's tomorrow's conversation. Good night."

"Night, Jack," said Ben.

He waited until Logan had left the room before picking up the glass and raising it to his lips. He jumped when the DCI's head appeared around the door frame again, spilling a third of the glass's contents down his front.

"And for fuck's sake, don't forget the dishwasher," Logan warned him.

And with that, he was gone.

CHAPTER EIGHT

"Hey, boss! Welcome to the madhouse!"

Logan gazed impassively at Detective Constable Tyler Neish. The younger detective stood with a hand raised, poised to do one of those best-bud handshake slaps with the interlocking thumbs that Logan had never had any time for. He regarded the hand, the irritatingly groomed appearance, and Tyler's cocky grin for a moment, then turned to Ben.

"Don't tell me he got *more* annoying."

"You wouldn't have thought it was possible, would you?" Ben sighed. "And yet..."

Tyler laughed it off. "Funny stuff." He lowered his hand. "Seriously though, boss. Good to see you."

"Thanks," said Logan. He offered up a handshake. A proper one. Tyler accepted it. "You too."

The team had been assigned the largest of the Incident Rooms at Burnett Road station, and Logan had been pleased to see plenty of activity going on when he'd first entered. It had all come to a halt almost immediately after he and Ben had arrived, though, with the team stopping what they were doing to come over and say hello.

"Good to see you up and about, Hamza," Logan said, shaking hands with a darker-skinned man with a neatly trimmed beard. The last time Logan had seen Detective Constable Khaled, the DC had been in the

Intensive Care Unit at Glasgow Royal Infirmary, recovering from a series of stab-wounds to the back.

"Well, it was touch and go for a while they tell me, sir," Hamza said, his Aberdonian accent momentarily taking Logan by surprise just as it did every time the man opened his mouth. "But no real lasting damage."

Ben patted him on the shoulder. "It'll take more than some bastard wi' a dirty great knife to keep Hamza down. Right, son?"

"Well, aye. But I'd rather not put that to the test by having another go," Hamza said.

"No, maybe best not," Logan agreed. "Any pain still?"

"Only when I laugh, sir," Hamza replied.

"That's why we sat him next to DC Neish," said Ben.

It took DC Neish a moment to pick up on the slight.

"Hey!"

Logan turned to DS McQuarrie next. She was only half invested in Logan's arrival, and was the one member of the team who hadn't yet put down the paperwork she was holding. Even now, when Logan was talking to the others, her eyes were darting left and right as she read over the top page of a report.

This was more like it.

"DS McQuarrie," Logan said.

Caitlyn looked up and they briefly shook hands.

"Sir."

"What have we got?" Logan asked, seizing this opportunity to get down to business.

He'd lain awake in Ben and Alice's spare room, unable to flick the switch in his head that would've let him get some sleep.

Whenever he'd closed his eyes, he'd come face-to-eyeless-face with Mairi Sinclair, and his nostrils had been filled with her death-stench again.

Or he might just have been smelling the lingering after effects of Alice's cooking. He hadn't been able to tell for sure.

At five o'clock, he'd concluded that he wasn't going to get any more sleep, and had dug out Dr Maguire's report from his phone's email inbox. The picture the report had painted of the victim's last few hours had done nothing to set him at ease, and by the time Ben had risen at seven, Logan was up, dressed, and ready to get going.

"Just looking it over, sir," Caitlyn said, indicating the report. "Can you give me five minutes?"

Logan nodded, appreciating the lack of time-wasting waffle. "Five minutes, then."

"By the way, case made the papers, boss," Tyler said. "Further back, though, nothing major. Got a few days until the local goes out, too, so with a bit of luck this one should be more low key than the last one."

"Hopefully," Logan agreed. He'd never really seen eye-to-eye with the press, and the circus that surrounded the kidnapping case in Fort William had done his blood pressure no favours whatsoever.

While Caitlyn continued to work her way through the report, Ben gave Logan the official tour. It lasted just a few seconds, beginning with, "Toilets are that way," and finishing again almost immediately after with, "and this is your office through here."

Logan had seen plenty of Incident Rooms over the years, and they were all much of a muchness these days. He'd also visited the Burnett Road station enough times that he could find his way around it without too many problems, so Ben hadn't seen the need to dwell too much on any of it.

Logan's office was a decent enough size, with a window looking out over the rest of the Incident Room, and a clean desk that was positively crying out to be covered in paperwork, Post-Its, and coffee mugs. There were In and Out trays on a smaller table that ran at right angles to the main desk. The Out tray was empty, while the stack of paperwork in the tray beside it was already displaying some structural integrity issues.

"Alright?" Ben asked. "They were supposed to give it a lick of paint after Snecky left, but..." He flicked his gaze around the room. "They didn't."

"No, I see that," Logan said, picking at a chip in the magnolia paintwork with a fingernail. "It's fine, though."

"For all you'll use it," Ben said. He had worked with the DCI enough to know that separating himself from the rest of the team wasn't really his style.

"Somewhere to put the coats, though," Logan said.

Ben chuckled. "Aye."

He glanced back over his shoulder, then quietly closed the office door behind them. Logan crossed his arms and leaned against the desk, recognising the incremental change to the atmosphere in the room.

"What's up?"

"I've been meaning to ask..." Ben began.

Quite what he'd been meaning to ask, he didn't go on to say.

But then, he didn't have to.

"Petrie," said Logan.

Ben nodded.

Owen Petrie. *Mister Whisper*. The serial child-killer who had haunted Logan's life for years, and whose shadow had loomed large over the recent Fort William case.

Logan puffed out his cheeks. "I went to see him in Carstairs," he said. "Afterwards, I mean."

He spoke slowly, either because he was carefully picking his words or because he was having to force them out of his mouth. "I wanted him to know what had happened with... You know. The abduction case."

"Aye. I know."

"I showed him a front page about the aftermath," Logan said. "And he reacted. I saw it in his eyes."

Ben's expression turned doubtful.

"I know, I know, he's meant to be..." Logan tapped himself in the centre of the forehead a few times. "But he's not. He's faking it, Ben. I'm sure of it."

"Well, he's managed to fool all his doctors, then," Ben said, trying not to make it sound like the opening salvo of an argument. "But you got closure, though?"

Logan shrugged. "As much as I'm ever likely to," he said. "But aye. I'm done with him. Hence me wanting to get out of Glasgow. Too many bad memories."

Too many failures.

"And here was me thinking you just missed me," Ben said.

"You should be so lucky," Logan replied, then Caitlyn caught his eye through the window and he gave her a nod. "Looks like she's ready for us."

Ben put a hand on the door handle, but didn't open it yet. "You'll be doing a wee speech first though, aye?"

Logan frowned. "Wasn't planning to, no."

"Ah well," said Ben, grinning. "The best laid plans, and all that..."

LOGAN STOOD with his back to the Big Board, looking out at the rest of the team. There were only the four of them, so it wasn't exactly a sea of faces. More of a puddle, really.

He wasn't one for speeches. Aye, he could carry them off if he had to, but that had never really been his leadership style. He'd much rather inspire through action than by spouting off a few half-arsed words of encouragement here and there.

Still, it was his first day in a new patch, and the team apparently needed a bit of a boot up the backside after serving under Snecky for the past few years, so Ben had talked him into it.

"Unlike my predecessor, I'm here entirely of my own free will," he said. As openings went, it wasn't exactly '*I have a dream*,' but it was good enough, and raised a couple of weak chuckles from the tiny audience. "I asked for a transfer here because every single one of you impressed me on the kidnapping case we worked back in March."

"What, even DC Neish?" asked Ben.

"Well, not so much DC Neish, no. But the rest of you."

"Cheers for that, boss," said Tyler.

"The fact is, I'm here because I can see the potential of this team. You might not be able to tell from my face, but I'm excited by it," Logan continued. "And so should you be. You've all done some good, solid work in the past, even with... certain parties potentially holding you back. But you could do *great* work. *We* could. Together. And, we will."

He tapped a photograph on the Big Board with the back of his hand. It showed Mairi Sinclair, smiling and vibrant and very much alive.

"We're going to start by finding the bastard who killed this lassie," Logan said. "We're going to do it quickly, we're going to do it efficiently, and we're going to get her family the justice they deserve."

He looked from face to face. "I'm assuming no one has any objections to that?"

"No, sir," said Caitlyn, amid a more general murmur of agreement from the others.

"Good."

Logan clapped his hands and rubbed them together.

"Then somebody get the kettle on, and let's see where we're at."

CHAPTER NINE

DS McQUARRIE HAD REPLACED LOGAN IN FRONT OF THE BIG BOARD, and was going through everything that had been pinned to it. It was mostly for the DCI's benefit, although a recap wouldn't do the others any harm, either.

"Mairi Sinclair. Aged thirty-one at estimated time of death," Caitlyn announced. There was occasionally a hint of her Orcadian heritage in her accent, but she was always quick to suppress it for reasons Logan hadn't yet been able to fathom. "Last seen Sunday morning by her son, Stuart, aged fourteen, when she left the house to go to the shops. A small cashline withdrawal was made from her account around eleven-twenty, and that's the last trace we have of her until her body was discovered in the early hours of yesterday morning."

"Where was the money taken out?" asked Logan.

"A Spar on Montague Row. About quarter of a mile from the house, sir."

"Any CCTV?" asked Hamza. The others were standing through the presentation, but he'd taken a seat and was scribbling notes in an A4 notepad he had open on the desk.

Caitlyn shook her head. "Cameras inside the shop, but the machine's on the outside. Doesn't have built-in surveillance. It's one of those ones you pay a fee to take money out, so not your typical ATM."

"I hate those," Tyler remarked. "It's my money, why should I have to pay to get it out?"

"You're paying for the convenience, aren't you?" Ben told him. "It's a penalty for being a disorganised bastard and not getting the money out somewhere else."

"No, I get that, it's just—"

He felt Logan's stare burning into him before he saw it. Tyler smiled sheepishly, then motioned to Caitlyn.

"Sorry. Continue."

"*Thank* you," she replied, with a degree of sarcasm that impressed Logan no end. "No CCTV between her house and the shop, although we're still checking for private cameras."

"What about dash cams?" Logan asked. "Have you put out a call for people who might've been in the area to check those?"

For the first time since beginning the presentation, Caitlyn glanced down at her sheet. "I'm not... No, sir. We haven't."

"I'll get onto MFR and the papers," said Hamza, jotting it down. "Put a call out."

"What's MFR?" Logan asked.

"Oh. Sorry. Moray Firth Radio, sir," Hamza explained. "Local station."

"Right. Good," Logan said. "Anyone remember seeing her in the shop?"

"No, sir," Caitlyn reported. "We've spoken to staff and put notices up for customers, but no one has come forward. Internal CCTV shows no signs of her on the day, either, so it doesn't look like she went into the shop itself."

"The question is, where did she go?" Tyler wondered.

Ben tutted. "Aye, we know that's the question, son. That's why we're all standing around here, isn't it?"

Tyler shifted on his feet. "No, I mean... Aye, but—"

"Kind of the entire point of our job, really," said Hamza, enjoying his fellow DC's obvious discomfort.

"No, I know. I was just saying."

"Maybe only say something if it's worth us listening to next time, eh?" Ben suggested. There was no real malice to it, though, and while Tyler's face had reddened in embarrassment, he gave a nod and a thumbs-up, before surreptitiously giving Hamza the finger behind his back.

"Is that normal behaviour for her?" Logan asked, getting back to the matter at hand. "Using that cashline, I mean?"

"Not as far as we can tell, sir. She usually just swipes everything. Last time she used an ATM was..." Caitlyn checked her notes. "...over eight months ago. She withdrew a grand over three transactions. She was buying a car, her sister tells us. That checks out. Which reminds me, we haven't found her car yet, either. It's a light blue Citroen C3. Been missing all week. Everyone has their eyes open."

"Mark that as a priority," Logan said. "It could tell us a lot."

"How much did she take out on Sunday?" Ben wondered. "From the cash machine, I mean."

"Ten pounds."

Logan frowned. "A tenner? That's it?"

"Aye, sir. That's it. A tenner."

There was a moment of silence as they all contemplated this small, yet potentially telling, detail. It was broken only by the sound of Hamza's pen nib on his notebook page.

"What else have we got?" Logan asked. "Anything on the material she was wrapped in?"

"Forensics is working to identify it at the moment, but the water will most likely have washed away anything useful," Caitlyn said. "Early indicators are that the plastic probably came from a building site. Bright green, so pretty distinctive, which is good. It was tied with climbing rope. We're trying to pin down the make to see if we can find a local supplier. But, you know, it's the Highlands. There are a lot of places to buy climbing rope."

"Any building sites in the area?" Logan asked.

"Aye, a few, sir," said Caitlyn. She turned to a map that took up a full third of the board, and indicated six blue pins. "Three new house builds, two extensions, and some repair work on a path. There's roadworks, too, but we haven't included those at the moment."

"That's in the immediate area around where the body was found?" Ben asked.

Caitlyn nodded. "Aye."

"But the body could've drifted in from somewhere else on the loch," the DI continued. "That's a big stretch. How many construction sites are there along both sides? Must be dozens."

"We've been able to identify over forty within a mile of the water," Caitlyn said. "There's a bit of a boom on, they tell me."

"It's not tidal, though, is it?" said Tyler.

Logan turned to him, an eyebrow raised.

"The loch, I mean. It's not flowing in and out, so the body probably hasn't moved that far. Right?" He looked around at the others, his cocksure swagger replaced by something a little less certain. "I mean, I'm no expert, but that makes sense, doesn't it?"

"Aye. Makes sense," Logan agreed, and the relief was immediately evident on Tyler's face. "Let's stick with those closest for the moment. Anyone been to look at them?"

"Not yet, sir. Didn't want to send uniform trampling in until we had a better idea of what we were dealing with," Caitlyn said.

Logan approached the map and considered the blue pins. One in particular caught his eye. It was closest to the water. Almost right on the edge.

"What's this one?" he asked, tapping the end of the pin.

"Repair work on the tourist path. Pretty minimal presence. Mostly just a couple of lads with spades and cement, I'm told."

There was a red pin along the shore next to the campsite, identifying the spot where the victim's body had been discovered. A green pin a mile or so along the road struck Logan as unusual.

"What's this one for?"

"Boleskine House, sir," said Caitlyn, which prompted a quick blast of the theme to *The Twilight Zone* from Tyler.

"What's Boleskine House?" Logan asked.

"It's a ruin now, mostly. Burned down a few years back," Ben explained. "Used to be owned by Aleister Crowley."

Logan's face suggested the name meant nothing to him.

"Big occultist, sir," said Caitlyn. "Black magic, devil worshipping, all that stuff."

"Is he worth bringing in?" Logan asked.

"Well, considering he died in the nineteen-forties," Ben said, smiling smugly. "He's not high on our list of suspects, no."

"It's not technically a building site, but there are some construction materials on the grounds," Caitlyn said. "And people with an interest in that sort of thing travel from all over to see the house, so I thought with the markings on the victim's body..."

"Worth looking into," Logan agreed. "Anything on the symbols themselves?"

"Not yet," Hamza volunteered. "I've got some people looking into it."

"CID?"

"No, sir," said Hamza, shifting a little uncomfortably in his chair. "Reddit. I did some drawings and posted them on a few Subreddits. Anonymously, like. No details. Thought that was our best chance of getting a quick hit on them."

"Subreddits?" Logan said, repeating the word in the same way that a parrot might. He shot Ben a sideways look. "Do I approve?"

"Don't look at me. Buggered if I know."

"Right. I'm going to assume it's fine, then," said Logan, turning back to Hamza. "Good thinking. Just keep an eye on it. I don't know what it is, but I don't like the sound of it."

Tyler opened his mouth.

"I don't care what it is, either," Logan said, cutting him off. "DC Khaled is responsible for it. If it blows up in some way, you're the one with his balls in the vice, Hamza, and I'll be the bastard cranking the handle. Got that?"

"You might want to write that down," Tyler told the other DC, gesturing to his notebook. "Balls... in... vice."

"Got it, sir," Hamza said, ignoring Tyler completely. "I'll keep a close eye on it."

Logan nodded, then turned his attention back to the Big Board.

The map took up a third of it, and around another third was currently empty. The space between these was mostly filled with photographs of Mairi Sinclair. There were four in total, only one of which showed her alive. A few Post-It notes had been stuck around the photographs with various comments and questions on them, and there was a list of addresses stuck with a magnet to the board's shiny white surface.

Hamza's drawings of the symbols that had been carved into the victim's skin were stuck down near the bottom of the board, and there were two other photographs to the left of the pictures of Mairi, both joined to her by lines of red marker pen.

"Who are these two?" Logan asked.

"That's the son, Stuart," Caitlyn said, indicating a school photograph of a boy aged around twelve or thirteen. "And that's his father, Robbie Steadwood. He and Mairi were never married, and have been separated since just before Stuart was born."

"What's the relationship like?" Logan asked.

"Dire. History of domestic call-outs when they were together. She's made a couple of complaints against him over the years since then. Harassment stuff, mostly. No charges ever pressed," Caitlyn said. "CID have tried to get hold of him all week, but they haven't had any joy. They're keen to talk to him about some potential drugs charges, too, unconnected to this case."

"Got a home address?"

"Aye, but he's not there. He's not working, as far as we know, and the few known associates we've been able to identify have all denied seeing him."

"Surprise, surprise," Ben muttered.

Based on his photo, Robbie Steadwood wasn't much of a family man. His head was shaved down to the bone, and his neck and face were like a gallery of bad tattoos. The picture they'd been able to source of him was a police mugshot. This didn't exactly come as any surprise.

"What's his previous?"

"Did a stretch in Peterhead. GBH and attempted sexual assault," Caitlyn said. "Neither on Mairi Sinclair."

"Charming lad. Chief suspect, then," Logan said.

"We've got the feelers out for him," Ben said.

"Fine tooth comb. And get me a report on the progress," Logan said. He rapped his knuckles off the man in the photograph's forehead. "I want this arsehole found and brought in today."

"I'll get on that, boss," Tyler said.

Logan turned away from the board. "Right, then. Caitlyn, I want you with me. We're going to go talk to the son, see if there's anything else he can tell us. Ben, I'm saddling you with DC Neish. Get those building sites locked down and checked out. Hamza, you're Office Manager. Get someone from CID brought in for Exhibits."

Hamza blinked in surprise. "What? I'd rather be out and about, sir."

"I get that. I do," said Logan. "But you're just back. You need to take some time and get back in the swing of things."

"That's bollocks, sir," Hamza said. His eyes widened, like he was surprised by his own outburst. "I mean... with all due respect."

"He's right, Jack," said Ben. "He needs to get back on the horse. I can run the office."

Logan rubbed a hand across his unshaven chin, then turned away from the others and motioned for Ben to do the same. "You sure about this?" he asked, dropping his voice to a low murmur.

"Sitting on my arse with a nice cup of tea? What's not to be sure of?" Ben asked. "Right up my street, that."

"You know what I mean."

Ben nodded and smiled. "He's grand. It'll be good for him."

Logan sighed, then both men turned back to the rest of the team. "Fine. Hamza, you're out and about."

"Thank you, sir. I appreciate it."

"But you're doing all the boring shite. I'm not having you overdoing things," Logan warned. "DS McQuarrie, you'll take Hamza on a drive-by of those building sites. Take a look, see if you get a feeling from any of them.

Don't go poking around too much at this stage, though, we don't want to draw attention."

"Got it, sir," Caitlyn replied.

Logan exhaled slowly through his nose. "Which means..."

Tyler's face split into a grin. He jumped up from where he'd been half-sitting on the edge of a desk. "Which means I'm with you, boss."

"God help me. But aye. You're with me."

"You'll no' thank yourself for that, Jack," Ben warned.

"Probably not, no," Logan agreed. He took another look at the Big Board, then nodded. "Everyone know what they're doing?"

"We're on it, sir," said Caitlyn, after a quick glance at Hamza.

Tyler rubbed his hands together, playing up his excitement. "Ready when you are, boss!"

"As for me, I'm already working on prioritising next steps," said Ben. He picked up his mug. "I'm thinking tea *then* biscuits, but it's early days and that's still liable to change."

Before anyone could reply, there was a knock at the Incident Room door, then a *squeak* as it was opened. A uniformed sergeant put his head around the door, looked across the faces of the team, then settled on Logan.

"Sorry to interrupt. There's a woman here says she has information about the murder. Wants to talk to the SIO."

Logan felt a little rush of hope, but quickly squashed it back down.

"Is there an interview room free?" he asked.

"They're all free, sir. But someone chucked their guts up in Room One last night, and it's still a bit ripe. I'd suggest Two," the sergeant told him.

"Right. Stick her in there, then," Logan said. "I'll be through in a minute."

The door swung closed as the sergeant retreated.

"DS McQuarrie, I want you in there with me. Tyler, get me that update."

Tyler's face went momentarily blank, before he remembered. "Oh! The ex. Right. I'll check up."

"Hamza, you do the... thing. Whatever that thing was you said."

"Subreddits, sir."

"Aye. That. You check that. See if anything's come in," Logan said.

He turned to the door, made a vague attempt at making himself presentable, which essentially just involved smoothing down his hair, then nodded.

"Right, then. Let's go see what's fallen into our lap."

CHAPTER TEN

MARION WHITEHEAD SAT ACROSS THE TABLE FROM LOGAN AND Caitlyn, looking borderline beside herself with excitement.

Before they'd entered the Interview Room, the uniformed sergeant had remarked that the woman looked like 'Doctor Who after a night on the lash,' and Logan couldn't fault the man on his observation skills.

She was in her late sixties, with a shock of silver-white hair that stood out from her head, no two strands of it going in the same direction. The contrast of the hair colour highlighted her skelping red cheeks, and there was a sense about her of someone who had recently come in from a bitingly cold winter's day.

This impression was backed up by her clothes. She wore a long camel hair coat and a longer scarf that looped around her neck and chin, then hung down below the top of the table at both ends. On her hands were a pair of fingerless gloves, with a little mitten-covering buttoned back so her fingertips remained exposed.

She was thick-set and sturdy, but there was a lightness to her movements that didn't quite fit with her appearance. Marion nursed a cup of tea close to her chest, her eyes swinging between the two detectives like she couldn't quite decide which one she should be looking at.

Logan made the introductions while Caitlyn took out her notebook and sat back a little, focusing the spotlight on the DCI and helping the older woman make up her mind.

"The front desk tells me you have some information for us, Miss Whitehead."

"*Ms*," Marion corrected. Her accent was from south of the border. Quite a bit south, in fact. "I prefer *Ms* Whitehead. But Marion's fine. Should you have a tape?"

Logan raised his eyebrows. "Sorry?"

"A tape. You know. 'State your name for the benefit of the tape.' That's what they do, isn't it? On the telly."

"That won't be necessary at this stage," Logan told her. "DS McQuarrie will just take a few notes as we're talking."

"Oh." Marion looked disappointed. Her eyes went to the spot where she presumably assumed a tape recorder should be, then she gave herself a shake. "Right. Yes. I suppose you know best."

"So, what was it—"

"I have a phone," Marion said. She leaned back in the chair and began fishing in the pockets of her coat. "We could record it on that, if you like?"

"Honestly, Marion. Not necessary. We only tend to do that if you're a suspect, and we have no reason to believe you are," Logan said. "So, please. What was it you wanted to tell us?"

Marion continued rifling through her pockets. "Not *tell* you, Sergeant," she said, reaching inside her coat. "Show you."

Caitlyn smirked and met Logan's eye.

"Sergeant," she mouthed, then they both turned their attention back to Marion as she let out a little cheer of triumph.

"Aha! Here we are."

She slapped a small bundle of six-by-eight photographs down on the desk then sat back, arms folded like she'd just won a game of chess and wasn't about to be particularly gracious in victory.

"What do you think of *that*?" she asked.

Logan looked from the photographs to the old woman, then back again. He leaned over and studied the top picture. It was blurry and slightly pixelated, like it was a blown-up section of a wider digital photograph that had been printed out.

From what he could tell, it showed a stretch of water, with a dark shape sticking out near the centre of the image.

Sliding the top photograph aside, Logan glanced at the one below. It was almost identical, but zoomed out a fraction so the shape in the middle was even more impossible to clearly make out.

"What am I looking at?" he asked.

"Exhibit A for the prosecution," said Marion, looking pleased with herself. "Do you know when I took these photographs, Sergeant?"

Logan gave a shake of his head to indicate that he did not.

"Tuesday!" Marion cried, then she banged the flat of her hand on the table for emphasis. "Tuesday morning. Six-twenty-seven, to be exact. I always write the date and time on the back."

Logan turned the photograph over. Sure enough, the details were written there in studious, but slightly shaky, handwriting.

"Up at the Drum end of the loch," Marion continued. "Not my usual spot. I'm usually down at the other end, but you know what they say. A change is as good as a rest. And how right they are!"

She gestured to the photographs with both hands, then sat back again triumphantly.

When it became clear that neither Logan nor DS McQuarrie were appreciating the significance of the images, she gave a wry little chuckle. "Well, it's the monster, isn't it? It's Nessie. I got her."

Logan flicked his eyes down at the pictures again, then brought them back up to meet the beaming smile of the woman opposite.

Beside him, Caitlyn quietly closed her notebook.

"Nessie?"

"A real beaut, isn't she?" said Marion, her eyes blazing with excitement. "Beautiful, yet deadly, it seems."

Logan wasn't bothering to look at the photographs now. Caitlyn picked up the top one and regarded it for a moment as Marion watched on eagerly.

"There's a whole pile there from all around the loch, although those are the most interesting," Marion said. "I managed to get a glimpse of her earlier in the week, too. Not far from where the body was found. Although, the photograph is nowhere near as good as this one."

"It's a stick, isn't it?"

"A *stick*?!" Marion's tone was scornful. Mocking, even. "Of course it's not a stick, you silly girl. Look at it! It's curved at the end."

Logan felt DS McQuarrie bristle beside him. To her credit, she didn't bite.

"It's a bendy stick, then," she said, putting the photo back on the pile.

"It's a head. It's clearly a head," Marion insisted. She leaned forward and tapped the bundle of pictures. "I've been living out there by the loch for twelve years and have never caught a whiff of her. And now this, right before that poor woman's body washes up? That can't be coincidence."

"You're right. When you put it like that it does sound pretty conclusive," said Caitlyn, making no effort to hide the sarcasm. The old woman didn't seem to pick up on it.

"Precisely."

Marion leaned in closer, clasping her hands in front of her. She lowered her voice, as if letting them in on a secret. "My theory is that she went in swimming."

"The monster?" said Logan.

Marion rolled her eyes. "Come on, man, keep up. The woman. She went swimming. Or possibly fell in. Was she found clothed?"

"I'm afraid I'm not at liberty to disclose that information," Logan told her.

Marion twitched in irritation. "I can't very well help you if you don't give me the details, Sergeant," she scolded. "No matter. I think she went in the water, disturbed Nessie in some way, and then... *Snap*. Dead. Just like that. She's lucky she wasn't eaten, really."

Logan met DS McQuarrie's eye. The expression on her face mirrored the one he could feel he was wearing on his own.

"It's tragic, of course, and I almost feel guilty for saying it, but this is all *very exciting*," Marion continued in a slightly breathless whisper. "I posted the photographs in some online groups I'm a member of and there's a real buzz about it all. People are *thrilled*."

This time, Logan felt himself bristle.

"A woman died."

"Of course. And, like I say, it's utterly tragic. *Utterly* tragic," Marion conceded. "But think of the bigger picture. We've got evidence! We've finally got proof that the Loch Ness Monster exists!"

She indicated her photographs again and settled back, arms folded once more. "I bet you wish you'd recorded this now, don't you, Sergeant? History in the making."

Logan blinked a couple of times, then puffed out his cheeks.

"Well."

He put both hands on the table and pushed his chair back, standing up.

"Thank you for the information, Ms Whitehead. You've given us an interesting new line of enquiry."

Marion looked a little confused. "Oh. Is that it? Don't you need me to sign anything, or...?"

"It's fine. We have all we need," Logan told her.

"You can keep the photographs. They're copies, I have the originals,"

Marion said. "Safely under lock and key," she added, eyeing both detectives with a degree of suspicion.

"It's fine. We have all we need," Logan reiterated. "You keep them."

"Won't you need them? You know, as evidence, or what have you?" Marion asked.

Logan shook his head. "We can hardly prosecute the Loch Ness Monster, can we?"

"Wouldn't fit in the court for a start," Caitlyn pointed out.

Marion picked up the photographs and flicked through a few of them. "No. No, I suppose not," she said, missing the sarcasm once again.

She held the bundle out to Logan. "I really think you should hang onto them. I had copies made special."

Logan relented with a barely contained sigh. "Fine. We'll hang onto them. Thanks," he said.

He took the photographs without looking at them.

"Hang on there for a few minutes, Ms Whitehead," he instructed. "I'll have someone take your details, then see you out."

"Have I been helpful, Sergeant?" Marion asked, and there was an earnestness there that stopped Logan stating the obvious.

"Aye. It's been... eye-opening," he told her, and her face lit-up. "Thank you for your assistance."

Marion was still beaming when Logan and Caitlyn left the room and pulled the door behind them with a *click*.

"Nicely handled, *Sergeant*," Caitlyn said, smirking. "We'll make a DI of you yet."

"Fingers crossed," Logan said. He looked down at the photos, shaking his head. It was a stick. It was *clearly* a stick. "What a nutter."

"Oh, God, aye," Caitlyn agreed. "Still, harmless enough, I suppose."

"Aye," Logan agreed. He set off along the corridor, but stole a glance back at the door to the Interview Room. "We'll see."

CHAPTER ELEVEN

"Useful chat, was it?"

Ben had a hopeful expression on his face, like he was envisioning a quick wrap-up to the case, followed by a slap-up lunch at the Chinese Buffet over by *Johnny Foxes*.

"We've cracked it. Case closed," Logan told him, briefly waving the photos before tossing them onto the desk that had been set aside for the Exhibits Officer. "The monster did it."

"The bastard. Had to happen sooner or later," Ben said, almost, but not quite, managing to hide his disappointment.

"Anything back for me, yet?" Logan asked, raising his voice to the rest of the room.

"No sign of Robbie Steadwood yet, boss," Tyler reported, visibly steeling himself for a bollocking. Instead, Logan just grunted and turned his attention to the team's other Detective Constable.

"Couple of replies on Reddit, sir, but nothing overly useful," Hamza said.

"What have we got?" Logan pressed, hoping for *something* they could use.

"Spoiler for the new Marvel movie, and some guy called me a paedo," Hamza said. He raised his eyes above his monitor and smiled apologetically. "The internet, sir."

Logan sighed. "No' exactly the most auspicious start."

He grabbed his coat, then beckoned to Tyler with a crooked finger. "Right. Let's crack on. Everyone knows what they're doing."

"We'll do the drive-by of those sites, sir," Caitlyn said. "Hamza, grab a photo of the map before we go, will you?"

"No bother."

Logan nodded. "Good. And be careful. No unnecessary risks," he reminded them. "We'll meet back here when we're done and see where we are."

"Best of luck," said Ben, dipping into a pack of chocolate digestives. He raised one in salute, then dunked it in his tea. "Oh, and Jack?"

Logan pulled on his coat, then looked back at the DI. Ben smiled. It wasn't his usual smile, exactly. There was something deliberately coy and mysterious about it, Logan thought. It made him vaguely uneasy.

"When you go meet the family, say hello to the liaison officer for me."

LOGAN AND TYLER sat in Logan's Ford Focus just down from the house where the victim's sister, Michelle Sinclair, lived. With a name like Druid Road, Logan had been half-expecting some quaint old witch's cottages, but instead the street was lined with rows of boxy terraced houses with postage stamp gardens.

The houses had all been clad in that exterior insulation material that made them all look even more uniform than they previously might have. Wooden pallets and blue plastic ties in some of the gardens suggested it had all been done fairly recently.

"So, what's our plan?" Tyler asked.

"The plan," Logan began, unclipping his belt, "is for me to do the talking and you to keep your trap shut."

"Right," said Tyler, a little flatly. "I could just stay here, if it's easier? Or, there's a pub around the corner. I could wait for you there. I mean, if you don't need me in there, boss."

"Did I say I didn't need you in there?" Logan asked. "Keep your mouth shut, but your eyes open. Watch how they respond. Listen for inconsistencies. Get a feel for them while I'm talking."

Tyler nodded, suitably chastised. "Right. Aye. Will do, boss."

Logan reached for the door handle, then stopped. "And stop humming that tune."

DC Neish blinked. "What tune?"

"The tune you've been humming all the way here."

Tyler continued to look blankly back at him.

"The tune. The bloody... the tune. You've been humming a tune."

"Have I?"

"Yes!"

Tyler thought for a moment. "Was it that Marshmello one?"

"Was it *what?*"

"Marshmello. You know? The DJ," said Tyler. "Huge on YouTube. Head's a big marshmallow."

It was Logan's turn to just sit and stare.

"No' an actual marshmallow, like."

Logan tutted. "Aye, funnily enough I guessed he didn't have an *actual marshmallow for a head*," he scowled. "Just stop it, whoever it is. It's getting on my nerves."

"Will do, boss," Tyler said.

"Good. Right, then. Game face on," Logan said. He checked the wing mirror, then opened the car door. "And remember—eyes peeled, ears open."

It was the Family Liaison Officer who opened the door. Logan took half a step back, not quite believing what he was seeing.

"Hello, sir."

"Sinead?" the DCI said, looking the uniformed constable up and down. "What are you doing up here?"

"Transferred up, sir," said PC Bell. "DI Forde convinced me. Too many bad memories down the road, so it made sense."

Logan knew exactly what she meant.

PC Bell had handled herself well during the child abduction case in Fort William. Exceptionally well, in fact. She was young, but she had a tough few years behind her, and probably more to come, and Logan had been impressed by the way she was handling things. He'd mentioned to DI Forde that she was going to go far, but he hadn't expected the crafty old bugger to take it literally.

"What about your wee brother? Harris, wasn't it?"

"Aye. He's loving it," Sinead said. "Already made some pals, and there's a breakfast club and loads of after-school stuff, so it works out well for work."

"Good. That's... I'm really pleased for you," Logan said. He jabbed a thumb back over his shoulder. "If I'd known you were here I wouldn't have bothered bringing this one along."

"Hiya," said Tyler, flashing Sinead a smile that Logan didn't see, but still somehow disapproved of. She nodded and smiled back at him.

"DC Neish."

"Call me Tyler."

"Call him DC Neish," Logan suggested. He looked past her into the hallway. "Family in?"

"They are, aye. Just in the living room. I was making them a cup of tea." She gave a backwards tilt of her head. "Want one?"

"Aye, go on then," said Logan. He moved to step inside, but Sinead blocked him.

"Shoes."

"Eh?"

Sinead pointed to the rough mat the DCI was standing on. "She's quite... particular. You have to wipe your feet out there, and then again in here."   •

She indicated a second, thinner mat just inside the front door.

"Trust me. Someone trudged in some dirt yesterday and she spent the next twenty minutes hoovering the same three foot section of the living room."

She glanced back over her shoulder, then leaned out of the doorway and dropped her voice further. "I wouldn't mind, but it's laminate flooring."

"Christ, one of those," Logan muttered. He wiped his feet. "Happy?"

"Ecstatic, sir," Sinead smirked. She stepped back. "Now this one, then I'll introduce you and go get the kettle on. You don't take milk, do you?"

"No, just black," Logan confirmed, stepping inside.

Sinead leaned around his tall, broad frame until she could see Tyler.

"DC Neish?"

"Is there any Earl Grey?" he asked.

Logan replied before Sinead could open her mouth. "No, there is not," he said. "You're on duty. You'll have proper tea. You can drink your bloody potpourri on your own time."

He was too busy wiping his feet on the second mat to notice the little nod that passed from Sinead to Tyler, or the wink and the thumbs up he gave her in reply.

"They're just through in the living room," Sinead said. She gestured ahead to a door at the end of the hall, through which Logan could hear the sound of gunfire coming from a TV. "I explained you were coming."

"How do they seem?"

"Are you asking how they're holding up, or what I think of them?" Sinead asked, keeping her voice low.

"Bit of both," Logan replied.

"They're holding up as well as can be expected, I suppose," Sinead said. She narrowed her eyes and ran her tongue across her teeth, thinking. "And can I get back to you on the other bit? Maybe best that you see what you think yourself first."

"Good idea," Logan said. "And it's Michelle, isn't it?"

"Aye. Not *Chelle* though. She hates that," Sinead said.

"OK. Good to know."

"*Mish* is fine, apparently, but don't call her *Chelle*," Sinead explained. She smiled and did the tiniest of eye rolls. "Like I said, she's a wee bit..."

"Of an arsehole?" Tyler whispered.

"*Particular*," Sinead corrected. She took a moment to compose herself, stifling a laugh, then closed the door behind the detectives and gestured along the hallway. "In you go. I'll come and introduce you all."

CHAPTER TWELVE

MICHELLE SINCLAIR WAS HOVERING BY THE WINDOW WHEN SINEAD brought Logan and Tyler into the living room. Even from behind, Logan recognised her as the woman he'd seen with Malcolm Sinclair back at the campsite.

At the sound of them entering, she quickly turned, and Logan noticed that her eyes went right to their feet before flitting up to check out the rest of them.

She was the type of woman who might normally be 'bubbly,' were it not for the fact her sister had recently been brutally murdered and dumped in a loch. She was in her mid-twenties, with hair so blonde it could only have come from a bottle. Her nails were long red talons that she picked at while Sinead made the introductions. She was in pretty decent shape, but probably a stone or so heavier than she'd like to be.

Michelle wore jeans and a dark blue shirt that she hadn't tucked in. Logan got the impression that it wasn't her usual style, although he had nothing to really base that on at the moment besides the hair and nails.

Her eyes were ringed with red, and there were some telltale mascara streaks that she hadn't quite managed to dab away. She offered up a smile to the detectives as they entered, but it was a hollow and lifeless one. An automatic rearrangement of her facial features. Nothing more.

"Michelle. Stuart," said Sinead, addressing the woman and the back of an armchair positioned to face a big telly that was mounted on the wall. A fifty-incher, Logan reckoned. Maybe more. "This is DCI Logan and DC Neish, who I told you about. They're just here to ask a few questions."

"Hello," said Michelle. "Although, we met, didn't we? With my dad?"

"We did," Logan confirmed. "How is he doing?"

"You know."

Michelle's voice was thin and flat. Absent, almost. She looked over to the armchair and forced her face into a more convincing smile. "Stuart. The police are here. Can you pause that, sweetheart?"

"No, I can't pause it," a voice grunted. "It's online. I can't very well pause everyone else in the world, can I?"

Michelle turned her smile towards the detectives, but her eyes told a very different story. Logan gave her an almost imperceptible shake of his head, dismissing her non-verbal apology as unnecessary.

"Well, can you come out of it?" Michelle pressed. "These detectives would like to talk to us."

The video game that had been playing on the TV screen froze. There was a heavy sigh, then a teenage boy stood up, an Xbox controller clutched in one hand.

Logan knew from the report that he was fourteen, but he looked a couple of years older. His face was a dot-to-dot puzzle of plooks, with some coarse hairs sprouting here and there from his jaw. He wore a t-shirt with a print of some sort of green blob with eyes on the front, and while he looked in Logan's direction, he didn't look *at* him, exactly.

Logan was almost relieved about that. There was a deadness to the boy's eyes—a haunted, faraway look that Logan had seen on too many people in too many living rooms over the years.

"This is Stuart," Sinead said again. The boy did manage to bring himself to look at her, and his eyes spluttered back into life a little. "He's Mairi's son."

"*Was* Mairi's son," Stuart grunted. His voice was tight. Hoarse. Like he was keeping the words on a firm leash.

"You still are," Logan told him. "Always will be."

Something in the boy's expression softened then hardened again, but he said nothing. After a moment, he gave the tiniest of shrugs, before his shoulders sagged back to their original position.

"Sorry, where are my manners?" fretted Michelle. She lifted a big sequined cushion from the couch, plumped it up, then set it back down. The couch was a small two-seater with high arm rests and a straight back. It looked just about the most uncomfortable bastard of a thing Logan had ever seen. "Take a seat, please."

Stuart wasted no time in doing just that. He slumped back into the armchair, and the room was filled with the sound of gunfire as he rejoined the game.

"Stuart, can you not?" Michelle said through a smile that was all teeth. "Just for five minutes, can you... Can you not?"

He didn't bother to sigh this time, and Logan got the impression he knew he'd been pushing his luck. As the detectives took a seat on the couch, the boy turned the armchair around with his feet so he was facing them. The couch was exactly as uncomfortable as Logan had been expecting, and the size of it meant he and DC Neish were practically pressed against each other.

"Cool. A spinny one," Tyler remarked, watching Stuart turn in the chair. He nodded to the telly. "Was that Blackout mode on Black Ops Four?"

Stuart looked at his Xbox controller, then up at his auntie, as if one or the other might answer on his behalf.

"Well, I don't know, do I?" said Michelle, rubbing his hair as she walked behind him. "It's all just shooting to me."

Stuart looked vaguely in Tyler's direction, then nodded. "Yeah."

"Nice. You played Fortnite?" the DC asked.

"Don't really like it."

"Nah, nor me. It's all eight-year-olds. Blackout's better."

While they'd been speaking, Michelle had perched herself on the wide arm of Stuart's armchair. It tilted ever so slightly, but she draped her right arm across the chair's back, better distributing her weight and keeping it all balanced.

"I'll go get that tea," Sinead said, slipping out of the room and leaving them to it.

In estate agent speak, the living room could be described as 'cosy'. Which, in the real world, meant there was barely room to swing a cat. There was just enough room to fit the armchair and two-seater couch, a small coffee table, and a three-shelf bookcase. The bookcase was filled with a row of *Dan Browns* and assorted *Fifty Shades*, a row of DVDs, and a larger section at the bottom with four cookbooks and a lot of empty space.

A six-inch wooden cross with a little ceramic Jesus on it was fixed to the wall above the bookcase, and now that Logan looked more closely he could see a Bible rammed in between the thrillers and the soft porn, like Moses pushing apart the Red Sea.

The walls were a very pale blue, aside from the one the TV was mounted to, which was patterned with a print of looping silver flowers. Logan had heard such things referred to as 'feature walls,' although this one was nothing but a bloody eyesore.

"They flooded the map recently," Stuart volunteered.

Logan was momentarily confused by this revelation, before realising the boy was still talking to Tyler.

"No! Did they? I'll have to check that out. Thanks for the tip," said the DC with what sounded like genuine enthusiasm.

Stuart gave a little nod and the slightest upturning of the corners of his mouth that suggested there was a smile still in him somewhere.

"No problem."

On the arm of the chair, Michelle rolled her eyes, then kissed the boy on the top of his head. Considering how greasy his hair was, Logan hoped she was up to date with her jags.

"We appreciate you both seeing us," Logan began. "I understand what a difficult time this must be for you."

"Very difficult," Michelle agreed. She sniffed, and took one of Stuart's hands—the one not currently clutching the game controller—and clasped it in her own. "But we're both determined to do whatever we can. Aren't we, sweetheart?"

Stuart gave a nod of what could, Logan supposed, be generously described as 'broad agreement.' His eyes had glazed over into a thousand-yard-stare again, and he was looking between the detectives rather than at them.

"I was brought in to lead the case yesterday," Logan explained. "So I wasn't involved in the original search for..."

He stopped himself saying 'the victim' just in the nick of time.

"Mairi. As such, I'd like to just go over a few things to make sure I have the clearest possible picture."

"Of course. We understand," said Michelle. She rubbed the back of Stuart's hand with a thumb. "You were the one who found the boy down in Fort William, Sinead tells us."

Logan glanced to the door. Luckily for Sinead, she was still through in the kitchen and so managed to avoid the dirty look he would otherwise have thrown at her.

"Aye. That's right," he confirmed, then swiftly brought the conversation back on track. He leaned forward a little and offered Stuart a well-rehearsed smile of sympathy. "I know this is difficult, Stuart, but I'd like to talk about the weekend. About the last time you saw your mum. Is that alright?"

Michelle kneaded his fingers between her own. "Go on, sweetheart," she whispered, giving his shoulder a squeeze with her other hand. "Just tell them what you know."

Stuart shrugged. "Just... Like I already said."

"It's a pain in the arse to keep going over it, isn't it?" said Tyler. He gestured to his notepad. "Imagine how I feel. I've got to write it all down."

"Can't you just record it?" Stuart asked.

Tyler straightened, his eyes widening. "Shite. Aye! That makes much more sense. Great idea." He took his phone from his pocket. "Is that alright with you?"

Stuart glanced at his controller again, like he might see the answer written there, then looked up and nodded. "Yeah. It's fine."

"Nice one. That makes things much easier," Tyler said, hitting the big red button on his audio recording app. The briefest of glances passed between the detectives, then Tyler gave Stuart the nod. "Right. Up and running. In your own time, mate."

The boy shuffled around in the chair, getting comfortable. Michelle continued to hold his hand.

"What do you want to know?" Stuart asked.

"You said you last spoke to her on Sunday morning. Around... when, would you say?" Logan asked.

"About eleven."

"You're sure?"

Stuart nodded. "She woke me up. I remember checking the time on my phone. It was three minutes past eleven."

"Did she say where she was going?"

A shake of the head.

"Would she normally go out on a Sunday morning?"

Another shake.

"I've tried to get her to come to church for years," said Michelle. "But she's not interested."

Her use of the incorrect tense struck her. She didn't mention it, but Logan saw the moment it dawned on her.

"So, it was unusual for her to be heading out on a Sunday morning, you'd say?" Logan pressed.

A nod, this time. "Yeah," Stuart said. His throat was tight, and the word took a couple of attempts before it came out.

"You're doing really well, mate," Tyler encouraged.

"Did she take the car, do you know?" Logan asked.

"Think so, yeah," said Stuart.

"But you didn't see?"

"No."

"Didn't hear the engine, or anything?"

"No, but it's gone, isn't it? So she must've," said Stuart, his tone becoming a little impatient.

Logan nodded. "Did you see it outside the night before?"

"What?"

"The night before. Saturday. Did you see the car then?"

Stuart's unibrow knotted above his nose. "I don't... I'm not sure."

He looked up at his auntie. She smiled and gave his hand another squeeze. "You're doing really well."

"She sometimes couldn't get parked outside the house," Stuart explained. "So she had to park down the road a bit. I didn't see. But why wouldn't it have been there?"

"No reason, son. Just trying to get as full a picture as possible."

He became aware of Sinead hovering outside the living room door, and sat back a little. "In you come, constable."

Sinead entered carrying a tray laden with three mugs, a milk jug, sugar bowl, and a can of Irn Bru. She sat them down on the coffee table, and passed one of the mugs to Michelle.

"There we are," she said.

"Thanks, Sinead," Michelle said. She looked past the constable to where Logan was reaching for one of the other mugs.

"I don't know what we'd have done without her. Isn't that right, Stuart?"

Stuart gave a non-committal shrug. "Yeah."

"It's nothing. Don't be silly," said Sinead. She turned back to the tray, spent a second or two just staring at it, then raised her eyes to Logan just as he took a sip of his tea.

His mouth twisted into a grimace of disgust and he looked down into the mug.

"That's DC Neish's, sir," Sinead told him.

Logan drew the constable a foul look, then set the mug of Earl Grey back down on the tray. His tongue moved inside his mouth, like it was trying to scrub the taste away, then he washed what was left of it down with a mouthful of proper tea from the other mug.

The questioning continued. Gentle. Probing. Michelle held Stuart's hand through most of it, but as he relaxed, the boy became more forthcoming with his answers.

It was only at that point that Logan began with the questions he'd come there to ask. He finished his tea and set the cup down on the tray and cleared his throat. He shot a glance at Tyler's phone to make sure it was still recording before leaning forward just a fraction.

"One more thing, son," he began.

His gaze flitted from Stuart to Michelle, then back again.

"What can you tell me about your father?"

CHAPTER THIRTEEN

Hᴀᴍᴢᴀ ѕᴀᴛ ɪɴ ᴛʜᴇ ᴘᴀѕѕᴇɴɢᴇʀ ѕᴇᴀᴛ ᴏꜰ Cᴀɪᴛʟʏɴ'ѕ ᴄᴀʀ, ᴛʜᴇ ᴇɴɢɪɴᴇ humming its impatience for them to move on.

He knew how it felt. This was the fifth site they'd checked out, and it was already shaping up to be as much of a bust as the previous four.

"This is the other extension job," Caitlyn said.

"Aye," Hamza agreed, looking across the front of the house. The main building was a traditional stone cottage, but the extension was much more modern. Offensively so, in fact. "Someone's got *Grand Designs* on Series Link."

There was an open bag of mints sitting in a dookit in front of the gearstick, and he'd been gradually working his way through them since they'd left Inverness over an hour ago. He reached for another, then yelped when his hand was slapped away. "Hey!"

"Hey nothing. You've had nearly the whole bloody packet," Caitlyn retorted.

"I've had about three!" Hamza protested.

"My arse you've had three," said Caitlyn. She relented with a tut. "Go on, then. But you're buying me another bag."

Hamza took one of the mints and unwrapped it. He popped it in his mouth and they both sat for a while watching a couple of workmen clambering about on the roof of the house extension. It was a B&B located just back from a single track road. The front looked out over the loch, and judging by the size of the windows in the new part, they were taking full advantage of it.

"Cracking view, right enough," Hamza said.

Caitlyn turned and looked out across Loch Ness. The edge of the road was lined with trees, but the house was raised up on a hillside enough that it peeped over the top of them.

"Not far to carry a body," the DS remarked.

"Have to cross the road, though," Hamza pointed out.

"Hardly a road, though, is it? It's barely a wide path."

"Risky, though." The mint *clacked* off Hamza's teeth as he moved it around in his mouth. "And then there's the trees. Probably a drop down into the water." He shook his head. "Last site was better. If I was going to kill someone, I'd have killed them there."

Caitlyn couldn't dispute that. The last site had been a new-build and stood right down by the water's edge. One of the balconies even hung out over the banking. It would've been easy for someone to wrap a body and just dump it straight into the loch without even setting foot outside the house.

Unfortunately, Caitlyn's information had been a little out of date. Construction had finished on the house six weeks previously, and the place was now a family home, complete with three kids and at least a couple of dogs. Hardly the place for a ritualistic murder.

"Nice place that one," Hamza remarked, not for the first time. "Wonder how much a gaff like that costs."

"More than we'll ever make," Caitlyn said.

"Heh. Aye. Fair point," Hamza agreed.

He reached for another mint, ignoring the glare it drew from DS McQuarrie, then snapped off a couple of photos of the site on his phone.

"Should we go talk to them?" he wondered.

Caitlyn checked her mirrors, then indicated to pull out from where they were stopped across the entrance to the house's driveway. "No, it's just a drive past," she said. "What's left?"

Hamza consulted the notepad on his lap. "Path repair."

"That's it?"

"That's it. Unless... Hang on."

He consulted his phone's map, then nodded ahead. "Boleskine House is straight along this road. We'll pass it in five minutes. We should swing in there and check it out." He sat up a little straighter in his seat. "They say you get a really weird vibe off it. You know, because of all the demon stuff."

After checking both directions for oncoming traffic, Caitlyn pulled out onto the narrow road.

"Do you believe all that stuff?" she asked.

Hamza side-eyed her. "Why, do you?"

"Obviously not."

"Nah. Nor me," Hamza said, just a little too quickly. "Still, interesting though, isn't it?"

"In what way?"

"Just, you know..."

He helped himself to another mint.

"Interesting."

Caitlyn waited for Hamza to unwrap the sweet, then plucked it from his fingers before he could do anything with it.

"Aye, suppose," she said, quickly shoving the mint in her mouth. "But if your head starts spinning and you projectile vomit pea soup on me, I will *not* be bloody happy."

CHAPTER FOURTEEN

AT THE MENTION OF HIS FATHER, EVERYTHING ABOUT STUART'S demeanour changed. His face hardened. His body language became stiff. His eyes shone with something that might have been contempt, but might equally have been fear.

"What can he tell you about his father? Not a bloody lot," said Michelle, answering on the boy's behalf. She shot an apologetic look to the porcelain Jesus on the wall, and slowly traced the back of her nephew's hand with her thumb. "Stuart hasn't had much to do with Robbie over the years."

"I understand. And I'm sorry to have to ask these questions. I wouldn't be asking if it wasn't important," Logan said, his attention still firmly on the boy. "When did you last see him?"

Stuart looked to Michelle for reassurance. She gave him an encouraging nod. "Go on."

"Like... six months ago. He turned up the day after my birthday."

"He had the wrong date, can you believe?" said Michelle. Her expression suggested she not only *could* believe it, but expected nothing less from the man. She shook her head. "His own son, and he had the wrong date."

"What did he say?" Logan pressed.

Stuart shrugged. "The usual. Sorry, he'd make it up to me, whatever. Same stuff he always says when he shows up. Wanted to take me to the pub to celebrate."

"His *fourteenth birthday*," Michelle stressed. "I mean..."

"He gave me a card with five hundred quid in it," Stuart said. His cheeks reddened a little. "Mum wanted me to give it back, but..."

"Five hundred quid's five hundred quid," said Tyler. "Least he could do."

"That's what I said," Stuart replied, and the reassurance from the detective constable seemed to encourage him. "Exactly."

"What about your mum? Do you know when she last saw him?" Logan asked.

Stuart shook his head. "No. Why?"

Beside him, Michelle sat up a little straighter. "Oh," she said. She looked and sounded a little surprised but not, Logan noted, particularly shocked. She recovered quickly and smiled around at everyone. "We should have some biscuits! You'll have a biscuit, won't you, Mr Logan?"

"Aye. Aye, I wouldn't say no," Logan said.

"You know where they are, sweetheart," Michelle said, smiling down at Stuart from her perch on the arm of his chair. "Get the nice ones, will you?"

Sinead, who had been standing quietly by the door, beckoned Stuart over. "You can show me where they are so I know for next time."

Stuart grunted, then stood up. "I know what you're doing," he said, but he trudged out anyway. Sinead bustled out after him, then closed the door behind them.

"You think Robbie did it, don't you?" said Michelle, taking Stuart's place in the armchair.

"We're keeping an open mind at this stage," Logan replied. "But we're keen to speak to him."

Michelle looked to the door, then lowered her voice. "She met him recently, I think. Or, she was going to. I don't know if she did."

"When was this?" Logan asked.

"About... Three weeks ago, maybe?"

"Did she say why?"

Michelle shook her head. "No. She seemed annoyed at him, but then there was nothing unusual there."

She dropped her voice further until it was scarcely a whisper. "He ruined her life. I mean, she wouldn't be... She wouldn't *have been* without Stuart, but... Robbie ruined her life."

"In what way?" Logan pressed.

"Sent her right off the rails. Messed with her head. Turned her against us all for a long time," Michelle explained. "She was sixteen when he got her pregnant. Sixteen! Had his way on her birthday, she eventually told me. Years later, I mean."

Michelle looked up at the ceiling, as if it were a screen replaying all the murky details of the past.

"She saw sense eventually, but only after she caught him having his way with some other poor unsuspecting lassie."

"Any reason to think he might do something like this?" Logan asked.

Michelle puffed out her cheeks. "Oh, I don't know. There's no predicting that man. Maybe, yes. I mean, if I had to pick someone?" She made a head gesture than was neither one thing nor the other. "Maybe."

Logan glanced at DC Neish, then back to Michelle. "Thanks. Very useful. We've got people looking for him now, so hopefully we'll find him soon."

"He not at work, then?"

Logan felt a flutter in the pit of his stomach. "Work? I didn't realise he had a job."

"He probably doesn't officially. It'll be cash in hand, I'm sure," she said, with a venom that suggested she considered this to be almost as bad as the other crime he was implicated in. "It's that building company. Bunch of cowboys. What are they called?"

"Not Bosco Building, is it?" asked Tyler.

"Yes! That's them," said Michelle. "You've heard of them?"

"Aye. You could say that," said Tyler.

Logan turned to him, an eyebrow raised.

"Explain later, boss. Long story."

There was a knock at the door, then Sinead's head appeared around the doorframe. Logan noticed, for the first time, another cross fixed above the doorframe.

"Just checking if you're ready for the biscuits?"

Logan nodded, beckoned for her to come in, then got to his feet.

"You've been very helpful, Miss Sinclair," Logan told Michelle. "And you too, son," he added, as Stuart trudged into the room behind Sinead, carrying a plate on which an array of biscuits had been half-heartedly arranged.

"Ooh, I'd like a little *Drifter*," Tyler said, helping himself to one of the brightly-wrapped chocolate fingers. He gave Stuart a beaming smile, then tucked the *Drifter* into the top pocket of his shirt. "Thanks."

"As soon as we have anything to pass on, we'll be in touch," Logan said.

Michelle jumped up from the armchair, took a moment to smooth the seat, then took the plate from Stuart and motioned for him to sit down.

Stuart hovered by the armchair, not yet sitting.

"You alright, mate?" Tyler asked.

"I forgot something," he said.

Michelle gave a little laugh. "Don't worry. It's just biscuits."

"No. About mum. I just remembered."

A hush fell.

"What was it you remembered, son?" Logan asked.

"She was arguing with someone. On the phone. Thursday night, I think it was."

Michelle frowned. "You never mentioned."

"I just remembered. I was in the kitchen. On Thursday, I mean. Her bedroom's right above it, and I could hear her arguing."

"Do you know who it was with, or what she said?" Logan asked.

Stuart shook his head. "No. Sorry. It was muffled. She didn't come downstairs for a while after it, and I forgot to ask her." He blinked several times, each one faster than the last. "I should've asked her."

"It's not your fault, mate," said Tyler, putting a hand on the boy's shoulder. "Alright? You weren't to know."

"Do you know what time you heard her arguing?" Logan pressed.

Stuart's eyes narrowed in concentration. "Not really. Between six and eight, maybe. I think."

"That's really helpful, son. Well done," Logan said. He looked from the boy to his aunt. "If either of you remember anything else, please let Sinead know."

"We will. And thank you. We're grateful for everything you're doing," Michelle replied. "Both of you. Sinead, too. It's..."

Her voice took on a note of hoarseness, her throat constricting. "We appreciate it. We... It's..."

Logan gave her a nod that told her he understood. Whatever it was she was trying to say, he understood.

"We'll be in touch," he told her. "And if there's anything you need, Sinead will take care of you."

He caught the constable's eye. "Call into the station later. We'll catch up."

"Will do, sir," Sinead said, as Logan brushed past her out of the room.

Tyler hung back with Sinead for a moment. "So, yeah," he began, shuffling on the spot and clicking his fingers down by his sides. "Thanks for the tea. Don't forget, if there's ever anything—"

"Get a move on, Detective Constable," came a gruff voice from the hallway. "We don't have all day."

LOGAN WAS ALREADY SITTING behind the wheel of the Focus when Tyler climbed into the front passenger seat. He waited until the DC had closed the door before voicing what was on his mind.

"Bosco Building?"

"Hmm? Oh, aye. They've been on the radar for a while," Tyler said. "CID reckons it's—"

"A front for a drugs operation. Russian led. Bosco Maximuke."

Tyler blinked. "Aye. That's right. You read the report?"

Logan shook his head. "He used to be based in Glasgow. He upped sticks and relocated his whole operation up to this neck of the woods."

"Oh. Right," Tyler said. "What made him do that?"

Logan slid the key into the ignition and fired up the engine.

"Me," he said.

DC Neish whistled through his teeth. "Oh. OK. So... we going to pay him a visit?"

"I am. You're not," Logan told him.

"What? Why not?"

"Because I said so. You can go back to the station and check in with Ben."

Tyler chewed on his bottom lip for a moment. "You don't think I should come, boss? Strength in numbers, and all that."

"I'm sure I'll cope," Logan said. He looked very deliberately to DC Neish's door handle. It took the younger detective a moment to figure out the meaning.

"Oh. You want me to get...?"

Logan nodded. "Aye."

"Right. Aye."

Tyler hesitated, then opened his door and got out. Logan pressed the button to wind down the window as the DC closed the door behind him.

"How am I supposed to get back?" Tyler asked, leaning down.

"Call an Uber," Logan told him.

"Uber doesn't do Inverness."

"Oh. Don't they?" said Logan. He mulled this over, filed it away, then clicked the button to wind up the window again.

Tyler watched from the kerb as the Focus pulled away and drove off down the road.

"Nice one, boss," he muttered. He kept watching until the car had turned the corner at the end of the street. "Cheers for that."

CHAPTER FIFTEEN

"You alright?"

Hamza stood halfway up a grassy hill, massaging his lower back with both hands and labouring for breath. The sun had found a route through the clouds just as they'd arrived at Boleskine House, and the direct heat coupled with the steep hike up the hillside wasn't doing him a lot of favours.

"Be fine in a minute," he puffed, looking up to where DS McQuarrie had been powering ahead.

She headed back down to join him, but he waved her back. "Seriously. It's fine."

"I told you you should've waited in the car."

"What, and miss the devil house?" Hamza said. He gulped down a couple of big breaths. "No chance."

Boleskine House was too far back and too well-hidden by trees to be seen from the road. The driveway leading up to the house had been blocked off with boulders, and a sign warned that trespassers would be prosecuted. The same sign also claimed that the site was protected by CCTV, but Caitlyn was sceptical. It was much cheaper to buy a sign claiming there was a CCTV system than it was to actually fit one, especially in a ruin this remote.

It wasn't impossible, of course, and she'd be delighted if she was wrong, but she'd also be very surprised.

Fortunately, there was a well-trodden path and a big hole in the fence close to where she'd stopped the car. The parking space probably belonged to the little graveyard across the road from the house, but none of the residents were in any real position to voice their objections, and there was nobody else around.

Hamza gave his back another rub, and felt the lines of scarring through his shirt. They stung when he got hot. Or cold. Or sometimes when he got tired. In fact, there was rarely a day went by when they didn't make their presence felt at some point or another.

He winced down another couple of breaths, then nodded to Caitlyn. "Right."

They resumed the climb, DS McQuarrie setting a slower pace this time. She tried to disguise it by making a show of looking out across the loch behind them, and to the open field over on the right, but Hamza saw through it and was only spurred on to walk faster.

As they approached, they were able to see more of the house. Or what was left of it, anyway. Fire had ravaged the place a few years back, consuming the roof and gutting the inside, but leaving most of the old stone walls standing.

A couple of chimney stacks stood steadfast and upright, the brickwork scorched but otherwise unaffected by the flames that had done a number on the rest of the place.

It was when Hamza saw the boarded windows that he felt the first fluttering of panic in his chest, and the scars on his back nipped at him in protest. He stopped, his legs turning to lead, memories of another ruined house not far away or long ago spinning around in his head.

"You OK?" he heard Caitlyn ask, and he forced his feet to move, to carry him on up the rest of the hill, ignoring the way his breathing was becoming erratic and his head was going light.

"Fine."

He felt her looking at him, saw her concerned expression from the corner of his eye. He ignored that too, and powered on past her up the hill, then through the gap in the fence that marked the boundary of Boleskine House.

Hamza stopped then, chest heaving, dark sparkles colouring the corners of his vision. Was it exertion, or panic? He couldn't tell. Both? Neither?

Or something else entirely?

The route had led them to the front of the house, where...

No. Not the front. This wasn't the front. He'd seen the plans. He knew this.

He thought about the floorplan he'd found online. Focused on it until he could see it in his mind's eye. He tried connecting it with the ruin in front of him now.

Beside them on the right was the library. The boarded windows made it impossible to see inside, but a big room full of books was unlikely to have fared well in a fire, Hamza thought.

To the left of that, a curved wall belonged to the... What was it? What was it?

He closed his eyes and tried to conjure up a clearer picture of the map.

"Drawing room!" he said aloud.

Caitlyn, who had been watching him with concern, switched to staring at him in confusion. "Huh?"

Hamza pointed to three different parts of the building ahead of them. "Drawing room, dining room, lounge."

DS McQuarrie regarded the house. "How do you know that?"

"It was on the plans," Hamza said. The icy fingers that had been squeezing the air from his chest were slackening their grip now, and colour was gradually returning to the edges of the world.

The wing of the house where the library was situated had fared better than the rest of the place. It still had some of its roof, and was the only section where anyone had bothered to barricade the windows. Presumably, it was to keep out squatters, although a few pieces of chipboard were unlikely to deter the buggers in Hamza's experience.

The rest of the place was so utterly destroyed that blocking the windows up was pointless. Through the holes in the walls, Hamza could see the blackened detritus of a family home. Most of the furniture had been entombed by the collapsing roof, but the skeleton of an armchair was visible amongst the wreckage. Something that might once have been a TV was now warped and buckled into some sort of modern art reimagining of its original form.

"Small rooms," Caitlyn observed.

Hamza gave himself a shake. Pulled himself together.

"What?"

"The rooms. They're smaller than I'd have expected."

Hamza managed a smile. "It's the home of the guy they called 'the wickedest man in the world.' He's supposed to have unleashed demons who still inhabit the grounds," the DC said. "And the thing you're worried about is that the rooms are a wee bit pokey?"

"Well, they are," Caitlyn said, raising herself up on her tiptoes to see in through one of the gaps where a window used to be. "The living room in my flat's bigger than this one."

"Aye, but your flat doesn't have a drawing room or a library, does it?"

"How do you know?" Caitlyn asked him. "It might have."

She stepped back from the house, looked it over, then they both started walking around to the other side of the building.

"What's a drawing room for, anyway?" Hamza asked, as they ducked under a solitary piece of 'Keep Out' tape strung across a pathway. "It's not for, like, *drawing* drawing. I know that."

"Well, it's for... You know."

"What?"

"Like... receiving guests."

They stopped at what would once have been a side door, but which was now just another hole in the wall. The floor beyond had fallen into the foundations, exposing some ancient-looking plumbing.

"Kitchen," Hamza said. "And what do you mean 'receiving guests?'"

Caitlyn shrugged. "Just, like, when you have guests, you put them in there."

"For how long?"

"What do you mean? There's not a set time. You're not roasting them in the oven."

"*He* might've," said Hamza, gesturing to the house beside them with a thumb. "Crowley. That was probably right up his street."

Hamza swore below his breath as he tripped on something. A *Sanyo* DVD player went skidding along the path, its once shiny-silver casing now marbled with black and grey. Down on the path by Hamza's feet, next to where the device had been, was a plastic DVD slip-case. The face of actor, Adam Sandler, had been partially melted, giving him an Elephant Man-like appearance.

"Ha. The Wedding Singer," said Hamza, recognising what was left of the DVD's cover. "Good film."

Caitlyn snorted. "What are you talking about? It's shite."

"It's not shite. It's decent. Drew Barrymore's in it."

"Drew Barrymore's been in a lot of shite."

"She was in a lot of good stuff, too!" Hamza protested.

"Alright, Adam Sandler, then," Caitlyn said.

Hamza stopped at the corner of the house and considered this.

"Aye, OK. He's shite, right enough," he conceded, then they stepped off the path and found themselves at the front of Boleskine House.

The first thing they saw was a stack of building materials. Concrete blocks. Wooden beams. That sort of thing.

The very next thing they noticed was the tarpaulin. It was tucked in close to the house's double front doors, which had partially survived the blaze. It was green. Bright green.

The same bright green that had been wrapped around Mairi Sinclair like a shroud.

"Oh-ho," Hamza remarked. "That looks familiar."

Caitlyn took a look around them. Her gaze followed the front of the house, tracked across to the moss-covered steps that led up to an overgrown garden, then returned to the bundle of plastic sheeting.

"Sure does."

She approached the tarp slowly, raising a hand for silence when Hamza started to remind her of the 'look, don't touch' order she'd been only too quick to remind him of back at the last couple of places.

There was a faint *snap* as Caitlyn pulled on a thin vinyl glove she'd produced from one of the pockets of her coat. Glass *crunched* beneath her feet as she closed in on the tarpaulin.

There were no birds, Hamza realised. No cheeping or twittering from the trees. Had they been silent since they'd arrived? Or had they just fallen quiet now, holding their breath just like he was as DS McQuarrie crept closer to the tarpaulin.

It was probably just the angle, but there was a bulge in the middle of the plastic. A lump. Big, too. Big enough to be a person.

There was no reason anyone would be hiding under a sheet of tarpaulin out here, of course. Hamza knew that. And yet, his gut twisted and his scars burned as Caitlyn took hold of the tarpaulin sheet.

Besides, if there was someone under there, there was no saying they were hiding. There was no saying they were alive.

The plastic crinkled as Caitlyn lifted a corner. She exhaled, suggesting her thoughts had been roughly along the same lines as Hamza's.

"Cement," she said, giving one of the heavy-looking bags a prod with her foot. "It's just cement."

"Well, *obviously*," said Hamza, the words coming out as a throaty giggle of relief. "What else would it be?"

He was still grinning when a shape exploded through the remains of the doorway beside him. Still smiling when a shoulder clipped him, sending him into a spin.

And then, a moment later, the impact with the ground finally wiped the smirk off Hamza's face.

CHAPTER SIXTEEN

LOGAN SAW THEM WATCHING HIM AS HE TRUDGED ACROSS THE YARD towards a Portakabin marked 'Office' tucked away at the back. There were three men, although they could easily have been mistaken for three clones of the same guy. Same bald head, same piggy eyes, same bulky frame. Same accent, too, Logan guessed, although they were currently still too far away for him to hear what they were muttering to each other.

One of the men broke ranks and moved to intercept. Logan didn't slow. Instead, he eyeballed the bastard, daring him to challenge him. One of the other two duplicates started walking in the direction of the office, while another took out a phone and pecked away at the screen with a sausage-like finger.

"Yes?"

The voice of the man approaching was pretty much exactly what Logan had been expecting. Eastern European. Russian, possibly. It was curt and gruff, the word coming out as more of a demand than a simple question.

He stepped fully into Logan's path. The detective sighed impatiently, but stopped walking.

"I'm here to see Bosco."

The guard—because he was a guard, no matter what his contract of employment might state—looked Logan directly in the eye, like he could make him turn around and leave through sheer willpower alone. It had probably worked on plenty of people in the past, too.

Not today.

"Aye, very good, son," Logan told him. "You been rehearsing that with your pals, have you?"

The guard's smooth brow furrowed.

"All squinting at each other, an' that. Giving it the big I am."

He produced his warrant card while the guard was still running the translation in his head. Judging by the rate at which recognition spread across the brute's face, it wasn't the first time he'd had one flashed at him.

"Just go tell your boss there's an old friend here to see him, alright?" Logan instructed. "And save the Clint Eastwood act for the tourists."

The clone who'd been texting on the phone during the conversation hollered something in a language Logan didn't understand. He understood the hand gesture well enough, though, indicating that Logan should be allowed past.

Smiling, Logan raised both eyebrows and waited. The man in front of him grunted, then reluctantly shambled aside, giving the detective room to pass.

"Good effort, though," Logan said, patting the man's broad chest. "Keep it up."

And with that, he thrust his hands in the pockets of his coat, and swept on past the man towards the office.

The door opened at his approach, revealing the third guard. He was bigger than the last one, with a scar that ran from one side of his mouth almost all the way up to his ear. Now that Logan was seeing him up close, he reckoned there was a good chance that he was actually related to the last guy. Not twins—they weren't that similar—but brothers, almost certainly.

Bosco always did like to keep things in the family.

"Through back," the guard instructed, gesturing to a door marked 'Manager.' He blocked Logan's path before he could move. "Are you alone?"

Logan looked the other man up and down. "That depends. Are we counting you?"

There was a moment of confused silence.

"What?"

"Aye. I'm alone," Logan said. He indicated the door with a nod of his head. "Now, d'you mind?"

"Let him through, Valdis."

Logan recognised the voice, even muffled by the door. He felt his fingers automatically ball into fists at the sound of it, but shook them loose again.

"You heard him, Valdis," Logan said, holding the brute's gaze. "Best do as he says."

Valdis' lips pulled back, revealing a row of yellow-brown teeth. He made a sound at the back of his throat that could've been a grunt or could've been a growl, but then the flooring of the cabin creaked as he stepped aside.

"I'll be waiting right here."

"Aye. Well." Logan looked the man up and down. "Have fun with that."

Bosco Maximuke was on his feet when Logan entered the office, arms held out in a gesture of welcome. "Jack! Look at you! Here!"

The Russian was half a head shorter than Logan, and a full third wider. He was dressed in a red nylon tracksuit he must've somehow had transported through time from the late 80s, and someone had attempted to perm what little hair he had left, with predictably awful results.

"Bosco. Almost didn't recognise you."

"Ha! Yes! The moustache? You like?" Bosco asked, smoothing down the clump of dark hair that crouched above his top lip.

"No' really," Logan told him.

"No? My wife, she agrees. She not like. Me? I like. My daughter? Oy. She *hate*."

Logan followed the Russian's gaze as he looked to the corner of the cabin. A girl of maybe seven or eight sat at a desk, headphones on, her attention focused on an iPad on a stand in front of her.

"She off school. *Sick,*" Bosco explained. "To me, I not think she is sick. I think she is..."

He concentrated, trying to summon the word from somewhere.

"*Chancer.* Yes? I think she is *bloody chancer.*"

He looked very deliberately from Logan to the girl and back again.

Logan nodded his understanding.

"So, as you see, now is not good time for me," Bosco said. "Although, it is good to see you. You must come by again when you are next in town. Yes?"

"Oh, I wouldn't worry about that. I've moved up here," Logan told him.

He enjoyed the subtle change to Bosco's face. The way the crow's feet around his eyes deepened. The way a shadow seemed to pass across him. The way he tried so very hard to keep his smile in place.

"What, did you miss me?" the Russian eventually managed to ask.

"Something like that, aye," Logan confirmed.

"And here, I thought I had seen last of you. 'No way he finds me up here,' I thought. 'No way he track me down.'"

"It wasn't exactly difficult. You called the company *Bosco Building,*"

Logan pointed out. "I mean, what's your logo? A big arrow with 'We Are Here' written on it?"

Bosco made a sound that was a bit like a laugh, but very clearly wasn't one.

"Anyway, I won't keep you long this time, but I'll make sure I pop back in soon," Logan told him. "Have a good look around the place. Be like old times."

He let the thought of that sink in.

"For now, I'm hoping you can help me out."

Bosco lowered himself into his chair and shot the briefest of looks in the direction of his daughter.

"What do you want?" he asked. He was still making an effort to sound amicable, but it was so paper-thin as to almost be see-through.

"Robbie Steadwood. He works for you."

Bosco shook his head. "No."

"What do you mean, 'no?'"

"I mean no. He does not work for me. He *did*," Bosco said. "But now, he does not."

"And why's that?"

"Because I no fucking see him, that's why not," Bosco snapped.

He shot a sideways look to his daughter, but she was still focused on a YouTube video playing on her iPad, and hadn't heard a thing.

"He vanish. Poof," the Russian explained, adding a little hand gesture for emphasis. "I no hear from him, I no see him. Not since his bitch-whore go missing."

The floor *groaned* beneath Logan as he shifted his weight on his feet. Bosco picked up on the impending danger and raised both hands.

"His words, not mine. 'She is bitch-whore,' he always say. Bitch-whore this, bitch-whore that. 'Bitch-whore won't let me see my kid!' You know? He says this about her, not me," Bosco explained. "And then she go missing, and he go missing, and now here you are. Looking."

He gave a dismissive wave, the movement curt and angry. "Well, they not here. Neither one."

"Aye. I know she's not here," Logan said. "She's dead."

Bosco's reaction was one of surprise. Logan couldn't quite figure out if it was real or not. He could usually get a pretty good bead on the Russian, but that stupid bloody moustache was throwing him off.

"Bitch-whore is dead?"

"Robbie Steadwood's ex-partner is dead," Logan corrected.

"You think Robbie did this?" Bosco asked.

"I don't know yet. Do you?"

The Russian leaned his chair back, then rocked it a little. His bottom lip came up and sucked on his moustache as he thought. "Could be. Maybe. They did not get on, I think. When she came round here one time, they had argument. Big argument."

Logan's eyes narrowed. "What did she want?"

"I do not know. I do not pry into things that are not my business."

Logan knew that was far from the case, but knew there was no point in pushing.

"When was she here?"

Bosco shrugged. "I do not remember."

Logan moved a little closer to the desk. The light from the window cast his shadow across the man in the chair.

"Try."

Bosco tutted. "Olivia, sweetie-heart?" he said, turning to the girl in the corner. When she didn't respond, he slapped his hand on the desk a few times and tried again. "Olivia!"

The girl tapped the screen a couple of times, tutted, and then turned to her father. The look on her face made her thoughts on being interrupted very clear.

"What?"

A conversation followed in Russian. It started off quite measured, but both parties grew increasingly agitated as it went on.

Eventually, Bosco seemed to get what he was after, and the girl turned back to her device.

"She thinks two weeks ago. Maybe fifteen, sixteen days."

"She off school then, too, was she?"

"Like I say. She is chancer," Bosco said. "Oh! Bitch-whore also phone me. Around same time, maybe. Day after."

"Phoned you? Why?"

"Asking where Robbie was working. Asking where she could find him."

"Did you tell her?"

"Not on first call. Third call? Yes. Third call, I have enough. I tell her. Get her out of my hair."

He stood up and gave an apologetic sort of shrug. "I wish I could help better, yes? But I know nothing. Where Robbie is now? It is mystery."

"Aye. Well. We'll find him," Logan said.

Bosco smiled, showing a little too many teeth. "Or, we might find him first," he said.

A silence hung between them for a moment. An unspoken under-standing that this would not be in Robbie's best interests.

Then, the Russian laughed and thrust a hand out for Logan to shake. "Good to see you again, my friend. But, you will give me warning before you come around next time, yes? You will call on the telephone."

Logan regarded the offered hand for a moment, then grasped it with his own much larger one.

"No," he said, squeezing good and hard. "I won't."

CHAPTER SEVENTEEN

As he hit the ground out front of Boleskine House, Hamza instinctively curled himself into a tight ball, wrapping his arms over his head for protection. He shut his eyes, bracing himself for the pain that had screamed through him when the blade had been buried in his back all those weeks before, and every night again since, when he'd eventually given in to sleep.

Instead of the pain, he heard crunching footsteps. Panicked breathing. A shout from Caitlyn, ejected mid-run.

"Police! Stay where you are!"

The voice that replied was frantic. Desperate-sounding.

"Don't shoot! Don't shoot!"

Hamza opened his eyes. A small, slight figure dressed all in black stood with his back to DS McQuarrie, both hands raised to the sky. A boy. Even from this distance, Hamza could see he was visibly trembling.

"Put your hands down," Caitlyn instructed.

The boy did as he was told, dropping his arms to his sides but not yet daring to turn.

"You alright?" Caitlyn asked, shooting a look back over her shoulder at Hamza as he clambered to his feet.

"Fine. Aye. Wee bastard just caught me off guard."

She nodded, then turned her attention back to the kid. "Turn around."

The boy shuffled anxiously, like this might be some kind of test he didn't dare fail.

Caitlyn sighed. "We can do this the hard way or the easy way. And, just so we're clear, the hard way involves you being face down on the ground with my knee between your shoulder blades. The easy way doesn't. Up to you."

The boy turned around. Hamza groaned.

"He looks about twelve. I got knocked on my arse by a twelve-year-old."

"I'm thirteen," the boy squeaked.

Caitlyn looked back at Hamza, smirking. "Hear that? He's thirteen. Nothing to be ashamed of."

Hamza flashed a sarcastic smile back at her, then they both approached the kid.

"What's your name?" Caitlyn demanded.

The boy straightened, as if standing to attention. "Lucas."

"Lucas *what?*"

A pause. A furrowing of the brow. "Lucas, *Miss.*"

Hamza bit his lip to stop himself laughing. Caitlyn rolled her eyes.

"I'm not your teacher. I meant what's your surname?"

"Oh. Sorry. Lucas Findlay."

Caitlyn gestured to the house. "What were you up to in there, Lucas Findlay? It's off-limits."

"And what did you knock me over for?" Hamza asked. He turned the sleeve of his jacket to reveal a big dirty mark. "Look at this."

Lucas shifted awkwardly. "Sorry."

"*Sorry* doesn't answer my question. What were you up to in there?" Caitlyn demanded. She drew herself up to her full height. "Or would you rather answer down at the station?"

Lucas shook his head so frantically Hamza worried it might come off.

"No, I was just... It was just..."

The boy swallowed, composing himself, then spat the rest out in one big breath.

"Barry Madsen dared me."

Caitlyn put her hands on her hips. "What?"

"Barry Madsen. He's in my school. He said I was too much of a chicken. And... and..."

He looked down at his feet. "Everyone laughed."

"Too much of a chicken to do what? Crouch in a house?" asked Caitlyn, growing visibly impatient.

Lucas shook his head. "Ouija board. I was meant to take a selfie," he said. "They say the place is full of—"

"Aye, I'm familiar with what they say," said Caitlyn, and Hamza got the distinct impression that was aimed at him.

"There was a girl who did it years ago," Lucas said. "She went mental. They think she got possessed."

Caitlyn sighed. "Do they really? So, you thought you'd do the same, did you?"

Lucas' eyes widened, like the implications of what he was doing had finally occurred to him.

"Where's your Ouija board, then?" Hamza asked.

"That's a point. If that's why you're here, where is it?"

Hesitantly, and without a word, Lucas reached into the back pocket of his trousers. He unfolded a piece of paper, on which he'd drawn something that might, with a bit of imagination, be a Ouija board.

"Did it work?" asked Hamza.

"Shut up. Of course it didn't work," Caitlyn interjected. "It's not real, and he shouldn't be messing around with the bloody thing up here."

"If you're so sure it's not real, then what's the problem?" Hamza asked. He looked pleased with himself, as if he'd just ensnared the DS in a cunningly set trap.

"Well, maybe because the roof's caved in, the place is full of broken glass, and the whole site's off-limits?"

Hamza's face fell a little. He considered the wreckage of the house. "Oh. Aye. Fair enough."

Caitlyn crossed her arms and looked the kid up and down. He was short and skinny, with fair hair poking out from beneath the hoodie he wore. If he really was thirteen, then he didn't look it. She'd have put him a year or so in the other direction.

He was doing his very best to stand still, but nerves were making him shift from foot to foot, his hands fidgeting down by his sides. When he wasn't talking, his mouth was a thin line, lips clamped together through the effort of not crying.

"Right. Cuff him," Caitlyn decided.

Hamza frowned. "What, seriously?"

"Sorry! Sorry! Please!" Lucas begged, his eyes filling.

Caitlyn held a hand up, calling for calm.

"Look, do you want your bloody photo or not?"

Hamza and the boy both blinked in surprise.

"What?" Lucas croaked.

She jabbed a thumb back over her shoulder in Hamza's direction. "Give him your phone," she instructed. "You can show Barry what's his name that not only did you do the Ouija board, thank you very much, but you got lifted for it, too."

The already panicky expression on Lucas's face ramped up a notch.

"We're not actually arresting you. Relax." Caitlyn raised an index finger and held it close to the boy's face. "But don't say I'm not bloody good to you."

Lucas didn't argue. He handed over the phone, the cuffs were applied, and Hamza then took a full three minutes to get 'the perfect picture' set up. This involved the careful positioning of the Ouija board—or Ouija *sheet*—if you wanted to get technical about it, plus some clever framing to get enough of the house in to make the place recognisable.

They'd cuffed the boy's hands in front of him so they could be seen in the picture. Caitlyn stood behind him with a hand on his shoulder and a scowl on her face, like she was about to huckle him to the ground.

"Right, are we ready now?" she asked.

"One sec," said Hamza, pinching the phone screen.

Lucas gently cleared his throat. "Can... can you swap?" he asked.

"What?"

"It's just... Barry Madsen will be more impressed if it's a man who's arrested me."

Caitlyn tutted. "Aye, well Barry Madsen's a sexist wee bastard," she said, clamping her hand on the back of Lucas's neck and grimacing at the camera. "Now, shut up and say cheese."

CHAPTER EIGHTEEN

"THE WANDERER RETURNS," SAID BEN, AS LOGAN ENTERED THE Incident Room.

The DI motioned with his mug to where Tyler sat behind a desk, combing through a few pages of printouts.

"The boy tells me you went to meet an old pal of yours."

"Aye. Could say that," said Logan shrugging off his coat.

"How is the mad Russian bastard?" Ben enquired.

"Same as ever. Except he's got a moustache now," Logan said.

"That's nice for him. Did he give you anything useful?"

Logan shook his head. "No. Just the usual spike in blood pressure. He hasn't seen Robbie Steadwood in weeks."

"And you believe him?" Ben asked.

"As much as you ever really can. I got the distinct impression he wants to find him for reasons of his own. I think it'll be very much in Mr Steadwood's best interests if we find him first."

Logan recounted what little Bosco had told him about Robbie, about Mairi Sinclair turning up at the yard, and about the argument that had followed.

"Things are no' looking good for young Robert, are they?" Ben remarked. "Still no sign of the bastard. I've asked for some extra resources to find him, and the call's going out on MFR within the hour. They're going to repeat it after every news bulletin."

"Good. He'll know we're looking for him, anyway. It's not going to hurt."

Tyler looked up from the sheets of paper spread out in front of him. "I made it back alright, Boss. You know, in case you were worried."

Logan shook his head. "I wasn't. It's a small city, and you're a grown man."

"Almost a grown man," Ben corrected.

"You're almost a grown man. I was confident that even you could find your way back, eventually."

Tyler smiled. "Wow. Is that a compliment, Boss?"

Logan briefly considered this. "I mean... no. Not really."

"You could argue it's the opposite, really," Ben added.

Logan approached the younger detective's desk. "What I will say..." he began. "Remember how I said that you should take notes and let me do the talking back at Michelle Sinclair's house? You remember us having that conversation?"

Tyler winced a little.

"I do."

Logan gave a nod. The lines of his face tightened, like it pained him to say this next part.

"Aye. Well. Good work in there with the boy. With the..." He made a vague gesture with a hand. "...whatever shite it was you were talking about. It was a big help."

Tyler's face widened into a grin. "OK, *that* was a compliment!"

"More or less," Logan conceded. He picked up a stapler from the DC's desk. "But, just so we're clear—the next time you disregard one of my direct instructions, I am going to shove this stapler right up your arse."

He held it horizontally.

"That way. Is that clear?"

Tyler eyed the stapler for a moment and squirmed in his seat, then he touched a finger to his forehead in salute. "Aye-aye, cap'n."

Logan set the stapler back down and indicated the documents spread out on the desktop around it. "What have you got?"

"It's phone records, Boss. Mairi Sinclair's. Waiting for more, but this covers the last couple of weeks."

"Got them already? That was quick."

"CID put a request in when she went missing. They just arrived."

"Ah, right, that sounds more like it," said Logan. "Anything coming up?"

"Possibly. There are three numbers that stood out. I've been able to identify two of them," Tyler said, consulting the notes he'd been making in a pad. His writing was impeccably neat, Logan noticed. He half-expected to see little bubbles above the lower case letter i's.

"Christopher Boyd's the one you'll be most interested in," the DC continued. "I counted six-hundred-and-twenty-seven texts, plus sixteen phone calls."

"Over what period?"

"About a fortnight, Boss. Just under."

Logan whistled. "Right. Aye, that's interesting."

"And get this," Tyler said. "I checked him out. Guess what his job is."

"No."

Tyler looked a little crestfallen. "Oh. Right. Well, he's a climbing instructor."

Ben strolled over to join them, coffee cup still in hand. "And what's that got to do with the price of cheese?" he asked.

"Climbing rope," Logan said. "Mairi Sinclair's body was tied with climbing rope."

"Last message was on Saturday morning," Tyler said. "It was pretty constant until then, then nothing after that. He texted her back and tried to call a couple of times, but no response."

Logan twisted his neck to get a better look at the phone records. "Was that message to him the last one she sent?"

"No, boss. That would be the other number that might be of interest. Shayne Turner. Female," Tyler said. "I looked her up. Pretty fit, actually."

He caught the look of disapproval from both senior officers, then quickly moved on. "Colleague of the victim. They worked together at the primary school. Shayne's a teacher, too."

"Friends, then," Logan said.

"Not exactly. Mairi sent four texts to her over the same nearly-two-week period. No calls."

"Why's she of interest, then?" Logan asked.

"Two reasons. First, Shayne was the last person she messaged. Sunday morning. Just before ten."

"Not long before she left the house," Logan remarked.

"Exactly. Secondly... I've compared incoming and outgoing records. With Christopher Boyd, they're pretty balanced. Back and forth, sort of thing. With Shayne Turner, that's not the case."

He consulted his notes again. "Like I said, Mairi sent four texts over the twelve days. Shayne Turner sent two-hundred-and-seventy-two. She also made three phone calls. None of them were answered."

"Have we got the contents of the messages?" Logan asked.

"Working on it, but it'll take time. The phone company's being a bit of a dick about it. We're having to go through the..." He made quote marks in the air. "...proper channels."

"No surprise there, then. They can be pernickety bastards," Logan remarked. "What about the other number you mentioned?"

"We haven't been able to identify it yet. Unregistered Pay as You Go. She called it twice in the week before she went missing. It's the only number we haven't been able to identify as friends or family," Tyler explained. "We're working on trying to trace its location, but haven't had a hit yet."

"OK. Well, keep doing what you're doing," Logan said. He tapped a finger on the paperwork. "And good work on this."

Tyler winked. "Two compliments in one day, Boss? I am on a roll."

Ben leaned over the desk, a hand extended, palm down. "Speaking of rolls."

Tyler took the offered item and unrolled it. It was a five pound note.

"One bacon and one black pudding," Ben said. He turned to Logan. "You having anything?"

Logan opened his mouth to decline, but his stomach chose that moment to loudly voice its objections.

"Aye, I should probably eat something, right enough," he conceded. "Flat sausage. Brown sauce."

"From the place across the road," Ben said. "No' the canteen here. They don't do black pudding."

For a moment, it seemed like Tyler might refuse, but then his shoulders slumped and his chair trundled back away from the desk as he got to his feet.

"Right. Fine," he said. "But someone else is getting it next time."

Ben watched him pick up his jacket and start trudging towards the door.

"Tyler, hold on, son. Wait up," he called after him.

DC Neish turned to find Ben smiling at him in his usual good-natured sort of way. Ben put a hand on the younger man's shoulder and squeezed.

"Get yourself a wee sweetie with the change, alright?"

Despite his irritation, Tyler couldn't help but smirk. "Too bloody right I will," he said.

Logan and Ben both watched as he left the Incident Room, and waited until the door had swung closed again.

"There's no' going to be any change, is there?" Logan said.

Ben shook his head. "No."

The door swung open again. Logan expected DC Neish to come storming back in again, but a woman entered, instead. He didn't recognise her at first, probably because she looked markedly less dishevelled than she had the first time they'd met.

Dr Shona Maguire's hair pulled back into a loose ponytail, and she'd swapped the crumpled lab coat and *Batman* t-shirt for a satiny blue shirt and a pair of jeans. The fact that she wasn't currently slurping down a *Bombay Bad Boy* Pot Noodle also helped smarten her up a bit.

"Aha. There you are," she remarked, sidling through the door and into the room. She carried a *Smyths Toys* bag that looked reasonably full, if not very heavy. "Sorry, was going to just email you the latest, but I was passing anyway so I thought I'd come in and tell you in person."

She smiled at both men in turn.

"Hello, by the way." She held a hand out to Ben. "Shona Maguire. Pathologist."

"Aye, we've met," said Ben, but he shook the hand anyway.

"Aha! So we have," said Shona. "It's..."

She made various shapes with her mouth, like her brain was running through all the possible syllables his name might start with.

"DI Forde. Ben," he said, putting her out of her misery.

"Ben! Yes! Ben Forde!" Shona said, pumping his hand with almost demented enthusiasm. "That's you."

"It is," Ben confirmed, taking his arm back.

"What have you got for us?" Logan asked.

"Cannabis," said Shona.

Logan raised his eyebrows and whistled quietly through his teeth. "That's a bold move," he said.

"Go on then, we'll take half an ounce," Ben whispered, furtively glancing around.

"Huh?" Shona looked momentarily confused, then it clicked. "Oh. Funny. Good one," she said. Her expression rapidly cooled. "No. I'm talking about the victim. About the young woman who was brutally murdered not far from here. Tragically cut down in the prime of her life."

She looked from one detective to the other.

"Hardly seems like a joking matter, does it?"

Ben shifted uncomfortably. "Well... No. I mean, obviously—"

"Ha. Got you back," said Shona. Her smile returned and she fired a finger-gun at DI Forde while simultaneously winking and making a *click-click* noise out of the corner of her mouth.

She quickly became more serious again.

"But yes. Toxicology reports show the victim had used cannabis in the days leading up to her death. Probably quite regularly, in fact, judging by the build-up in her system."

Ben looked up at Logan. "She's a teacher, isn't she? I thought they did checks?"

Logan shrugged, but said nothing.

"Anything else?" he asked the pathologist.

"I think that's about your lot," she said. She looked apologetic, like she'd let them both down in some way. "Couldn't retrieve any useful DNA. Water took care of that, like I thought it would."

She shook a fist and pulled an angry face. "Bloody water."

Shona lowered her fist again. "Anyway, thought you should know about the drugs. I've stuck it all in an email."

"I thought you said you hadn't emailed," Ben remarked.

Shona hesitated. "Hm?"

"You said you decided not to email and just swing by," Ben reminded her.

The pathologist briefly met Logan's eye, then looked away again. It was hard to tell with the harsh glow of the overhead strip lights, but Logan thought he detected a slight reddening of her cheeks.

"I decided to stop by *and* email," she explained. "You should always try to double-up on important messages. You know who said that?"

Ben shook his head. Shona gave him a bump on the shoulder with the side of a fist.

"Well, there's something for you to find out," she said, then she flashed them another smile and backed towards the door. "Good luck with it all. Anything else you need. You know, corpse-wise, you know where to find me."

She waved at them both as she reached the exit. "Until next time, gentlemen," she said, and then she nudged the door open and slipped out into the corridor.

It was Ben who eventually voiced what was on both their minds.

"She's a strange one."

"Aye," Logan agreed, still watching the door. "She's that, alright."

CHAPTER NINETEEN

THE NEXT COUPLE OF HOURS WERE FILLED WITH THE MEAT AND potatoes of polis work. Or, as Ben insisted on calling it, the mince and tatties.

He had a knack for co-ordinating that sort of thing. Possible car sightings were chased up. The additional resources the investigation had been allocated were put to work hunting for Robbie Steadwood. Phone calls were made to everyone who'd been staying at the campsite in Foyers around the time Mairi had gone missing, and a team was set up to handle the influx of phone calls they were expecting after the MFR broadcasts started going out. Plenty of them would be nutters, but there might be something useful in amongst it all.

Caitlyn and Hamza came back, and filled the others in on the green tarpaulin they'd found at Boleskine House. They'd already arranged for uniform to cordon the place off, and a forensics team was dispatched to give the place a going over.

They mentioned the boy with the Ouija Board but not, to Hamza's relief, the fact that he'd been unceremoniously knocked on his arse when the kid had tried to flee the scene.

Caitlyn updated the Big Board with all the new information they'd gathered, while Hamza and Tyler ran some cursory background checks on Shayne Turner and Christopher Boyd.

"I want to talk to the victim's parents, too," Logan announced, midway through reading over the typed-up version of the recording DC Neish had made at the victim's sister's house. "Can someone get me their details?"

"It'll be on HOLMES, sir," Caitlyn said.

"Can you print it off for me?" Logan asked. "Bloody thing always crashes as soon as I go near it. I don't think it likes me."

"God, and you such an affable fella, too," Ben remarked.

A bit more digging later, Hamza and Tyler gave a rundown on Shayne Turner and Christopher Boyd. Hamza took the floor first, and was almost blinded when Tyler clicked the projector on. He hissed for a moment like a vampire caught in sunlight, blinking and shielding his eyes until he found a route out of the projector's beam.

"Sorry," Tyler said, although it was immediately apparent to everyone in the room that he wasn't really.

Hamza scowled at him, then indicated the slightly fuzzy image of a young woman with jet-black hair and deep brown eyes that was projected onto a blank area of wall.

"Shayne Turner. Age twenty-three. Moved with her family from Australia eight years ago, now teaches Primary Four at the same school Mairi Sinclair taught at."

"My teachers never looked anything like that," Tyler remarked, his tongue practically hanging out. "Pretty sure they were all in their eighties."

"She started at the school in September last year," Hamza continued, ignoring him. "The head runs a sort of staff mentorship programme, where new members of staff are paired up with someone who's been there a while."

Hamza gestured to the soft-focus image. "Guess who she was paired up with."

"Mairi Sinclair," said DS McQuarrie.

"Right."

"What else do we have on her?" Logan asked.

Hamza consulted his notes. "Not a lot. No previous. Looking at her social media, she lives alone, has a couple of dogs that look like big rats, and buys a *lot* of stuff off Etsy."

He looked very deliberately at DC Neish.

"She's also gay."

"Gay?" A battle raged on Tyler's face as he tried to work out how he felt about this new piece of information. "I don't know if that's better or worse."

Hamza didn't have much more to add about Shayne, so he sat down and gave the floor to Tyler.

Christopher Boyd's photo was taken from the website of his climbing instruction business. It showed him hanging off an icy wall by a length of rope that looked not dissimilar to the type used to tie up Mairi Sinclair's body. The shadow of his climbing helmet obscured the top part of his face a little, but he was smiling broadly and offering a thumbs-up to the camera with his free hand.

Tyler rattled through his basic stats—age forty-two, divorced, father of two. He'd set up a family-friendly climbing wall in the Eastgate Centre a few years back and won a local business award for it. There were a couple of call-outs for alleged domestics at the house he'd shared with his ex-wife, but no charges were ever pressed, and they divorced a year and a bit later.

"Anyone spoken to him since Mairi went missing?" Logan asked.

"No. No one CID spoke to mentioned him," Tyler said. "If they were having a relationship, I reckon it was on the sly."

"And he hasn't come forward himself?"

Tyler shook his head. "Doesn't look like it, Boss."

Logan's chair creaked as he sat forward and regarded the man's grinning image. "Interesting."

He ran his tongue across the front of his teeth, then looked between both DCs. "Any suggestion that either of them are into that supernatural guff?"

"Nothing on Shayne Turner, no."

Tyler shrugged. "Looks like he went as Harry Potter to a fancy dress party in October. Does that count?"

"No. That doesn't count," Logan said.

"Maybe if he went as Voldemork," Ben remarked.

When the others turned to look at him, he rocked back on his heels, looking pleased with himself.

"Ha. You think I don't know about this stuff," he said. "Finger on the pulse, me."

"It's 'Voldemort,' sir," Caitlyn told him.

Ben's eyebrows twitched.

"Hm?"

"It's *Voldemort*. Not Voldemork."

"Is it?" Ben cleared his throat. "Aye. Well. You know which one I meant."

"Finger on the pulse? Head up your arse, more like," Logan muttered. "Right, I want to talk to both of them."

"Want me to have them brought in, sir?" Caitlyn asked.

Logan drummed his fingers on the desk in front of him, considering the options. "Bring the teacher in. But after school finishes, don't go making a scene."

Ben checked his watch. "Should be done now. It's twenty to five."

"Already? Jesus," Logan muttered. "But aye. Fine. Get her in."

"And Boyd, sir?" Caitlyn asked.

Did you say his place is at the Eastgate? Does he work out of there?"

"Yeah, Boss," Tyler confirmed. "Based there through the week. Part-time staff run the place at weekends."

"Right. Good. We'll go to him, in that case. See how he likes having me traipsing through his place of business. Might give us more of an insight into him."

He cast his eye across to the Big Board, running through a quick mental recap.

"Symbols," he said, his gaze falling on the sketches Hamza had made. "Where are we with that?"

"Hang on, I'll check, sir," Hamza replied, turning his attention to his computer. A couple of mouse-clicks later, he sat up straighter. "Got something. The symbols are..."

He hesitated, as if taking a run-up to the word.

"Apotropaic, apparently."

Based on the complete lack of expression on the faces of the others, Hamza decided to read on.

"It says that Apotropaic magic is a branch of magic designed to ward off evil influences. Misfortune, demonic possession, the evil eye. That sort of thing. This guy reckons the symbols are a real mish-mash of cultures. Egyptian, Greek, Roman, Serbian."

"A big old mixed bag of bullshit," Tyler commented.

"Anything connected to Crowley or Boleskine House?" Caitlyn asked.

Hamza used his mouse wheel to scroll down the page a little. "Nothing I can see, no," he said. "I'll have a proper read and see what else it says."

"Good. The rest of you, find me Mairi's car, and find me Robbie bloody Steadwood," Logan said, getting to his feet. "Ben, once Forensics have any news from Boleskine—"

"You'll be the first to know," DI Forde confirmed.

"DS McQuarrie, you're with me," Logan told Caitlyn. "We're going to go pay Mr Boyd a visit."

He turned to Ben, a thought striking him. "Any word on the rope used to tie up the vic?"

"Aye. I think I saw they've got a match. I'll text it to you," Ben said.

He checked his watch again, then shot Logan a warning look. "Just don't take too long," he said. "Alice tells me she's doing something nice for dinner."

"What, is she getting someone else to make it?"

"Chance'd be a fine thing," Ben replied. He called after the DCI as he and Caitlyn headed for the door. "Just don't be bloody late!"

CHAPTER TWENTY

BOSCO SAT BEHIND HIS DESK, SMILING AND NODDING AS HIS DAUGHTER explained every intricate detail of the latest round of YouTube videos she'd just been watching.

He wanted to be interested. Sort of. He wanted to support her in what she chose to do, but it wasn't easy when all she chose to do was watch groomed twenty-somethings of indeterminate genders applying make-up, or making slime, or opening little bags with toys inside, or whatever else they had moved onto these days.

Where was the conversation to be had there? Where was the common ground?

God, he wished she was back at school.

"Uh-huh. Uh-huh," he said. His eyes were pointed in her direction, but he wasn't looking at her. Not really. Nor was he listening. He was hearing, yes—just enough to be able to nod and smile at the right time—but not actively listening.

His thumb rubbed along the length of a badly-chewed pencil he'd picked up off his desk, and which he now held clutched in a white-knuckled grip. He could feel the wood bending under the pressure, hear the little groans it made, even over the *quack-quack-quack* of whatever inane bullshit his daughter was blabbering about now.

It would've been easier for him if she was talking in Russian, but she felt more comfortable using English, and it was important that she kept practising. He was pleased at how well she spoke the language. He just wished she'd stop with that upward inflection at the end of each and every fucking sentence.

Another gift from YouTube.

A knock at the door offered some momentary respite.

"Come," Bosco said.

Olivia appeared mortally offended by this, and glared daggers at her father.

"What? I have work, yes?" Bosco told her. "I not get to be sick."

The door opened, and Valdis, the guard with the scar on his face, ducked through.

"What you want now?" Bosco asked.

Valdis looked very deliberately at the girl. She managed to hold his gaze for almost a full three seconds, before blinking and looking away.

"Sweetie-heart. Daddy has business to talk. You go..." He mimed putting on headphones. "Yes? Yes."

The girl wheeled her rolling chair back over to her iPad, pushing herself along on her feet. Once there, she chanced another quick look up at the towering Valdis, before pulling on her headphones. She tapped the play button on the tablet's screen, and her eyes glazed over at once, like a junkie getting a long-overdue fix.

"What is problem?" Bosco asked, once Olivia was fully engrossed in the screen.

Valdis still looked a little uncertain, but Bosco dismissed his concerns with a twitch of irritation. "She is fine. She not hear nothing. What is problem?"

"There was a message on the radio. About Robbie," Valdis said. While different, his accent was just as thick as Bosco's, although his grasp of the language was better.

Bosco's face darkened. "They found him?"

"No. It was asking people to help look for him."

The Russian relaxed a little. "Good. I mean, not good they are looking. Good they not yet found him."

He jabbed at the desktop with a finger. *Thunk-thunk-thunk.* "We find him first. We find piece of shit Robbie before police."

"We're trying."

"*Try fucking harder!*" Bosco roared, leaping to his feet.

Over in the corner, Olivia jumped in her seat, but didn't turn. She quickly turned up the volume and pressed her headphones tighter to her ears as her father continued to shout.

"Don't come here and give me excuse! *'We can't find him. We try our best!'*" He brought his clenched fists to his eyes and mimed crying. "*Waah. Waah. Waah.*"

Not just Olivia, but everything on Bosco's desk jumped this time as he slammed both hands down on it. "I don't want excuse. I want piece of shit Robbie before he talk to police. I want to..." He mimed gripping something between both hands. "...what is word?"

"Strangle," Valdis said.

"I want to strangle him with my two hands until his piece of shit eyes come out of his head!"

Valdis's eyes darted to Olivia again. Bosco's body language remained furious, but he lowered his voice by a few dozen decibels.

"She not hear. Her brain is fucking rotted by that shit," he scowled.

He took a breath, composing himself, then dropped back down into his chair.

"You find Robbie. Tear city apart if have to. Put tail on Logan."

He scowled at the thought of him.

"Fucking Logan," he muttered. "Put tail on him. Someone good. Follow and report. I want to know everything he does. If he goes for shit, I want to know what it smells like. Yes?"

Valdis nodded. "Understood."

"Good. Because, if piece of shit Robbie talks to police," Bosco said. His eyes fell on his daughter and stayed there for a moment, before flicking back to the towering skinhead standing before him. "Then we all are fucked."

CHAPTER TWENTY-ONE

"GREAT, CARRIE. WELL DONE. YOU'RE DOING BRILLIANT. NOW, LEFT foot over. No, left foot. That one, not... There. See, that was easy, wasn't it?"

"Christopher Boyd?"

The climbing instructor turned away from the artificial rock face at the sound of his name, a big welcoming smile plastered across his mug. It wilted a little when he saw DCI Logan and DS McQuarrie standing there, all-business.

"Yes?"

The detectives flashed their warrant cards and Logan quickly ran through the introductions. Around them, half a dozen children and a couple of adults traversed the wall, manoeuvring themselves across a series of brightly coloured rubber hand and footholds.

Two other staff members were on hand to offer advice to those climbing. Logan reckoned Boyd could spare himself for a few minutes.

"We'd like to talk to you, Mr Boyd," Logan said. "Somewhere private would be best."

"Chris?" came a voice from the wall behind him.

"One second, Carrie," Christopher said. He pulled a perplexed sort of smile for the benefit of the detectives. "Why? What's this about?"

"We should probably talk in private," Logan reiterated.

"Chris!"

"One *second*, Carrie," Christopher said. The words snapped out of him, but he quickly brought the smile back. "I'm in the middle of a lesson. Can you come back at another—"

"It's about the murder of Mairi Sinclair," Logan told him. He watched the expression on the instructor's face go from fake smile to genuine terror, then leaned in a little closer. "Would you like me to say that again, but louder?"

Christopher shook his head. "No."

"Chris, I'm going to fall!"

"You're three feet off the ground, Carrie!" the instructor hissed. "Just jump. That's what the mats are for."

He turned back to the detectives. Behind him, there was a "Waah!" and a *thwack* as an eight-year-old girl dropped onto the crash mat.

"We can talk in my office," Christopher said. He gestured in the direction of a *Staff Only* door nestled in an artificial rocky crag. "This way."

ALTHOUGH THE CLIMBING wall area of the business was impressive, the manager's office was less so, and looked like it had been added as something of an afterthought. The only thing that identified it as an office was a desk, a chair, and an In Tray that had overflowed to the point where much of the paper had cascaded out and onto the floor.

If Christopher hadn't specifically referred to it as his office, it could've been almost any kind of room, with *Random Junk Storage* being the most likely candidate. Boxes of flyers, membership forms, and other assorted paperwork were stacked haphazardly around the room, a brief description of their contents scribbled on the partially collapsed cardboard walls in black marker.

One of the boxes had caught Logan's eye almost immediately, thanks to the end of a purple and black rope that hung over the top and down the side of it. The branding on the box said 'Edelweiss.' Logan had received the same word via a text from Ben during the drive over.

The desk was positioned up against one of the few patches of wall not stacked high with cardboard containers. A year planner was tacked in place above it, hundreds of sticky coloured dots making it look like some sort of collage.

There were two seats in the room—a threadbare office chair by the desk, and something that would've looked more at home in a 1970s kitchen. Logan chose to sit on neither. As standing in the cramped space forced all three of them awkwardly close together, Christopher sat on the one by the desk.

He then realised that he had to crane his neck to look up at the towering detective, and so perched himself on the desk, instead.

"*Murdered?*" was the first thing the instructor said, once he'd got himself into a position he felt comfortable with. "I knew she was missing, but... murdered?"

Logan nodded. Behind him, Caitlyn had her notebook out, pen nib poised above a blank page.

"Body was discovered in the early hours of yesterday morning," Logan confirmed. "It was in the papers."

"I don't read the papers," Christopher said. He stared at the floor by Logan's feet for a while, then muttered, "Shit," and raised his head again. "Do you know who did it?"

"Not yet. We're still trying to ascertain what happened."

Christopher's eyes widened. "Wait. Wait. Hold on. Why are you here, exactly?" he asked. "You don't think I had something to do with it?"

"Like I say, we're still trying to ascertain what happened," Logan said. "We're hoping you can help us paint a better picture of Mairi's final days."

"I didn't see her," Christopher said. The words rushed out a little too quickly, and he spent the next few seconds trying to make himself appear more relaxed than he was. His shoulders lost some of their tension, and he managed to arrange his expression into something suitably sad.

And yet, his hands gripped the edge of the desk so hard that Logan could see his knuckles turning white.

"But you spoke to her," said Caitlyn. Her voice was softer than Logan's. Encouraging. Comforting, almost.

Logan didn't know the DS very well, but he suspected this was a voice she saved especially for just this sort of occasion. He couldn't imagine her speaking like that in many other circumstances.

"Right?" she said, egging Boyd on with a nod of her head.

"Yes. I mean... Yes. But not in person. Just a few texts and a couple of calls."

"A few texts?" said Logan, seizing on the phrase. "How many texts would you say you'd exchanged? Roughly?"

Christopher puffed out his cheeks, buying himself some time. "I don't know. Quite a lot."

"Aye. Well, you're not wrong there," Logan agreed. "In fact, I'd go so far as to say it wasn't *quite* a lot. It was a lot."

He turned to Caitlyn. "DS McQuarrie, would you agree with that description?"

"Aye, sir," Caitlyn said. "It was a lot."

"It was a whole lot," Logan said, turning his attention back to the instructor. "Seems like you were close."

"No. I mean, not really. I mean... it was early days, you know?" Christopher said. "We weren't, like, what you might call... exclusive."

Another turn of the head in Caitlyn's direction. "What does he mean by that?"

"He was shagging other women, sir," said Caitlyn. Her softly-softly tone had hardened already. Logan was surprised it had lasted as long as it had.

"Aye. Thought that's what he was saying," Logan agreed. He looked back at Christopher and gave a disapproving shake of his head. "Did Mairi know?"

"Yes! We weren't... It wasn't like... It was just a thing, you know? Just, like, I don't know. Flirting, I suppose."

"Six hundred plus texts in a fortnight? That's a lot of chat-up lines," Logan said. "What were you doing, sending them one letter at a time?"

"No, I—"

"She texted you on Saturday morning," Logan said.

Christopher hesitated, expecting a question to follow.

"Yes," he said, when one didn't arrive. "We were supposed to be meeting up."

"Why?" Logan asked.

"Just, like, lunch. I was going to give her a lesson, then we were going for lunch."

Christopher looked suddenly flustered, like he might've just incriminated himself. "But she cancelled. That was the text. She said she had a headache, and couldn't come."

He fumbled for his phone. "Here, look. I kept it."

With a few taps and swipes, he brought the thread of messages up and passed the phone to Logan. The DCI kept drilling into the instructor with his stare, and passed the phone over to Caitlyn.

"He's right, sir," the DS said, skimming through the last few messages. "They arranged it on Friday morning, but she cancelled on Saturday. He sent a few follow-up messages, but no reply."

"And through the following week!" Christopher said, directing her attention further down the thread. "Look, I tried messaging and calling her half a dozen times to ask where she was! If I'd killed her, I wouldn't do that, would I?"

Logan continued to hold the man's gaze. Christopher seemed to shrivel before his eyes.

"Well, I mean, I suppose I might," he muttered. "But I didn't! I didn't see her since her lesson the week before."

"Too busy with your other lady friends?" Logan asked.

"Too busy with work. We both were," Christopher protested. "She wanted to keep it low key. Said she didn't want her son getting confused. She was worried about her ex, too."

Logan's ears pricked up. Caitlyn stopped scrolling through the phone.

"In what way?"

Christopher shrugged. "I don't know. I think she was scared of him. I got the impression he was a nasty piece of work. They hadn't been together for years, but he still seemed to want to control her. I mean, that was the impression she gave me, anyway. I never met the guy myself. Don't think I really want to."

"So, you made arrangements on Friday morning, then the next message was... when?"

"Saturday," Christopher and Caitlyn both said at the same time.

"There's dozens of messages on Thursday, Wednesday..." Caitlyn said, scrolling back through the texts while Christopher squirmed on the desk.

"Should you be...? I'm not sure you—"

Caitlyn held up the phone. On screen was a close-up of a fully erect penis. From the expression on the DS's face, she was unimpressed on a number of levels.

"Seriously?" she said.

"It was just... She asked for it."

Logan raised an eyebrow. "Interesting choice of words, Mr Boyd."

"What? *No!* I mean... look at the messages. She egged me on. I don't just send... Just send..."

"Dick pics," said Caitlyn, finishing the sentence for him.

"Yes. Exactly. I don't just do that without... You know? Being asked."

"You're saying you don't just send pictures of your penis willy-nilly?" asked Logan. "I should hope not."

He motioned to Caitlyn. "Put that thing away, DS McQuarrie, before you have someone's eye out."

He returned his attention to Christopher. "So, dozens of messages every evening, but nothing on Friday?"

Christopher took his phone back from Caitlyn and hurriedly stuffed it in his pocket, his cheeks burning red. "No. She didn't send anything."

"And nor did you?"

"I was... out. On a... I was meeting someone."

"You were on a date," Logan said. He glanced back over his shoulder. "Is that still a thing young people do?" he asked.

"I believe so, sir."

"Although, you're nearly as old as I am, Mr Boyd," Logan said. "You'd think a man of your age would know better than to go sending photos of his boaby to women. Especially ones ten years younger."

"And a primary school teacher, sir," Caitlyn added.

"Aye. And a *primary school teacher*, at that," Logan said. He inhaled deeply through his nose, making his displeasure obvious. "Can you confirm your whereabouts over the weekend, Mr Boyd?"

Christopher's eyes blazed with panic. His hands gripped the desk again, knuckles quickly turning the colour of snow. "Uh, yes. I was here most of Saturday. One of the part-timers is off, so I'm doing Saturdays to cover."

"And Sunday?" Logan pressed.

"Sunday? Sunday. *Sunday*," Christopher said, his voice becoming lower. "What did...? Oh! Yes. Aviemore. I went across to Aviemore. There was a talk on at one of the hotels, organised by Waterstones. You know, the bookshop?"

"I'm aware of Waterstones."

"Well, I was there. I left at about ten and didn't get back until about eight."

The expression of utter relief on his face told Logan what the answer to the next question would be.

He asked it, anyway.

"Can anyone confirm that?"

"Yes! Loads of people. A few of us went over from the climbing club. We went in John's car. Maitland. John Maitland. Mountain Rescue. You might know him?"

Logan's demeanour gave nothing away.

"Well, anyway. Him. I can get you his details."

Reaching into his coat pocket, Logan produced a card. "Please do that, Mr Boyd. And, if anything else occurs to you that you think might be useful to us, be sure to pass it on."

Christopher took the card and turned it over in his hand a couple of times, looking at it, but not really seeing. "Is... is that it?"

"For now. But I wouldn't leave the country," Logan told him. He reached over to the box with the Edelweiss branding, and tapped the cardboard. "Do you mind if I take one of these?"

Christopher's eyes went to the box, then back to the detective. "A rope?"

"Aye. Would you mind?"

The request had clearly caught the instructor off guard. After a few moments spent alternating between different confused looks, he shrugged and nodded. "Sure. If you like."

Logan nodded to Caitlyn, and Christopher watched as she pulled on a pair of rubber gloves and fished out a clear plastic evidence bag.

"Much appreciated," Logan told him, as Caitlyn carefully placed the rope in the bag. "I've always wanted one of these."

Christopher watched, silent and impassive, as Caitlyn ziplocked and tagged the bag.

That done, Logan nodded his approval. "Nice to meet you, Mr Boyd," he said. He regarded the man and his office for a moment. "We'll be in touch."

CHAPTER TWENTY-TWO

MAIRI SINCLAIR'S PARENTS LIVED IN ONE OF THE NEW HOUSES OUT near ASDA. With a bit of imagination, you could almost convince yourself it was on the way back to Ben Forde's house. And, after dropping Caitlyn back at the station car park and telling her to knock off for the night, Logan did exactly that.

"Is that Mairi?" Logan asked, motioning with his cup and saucer to a framed photo on the wall. It showed a young woman in her late teens or early twenties. She looked unimpressed at having her picture taken. Possibly embarrassed by the inch-thick black eyeliner and brows that could've been drawn on with a Sharpie, Logan reckoned.

"Her *Goth phase*," sighed Mr Sinclair. Clearly, he hadn't approved at the time, and Mairi's death had done nothing to change his opinion. "The less said about that, the better."

Malcolm looked better than he had when Logan had met him at the campsite earlier. Logan had been braced to find him sitting rocking back and forth in the corner, but he'd clearly had a talk with himself and now looked more angry than upset. He hadn't mentioned their previous meeting, and Logan had made a point of not bringing it up, either.

Elaine Sinclair, Malcolm's wife, was sitting on the couch beside him, a few-feet-wide gulf of couch between them. She crossed it just long enough to slap him on the thigh and tut her disapproval.

"Oh, shut up, Malcolm," she snapped. Her face was thin and gaunt. Not a recent development, Logan thought, but he doubted the past few days had done much to help. "She was only into it for a year or so," Mrs Sinclair explained to the detective. "Snapped out of it shortly after Stuart was born."

"When she got shot of that arsehole, you mean," Malcolm Sinclair grunted.

Logan cocked his head back a little.

"Steadwood," Malcolm said. He spat the word out, like he couldn't bear the taste of it. "Ruined her bloody life, he did."

"Oh, behave. You're being dramatic."

"Dramatic? What are you talking about, Elaine?" Malcolm blustered. "He turned her against us. Against all of us."

"She was a teenager. They all turn against their parents sooner or later!"

"Michelle didn't!"

"Yes, she did. Just in a different way," Elaine insisted. "She went all... churchy."

"What's wrong with that?"

"I didn't say there was anything *wrong* with it."

"Better a Christian than a bloody ghoul!"

"Goth, Malcolm. *Goth!*"

Malcolm scowled across the desert of couch that lay between them. "You know what I meant!"

Logan watched the argument unfolding over the rim of his cup. Malcolm Sinclair wasn't coming across particularly well at this point, but there was no denying that the man made a fine cup of tea.

Elaine Sinclair took a cushion that was wedged between her and the arm of the couch, plumped it up on her lap, then set it back down, this time between her and her husband so there was no longer just a gulf between them, but a wall.

They'd been like this since Logan had arrived. Picking away at the scabs of a relationship he suspected should have been over years ago. The death of a loved one—particularly under such horrific circumstances—was often a 'make or break' point in a relationship. Sometimes, it brought families closer, strengthening bonds that were already there, and helping to heal any cracks that may have started to appear.

Often, though—more often—it went the other way. Grief took those hairline cracks and made them fractures. Over the course of longer investigations, Logan had seen even the strongest relationships fall apart. Given that the Sinclairs didn't seem to be on a particularly solid footing at this stage, he didn't fancy their chances.

"Do you mind me asking what happened?" said Logan, sitting his cup back in the saucer, then setting them both down on the side table Mrs Sinclair had dragged out of the corner for his benefit. "With Robbie Steadwood, I mean?"

"Ugh. He got her pregnant for a bloody start," Malcolm said. "She was sixteen. He was, what? Twenty?"

Malcolm breathed deeply, forcing himself to relax. His head was shaking from side to side, as if denying everything he was saying.

"He'd got her into drugs before that, of course. Oh, yes. *Cannabis*. She used to reek of it."

"She said it was only once," Mrs Sinclair told Logan. "And I believed her."

"Because you're a gullible bloody idiot," her husband muttered.

"Oh, *shut up*, Malcolm."

Logan decided not to tell them about the toxicology report on Mairi's body, if only to stop Malcolm Sinclair lording it over his wife as some sort of victory.

"They were only together about a year," Elaine said. "They broke up while Mairi was pregnant with Stuart."

A fond expression played briefly across her face as she thought of her grandson. It was the closest Logan thought he'd get to seeing her smile. It was probably the closest she'd come to smiling in a very long time.

"*He* dumped *her*, would you believe?" Malcolm said. "Him a bloody... I don't know... child-molesting junkie, and her from a good family. And she *was* a child, Elaine," he stressed, anticipating an interjection from his wife. "She might've been sixteen when she got pregnant, but do you think he hadn't had his way with her before then? Honestly? You ask me, he should've been bloody jailed."

Mr Sinclair leaned forward, locking eyes with Logan. "He was, eventually, you know? Locked up, I mean. Not for what he did to Mairi, but he was thrown in jail."

"I was aware of that, Mr Sinclair, yes," Logan confirmed.

"You should've kept him in. You should've thrown away the bloody key. Maybe if you had, then Mairi wouldn't—"

A sob caught in his throat. No, not a sob. A *sound*. It was something primal. Something broken. The kind of sound a wounded animal might make when it realised that all hope was lost.

His movements, which had been driven by anger, suddenly lost all their energy. His hands fell onto the cushions beside him, and everything about him just sort of sagged into the couch, like whatever strings had been holding him up had all been cut at once.

He coughed and cleared his throat several times. It reminded Logan of someone desperately trying to turn over an engine that was refusing to kick in.

Elaine's hand slid across the cushion and rested on top of her husband's. Her fingers interlocked with his and squeezed. They didn't look at each other. They didn't have to. That touch had said it all.

Maybe those cracks didn't run too deep, after all.

Logan's phone buzzed in his coat pocket. He checked it quickly, saw a message from Ben asking him where the bloody hell he was with a lot of question marks on the end, and slipped the phone away again.

"News?" asked Elaine.

"No. Sorry. Another matter," Logan told her. His eyes went back to the wall again. There were dozens of photos in all, each one individually framed in mismatching styles and colours. Younger incarnations of Mr and Mrs Sinclair appeared in a few of them, but mostly they showed Mairi and Michelle, with a couple of Stuart's school photos in amongst them.

"The girls were inseparable when they were younger," Elaine said, following the DCI's gaze. "So alike, too. When I look back at some of the pictures I have to stop and think which one I'm looking at. They've always stayed similar. Even on the phone, you can never tell who's who, they sound so much alike."

She glanced down for a moment.

"Sounded."

"Of course, Robbie Steadwood put paid to that, too," Malcolm grunted.

Elaine sighed. Her hand returned to her side of the barricade. "God, what are you talking about now? How on Earth did Robbie Steadwood stop them looking and sounding alike?"

"Not that! Being close, I mean. Ruined their relationship, he did. After he came along, Mairi had no interest in Michelle. None."

"Because she was sixteen, and Michelle was ten, Malcolm," Elaine explained. To her credit, she was trying to be patient. She just wasn't being particularly successful. "She was becoming an adult, and Michelle was still just a child. Of course, they were going to drift apart."

"It wasn't a drift, it was a bloody schism!"

"Oh, shut up."

Malcolm muttered under his breath and shifted around in his seat, but chose not to argue any further.

"Michelle was always so good with Stuart, though," Elaine said, smiling fondly. "They've always been very close. More like brother and sister than nephew and auntie."

"We told him he could come stay here, of course," said Malcolm, sounding maybe a touch put out. "When Mairi went missing. We've got a spare bedroom. But he opted for Michelle's, in the end."

"She's closer to his age. And, like I say, they've always got on. More like brother and sister, than anything," she reiterated.

The rest of the conversation played out pretty much as Logan had been expecting. Mr Sinclair had some very strong thoughts when Logan asked if they could think of anyone who might have wanted to hurt their daughter. They concerned Robbie Steadwood and involved what was, to Logan's ears, some fairly light swearing, but which seemed to shock Mrs Sinclair no end.

"Malcolm!"

"Well, he *is* a wee arsehole, Elaine. There's no two ways about it!"

Logan had quickly steered the conversation back on track, while ignoring the insistent buzzing of his phone in his pocket.

"When did you last see Mairi?"

"A few weeks ago," Elaine said. "She usually popped around a few times a month, but she hadn't been around in a while."

"Any reason for that you can think of?" Logan asked.

"No."

"No fallings out?"

"No. What are you saying? Nothing like that!" Elaine said, visibly offended.

"I'm not saying anything, Mrs Sinclair. Just trying to get a full picture," Logan said.

After a couple of further questions, he decided that enough was enough. The Sinclairs were flagging now, their grief wilting them before his eyes. There was more to be had from them, he was sure, but he'd heard all he needed to for the moment.

"I'll see myself out, you're fine," he said, waving Elaine back into her seat when she made a move to stand and show him the door. "If you think of anything else, or there's anything you need, just give us a call. Either I or one of my team will be right out with you."

"Thank you, Mr Logan," Elaine said, clutching the card he'd given her right before he'd stood up. "We will."

"Please," Logan said, smiling grimly. "Call me Jack."

THE DOOR to the Focus shut with a comforting *thunk* as Logan pulled it closed behind him. A quick glance at his phone showed two missed calls from Ben and four texts, each one less amused than the one before. Logan's dinner was now 'in the dog,' apparently. Considering the Fordes didn't have any pets, Logan wasn't quite sure whose dog it was in, but it was in someone's.

Chippy on the way back, then. He dimly recalled there being a *Harry Ramsden's* nearby somewhere, although he couldn't quite place where.

He was about to type out a quick apology when the screen lit up with an incoming call from a local 01463 number he didn't recognise.

"Logan," he said, pressing the phone to his ear.

The voice on the other end hesitated, caught off-guard by the speed of the response. "Uh, hello, sir. It's Sinead. PC Bell, I mean."

"Sinead. Hello."

"I swung by the station, sir. You weren't there, so I thought... I hope you don't mind me calling? It just seemed like you wanted to ask me something."

She was good.

"Aye. Thanks. It was just a general thing, really. Just..."

He glanced up at the Sinclairs' house, then checked his rear-view mirror, like he might find someone there listening in. There was only one other car parked on the street—a black Audi—sitting a good forty feet behind him. Someone was in the driver's seat, but short of maybe the Six-Million Dollar Man, nobody could be listening in from that distance.

"I feel bad even asking it, but did you think—"

"That Michelle is a bit touchy-feely with Stuart?"

Logan exhaled, like all his nasty little suspicions had somehow just been vindicated.

"Aye! Exactly. There was a lot of patting and stroking going on there, wasn't there?"

"It's pretty constant, sir, yeah," Sinead agreed. "Caught me off guard a bit to start with, but I think it's maybe just how she is with him. But probably amplified, given the circumstances."

Logan ran his tongue across his teeth. She was probably right, of course. The Sinclairs had told him that Michelle and Stuart had always been close. 'Like brother and sister,' Elaine had said. Emphasised it twice, in fact.

She was comforting the boy, that was all.

Almost certainly.

"The sister's got an alibi for the Sunday, aye?"

"Church in the morning, then Aerial Hoop in the afternoon."

Logan's silence spoke volumes.

"It's a fitness thing, sir. They do it at the leisure centre. And Stuart was streaming online on Twitch from around twelve through until five."

Another silence.

"It's like TV for gamers. He was broadcasting live most of the day."

"Right. Aye. Fair enough," Logan said, briefly wondering when he became so completely out of touch with... well, everything, it seemed. "And you're probably right about all the physical contact stuff. It's probably nothing. But keep an eye on it, will you?"

"I'm not back in until Sunday, but I've already passed it on," Sinead said. "I'm going with them to Mairi's birthday thing in the afternoon."

Logan wracked his brain for information on a birthday thing, but drew a blank.

"Some of the teachers at the school arranged it. It's at four o'clock. The kids from Mairi's class are all going to release paper boats they made into the loch. They've invited her family along."

"Right. Sounds... nice, I suppose."

"Maybe if they weren't doing it from the spot the body was found."

"No!"

Sinead gave a chuckle. "Aye. Someone at the school thought it was a good idea."

"And nobody thought to dissuade them?" Logan asked. "I mean, Jesus Christ. 'Say goodbye to your teacher, kids. Oh, and by the way, this was where her eyeless mutilated corpse was first dragged ashore.'"

"I doubt that's the wording they'll use, sir," Sinead said. "They'll probably paraphrase it a bit."

"Aye. Maybe for the best," he agreed.

"I'll let you know how it goes. And, like I say, I've passed on the touchy-feely thing. Whoever's on tomorrow should take note."

"Good. You're doing well," Logan told her, and he could practically hear her shoulders straighten all the way down the line. "Keep it up," he added, then immediately felt like a patronising old bastard and wished he could take it back.

"Will do, sir."

"Right. Good. Well, enjoy your day off, constable."

"Harris has friends coming over. I'd rather be on traffic duty, to be honest," Sinead said.

"I'm sure that could be arranged," Logan told her. "Have fun."

"Definitely won't."

Logan gave a dry little chuckle. "No. I wouldn't imagine so. Bye, Sinead."

"Bye, sir," she said. Then: "Oh, sir?"

"Aye?"

"Did you...? You know? Your daughter? You said you were going to get in touch."

When Logan didn't answer immediately, she jumped back in.

"Sorry. Shouldn't have asked. None of my business. Sorry."

"I did get in touch, yes," the DCI told her, although he wasn't entirely sure why. "We... made arrangements to have lunch."

"That's great!"

"She didn't turn up."

It was Sinead's turn to miss a beat.

"Oh," she eventually said. "I... Oh."

"Goodnight, constable."

"Goodnight, sir."

And with that, Logan jabbed the button to disconnect the call. He rattled off a quick 'on my way,' text to Ben, then tossed the phone onto the passenger seat.

"Right," he breathed, firing up the engine. "Where's that bloody chippy?"

Logan pulled away from the kerb and drove off down the street, leaving the Sinclair's house behind.

A few seconds later, the only other car on the street hummed into life and came creeping after him.

CHAPTER TWENTY-THREE

THERE WAS A SOLEMN AIR ABOUT THE INCIDENT ROOM THE NEXT morning that immediately made Logan uneasy.

He'd had another sleepless night spent in the Fordes' spare room. The first few hours had been spent running over the details of the case, then the deepening darkness and increasing tiredness had conspired to drag his mind back to past failures, both personal and professional.

He thought of the Sinclairs' house, with all those family photos on the walls. He had a couple of photos of Madison when she was younger, he thought, but they were in a box somewhere, and she hadn't looked particularly happy.

But then, none of them had. Not then.

And, in his case, not since.

Jumping back into things at the station was going to sort him out, he'd thought, but the long faces of the rest of the team, and the way none of them were meeting his eye told him that things were not about to start well.

"What?" he demanded. "What now?"

DS McQuarrie looked to Tyler and Hamza to see if either of them were going to volunteer the information, but neither of them showed any signs that they might be about to open their mouths.

"Guessing you haven't seen the papers, sir?" she said.

"What papers?"

Caitlyn winced. "All of them."

Tyler held up a copy of *The Sun*. The sight of that rag got on Logan's tits at the best of times, but the headline splashed across the front now almost brought his blood to an immediate rolling boil.

"Monster attack?" he spat. "Fucking *monster attack*? What's this shite?"

"You're joking," Ben groaned, taking the paper from Caitlyn. He held it at arm's length, either because of his eyesight, or because he didn't want to get too close to the bloody thing.

"Your woman that was in yesterday, sir," said Tyler. "The Nessie hunter. With the photos. She went to the press."

"Big time," added Hamza.

He held up copies of *The Daily Record* and the Scottish edition of *The Daily Mail*. Both sported similar headlines and scenic images of Loch Ness, although neither had gone as far as *The Sun*, which had an artist's impression of the monster leering out from the water right below the headline.

"Bastards!" Logan barked.

"Is that... Is that blood around its mouth?" Ben asked, studying the image more closely.

"Utter *bastards*!"

Caitlyn quietly cleared her throat. "Would now be a bad time to tell you it's all over the internet, too, sir?" she ventured. "They're running with the story in the foreign press, too."

A vein on Logan's temple pulsed a troubling shade of purple. He clenched and unclenched his fists, his nostrils flaring as he fought to compose himself.

"Still, at least—" Tyler began brightly.

Logan stabbed a finger at him.

"Don't!" he warned. "I want you to think very carefully about what you were going to say. *Very* carefully."

Tyler hesitated. He gave a little cough.

"Nothing, boss," he said.

"That woman and her fucking photos!" Logan spat. He looked around. "What did we do with them, anyway?"

Ben folded up the newspaper he was holding, then filed it in the bin.

"Exhibits Officer we borrowed from CID has bagged them and checked them in," he said, motioning to a cluttered desk in the corner of the room. There were assorted sizes of plastic bags laid across it, each containing something pertinent to the case.

Even in a case like this one, where they had almost bugger all in the way of clues, let alone actual evidence, the amount of clutter in wee plastic bags soon started to pile up. Logan was in no mood to sift through that lot just to find some photos which he was essentially just planning to glare angrily at, so he just shot a vague look of contempt in the direction of all the wee bags, instead.

"Right. It is what it is," he said, after a bit more deep breathing. "That's the bad news, what's the good news? Because I'm *really* hoping you have some good news to give me."

A few wary looks were exchanged. Logan's deep-breathing became a groan.

"What now?"

"Tests on the tarp taken from Boleskine House came back," said Ben, offering himself up as sacrifice. "No match to the one used to wrap Mairi Sinclair."

Logan buried his face in his hands, and the Incident Room was filled with the sound of muffled swearing.

The others waited for him to emerge from behind his hands again. He raised and lowered his shoulders and cricked his neck around, trying to ward off the tension that was building there.

"It is what it is," he said again. It hadn't sounded particularly convincing the first time, but that performance had seemed Oscar-worthy compared to the second attempt. He turned to Caitlyn and Hamza. "And there was nothing at any of the other sites?"

"No, sir," Hamza confirmed.

"You checked them all?"

"Yes, sir."

Beside Hamza, Caitlyn's face fell. "Shit."

"DS McQuarrie?" asked Logan. His voice was flat and level, but carried a distinct promise that this could change quite quickly. "What's the problem?"

Caitlyn shot Hamza a sideways look. "The path, sir. The path repairs. We didn't check there."

Logan consumed half the air in the room in one big sniff. DC Neish sidestepped away from Caitlyn and Hamza as quietly and casually as possible.

"What?" Logan asked.

He didn't need to ask the question. He already knew the answer. He was asking for their sake, not his. He was giving them a chance to change their mind. To correct their statement. To tell him that they were 'just joking, sir,' and reveal that they weren't actually the pair of useless bastards they were currently claiming to be.

"My fault, sir," said Caitlyn. "Once we had the tarp at Boleskine, I thought—"

"Bollocks. It was my fault," Hamza said. "I was struggling, and it's a steep walk down to the site. I'd been moaning about it the whole way there."

"He hadn't, sir," Caitlyn insisted. "I was the senior officer, I should've—"

"Aye, too fucking right you should've!" Logan barked, throwing his arms up. "I mean, Jesus Christ, what were you thinking? You had one job. *One.* 'Check out all those building sites.' Remember me saying that to you? Remember that? Key word, 'all.'"

"Jack," said Ben. "Mistakes happen. You know that."

Logan spun, eyes practically bulging. "*What?*" he asked, for much the same reason as he had the last time.

Ben, however, wasn't having it.

"You heard me. And you know I'm right," the DI said. He rocked back on his heels and crossed his arms across his barrel-like chest. "Now, do you want to keep storming about and ranting, or will we crack on with being the polis and try to solve this case?"

They faced each other down. Logan was much taller than Ben, but the sight of him there all red-faced and with steam practically billowing from his nostrils didn't seem to faze the older detective in the slightest.

"Your wife's cooking is shite, by the way," Logan told him, but the bluster had already started to fade.

"Aye. You're not wrong," Ben agreed.

He gave the DCI a clap on the arm, then walked past him and addressed the others.

"Right. Obviously, there was an issue on this occasion. All those sites should've been checked."

Caitlyn and Hamza both nodded.

"Of course, sir," the DS said, folding her hands behind her back. "Won't happen again."

"Oh, it probably will," Ben said. "Not this, specifically, but mistakes happen. Wasn't the first time, certainly won't be the last. There's no avoiding that. What matters is how we deal with those mistakes afterwards."

He gestured to the two officers responsible for this particular balls-up. "DS McQuarrie, DC Khaled, you two will go back to Foyers and check out that site. Snoop around, see what's there to be seen, but don't get too involved."

"Yes, sir," Caitlyn said.

Hamza didn't look overly excited by the prospect, but nodded his agreement. "Sir."

Ben turned his attention to Logan. "Jack, we've got the teacher coming in this morning. Shayne Turner."

"The fit one," Tyler added. He rubbed his hands together, then stopped when he saw the vein on Logan's temple double in size again.

"I thought she was coming in yesterday?" Logan said.

"Aye, well, maybe if you hadn't been out gallivanting until the wee small hours, you'd have known she couldn't make it in yesterday. Parents evening. We told her this morning would be fine."

"I was back at yours by quarter to nine," Logan protested, but it fell on deaf ears.

Alice Forde had given him the cold shoulder when he'd arrived at the house with a *McDonald's* brown paper bag. He hadn't been able to find a chip shop, and while he knew there was one across the road from the station, he also knew that if he went there he'd only end up heading back to work.

Her husband hadn't been overly impressed by Logan's later-than-expected arrival, either, and Logan's peace offering of a Creme Egg McFlurry had done nothing to ease the tension.

Ben had eaten it, mind. Wolfed it down, in fact. It just hadn't stopped him being a miserable bugger for the rest of the evening.

Logan shook his head. "Change of plan. Ben, you and DS McQuarrie handle the interview. I'll take the boy and check out the site."

Tyler snorted and shot Hamza a patronising look. "Ha! 'The boy.'"

He felt Logan's eyes on him. His smirk fell away as the penny dropped. "Wait. Who's the boy? I'm not the boy, am I?"

"Aye, son," said Ben. "You're the boy."

"Why am I the boy?!" Tyler yelped.

"We were all boys once," Ben said. He looked Tyler up and down. "Some of us just grew out of it quicker than others."

"I'm not having you mooching around the place when the teacher's in, oozing hormones behind you like a slug," Logan told him. "So, you're with me."

It looked like it was taking all Tyler's effort not to throw up his hands and stamp his feet, but he managed to keep a lid on it. "Right, boss," he said, the words coming out as a sort of hollow sigh. "Fair enough."

"Hamza, follow up on those symbols. See if anything else has come in.

And get me an update on Robbie Steadwood. The more I hear about that wee scrote, the keener I am to meet him."

"Right, sir. And I found something already," Hamza said. "The holes in the skull? More occult stuff. It's meant to be a way of letting demons out."

"Sounds scientific," said Tyler.

"Aye, I'm not saying it actually works, like," Hamza replied. "Just that's what people used to believe, and some civilisations still use it to cure cases of demonic possession." He looked slightly embarrassed by the explanation. "Note, there should've been quotation marks around a lot of the words in that last sentence."

Logan's frown, which was never far away, took up residency on his face. "So, what are we looking at? Some sort of Exorcism?"

"Very possibly, sir. Might even be possible to tie in the missing eye thing. I mean, if you're a believer in that sort of thing, what do you do if someone's giving you the literal evil eye?"

"Pop 'em out," said Tyler.

Hamza nodded. "Pop them out."

Logan took a few moments to consider all this, but remained non-committal.

"Right. All interesting stuff," he said. He clicked his fingers at DC Neish. "Tyler, with me. Let's go."

"You'll need to be back by one," Ben told Logan. "Hoon wants to see you."

"Hoon? Bob Hoon? Is he up here now?"

Ben nodded. "Aye. He made Detective Superintendent."

Logan tapped himself on the side of the head. "Shite. Aye. Of course he did. I knew that."

"He's suggesting a press conference to try to nip the monster business in the bud. Emailed me about it in the early hours of the morning. Wants to see us both."

"Right. Fair enough," said Logan, nodding. "Wait a minute. So, you knew about all the monster shite in the papers before we got here?"

"Hm? Oh, aye," said Ben. He glanced across to the others and smiled. "But there was no bloody way I was going to be the one to break it to you."

CHAPTER TWENTY-FOUR

DC NEISH HAD NEVER HEARD A HUMAN BEING GROWL BEFORE. NOT really.

Sure, he'd heard people say things in a way that *implied* growling. He'd heard people pretend to growl. *Attempt* to growl. He'd even once had a girlfriend who used to make all manner of animal noises in the right sort of situation.

But he'd never *actually* heard another human being growl before.

Until now.

It started when Logan saw the press photographers, then rose in his throat when he realised what they were taking pictures of.

A group of twenty or so men and women stood posing in the campsite car park, their arms filled with cuddly Nessie toys, fishing nets, and various other props. The loch formed a backdrop, framed on either side by the conifers that marked the edge of the campsite.

It had barely been forty-eight hours since Mairi Sinclair's body had been found, and now this... this *pantomime* was taking place just metres from where she'd washed ashore.

Logan roared the Focus up behind the photographers, then slammed on the brakes, spraying gravel behind the car as he skidded it to a stop.

He was out of the car before Tyler had unclipped his belt, and didn't have time to warn the photographer who'd come closest to being hit before the man could open his mouth.

"What's your fucking game, mate?" the photographer demanded. "Driving like a bloody maniac."

Tyler unfastened his belt, but decided it was probably safest to stay in the car for now.

"Who are you?" Logan demanded, pointing at the man who had spoken to him.

"What?"

"You heard me. Who are you? What's your name?"

"None of your business, that's who."

A female photographer turned to Logan, camera raised. His head snapped in her direction, anger blazing behind his eyes. "Press that button. I dare you."

The woman's finger hovered over the camera's shutter release, but then she sensibly lowered it without taking a picture.

"Aye, thought so," Logan said, scowling.

Tyler got out of the car and stood behind his boss as Logan produced his warrant card and held it up for everyone to see. "Detective Chief Inspector Logan. Senior Investigating Officer in the murder of Mairi Sinclair," he announced.

Once he was sure they'd all had a good look at the card and knew he was telling the truth, he closed it over and put it back in the pocket of his coat.

"I'm going to say this once and once only," he said. "So, it's in all your best interests if you listen, and listen carefully."

He cleared his throat, glanced across their faces to make sure they were all paying attention, then jabbed a thumb back over his shoulder. "Fuck off."

There was some silence from the press, some anxious murmuring from the people with the props.

"Did I stutter?" Logan asked Tyler. The younger detective shook his head.

"No, boss."

"No, I didn't think so. And yet, they haven't fucked off like I told them to," Logan said, turning his glare back on both groups.

It was then that he spotted her. The instigator of this whole bloody thing. The madwoman with the monster photos, Marion Whitehead.

"You. You caused all this... this... Whatever this shite is," Logan snapped, eyes boring into the woman while his hands gestured vaguely at the gathering of people and press.

Logan didn't consider the press themselves to be 'people'. They were cockroaches. Lower than that, even. If cockroaches got parasites, that's what the press were.

"Good morning, sergeant!" Marion chirped, elbowing her way through her gaggle of cronies. "I am indeed responsible for all this excitement. See? I told you those photographs were dynamite!"

She stood in front of Logan, barely two-thirds his height but all peacocked up with pride.

"It's my pleasure, though, sergeant. You don't have to thank me."

One of Logan's eyes twitched.

"*Thank you?*"

"Like I say, no thanks necessary," beamed Marion.

Tyler jumped in before Logan exploded.

"Hi. Detective Constable Neish," he said, smiling at both groups in turn.

None of the press pack had started firing out questions, suggesting they were all photographers and not reporters. This was a staged photo-opp at the moment, and nothing more.

The crowd with the props were a mixed-bag. Weirdos mostly, but a couple of oddballs in there, too. You could see it a mile away.

"And you are... monster hunters, is that right?" Tyler asked.

There was some excited chattering from the group, but none of them actually confirmed or denied this until Marion piped up.

"Bang on, sonny! We're all members of the same Facebook group. We are the Paranormal Investigation Society Scotland."

"Right. Very cool," Tyler said. "It's just—"

"Piss," said Logan.

Tyler hesitated. "Boss?"

"Paranormal Investigation Society Scotland. *PISS.*"

The younger detective snorted, but Logan wasn't amused. Tyler's interjection had bought him a few seconds to bring his temper under control, but it was still bubbling away below the surface, ready to erupt at one wrong word.

"A woman died here. A mother," Logan said. "She was murdered by a human being, no' a monster."

"How can you be so sure?" asked a man from the Nessie-hunting group. His accent was North of England, but he wore a tartan bunnet with a ginger wig attached, and carried a cuddly Loch Ness Monster under one arm.

"Because there's no such fucking thing," Logan barked, feeling the fury surging through his veins again.

"Obviously, you didn't look at those photos," sniffed Marion. "I knew you wouldn't. None are so blind as those who will not see."

"Well, unless you lot want to see the inside of a jail cell, I suggest you pack up all your shite and go back to where you came from," Logan said. He glowered at the photographers. "And that goes for you, too."

"You can't do that," the female photographer who'd briefly considered taking Logan's picture said. "You can't arrest us."

"Can't I? You think? Will we find out?" Logan asked her.

His head tick-tocked between both groups. Marion was still standing at the front of the PISS Squad, or whatever the hell they were calling themselves, but she was less puffed-up now than she had been a moment ago.

"No, thought not," Logan said. "If you want to go play dress-up, do it somewhere else. A woman died."

He yanked the *See-You-Jimmy* hat off the Northerner's head and threw it to the ground. "Have some damn respect."

He marched through the group, shouldering them aside and forcing them to stumble out of his path. Tyler scurried along behind him, and almost collided with the DCI's back when he stopped and turned.

"And if any of you get in the way of my murder investigation," he spat, "I'll drown you in your own fucking acronym."

TYLER HURRIED along the uneven path, struggling to keep up with Logan's much longer strides. The DCI had spent the first twenty seconds of the walk ranting about 'those sad bastards,' but had then fallen into a sort of seething silence that had lasted for the past several minutes.

At first, Tyler had tried making conversation, but Logan hadn't risen to any of it, and now the pace and the uneven terrain were taking their toll, and Tyler was more focused on breathing than making small talk.

Most of the path had been hewn out of the side of a hill that ran alongside the loch. They'd been climbing for a while, picking their way across rocky stretches, and striding across channels made for little streams that ran down the hillside to the water below.

Occasionally, they'd come to a bridge, or a stretch of the path that had clearly been worked on in recent months, and would enjoy a few moments of strolling on flat ground, before the surface fractured into another few hundred yards of wobbly rocks and gravel.

But the views, though. God, the views.

Now they were that bit higher, they could see a good couple of miles along Loch Ness in both directions. The sky was overcast, and the water was more grey than blue, but it still would've been breathtaking, had either of them any breath left to give.

"You sure... this is... the right way?" Tyler wheezed, each little clump of words punctuated by a heave of his chest.

"So Hamza tells me, aye," Logan said, his own breathing almost as laboured as Tyler's.

He stopped at a bend and leaned on the railing that had been erected along the side of the path that overlooked the water. It was a nasty drop from here. A couple of hundred feet, with a few bounces on the way to the water. If you were lucky, you'd hit the grass, but more likely you'd be smashed against one of the big boulders that dotted the hillside below.

"There must be an easier way than this," Tyler complained. "We must've walked miles."

"Yer arse. Less than a mile," Logan said. "And, aye, there is an easier way."

Tyler blinked. "What?"

"There's a path from up top. By the cafe. Leads you right down."

"What?" Tyler said again. "Then why did we come this way?"

"Wanted to see how far it was from the camp to the building site," Logan said. He was bringing his breathing back under control now, and Tyler groaned when the DCI set off marching again. "This is the most direct route."

"Why does that matter?" the younger detective asked.

"Because we're assuming the body was dumped elsewhere," Logan said. "For all we know at the moment, she was killed on-site or nearby, then dumped right where she was found. You said yourself, it's not tidal, so there's not a huge amount of movement in the water."

"So, what...?" Tyler panted. "You think someone could've killed her up here, then carried her down?"

"No, I don't think that. I'm ruling out possibilities," Logan corrected.

"Aye, well, I think we can safely rule this one out, boss," Tyler said. "No way anyone's lugging a corpse all this way."

Logan didn't like to agree with DC Neish if it could be helped, but there wasn't much else for it on this occasion. "No. Can't see it," he agreed. "Now, keep up. We should be almost there."

CHAPTER TWENTY-FIVE

"Thanks for coming in," said Ben, smiling warmly at the woman in the chair on the other side of the table. "Tea? Coffee?"

"Uh, no," said Shayne Turner. "Thanks."

Her accent was Australian, with that implied question-mark on the end of everything that came out of her mouth. Her hair was dark, cut short and choppy, and perfectly complimented the golden-brown of her skin tone. Everything about her was small and slight, except her eyes, which seemed cartoonishly wide.

Not for the first time since Shayne had arrived in the building, Ben was thankful that DC Neish wasn't here.

Shayne's cartoon eyes went from DI Forde to DS McQuarrie, who stood just behind and off to the side of the seated senior officer. Caitlyn's arms were crossed, and her expression carried none of the warmth that Ben's did.

"Should I... Should I have a lawyer?" Shayne asked.

"You can do, if you like. We may use some of what you tell us in court," Ben said. "But you're not under arrest or any of that stuff, Miss Turner. You're not suspected of anything. This is just a chat. We're just hoping you can help us clarify a few things about Mairi Sinclair. Square away a few details, sort of thing."

At the mention of the victim's name, Shayne stiffened. At the same time, her face seemed to crumple.

"I still can't believe what happened," the teacher said.

"What *did* happen?" asked Ben. The question took her by surprise, and he cranked up his smile a little. "From your point of view, I mean. When was the last time you saw Mairi?"

"Friday," Shayne said. "Not... I don't... Last Friday, I mean. Not yesterday."

"We understand," said Ben. "Last Friday...?"

"After school. Well, at the end of the day. We were just, you know, like chatting? Just catching up, or whatever. Then, she left, and... Well. I guess she died."

"How did she seem?" Ben asked. "And are you sure I can't get you something? Water, maybe?"

Shayne shook her head. "I'm fine, thanks. She seemed fine. A little stressed, maybe, but it had been a long week. We've got OFSTED coming in in a couple of weeks, so it's all a bit hectic."

"Gotcha. I don't envy you that. Good luck with it."

Shayne allowed herself a brief smile. "Thanks," she said, then she flicked her gaze to Caitlyn, and the smile fell away again.

"Was she more stressed than usual, would you say?" Ben pressed.

Shayne considered this, then shrugged. "Dunno. Hard to say. Maybe a little. She said something about her ex. I think he was back on the scene in some way. Think she'd had a fight with her dad about it."

"Her dad?"

"Yeah. Reckon that's what she said. I think there's some history there. Don't think her dad likes her ex much."

She gave a sort of half-shrug and a little wave of a hand. "But, I don't know. Just how it seemed. I might be wrong."

There was a scratching of pen on paper. Caitlyn had unfolded her arms now, and was jotting down notes as the conversation unfolded.

"I don't mean a *fight* fight," Shayne clarified. "Just, like, an argument. And maybe not even that. It was just the impression I got, you know?"

"We understand," Ben said again. He sighed, good-naturedly. "Families, eh?"

"Yeah. Families."

"Would you say that you and Mairi were friends?" asked Caitlyn. Her tone was more abrupt than Ben's, like she was in more of a hurry to get down to business.

Shayne hesitated. She looked from Ben to Caitlyn and back again. Ben nodded encouragingly.

"Go on."

"Uh, yes. We were friends," Shayne said.

"Close friends?" Caitlyn pressed.

"Yeah. I think so. Pretty close. She really helped me when I started at the school. Totally took me under her wing. She was pretty cool."

"More than friends?"

A frown troubled Shayne's carefully sculpted eyebrows. "What? What's that supposed to mean?"

"Were you in a sexual relationship with Mairi Sinclair?" Caitlyn asked bluntly.

"No! What? No. Nothing like that."

"But you wanted to be?"

Shayne looked to Ben for support, her already large eyes widening further. He said nothing, just waited patiently for her to answer.

"I'm not... I don't..."

She rallied, pulling herself together, and looked Caitlyn right in the eye. "No. She was my friend. That was all. I didn't think of her in that way."

Ben took up the reins again. "Right. No. You were just friends. Close friends, like you say."

"Yeah. Exactly," said Shayne, but the way she shifted in her seat suggested she knew something more was coming. Her eyes followed a sheet of paper that Caitlyn slipped onto the desk in front of Ben.

"You kept in contact regularly?" Ben said. "Texts. Phone calls. That sort of thing?"

"Sure. Yeah. I mean, I guess so."

"You did," Ben said. He gave the paper a little wave in front of her. "We've got the records. You kept in near-constant contact, in fact."

He peered down his nose at the paper, regarding it as if for the first time. "Her? Not so much. In fact, in the twelve days prior to her disappearance, you sent her a total of two-hundred-and-seventy-two text messages."

Ben sucked air in through his teeth and looked up at Caitlyn. "Is this right, DS McQuarrie?"

"It's correct, sir, yes," Caitlyn confirmed, not taking her eyes off Shayne.

"Two-hundred-and-seventy-two. Wow. That's a lot. Isn't it? That seems like a lot."

Shayne shrugged. It came off nowhere near as nonchalantly as she was evidently aiming for.

"I text a lot."

"You do."

"I used WhatsApp back before I moved up here, but the data connection's not great out where I am," Shayne said, as if this somehow explained everything.

"Oh, aye. It can be a nightmare up here," Ben confirmed. "Government's working on it, but they've been saying that for a while. You're fine in the city centre, but once you go outside, forget it."

Ben peered over the top of the paper at the woman across the table. "Where was it you lived again?"

"Out by Dores," Shayne said. "Private rent."

"Oh, lovely. Lovely spot, that," Ben said. He sucked in his bottom lip, giving this some thought. "That's out on the Foyers road, isn't it?"

"It is, sir," Caitlyn was quick to confirm.

DI Forde sighed sadly. "Not far away from where poor Mairi was found, then."

He let that hang there for a few moments, then went back to the printout he was holding.

"So. Two-hundred-and-seventy-two text messages over twelve days. Can you remember how many times Mairi replied?"

Shayne shrugged again. This time, there was no mistaking the tension in it. "Not sure."

"Rough guess?"

"Like, I don't know, a hundred?" Shayne ventured.

"Four," said Ben.

He gave that one a few seconds to sink in, too.

"She texted you four times."

Silence.

"During that same twelve day period. Four."

"That can't be right. I'm sure it was more than that," Shayne said.

She was leaning back from the table a little now, her hands crossed in front of her, the lines of her body all straight and stiff.

"Nah, it was more than that."

"Not according to her phone records," Ben said. "Four. See?"

He turned the page around for Shayne to see. The same number had been picked out four times in yellow highlighter. "That's your number, isn't it? The last message she sent you was Sunday morning. An hour before she was last seen alive."

Shayne barely glanced at the page. "I think I should have a lawyer."

"Why? You haven't done anything, have you?" Caitlyn demanded. "What are you worried about?"

"No, but—"

"It must've been frustrating," Ben said.

Shayne's brow furrowed. "What?"

"Four replies. To all those messages. And three phone calls that she never picked up." Ben clasped his hands in front of him and offered up a sympathetic smile. "How did that make you feel?"

"Fine. She was busy. I got it."

"Did you?" asked Caitlyn. "Because you sent two-hundred-and-seventy-two messages. At what point did you *get it*, exactly?"

"It was just silly stuff. Jokes, mainly. Me bitching about the job. Most of it wasn't even looking for a reply," Shayne said. "The jokes I sent to loads of people at the same time."

"I love a good joke," said Ben, rubbing his hands together. "What sort of thing was it?"

Shayne shrugged again. "Can't remember."

"What, none of them?" asked Ben. "You can't remember a single joke you sent?"

"I don't know. Only a few were, like, jokes or whatever."

"You said 'mainly,'" Ben told her. "You said you sent, 'jokes, mainly.'"

"Are you changing your story?" Caitlyn asked.

"What? No. I mean... I just mean... They weren't *joke* jokes. Just, you know, messages about funny stuff that had happened at school. Things the kids had said. That kind of thing."

"And her message to you on Sunday?" Ben asked.

That seemed to catch the teacher off-guard a bit. "Yeah, I don't know. She replied to a joke. Just said, like, 'good one,' or whatever."

"And that was unusual?" Ben asked.

"Yeah. I guess so."

"Would you mind showing us your phone?" Caitlyn asked.

"Yes, I fucking would mind, actually," Shayne snapped. Her cheeks reddened as she focused her attention on Ben. "You said this was just a chat about Mairi, so why do I feel like I'm being interrogated by Good Cop and Bitch Cop all of a sudden? I should have a lawyer for this. You're not allowed to just keep me here without a lawyer."

"I can assure you, no one is keeping you anywhere, Miss Turner," Ben said. "We're just—"

"Oh, so I can go, then?"

Ben's hesitation lasted only a half-second, but it was enough.

"Sweet. Then see ya. I'm going," Shayne said, pushing back her chair and standing up. "If you want to speak to me again, you can go through my lawyer."

"Who would that be?" Ben asked.

This took the wind from Shayne's sails a little. "Well, I don't have one yet. But I'll get one."

She motioned to the door and shot daggers at Caitlyn. "Can you let me out?"

Caitlyn waited for the nod from DI Forde, then knocked on the door. She stepped aside as it was opened from the other side, and Shayne went thundering past her.

"See Miss Turner out, would you?" Caitlyn said to the uniformed officer in the corridor.

She turned back to Ben to find him laughing quietly.

"*Bitch Cop*," he chuckled. "Aye, she got the measure of you, alright."

CHAPTER TWENTY-SIX

THE SIGN ON THE DOOR OF THE HUT DID NOTHING FOR LOGAN'S MOOD. Tyler had seen it first, and had a full second to groan inwardly before the DCI spotted it.

"Bosco Building," he spat. "*Bosco fucking Building*! Did we know this was them? If not, why not?"

"Not sure, boss. I'll check," Tyler said.

"I mean... Jesus Christ! That's been sat here this whole time!"

"I guess so, boss."

Logan looked straight up at the sky overhead, chewed over a few angry insults, then swallowed them back down.

"Right. Well. It is what it is," he said. "Gloves and shoe coverings on."

The works hut was a small Portakabin style construction, with a flat roof, no windows, and a single door that had been secured by a sturdy-looking padlock. It was at the very end of the path, situated right on the Falls of Foyers viewpoint. Had the hut been built with windows, it would've had a cracking view of the falls as they cascaded down the steep stone wall directly across from the viewpoint.

"Where does this go?" Logan asked, as he and Tyler both pulled on gloves. "The waterfall?"

Tyler leaned over the metal barrier and peered down into the water fifty or sixty feet below. A spray of white mist rose up from where the tumbling water pummelled against the rocks. "Dunno. Into the loch, I suppose."

"Aye. That's what I was thinking," Logan said. He produced a pair of shoe coverings from his pocket and slipped them over his feet.

"I haven't got any shoe ones, boss," Tyler said.

"For f—" Logan sighed. "Fine. You'll have to stay outside. Be careful where you step."

The DCI picked his way over to the hut, gave it a quick once-over, then checked the padlock. Up close, it was even sturdier than he'd thought. Someone was keen to keep people out.

Still, way out here, unguarded like this? There was no saying what might happen. Opportunistic thieves. Teenage vandals. Anyone could come along and put a door like this in.

Logan stepped back, took aim at the lock, then drew back a foot.

"Boss!"

Logan stopped. "Look away if it bothers you, son," Logan told him.

"What? No, it's not that," Tyler said. "I was just going to say..."

Logan looked back at him over his shoulder. Tyler held up a little leather pouch that was open at the top. Several curved pieces of metal stuck up from the opening.

"...there are alternatives."

"My way would've been quicker," said Logan.

He was watching Tyler kneeling in front of the door, digging around inside the padlock with his tools. His brow was furrowed, and his tongue was sticking out in concentration.

"You have done this before, yes?"

"Yeah, boss. I do it all the time," Tyler said. He glanced up at the DCI. "For fun, I mean. I'm not a cat burglar."

"Evidently," Logan said. "I mean, you'd struggle to make it as a sloth burglar at this rate."

He looked around, glanced at his watch, then sighed. "Watch out. I'm going to kick it in."

"Hold on... I think..."

There was a *clunk* as the top part of the lock sprung open. "Bloody hell, it worked!" Tyler exclaimed.

"What do you mean, 'it worked'? I thought you'd done it before?"

"Well, yeah, but I've got this see-through lock that lets you see what you're doing," Tyler explained, standing. "I've never tried a proper metal one before."

Logan tutted. "Now you tell me."

"Worked, didn't it?" Tyler said, slipping the tools back into the pouch.

"Aye," Logan begrudgingly conceded. "It did. Good job." He indicated the lock-picking set with a nod. "How long you been carrying that about for?"

"About two years," Tyler admitted. He slipped the set back into the pocket of his jacket and gave it a pat. "Eight quid off eBay. Worth every penny."

"Bargain," said Logan. He took hold of the door handle and motioned for the DC to keep back. "Right. Let's see what we see."

The door opened with a long theatrical *creeeeak*. Weak sunlight spilled in through the widening gap, barely making a dent in the darkness painting the walls.

There were three cords hanging from the ceiling like old-style bathroom light switches. Logan pulled one, and a fan roared into life. He pulled it again, then tried the next one. A blast of heat rolled down on him from above the door.

Muttering, he tried the third cord. With a *ka-klack*, an overhead light came on, and the hut's secrets were revealed.

Even before his brain had processed the details of what he was seeing, Logan knew this was it. This was the place.

This was where Mairi Sinclair had died.

The inside of the hut was a clutter of tools and equipment with space left over for two people, maybe three if they all knew each other well enough.

There was a chair by the back wall—a metal number with a torn padded seat and sturdy-looking arm rests. Logan's eyes were drawn instinctively down. They spotted the cable-ties almost immediately, a split in each one where they'd been cut off.

The floor itself was a square of uncovered plywood. Stains marked it below and around the chair. A variety of fluids, all now dried into the fibres of the wood. Logan could identify one of them immediately, and could hazard a good guess at the nature of the others based on what he knew of Mairi Sinclair's final hours.

Logan had been braced for this. Of course he had. After everything he'd seen, he was *always* braced for this.

And yet, his throat tightened, his stomach twisted into a knot, and the skin on his face prickled at the thought of the suffering that had been inflicted here.

"Boss," said Tyler. His voice was low and measured, and came from right behind Logan.

The DC pointed past Logan and up at the hut's ceiling. There was a shelf fixed to the wall just below it. A roll of green tarpaulin sat there, one uneven end hanging down.

"Aye," was all Logan said.

He clenched his teeth, forced himself to take another look around the hut, then pulled the door closed.

"Call it in, son," he instructed.

He inhaled deeply, hurrying along the departure of the hut's air from his lungs. "Tell them we found it."

CHAPTER TWENTY-SEVEN

"WHERE THE SUFFERING FUCK HAVE YOU BEEN?"

Logan closed the door to Hoon's office and joined Ben in front of the Superintendent's desk. Hoon sat on the other side of it, perched on a wooden chair that creaked and groaned whenever he shifted his not-inconsiderable weight. The office was windowless, with the only light coming from the overhead strips. They cast a clinical white glow directly down on the Superintendent, picking out all the old acne scars that pitted his face like craters.

Big Boaby Hoon, wi' a face like the moon.

Logan had always got on well with Hoon. Or, as well as anyone could get on with the venomous old bastard, at any rate. They had never been friends, exactly, but they had shared a mutual respect. Hoon had accepted promotion grudgingly, and Logan suspected he'd like nothing more than to be back out on the streets, taking names and—if the rumours were to be believed—cracking heads.

They were alike in a lot of ways. Hoon had played on some of the meaner streets of Glasgow as a child, then policed them as an adult. He was an East End lad, grew up somewhere off Duke Street, Logan dimly recalled.

Hoon'd had some high profile collars in his time, but his share of balls-ups, too. After Logan's failure to save yet another of Owen Petrie's child victims a few years back, he'd been considering jacking everything in, until Hoon had cornered him and talked some sense into him.

Or maybe some sense out of him. The jury was still out on that one.

Either way, the man had shown a softer side to the gruff, foul-mouthed persona he'd become famous for as he'd moved up through the ranks.

"One o'clock, I said," Hoon barked. He pointed to a clock on the wall. "Does that look like one o'fucking clock to you?"

"No, sir," Logan said.

"What time does that look like to you?"

"Twenty past one, sir."

"Does it? Really? Look closer."

Logan tried not to show his irritation. "Twenty-two minutes past one, sir."

"Bingo. Fucking *well done*. Twenty-*two* minutes past one," Hoon said. He smiled broadly, showing off his yellow teeth. It was, perhaps, the most unauthentic smile Logan had ever seen. "Well, thanks for eventually gracing me with your presence. So nice of you to squeeze me into your busy schedule."

He splayed his hands out in Logan's direction, palms upwards, in an abrupt gesture. "Well?"

Logan knew this game. He'd played it before. Hoon was looking for an excuse. Ideally, a feeble one he could rip apart.

Fortunately, Logan had an absolute belter.

"We found the murder scene, sir," he said. "That's why I was held up."

"You found it?" Ben asked.

"Did he no' just fucking say that, Benjamin? Did you no' just hear those words come out of his fucking mouth?" Hoon spat.

He glowered at DI Forde to make his feelings on any further interruptions very clear, then turned his attention back to Logan.

"Where?"

"It's a works hut. Down by the Falls of Foyers. I've got a team there now going over it."

"The Falls of Foyers? Then why in fuck's name has it only been found now?" Hoon demanded. "That's, what? Half a mile from where the body washed up? For fuck's sake, Jack."

"It was... overlooked, sir," Logan said.

Hoon's chair groaned as he leaned forward, like it knew what was coming next.

"*Overlooked?*"

Out of the corner of his eye, Ben saw Logan nod.

"Bad call on my part, sir," the DCI said. "Won't happen again."

"See that it fucking doesn't," Hoon warned. "You're just in the door here, Jack, you can go straight back out it just as fucking quick."

He gave that a moment to sink in, then leaned back. "We have any idea who was working out of the hut?"

"We do," Logan confirmed. "According to Bosco's secretary's records..."

He braced himself.

"Robbie Stead—"

"Don't fucking finish that sentence," Hoon warned, slamming a hand on the desk. "Seriously, Jack? The victim's abusive ex-partner working half a mile from where the body was found and nobody fucking noticed?"

"Like I said, sir. An oversight on my part."

"I'll fucking 'oversight' you," Hoon muttered.

His face contorted and his nostrils flared, like he'd just caught wind of a daud of dogshite on his top lip.

"Well, what's done is done, I suppose. But these monster-hunter pricks. What do we make of them?" he asked. "Because I know what I'd like to make of them. A big pot of fucking soup."

"DC Neish and I met some of them at the campsite on our way to investigate the hut. They were doing some sort of photo call."

Logan saw the colour of Hoon's face change. There was always a vague sort of reddish tinge to the man, but he was literally going purple before their eyes as his temper rose.

So, that's what that looked like from the outside.

"*A fucking photo call?!* A woman was murdered!"

"Aye. That's what I said before I chased them off," Logan said.

"Next time you see them, arrest them. Fucking arrest the fucking lot of them," Hoon instructed. He anticipated Ben's question before he could open his mouth to ask it. "I don't care how. Think of something. Shove a kilo of coke up their collective arses, if you have to. I don't want those pricks parading around for the tabloids, got it?"

"Got it, sir," said Logan.

Hoon exhaled through his gritted teeth. "Right. Good," he said. He looked Logan up and down. "How you settling in?"

"Hitting the ground running," Logan said.

"Good. Well..." He gestured vaguely. "You know where I am."

He turned his attention to the computer beside him and started to peck at the keys with his fingertips.

"You can fuck off now," he said. "Ben already gave me everything I need for the press conference. He bothered his arse to get here on time."

Logan glanced at Ben. The DI rocked back on his heels, looking pleased with himself.

"Right, sir. Let us know if you need more."

Hoon gave the detectives the briefest of looks which successfully managed to convey the phrase, "Aye, you're fucking right I will," without him saying a word, then went back to typing.

Logan and Ben were at the door when the Superintendent spoke again.

"Jack?"

"Sir?"

Hoon tore his eyes away from his screen. "Nail this bastard quickly for us, eh?"

Logan nodded. "Aye," he said. "That's the plan."

CHAPTER TWENTY-EIGHT

LOGAN AND THE OTHERS STOOD AND SAT BY THE BIG BOARD, EACH OF them chipping in their own findings from the past few hours.

DS Joyce, the Exhibits Officer they'd temporarily nicked from CID, sat by her desk, alternating between typing on her computer terminal and peering over the top of her glasses at one of the sealed evidence bags piled up in front of her.

"So, while you two were living the high life doon by the water, some of us were doing some proper polis work," Ben told Logan and Tyler. "First up, me and Bitch Cop over there spoke to Shayne Turner."

Tyler's ears practically pricked up. "What was she like?"

"A bit cagey. Got riled in the end and stormed off."

"That's not really what I meant," Tyler said.

Ben sighed. "No, I know. But that's all I'm telling you."

"You ask her about all the messages she sent?" Logan asked.

"Well, since that was the whole point of getting her in here, aye," said Ben. "Been a bit of a wasted opportunity if not, eh?"

"And?"

"She says they were mostly 'jokes.'"

"Jokes?"

"That's what she said," Ben confirmed. "Jokes."

"Did you buy it?"

Ben and Caitlyn exchanged glances. Both shook their head at the same time.

"Not really, no," Ben said. "But she said something else interesting."

Logan crossed his arms and half-sat on the edge of a desk. "Go on."

"She says Mairi had been a bit on edge lately. She'd been fighting with her dad because, and I quote, 'Her ex was back on the scene in some way.'"

"In what way?"

"That was all she seemed to know," Ben said. "We can haul her in and press her properly, if you like."

"We'll see," Logan said.

He looked over at the Big Board, and was heartened a little by it. He'd felt like they hadn't been making much progress on the case so far, but the board was barely recognisable from what it had been yesterday. Caitlyn had pinned up printouts of the pictures Tyler had taken of the murder site, and she and Hamza had put together a timeline of everything they knew so far. At last, some kind of picture of Mairi Sinclair's last few days seemed to be emerging.

"There's been a fair bit of new information," said Ben, reading Logan's expression, if not his mind. "I think it'd be good for everyone if we did a quick recap."

"Aye," Logan agreed. "Good call."

"But first, the big news," Ben said.

"You're pregnant, sir?" Tyler guessed, placing a hand on his chest and gasping with delight.

Logan flinched, all too aware of Ben and Alice's painful history with pregnancy. Ben, for his part, glossed right over the comment and carried on.

"The rope taken from Christopher Boyd's office? Exact match for the one used to tie up Mairi Sinclair's body. Same make, same model, same colour. Same rope."

Logan's eyes widened just a fraction at this new information, but he said nothing.

"So... it was him, then?" said Tyler. He looked around at the others for confirmation. "It must've been him, then. Right?"

"Not necessarily," said Hamza. He was sitting behind his desk, the glow from his computer monitor casting half his face into shadow. "Could be coincidence."

"Hell of a coincidence," said Caitlyn.

"Want me to have him brought in?" Ben asked Logan.

The DCI gave this some thought, then clicked his tongue against the roof of his mouth. "Not yet. Get eyes on him. Find out where he is and what he's up to. But subtle. Let's not spook him if we can help it."

He gestured to the board. "Where are we otherwise?"

"Caitlyn," said Ben, perching himself on the desk beside Logan. "Would you do the honours?"

Over the next few minutes, DS McQuarrie went over the timeline they'd been able to put together covering Mairi Sinclair's final days. Logan knew all of it. He'd gone over the timeline a dozen times the night before while lying awake in Ben's spare room, and had been able to slot in the new pieces of information as they'd come up.

He listened, anyway. It was sometimes useful to hear someone else talking it through. Occasionally, it would trigger some new thought or idea that could help crack a case wide open.

Mairi Sinclair had been agitated in the days leading up to her death, and was possibly seeing her ex-partner, Robbie Steadwood, which had led to conflict with her father, although Malcolm Sinclair hadn't mentioned this to Logan or any of the other officers he'd spoken to.

Phone records for Thursday evening, when Mairi had been overheard arguing, showed three calls, two incoming, one outgoing.

The outgoing call was to the Pay As You Go number they hadn't yet been able to identify, and had lasted just shy of seven minutes.

The incoming calls were from Mairi's sister, Michelle—a short call of under five minutes—and her parents' landline number. That call had gone on for almost twenty minutes. Any one of the three of them could've fit with Stuart's vague estimate of the timing, and he hadn't heard enough about the argument to help them pinpoint who she'd been speaking to.

Caitlyn's money was on Malcolm Sinclair, though, and the rest of the team were leaning towards being in agreement. Based on the length of the call, and Shayne Turner's information regarding the friction between father and daughter, it was by far the most likely possibility. Not a dead cert, but as close as they were likely to get to one.

She'd gone to school on Friday, as normal, but hadn't returned texts or calls until Saturday, when she'd cancelled her lunch appointment with Christopher Boyd. The text messages they'd seen on his phone confirmed this, and corroborated the lack of response seen on Mairi's phone records.

According to Stuart Sinclair's first statement, she'd 'mooched around the house' on Saturday, but hadn't seemed particularly upset or out of sorts.

He'd spent most of the day in his bedroom, though, and had only really seen her when she'd shouted him down to eat. He'd had headphones on, and had been talking to people online, so it was possible she'd gone out for anything up to three or four hours without him realising. Neighbours hadn't seen her come or go, though, and there was no other evidence to suggest she'd gone anywhere.

Stuart hadn't heard her go to bed, and the last interaction he'd had with her was the following morning, at three minutes past eleven, when she'd said she was going out. She'd then either walked or driven to a nearby Spar shop, taken ten pounds from the ATM, and that was where the trail went cold.

At some point shortly after that, she'd been taken to the works hut at the Falls of Foyers, tortured, mutilated, then murdered. Her body had been wrapped in plastic sheeting from the hut, tied up with a rope matching the one taken from Christopher Boyd's office, and—an educated guess—dumped over the railings into the tributary below, where the fast-flowing water carried her out into Loch Ness.

"Aye, that's about the size of it," Ben said. He looked around at the rest of the team. "Anyone have anything to add?"

"Why did she stop texting?" Logan wondered. "We've seen her records, she was never off the bloody thing. Why the big hole from Friday afternoon until she was killed?"

"Still waiting for the rest of the records to come though, sir," said Hamza. "But based on what we've got, it looks like she texts into the competition on one of the Saturday morning cooking shows every week. She didn't that day."

"Bad mood, maybe?" Tyler guessed. "Time of the month?"

"Jesus," Caitlyn muttered.

"What? It affects the mood, doesn't it?" Tyler protested.

"It doesn't stop your fingers working," Caitlyn said, miming tapping out a message on a phone.

"No, but she might've just been, you know, in a huff, or whatever."

Logan sucked in his bottom lip. "It's an extreme behaviour change, whatever the reason behind it. There's something there. We should dig deeper."

"Uh, sir."

The voice was an unexpected one, and it took Logan a second to place its source.

DS Joyce sat up straight behind her desk, one hand on her mouse, both eyes fixed on the screen.

"Yes, Detective Sergeant?"

"Message just in, sir. It's Mairi Sinclair's phone."

She looked up at him over the top of her spectacles.

"It's just been switched on."

CHAPTER TWENTY-NINE

Merkinch—or The Ferry, as it was known locally—had a reputation as being one of the rougher areas of Inverness. A reputation that, as anyone who'd had the misfortune of finding themselves there after closing time would attest, was well-deserved.

Originally home to Inverness's ship-building industry, the area had steadily declined over the past couple of decades to become the husk of a place it now was. On the drive over, Tyler had described the place as 'Dundee, without the good bits,' and now that he was here, Logan felt the DC had done Dundee a great disservice.

It must once have been a thriving area, but now it was all bookies and charity shops, plus a wide selection of takeaways that each looked as toxic as the one before. Evidence of its industrial past still shone through in the architecture, but the buildings were faded and tired, and no amount of mobile phone accessory shops could disguise it.

It was the feel of the place that struck Logan most, though. He knew places like this all too well. Places where desperation oozed from the fabric of the buildings. Where the evidence of deprivation wasn't just there to be seen, it was hanging around in the very air itself to snag at the back of the throat. A tangible *thing* that blighted the landscape and the lives of everyone within its boundaries.

Logan had never set foot in the area before, but he already felt he knew it like the back of his hand.

The Ferryman was what might be described as 'a working man's pub,' although only by someone with a keen sense of irony. It was standard enough fare from the outside—faded red frontage, hand-painted sign, and frosted glass windows that were too caked with grime to see through.

An attempt had been made to tart the place up a bit by adding some uplighters just beneath the sign, but the effect had been somewhat counteracted by the crude picture of an ejaculating cock that had been scrawled in marker pen across the wall.

It was a shitehole. No two ways about it.

And whoever had Mairi Sinclair's phone was somewhere on the premises.

"Everyone else in position?" Logan asked. "Back way covered?"

"Yeah, boss," Tyler confirmed.

They were sitting in Logan's car thirty feet past the pub, watching the front door in the side and rear-view mirrors. A couple of jakey-looking bastards were hanging around out front, smoking tight rollies, the fags hidden in the cup of their hands whenever they brought them to their mouths.

"Hamza and DS McQuarrie are out back. Uniform are on standby but keeping their distance until we give the word."

"And it's still in there?"

Tyler gave a nod to confirm. "Last pinged three minutes ago. No one in or out since then."

"Right. Good. OK, then."

Logan put a hand on the door handle.

"Like we planned. Give it a couple of minutes after I go in, then phone."

He started to move, then hesitated.

"And don't fuck it up."

Tyler pulled a 'come on,' face. "What do you take me for, boss?"

Logan opened the door.

"Trust me, son," he said. "You do not want me to answer that question."

THERE WAS something of the Old West saloon about *The Ferryman* when Logan pushed open the heavy door and stepped over the threshold. It wasn't so much the design of the place as the atmosphere. The way the music seemed to quieten, and the punters sitting gathered around their little round tables all turned and scowled in his direction.

A man in his mid-fifties stood behind the bar, polishing a glass with a dishcloth. He'd been in good shape once, Logan guessed. You could still just make it out in his frame. The bulk of him had slipped downwards, though, and now gathered around his middle like a big rubber ring.

His face was pale and pasty, like he hadn't seen the sun in years. Given the state of those windows, this would not be much of a stretch. His hair was an obvious dye-job, too black to be natural. He'd touched up the eyebrows, too. Between the coal-black hair and sickly white face, he bore an uncanny resemblance to a—

"Badger!" called a voice from one of the booths in the corner. "Gonnae bring us another drink, eh, man?"

The barman, who had been watching Logan from the moment he'd opened the door, continued to study him. "Gonnae get up off your arse and get it yourself?" he suggested. "I'm no' yer mum."

No one else in the bar had spoken. Instead, they all watched Logan. Some of them were sneaky about it, peering at him over the top of their pint glasses, or squinting through their whisky-haze. Others were more brazen, sitting up straight and eyeballing, trying to scare this stranger off.

Logan's instinct was to study the faces, to see how many he recognised, and figure out which of them would have a knife, or a gun, or a big bag of pills stashed somewhere about their person. It was habit for places like these, and it took a concentrated effort for him to ignore the punters and make for the bar.

He reached for his inside coat pocket, and saw the barman bristle. Badger was clearly anticipating a warrant card, and appeared momentarily surprised when Logan produced a wallet with a couple of twenties poking out of the fold.

"Pint, thanks."

Badger kept polishing his glass. "Tennent's do you?"

Logan nodded, then watched as Badger gave the glass he was holding a final wipe with the cloth, blew inside it to blast all the little fluffy bits away, and started to fill it from the Tennent's tap.

The smell of it swirled up Logan's nostrils, filling his head and making something that had lain dormant there stir back into life.

He'd been expecting this, of course. He knew himself well enough to know this was always going to happen. The conflict. The internal battle. The little voice telling him that a sip would be a fine. A sip wouldn't do him any harm. A sip would be *necessary*, in fact, to set everyone's minds at ease that he wasn't here to lift them.

He could still feel their eyes on him. Watching him. Accusing him of being something he most definitely was.

The amber liquid glugged into the glass, foam creeping up the sides.

He didn't even like Tennent's—no one actually *liked* Tennent's—and yet he could feel his tongue rasping across his dry lips, and a prickle of anticipation on the back of his neck.

Over in the booth, a phone rang.

Thank Christ.

Logan could see the guy reflected in the bar's mirror. He was a lanky scrote in a hoodie that had once been white but was now an atlas of colourful stains. He glanced around before fiddling with the phone, eventually silencing it.

The foam reached the top of the pint glass. There was a *clunk* as it was deposited on the bar in front of him.

"Two eighty."

Logan fished three pound coins from his pocket and dropped them on the bar. "Keep the change," he said.

The glass was icy-cold as his fingers wrapped around it. He could feel condensation forming already, hear the faint *pop-pop* of the foam bubbles bursting on the pint's head as he carried it over to the booth in the corner.

A few eyes were still on him, but a low murmur of conversation had returned to the pub. He wasn't a 'kent face' locally—not yet—and while the hackles had gone up when he'd made his entrance, he could feel the tension easing in the air.

"Alright, pal?" he asked, arriving at the booth. It was a horseshoe-shaped number, with leather seats that were more holes than actual material. The only way out involved sliding around the table to one end of the curved bench. Either one was a simple side-step away from Logan's current position.

Bloody amateurs. Wouldn't last five minutes down the road.

The scrote on the other side of the table looked up, his brow furrowed, eyes filled with the glassy gaze of someone who'd been dished out their methadone prescription in the past few hours. He was young—late teens, early twenties—and sported a beard so patchy it could've been put together out of sweepings from a barber shop floor.

"Eh?" the scrote asked, his eyes narrowing. Logan couldn't tell if this was an attempt to look threatening, or if he was just making an effort to focus. "Fuck you say?"

"Nice phone. Where'd you get it?" Logan asked.

The pint glass was heavy in his hand. Heavier than it should've been.

He was more aware of it than he should've been, too. Part of his brain was focusing exclusively on the weight of it in his grip. The feel of it in his hand. The thought of it in his mouth.

He forced himself to focus on the phone, instead. It was sitting on the table between them, much closer to the younger man than it was to Logan.

Still, given the state of the guy, Logan fancied his chances.

"Fuck's it to do with you, eh?" the scrote hissed.

"Nothing," Logan admitted. He leaned over and placed the pint down next to the handset. "Here. Bought you a drink."

"Fuck you do that for?"

Logan picked up the phone. By the time the streak o' pish on the other side of the table noticed, he was examining the screen.

The phone was an older model than he'd been expecting. An Alcatel, with buttons on the front and a screen not much bigger than a postage stamp.

"Here! Gie's ma phone back."

A burner. That's what this was. A burner.

At a table somewhere behind the DCI, another phone began to chime.

Ah, shite.

Logan turned. His eyes met those of a dead-eyed thirty-something wearing a baseball cap and a tracksuit. He had a phone in his hand, and a look on his face that told Logan exactly what was about to happen.

"Don't even think about it!" Logan roared, but the guy was already up on his feet. He toppled the table in the DCI's direction, then was off and running, weaving past the other punters and launching himself out through the double doors.

Logan set off in pursuit, shouldering past a couple of the runner's cronies who tried to get in his way and slow him down. He hit the doors just as they swung shut, throwing them wide and barrelling out onto the street.

He heard, but didn't acknowledge, the shout of, "Ma phone! 'At's ma fuckin' phone!" as the doors closed behind him again, and then he was off, powering along the pavement, his coat swishing behind him.

Tyler was out of the car and running, on a direct intercept course with the fleeing bam.

"Police! Stop where you are!" he bellowed, and Logan was almost impressed by the lad's authoritative tone.

Almost.

The bam was considerably less so. Ignoring the DC completely, he dodged down a side street and set off at a fair clip, knocking over a couple of wheelie bins and spilling recycling across the road behind him in an effort to slow his pursuers down.

"Get after him," Logan ordered, letting Tyler take the lead. Logan was a big man, but had a turn of speed about him when he really needed to.

Still, Tyler was younger and faster, and had more chance of catching the bastard. And, ultimately, why have a dog and bark yourself?

Catching his breath, Logan took out his radio and watched as Tyler threw himself into a controlled sprint, bounding over the scattered cans and newspapers, and already starting to close on the target. There were a few other openings to side streets ahead, though, and probably a network of alleyways that would offer multiple escape routes for someone who knew the area well. Tyler was gaining ground, but not quickly enough. The bam would reach a side street any second and be out of sight.

"He's running," Logan barked into the radio. "Down..."

He looked up, searching for a street name.

"Brown Street. Repeat, target is fleeing down Brown Street."

Suddenly, Hamza was in front of the guy, skidding around a corner just in time to make a grab for him. The scrote barrelled into him, shoulder-first, and Hamza's attempts at interception became a clumsy scramble to stay on his feet. He hit the wall backwards, the force of the double-impact knocking the air out of him, and forcing him to cling to the wall for support.

"Shite," Logan hissed, as the suspect set off again, Hamza barely having slowed his escape.

There was a screech of tyres and a black Ford Mondeo backed into the street directly in front of the runner. He hit the back of the car at speed, rolled up and over the boot, then hit the ground on the other side with an impact so loud that Logan heard it all the way back at the corner.

DS McQuarrie was out of the driver's seat in a heartbeat. Logan watched as she raced around the front of the car just as Tyler reached it and ran around the back.

It's alright, sir," said Hamza's voice from the radio. He pushed himself away from the wall, rubbed his lower back, and raised a thumb in Logan's direction. "We got him."

CHAPTER THIRTY

LOGAN STOOD AT THE BACK OF INTERVIEW ROOM THREE, OUT OF sight of the whining wee bastard in the chair.

He'd demanded to be taken to hospital with the light graze he'd sustained to the palm of one hand when he'd hit the ground on the other side of the car. Logan had refused, and not particularly politely, and they'd placed him under arrest.

DI Forde had recognised him on sight. Chris Hamilton, well-known local irritant with a long list of petty—and some not so petty—offences to his name. He'd waived his right to a solicitor, almost certainly on the basis that having one had never helped him before.

Ben sat directly across from him, the recorder running. He was playing it 'disappointed father-figure,' rather than 'hard-nosed polis.'

Logan would handle that role.

"Come on, son. We're going around in circles here," Ben told him. "Where did you get the phone?"

Hamilton shrugged. He had a facial tic that made him wrinkle his nose and draw up his top lip every few seconds, revealing a horror-show of mahogany teeth so worn down there were gaps between each one.

"I telt ye already, man," he said. His voice was slurred and nasal, like it couldn't bring itself to go via those teeth. "A guy."

"What guy?"

"I don't know, do I? A guy, man. Just a guy."

"So, some random guy just gave you an expensive phone?"

"Aye. That's what I've been tellin' ye. Just some guy."

Ben looked past Hamilton to where Logan was leaning his back against the wall. "There you go. Just some guy. We happy with that, Detective Chief Inspector?"

"No."

Ben turned his attention back to Hamilton.

"No. Apparently we're not happy with that, Chris. You'll have to be a wee bit more specific," Ben said. "What guy?"

"He was like... You know."

"We don't know. That's why we're asking."

"Like *a guy*. What else d'ye want me to say?"

Logan was across the room in two big strides. He slammed the flat of a hand on the table. The *bang* raced around the room, with a little shriek of fright from Hamilton in hot pursuit.

"Fuck's sake, man! What was that for?"

Ben glanced at the recorder. "For the record, DCI Logan struck the table, not the suspect."

"I'll tell you what else I want you to say, Mr Hamilton. I want you to say, 'I confess to the murder of Mairi Sinclair.'"

Hamilton's eyes blinked independently of each other for a moment. His tic stopped for a few seconds, like processing what Logan had said was drawing too much brainpower to keep it going.

When it returned, it was more frequent than ever, determined to make-up for lost time.

"Eh?" was the best response Hamilton could come up with.

"Mairi Sinclair," said Logan. "Body was found recently."

"Murdered, like?"

"Mutilated by some sick wee bastard," Logan said. "And you were found in possession of her phone."

"Eh? Naw. Wait."

Ben sucked air in through his teeth. "Doesn't look good, son."

"Naw. Hang on. I didn't murder anyone," Hamilton insisted. He was twitching so hard now he inhaled sharply up his nose each time it scrunched up.

"Aye, you did," Logan told him. "You've got her phone. You must've."

Hamilton shook his head vigorously. "Naw. I told you, I got it from—"

"There was no guy," Logan barked. "Don't say you got it from 'some guy.' You abducted Mairi Sinclair, you killed her, then you disposed of her body."

"You'll be put away for life for this, son," Ben said. "Nothing I can do about it."

Hamilton's head whipped left and right, tick-tocking from Ben to Logan and back again. "I didn't... Naw. I'm no'..."

"Last chance," Logan said. "Where did you get the phone?"

The tic was near-constant now, one every half-second. It was exhausting to even look at.

Hamilton's voice was a dry croak. "I telt ye, man. It was—"

Logan turned away from the table. "Interview terminated. Chris Hamilton, I am arresting you on suspicion of the murder of Mairi Sinclair. Anything you—"

"A car!"

Logan stopped.

"I got it from a car. Alright?" Hamilton said. "I didnae kill nobody."

Logan approached the table again, leaned both hands on it, and drilled a stare right between Hamilton's eyes.

"*What* fucking car?"

LOGAN STOOD in the car park of Raigmore hospital, watching a man and a woman in white paper suits carefully check over the exterior of a light blue Citroen C3. The car was near the back of the parking area, tucked between a people carrier and one of those stupid wee city cars that were barely big enough to hold one person and two days' worth of shopping.

"Can't believe it's been here this whole time," Logan muttered. "How did we not find this?"

Ben gestured around at the car park, and the thousand-odd cars crammed into its white lines. "Busy place. Hospital's always got folk coming and going. Then, there's all the arseholes who chuck their car here in the morning and get the bus into the city centre. Treat it like a Park & Ride. Meanwhile, people wanting to use the actual hospital facilities are stuck circling around and around, trying to find a space."

Logan shot him a sideways look. The DI cleared his throat.

"Aye. Well. I'm just saying. It's out of order."

"What's out of order is that this car has been here for a week, and we didn't notice," Logan said. He sighed. "Hoon's going to lose the rag. And rightly bloody so."

Ben checked his watch. "He'll be making his press statement soon. Maybe we can slip this past him without him noticing."

Logan raised an eyebrow.

"No," Ben sighed. "You're right. There's hee-haw chance of that happening."

"Get uniform asking questions. Has anyone in the hospital noticed the car sitting here? If so, when?"

"Caitlyn's already co-ordinating," Ben said. "Can't say I'm overly hopeful, though."

They watched the SOC officers do their stuff. A fine drizzle had started to fall, and they'd had to work fast to erect a little tent over the car to try to keep it dry. A futile gesture at this stage, Logan thought. By all accounts, it had been lashing down for three days solid earlier in the week.

"How's Hamza doing?" Logan asked.

"Pride's hurt, more than anything."

Logan nodded. "He panicked. I could see it in the way he moved. He's lost confidence."

"Can you blame him?"

"No. It's a miracle he came back at all."

"It's a miracle his wife bloody lets him," Ben said. "He pulled me aside when he got back to the station. He's feeling pretty bad about messing up. Reckons he should've caught the guy."

"It happens," Logan said.

"Aye. That's what I told him. He'll get back in the saddle sooner or later. Until then, every day we send that boy home in one piece is a good one in my book."

A black Audi drove past behind them, engine purring as it made its way between the rows of parked cars. Logan turned to wave it on, and it immediately sped up, pulling past the scene and continuing quickly along to the end of the row.

"See what I mean?" said Ben.

Logan frowned. "What?"

"Poor bugger's been circling for the past ten minutes trying to find a space. That's the fourth time he's passed us."

Logan looked back in the direction the car had gone, but it had already rounded the corner and was lost to him somewhere between the rows.

One of the Scene of Crime officers pushed back her hood as she crossed to the detectives. "We've got what we can from the outside."

"Not much, I'm guessing."

"No, sir. Not a lot. Confirmed the forced entry, though, and looks like the clothes hanger he used is still inside. We want to bring it in to do the interior. Permission to arrange a recovery?"

Logan nodded his approval.

"We'll have to get some of the other cars shifted," the SOC officer said.

"Give the registrations to one of the uniforms," Logan instructed. "They can check with the hospital, see if they can find any of the owners."

"And if they can't, then just break the windows and shove them out of the way," Ben said, rubbing his hands with glee. "Park & Ride bastards."

CHAPTER THIRTY-ONE

FOR A FOUL-MOUTHED ANGRY OLD BASTARD, HOON HAD A REAL KNACK for press conferences.

He shared Logan's contempt for the media, but managed to hide it better than the DCI did. Of course, he actually made the effort—something Logan had never bothered to do.

Hoon had always had a knack of knowing when a camera was pointed at him, and could slip effortlessly into the media training Police Scotland had started inflicting upon its senior officers over the past few years.

Logan himself had been booked into three of the training sessions over the past six months, but had always been able to dream up some excuse that got him out of it at the last minute.

The Superintendent opened with a prepared statement thanking the public for their interest and help with the case, then revealed some of the less-juicy details about the manner of death, focusing mostly on the stabbing and the bit where Mairi Sinclair had been tied up in plastic sheeting—two things that would be difficult to achieve with a pair of monster-sized flippers.

He also spoke about her family, about the son she'd left behind, and the children she had taught. Marion Whitehead and her PISS pals had turned Mairi's death into a joke, with the press only too happy to deliver the punchline. In a few concise sentences, Hoon had made her human again, and the gag suddenly didn't seem so funny.

After that, he put out an appeal for information on the whereabouts of Robbie Steadwood. He didn't say why, but the 'do not approach' disclaimer would paint enough of a picture for folk to come to a reasonable conclusion.

Between the statement and the shout-out, Hoon had neatly turned the press from an enemy to an ally. Robbie Steadwood's face would be everywhere by morning. There'd be nowhere for the bastard to hide.

Logan watched him take a couple of questions from the floor, then turned the TV off.

"Aye. He's got a knack for it," he said, turning away from the screen.

Ben Forde nodded his approval. "He's a better man than I am."

"Not exactly hard, boss," Tyler called from his desk.

Ben smacked his lips together a few times. "Anyone else thirsty?" he asked. "I could just go a nice cup of tea."

Tyler groaned and got to his feet. "Fine."

While Tyler took the tea order and set off to make it, DS McQuarrie filled them in on Christopher Boyd's movements.

He'd been at his climbing wall in the Eastgate that afternoon, had met a young blonde woman for lunch in the food court, then had headed home at just after four. He was still there now, although a report had just come through of a different woman turning up at the house, and being very warmly greeted at the front door.

"I'd say he's a player," Caitlyn said. "His relationship with Mairi Sinclair doesn't seem to have held any particular special meaning for him. Certainly moved on quickly enough."

"If it was him who killed Mairi, these women could be in danger," Ben remarked. "We should think about bringing him in."

Logan mulled this over. "Hamza?"

Over at his desk, Hamza looked up from Mairi's mobile phone. It had been checked for prints and other forensic evidence, then given back to the MIT for further investigation. Unfortunately, the phone was locked. Hamza had taken a few stabs at pincodes based on the dates of birth of Mairi and her closest family, but had come up blank.

"Still struggling to get into it, sir," he said. "Might have to turn it over to the tech bods, see if they can do something. Could take a while, though."

"Let's have a look," Logan said, approaching the desk and holding a hand out.

Hamza passed over the phone, and Logan regarded it with something between curiosity and suspicion. He gave the screen a prod, examined the message that appeared, then nodded and slipped the phone into his pocket.

"I might know someone," he said, heading for the door. "Give me twenty minutes."

"Don't tell me you know a phone hacker in Inverness, Jack," Ben said.

Logan paused briefly by the door. "Something like that."

"THIS IS SO WRONG. This is a whole other level of wrongness. Is this even allowed? Legally, I mean?"

Logan gave the coroner an emphatic nod. "Oh, God, aye. It's practically standard operating procedure."

Shona Maguire wasn't buying it. That much was clear from the look on her face. She stood with one hand on the handle of the drawer in which Mairi Sinclair's remains currently rested.

"Morally, then?" she asked.

Logan sucked in his bottom lip. "Morally, it might be a greyer area. But what would she want?" he asked, gesturing towards the drawer. "I think she'd want us to find who killed her, don't you?"

Shona conceded that point with a tilt of her head.

"And it's no' like I'm asking you to cut one of them off. I just need to borrow a finger for a few seconds, and job done. No one will ever know. And least of all her."

With a sigh, Shona moved to pull the handle, but then stopped.

"Fine. But you owe me one."

"Fair enough," Logan agreed. "Next time you want access to one of the dead bodies in *my* fridge, you'll be more than welcome."

"Or, you could buy me lunch."

Logan glanced at the clock. It was now comfortably past dinner-time.

"Not today, obviously," Shona said. "But sometime."

"Oh. Right," said Logan. "Lunch."

He looked down at the phone and tapped the screen. "Maybe I can guess the code."

"Funny," said Shona. The drawer *ker-thunked* as she pulled it open. "*Really* funny."

BEN HAD ACCEPTED the fact that his dinner would now almost certainly be inside some dog or another, but he hadn't even mentioned heading back to the house. The phone was a major breakthrough, and that buzz was in the air. That feeling that something was about to fall into place. That something that had been holding them back was about to give.

Alice would have a moan. Of course she would. But she understood. After all these years, she understood.

"Still a lot to go through, sir," Hamza said, after Logan jarred him about the phone's contents for the third time in as many minutes. "She's quite prolific when it comes to texting. I haven't even started on the emails."

Tyler entered from yet another tea run, balancing a tray laden with mugs. He'd made a point of bringing a half-open pack of Digestives, knowing they'd only send him back for biscuits if he turned up empty-handed. His face was a picture of concentration as he made his way across the Incident Room, trying not to spill a drop.

"Overfilled some of these," he said by way of explanation for his cautious creep from the door.

Ben glanced his way, rolled his eyes in a vague sort of disapproval, then turned his attention back to Hamza.

"Voicemails all deleted, except a couple of old ones from her boss about school-related stuff," DC Khaled continued.

"Don't tell me what we haven't got, tell me what we *have*," said Logan, growing impatient.

"Right, sir. Aye. Sorry," Hamza said. He consulted his notes. "Big headlines, then. She was sleeping with Robbie Steadwood. It had been going on for a couple of weeks, from what I can tell. There's not a lot of interaction between them, but what's there is... revealing."

"He wasn't sending dick pics, too, was he?" Caitlyn groaned.

Hamza snorted, then shook his head. "No. Not revealing like that. He was supplying her with cannabis."

"So, he was her dealer," Ben said.

"Aye, but, there's more to it than that," Hamza said. "It's like she's blackmailing him. Like she's holding some sort of secret over him. It's never specified what, but he warns her not to say anything. I quote: 'Blab, and you're a dead woman, Mairi. A fucking dead woman.' Only, without the punctuation, and half of it is spelled wrong. But you get the gist."

Ben sucked in a breath. "Not looking good for our Mr Steadwood, is it?"

"Not looking great, no," Logan agreed. "Be handy if he hadn't vanished off the face of the Earth."

"Press coverage should help."

Annoyingly, Logan had to concede that it might.

"Aye. What else do we have?"

"Shayne Turner's story seems to check out," Hamza revealed. "There are an insane number of texts from her, but almost all of them are shite. Inspirational quotes, mostly about feminism. Links to quizzes—'Which Hogwarts House are you in?' sort of stuff."

"Harry Potter," said Ben, displaying his in-depth knowledge of the franchise once again.

"Uh, yeah. So, that stuff, some jokes. Lots of jokes, actually, none of them very funny. Some chain letter type shite—'Forward this to five friends or you'll go blind' or whatever—and a couple of genuine work questions which Mairi replies to. Mostly just noise, though. Nothing incriminating. The text Mairi sent on Sunday morning was a reply to a meme Shayne sent a few minutes before."

"A what?" Ben asked.

"Like a funny picture, sir," Hamza said. "She just replies, 'Good one!' That's it."

Tyler set the tray on the desk and started passing out the cups. "So, the teacher's in the clear, then?"

Logan took his tea and blew on it. "Looks like it, aye. She was never exactly up there as a suspect, though."

"Someone should phone her and let her know," the DC suggested. He passed Ben his mug and offered up the Digestives. "Want me to do it?"

"I'll do it," said DS McQuarrie.

"It's hardly DS work, that," Tyler said, smiling eagerly. "Honestly, I can do it. I don't mind."

"No, son," Ben said. He gave Caitlyn a solemn look. "This looks like a job for Bitch Cop."

He regarded the offered biscuits. "But *Digestives*? Is that the best you could do?"

"There were a pack of Kit-Kats, but CID had put a sticky label on the front with their name on it."

Ben tutted. "Bastards," he said, then he glumly helped himself to a couple of the stale biscuits.

"There's some back and forth between Mairi and her sister, mostly about Stuart. The son."

"What about him?" Logan asked.

"Nothing major. Looks like he stayed at Michelle's house a few times. Reading between the lines, I'm not sure Mairi was all that happy about it, but I'm purely surmising," Hamza said. "Their messages feel a bit standoffish, though. If I didn't know they were sisters, I wouldn't have been able to figure it out from those."

"Parents said they were close when they were younger, but drifted apart when Mairi hit her Robbie Steadwood phase," Logan explained. "If Michelle suspected he was back on the scene, that could explain it."

"One story that doesn't check out is Christopher Boyd's," Hamza continued.

There was an almost-audible change to the tone of the room. Logan set his mug down on the desk beside him. "Do tell."

"It's mostly what he said. The texts between them are flirty all week. There's also the now-infamous penis photograph, of course."

"Let's have a look," said Tyler.

Hamza turned the phone DC Neish's direction. Tyler regarded it for a moment with a mixture of horror and wonder, then swallowed and shrugged. "Not that impressive."

"Do you mind?" Logan snapped, glaring at them both in turn.

Hamza quickly set the phone back down on the desk.

"DS McQuarrie has already seen all this on Boyd's phone. I thought you had something new?"

"Aye, sir. It's a message he sent after she cancelled their meeting," Hamza said.

"I saw the messages he sent after," Caitlyn said.

"I think maybe he deleted one," Hamza said. "There were four messages asking why she couldn't come, if he could see her later, if everything was OK. That sort of thing."

"I know. I saw them," Caitlyn reiterated.

"And then, there's the fifth message," Hamza said. He circled something on the top page of his notepad, turned the pad around, and slid it across the desk.

Caitlyn read it in silence, then looked up. "That's the full thing?"

Hamza nodded. "Word for word."

Logan reached past her and took the pad. His face darkened as he read it.

"Well? What does it say?" Ben asked, standing on his tiptoes to see over the DCI's shoulder. "For God's sake, man, don't keep us in suspense!"

CHAPTER THIRTY-TWO

CHRISTOPHER BOYD LOWERED HIMSELF ONTO THE MIDDLE SEAT OF the couch, two glasses of wine in his hand. After these, they'd have polished off the whole bottle. He had a second one on standby, but the way things were going, he wouldn't need it.

He loved the single mothers. Always a cheap date.

This one was in her early-thirties, but could've passed for younger if she put a bit of effort in. She'd tried tonight, bless her. The make-up had been applied a little clumsily, the foundation inexpertly blended in around the neck.

A mother, maybe, but also a child playing dress-up.

He'd endured all her stories about her little boy. He was nine now —"Not so little anymore!"—and sounded, if Chris was being honest, like a right wee prick. He didn't tell her that, of course.

He never told them that.

Chris smiled as he handed her the glass, their fingers brushing together as he passed it from his hand to hers.

"Thanks," she said, mirroring his smile with one of her own. "I probably shouldn't, but..."

He clinked his glass against hers, and what little resistance was there, melted away. The *chink* the glasses made rang like a ringside bell around the living room.

Seconds out. Final round. Soon, he'd be moving in for the kill.

He watched her take a big sip. She winced, just a little, at the taste of it. He could hardly blame her. It was some Lidl shite. Cheapest of the cheap.

Good enough for her.

"Is it just me, or is it really warm all of a sudden?" she asked, blowing upwards onto her face, and making her fringe twitch.

Chris was sitting half-turned to face her, one elbow propped on the back cushion. He swirled his wine around in the glass, watching her. He'd set the heating timer to click on half an hour ago and rapidly ramp up the temperature. They usually blamed it on the wine.

"No. I'm alright," Chris said, his voice soft and low, like the *Best of Motown* album currently streaming from the living room Smart Speaker. "Want me to open a window?"

She pulled the collar of her shirt away from her neck and wafted it back and forth. "No. It's OK." She blew on her reddening face again and smiled at him. "Probably just the wine."

He clinked their glasses together again and took a drink, compelling her to do the same. They each had a gulp left.

Wouldn't be long now.

"I'm usually too cold. David's usually moaning that I've always got the heating on," she babbled.

He laughed falsely, trying not to show his irritation. Another David story. How *wonderful*.

"Kids," he said.

"You can say that again."

He sipped.

She sipped.

Soon. Very soon.

He slid a little closer, bringing the arm that was propped up on the back of the couch, right behind her head. She stiffened, but tried not to show it, as he idly curled a finger in her hair. She reddened further, her eyes gazing straight ahead, and brought her wine glass back to her lips.

"You have beautiful ears," Chris said, and she snorted a laugh into her glass.

He grinned, polished off the rest of his own drink, and set the glass on the coffee table.

"Do I really?" she asked, turning to face him.

Chris nodded. "Totally. The swirly bit. The sort of... dunkle thing. The *lobes*. Sweet Jesus, the lobes."

"I have good lobes?" she asked, smirking at him behind the rim of her glass.

"You have *exceptional* lobes," he told her. "I mean, sure, not as good as mine, but still. First class."

"You don't even have lobes!" she giggled.

"What? Yes, I do!" Chris protested. He felt his ears, his eyes widening in panic. "Shit. Where did they go?"

She laughed at that, the sound reverberating around inside her glass. She drained it, and he took it off her, sitting it on the table so it was touching his own.

He felt her tremble when he went back to toying with her hair. She was looking at him now, but it was taking an effort on her part. She was an introvert. He'd seen that at their first lesson together. He'd also seen the curve of her arse as he'd guided her up the wall ahead of him, and had been planning this moment ever since.

And not just this moment, of course, but all the moments to come over the next hour or so. He'd thought about those *a lot*.

It hadn't taken much to get her here. A few jokes. The odd compliment. A tiny bit of attention that didn't start with, "*Mu-um...*" That was all it took. That was all it ever took.

Pathetic, really.

He slid closer still, until his knee was touching the side of her leg. The jeans were from ASDA. He recognised the brand. They looked new.

Bless her. She was trying. Between the new outfit and the make-up, she really wanted to make an impression. She really wanted this to *work*.

And it would work. He'd make sure of it.

Tonight, at least.

She exhaled, and spoke in a fast whisper, as if confessing some deep, dark secret.

"It's been ages since I've done this."

She followed up with an embarrassed smile, like she couldn't quite believe she'd shared that information.

"Me, too," he told her, fingers still tickling down the back of her hair.

Her eyes went wide. Doubting, but hopeful.

"Really?"

"Mm-hm," he said, pressing the lie.

"Bullshit!" she scoffed. "I bet you do this all the time."

He shook his head, his eyes still fixed on hers. "Nm-mm. No."

She still looked doubtful, but he'd convinced her enough. Not that she'd needed much.

He heard her breath catch in her throat as he leaned in, still holding her gaze. His hand slipped onto her thigh. She closed her eyes, painted cheeks flushing with embarrassment, or arousal, or some heady mix of the two. Her lips were soft, welcoming.

Grateful.

His hand caressed her thigh, fingers kneading the flesh. She'd kept in shape. Total fucking personality vacuum, but she'd kept in shape. He'd give her that much, at least.

She didn't fight him as his hand slid down between her thighs. Didn't protest as he moved it upwards. Didn't resist as—

There was a knock at the front door.

No. More than that. A thumping. A hammering that threatened to shake the thing off its hinges.

"What the hell?" Chris said, reluctantly pulling away from his conquest.

The hammering came again, even louder this time than before. Who was out there knocking? A fucking gorilla?

"Alright, alright," he said, jumping up. He hurried past the coffee table, then stopped and picked up the bottle, holding it by its neck.

"What's going on?" asked the woman on the couch.

"I don't know. Wait here. Don't go anywhere," he instructed.

Another round of thumping filled the hall as Chris crept through it. He quickly and quietly slid the door security chain in place, tucked the bottle down beside him so it was out of sight, but ready to swing, and turned the snib of the lock.

"What the hell's the matter with you?" he demanded, pulling the door open until the chain went tight.

A bear of a man in a long overcoat stood on the step, two uniformed police officers flanking him a step behind. A police car was parked right outside his gate, the flashing blue lights licking across the fronts of the buildings on either side, picking out half a dozen faces that watched from around their curtains.

Chris recognised him at once. He'd met him just the day before.

"Christopher Boyd," said DCI Logan. He held up his warrant card, presumably in case the man on the other side of the door needed a refresher. "You're under arrest on suspicion of the murder of Mairi Sinclair."

CHAPTER THIRTY-THREE

DS McQuarrie slid a sheet of paper across the table until it was directly between Christopher Boyd and his solicitor, Lawrence Cairns, who had been brought in while Boyd was being fingerprinted and photographed.

The page showed a blown-up screenshot of a single text message from Mairi Sinclair's phone, with the sender's name above it, and the date and time below.

Christopher's gaze flicked over it far too quickly to have read it. "What's this? What are you showing me?"

Caitlyn eyeballed him across the table. "You know what this is, Mr Boyd. It's a text message you sent to Mairi Sinclair the day before she went missing. For the benefit of the tape, can you please read the message aloud?"

Christopher's gaze went from the DS to the page and back again. "I don't... I don't want to."

"Well, I'm asking you to," Caitlyn said.

She edged the paper closer to him.

"For the tape."

Christopher licked his dry lips. His eyes were bleary, and he held himself like someone suffering from an early onset hangover. He looked to his legal counsel, and Cairns gave a tiny shake of his head. The solicitor had a face like thunder on him. Clearly, this was not how he envisioned himself spending his Saturday evening.

"He doesn't have to read it out loud, Detective Sergeant. We both know that," Cairns said.

The chair beside Caitlyn's creaked as Logan leaned over and snatched up the paper. "Fine. I'll read it, then," he said.

He cleared his throat, and read the message in a flat, matter-of-fact voice.

"'What the fuck? You ungrateful cunt. What are you fucking playing at? Don't fucking ghost me, or you'll be fucking sorry. You fucking ungrateful slut.'"

Logan didn't look at Christopher yet. Instead, he turned the page so it was facing the solicitor. "Mr Cairns, can you confirm what I read is what is written on this printout?"

Cairns slid his glasses up the bridge of his nose and regarded the message on the paper. "Yes. That's what it says," he said. "But we don't know if that's an actual message that was sent to the victim. And, even if it was, anyone could have sent it."

"Oh, it was a real message, alright," Logan confirmed. "We have Mairi Sinclair's phone, and the phone records back it up. We've got the bods going through Mr Boyd's phone now. I'm sure they'll be able to confirm he deleted this message some time after it was sent."

In fact, Logan had no idea if they'd be able to confirm that or not. Still, it seemed to put the wind up the bastard, and that was the main thing.

"Even if it was sent from my client's phone, again, there's no saying he was the one who sent it," Cairns said. "It is entirely possible that someone else used his phone to send that message."

"Possible, I suppose, aye," Logan conceded. "Not exactly likely, though, is it?"

"It doesn't matter what you consider to be likely or not, Detective Chief Inspector. It matters what you can prove," Cairns said. "And I defy you to prove that my client sent that text message."

He smiled, showing off a set of teeth far too white and regimented to be natural.

"Now, unless you have something else, I think we'll be bidding you both a good evening and being on our way."

Logan glowered at the brief. "Well, then, looks like you won't be going anywhere for a while," he said. He let his gaze creep across to Boyd, who tried very hard not to wilt under the weight of it, but failed. "Because that's not all we've got. Is it, DS McQuarrie?"

"No, sir," said Caitlyn, adding her own stare to Logan's. "It is not."

"Where was it you said you were on Sunday, Mr Boyd?" Logan asked.

"I told you."

"Aye. I know. But I want you to tell me again."

"Aviemore," Christopher said. "There was a climbing talk. Bookshop organised it."

Logan leaned back and nodded. "Right, right. I remember now. A group of you went, didn't you? Who was it who drove again? John someone?"

"Maitland. That's right. He's in the Mountain Rescue."

"How was the talk? Good?" Logan asked.

Christopher's brow creased. He could sense a trap approaching, but had no idea how to stop himself walking straight into it.

"It was alright."

"About height or something, wasn't it?" Logan said. He flipped a page on the notepad in front of him. "Here we go. Highest vs Tallest: The Case for Redefining the World's Great Summits."

He folded his arms and looked to Caitlyn for her thoughts. "Sounds fascinating, eh?"

"Not really, sir," DS McQuarrie countered.

"No. No, I see what you're saying," Logan agreed. "Still, if you're into that sort of thing, I'm sure it's fascinating. Right, Mr Boyd?"

Christopher looked to his solicitor for support, but Cairns looked as much in the dark as his client.

"Yeah. It was interesting."

"You know what else is interesting?" Logan asked. "You know what else is *very* interesting indeed?"

Christopher shook his head and swallowed, sensing the trap was about to be sprung.

"We checked with the bookshop. They confirmed the talk took place. Someone there even checked that you were there. Found your ticket, confirmed it had been used."

Boyd almost giggled with relief. "See! I told you."

"The previous Sunday."

The words hung in the air between them. Logan let them settle in, enjoying the way the expression of glee that had briefly inhabited Boyd's face was now crumbling.

"N-no," Christopher said. "What? Was it?"

"Sunday fourteenth of July," Caitlyn said. She presented a printout of an Eventbrite page showing details of the event. "One week before the murder of Mairi Sinclair."

Boyd snatched up the page, hands trembling.

"You know what this means, don't you, Mr Boyd?" Logan asked. He waited until Christopher had lowered the page and raised his eyes to meet the detective's gaze. "You're alibi's a load of old shite."

Across the table, Christopher massaged his temples with the index and middle fingers of each hand. "Wait. Wait. It was... I just got mixed up. I'm sure it..." He inhaled, his breath a shaky quiver in his throat. "Give me a minute."

"Take your time," Logan said. "We've still got... what? Twenty-three hours until we have to charge you. Thereabouts. No rush."

He held a hand out to Caitlyn. She placed a clear plastic evidence bag in it without saying a word. A nurse, passing the surgeon his tools.

Logan deposited the bag on the table. "Can you tell me what that is, Mr Boyd?"

Christopher's eyebrows danced up and down on his forehead as he stared at the bag.

"It's a rope."

"You're right. It is a rope. Well done," Logan said. "It's the rope I took from your office yesterday, to be precise."

Boyd regarded it again, then gave the faintest of shrugs. "So?"

"It's also an exact match for the rope used to tie up Mairi Sinclair's body," Logan continued. "And I mean an *exact* match. They compare them both very close up, I'm told. Magnifying glass, probably. I don't know the science."

"Microscope, sir," Caitlyn corrected.

"*Microscope!*" said Logan, folding his arms and leaning forward so they rested on the table. "Hear that, Chris? A *microscope*. Amazing what they can do these days."

He clicked his tongue against the roof of his mouth. The *pop* sound it made was enough to make Boyd jump in fright.

"So, what have we got?" Logan said. "Motive? You were evidently angry at her for cancelling your date. You could argue—and believe me, we will—that the message you sent her was a threat of physical harm. The fact you deleted it suggests a measure of guilt on your part, but we'll come back to that.

"Alibi? Fuck all. That's gone," the DCI continued, waving a hand. "Opportunity? You knew where she lived, you haven't been able to tell us what else you were doing on the day she went missing, and you've got a fancy motor with a big boot. So, I'm going to say 'yes' to that one."

He tapped the plastic bag with a finger. "And then there's this, of course. Can't forget this, can we, Detective Sergeant?"

"No, sir. Can't forget that," Caitlyn agreed.

Logan leaned further across the table and dropped his voice into a conspiratorial whisper. "And I'm betting when we compare the DNA samples we took from you with what we've found in Mairi's car, we're going to get a nice big fat match."

"Conjecture," Cairns protested.

"Overruled," Logan told him. He smiled, or maybe bared his teeth. It was hard to say for sure. "See? I know the lingo, too, sunshine. And you're in my court now."

He let Cairns stew on that for a moment, then turned his attention back to Christopher. The smile fell away as suddenly as it had appeared.

"Why'd you do it, Chris?"

Boyd shook his head. "I didn't."

"I mean, I get the crime of passion angle. You were angry. Fine. We've seen that before," Logan continued. "But fuck me. The symbols. Her *eyes*? That was going above and beyond. What were you thinking?"

Boyd's mouth flapped open and closed. A fish out of water.

"What? I didn't do anything. What about her eyes?"

He looked to his brief for support. "What's he talking about? What about her eyes? What symbols?"

"You know fine well what I'm talking about, Chris," Logan hissed. "You mutilated her, you killed her, you tied her up with climbing rope, and then you dumped her over the falls. Right?"

"N-no. That's not what happened!"

"Oh? Then tell me how it did happen," Logan said. "Did you kill her first and then mutilate her?"

"No! I didn't do any of it! It wasn't me!"

His breathing was coming in short, unsteady gulps. His eyes were wide, the pupils dilating.

"Sunday. Sunday. Sunday," he said, the word babbling out of him over and over again. "What was I...? I must've..."

"Cut the shite, son," Logan barked. "We both know what you were doing on Sunday. You were torturing and murdering an innocent woman. You were disposing of a body. You were—"

There was a knock at the door. It opened a crack without waiting for the instruction.

"Boss?"

Logan flinched, then bit down on his lip, stopping an outburst before it could start.

"DC Neish. We're kind of in the middle of something here."

"Uh, yeah. There's a phone call. Asking for you, specifically."

"Take a number. I'll call them back," Logan said, still not turning towards the door.

Tyler shuffled awkwardly from foot to foot. Caitlyn had turned in her chair and was glaring daggers in the junior detective's direction. It wasn't anywhere near the standard of Logan's stare, but it was still pretty damn fierce.

"You're going to want to take this one, boss," Tyler insisted.

Logan's chair creaked as he turned. Tyler smiled weakly.

"Trust me."

CHAPTER THIRTY-FOUR

The wipers of Logan's Ford Focus THWUMPED BACK AND FORTH, fighting a losing battle against the downpour that was currently launching a diagonal assault on the windscreen. The full-beam of the headlights painted two overlapping cones of light on the road ahead, and the trees that lined it on the left.

Logan tore his eyes from the road long enough to glance at his satnav. Close now. Three minutes.

Another car rounded a bend in the road ahead. Both drivers dipped their headlights until they'd passed each other, then clicked them back up to full power. Logan caught a brief glimpse of Loch Ness through the line of trees that rounded the curve in the road. Or rather, he caught an *impression* of it—a vast darkness looming beyond the tree-line, into which the car's headlights couldn't possibly penetrate.

Two minutes.

He replayed the call in his head, as he powered on through the rain. *Calls*, technically. The caller had hung up four times during the conversation, convinced he was being traced, and that this would somehow throw them off the scent.

Hollywood had a lot to answer for.

Once all the initial 'pleasantries' had been exchanged, the actual point of the conversation had been simple enough. An address and an instruction.

"Come alone."

Ben had protested about that part, of course, but Logan had given his word. He'd eventually set Ben's mind at rest by letting Hamza set up some sort of tracking app on his phone, which meant they could follow its location. Hamza, Tyler, and Caitlyn would follow a couple of miles behind, and only move in if they smelled a rat.

At least, that was the theory. But the address had led him to a phone box in the arse-end of nowhere, and the note inside had given him a second location, along with instructions to leave his phone in the booth.

There was a small wireless video camera fixed to the corner of the phone box. Logan had no idea if it was genuine, but he decided it wasn't worth the risk. He'd held his phone up to it, then placed the device on the ground before showing his hands were now empty.

That done, he'd got back in his car, programmed the new address into the satnav, and set off into the night.

"You have arrived at your destination," chimed a female voice, snapping Logan back to the present.

He clicked on the indicator, tapped the brakes, and steered the car onto the driveway of a darkened house. It was a new build. Close to being finished, but not quite done. The walls and windows were all in, but the roof was covered in black plastic, and the grounds were still mostly builder's rubble.

Of course. The address had seemed vaguely familiar when Logan had seen it written down, and now he knew why. It was one of the sites from Caitlyn's list. Its placement on the opposite side of the loch to where the body had been discovered had bumped it down the list of priorities, though, and there would have been nothing obvious from the drive-by to suggest anything about the place might be amiss.

The car's headlights shone in through the window as Logan pulled up, casting the impossibly large shadow of a figure across the unpainted wall of the room beyond.

He cut the engine. The lights stayed on when he opened the door and stepped out, only dying once he'd reached the house's front door. He entered without knocking, finding himself in a space that would eventually be a hallway, but wasn't quite there yet.

Three empty doorways and an unfinished staircase led off from it. Only one of the doorways could feasibly lead to the room at the front where Logan had seen the figure. The glow of candlelight flickering from within that room confirmed this, and Logan's feet *clumped* on the bare floorboards as he advanced in that direction.

A man stood in the centre of the room, silhouetted by the candle sitting on a stack of cement bags behind him. He was big. Well-built. Probably wouldn't need the sledgehammer he clutched in both hands, but he'd brought it along, anyway.

Logan looked him up and down for a moment, then around at the unfinished room. Finally, he put his hands in the pockets of his overcoat and gave a disinterested sort of shrug.

"Well, Mr Steadwood?" he asked. "What can I do for you?"

CHAPTER THIRTY-FIVE

"I SHOULD HAVE DRIVEN."

Caitlyn turned in the driver's seat to look at Tyler.

"Why should you have driven?"

"Well, I've done the advanced course," Tyler said.

"We've all done the advanced course," Caitlyn countered.

"I've done it twice," Hamza chipped in from the back seat.

"No, but... I know. I just think I should have driven," Tyler said. "It's technically my car."

"But it's not, though, is it?" said Caitlyn. "Not really."

"It sort of is. And I should've driven. I'm not making a big fuss about it. I'm just saying."

Tyler shifted in the front passenger seat and crossed his arms. "I think I should've driven."

They sat in silence for a while. The screen of Hamza's phone lit up as he tapped it. Caitlyn looked back at him in the mirror.

"Anything?"

"He hasn't moved in a while," Hamza replied. The light from the phone screen picked out the lines of concern on his face. "Reckon he's alright?"

"I'm sure he's fine. He can handle himself."

"Steadwood's a big bastard, though," Hamza pointed out.

Tyler turned in the passenger seat. "Have you seen the size of the boss? It's the other guy I'm worried about."

"Won't do him any good if he gets taken by surprise, though," Hamza pointed out. "Nothing you can do then."

Tyler groaned. "'This isn't going to be another story about you getting stabbed, is it?" he asked.

Caitlyn smirked. "Did DC Khaled get stabbed?" she asked. "He's never mentioned it."

"No, he doesn't like to talk about it," Tyler said. "Except at every available opportunity."

"Ha-fucking-ha," Hamza said. "I'm just saying. It happens. You can be the strongest, toughest person in the world, then some wee bastard sneaks up behind you and..."

"Stabs you repeatedly in the lower back?" Caitlyn said.

"For example, aye," Hamza said. "Not specifically that, necessarily, but aye."

"Sorry, I'm still on the 'strongest, toughest person in the world' thing," Tyler said. "You weren't seriously describing yourself there, were you? Because no offence, mate, but you're not even the toughest person in this car."

"Aye, but neither are you," Caitlyn told him.

"Close second, though," Tyler said.

"Distant second."

A white van flew past, headed south past the layby they were parked in, far too fast for the road and the conditions. The speed and the closeness of it rocked the car.

"Twat," Tyler muttered.

Caitlyn reached for the keys in the ignition, the instinct to give chase kicking in. She caught herself before she could fire up the engine, and forced the urge back down. Now wasn't the time.

They sat in silence for a while. It was Tyler who eventually broke it.

"I spy, with my little eye, something beginning with..."

"Rain," said Caitlyn.

Tyler tutted. "Right. Your turn."

"Nah. You're alright," Caitlyn said. She looked at Hamza in the mirror. "Anything yet?"

His face lit-up in blue-white light as he opened his phone again. He studied the screen for a moment, then shook his head.

"No," he said. He gazed out through the side window. The world beyond seemed twisted and warped by the streaks of water meandering down the outside of the glass. "Nothing yet."

"SIT DOWN," Steadwood instructed.

"I'm fine where I am, thanks," Logan replied, but the other man was having none of it.

"Fucking sit down," he hissed, brandishing the sledgehammer. He nodded towards another stack of concrete bags. "Sit there."

Logan considered his options, starting with the bunch of keys one hand was clutching in his coat pocket, the keys themselves poking up between his fingers. Steadwood was big, but the sledgehammer was a heavy and clumsy weapon. There was a reasonable chance Logan could get in close before the other man could complete a swing.

Still, jamming a Yale into the side of Steadwood's face was hardly going to convince him to start talking. And he clearly wanted to talk, or he wouldn't have called in to set up the meeting.

Logan sat, but kept the keys in his hand and his options open.

"Right. I'm sitting. What do you want?"

"Did you come alone?"

"What do you think?"

"*Did you fucking come alone?*"

Logan sighed. "Aye. I came alone." He motioned to the darkened grounds in front of the house. "See for yourself."

Steadwood backed towards the window, not taking his eyes off Logan.

Once he was close enough, he shot a couple of brief glances out into the gloom, then returned to somewhere just beyond hammer-striking distance.

"Good. That's good. That's good. What about your phone?"

Logan groaned inwardly. Fake camera, then.

"In the phone box, as instructed. I showed it to the camera."

"Oh. Aye. Aye, right. Good," Steadwood said.

He half-turned for a moment, and the candlelight picked out some of the detail of his face. That dead-eyed sneer of contempt that he'd worn in his mugshot photo had been replaced by something raw and desperate.

Logan recognised the tell-tale signs of a man who hadn't slept properly in days. God knew, he'd seen them in the mirror often enough.

"They're saying I killed Mairi. Your lot. That's what they're saying, isn't it?"

Logan shook his head. "No. We said we wanted to talk to you in connection with her murder."

"Same fucking thing."

"You have to admit, Robbie, it doesn't look great, does it?" Logan said. "You two don't exactly have the most auspicious past. Then, you get back together, and a little while later she turns up dead and you vanish off the face of the Earth. Tongues were always going to wag and fingers were bound to start pointing."

"We weren't back together. We shagged a couple of times, that was it."

"Oh, well that changes everything," Logan told him. "You should've just said. That would've cleared everything right up."

Steadwood looked confused. He tightened his grip on the sledgehammer's handle, as if taking comfort from it.

"I was being sarcastic there," Logan felt compelled to point out. "It doesn't change anything."

"What if I told you she was fucking blackmailing me?" Steadwood spat. "Would that change anything?"

Logan considered this. "Aye, maybe," he conceded. "But not in your favour."

He watched the other man, waiting for the penny to drop. It didn't.

"In that it would give you a pretty clear motive for killing her," he explained.

"I didn't fucking kill her! I told you!"

"Then why hide, Robbie?" Logan asked.

"Because I knew you lot would try to pin it on me. And I didn't do it. I didn't kill her."

He gripped the sledgehammer even more tightly until his knuckles turned white. He was one good swing-length away, and the odds of Logan making it to him in time were substantially worse now that he was sitting down.

"Alright. You didn't kill her. Let's go with that for the moment," he said. "Tell me about the blackmail."

Steadwood glanced to the window and the door as if to make sure no one was listening in.

"She'd been getting some stuff off me."

"Hash," Logan said.

Steadwood looked briefly surprised, but then nodded. "Aye. Just a bit here and there. Didn't want to do too much because of her job, an' that. She was pretty skint, so she couldn't really pay for it. We came to an... arrangement."

A jigsaw piece clicked into place.

"The sex."

"Aye," Steadwood admitted. "That was the deal."

"Whose idea was that?" Logan asked.

"Mine," Steadwood said, without any hint of regret. "But she was right up for it."

"That can't be what she was blackmailing you about."

"What? No. I fucking wish," Steadwood said. "She found out where I was getting the stuff from."

Another piece. Another click.

"Bosco. She threatened to tell him you were nicking from him?"

Steadwood nodded. "At first, aye. But that was just the start of it. She started getting these ideas. These stupid fucking ideas. I told her to cut it out. Told her what would happen."

"What kind of ideas?" Logan asked.

"She wanted to talk to Bosco directly. She said she was going to threaten him. Said she'd grass us all up if Bosco didn't give her a payoff."

Jesus. Obviously, the woman didn't know Bosco Maximuke.

"Did she ever speak to him?"

"I don't... I don't know," Steadwood admitted. "But if she did, or if Bosco found out what she was planning..."

He let out a shaky breath. The candlelight picked out the sudden wetness of his eyes.

"I wasn't hiding from your lot. I was hiding from him. If Bosco killed Mairi, then he knows. He fucking knows. And I'm a dead man."

Logan nodded. "Aye. Probably."

He stood up.

"Best of luck, Mr Steadwood."

Robbie blinked. "What?"

"It's late. I should be getting back," Logan said. "If I don't show face back at the station soon, we'll have a dozen armed response bastards kicking in the door before we know it."

Steadwood tensed. "What? You said you were alone. You left your phone at the phone box."

"Aye," Logan confirmed. "But I left your note, too. The one with the address on it."

Even in the dim light, he saw the other man's face go pale. It really made his tattoos pop.

"Seems like an oversight that, Robbie. Shame, because it was textbook stuff, otherwise," Logan said.

He made for the door, his hands still in his pockets, the keys still bunched in his fist.

"Thanks for the information, though. Good chat. If you start running now, you might get away before Bosco finds you. Buy yourself a week or two, anyway. Give you time to get your affairs in order. That sort of thing."

"What? No. Stop!" Steadwood warned, his voice rising. "Don't fucking move. You can't just leave me."

"Aye. I can," Logan said. "Goodbye, Mr Steadwood."

He stopped by the door. Only then did he look back.

"I'd say it's been a pleasure but, well, you're an arsehole, so I'd be lying."

He nodded, and tapped a finger to his forehead in salute. "Seriously, though. Why are you still here? You need to get going, and get going fast. If Bosco did kill Mairi, you don't want to go through the same thing. Trust me."

Robbie stood rooted to the spot, his mouth hanging open, his fingers twisting the sledgehammer handle like it was a stress toy.

"Or, you could put down the hammer and come with me," Logan suggested. He took the keys from his pocket, spun them around one finger, and headed out into the hallway.

His voice drifted back in through the doorway, and echoed around the bare room.

"Your choice, son."

CHAPTER THIRTY-SIX

LOGAN EASED DOWN ON THE ACCELERATOR, HOPING TO BEAT THE lights. He tutted quietly when the watery splash of green on the windscreen became orange, then red.

Steadwood fidgeted nervously in the seat beside him as Logan brought the car to a stop. They were by the Abriachan junction, the steep road running up the hill to the left of the car, a wide turning area just off the road on the right.

The wipers were going full-tilt, a steady percussion of *ka-thunk-ka-thunk* as they valiantly battled the rain.

"Bloody roadworks. This time of night," Logan muttered.

"It's quieter. Everyone bitches about it being done during the day, so they try to do it at night," Steadwood explained through a mouthful of his own thumbnail. He'd chewed the nails of the other nine digits down to the quick, and was going for the full house. "Picked some night for it, though."

"Aye," Logan agreed. He tapped his fingers on the wheel and dipped his headlights in anticipation of something coming the other way. No sign yet, but presumably the sensor at the other end had picked up something approaching. "Some night."

They sat in silence for a while, waiting.

"One thing I don't get," Logan said, keeping his gaze fixed ahead.

"What's that?"

"Bosco. I've been involved in murder cases before that we suspected he had a hand in. Couldn't prove anything, though. He never did anything like this."

"What, kill a woman?" Steadwood said. "I don't think he'd have a problem doing that."

"Oh, no. He's an equal opportunity bastard, alright. No, not that," Logan said. "I mean the... voodoo stuff. Whatever it is. The symbols. The eyes."

He heard Steadwood shift in his seat, saw the look of confusion out of the corner of his eye.

"What?"

Logan spared him the briefest of looks. Steadwood's expression seemed genuine enough. He had no idea what the DCI was on about.

"Mairi's body was covered in symbols. Carved right into her," Logan said. "And her eyes had been removed."

"Fuck. What? Fuck!" Steadwood ejected. The words became a wheeze, like his airways were tightening up. "What kind of symbols?"

Logan shrugged. "Just symbols, really. We looked into them. Something to do with warding off evil spirits. Demons, or whatever."

"Jesus," Steadwood hissed. He put a hand on the dash, as if having to steady himself. "Jesus Christ. Seriously?"

"Not really something I'd joke about, son," Logan said.

He craned his neck, looking along the empty stretch of road for any sign of an approaching vehicle, but finding none.

Another vehicle had drawn up behind them. A van, judging by the way the beam of its headlights filled the inside of Logan's car. He muttered something uncomplimentary, and angled the rear view mirror up towards the ceiling to stop himself being dazzled.

"It's about the house. That fucking Ouija board," Steadwood said.

Logan shot him a look and held it this time. "What?"

"When we were kids, we went to this house. Boleskine. Supposed to be all black magic, or whatever."

"So I've heard."

"We drove out there one day years back. Did the Ouija board. Mairi was right into it. She went all, like, Gothy, or Emo, or whatever you call it. Used to get her proper horny, too," Steadwood said. There was a wistful sort of look on his face as he trawled back through some memorable moments. "She kept saying she'd been possessed by one of the demons. Complete bollocks, obviously, but I went along with it for all the freaky shit."

The sound of the van's engine reverberated around the inside of the car.

The lights were still red, and there was no sign of anything coming in the opposite direction.

The fine hairs on the back of Logan's neck stood on end.

It had been half an hour since he'd driven this road in the opposite direction. He hadn't been stopped then. Had the lights even been on?

"But it wasn't just the two of us. At the house, I mean. Doing the Ouija board stuff. It wasn't just us."

"What are you saying?" he asked, only half-listening.

"I'm saying that Bosco didn't kill her," Steadwood said. It came out like a giggle of relief. "It wasn't Bosco. And that means he isn't after me."

"Not Bosco? Then who was it?" Logan asked, turning in his seat to look in Steadwood's direction.

That was when he saw the headlights rapidly approaching down the hill.

Big. Bright. Blinding.

Close.

"Shite!"

The gearstick crunched. Logan's foot hit the floor.

Before it could move, an ear-splitting impact filled the car with glass and thunder.

The world slammed sideways.

Tumbled. Rolled. Flipped upside-down.

The horn blared—a long, continuous tone, like the mournful cry of a grieving whale.

Logan heard shouts from nearby, whimpers of pain from closer still.

He heard doors slam. Footsteps racing.

Felt blood tickle down his face.

And then, darkness rushed in, swallowing him whole.

CHAPTER THIRTY-SEVEN

Lights. Voices. Movement.

Pain.

A hand on his forehead. A pinprick in his arm. A comforting word in his ear.

Darkness again. Deeper than before.

Deeper than he'd ever thought possible.

He revelled in it for a while, licking his wounds. How long, he couldn't say, but long enough. Too long, maybe.

He kicked for the surface, latching onto a sound. Repetitive. Familiar.

Bloody annoying.

He followed it through the chasm of black that surrounded him, sticking close to it as the black became shades of grey, then white.

His eyelids fluttered. Blinked. Opened.

The coroner, Shona Maguire, leaned over him, smiling down.

"Christ. That can't be a good sign," Logan croaked.

Shona appeared momentarily confused, then it clicked.

"Oh. Yes. Haha. No, don't worry, you're not dead."

She looked him up and down. "I'm told it was a close-run thing, mind you. But you're still in the land of the living."

Logan moved to sit up. It quickly became apparent that this would be a terrible mistake on his part, and he fell back onto the pillow with the room spinning in big looping circles.

He was in a bed in a private room, assorted cables and tubes hooked up to various parts of his anatomy. He hurt. A lot. So much so, in fact, that it was difficult to pinpoint any one specific pain. Instead, his whole body felt like one big bruise, while the worst hangover he'd ever had played a drum solo inside his skull.

Over the din of all that, Logan heard the sound that had led him out of the darkness. It came from a phone that sat on the smooth plastic table beside his bed.

"See? Computer generated non-binaural audio," Shona said, following his gaze. She tapped the phone, silencing it. "Thought it was worth a go. Besides, I couldn't find *Come on Eileen*."

"You don't find *Come on Eileen*," Logan said. "*Come on Eileen* finds you."

It was only after he'd said this that it occurred to him he had no idea what he meant by it. Clearly, his brain had taken a fair old rattling.

He decided to gloss over it and pretend it hadn't happened.

"What do you remember?" Shona asked. She leaned in closer, studying his eyes. In a medical sort of way, he thought. Nothing more.

His initial instinct was to answer the question with *not a lot*, but then an image popped into his head. A series of them, in fact, flashing up one after the other.

Lights growing larger. A vehicle closing in. A man, silhouetted in the passenger seat.

"Steadwood!"

Shona flinched. "Aye. I've seen him, already," she said. "In a more... professional capacity."

The migraine drilling through Logan's skull made him miss the nuance of this.

"What do you mean?"

"Let's just say, he's not looking as good as you are," Shona said.

Logan spent the next few seconds cursing at the polystyrene tiles of the ceiling. This quickly tired him out and he sunk into the pillow, breathing heavily.

"You done?" Shona asked.

"Aye. For now," Logan wheezed.

"Good. He died at the scene, if you're wondering. Pretty instant. And I ate your sandwich."

Logan's eyes flicked left and right, processing everything she'd just said.

"What sandwich?" he asked.

Shona held up an empty plastic wrapper. "Nurse brought it in on a tray earlier, in case you fancied it. Didn't look like you were going to wake up anytime soon, and we did agree you owed me lunch..."

Logan wasn't sure if he had actually agreed to that or not, but he... Wait.

"Lunch? What time is it?"

"Just after half two," Shona told him.

Logan looked around the room until he found the clock on the wall.

"But, you know, check for yourself, don't just take my word for it," Shona told him.

"Half two?" the DCI grimaced. "On what?"

Shona hesitated. "Uh... On my watch?"

"What day?"

"Oh. Sunday. Twenty-eighth of July," Shona told him. Logan let out a little sigh of relief. "In the year twenty-forty-seven!" Shona concluded. "Dun, dun, *duu-uun.*"

Logan looked largely unimpressed by this, so Shona shook her head. "It isn't. That was Fake News. Sorry. The accident was yesterday."

"Sleeping Beauty up and about, is he?"

Logan and Shona both looked over to the door in time to see Ben Forde chapping on its little glass window. He carried a copy of *The Sunday Post*, and looked ever-so-slightly disappointed that he might not get a chance to sit and do the crossword, after all.

"Sure is. Doctors haven't been in yet," Shona said. She stepped aside, making room for Ben to take her place. "I'll go corner one and get them to come in and check you over."

Ben nodded and smiled at her as she passed him on the way to the door. He waited until she was safely out of earshot before taking a seat on the plastic chair beside Logan's bed.

"What was she doing here?" he wondered. "Touting for business, was she?"

"Something like that," Logan said. He coughed. It hurt tremendously—a sharp, stabbing pain that cut through the fug in his head and snapped him back into some semblance of focus. "Tell me you got them."

Ben tapped his newspaper on his knee a couple of times. "Cleared off before we got there. Doused the insides and burned it out. Scene of Crime team had a look, but there wasn't much of it left."

"Shite. What about the other one?"

The creases on Ben's brow deepened. "Other one?"

"There was a van behind. White, I think, but the lights made it hard to tell."

"No sign of it at the scene. We'll get on it."

Logan knew there wasn't much point, but made some vague noises of approval all the same.

"Alright there, boss?"

Tyler stuck his head around the door, all smiles. Logan and Ben both simultaneously smacked their lips together, indicating their thirst.

"Fuck's sake," Tyler muttered, before disappearing outside again.

"He's a good lad," Ben said. "Everyone was worried about you. I told you not to go off yourself. I should've gone with you."

"Aye. You could've been in the bed opposite," Logan said. He shook his head. "Nothing anyone could've done."

Ben conceded the point with a nod. "Suppose so. We're looking out for Robbie Steadwood's next of kin. The only one we can find at the moment is Stuart Sinclair."

"Jesus. Of course," said Logan, closing his eyes. "God. He's had some week of it, eh?"

"Poor kid," Ben agreed. He shifted in the chair, opened his mouth to say something, then closed it again.

Despite having his eyes closed, Logan somehow picked up on it.

"What else?" he asked.

"Hmm?"

"What were you going to say?"

Ben puffed out his cheeks and scratched his head, as if trying to recall.

"Spit it out," Logan told him, finally opening his eyes.

"It's Christopher Boyd."

"Don't tell me he's dead as well?"

"No. Worse, maybe," Ben said. "He's got an alibi. Remembered it once you'd, and I quote, 'stopped bullying him.'"

"Bullying him? What is he, twelve?" Logan grunted. "What's the alibi?"

"Work."

"Work? That's it? 'Work.'"

Ben nodded. "Aye. Says he's been working so much lately he lost track of the days. Short staffed."

"Did we verify it?"

"Afraid so. Security cameras show he was there the whole weekend. Checked lesson logs and confirmed with a couple of the students that he'd been the one giving the lessons. All checks out."

"And the rope?"

"Same rope they sell at the climbing place. Bank statements show Mairi made a purchase there a couple of weeks ago that matches the price they sell it for."

"So, she was tied up with her own rope?" Logan sighed. "Aye, well. To be honest, I wasn't really feeling it, anyway. I think Boyd's a horrible bastard, but I don't peg him for a killer."

"So, we're back to Robbie Steadwood," Ben concluded.

Logan said nothing.

"Right?"

"Hmm? Aye. Maybe. I mean... I suppose it fits."

"But?"

"He said he didn't do it."

"Oh, well then. In that case..."

Logan rolled his eyes. It hurt quite a lot, and he made a mental note not to do it again. "It's not just that. Mairi had been threatening to grass up Bosco. She wanted a pay-off."

Ben choked on his own saliva. He spent a few seconds coughing, his eyes almost bulging out of his head. "She threatened Bosco Maximuke? For *money*? Jesus Christ. We should get her cause of death verdict changed to 'suicide.' What the bloody hell was she thinking there?"

"Steadwood didn't think she'd actually spoken to Bosco. She was trying to do it all through him. He was understandably reluctant to be the go between," Logan explained.

"No bloody wonder. Probably didn't want to end up eating his own bollocks."

"Who's eating their own bollocks?" asked DC Neish, carrying a couple of paper cups into the room with near-superhuman levels of concentration.

"Will you learn no' to fill them right to the top?" Ben tutted, watching Tyler shuffle across the floor.

"It wasn't me this time. It was the machine," Tyler protested.

Ben glared at him, aghast. "Machine? Don't tell me you used the machine."

Tyler looked from Ben to Logan and back again. In order to do this without spilling any of the tea, he stopped walking.

"Uh, yeah. Why?"

"There's a perfectly good tearoom just... what?" Ben said. "Three floors down."

"But the machine's just down the hall," Tyler pointed out.

"Aye, but the tea'll be shite from a machine, won't it?" said Logan. "Away you go down and get us some proper tea."

"And they do good cakes down there," Ben added. "I'll have something with cream in it. An eclair, maybe."

He turned to Logan. "Wee eclair?"

"Aye," said Logan. "Aye. I could go a wee eclair."

They watched Tyler expectantly.

"Well?" said Ben. He made a shooing motion. "Go on, then."

Tyler peered down at the paper cups in his hand, then back over his shoulder at the door.

"Is there something you want to say, DC Neish?" Logan asked, his voice dropping into something not far off a growl.

Tyler swallowed and squared his shoulders, pulling himself up to his full height. "No."

Ben's eyebrows drew closer together. "No? No what? No, there's nothing you want to say?"

"No, I'm not going to get more tea," Tyler said. The first few words came out slowly, then the rest all at once in a slightly panicky gasp. He held up the cups. "I got you tea. If it's not good enough, go get it yourself."

Logan and Ben both stared at the younger officer.

There was a low groaning sound as the leg of Ben's chair scraped backwards across the vinyl flooring and Ben stood up. He eyeballed the junior officer, squaring up to him as if ready to fight.

And then, Logan and Ben both brought their hands up and clapped. Tyler's face, which had adopted a sort of rabbit-in-headlights expression, crinkled in confusion.

"High bloody time," Ben said, still clapping.

Tyler looked between both men, the cups still in his hand. He looked like he had a hundred questions running through his head, but he settled on a generic, "What?" presumably in the hope that it would cover everything.

"You're no' a tea bitch, son," Logan told him. "It was high time you realised that."

"What? So..." Tyler's head continued to tick-tock between them. "What?"

Ben chuckled and both men stopped clapping. "Don't worry about it, son. Just put the cups down on the table."

"Oh. Right, yeah," said Tyler. He continued his slow shuffle, then sat the cups down. "That one's yours," he said, placing one of them nearer to Ben.

"You're alright. I'm not really a tea hand."

Tyler laughed for a moment, but then realised DI Forde was being serious. "What? You didn't want tea?"

"No. We just wanted to see if you'd go get it," Ben said. "I could murder a coffee, though."

"Ha! Yeah. Good one," said Tyler.

Ben held his gaze. "No, really. Just the machine will be fine."

DC Neish searched Ben's face for any indication as to how he should respond to this. He saw nothing there but honest sincerity.

"Coffee?"

"Black. Two sugars," Ben said. "Thanks, son."

He turned in his chair to face Logan. Tyler hung back for a few seconds, considered all his options, then backed out of the door.

"Ah well. One step at a time, I suppose," said Ben, sounding just a little disappointed.

"The truck that hit me," said Logan, steering the conversation back on track. "One of Bosco's?"

"No. Different building firm. Not related," Ben said. "We've checked driver records, but they're saying it was stolen off one of their sites yesterday evening. Shouldn't have been anyone driving it."

"Bosco always was a slippery bastard," Logan muttered. He pushed back the covers of his bed, revealing an unflattering hospital gown. "We'll see what he says when I ask him face to face."

"I think you should be staying where you are, Jack," Ben protested. "At least speak to the doctor."

Logan swung his legs out of bed. The floor felt icy cold against his bare feet, and immediately sent his head into a spin. He swallowed down something that might have been bile and might have been vomit, then reached under the gown, feeling for the ECG pads stuck to his chest.

"I'm sure they've got my number," he said. There was a *rrrip* as he tore one of the pads free. "They know where to find me."

CHAPTER THIRTY-EIGHT

"Aha! Detective Logan. Please. Sit. Come. Sit. You do not look well."

Logan stood just inside Bosco's office, fighting the urge to lean on the door frame for support.

A flustered-looking doctor had cornered him for a brief conversation on his way out of the hospital, and had made a pretty rock-solid case for Logan taking a couple of days to rest and recover. He'd suffered three broken ribs, a few nasty head cuts, and a hefty concussion in the crash. He had no business being up and about, the doctor had insisted. No business at all.

Logan had thanked him for his concern and then gone ahead and checked himself out. He elected not to mention the neck stiffness, shoulder pain, or the way his right knee now *clunked* whenever he tried to straighten the leg.

He could cope with it. Most of it was fine, in fact, provided he didn't make any sudden movements. The ribs were just a dull ache as long as he stood perfectly still and didn't do anything stupid.

Like breathing, for example.

Larger movements made pain burn through his left side—a kettle-full of boiling water that poured from his armpit down to his waist, and made him hiss through his teeth. He'd sneezed earlier. That had been an experience he had no desire to ever repeat again.

"What happened to you?" asked Bosco. He was sitting behind his desk, fiddling idly with a stress ball shaped like a single breast. "Was it accident?"

Logan shook his head. Something in his neck went *twang*. He ignored it.

"No."

"Oh?" Bosco looked him up and down. "Someone did this on purpose? But who would wish to hurt you?"

"I'm pretty sure we both know the answer to that."

Bosco stuck out his bottom lip and looked blankly at him. "No. No, I cannot imagine. An upstanding law figure like you?" He shook his head. "It is disgrace anyone would do this."

With a *haach-phtu*, he spat on the floor.

"Disgrace."

He motioned vaguely in the direction of the window. "My advice to you? You should get away. Take holiday. Rest. I would be happy to contribute to cost of this. For old time sake."

"You killed Robbie Steadwood," Logan said.

"Robbie Steadwood? Robbie Steadwood?" said Bosco, stroking his chin. He straightened and clicked his fingers. "Ah! *Robbie* Steadwood. I remember. Yes."

He adopted an expression of surprise. It was even more fake than the bastard's tan. "Wait, Robbie is dead? Oh dear. This is first I hear of this sad news. My condolence to his family."

"You knew he was going to co-operate with us," Logan said. "You knew he was going to tell us about the drugs."

"Was he? I guess we will never know," Bosco said. "Besides, he is murderer, yes? He killed bitch-whore woman. I am respected businessman."

He thumped a fist against his chest. "I am Bosco Maximuke! If is my word against his, I think my word is winner, yes? And I say there are no drugs here. No drugs anywhere I go. Clean. Yes? Spotless clean. No drugs anywhere."

Bosco got up from his chair, gave the stress-boob another squeeze, then set it on the desk. He hummed quietly as he approached the cabin's single window and looked out at the yard. Four police cars were spread out across it, lights flashing. He could see half a dozen uniformed officers in high-vis vests. A couple of them followed spaniels on leads, the dogs' noses pressed to the ground as they zig-zagged left and right.

"Aw. Puppies," Bosco remarked. "So cute and adorable."

He turned away from the window. "They will not find anything. You know this. This is legitimate business. There is nothing to find."

Bosco looked so unconcerned, so unshakably full of confidence that Logan knew he was right. They were wasting their time. The bastard had already covered his tracks.

"I'm going to be watching you, Bosco," Logan warned. "You won't be able to blow your fucking nose in this town without me hearing about it. It'll be just like the old days."

"No. Not like old days. You are new to city, detective," Bosco said. "Me? I know many people. I have many friends. Everywhere, the eyes and the ears. Some within your own organisation."

He beamed and held his arms out at his sides. "I am popular man. What can I say?"

The smile fell away. "You? You have nothing. No car. No family. And I hear even the apartment you were due to rent has fallen through."

Logan bristled, his eyes narrowing.

"Oh. You did not know? Shame. Someone outbid you, I believe." His smile returned, broader than ever. "I wonder who that could have been?"

Bosco sat down in his chair, interlocked his fingers, and rested his hands on his belly. "You look tired. Take a holiday, detective," he said, the chair complaining loudly about his weight. "And, I suggest you do not come back."

CHAPTER THIRTY-NINE

THE GENERAL CONSENSUS BACK AT THE STATION SEEMED TO BE TO keep out of Logan's way. He paced back and forth across the Incident Room, muttering below his breath and occasionally letting out a grunt of pain when he turned the wrong way, or put too much weight on his injured leg.

Caitlyn, Tyler, and Hamza sat at their desks, busying themselves at their keyboards, or staring intently at documents. All of them—even Tyler—had taken one look at the DCI and concluded that now probably wasn't the best time to open their mouths about... well, anything whatsoever.

DI Forde didn't share the same sentiment. None of them could figure out if he was brave, or just stupid.

"You shouldn't be here, Jack. You should still be in hospital," Ben told him.

Logan's head snapped angrily in Ben's direction. Pain raced up the side of his neck, forcing a hiss through his teeth.

"See? You need to get some rest. You're doing yourself no favours."

"I need to solve two murders, is what I need to do," Logan bit back.

"Aye, well. We can handle that, until you get back," Ben said. "Besides, as far as Hoon's concerned, we've already cracked one."

Logan stopped pacing. His knee and ribcage both thanked him for it.

"What?"

"He's looked over what we have. Reckons Robbie Steadwood murdered

Mairi Sinclair," Ben said. "He had a solid motive, history of violence, and she was killed in his hut. DNA came back showing he'd been in her car. He reckons that's enough to build a case around."

"Oh he does, does he? And what's he saying about the fact that Robbie Steadwood was just murdered?"

Ben shrugged. "Not a lot. Doesn't think the two deaths are necessarily connected. If Bosco knew you'd taken Robbie in, and thought Robbie had information he was going to share, it's no great surprise that he'd want to shut him up."

"So, Hoon knows Bosco was behind this?"

Ben shook his head. "Hoon *believes* Bosco was behind it. But you know yourself, Jack. What we believe and what we can prove are not the same thing. We found nothing at Bosco's place, there was nothing to tie any of his guys to the crash scene..."

He shrugged.

"What else can we do?"

A flush of rage went rushing through Logan, but caught in his throat before it could come out as a lot of angry ranting.

What was the point? Everything Ben was saying was right. Infuriating, but right.

Bosco had done this sort of thing before, and always managed to get away with it. Even if they could link one of his men to the scene, they were fiercely loyal to the Russian. The chances of getting one to talk were so slim as to be almost non-existent.

His shoulders sagged. The worst of the pain, which adrenaline had been keeping at bay, came rushing in to fill the gaps his fading temper left behind.

He thought about retreating to his office, but it seemed ridiculously far away. Instead, he hobbled to the closest available chair, and practically fell into it.

For a while, he just sat there, saying nothing. The only sounds in the Incident Room were the tap-tap of Hamza's keyboard, and the slow, rhythmic flicking of Tyler looking through a bundle of photographs.

These were joined by another sound, when Ben fished his car keys out of his pocket.

"Come on. I'll take you back into Raigmore. You look like shite."

Logan showed no signs of resistance. He gave a sigh that whistled as it came out of him.

"Give me a minute," he said.

DS McQuarrie briefly glanced up at him, then went back to studying a report. DC Neish briefly paused in flicking through the photographs, opened his mouth as if to speak, but thought better of it.

"We'll handle everything while you're gone," Ben said, picking up his coat. "Caitlyn can get the report done. I'll talk to the family."

"Aye," was all Logan had to say.

His chair *squeaked* as he used his feet to rotate it in the direction of the Big Board. He stared at it in silence for a while, taking in the information that had been assembled there.

It made sense, right enough. Steadwood. Sure, Christopher Boyd had been a distraction for a couple of hours, but Steadwood had always been almost the most likely suspect. It fit. *He* fit.

And yet.

"If not him, who else?" Logan wondered aloud.

Ben hesitated, his coat half on. "Eh?"

"Assuming it wasn't Steadwood. Who else?"

Ben regarded the board, then shrugged. "No one obvious. Everyone else has alibis for Sunday. Could've been some randomer, I suppose."

Logan shook his head. The jolt of pain cut the movement short. "I don't think so. If she was randomly snatched, why the change in behaviour? Why cancel the date with Boyd? Why stop texting everyone? Why take ten quid out of a cash machine she's apparently never used before?"

With some difficulty, he stood up, his attention still focused on the board. "Something was different. Her behaviour was different. It was like she knew something was coming. And, if she knew that, then she knew her killer."

"Which brings us back to Robbie Steadwood," Ben reasoned. "She was blackmailing him, Jack. She was killed in his hut. He has a history of violence against women. Against that specific woman, in fact. I know nothing's ever open and shut, but this feels pretty damn close."

"Boss?"

If Logan heard him, he didn't let on.

"It's the manner of death, though. What he put her through. There's nothing in his history that's anything like that," the DCI reasoned. "It's not his style."

"It's not really anyone's style though, is it? None of them has exactly struck me as some sort of devil worshipper."

Behind them, Tyler stood up. "Boss!"

With a grunt and a fair amount of difficulty, Logan turned. "What?"

DC Neish thrust a photograph towards him. "You're going to want to look at this."

Taking the picture, Logan studied it. It was ever so slightly out of focus, but showed a big stretch of Loch Ness. The angle of the sun and the colour of the light suggested it had been taken early in the morning.

"It's one of the photos that mad old bat brought in. The Nessie-hunter," Tyler explained. "What was her name?"

Logan tore his eyes from it long enough to shoot the junior officer a questioning look.

"You not seen it yet?" Tyler asked, looking annoyingly smug.

Logan flicked his gaze down again, and this time he spotted it immediately. A shape in the loch, twenty or thirty feet from the shore. A green hump, just cresting above the glassy surface.

"Jesus Christ," he muttered. "No way."

He squinted, bringing the photo closer, then moving it further away as he tried to better focus. "Is that... Is that what I think it is?"

"I reckon so, Boss," Tyler said. "I can get some bigger copies made, but... aye."

"Well? Don't keep us hanging on. What is it?" asked Ben. Hamza and Caitlyn were both watching the DCI, too, Hamza's fingers poised on his keyboard and Caitlyn's report held open, as if they had both been frozen in place.

Logan held the photograph up for the others to see, then tapped the spot where the shape broke the surface of the water.

"What am I looking at?" Ben asked, doing a more exaggerated version of the squint Logan had been doing. "It's no' the monster, is it?"

"Green tarpaulin," Logan said. "Pretty sure I can make out a rope around it, too, which means—"

He stopped talking as he read the studious handwriting on the back of the picture. Had there been any colour left in his face that wasn't just black-and-blue, it would almost certainly have all drained away.

"Clocked it, have you, boss?" Tyler asked.

The DC rocked back on his heels and looked around at the others, determined to take at least some of the glory for himself.

"That photo was taken on Sunday morning. Just after seven," he said.

He gave them a moment to digest this, before following up with the clincher.

"Five hours before Mairi Sinclair disappeared."

CHAPTER FORTY

"I DON'T CARE IF YOU HATE GETTING YOUR PICTURE TAKEN. IT'S happening. Sinead, would you?"

Michelle Sinclair handed Constable Bell her phone, then put an arm around Stuart's shoulder and pulled him in close. He was several inches taller than she was, and although he made a few vague grumbling noises, he didn't physically resist.

They were all gathered in Michelle's living room, gearing up to make the drive to Foyers for the birthday service the school had organised. Michelle hadn't changed out of the clothes she'd worn to church that morning, and looked dressed for a funeral.

Stuart wore jeans and a hoodie, which Michelle had resigned herself to being the best she was going to get out of him. At least it was clean and freshly ironed, she'd reasoned.

"Right, do I just...? I've got it," said Sinead, studying the buttons on the phone's screen. She lined up the shot and fired off a couple of snaps, then rotated the device. "We'll do a tall one. Cheese."

Michelle let her arm drop down to around Stuart's waist. He was angled towards her a little, and she put the other hand on his chest.

"Cheese."

Sinead tapped the screen and passed the phone back. "You might want to check them. It's not my strong point," she said.

Michelle swiped through the pictures. "Oh, these are lovely. Look, Stuart. Look. Are they not lovely?"

Stuart nodded, but in a way that made it clear he couldn't really care less. "Don't put them on Facebook," he said.

"Oh, but—"

She caught the look on his face. There was no winning this argument.

"Fine. Fine. I'll keep them for my *personal collection*."

She winked at Sinead, laughing, then checked the time at the top of the screen. "Oof. We'd better get going. Did we decide who's driving?"

"I can do it," said Sinead.

Michelle gave a little wince. "Would you mind if I do it? I get travel sick on that road as a passenger. Something about the windy bits. They go right for my stomach."

"Inner ear," Stuart corrected.

Both women looked at him, which instantly made him visibly uncomfortable.

"It's the inner ear that gets car sick. Not the stomach."

"Oh. Right. Well... that's handy to know," said Michelle. She rolled her eyes at Sinead, then smiled. "So, OK with me driving?"

"No problem at all," Sinead said.

"We really appreciate you coming with us," Michelle said. "It's going to be a challenging day. We've both grown very fond of you, Sinead. Haven't we, Stuart?"

Stuart appeared to become even more uncomfortable with this, and just sort of shrugged in response.

"It's no problem, honestly," Sinead said. "Anything I can do to—"

The buzzing of her phone interrupted her. She checked the screen, and saw DCI Logan's name emblazoned across it. "Sorry. Just one sec, OK?" she said, retreating out into the hall. "I have to take this."

Logan started speaking before Sinead even had a chance to offer a greeting.

"Are you with the boy?"

Sinead glanced at the living room door. She could hear Michelle and Stuart's voices in there, low and quiet.

"Uh, yes. Why?"

"I need you to double-check something for me. Don't make a big deal of it," Logan said. "I need you to ask him when he last saw his mum."

"Sunday morning, wasn't it?" Sinead offered.

"Aye, that's what he said, but things have come to light. I need you to ask him. Now. While I'm on the phone," Logan said. "Can you do that without arousing suspicion?"

"Uh, yeah. Aye. I think so. Hang on."

At the other end of the line, Logan waited. He had his phone on the desk in front of him, the speakerphone activated. The rest of the team had gathered around to listen in silence to the conversation.

There was a rustling sound. Movement.

Sinead's voice came again, more muffled this time.

"Stuart? Quick question. Sorry. I know this is the last thing you need, but they're just finishing up some paperwork and need to double check when the last time you saw your mum was."

Stuart Sinclair's voice was indistinct, but just possible to make out. "About eleven."

"On Sunday?"

Silence. Logan presumed a nod.

"Right. Thanks."

"Ask him if he saw her. Actually *saw* her," Logan urged.

"And you actually saw her then, yeah?" Sinead asked.

There was a pause. Logan held his breath.

"You mean *saw* saw her? Like actually saw her?" Stuart asked.

Logan stared intently at the phone, like he could somehow see through it into Michelle Sinclair's living room, if only he tried hard enough.

"Tell him yes," he said. "Or did he just hear her?"

"I mean did you see her, or just hear her? Did you say you were in bed?"

"Um... Yeah. I just heard her, actually. She shouted up."

Logan leaned both hands on the desk, supporting himself as the conversation he'd had with the victim's mother, Elaine Sinclair, came rushing back to him.

Even on the phone, you can never tell who's who, she'd told him.

They sound so much alike.

There was more rustling from the phone, then Sinead's voice returned sounding much closer again.

"He says—"

"We got it," Logan told her. "Are you somewhere out of their earshot?"

"One sec."

More rustling.

"Do you two want to head out to the car? I'll just be a minute."

"Everything alright?"

That was Michelle Sinclair's voice. The concern was clear for all to hear.

"Aye. I just messed up a report. I need to explain a few things on it."

"Oh. Well, don't let them give you a rollicking," Michelle said. Her voice grew louder, and Logan could picture her leaning in closer to the phone. "She's doing a very good job, I'll have you know. She's an asset to the force."

"Thanks," Sinead told her. "I won't be long."

"I'll leave the keys in the door," Michelle said, her voice fainter and farther away. "Come on, Stuart."

There was silence for a few seconds, then Sinead spoke again.

"OK. All clear," she said. "Now, what's up?"

SINEAD HAD BEEN UPSTAIRS in Michelle's house a few times, but only to use the bathroom. She'd already identified Michelle's room by the 'Rise Up and Pray, Luke 22:46' embroidery fixed to the door in a round frame.

The spare room, where Stuart slept, was directly across the hall. Sinead took a quick check in there first, and was surprised to find the bed pristinely made. Michelle's doing, she thought. No way Stuart would've bothered his arse.

This room was at the front of the house, and Sinead risked a look out through the window. She could see Michelle and Stuart standing beside Michelle's car a little along the street. From this distance, it looked like they were arguing about who was sitting where.

Sinead quickly leaned back out of sight when Michelle started to look back in the direction of the house. She crept hurriedly out of the room and pulled the door closed behind her.

She crossed the hall, hesitated just briefly at the door to Michelle's room, then pushed down the handle and slipped inside.

If Stuart's room had come as a surprise, Michelle's was even more so.

Not the decor. That was exactly what Sinead would've imagined. It was done out in floral print wallpaper, with various religious images artfully set out around the room.

The most striking of these was a large portrait of Christ on the cross. Down at the bottom of the image, at the foot of the cross, various dark, long-limbed creatures writhed together in what looked like some sort of orgy. Sinead didn't imagine it was the sort of image that would be conducive to a good night's sleep, but it felt 'on brand' for Michelle Sinclair, and Sinead didn't think it was particularly noteworthy.

What was surprising was the mess of the place, which starkly contrasted the room across the landing. The bed was unmade, the duvet all bunched up in a big knot. There were clothes on the floor. Jeans, one leg turned inside-out. A t-shirt. Underwear.

None of it Michelle's.

The curtains were still drawn, painting the room in a gloomy half-darkness that made the Jesus painting feel even more oppressive.

The top pillows on either side of the bed were crumpled, suggesting they'd both been used. The sheet backed that up, both sides creased, and partially untucked from beneath the mattress.

From the placement of the clothes on the floor, Sinead worked out which side Michelle had been sleeping on. She moved around the foot of the bed until she reached the other side, and eased open the drawer of the bedside table.

A box of condoms sat in a nest of silky underwear. Opened.

There was something else in there, too. Something white, right down at the bottom, almost completely hidden by the underwear.

Taking her pen from her pocket, Sinead used it to move the garments aside. A notepad was revealed, the top page covered in drawings of strange shapes.

No. Not shapes, she realised.

Symbols.

Downstairs, the front door opened. Sinead quickly closed the drawer and turned. As she did, her foot caught something under the bed.

Three books came sliding out onto the floor in front of her. Sinead wasted a moment reading the title—*Wisdom of Eosphoros: The Luciferian Philosophy*—then hurriedly shoved the books back out of sight with her foot.

She made it back out onto the landing, closed the door, and had just opened the door to the bathroom when Michelle appeared at the top of the stairs.

Sinead summoned up the most natural smile she could. "Hey. Sorry."

Michelle regarded her in silence for a moment, then her eyes crept to her bedroom door. She looked it up and down, minutely adjusted the tapestry hanging from it, and then looked back at Sinead.

"Everything alright?"

"Yes. Sorry, I just had to run to the loo before we set off," Sinead said.

Michelle peered past her through the open door of the bathroom. "Oh," she said. "Right."

"Didn't want to stop on the drive down," Sinead said.

"No," Michelle agreed. She looked at her door again, then back into the bathroom. "I didn't hear it flush."

"Hmm? Oh. God. Sorry," said Sinead.

She turned and entered the bathroom, flushed the toilet, then returned to the landing.

"So rude of me. Sorry," she said, then she motioned past Michelle to the stairs. "Shall we?"

STUART WAS SITTING in the front passenger seat when they reached the car.

"I told him to get in the back," Michelle muttered.

"It's fine," said Sinead. "I'll sit in the back."

She already had her phone in her hand, ready to fire off a text to DCI Logan.

Michelle blocked her as she reached for the handle on the car's back door.

"Actually, Sinead, would you mind if I let you drive, after all?" She wrinkled her nose. "Not really feeling up to it."

"Uh, yeah. Yeah, OK," said Sinead. "What about the travel sickness, though?"

"I'll be fine."

"Don't you at least want to sit up front?"

Michelle opened one of the car's back doors. "It's fine," she said, squeezing into the car directly behind the driver's seat. "I'll be good right here."

Sinead stood outside the car, rolling her phone over in her hand a few times as she tried to think of a way to send a message without being noticed.

She had just concluded it was going to be impossible when Michelle rapped on the window with a knuckle.

"Come on, then," she urged. "We don't want to be late."

With a final glance at her phone, Sinead slipped it into one of the pockets of her uniform, opened the door, and climbed in behind the steering wheel.

Adjusting the rear view mirror, she saw Michelle in the back. Half of her face was hidden by the driver's seat headrest, and one eye stared back at Sinead through the reflection.

"Take the back road," Michelle instructed.

"The back road?"

"Out past the hospital, then down by ASDA."

Sinead took out her phone, spying an opportunity. She shot a glance across to Stuart, but he was engrossed in his own phone, not paying any attention.

"I'll find the postcode and programme it in," Sinead said, opening the messaging app.

"No need. I'll talk you through it."

A hand appeared over the back of Sinead's chair, and she quickly clicked out of the app before Michelle leaned forward.

"Straight on, and right at the end of the road," Michelle instructed, her voice close by Sinead's ear. "I'll have us there in no time."

CHAPTER FORTY-ONE

LOGAN CHECKED HIS PHONE. AGAIN.

Nothing.

Where the hell was she?

"She was supposed to be in touch before now," he said. "She told me five minutes."

He looked up at the clock. Almost twenty minutes had passed since he'd told Sinead to have a quick snoop around in Michelle Sinclair's room. She'd assured him it was safe, that she had the perfect opportunity.

So, where the hell was she?

"Should we phone her?" Tyler asked.

Logan shook his head. "No. She'd have been in touch if she could talk to us. Phoning might put her at risk."

"You don't think she's dangerous, do you, boss? Michelle, I mean."

Logan scowled. "Well, there's a very real possibility that she gouged her sister's eyes out and drilled holes in her skull, so I'd say she's no' without risk."

"Yeah, but I mean she's not going to kill one of us, is she? She wouldn't be that mental."

"You didn't get an up-close with the body," Logan grunted. "Trust me, the photos don't do it justice."

"We could get uniform round to the house." Ben suggested.

Logan sucked in his bottom lip. "I don't want her getting spooked. We don't have enough on her yet."

"To be fair, sir, we've barely got anything on her," Caitlyn pointed out. "It's all speculation."

"That's why we need PC Bell to hurry up and get back to us," Logan said.

He checked the phone again.

Still nothing.

"I could take a drive by," suggested Tyler. "Low key, like."

"They know your face," Logan pointed out.

"They don't know mine, sir," said DS McQuarrie.

"No, but you've got Polis written all over you," said Tyler. He cleared his throat when Caitlyn glared at him. "That's... I meant that as a compliment."

Logan straightened, ignoring the series of stabbing pains the movement brought with it.

"Hold on. What day is it?"

"Sunday, boss," said Tyler, grateful for the change of subject.

"The service."

"What service, sir?" Hamza asked.

"They're doing a service thing for Mairi's birthday. Down at the campsite in Foyers," Logan explained. "A load of kids from the school are releasing a paper boat or something."

Ben's face contorted in a sort of shocked horror. "Where her body was found? Who thought that was a good idea?"

"Aye, I did wonder the same thing myself," Logan replied. "It's on at four."

He glanced at the clock.

"We can still make it. Ben, you swing by Michelle's house," Logan instructed. "Take Hamza. See if anyone's still there. If not, head down the road and meet us."

He gestured to Tyler and Caitlyn.

"You two, get your coats. You're coming with me."

"Sir," said Caitlyn, already on her feet and ready to go.

Everyone else began to move, too, reaching for jackets and hunting pockets for car keys.

"Tyler, we'll take your car. Mine is—"

"In fucking ruins, boss?"

"*Out of action.* So, we'll take yours," Logan said. He held a hand out. "But I'm driving."

Tyler took the keys from his pocket, but didn't hand them over. Instead, he looked the DCI up and down. "You sure you're fit enough, boss?"

"I'm fine."

"My arse you're fine," Ben said, giving a derisory snort. "You can barely walk, man. Can you even see out of that eye? You're not driving anywhere."

He turned to DC Neish. "Don't give him your keys. That's a direct order. I don't care if he trumps me, give him those keys and you won't just be directing traffic, you'll be bloody washing it. "

Tyler spun the keys around his finger like a cowboy with a six-shooter, and grinned. "Nice one. Looks like I'm finally in the driver's seat, boss."

"Give them to DS McQuarrie," Ben concluded.

"Aw, what? But—"

Caitlyn snatched the keys from him as she walked past.

"Thanks for those," she said, marching over to the door. She stopped there and shot a look back at Logan and Tyler. Tyler was still staring sadly at his empty hand. Logan was trying to summon the energy to argue with Ben, but his injuries were very much siding with the Detective Inspector.

"Well?" said Caitlyn. She twirled the keys around her finger, exactly like Tyler had done, only with substantially more panache. "We going to arrest this bitch, or what?"

CHAPTER FORTY-TWO

LOGAN ARRIVED AT THE SERVICE JUST IN TIME TO CATCH THE percussion interlude. The head teacher, a prissy-looking man with burgundy trousers that immediately marked him out as a dyed-in-the-wool Tory voter, stood by the water, addressing the assembled onlookers.

Miss Sinclair had been instrumental—pun intended, Logan thought—in getting the class band project off the ground, and so he'd thought it appropriate that the band give her a send-off in 'their own inimitable style.'

Logan wasn't sure it technically qualified as 'a band' if every instrument was a drum or a shaker of some description, but the kids were all seven or eight, so he wasn't about to split hairs.

He'd clocked Sinead as soon as he'd pulled up. She stood with Michelle and Stuart down near the front of what was a surprisingly large audience. There were fifty to sixty adults gathered by the water's edge. Mostly parents, probably, although he saw the teacher, Shayne Turner, and Mairi's parents there, too.

He'd indicated for Tyler and Caitlyn to spread out and try to blend in with the crowd. This was partly so they could better keep an eye on Michelle Sinclair, and partly because Logan couldn't be arsed listening to Tyler anymore.

It had been a long drive down.

The crowd watched on, smiling appreciatively, as the band began to hammer and shake their instruments. It sounded, Logan thought, like a kitchen being turned upside-down. If Mairi Sinclair was responsible for this, then maybe there *had* been something demonic about the woman, after all.

He told himself off for that one. Or rather, he imagined Ben telling him off for it.

Inappropriate, Jack.

From his vantage-point at the back, he watched the family. Mairi's parents stood on Sinead's left, a few feet away. Michelle was on the constable's immediate right, one hand on Stuart's shoulders, her fingers kneading at the muscle. The boy stood with his head down, staring at his feet. Occasionally, he'd draw his sleeve across his eyes, but otherwise he wasn't moving much.

He saw Sinead turn and look across the crowd. She spotted Tyler first, and relief briefly painted the lines of her face. She twisted further until she found Logan. They exchanged almost-imperceptible nods, then she faced front again just as what was presumably the chorus kicked in and the clumsy crashing became even louder and more insistent.

And then, mercifully, it stopped. There was no warning, or anything to suggest the tune had reached any sort of conclusion. Ninety-percent of the band just stopped playing, with only a couple of stragglers left embarrassedly shaking their maracas in the silence that followed.

The performance was met with a round of applause that sounded infinitely better than any of the instruments had, then Shayne Turner stood up to make a speech. It was short and to the point, and she spoke with emotion choking her voice.

She spoke of a much-loved teacher, and a considerate friend. She told a few funny stories about things that had happened in various classes, about all the parts of the job that Mairi loved, and touched on how much she'd be missed by everyone who had known her.

By the end of it, there was barely a dry eye in the house. Mairi's pupils were all in ruins. Their parents, too. Stuart's face was buried in his hands, and Michelle's shoulder-rub had become a full on hug.

With the speech done, the head teacher invited the children down to the shore. They went armed with little origami boats, some enthusiastically, others hanging back with their parents for a while, summoning the courage to make a move.

With some encouragement and corralling from the school staff, the children all gathered at the water's edge, boats clutched close to their chests.

They'd all written messages, the head explained. Private thoughts.

Things they wished they could say to their teacher. Some had drawn pictures of her favourite things.

One had written an acrostic poem using the letters in 'Miss Sinclair.' He'd apparently used 'Super Teacher' three times, which the head suggested was a testament to how well thought-of she had been. Logan suspected it was more a testament to a lack of imagination on the boy's part, personally.

Still, the thought was there.

Once the children were all lined up, the head invited Mairi's family down. Elaine and Malcom were quick off the mark, and soon joined the children at the shore. It was hard to tell for sure from the back, but they seemed genuinely touched when Shayne handed them both a paper boat. They locked hands and stood together, gazing out across the loch.

Stuart wasn't so keen. He stood shaking his head, not looking at the offered boat. Michelle was doing her best to cajole him into taking it, but his feet were planted and he had no intention of going anywhere.

Logan watched Sinead whisper something in Michelle's ear. After a moment, Michelle unhooked her arm from Stuart's shoulders, and accepted the offered boat. She joined her parents at the shore. Without a word, her dad pulled her in for a hug, and kissed the top of her head.

Elaine Sinclair turned to Stuart and reached a hand out for him. He kept his head down, his shoulders heaving as he sobbed.

"Poor bugger," Logan muttered. Stuart didn't know about his father yet. And that was only the second biggest bombshell he was likely to be hit by today.

"Would anyone else like to release a boat for Miss Sinclair?" the head asked, casting his gaze across the crowd.

A few of the parents looked at each other, hesitant and uncertain. One voice rang out confidently, though.

"I'll take one."

Logan's head whipped around at the sound of DC Neish's voice. Tyler approached the front through the crowd, all heads turning his way.

"What the hell is he doing?" Logan spat. He caught the eye of DS McQuarrie, but she just shrugged in response.

Tyler stopped beside Sinead, touched her briefly on the arm, then leaned past her and said something to Stuart. The boy shuffled from foot to foot, saying nothing.

And then, to the visible delight of his grandmother, he stepped away from PC Bell and followed Tyler down to the water's edge.

Once there, they both took boats from the head teacher. Tyler looked back over his shoulder and shot Logan an apologetic look. Logan wanted to be angry. He really did. Instead, he sighed and nodded.

And then made a mental note to give him a bollocking about it afterwards.

Tyler wasn't the only one looking at Logan. Michelle Sinclair was staring at him, too. There was a look on her face that Logan couldn't quite place. Confusion, certainly, but something else, too. Betrayal, maybe.

Michelle shot a look at Sinead, and Logan realised the constable wasn't necessarily out of danger yet.

He moved through the crowd, picking his way across the rocks the way he and Ben had done on his first day here. His injuries slowed him a little, and it took him almost half a minute to reach the front.

"Thanks," he said, accepting a boat. He offered up a thin smile to Mairi's family. "We wanted to pay our respects."

"Oh, that's very kind of you," said Elaine Sinclair. "Isn't it, Malcolm?"

"Very kind," Malcolm agreed. His voice was raw and hoarse. "Thank you."

A few parents came forward to collect boats. The teachers all produced their own. Soon, a long line of adults and children had formed along the shoreline.

"Ready, mate?" Logan heard Tyler whisper. Stuart's reply was a wipe of his eyes and a nod.

A breeze tickled along the back of Logan's neck, and sent ripples rolling across the surface of the water.

"Perfect timing," Michelle said, glancing skyward.

The head teacher gave the word, and everyone knelt, bent, or crouched. The boats entered the water one by one, the breeze catching their pointed sails and rocking them out into the loch.

There was silence then, broken only by the occasional sob from the children, and the calling of the gulls far overhead. The boats drifted along, an unsteady armada venturing across the waves. One by one, the currents caught them, guiding them first into groups, then into individual explorers all striking out on their own.

There had apparently been a song planned to finish, but none of the kids were much in the mood to perform, and so it was agreed—to everyone's visible relief—that it wouldn't go ahead.

Instead, some final words were said by the teachers, Malcolm and

Elaine Sinclair struggled through some words of thanks, and then the whole thing was drawn to a slightly anti-climactic close.

Logan stood back with Sinead during the Sinclairs' speech. Michelle glanced their way a few times, but they were too far back and she was too close to her parents for her to hear anything of what Sinead was saying.

"Well done," Logan mumbled, once Sinead had finished telling him what she'd found.

Sinead shook her head. "I should've seen it."

"No one saw it," Logan told her.

"No one else was in the house with her all week."

"Aye well, that's true, right enough," Logan conceded.

Sinead flinched, like the words had physically stung.

"I'm kidding. You've done well. You couldn't have known."

"Thanks." Sinead shot the DCI a sideways glance. "Mind if I ask what happened to your face, sir?"

"Wind changed and it stuck like this," Logan said. "My mother did warn me."

Sinead smiled, sensing that was all she was going to get out of him right now.

They both watched Michelle sidle up to Stuart again. Tyler had been standing by the boy, but gave him a pat on the back and tactfully withdrew when his aunt joined them.

"Did you send him to talk to Stuart?" Sinead asked.

"Did I hell," Logan spat. "I told him not to get himself noticed."

"Oh."

Sinead chewed her tongue for a few moments.

"Nice of him, though," she said. "I think Stuart would have really regretted not doing it."

Logan groaned, but had to concede the point.

"Aye. I suppose," he said. He shot her a sideways look. "And I suppose you could do worse."

Sinead's face turned a shade of deep pink.

"Not *much* worse, granted," Logan added. "I'm actually struggling to think of anyone worse, off the top of my head who isn't currently in jail. But theoretically, I mean. You could theoretically do worse."

Sinead's face was a shade of beetroot now. She cleared her throat and kept her eyes to the front. "I don't know what you're talking about, sir," she said.

To her relief, DS McQuarrie appeared beside them and immediately steered the conversation back on track.

"What's the plan, sir?"

The audience was thinning now, the parents leading their children back up towards the campsite's car park. Michelle was hugging her parents, then Stuart was forced to reluctantly endure the same treatment, this time accompanied by some kissing from Elaine, and a gruff, "Your mum would've been very proud," from Malcolm.

"Sinead, there's a cafe up at the top of the path leading down to the falls. You and Tyler take the boy there. Get him something to eat."

"What about Michelle?" Sinead asked.

Logan gazed down the shore at Michelle Sinclair. He flexed his fingers in and out. One of them *clicked* painfully.

"Leave her to me."

CHAPTER FORTY-THREE

THE PATH WAS HARDER GOING THAN LOGAN REMEMBERED.

Of course, the last time he'd walked it he hadn't been sporting broken ribs and a knee injury. Now, every breath was like a blast of fire filling his chest and scorching him from the inside-out. His knee had stopped *clunking* and was now making an audible *crack* every few steps. He wasn't sure if this was better or worse.

It felt worse.

It didn't help that Michelle Sinclair whinged even more than Tyler had. Mind you, in the woman's defence, Tyler hadn't done the walk in heels and a skirt.

DS McQuarrie was hanging back, close enough to listen in, but far enough away that she didn't seem to be part of the conversation.

"Sorry, what is the point of this?" Michelle demanded, leaning on a wooden handrail as she heaved herself up a rocky incline. It was mostly downhill, but the path occasionally climbed to get over some unmovable boulder or other obstacle. "I should be with Stuart. He needs me."

"It won't take long, Miss Sinclair," Logan wheezed. "Believe me, I'm enjoying it even less than you are. But, there's something I need you to see."

She shot a look past him at the path ahead. Trees leaned down over it, an ever-moving canopy of green that sent shadows scurrying across the rocky ground. Michelle's words and tone may have been angry, but it was worry that was written in that look.

"Can't you just tell me?" she asked, stopping dead. "I don't... I don't want to go down there."

Logan stopped, too, grateful for the breather.

"Why not? Do you know what's down there?" he asked. His stare bored into her. Shrank her.

She shook her head. "N-no. I just... It's a long way."

"It's not much further," Logan assured her. He set off limping again. "Almost there."

He looked back up the slope at her.

"Won't be long now."

TYLER LOOKED up from the menu, a big smile on his face. "They do Coke Floats! I haven't had one of them in years."

Across the table, Stuart searched the menu. It was lying flat on the plastic tablecloth in front of him, the effort of holding it apparently proving too much.

"What's a Coke Float?"

"What's a...? You've never had a Coke Float?" Tyler gasped. He looked to Sinead, who sat on his right, between him and the boy. "He's never had a Coke Float!"

"I've never had one, either," Sinead said. "It's the ice cream thing, isn't it?"

"Jesus," Tyler said. "You're both in for a treat. It's Coke, right, then a big dollop of ice cream on top, then..."

He thought for a moment.

"Actually, that's pretty much it. But it's amazing."

"It sounds horrible," Stuart said.

"What are you talking about?" Tyler said, the volume of his voice rising enough to draw looks from the handful of other people in the cafe. "It sounds brilliant. And it is. That's it decided. Three Coke Floats."

Sinead and Stuart exchanged wary looks.

"Don't pull that face! Trust me, you're going to love it."

Sinead raised her eyebrows. "What do we think? Do we trust him?"

Stuart looked deeply sceptical, but then gave a nod. "Fine. I'll try it."

"That's my boy," Tyler said, high-fiving the boy across the table. "Constable Bell? You joining the Coke Float Club?"

"Are you paying?"

"No, he is," said Tyler, jabbing a thumb in Stuart's direction.

"Wait, what?" Stuart asked, straightening.

"I'm kidding. Yes. My treat."

He stood up, reaching for his wallet. "Three Coke Floats it is. Then we'll see about food."

Sinead and Stuart watched him approach the counter, swaggering like he owned the place. They didn't catch what he said to the grey-haired woman behind the counter, but from the way her face lit-up it was clear he'd turned on the charm.

"He's pretty funny," Stuart remarked.

"He has his moments," Sinead agreed.

Stuart's eyes went to the cafe's front door. It was mostly glass, and looked out over the road to where a steep path led down to the Falls of Foyers.

"Where's Michelle?"

Sinead hesitated, then smiled. "I'm sure she won't be long."

She tapped the menu in front of him. "Now, what do you fancy for eating?"

MICHELLE SINCLAIR HADN'T SPOKEN in almost a minute. Hadn't grumbled. Hadn't complained. Hadn't uttered a single, solitary word.

Instead, she just stood perfectly still, eyes locked on the nondescript workman's hut that stood at the end of the path, overlooking the falls. A mist of moisture swirled in the air, as the water crashed like thunder just a few dozen feet away.

"Something you'd like to tell us, Michelle?" Logan asked and, for a moment, it looked like she might.

But then she shook her head, pulled herself together, and looked the DCI right in the eye. "What is this?"

Logan shrugged. So, that's how she wanted to play it.

"This? This is where Mairi was murdered," Logan told her. He gave the nod to Caitlyn, and she cut the *Police: Do Not Cross* tape that had been cordoning the place off. The ends fluttered briefly on the breeze, then fell to the ground.

"Robbie Steadwood was working out of this hut," Logan continued.

Michelle tried to keep the relief from showing on her face, but did a very bad job of it.

"Oh. Was it? And, so..." She swallowed. "This was where he killed her?"

"This was where she died, yes," Logan said, side-stepping the question.

He opened the door, stepped inside the gloomy hut, then beckoned for Michelle to follow.

"No. I don't want to," Michelle said. She shot Caitlyn a pleading look, but found no comfort there. "I don't want to go in."

"It's very important, Miss Sinclair. It won't take a second, but it'll help your sister get justice."

Michelle looked at the shadowy shape of Logan inside the doorway, then across the front of the hut. Even from this distance, Logan could practically see her skin crawling backwards, trying to pull her away from the place.

"Have you found him yet? Robbie, I mean," she asked.

"We have. I took him into custody myself last night," Logan confirmed. "Turns out Mairi was mixed up in some bad business with one of the local thugs. She was playing a very dangerous game."

"Oh. God. I had no idea," Michelle said, but she looked emboldened by the news, and took a step closer to the hut. "Do you think they did it? Or Robbie?"

"We have a few theories at the moment," Logan told her. "That's what I could use your help with. Please."

He disappeared into the hut. Caitlyn gave Michelle an encouraging nod, then gestured for her to follow Logan inside.

The hut's chipboard floor dipped a little under Michelle's weight as she stepped inside. The only light in the place seeped in around her through the doorway, the lack of windows meaning most of the hut was lost in shadow.

Her breathing echoed off the wooden walls, fast and erratic. She wrung her hands together, and even in silhouette, Logan could see how uncomfortable she was to be standing there in the half-darkness.

"Do me a favour, will you, Miss Sinclair?" he asked from the other end of the hut. "Stick the light on."

Michelle seemed almost grateful as she reached up and pulled the cord. There was a *ka-klack* from the ceiling-mounted switch, and the hut was flooded with light.

Logan sucked in his bottom lip. "Detective Sergeant McQuarrie. Did you see that?"

"I did, sir," said Caitlyn. She was standing in the doorway at Michelle's back, looking in through one of the gaps.

"See what?" asked Michelle.

Logan gestured to the three cords that hung by the door. Michelle was still holding onto one, like a child with a helium balloon.

"You knew which one to pull," Logan said.

Michelle frowned, then looked at the cord she was holding. She released it immediately, like it had just given her an electric shock. It swung back and forth, entangling itself around the others.

"What? What do you mean?"

"You knew which one was the light," Logan said. "How?"

Michelle's mouth flapped open and closed. "I mean... What do you mean, 'how?' I just... I just guessed."

"That was lucky. First time I was here, I pulled the other two first," Logan said. "They just look more, I don't know, inviting, I suppose. The one for the light is sort of hidden at the back, isn't it? Looks the least likely. And yet, you managed to pick it out. First time."

Michelle said nothing. Her face went through a range of expressions but couldn't settle on any one in particular.

"But then, it's not your first time here, is it? You were here last week," Logan said.

"You were here the day you killed your sister."

CHAPTER FORTY-FOUR

"It was you, wasn't it, Michelle?" Logan asked. "You were the one who went to Boleskine House with Mairi and Steadwood. You were with them when they did their... occult whatever."

"What? No. No, I'm not... I didn't kill her. I don't know what you're talking about," Michelle said. "I'm not... I don't have to listen to this. I want to go."

She tried to leave, but DS McQuarrie blocked the doorway.

"Get out of my way, I want to go!"

"That was the night everything changed, wasn't it?" Logan pressed. "Your parents told me. You'd been close before then, the two of you. But that's when you started to drift apart."

"No. No, this isn't... It's not..."

"The three of you went up to Boleskine and you did the Ouija board together. I'd imagine that must've been pretty scary, considering your age at the time."

"How did you...?" Michelle began. She shook her head. "I didn't want to. They said it'd be funny. They said I was being stupid, but... I didn't want to."

"Afterwards, she told you there was a demon in her," Logan continued. "That's right, isn't it?"

A sob. A nod.

"A load of shite, obviously, but how old were you at the time? Ten? Eleven? You believed her, didn't you? You believed what she was saying."

Michelle clenched her jaw, her eyes filling with tears.

"You thought she was telling the truth. Didn't you, Michelle? You thought she really had been possessed, or whatever it was she was claiming," Logan continued. "Is that where all the holy-moly stuff comes from? Your parents aren't religious, but you are. Is that why? Was it to protect you from her?"

Michelle shook her head. "N-no," she said. "Not from her."

Her voice became a whisper. "From *it*."

"It?"

"The demon!"

Michelle looked around at Caitlyn, then back to Logan. There was a resignation to the way she moved now, an acceptance of what was to come.

"I know what you're thinking. It sounds crazy," she said, her voice flat and measured. "And it does. I know that."

"What sounds crazy?" Logan asked her. "Tell us what happened."

Michelle drew in a shaky breath. "Everyone keeps saying she changed back then, like it was a phase or something. But it wasn't. She didn't change."

"What, then?"

"She *left*. That thing took over. It... it... swallowed her, so that it wasn't her anymore."

Michelle took a step further into the shed, her eyes wide and blazing. "It looked like her. It sounded like her. But it wasn't her. Not really. She wouldn't do those things. Mairi wouldn't be like that."

"Like what? What things?" Logan asked. "Get pregnant? Do drugs? I hate to break it to you, Michelle, but plenty of teenagers do those things without the need for any demonic intervention."

"Not those," Michelle snapped, her pitch rising. "That's not what I mean."

"What, then?"

"Nothing. Forget it."

"What did she do?"

Michelle was shouting now. "I told you, it wasn't her! It wasn't her! Mairi wouldn't have done that!"

"Done what?" Logan demanded, raising his own voice to match.

Her scream shook the walls of the hut.

"*She wouldn't have let him touch me!*"

The words echoed in the silence that followed. Even Michelle seemed shocked by them, flinched away from them, like she hadn't heard them spoken aloud before.

"Mairi wouldn't have let him do those things," she said, her volume a fraction of what it had been just a moment before.

"Steadwood?" Logan asked.

Michelle made no move to answer. She didn't have to. The look on her face said it all.

"It couldn't have been her. Even after, when everyone else thought she was back to normal, it couldn't have been her."

Her voice was a whisper, so low that Logan could barely hear the words.

"Because she never even said she was sorry."

She jammed the heels of her hands against her eyes and screwed them in, like she could physically manhandle the tears back into her eyes.

"I actually thought she was back, for a while. She almost had me fooled," she whispered.

She snapped her hands down to her sides, clenching her fists and stamping a foot. "And then she started to see him again! After everything he did. To her. To me."

Despite everything, despite what she'd done, Logan almost felt sorry for her.

"And that's when I knew. That's when I knew I had to do something. I had to get rid of it! I had to get it out of her."

"So, you phoned up Bosco pretending to be Mairi and found out where Steadwood was working, then you brought her here and killed her. Why here? Did you hope you could frame him for it."

"That wasn't... I didn't..." Michelle said, shaking her head. "I was trying to cure her. I just wanted it out of her. Before her birthday. I couldn't stand the idea of that... that *thing* being in her skin longer than she was."

Logan shot Caitlyn a look and could tell the DS was thinking the same as him. Insanity plea. No question.

"I wanted her back, that was all. I just wanted my big sister back," Michelle continued, the words punctuated by deep, throaty sobs. "There are methods. *Proven* methods. Rituals that work, that actually do work. You can read about it. It's in books. Rituals that would've saved her. Would've brought her back. It's real. It's all real!"

"I could maybe buy that, if it was just the Exorcism stuff," Logan told her. "But you stabbed her through the heart, Michelle. There's no coming back from that."

Michelle shook her head, her whole body trembling. "N-no."

"You did. You stabbed your sister through the heart," Logan insisted.

"No! I didn't!"

"You killed her, Michelle. You murdered your own sister right here in this room. Didn't you?"

"No! I didn't! I *didn't*!" she screeched. "That wasn't my idea. That wasn't me! I didn't want to!"

Logan hesitated. "What? Then who? Not this demon you keep talking about? Why would it want you to...?"

She shook her head, tears tripping her. Her expression told him everything.

Logan's words died in his throat. His stomach tightened. His heart sank.

God. No. Not a demon. Not a monster.

A man.

A child.

"Shite!" He looked past Michelle to DS McQuarrie. "Caitlyn!"

Caitlyn had her phone out, her fingers already stabbing at the screen, having come to the same conclusion that Logan had.

"No signal," she said.

"Christ. Well then, don't just stand there," Logan spat. He pointed out the door, towards where the path climbed steeply up to the road half a mile above. "Fucking *run!*"

CHAPTER FORTY-FIVE

"SEE? WHAT DID I TELL YOU?" ASKED TYLER. HE SWIRLED THE FOAMY white dregs at the bottom of his glass around with his straw. "Was that, or was that not, the best thing you've ever tasted?"

"I wasn't a fan," Sinead said.

Tyler held a hand up, blanking her. "You don't count. Your opinion is wrong," he said. "Stuart? Back me up here. You enjoyed it, right?"

"It was alright, yeah," Stuart said. There was a *shlurp* as he sucked up the last half-inch of liquid. "It was pretty good, actually."

"*Pretty* good? Or the best drink you've ever had?" Tyler pressed. He scowled briefly in Sinead's direction. "Don't let her influence you. Ignore her. She's an idiot and a liar."

Sinead flicked the end of her straw at him. "Bit harsh!"

Tyler sighed. "Fine. An idiot *or* a liar. Better?"

"Not really, no!"

Stuart looked between them, idly fiddling with his straw. He glanced up when a shadow passed over the table, then quickly cast his eyes down at the menu again.

"Who's ready for a wee bite to eat?" asked the waitress. She was a different woman to the one Tyler had charmed earlier, but radiated the same sort of jolly enthusiasm. She smiled down at them, notepad and pencil poised.

"Do you do just chips?" Tyler asked.

"A bowl or a basket?"

"Which one's bigger?"

"The basket."

Tyler returned the smile. "Then I'll have a basket."

"Anything else?"

"No, that's me. Sinead?"

The waitress turned her attention to PC Bell. "Can I get the ham and cheese toastie?"

She looked up from the menu at Tyler. "Can I steal some of your chips?"

"Absolutely not," he told her, but she chose to ignore it.

"I'll steal some of his chips. That's fine."

The waitress scribbled her note. "And for you?" she asked, turning to Stuart. She gave a little start. "Oh! Hello again."

Stuart didn't look up.

"Hiya," he replied. "I'll just have chips, too."

"Basket?"

Stuart nodded.

"No cake today?" she asked.

Sinead looked from Stuart to the waitress and back again.

"He was in a week or so back. Friday or Saturday, wasn't it? Red Velvet, you had. That's right, isn't it? Last piece, too. I remember, because I'd been eyeing it up myself."

She laughed and gave Stuart a little nudge on the shoulder. "I'm kidding. Last thing I need to be doing with my figure is eating cake."

Sinead and Tyler's eyes met across the table.

"You were here last week?" Tyler asked.

"With your mum and auntie, wasn't it?" the waitress said. She rocked back on her heels, looking satisfied. "We must've made a good impression!"

She tapped her pencil on her pad, then winked down at them all. "I'll go get this sorted. Just shout if you need anything else."

"Uh, yeah," said Sinead. "Thanks."

Neither of the police officers watched her go, their attention instead entirely focused on Stuart. He didn't make eye contact, just sat there fiddling with his straw and staring at the pattern on the plastic tablecloth.

"Stuart?" Sinead asked. "Is there something you want to tell us?"

The waitress appeared again, a rack of condiments in one hand, and some cutlery in the other. She set them down, then placed a steak knife in front of Sinead.

"For the toastie," she explained. "It's fresh bread, and a bit tough."

"Thanks," Sinead said, not taking her eyes off the boy.

They waited for the waitress to leave again before resuming their questioning.

"Mate?" Tyler asked. "Is that right? Were you in here with your mum and Michelle last week before your mum... Before everything happened?"

Stuart shrugged. "Don't remember."

Tyler crossed his arms on the table and leaned closer. "What do you mean? How can you not—"

The glass smashed against the side of his head, showering him in Coke-foam and backwash, and sending him tumbling to the floor, blood already beginning to pour.

Stuart had the knife before Sinead could react. They were both on their feet at the same time, but he caught the underside of the table and flipped it towards her, forcing her back and blocking her path. Around them, the other diners sat frozen in shock. They were mostly elderly, aside from a woman with a toddler, and mercifully none seemed like have-a-go-hero types.

"Stuart, calm down," Sinead said, holding her hands in front of her. "Put the knife down, OK? Let's talk."

"Fucking stay back!" Stuart warned. "I'll kill you, I mean it. I'll fucking do it! I'll kill everyone in here!"

There was some commotion then, as a couple of the elderly patrons and the woman with the child got up and made for the door.

"*Don't fucking move!*" Stuart screamed at them, spinning and slashing at the air with the knife. His knuckles were white on the handle, his hand trembling.

He yelped in shock when Tyler caught him by the legs and got a shoulder in at the back of his knees. There was a *thud* as Stuart went down, his forearms slamming into the floor.

Sinead struggled to manoeuvre the table aside, but the space between it and the furniture on either side was tight, and it was a slow process. Before she could reach him, Stuart had kicked a leg free. He drew the knee up and brought his foot down, first on Tyler's shoulder, then on the side of his head. Once. Twice.

Stunned, Tyler lost his grip and Stuart launched himself to his feet like a sprinter off the blocks. He flew at the door, threw it open, and went stumbling out into the world beyond.

After finally managing to get out from behind the table and scattered chairs, Sinead dropped down by Tyler's side.

"You OK?"

"Get after him," DC Neish groaned.

Sinead sprang upright again. "Make sure he's OK," she ordered the rest of the cafe in general, then she hurried to the door and raced on out after Stuart.

There was no sign of the boy outside, and too many directions to choose from. Across the street, the path led down to the waterfall. Another path led off to the left of the cafe, tucking in behind it before joining a track that led up into the woods behind. The road itself curved out of sight just a few dozen yards on the left. Part of the cafe building and an old-style red phone box blocked the view of the road to the right.

The boy could've gone anywhere.

A figure appeared at the top of the path over the road, hair wild, breath coming in big, frantic gasps.

"DS McQuarrie!" Sinead hollered.

Caitlyn put a hand on her chest, as if she could hold her racing heart steady. "Stuart. It's Stuart," she wheezed.

"Aye, we know," Sinead told her. "He's legged it."

Caitlyn put her hands on her knees, gulping down air. She straightened again almost immediately, and jabbed a finger off along the road to her left. "There."

Sinead jumped the steps in front of her, caught the edge of the phone box, and skidded out from the shadow of the building.

Stuart had a big head start, and was powering ahead. DS McQuarrie launched herself into a run, but the steep climb from the falls had taken its toll, and Sinead passed her almost immediately.

She thought about shouting, calling after him, pleading with him to stop, but he was in full-on fight or flight mode now, and seeing sense was unlikely to be on the cards.

Instead, she ran, throwing herself forward and hoping her legs would keep up. Stuart was younger, fitter, and had a solid head start, but...

Actually, there was no 'but,' she realised. The chances of catching the little bastard were tiny. She'd just have to hope he tired out before she did, or pray for some kind of miracle.

"Hmm. I don't know. Is that the spicy one?" asked DI Forde as he dropped a gear and guided the car toward yet another winding bend in the road.

"Piri Piri? Aye. It's fairly spicy," Hamza confirmed. "Nice, though."

Ben scrunched up his face. "I don't mind spicy, but Alice wouldn't like it."

"They do milder ones," Hamza said. "You can get just plain chicken, if you want.

Ben perked up. "Oh? She could have that."

"Aye, and you could try the—"

He hissed and gripped the handle above the side window as Ben rounded the curve and swerved to avoid someone sprinting past at the side of the road. He saw a uniformed officer running towards them, and the brakes screeched as Ben brought the car to a stop.

The gearstick *crunched* as Ben slammed it into reverse, then twisted around, one arm stretched across the back of Hamza's seat. Hamza gripped the handle tighter as the car whined backwards unsettlingly quickly. He saw the reflection of the running boy in the wing mirror and caught a glimpse of his face as the kid shot a look back over his shoulder at the car.

"Is that Stuart Sinclair?" Hamza asked, recognising the boy from his photo.

"Christ knows," Ben said. He accelerated past the boy, then swerved the car in front of him and skidded to a stop.

Stuart collided with the bonnet, rolled up onto the windscreen, then landed heavily on the driver's side of the car. DI Forde was already unfastening his belt, and after a momentary hesitation, Hamza did the same.

Both men jumped out of the car just as Stuart hauled himself back to his feet. Far behind the boy, the uniformed officer—PC Bell, Hamza realised—was shouting something, but she was still too far away for him to hear properly.

"Whoa, whoa, whoa!" Ben urged, blocking Stuart's path when he attempted to run. "Easy, son. What's going on? What's the big hurry?"

Hamza hurried around the car to block the boy's retreat. As he did, PC Bell's voice reached them, suddenly loud and clear.

"Knife!"

Hamza looked down. Light glinted off a sliver of metal in Stuart's hand as he drew it back, the blade pointed at DI Forde's stomach.

Panic ground the world into slow motion and turned Hamza's limbs to lead. He saw the blade begin its upward swing. Saw the exact moment of realisation on Ben's face, the tightening of the jaw as he braced himself, the fear in his eyes.

Hamza lunged, grabbed, caught, twisted. Stuart cried out in pain and shock and frantically tried to yank his arm free, but Hamza slammed it, wrist first, against the edge of the car door. The knife clattered across the windscreen and thumped onto the bonnet.

Stuart roared in pain and frustration. He grabbed for Hamza, but the DC twisted his arm up his back and shoved him against the side of the car.

"Let me go! Let me go, or I'll fucking kill you!" Stuart spat.

"Aye, good luck with that, son," Ben told him. He gave Hamza a pat on the shoulder and winked at him. "Bigger men than you have tried."

CHAPTER FORTY-SIX

DCI LOGAN LEANED ON A GATEPOST BY THE SIDE OF THE ROAD, watching as Stuart and Michelle were bundled into different cars. A crowd had been drawn by the flashing lights, and Sinead had been leading the effort to keep everyone back until a few more uniforms had turned up, and Logan had called her over to join him and DS McQuarrie.

"How's our boy?" he asked, and Sinead's eyes were drawn to the ambulance where DC Neish was—in the most literal sense—currently having his head examined. DI Forde and DC Khaled stood at the open back door, laughing and joking with one of the paramedics.

"Aye, he'll live. It's going to need stitches, though."

"Don't suppose they can do his mouth at the same time, can they?" Caitlyn asked.

Sinead shook her head. "No. I already suggested that. They were having none of it."

They all watched a couple of uniformed officers climb into the front seats of their cars. A constable pulled the cordon tape aside and stood back until both cars had passed. Michelle Sinclair had her head buried in her hands in the back of one car. Stuart sat in the other, staring blankly out at the world.

He briefly met Sinead's eye as he passed, but there wasn't so much as a flicker of recognition from him.

"I still can't believe it," she said. "I mean..."

"Aye. Takes some getting used to, this sort of thing," Logan said.

"But you do," DS McQuarrie added. "Unfortunately."

"But, I mean... Why? She was his mum!"

Logan shrugged. "I don't know. We'll find out. From what Michelle said, Mairi had found out she and Stuart were sleeping together. Understandably, she was less than impressed and put a stop to it. Or tried to, anyway. We know how that panned out."

"He killed his mum so he could shag his auntie?"

"That's fourteen year old boys for you," Caitlyn said. "Horny wee bastards."

"And I'll bet Michelle had been filling his head with all her demon shite for years," Logan added. "That can't exactly have helped with his mental stability."

"Think she believed it? The demon stuff?" asked Caitlyn.

Logan puffed out his cheeks. "Who knows? Maybe. Aye. She was a kid herself when it all happened. Sounds like it was the only way she could process what Mairi let Steadwood do to her."

Caitlyn nodded. "Better to blame a monster than your own big sister, I suppose."

Sinead's brow furrowed as she tried to make sense of it all. "So... when did they kill her?"

"Late Saturday, from what I can gather," Logan said. "They all came down here together on Friday, a nice wee family jaunt, then they took a walk down to the falls and imprisoned her in the hut. They used her phone on Saturday to cancel the date with Boyd, and when the text came in from Shayne on Sunday they replied. I suppose they didn't realise it was out of character for her. Then, Stuart took money out of the cash machine to make us think she was still alive, but she was already dead by then. They left the phone in the car, thinking that if we found it the texts would help back up their story."

"Why dump the car at Raigmore, though?" Caitlyn asked.

Logan shrugged. "Big car park, always busy."

"Easy bus back into town," Sinead added. "I sometimes park there and take the bus into work."

"For God's sake, don't let DI Forde know that," Logan said.

As if sensing his name being mentioned, Ben came away from the ambulance, and he and Hamza sauntered over to join Logan and the others.

"Alright there, Slugger?" Logan asked.

Hamza grinned—not proud, exactly, but something else. Relieved, maybe.

"Not bad, sir, thanks for asking."

"Ben?"

"Aye, I'm grand, Jack," DI Forde said. He put a hand on Hamza's shoulder and squeezed. "I phoned Alice and told her what happened. She's invited DC Khaled over for dinner."

"Aye, well they say no good deed goes unpunished, right enough," Logan remarked.

While Ben leapt to a half-hearted defence of his wife's cooking, Sinead found her eyes drawn back to the ambulance. This did not go unnoticed.

"PC Bell, will you do me a favour?" Logan asked.

Sinead turned, the formality of Logan's tone immediately straightening her shoulders. "Of course, sir."

"Will you accompany Detective Constable Neish to the hospital?"

Sinead cheeks reddened a fraction. She gave a little cough, clearing her throat.

"Of course."

"Thank you. And look after him, will you? He's one of the good ones."

"Yes, sir. Will do."

Logan caught her by the arm as she turned to leave.

"But for Christ's sake," he hissed. "Don't tell him I said that."

CHAPTER FORTY-SEVEN

Logan sat in another cafe at another time.

Waiting.

He'd been waiting for a while now. Twenty minutes. Thirty? He couldn't bring himself to check.

He sat with his hands around his mug, but there was no warmth there now. A thin puddle of tea lay at the bottom of the mug, the pot already drained dry. He'd resisted the little plastic-wrapped biscuit for the first ten minutes or so, but that was now long gone.

His phone buzzed on the table, the screen lighting up. His daughter's name filled the screen, along with a photo of her from ten years ago.

"Maddie. Hello!" he said, picking up the handset. The cafe was half-empty, but he kept his voice low. He couldn't stand people who shared their phone conversations with the rest of the world, and he was buggered if he was going to join them. "Everything alright?"

"Um, yeah. Fine," she said. "I just... Listen, I heard what happened. The accident."

"Ben," Logan said.

"Ben," Madison confirmed.

There was an awkward silence. Logan couldn't leave her floundering in it.

"I'm fine," he told her. "No harm done."

"Really?"

"Really." He traced his fingers across a cluster of little scabs on the side of his forehead. "I mean, I think my modelling days are over..."

She laughed. It was music, lifting him.

"But aye, I'm fine. I promise."

"Right. Good. That's... good," she said.

There was another silence, but a little less awkward this time.

"I'd better go," Madison said. "I just wanted to check."

"Right you are, sweetheart," Logan said. "Thank you. I'm fine."

"Good," she said again. "And, well, I'm up in Nairn in a couple of weeks. With work."

"Oh?"

Logan felt himself holding his breath.

"If you're free, maybe we could..."

"Aye. I'd like that."

"Right. Well. OK. Me, too," Madison said. "But I better run. I'll... I'll call you."

"I'll look forward to it."

"Bye, Dad."

"Bye, sweetheart."

The line went dead. Logan took the phone from his ear and looked at the screen, watching until Madison's photo was replaced by the phone's home screen. He raised his eyebrows in surprise, gave a little shake of his head, and had just sat the phone down on the table when the cafe door opened.

A woman entered, a gust of wind and a spray of rain shoving her inside.

"Sorry! Sorry! Traffic was terrible," gushed Shona Maguire, once she'd spotted him. "Am I late?"

"Cutting it fine, maybe," Logan told her.

The wind had made the pathologist's hair stand on end. She took a moment to smooth it down, then blew a raindrop off the end of her nose.

"You look happy," she observed.

Logan gave this some consideration.

"You know," he remarked. "I think I might be."

"Wow. Really?"

"In that neck of the woods," he said. "Don't worry. I doubt it'll last."

Shona wiped a hand across her brow. "Phew. Had me worried there."

She took the chair across from him. "You eaten yet?"

Logan shook his head. "No."

He passed her the menu.

"Decided what you're having?"

"About an hour ago, aye," Logan said.

She pulled a face at him. "Just for that, I'm going to take ages to choose." She tapped a finger against her chin. "What to have? What to have...?"

Her eyes met Logan's over the menu. She grinned, stuck her tongue out, then went back to reading.

Logan looked out through the cafe's big window at the street beyond. Academy Street. One of the few in the city he could name.

That would change, though, soon enough.

The rain was battering down. He watched pedestrians zig-zagging through it, dodging the spray from cars and buses that trundled through the puddles lining the road. Even the Chinese tourists weren't stopping to take photographs, which was practically unheard of.

"Right. I think I know what I'm..." Shona began, then she discovered the other side of the menu and shook her head. "Wait, no. I take that back. Give me a minute."

Logan was about to reply when his phone buzzed again.

Ben Forde.

Across the table, Shona patted her jacket pocket, then reached inside.

They both brought their phones to their ears at the same time.

"Ben? What's up?"

"Got a stoater for you, Jack. Just been called in," DI Forde said.

"Where?" asked Shona, pressing her phone against one ear and jamming a finger into the other one.

"Murder, I'm guessing," Logan said. His eyes met Shona's. She smiled grimly back at him, and they both stood up.

"No bother. On my way," the pathologist said.

"Text me the details," said Logan. "I'll be right there."

They both hung up.

"So, something's come up..." Shona told him.

"Aye. Snap," Logan said.

His phone buzzed. A text message flashed up. An address. Local.

"Another time?"

"Cool, yeah. Another time," Shona confirmed.

She looked down at her own phone as it bleeped, then jabbed a thumb over her shoulder.

"Race you there?"

Logan gestured to the door. "Ladies first," he said.

He followed her to the door, they said their goodbyes, then Logan stepped out onto Academy Street. The shops and restaurants that lined it were strange and unfamiliar to him. Even the buses weren't the same, or the people hurrying along the pavement. This wasn't Glasgow. This wasn't his city.

But it would be, soon enough.

Logan pulled the collar of his coat up around his neck. He fished in his pocket for his car keys.

And with that, he set off into the howling Highland summer, and to whatever lay lurking ahead.

THE KILLING CODE

DCI JACK LOGAN BOOK THREE

CHAPTER ONE

It had been twelve hours since Esme Miller had started her shift. Four since she had begun to watch the clock. Two since she had started counting down the minutes until she could finally clock off.

In less than one, she would be dead.

"You still here?"

Esme looked up from the flat-soled shoes she'd been in the process of untying and smiled through her exhaustion at the young man in the doorway. Kel was barely in his twenties and was usually a bouncy-ball of energy, but the shift had been a long one, and the aftermath of a traffic accident earlier in the day had taken its toll on all of them. Now, he just looked like he wanted to be at home, tucked up in bed.

Instead, he leaned on the handle of a mop, trying to hide the fact that he was currently relying on it for support.

"Aye, but not for long, thank God. That's me finished," Esme said. "You?"

"Nah. Been roped into staying on until midnight. A&E can't get cover."

He smiled, but the way he shook his head betrayed his true feelings on the matter.

"Bloody Brexit," Esme said.

Kel laughed at their little running joke and nodded. "Too right. Bloody Brexit."

Esme kicked off her comfies and began the process of wrestling her swollen feet into her regular outdoor shoes. "You must be due a break, though?" she said. "You look awful."

"Cheeky cow!" Kel protested. "Talk about pot and kettle. Have you looked in the mirror lately?"

"I tried, but it shattered."

"No bloody wonder."

Esme placed her work shoes in her locker and took out her jacket. The walk wasn't far, but she'd been reliably informed that the rain had been off and on all day, and she didn't fancy arriving home like a drowned rat.

"Make sure you get that break," she said, closing her locker and turning back to the door.

"Aye, they're giving me an hour to get my head down. But first..." Kel raised the mop and gave it a waggle. "Clean-up in Room Four."

Esme thought for a moment. "Albert?"

"Aye."

"Not again. What end?"

"Both ends. Simultaneously," Kel said.

Esme tried very hard not to laugh but wasn't entirely successful. "Yikes."

"It was actually one of the most impressive things I've ever seen. He was like a human fountain at one point. I was half-expecting Hugh Jackman to jump out in a top hat and start singing *The Greatest Show* at me."

Esme snorted. "You wish."

Kel gave a dreamy little sigh. "A boy can dream."

"Aye," Esme agreed. She jabbed a thumb in the direction of Room Four. "Once you've cleaned up the shitesplosion."

Kel gave a little tut and sagged against his mop again. "Way to bring that fantasy crashing to the ground there."

"You're welcome," Esme said, pulling her jacket on.

Kel stepped aside to let her out. "You back on tomorrow?"

"Nope! Two whole days off," Esme gloated, waggling a two-fingered peace sign in his face as she passed him.

"Two? Jesus. Who did you have to sleep with to make that happen? And, can you give me his number?"

Esme gave a little chuckle. The remark probably deserved more than that, but exhaustion was muting her reactions. She could hear a hot shower and her bed calling to her from a mile up the road.

"Goodnight, Kel," she said. "And make sure you take that break."

"Too bloody right," Kel said. "Night. See you on..." He puffed out his cheeks. "Whatever day is two days from now."

"God knows. I'm sure someone will keep us right," Esme replied. "See you then."

She shambled away from the changing room and along the corridor in the direction of the nurses' station. The usual alarms *bleeped* and *pinged* from the usual doorways as she passed them. The usual snores. The usual groans.

Not her problem. Not tonight, not tomorrow, and not the next day, either. Two whole days off. Even if she slept for one—which felt quite likely at the moment—she still had another spare. That was dream-come-true stuff.

There was no one at the nurses' station when she got there, everyone was off doing the final rounds for evening medication. Somewhere along the corridor behind her, she heard Kel's voice. It was bright and enthusiastic, stuffed full of fake cheer.

"Nice try on the redecorating in here, Mr French. But maybe best leave it to the experts next time, eh?"

Esme smiled, scrawled her name on the sign-out sheet, then hurried towards the ward exit before anyone could ask her anything. She swore some days a shift at Raigmore was like being Al Pacino in *The Godfather*.

Just when you thought you were out, they pulled you back in.

Tonight though, she made it to the ward door, out into the corridor, and over to the lifts without anyone calling after her. The lifts weren't there, so she took the stairs rather than risk hanging around to wait. It wouldn't be the first time a doctor or one of the senior nurses on duty had caught up with her while she waited for the lift to arrive and she'd found herself talked into working an extra couple of hours.

There were three flights of stairs to get down. Her feet didn't complain. They knew it was in their best interests to get the hell out of there quickly and with as little fuss as possible.

Two days.

More than that, even. Fifty-nine hours until she clocked back in again. Her feet were willing to take the hit.

She took the side door to the outside when she reached the bottom of the stairs, and the cool October air woke her up a little, sharpening her senses.

It was quicker to walk through the hospital and leave by the Outpatients door, but the longer she was inside the building, the greater the chance she'd be dragged into some unpaid overtime.

No, better to take the longer way around the outside of the building, enjoy the crispness of the air, and—hopefully—not meet another living soul.

Or, at least, none with any direct authority over her working hours.

With thoughts of the next fifty-nine hours filling her head, Esme Miller set off around the outside of the hospital and headed for a home she would never reach.

HE LOVES *the way she walks. So fluid. So smooth. She almost looks real.*

But then, he loves the way they all walk. Always different. Unique. Like a fingerprint. And yet, exactly the same in all the ways that count.

Her gait varies, just like the rest of them. Sometimes it's bright, like when she walks little Chloe to school, or sets off to meet her sister for lunch. Tonight, now, her footsteps are flat. Slow. Plodding. She's battling exhaustion. It isn't real, of course, but she feels it all the same.

She'll sleep soon.

He'll allow her that.

Her movements are so lifelike. Just by looking, it's almost impossible to know that she's on strings. Most people can't see them. Most people don't understand.

He is not most people.

He is different.

And yet, in all the ways that count, he is the same.

She comes around the back of the hospital, slumping her way past the big bins, then thacking onto the grass. That too seems so real, so alive, so here-and-now. But he sees the truth.

Or rather, the lies.

He wonders, just briefly, what she's thinking as she pulls her bag higher on her shoulder and sets off across the shaded lawn. Then, he reminds himself of the stark reality of it.

She isn't thinking. None of them are. None of them ever do.

Taking the shortcut across the grass will save her four minutes on her journey home. He knows this. He has timed her often enough.

Four minutes, even accounting for the way she'll pick up speed when she's halfway across, right in the middle of the darkest spot, hidden in the shadows of the trees lining the edges of the hospital grounds.

The trek across the grass will take her less than two minutes. Not long. But long enough.

Beyond the trees, the evening traffic trundles by. Pointless people leading make-believe lives. Fools. Liars. All of them.

They don't matter. None of them matter. Not now.

Not ever.

She's a third of the way across the grass. The darkness reaches out to embrace her.

The knife is heavy in his hand, its weight yet another deception in a never-ending list.

She is halfway now. Her pace quickens.

He loves the way she walks. She almost looks real.

But he knows different. He knows the truth. And soon, he'll show them. He'll show them all.

CHAPTER TWO

DETECTIVE CHIEF INSPECTOR JACK LOGAN PLODDED UP THE WINDING staircase that led to his top floor flat, his boots scuffing on the uneven stone steps. The day had been a long and exhausting one. Not physically, granted, but a stack of paperwork had finally caught up with him, and being stuck behind a desk for hours always took its toll on his energy levels.

Still, he'd broken the back of it, and what had been a stack was now just a couple of small bundles and an overflowing box file. He'd be through it all in a week or so. Sooner, if he could convince DI Forde to chip in. That shouldn't take too much in the way of bribery and corruption.

Ben Forde wasn't exactly a fan of the paperwork—no bugger was—but he didn't hate it in the same way that Logan did. There were even rumours that he'd once said he found it 'relaxing,' but he'd been quick to take that back after everyone in earshot had offered to help him get properly chilled-out by giving him their own to do.

After the paperwork was out of the way, Logan was hoping for a bit of breathing space. He might even take a couple of days off to get settled into the flat properly. He'd been in for almost two months now but was still living out of boxes.

Not many boxes, granted. He hadn't brought a lot with him when he'd left Glasgow. Still, it would be good to get properly set up. Even better to take a couple of days to unwind. Things had been more hectic than expected following his move north, and he felt like he hadn't caught his breath in weeks.

He might even finally get around to putting up that shelf he'd bought the day after moving in, although he wasn't committing himself to it quite yet.

There were eight flats in the block, each one staggered half a floor above the one before, on opposite sides of the stairwell. He was passing the floor before his own—eight steps from his front door—when he heard the shout and the sound of something breaking. A plate, he thought. Possibly a glass.

His desire to get home carried him up a step before a sense of... not duty, exactly, more common decency, stopped him.

"How was that me? Eh? How is that my fault?"

Male voice. Young-ish. Mid-twenties, maybe.

"It's no'. You're no' listening. That's no' what I'm saying!"

A woman. Younger still, he thought. Both voices were raised, albeit in different ways. His was angry. Aggressive. There was a pleading edge to hers. Not quite desperation, but not far off it.

"Well, what *are* you fucking saying then, eh?"

A crash. A thud.

"Come on, then? What are you fucking saying?"

Logan hadn't met any of his neighbours yet.

He stepped down onto the landing.

Now seemed like as good a time as any to introduce himself.

He knocked on the door. It was a policeman's knock, the type of knock that made it very clear the knuckles responsible for it weren't going to go away without getting an answer.

The man's voice dropped in volume but lost none of its anger. There were a few hissed comments too quiet for Logan to hear, then a series of thudding footfalls.

The door was yanked open. An unshaven twenty-something with crooked teeth and greasy hair scowled at him, chest all puffed out, fist clenched at his side. His eyes were set so far back in their dark hollows they looked like they'd been put there with a Black & Decker.

"The fuck you want?" the scrote demanded. He was shorter than Logan by a whole head, but his system was currently so flooded with testosterone that he didn't appear to notice his height disadvantage.

Logan held the man's gaze long enough to make an impression, then looked past him to where a skinny lassie with a hair colour that could only have come from a bottle stood at the far end of the hall. Her arms were wrapped around her middle, her weight shifting from foot to foot.

Pieces of a broken mug lay on the bare floorboards around her, a dark brown tea or coffee stain on the wall marking the spot where it had first made impact.

"Everything alright?" Logan asked.

"The fuck's that got to do with you?" the scrote demanded.

Logan flicked his gaze to him, just briefly. "Did I look like I was talking to you?" he asked.

The chest puffed out further. Logan could practically hear the *creak* of the bastard's joints as he tightened his fists.

"The fuck you say?"

"Miss?" said Logan, ignoring him. "Everything alright?"

She opened her mouth as if to reply, but then closed it again when the door started to close.

"She's fine. Fuck off."

The door stopped when it hit the toe of Logan's boot. He thought about reaching into his coat for his warrant card, but decided to keep that a surprise for now.

"Gonnae move yer fucking foot?"

"Gonnae shut yer fucking mouth?" Logan countered, eyeballing him.

It was a direct challenge. There were two ways this could go now, Logan knew. Either the scrote would double-down and come at him, or he'd back off. Chicken out. Shite the bed.

"What?" the man said. He seemed to shrink a little as his eyes furtively looked Logan up and down.

Shite the bed, then.

"Miss? Are you OK? I heard shouting," Logan said.

She stopped her shifting and slouched all her weight on one hip. Her face became a sneer. "Piss off, ya nosy bastard. What's it to do with you?"

Emboldened by this, the greasy wee bam started bumping the door against Logan's foot. "You heard her. She's fine. So, off ya fuck, eh?"

Logan looked between them, then sucked in his bottom lip.

"Fair enough," he said.

He was about to withdraw his foot when he spotted the well-trodden pile of mail on the floor. Brown envelopes, mostly, with red 'Final Demand' warnings stamped on the front.

"Tanya," he said, reading the name on one of the address labels. He met the girl's eye again. "I'm just upstairs, alright? If you need me."

She said nothing, just looked down at the floor and tightened her arms around her middle as Logan withdrew his foot. The door closed between them with a *bang*.

"Prick!" the man spat through the wood, and then there came the thudding of retreating footsteps, some low muttering, and the slamming of a door somewhere further back in the flat.

Logan grunted below his breath. "Welcome to the bloody neighbourhood," he mumbled, then he reached into his pocket for his keys, plodded up the remaining steps, and finally made it home.

With its dirty windows and peeling metal railing, the stairwell that ran up through the block of flats was tired and grim. Much the same could be said for the inside of Logan's flat, too.

He'd originally been set up with a decent place overlooking the river until Bosco Maximuke, a local property developer, drug-dealer, and long-time pain in Logan's arse, had interfered. Three other places had fallen through since then, and Logan was convinced Bosco was behind them all.

After he'd come for a viewing of this place, Logan had partly been hoping that Bosco would cause this deal to collapse, too. Unfortunately, his offer was accepted, his deposit taken, and the keys duly presented to him by a letting agent who had made no attempt to disguise the fact that she could hardly believe her luck.

It had come fully furnished, but Logan had insisted most of the stuff be taken out before he moved in, and preferably destroyed in a big fire somewhere far away. The couch, in particular, had been covered in so many dirty stains it looked like a map of some newly discovered country. And not one anyone in their right mind would ever want to visit.

He'd bought a few pieces of furniture to replace some of the stuff that had been chucked out. A new couch. A coffee table. That sort of thing. He'd since been informed by Ben's wife, Alice, that none of it matched, and that the couch was too big for the room. Annoyingly, she was probably right.

Logan groaned his way out of his coat, tossed it onto one arm of the couch, then flopped down beside it. The three-seater may well have been too big, but it was comfy. Bloody should be, considering what he'd paid for it.

He'd just kicked off his boots and put his feet up on the coffee table when two things occurred to him. The first, and most important, was that he should've put the kettle on before sitting down. Now, he was going to have to get up again, just as he was getting comfortable. It was a rookie mistake, and he cursed himself for it.

He could *not* have tea, of course.

He contemplated this idea for a moment, but quickly dismissed it as ridiculous. He was tired, aye, but he wasn't so tired that he was willing to forgo the unique pleasure of a post-shift cuppa.

Still, where was DC Neish when you needed him?

The second thing that occurred to Logan was that the red light on his phone was blinking, signalling he had a new message. He'd never had a message on the landline before. He didn't even think anyone had the number. It would be some shite about PPI, or a non-existent traffic accident he'd never been involved in, no doubt, but he had to pass the handset on the way to the kitchen, so decided to check it anyway.

It took him a full forty seconds of staring at buttons to figure out which one played the messages. He let it run as he continued through to the kitchen, jiggled the cord out of the back of the kettle, and began filling it from the tap.

"You have... one new message," the machine declared in an unconvincing female voice. "From... unknown caller. Received today at... six forty-nine... PM."

Logan put the lid back on the kettle and jammed the cord into the socket.

There was nothing more from the phone's base unit. He clicked the switch on the kettle, idly wondering if the message had started to play yet, or if he had to go and press some other button to set it going.

And then, he heard it. A soft hissing. A near-silence that suggested a void on the other end of the line. A breath. Two. In. Out. Slow and steady.

And then, a *click* as the handset was replaced at the other end, and a half-second of dead tone before the robotic voice piped up again.

"You have no more messages. To play these messages again, press one. To delete them, press—"

Logan leaned around the doorframe and jabbed a button on the base unit, silencing the machine.

He wondered, just briefly, about the message, but then the water in the kettle began rolling to the boil, and he pulled open the cupboard where he kept the mugs.

Then, when he found it empty, he turned his attention to the sink, and to the Jenga-style stack of dirty dishes contained therein.

By the time he'd picked the least dirty mug and swirled it under the tap, he'd stopped thinking about the phone message.

By the time he'd settled back down on his too-big couch with his size twelves up on the coffee table, he'd forgotten it had ever happened.

KEL YAWNED, stretched, and stepped out of the A&E department's makeshift sleeping quarters, directly into the path of an oncoming ambulance stretcher. Two paramedics were rattling off details of the patient to a frantic-looking nurse, their dark green uniforms made darker still by the smears of blood that covered their fronts.

One of the emergency department doctors was bent double beside the trolley, scuttling crab-like as he worked on the patient. He had his back to Kel, blocking the view of the person on the stretcher.

Kel stepped back into the room, making space for them all to pass. One of the older nurses—Cindy—was doing the same sideways scuttle as the doctor, but on the opposite side of the bed. She'd have done this a hundred times before, but there was a panic to her movements and a frantic edge to her voice.

"Esme? Esme? Can you hear me, pet?"

"Wait, what?" said Kel, stepping out as the trolley swept past. "Esme?"

One of the paramedics looked back over her shoulder. Her eyes were wide, her pupils dilated. A smear of crimson was wrapped across her throat like a scarf.

"Aye," she confirmed, recognition flitting across her face when she saw Kel. "It's Esme. She's been attacked."

"*Attacked?* What?" Kel spluttered. "You sure?"

The paramedic's lips went thin and colourless. She glanced down at the woman on the stretcher, then swallowed. "Aye," she said, throat tight, voice hoarse. "I'm sure."

LOGAN'S PHONE RANG, jolting him awake. His arm jerked, tipping the mug he'd been holding balanced on his stomach, and sloshing his shirt in a glug of cold tea.

"Shite," he spat, the cold cutting through the bleariness and peeling his eyelids all the way open.

After dumping the mug on the coffee table, he rummaged in his coat until he found the phone. He didn't bother to look at the number on the screen. There was no point. Who else would be calling him at this time?

"Logan," he grunted, stifling a yawn. He checked his watch. After eleven. He'd been asleep for over an hour.

He listened to the voice on the other end.

"When?" he asked, once it had finished. He listened for the answer, then checked his watch again. "OK. I'll head right there. Call in DS McQuarrie. Get her to meet me there. Is the scene locked down?"

He nodded at the answer.

"Good. Right, then. Keep me posted."

He hung up, let his head sink back onto the couch, and sighed.

Maybe take a few days off.

He snorted at the very idea of it now.

"Wishful bloody thinking."

CHAPTER THREE

THE ATMOSPHERE IN A&E BROKE THE BAD NEWS TO LOGAN BEFORE anyone could say a word. He caught the eye of a uniformed officer who was standing talking to a nurse, and received a brief shake of the head in response.

Damn it.

The waiting area was fairly small, with mismatched chairs and a table laden with dog-eared magazines. There were two people waiting to be seen, one nursing a swollen wrist, the other holding a cold cloth against her forehead. Neither looked serious, so Logan had no issue with keeping them waiting.

There was a sliding glass hatch in the wall that showed a corner of a little reception room beyond. A nurse spotted him and said something he couldn't hear. DS McQuarrie's face appeared at the glass a moment later, and she gestured to a door just to the left of the window.

"Sir," Caitlyn said, straightening as he entered the room. "Bad news, I'm afraid."

"Aye," said Logan. "What have we got?"

"Victim worked here at the hospital," Caitlyn began.

"Esme," said the nurse sitting at the desk. "Her name was Esme."

Caitlyn glanced back at her. "Esme. Yes. Sorry," she said, then she nodded past Logan to the door at his back. "Should we maybe...?"

"Aye. We'll step outside," Logan said. He smiled grimly at the nurse.

"Sorry for your loss."

"It's not our loss. It's Rowan's," the nurse said. Her hand went to her mouth, tears blurring her eyes. "And, oh God, Chloe. Little Chloe."

"Family," Caitlyn said, although Logan had already guessed as much.

The nurse drew in a steadying breath through her nose, shook her head, then raised her gaze to the detectives. "Right. OK. If you need anything else, just... I don't know. Someone will be able to... I'm sure."

"Thank you. We know it's difficult," said Caitlyn. "Are you OK? Would you like us to get someone?"

"I'm fine," the nurse said. "Honestly. It's just a shock. Go do what you have to do."

Logan led the way out of the room, and Caitlyn followed him to a quiet area of the corridor. There were four treatment areas leading off from the corridor ahead. Three of them were open, showing empty beds. A blue curtain was drawn across the fourth, concealing everything within.

A male nurse stood talking to a uniformed female officer over by a window. They kept their voices low, occasionally shooting glances at the curtained-off area.

"So?" Logan prompted.

Caitlyn had a notebook in her hand but rattled off the details without looking at it.

"Esme Miller. Age thirty-three. Nurse here. She was on her way home from her shift when she was attacked. Right outside on the hospital grounds. Another nurse found her on his way in. He was running late, and it's a common shortcut, apparently."

"Attacked how?"

"Multiple stab wounds," Caitlyn said. "She was alive when they brought her in, but she'd lost too much blood, and some of her organs had been punctured. There was nothing they could do. She died a few minutes before I got here."

There was some commotion from out in reception, and then the double doors that led through into the back area were thrown wide. A red-haired forty-something man with wide eyes and a dishevelled appearance came barrelling through, his movements sharp and agitated.

"Esme? Esme?"

"Rowan, wait," said a nurse, hurrying through the doors behind him.

"Where is she? Where's Esme?" the man demanded, powering along the corridor, head snapping left and right as he searched the area.

"Rowan, wait pet, please!" the nurse pleaded, but he was having none of it.

His eyes fell on the curtained-off area and he broke into a jog. Caitlyn moved quickly to intercept.

"Mr Miller? Mr Miller, stop."

He looked at the woman blocking his path, something like disgust contorting his features. "What? Who are you? Let me through. That's... My wife's in there."

"I understand that, Mr Miller," Caitlyn said. "But I'm afraid you can't go in there. I'm sorry. I know how you must be feeling, but we can't risk you contaminating potential evidence."

"*Evidence?*" Rowan spluttered. "She's not *evidence*, she's my bloody wife! She needs me. I should be in there with her. Who even are you, anyway?"

Logan groaned inwardly. He didn't know. The poor bastard. He had no idea.

But he was catching up quickly.

"Wait. Wait," he said, the force of the realisation forcing him back a step. He shook his head, tears cutting down his cheeks from nowhere. "No. No. She's not..."

He tried to step past Caitlyn, his voice rising. "Esme? Esme, sweetheart, it's... It's..."

"I'm sorry, Mr Miller," said Logan, moving in to stand with DS McQuarrie.

"She's not. She can't be," Rowan said, the words squeaking out of his narrowing throat. He looked from one detective to the other, eyes pleading, like they could somehow change it. Somehow fix it. "Please. *Please.* She's not."

The nurse who had come hurrying through after him put a hand on his arm. He stared down at it, frowning, like he couldn't quite figure out what it was.

"I'm so sorry, pet," she said, her voice almost as shaky as his. "We're all so very sorry. We did everything we could."

Rowan continued to stare at the hand on his arm. His Adam's apple was the only part of him that moved as he swallowed a few times, like he was choking back a mouthful of spew.

"I'm DCI Jack Logan, this is DS Caitlyn McQuarrie," Logan told him. "I won't insult you by saying we understand what you must be going through."

Rowan pulled his arm away from the nurse's hand. "I want to see her. I want to go in. I want to see her."

"I'm afraid that's not possible," said Caitlyn. "Like I said—"

"I heard what you fucking said! But that's my wife! I want to see her. I need to see her!"

"Mr Miller—" Caitlyn began.

Logan put a hand on her shoulder. "I think we can allow it," he said. He met Rowan's eye and held his gaze, drilling the importance of what he was saying into the man. "But I'm afraid we can only let you see her. Any contact will jeopardise our chances of catching the person responsible for this. Is that understood, Mr Miller?"

Rowan nodded without any hesitation. "I just... I just need to see her."

DS McQuarrie shot the DCI a look that suggested she had strong reservations. Logan acknowledged them with a nod, then placed a hand on Rowan's back and guided him to the corner of the curtain.

"Are you sure about this?"

"Yes," Rowan croaked, without an ounce of doubt.

Logan peeled the curtain aside and stepped through first. Caitlyn watched Rowan step through behind him, and the curtain fall back into place.

She met the nurse's gaze, then they both looked away at the sound of Rowan's sobbing. "No. Oh, God, no. Esme. No. No. God, no, please!"

"I'm sorry, Mr Miller. I can't let you go any closer." That was Logan's voice, soft and gentle, yet unmistakably rigid at the same time.

The nurse shifted anxiously, wringing her hands together as she waited by the curtain.

When it was pulled aside a moment later, she was quick to step in close to Rowan and put her arms around him. He let himself be pulled in, his own hands trailing limply at his sides, his face blank and expressionless, like a robot in the middle of a reboot.

"I'm so sorry. I'm so very sorry," the nurse whispered to him. "Come on, let's get you a cup of tea."

She looked to Logan for approval. "That's OK, isn't it?"

"Aye. Of course," Logan said. "Caitlyn, will you...?"

DS McQuarrie nodded. "Yes, sir."

She followed behind as the nurse led the still torpid Rowan towards an office tucked away at the back of A&E.

They were halfway to the door when Rowan stopped abruptly, his brain starting to process the enormity of how his whole life had been irrevocably changed.

"Oh, God. Chloe. What am I going to tell Chloe? What's she going to do without her mum?" he asked. He looked imploringly at the nurse and Caitlyn, like one of them might offer an answer. "What are we going to do?"

"We'll figure it out, pet," the nurse said, squeezing his arm. "Come on. Let's get you that cup of tea."

Logan watched Rowan resume his shell-shocked shuffle. Almost as soon as they'd disappeared into the office and closed the door, there was a tap on his shoulder.

He turned to find a woman in a parka jacket looking up at him, a circle of her face visible inside the synthetic fur edging of the hood.

"Ye alright there, Jack?" she asked, playing up her Irish accent. She looked past him in the direction of the door. "Was that her fella?"

"Uh, aye. Yeah, that was him," Logan said. To his immense annoyance, he caught himself straightening his shoulders a little. For the first time since he'd taken the phone call back at the flat, he wished he'd taken a moment to at least glance in a mirror.

The woman pushed back her hood and gave a little shake of her hair. "Thought so. That's why I hung back. I'm not great with the living ones. Give me the dead ones, any day. Much less small talk required."

She jabbed a thumb over her shoulder in the direction of the curtain. "Body in there?"

It had been a few months since Logan had first met the pathologist, Shona Maguire. He'd been struck then just how unlike the previous pathologists he'd worked with she was, and that opinion had not changed since. It had grown, in fact, to the extent he was now positive he'd never met *anyone* who was quite like she was.

Professionally, he meant.

That was all.

"Aye. She's in there," Logan confirmed.

"Stabbing, I hear."

"So it seems. I'll leave it to you to make the final call."

Shona tucked her thumbs into an imaginary pair of braces and rocked back on her heels. "That's why they pay me the big bucks."

"Do they?" Logan asked.

"Not really," she admitted, letting the non-existent braces *twang* back into place. "Piss poor, actually. I should probably strike."

"Aye, well, if you could leave it until you've dealt with this, that would be handy."

She tapped a finger to her forehead in salute. "Ten-four."

Shona beckoned to the male nurse who stood beside the uniformed officer over by the window. "Is there a porter available who can help me move..."

"Esme," Logan mumbled.

"...Esme around to..." She glanced at the office door, then lowered her voice to a whisper so that Rowan Miller wouldn't hear. "...*you know where?*"

The nurse blinked a few times, like he wasn't quite sure what was being asked of him, then gave a nod. "I think Kel's just taking a minute to himself. I'm sure he'll be able to help. I'll go check. If not, I can do it."

Shona gave the nurse a thumbs-up as he passed her, then turned back to Logan. "Want to come watch?"

"Not even remotely," Logan said.

The pathologist crinkled her nose. "Nah, that line very rarely works," she admitted. She backed away in the direction of the curtain. "You do still owe me lunch, though."

"How about breakfast?" Logan asked her.

Shona's expression became one of genuine surprise. "Detective Chief Inspector! What are you suggesting?"

"That I swing by your office in the morning to see what you've found," Logan said. "I'll bring you a bacon roll."

"Chuck an egg on top and it's a date," Shona told him, opening the curtain at her back. "Enjoy the rest of your night."

"You, too," Logan told her, then he winced.

"Well, it's unlikely to be a barrel of laughs," Shona said, after just a moment of hesitation. "But I'll see what I can do."

Then, with another little salute, she stepped through the curtain and closed it behind her.

Logan stood rooted to the spot for a moment, then shook his head.

"*You, too,*" he muttered. "Jesus."

He caught the Uniform smirking at him. She quickly glanced away when she realised she'd been rumbled.

Logan clicked his fingers and pointed at her. "You."

"Sir?"

"Any idea who found the body?"

The constable shook her head. "No, sir."

"Well, then," Logan grunted. He put a hand on the back of his neck and tilted his head, working out some of the knots. "Maybe you could make yourself useful and go find out."

CHAPTER FOUR

THE DOCTOR'S OFFICE WAS REASONABLY LARGE, BUT THE overflowing bookcases and industrial-looking shelves made it feel claustrophobically small.

The amount of clutter in the place didn't help. There was pointless shite on almost every surface. Stress toys. A *World's Best Surgeon* mug. Three cactuses in little pots.

The doctor who'd donated his office had made a point of telling Logan to, "Watch out for my trophies." Logan had expected them to be some sort of medical awards, but instead had been confronted by a half-dozen-strong army of little tennis figurines made of gold-coloured plastic. Runner-up prizes, mostly, according to the little etched plates on the front, but there were a couple of winners in there, too.

There had only been one chair—a battered old padded number with stuffing spewing out through a tear in the armrest—but one of the porters had brought in another at Logan's request. It was hard plastic on metal legs, and it had taken three attempts before Logan had found a way to fit it in the room in a way that wouldn't leave him playing footsie with the person sitting opposite.

The person sitting opposite at this particular moment was the nurse who had discovered Esme on the hospital grounds. He was older than Logan—mid-fifties or thereabouts—with greying hair, a day or two of stubble, and the demeanour of someone trying very hard to put a brave face on things.

Logan checked the notebook he'd been given by one of the Uniforms. "Mr... Brews, is it?"

"Bob."

"Bob. How are you doing?"

The question seemed to take the nurse by surprise. "Um... Aye. Bit shaken, if I'm honest. But, you know. We see this sort of stuff all the time."

He shook his head like he was annoyed at himself. "Not stabbings. Not really. But, you know, injuries." He swallowed. His bottom jaw juddered. "Death. It's all part of the job."

Bob attempted a smile. "Bit like you lot, I suppose."

"Aye. Different when it's one of your own, though," Logan said.

The nurse exhaled, puffing out his cheeks, and nodded in agreement. He didn't say anything, though, and Logan suspected that, right at that moment, he couldn't.

"Take a minute, Mr Brews. Bob. You've had a shock."

"You can say that again," Bob whispered. He became unable to hold Logan's gaze and looked past him instead, adopting that thousand-yard-stare that the detective knew only too well. He was replaying it in his head. Or rather, it was replaying for him, whether he wanted it to or not.

"Tell me what you saw," Logan encouraged.

"It was... I was late. Again. Fell asleep after dinner and woke up in a panic. The bus stopped at the traffic lights back along the road, so I asked to get off there. It's quicker to cut across the grass than wait for it to pull into..."

He smiled apologetically.

"Sorry. Not relevant."

"Don't worry. Just keep going," Logan told him.

Bob continued, hesitantly at first. The more he said, though, the more freely the words came.

"There's a gap. At the trees, where they meet the fence. There's a path. Aye, not a path, but a... It's been worn in. A track, I suppose. We all use it. Anyway, it's dark until you get closer to the hospital. I had the phone torch on. To see. Only, I didn't. See, I mean. Her."

He shook his head, annoyed at himself.

"I'm not explaining it. I heard her, is what I mean. This... noise. I thought it was an animal at first. I thought maybe a cat or a dog had been hit by a car and had crawled onto the grass. It's happened before."

"The sound was coming from the path ahead of you?" Logan asked.

"No. To the side. Over on the right. Nearer the fence," Bob said, gesturing in that direction. "I was late. Third time this month. I thought about not stopping, but... How couldn't I? I could tell it was in pain, whatever it was. It was suffering. I couldn't just... I wasn't just going to... Late or not, you know? I couldn't."

"I understand. It's to your credit, Mr Brews."

"Bob," he said again.

"It's to your credit, Bob. You couldn't leave it suffering. Then what?"

Bob bit down on his bottom lip, like he couldn't bring himself to say the words. Or maybe he couldn't face hearing them out loud.

"I think I realised before I saw her," he said, his voice a whisper. "Not that it was Esme, I had no idea, but that it wasn't an animal. The noises were... wrong. Different. I felt sick. Even before I saw her, I felt sick. Even before I knew, I *knew*."

He took a series of breaths, like a swimmer preparing to dive down deep. "She'd been gagged. There was tape on her mouth. Her eyes were rolling. She couldn't breathe. I took it off. There was a rag stuffed in there, right down into her throat. I took it out."

Bob's hands were twisting together, the veins on his forearms standing on end. "And the blood. There was so much blood. Too much. Far too much. I knew. She'd lost too much. But I shouted. I shouted and shouted, and then someone came. Paramedics. They'd been doing a drop-off. Luck, really."

Tears fell and *pluh-plinked* onto the front of his uniform. His voice had been wavering through the past few sentences and was now throaty and raw.

"But it was all too late. I knew that. They did everything they could, but I knew. All that blood. I knew."

"I'm sorry," Logan said. "I know how difficult this must be. You're doing really well."

Bob ran a bare forearm across his eyes, smiled weakly, and sat up straighter in the padded chair.

"Did you see or hear anyone else?" Logan asked. "Around where you found Esme, or maybe out on the pavement before you started across the grass?"

"No. I don't think so. I wasn't really paying attention, though. I was... With me being late and everything. I wasn't really looking, so I don't... I'm not... I'm sorry."

"You sure?" Logan pressed. "You didn't hear anything, maybe? When you were with Esme?"

The realisation of what the detective was getting at registered on Bob's face. "You think he was still there?" he gasped. "What, like, watching? You think he was there?"

"Almost certainly not, no," Logan said. "I'd be very surprised. But always worth asking. So, there was nothing that made you think someone else was nearby?"

"No. Nothing."

Bob's voice was flat, his face drained of colour. The initial adrenaline surge of the discovery was passing, and he was heading for a crash. Logan had seen it often enough to recognise the signs.

"I think we'll call it a night, Bob," the DCI said, flipping the notebook closed. "You don't need this right now."

Bob's relief wrote itself in large letters across his face. "Thank you."

"Do you have someone to get you home?" Logan asked.

"Home?"

Logan stood up. "Aye. Do you need a lift?"

"I'm on shift," Bob said. "We're... With Esme... We're short-staffed enough as it is."

"I'm not sure that's such a good idea."

Bob's mouth arranged itself into something that could almost pass for a smile. "No, nor me. But it is what it is."

He put his hands on the armrests as if to stand up, but then stopped.

"I think... If you don't mind, I'll just take another minute in here by myself."

Logan gave him a nod. "Of course. Take care of yourself. We'll be in touch, and if you think of anything else..."

He passed the nurse his card. "Just ask for me by name. Someone will get you through."

Bob took the card, glanced at it, then slipped it into the breast pocket of his tunic. "I will."

Logan side-stepped between the chairs, leaned to avoid a shelf overburdened with box files, then stopped by the door.

"All the best, Mr Brews."

"Bob."

"Bob," Logan corrected. Then, with a final nod of acknowledgement, he slipped out of the room and left the man alone with his grief.

CHAPTER FIVE

THE CRIME SCENE WAS THE STANDARD AFFAIR. SPOTLIGHTS. TAPE. White paper suits.

The usual.

The night was crisp and cold, and even with Raigmore spilling its light pollution towards the sky, Logan could make out a fair crop of stars winking down on the proceedings below.

A tent had been set up over the spot where the body had been discovered. Illuminated from within, its whiteness gave it a ghostly appearance against the dark trees standing guard at the edges of the hospital grounds.

Logan stood just outside the cordon tape, watching one of the paper suits come striding towards him. He didn't know many of the Scene of Crime team particularly well yet, but Logan would recognise Geoff Palmer's graceless lumbering anywhere. It was ironic that the only member of the team he really knew was the one he had the least desire to.

There was something about Palmer that rubbed Logan the wrong way. More than one thing, actually. Mainly, it was the fact that he always seemed annoyed at having been called in to do his bloody job. Even if the shout came in during office hours, he'd huff and grumble like it was all some big inconvenience.

Getting dragged out of his warm bed at this time of night had only served to make his mood worse.

"DCI Logan," Palmer said. The elasticated opening of the paper hood framed his face, turning it into a pudgy circle of flesh. It wasn't a good look on anyone, but Palmer's red cheeks and bulbous nose meant he appeared particularly grotesque and ridiculous in it.

Probably one of the reasons he hated showing up to these things, Logan reckoned.

"Geoff. What have we got?"

"Well, I'm hesitant to say, 'bugger all,'" Palmer spat. "But not far off."

He pushed back his hood and shot a look of distaste up at the hospital. "Maybe if half of NHS Highland hadn't gone trampling all over the place, we'd have been able to get something useful. No attempt made to preserve the crime scene. None at all."

"Well, they were more interested in preserving life at that point," Logan pointed out.

Palmer grunted, like he didn't consider this an acceptable excuse.

"I've seen how much blood she'd lost. They were obviously wasting their time," he said. "They should've known that."

Logan stared at the man in disbelief, grateful for the cordon tape between them.

"Preservation of life is top priority," Logan said.

"Well, it's made our job a lot more bloody difficult."

"Tough shite," the DCI snapped. The tone of his voice was enough to make Palmer reconsider voicing any further complaints. "What do we have?"

Palmer's suit rustled as he pointed to a spot about ten feet from the tent, where two other SOC officers were doing a fingertip search of the grass.

"We think she was grabbed there. Knocked over, then dragged closer to the fence. Marks suggest she was kicking at the time, so conscious."

His finger moved to the tent itself. "She was stabbed there. From the blood pattern, she was on the ground at the time. Either she tried to roll away, or he flipped her over at one point. He might've stabbed her again. You'll have to look at the body for that."

Palmer made a vague sort of gesture. "Looks like she tried to crawl back in the direction of the hospital after she'd been injured, but she didn't get far."

"What about the tape and the rag?"

Palmer's eyebrows knotted above his bulbous nose. "The what?"

"The nurse who found her, he said she had tape over her mouth. He took it off and took out a rag that had been stuffed in her throat."

"News to me."

"What? You haven't found it?"

"Haw!" Palmer shouted, cupping a hand to his mouth. The other SOC officers *meerkatted* up, all eyes turning his way. "Tape and a rag. We found anything?"

Glances were exchanged. Heads were shaken.

"Doesn't look like it, no," Palmer said, turning back to Logan. "Maybe your man took it. Or one of the paramedics. Not like they didn't fuck it all up enough already."

"Keep your eyes peeled for them," Logan instructed.

Palmer tutted. "Obviously."

For a moment, Logan considered grabbing the cordon tape and wrapping it around the bastard's throat, but common sense prevailed and he settled for glowering at him, instead.

"Anything else you can tell me?"

"Not a lot, no. It's a well-used path, and the scene was heavily compromised."

He pointed to the left of the tent, to where a fence divided the patch of grass from a neater, more landscaped area next door.

"If I had to guess, I'd say your killer went that way, over the fence into the grounds of Maggie's next door."

"Maggie's?"

"Cancer support," Palmer said. "You'll have seen the building. Looks a bit like a boat."

"Right, aye. I've seen it," Logan confirmed. He looked in the direction of the building now, but the view of it was blocked by a row of hospital vehicles.

"That's pretty much a guess, though," Palmer stressed. "There's some depression in the grass leading to the fence, but it could be unconnected." He shrugged. "Still, he had to go somewhere, so that's your best bet."

"He'd be bloody."

"Maybe not as bad as you think. There was no arterial spray, from what we can tell, and she was lying down, so beyond a bit of backsplash, he could've been reasonably clean, provided he was careful."

"And do you think he was?" Logan asked. "Careful, I mean?"

"Pathology would know more than me," Palmer said. "But he had the presence of mind to take her away from the track and, so you tell me, stick an efficient gag on her. No sign of the murder weapon either, so he took that with him. So, based on that, he certainly wasn't reckless."

"Have you got someone searching the grounds next door?"

"Not yet, no."

Logan tutted. "Why not?"

"Oh, hang on, and I'll just give the Magic Manpower Tree a shake, will I?" scoffed Palmer. He mimed shaking a tree. "Oh, look. Fuck all fell out."

He dropped his arms to his sides and scowled. "We're doing what we can with what we've got. If you want to talk to Hoon about getting more resource brought in, great. I won't stop you. Otherwise, it'll have to wait until we're done on this side of the fence."

Logan gave a grunt of annoyance. Mostly because Palmer was right. It was a relatively small department, and they couldn't do everything at once.

"You've cordoned it off, though?"

"Please," Palmer sneered.

"Right. Good."

"Can I get back to it now? Are we done?"

Logan briefly fantasised about throttling him again, then about-turned and started marching back in the direction of the hospital.

"Aye," he said. "We're done."

CHAPTER SIX

THE MORNING SUNLIGHT SEEPED INSIDIOUSLY THROUGH THE corridor's single window, weak and grey, and about as half-arsed as was to be expected for Scotland in October.

Logan paused outside the door to the mortuary for a moment, knocked twice, then pushed it open. *Ballroom Blitz* by Sweet hammered into him, almost forcing him back a step. He'd heard it from out in the corridor, but the door was heavy, and clearly had some impressive soundproofing qualities.

The volume of it trembled his eardrums and vibrated his internal organs in a deeply unpleasant way. Bracing himself, he stepped into the room just as *the man at the back* was instructing everyone to attack.

The song was blasting out from a cylindrical speaker that sat on a desk in the corner of the mortuary's outer office. There was a pencil holder beside it, the pens and pencils jiggling and dancing in time with the music's vibrations.

The swing door that led through to the actual business part of the mortuary opened, and Shona Maguire shuffled through. She was in the process of trying to peel off a pair of rubber gloves that seemed intent on making things difficult for her, and let out a little yelp of fright when she spotted Logan standing in the doorway.

"Jesus!"

"No' quite," Logan said, raising his voice to be heard over the racket.

"Alexa. Stop," Shona instructed.

The music kept blaring out.

"Alexa! Stop!" Shona shouted. "Alexa!"

The chorus kicked in, raising the volume in the room even further. Shona shot Logan a sideways look and had another go at shouting over it.

"ALEXA! STOP!"

The blitzing of the ballroom continued uninterrupted.

Logan reached the speaker in three big strides, and yanked the power cable out of the back. Silence fell so suddenly the impact of it almost shook the floor. A spinning blue light on top of the cylinder gave an indignant flash, then faded into darkness.

"Thanks. There's a volume button on top, though," Shona said. "You don't need to rip the cable out."

"It was that or kick it to death," Logan told her.

"It's one of those Amazon things. They're voice-controlled."

"Aye, I saw. Handy, that," Logan remarked. He considered putting the cable back in, then decided it wasn't worth the risk and hooked it in amongst the now stationary stationery.

"The volume might have been on the high side for it to work."

Logan nodded past her at the swing door. "I just assumed you were trying to wake that lot," he said. "Anyway, what happened to the brain music you usually listen to?"

"Long night," Shona told him. She gave a triumphant little cheer as she finally managed to remove the rubber gloves. "The brain music's good for concentration. It's not so good at keeping you awake."

She pressed a foot down on the pedal of a bin and dropped the gloves inside. "Don't suppose you remembered to bring...?"

Logan held up a white paper bag, and Shona's eyes lit up.

"Did you get an egg on it?"

The DCI smiled. "Don't say I'm not good to you."

A FEW MINUTES LATER, Logan and Shona sat on opposite sides of her desk. The detective was nursing a mug of tea, while the pathologist munched her way through the bacon and fried egg roll. The yolk had burst almost immediately and was in the process of dribbling down onto the paper bag Shona had placed on the desk directly in front of her as a makeshift napkin.

"Mm. 'S good," she said. "Want a bit?"

Logan considered the offered roll, and the puddle of yellow currently congealing in the paper bag.

"You're alright, thanks," he said. "I'm a vegan."

Shona almost choked. "You are not. Are you?"

"No. But I'm seriously considering it after watching you eat that, you clarty bastard," he said.

Shona laughed and dunked the edge of the roll in the pool of egg yolk. "It's the only way to eat it," she said, before cramming in another mouthful.

Logan took a sip of his tea and glanced impatiently at the swing door.

"So, late night, then?" he asked.

"Aye. Fairly. You?"

"Got home about three."

"But let me guess. You didn't sleep," Shona said. She crunched a crispy piece of bacon. "Just lay awake, thinking about how cruel a place the world is."

Her face lit up. "No. Wait. You stood by the window looking out over the twinkling lights of the city, all dramatic-like."

She narrowed her eyes and adopted a Clint Eastwood drawl. "*I'll show those criminal scum that crime doesn't pay. Not in my city.*" She smiled at him. "Am I close?"

"Was out like a light, actually," Logan told her. "Besides, my view's shite." He took another drink of tea. "Also, I'm not Batman."

"That's just what Batman would say," she said, eyeing him with exaggerated suspicion.

"Would he? Doesn't he literally say, 'I'm Batman' in the films?"

"Fair point," Shona conceded.

She finished the last bite of her roll, then brushed her hands together, dusting off the flour. After a glug of her tea, she tilted her head in the direction of the inner mortuary door. "Right. Want a look?"

Logan's eyes flicked very briefly to her stomach. "You not wanting to let that settle first? You know, before..."

"Hmm? Oh, no. It's fine," Shona said. She fished a piece of bread out from the back of her teeth with her tongue. "Wait, is that why you didn't have anything? Were you worried about...?"

She puffed out her cheeks and made a vomiting sound.

Logan gave a dismissive little wave. "If my stomach can handle watching you eating that, it can handle anything."

"Just as well," Shona said, standing up. "Because this one's *really* not pretty."

CHAPTER SEVEN

SHONA HADN'T BEEN KIDDING. ESME MILLER'S BODY HAD BEEN covered when they'd entered the mortuary, but when the sheet had been drawn back, Logan had been thankful he'd avoided breakfast.

You got used to them, of course. The corpses.

The first one was rough. No matter how prepared you thought you were, that first body on that first slab always hit you hard.

The apprehension made the second one worse. You built it up in your head beforehand, braced yourself for the horror to the point that you were panicking before you'd even set foot in the place. When you actually saw it, though, it wasn't as bad as your imagination had been preparing you for.

After that, it was easier. After that, it was just part of the job.

He wasn't sure how many down the line he was now. How many bodies had he seen? How many empty shells on cold slabs? How many of them could he remember the names of? Not many.

Not enough.

But then, it wasn't his job to remember them, he told himself. It was his job to avenge them. To get them justice. The remembering—the mourning —that was up to someone else.

Esme Miller lay on her back, naked and fully exposed. Shameless in death. Her torso was a pin-cushion of stab wounds, each dark hole standing out as a bloody affront against her pale, bloodless skin.

A single slit ran from below her sternum to just past her belly button.

Logan had seen similar incisions made during the autopsy process, but this one looked ragged and uneven. Either Shona wasn't as good at her job as he thought she was, or the killer had inflicted the wound himself.

"That wasn't me, by the way," the pathologist said, as if reading his mind. "She came in like that."

Logan nodded. Grunted. Said nothing.

"I'll run you through what I think happened," Shona continued. "Any questions, just ask."

She walked around the table until she was beside Esme's head. "There was an impact to the back of her head. A hard one, too. I reckon your man brained her from behind as she was walking across the path. Hilt of the knife, before you ask. Judging by the shape of it."

Shona took a pen from her pocket and indicated a couple of points on the top of the victim's skull. "There's hair missing and some damage to the scalp. I reckon he dragged her by the hair. Going by the state of her hands, she tried to resist being pulled. There's a lot of dirt under the fingernails. She dug in. Does that fit the scene?"

Logan nodded, and Shona made a satisfied little *click* sound with her tongue. At the same time, her face crumpled a little, like she hadn't really wanted to be right.

"Moving further down the body, there are some burst capillaries on the cheeks and elsewhere on the face that suggest asphyxiation. Nothing on the throat to indicate strangulation, though, and there's sticky residue on the cheeks that—"

"She was gagged. He put a rag in her mouth then taped it shut," Logan said.

Shona looked impressed.

"The witness told me."

"Oh. Right. Well, yeah, that's the conclusion I came to. I found some fibres in the throat and passed them to the Forensics lot, but I'd imagine they've already found the rag itself."

"Aye. You'd imagine," Logan said.

Shona raised an eyebrow. "They haven't?"

"No. We thought maybe the paramedics took it, but they say not. The nurse who discovered the body reckons he tossed it on the ground after he took it off her. Nobody has seen it since."

"So... what does that mean?" Shona wondered. "He came back for it? The killer, I mean?"

"That's the best I've got at the moment," Logan confirmed.

"He hung around, then? Nearby. While they were working on her. He didn't just run."

Logan shook his head. "He didn't just run."

"Bold," Shona said, then she continued down the body to where most of the obvious action had occurred. "And then, we have this. Fourteen stab wounds, various depths, mostly confined to the chest area. There's a lot of laceration on the forearms, too."

"She put up a fight."

"Tried to, anyway," the pathologist confirmed. "There are six other wounds on her back, but we'll come to that in a minute."

"Any thoughts on the knife?"

"Big bastard of a thing," Shona said. She held her index fingers about eight inches apart. "That size, roughly. Serrated. It's got a hilt. Is that the right word? Like a two-pronged little hand shield, an inch or so long on each side. They left an imprint next to some of the wounds."

"Jesus."

"Yeah. He put some force into it."

"Definitely 'he,' you think?"

"I tend to avoid definites so there's less chance of me looking bad later if I turn out to be wrong," Shona confessed. "But I'd say so. Could a woman put the same amount of force behind it? Probably. But—and I'm aware this isn't really my department—a knife that size? An attack like this? That's a man trying to compensate for something."

Logan couldn't really argue. Statistically, they were almost certainly looking for a man. He'd keep an open mind, of course, but right now he was just happy to narrow the search a little.

"Anything else you can tell me about him?"

"Nothing overly useful. Right-handed, I think, judging by the angle of the wounds. Probably a bit taller than the victim. The head impact was a downward strike from higher up."

"So why just 'probably' taller?"

Shona shrugged. "He could've jumped."

"Jumped?"

"He expended a lot of energy in the attack. Those stab wounds were pretty frenzied. And the head blow was hard. I mean, like, *hard*. Either he's big and *very* strong, or he didn't do it from a standing start," Shona explained.

Logan stepped through this in his head. "So, he runs up behind her, jumps, knife raised, and—"

"Bang. Cracks her on the skull," said Shona. "It's a theory, anyway. But, like I say, maybe he's just a big fella."

"And this?" Logan asked, indicating the slit in the stomach.

"Nasty one. I wish I could say it was done post-mortem, but judging by the wound, I think he cut her open while she was conscious."

"Why would he do that?" Logan asked. The question was more for himself than the pathologist, but she answered anyway.

"Not my area of expertise, I'm afraid," Shona said. She puffed out her cheeks. "He was mental, maybe? Probably one for the psychologists if you want a more thorough diagnosis than that. All I can tell you is that he cut her open, but her insides are all present and correct, if a little worse for wear. He didn't take anything, I mean."

"That's... good," Logan said.

"You know when 'she didn't have her organs harvested' is the most positive thing you can take away from a conversation that it's going to be a shitty day, don't you?" Shona said.

"Just the latest in a long line," Jack replied. He looked the victim up and down, then raised his eyes to meet Shona's. "Any sign of sexual assault?"

"No. Nothing. Although, from what the A&E guys tell me, her jacket and tunic had been removed," Shona said. "But I think that was so he could get to her back."

"Her back?"

"Yeah. Don't really want to turn her over again until I stitch her up, but I took some photos."

Logan followed her over to a large screen that was mounted vertically on the wall. A keyboard and mouse sat perched on a shelf that could've done with being a few inches longer and wider directly below the display. Shona gave the mouse a little dunt and the screen blinked into life.

Esme's body lay face-down on the slab in the image that appeared, several more puncture marks clearly visible around the middle of her back. They were bunched close together, like bullet holes clustered around a bull's-eye.

"I don't know if she turned herself over, or if the killer did it," Shona said. "I'd be surprised if she'd have had the strength, but it's not beyond the realms of possibility. Adrenaline would have been flowing pretty freely at that point." She indicated the stab wounds. "Obviously, these were him. As was this."

She clicked the mouse. The picture changed to show a closer shot of the upper back. Logan leaned in closer to the screen, his brow furrowing.

"What the hell's that?" he asked, peering at two marks on her skin just below and to the right of her left shoulder. "Not more bloody voodoo symbols?"

"Hmm? Oh, the Loch Ness woman? No. More straightforward than that."

She clicked the mouse again, and a similar image appeared. In this one, the wounds had been cleaned, and the markings were clearly visible.

"F A," Logan said, reading the letters aloud. He looked from the screen to Shona and back again. "What's that? F A?"

"Football Association? Folk Awards? Fuck All?" Shona guessed. She shrugged. "Could be anything."

"Aye. I suppose."

"Although..."

"What?"

Shona indicated the photo. "Look at the positioning of it on her back. It's all over on the left."

Logan studied the photo again. He was about to ask what she was getting at when the penny dropped.

"It's not finished."

"That's what I reckon. He was interrupted. Whatever he was writing, it's not finished. It's half a message."

"But what's the other half?"

Shona patted him on the shoulder. "I think that's your job, not mine," she said. She started to turn away, then stopped. "Oh, but one thing that might be useful?"

"Yes?"

"The knife he used? It couldn't have made those letters. Too big, there's no way your killer could've formed the shapes the way he did. Not using that thing."

"So, he had a smaller knife with him, too, then?"

Shona shook her head. "Not a knife, exactly," she told him.

She took a short metal rod from a tray and held it up. The overhead lights glinted off its thin blade.

"A scalpel."

CHAPTER EIGHT

"You should've phoned me, Jack."

Logan finished shrugging off his coat, then gave a dismissive wave in DI Ben Forde's direction. "You hadn't stopped in days. You needed to catch up with yourself," he said. "Guys your age, you need your rest."

"I'll 'guys your age' you, you cheeky bastard," Ben retorted. "Anyway, I was hardly relaxing. Alice had me in the bedroom all bloody evening. You should see the state of my knees."

Logan blinked, momentarily lost for words.

"No' like that. Get your mind out of the gutter, man," Ben told him. "We're putting laminate flooring down."

"Oh, thank God," Logan said.

"Well, I say, 'we,' but she assumed a strictly supervisory role," Ben continued. "I told her I'd happily pay for some other bugger to come in and do it, but oh no. 'Why waste money when we can do it ourselves?' she says. Then she just stands there in the doorway with a mug of cocoa and a judgemental bloody look on her face."

Logan gave a chuckle, then dumped his coat on the back of his chair.

"Sorry, if I'd have known, I'd have sent an Armed Response Unit to come get you out," he said. "Caitlyn was there though, so we got by without you." He looked around the Incident Room. "She in yet?"

"In and back out, boss."

DC Tyler Neish sat at his desk, the mouthpiece of a phone handset pressed against his shoulder so whoever was on the other end couldn't hear him.

"She said she was going back to the hospital to pick up some paperwork. Shift changes, or something."

The junior detective returned the phone to his ear and jumped back into the conversation. "Sorry about that."

"I'm just back from the hospital myself. I could've done it," Logan said.

Ben couldn't hide his smirk. His bushy eyebrows danced as he waggled them up and down. "Oh, aye? Hoping for a check-up with a certain Irish doctor, were we?"

"Well, considering all her other patients are all mutilated corpses, no. No' really," Logan said. "But aye, she took me through what she'd found on the body."

"Bad one?" Ben asked, noting the slight change in Logan's tone, and the way the lines of his face altered. Anyone else would've missed both, but Ben had known Logan longer than most.

"Aren't they all?" Logan asked, then he jabbed a thumb in Tyler's direction. "Who's Bawchops talking to?"

"The family liaison over at the Miller's house. He offered to be the point of contact."

"Did he now?" Logan asked. "And who's the liaison, out of interest?"

Ben glanced over at DC Neish, then shrugged. "Not sure, actually. Why?"

Tyler raised his eyes as Logan approached the desk with hand extended.

"Uh, boss?"

Logan made a beckoning motion. Tyler managed almost a full second of resistance, before caving in and passing the handset to the DCI.

"You alright there, Constable Bell?" Logan said into the phone.

For a moment, there was nothing but a soft hiss of static and a suggestion of surprise. Then, the voice of Constable Sinead Bell returned to him down the line.

"All good here, sir," she said, a little sheepishly.

"Great. Glad to hear that," Logan said, staring down at Tyler as he spoke. The DC wilted under his gaze and started flicking through his notebook like it was suddenly the most interesting thing in the world. "How's Mr Miller doing?"

"Um, not bad, actually, sir. He's got someone from Victim Support in with him now. A counsellor. Think they know each other through the hospital. I, uh, thought I'd take the opportunity to call and report in. They're talking to Chloe now. The daughter."

The daughter. Damn. He'd known about her from conversations at the hospital, of course, but there had been so much else going on, so much else to do, to think about.

"What age is she?" he asked.

"She's six."

Logan pinched the bridge of his nose. "Shite. And how is she coping?"

"Upset, obviously. But more sort of... confused, really. I don't think she quite understands."

Of course, she didn't. How could she?

"Poor wee bugger."

"She's that alright, sir," Sinead agreed.

"I'll get over this morning. Let me know when Vic Support's finished."

"Right, sir. Will do," Sinead said. He heard her take a breath before she continued. "Um, is that everything?"

Logan's eyes narrowed. "Aye. Why?"

"Can you... Would you mind putting me back onto Tyler? Onto DC Neish, I mean? I just... I need to check something with him."

Logan muttered something unintelligible, then held the phone out to Tyler. "You have thirty seconds. Make it quick."

Tyler regarded the phone with suspicion, like it might be some sort of trap.

"Twenty-five seconds."

Lunging, the DC took the phone, cradled it to his ear, and turned in his chair so he was facing away from the rest of the room. "Hey... Yeah, I know."

He flicked a wary glance in Logan's direction. "Uh, yes. That sounds like a plan, um, constable."

Tyler listened. Logan continued to loom over him, tapping his watch.

"Yes. I agree. Half-seven," Tyler said. He was clearly enunciating every word, like it somehow made the conversation he was having more legitimate. "That sounds fine."

"Five. Four," Logan announced.

"OK. You, too. Bye!"

"Three. Two."

Tyler pressed the 'end call' button and dropped the phone on the desk like it was suddenly too hot for him to hold. He cleared his throat and then gestured to the abandoned handset. "Work stuff."

"My arse," Logan said. He cast his gaze across the Incident Room, as if only just noticing how empty it was. "Where's Hamza?"

"He's still on that HOLMES course up in Aberdeen," said Ben. "They're doing a new update, apparently. Just as I was getting used to the last one."

Logan grunted. HOLMES—or, to be more precise, HOLMES 2—was a computer system that linked up all the UK police forces, allowed the sharing of information, and helped keep track of ongoing cases. The acronym stood for 'Home Office Large Major Enquiry System,' and it had been put together for the sole purpose of being an all-in-one crime investigation tool.

Unfortunately, it was a heap of shite. It had been barely usable when it had first come online, and every subsequent update had somehow found new and interesting ways of making it worse.

"When does it finish? Can we get him back?" Logan asked.

"We've already called him back in. He's on his way over."

"Right. Good. We're going to need all hands on deck for this one."

"Aye, reckon you're right there," Ben agreed. "And I say that as someone who's seen the Forensics report this morning."

Logan nodded grimly. "They didn't have a lot when I left last night."

"Things didn't improve much after you left, either," Ben said. "Not a lot to go on."

"Any mention of them finding the gag?"

Ben frowned. "Not that I saw, no. What gag?"

"There was a rag shoved in her mouth, then taped over the top," Logan explained. "The fella that found her took it off, but there's been no sign of it since. If we haven't found it, we have to work on the assumption the killer took it."

"You reckon he came back to the scene then, boss? Bit ballsy, that," Tyler said.

"Aye. But ballsy's good. We want ballsy."

"Means he's more likely to give himself away," Ben added.

"Exactly."

"Suppose," Tyler conceded.

"Forensics have anything else?" Logan asked.

Ben gave a non-committal shrug. "Not really, no. Said they couldn't be sure if he went over the fence or not but reckon it's the most likely escape route."

"Except he didn't escape. He waited until the victim had been taken away, then went back and cleared the scene."

"Worrying," Ben said, and Logan gave a grunt of agreement.

DC Neish looked from Logan to Ben and back again. "Why's that worrying? I thought it was a good thing? I thought we wanted him ballsy."

"There's ballsy and there's calculated," Logan said. "He attacked her yards from the hospital on a relatively busy path, dragged her a short distance away, then waited nearby while paramedics worked on her. The stab wounds were hard. Frenzied. And yet, he didn't run or panic after being discovered. He waited. Patiently. Then, he tidied up after himself."

"Calculated," Ben emphasised.

"And to be *that* calculated—to not panic like that—suggests it's not his first time," Logan continued. "There may be other victims."

"What, like a serial killer?" Tyler gasped, his eyes going wide.

"Look at the state of that," Ben said, glowering at the younger detective. "Like a kid in a bloody sweetie shop."

Tyler tried to dampen down his excitement. "What? I mean, obviously, it's terrible and everything. It's just... I've never been on a serial killer case before."

"Aye, well we don't know that's what this is," Logan pointed out. "It's only a hunch at this point. So, we keep an open mind."

"It almost certainly *won't* be," Ben said, shooting Tyler a chastising look. "So, try not to get your hopes up."

"I wasn't getting my hopes up! I don't *want* it to be," the DC protested. "I'm just saying, I've never worked one before. That's all."

"Aye, while frothing at the bloody mouth," Ben said. "It's a one-off. Let's hope so, anyway."

"No arguments there," Logan said.

He sat down at his desk. It was in the middle of the room, with the others circling it like wild west wagons. He had an office tucked away at the back of the Incident Room, but he had never been one for lurking around the edges. Much better to be slap-bang in the centre of it, even if that meant subjecting himself to Tyler's attempts at banter.

"Dr Maguire was going to email over the Pathology report when I left. I'll send it on and you can both have a read," Logan said, powering up his computer. "The big headline though, is that our killer had started to carve something into the victim's back, but we think he was interrupted."

Tyler groaned. "Not another occult thing?"

"That was my first instinct, but no. These were letters."

"Great. Just a good old *bog-standard* headcase then," said Tyler. "That's a relief."

Ben's brow furrowed. "Letters? What letters?"

"An F and an A," Logan said.

Ben sat on the edge of his desk. "F A?"

"Football Association?" Tyler guessed.

Logan shook his head. "We don't think it was an acronym. We think it's the start of a word. A short word. Like 'fat,' or 'fast,' or—"

"Fake," Ben said.

Logan looked at the DI over the top of his computer monitor. "Eh?"

"It says 'Fake.' Or would've done, anyway."

Tyler jumped in with the question before Logan could ask it. "How'd you know that, boss?"

"Because," Ben began. He exhaled through his nose, briefly glanced at the ceiling, then continued. "I've seen it before."

CHAPTER NINE

DS Caitlyn McQuarrie looked pointedly at her watch, then eyeballed the door across from where she had been sitting for the past fifteen minutes. One of the senior clerical staff members had vanished into the room to run off the shift schedules she'd asked for, and there had been a conspicuous lack of printer whirring sounds since.

Had it been a waiting room, there would at least have been a few magazines for her to flick through. Instead, all she had to look at was a stack of leaflets pointing out the warning signs of bowel cancer and stroke, and a chart showing the hospital's cleanliness rating over the past week. (Silver star: Room for Improvement.)

She didn't even have a signal on her phone, so couldn't check to see if the Forensics or Pathology reports had come in.

More to kill time than any desire to actually know what it said, she checked her watch again.

Sixteen minutes. Long enough.

Standing, she crossed to the door and gave a knock. The same member of clerical staff opened it immediately, like she'd been poised with her hand on the handle on the other side. The woman was short and stocky, and was rocking the classic half-moon-glasses-on-a-length-of-cord look favoured by women of a certain age and station.

"Yes?" she asked, peering up at Caitlyn like they'd never previously met.

"You were going to get me that printout."

"And I'm getting it," the woman said, bookending the sentence with a couple of tuts. "What does it look like I'm doing?"

Caitlyn resisted the urge to say, "Not a whole fucking lot, actually," and instead flashed something that could generously be described as a smile.

"Any idea how long it'll be?"

"I need to get clearance. Data protection," the woman replied.

"And how long will that take?"

"How long's a piece of string?"

"Roughly?" Caitlyn said, valiantly clinging to the last vestiges of her patience. "How long will it be, *roughly*?"

"Is there a problem here?"

Caitlyn turned to find a tall man with hawk-like features striding over to her. He wore a stethoscope around his neck, suggesting not only that he was a doctor, but that he wanted everyone to know it. She pegged him to be in his early fifties, with some grey streaks in his hair that gave him the sort of 'distinguished' look that would immediately see a woman of the same age consigned to the scrapheap.

"DS McQuarrie," Caitlyn said, producing her warrant card. She savoured the way the doctor's surly approach stuttered and came to an abrupt halt.

"Oh. Is this about Esme?"

Caitlyn nodded. "It is. We've requested shift records for who was on duty last night."

"I was just getting them," said the woman in the office, practically curt-seying when the doctor turned her way.

"Good. Let's speed it up. We don't want to keep this young lady waiting."

Caitlyn decided to let the 'this young lady' bit go, and instead just enjoyed the expression of defeat on the admin woman's face.

"Of course. I'll chase it up right away."

"Yes. Do that."

The doctor waited until the door closed, then smiled apologetically. "Sorry. They can be sticklers for procedure." He gestured to another door a little way along the corridor. "Here. You can wait in my office."

"I'm fine here, thank you," Caitlyn said.

"I'd like to talk to you, actually," the doctor told her. "Plus, I was on duty last night, so chances are you're going to want to talk to me at some point, anyway."

He made another gesture in the direction of the door.

"Shall we?"

"Here, let me shift those for you," said the doctor, moving a couple of tennis trophies that hadn't been even remotely in Caitlyn's way. He placed them in the middle of his desk, then motioned for Caitlyn to sit on the plastic seat Logan had dragged in the night before.

"Please," he urged, smiling encouragingly. He looked happy when Caitlyn sat, and lowered himself into the padded chair with the ripped arms. "Colin."

"I'm sorry?"

"Colin. Fletcher. *Doctor* Colin Fletcher."

"Right. Yes. DS McQuarrie. Caitlyn."

"Caitlyn!" he said, clasping his hands together. "Lovely. And 'DS,' that's Detective...?"

"Sergeant."

"Detective Sergeant!" Colin echoed. "Well done."

Caitlyn hesitated, not quite sure how to respond to that. She decided not to bother.

"You were on duty last night when Esme Miller was brought in?"

Colin's face became sombre. He pinched his chin between thumb and forefinger like a man deep in thought. "Indeed. Yes. Terrible business. Poor Esme. We did all we could, of course, but we were fighting a losing battle. Whoever attacked her, he made a bloody good job of it."

He caught the look on Caitlyn's face, and hurriedly clarified. "Not *good*. I'm not condoning it in any way, of course. I'm just saying. If he'd been trying to kill her, then he went the right way about it. Mission accomplished."

"Right," said Caitlyn, making a mental note of all that. She fished in her pocket and took out her actual notebook, then flipped it open. "What can you tell me about when she came in?"

"What would you like to know?"

"Was she conscious?"

"Barely. She'd lost a lot of blood by that point. Everything was in the process of shutting down."

"Did she say anything?"

"Nothing coherent. The odd mumble, maybe. Nothing I caught." Colin shrugged. "She may have said something to the paramedics prior to her arrival, but by the time I saw her she was almost gone. There was nothing anyone could've done. I did everything I could."

"I'm sure you did, Mr Fletcher."

Colin smiled. "Please. 'Doctor.' It's petty, I know, but six years of medical school and a mountain of student debt. I have to justify it somehow."

Caitlyn doubted the mountain of debt part. The guy would've been educated back in the student grant days, and his plummy accent—Oxford area, she thought—suggested Mummy and Daddy probably helped with the bills.

"Doctor. My apologies," she said, going along with it. "I'm sure nobody blames you for what happened."

"Well, they shouldn't. She was too far gone," Colin reiterated, and Caitlyn wondered just whose benefit he was saying it for. "I did all I could."

"Did you know Esme well?"

"Hmm? Oh, no. Not really. We've been short-staffed of late, so everyone has been moving around. I knew her, but only vaguely. Always seemed nice, though. Excellent at her job. Really excellent. Well thought of by everyone. An asset to the NHS. She'll be sorely missed."

It sounded, Caitlyn thought, more like a press statement than an honest account of his actual feelings on the matter. She made a note of it and clocked him watching her when she looked up from her pad.

"Is everything alright?" he asked.

"Of course. Just making a few notes."

"Important to keep records," said Colin. He gestured to the box files on the shelves surrounding them. His eyes went to the pad again. "Do I get to see?"

"Why would you want to see?"

The doctor shrugged and smiled. "Freedom of Information."

Caitlyn didn't return the smile. "You're free to put in a request through the official channels," she told him.

"Ouch," Colin said, then he gave a little chuckle. "I jest. Of course, you need to take notes. Feel free."

"I will," Caitlyn told him, her tone making it clear that she had no need for, nor interest in, his permission. "You said there was something you wanted to talk to me about."

"Hmm. Oh. Yes. Yes, I did," Colin said. He tapped idly on the head of one of his trophies. It was a little tennis player in the middle of a serve. "It's nothing, really."

Caitlyn waited for him to continue. Unfortunately, patience had never really been her strong point, and she urged him on with a, "Well?"

"I'm hoping this doesn't strike you as too forward, but, well..."

He stopped fiddling with the trophy and clasped his hands in his lap. "I can't believe I'm asking this. It's not entirely appropriate, given the... You know. With everything?"

Caitlyn frowned. "I don't follow. What are you trying to say?"

"OK. I'm just going to... I'll just say it," Colin said. He took a breath. "Would you like to go out sometime?"

Caitlyn blinked. Stared. Felt her jaw dropping open.

"Go out? You mean, like...? What?"

"Dinner. The cinema. Whatever people do these days."

"Mr Fletcher, are you... Are you asking me on a date?"

"Doctor," Colin auto-piloted. He winced, annoyed at himself. "I mean, yes. Yes. A date. Or just... You know. As friends?"

"Friends? I literally met you five minutes ago."

"No, I know. I know. But, I mean... And forgive me if this sounds..."

Colin shook his head, clearly getting flustered. "I saw you last night. And, well, I thought... You're quite striking, and I thought..."

"A woman was murdered, Mr Fletcher," Caitlyn said, putting emphasis on the 'mister' part. "A woman was stabbed to death. A woman you know. I hardly think this is appropriate, do you?"

"Well, I mean... But we deal with it all the time, don't we? Death. We're hardly strangers to that. And life doesn't just stop when someone dies, does it? I mean, it does for them, obviously, but not... That's not what I'm trying to..."

He sighed and seemed to deflate. He dropped his head, then raised his eyes to meet Caitlyn's.

"Is that a no, then?"

"Yes, Mr Fletcher," Caitlyn said. She got to her feet and stood above him, looking down. "It's very much a no."

"I really do... I know it sounds silly, but I really do prefer 'Doctor,'" he said.

"Aye," Caitlyn said. She closed her notebook and shoved it back down into her pocket. "I know you do."

CHAPTER TEN

LOGAN SAT FORWARD IN HIS CHAIR, STUDYING THE IMAGE ON HIS computer screen. It showed a woman's chest, from midway up her breasts to the bottom of her chin. She had some well-defined tan lines from a bikini, and a smattering of freckles blooming up from her cleavage.

He noticed neither, his attention instead focused fully on the four letters sliced into the woman's skin.

FAKE.

"Danni Gillespie," said Ben. He stood behind Logan's chair, leaning in so the glare of the overhead lights wasn't blocking his view of the screen. "CID case from a couple of years ago. I got asked to give them a hand."

"Oof. Looks nasty," said Tyler, who had rolled his own chair over to Logan's desk.

"That's not the half of it. She was attacked on the way home from a night out. Sexual assault. Bad one," Ben said. "I mean, they're all bad, but this one was different."

"Different how?" Logan asked.

"Just... God. I don't know. The things he said to her. The things he did. I don't really want to..." Ben gestured to the screen. "There's a report. But it doesn't make for pleasant reading, I'll warn you now."

Logan glanced over his shoulder at the DI. One look at the older officer's face told him not to push for the gory details.

He turned back to the screen and clicked through to the next image. It gave a closer look at the first letter.

Fishing out his phone, he opened up the images Shona Maguire had emailed over and pinch-zoomed in. The shapes of the F and the A weren't identical, but they were close enough to suggest that the same person was responsible for both.

"Bollocks," he muttered. "I'm assuming we never caught whoever was behind it?"

"They had a suspect. Donald... something. Sloane. Weird fella. He looked a dead cert, but it fell through. He came up with an alibi. Pretty cast iron, if I remember rightly," Ben said. "Victim's brother and a couple of his mates leathered shite out of him soon after we'd let him go."

"Oh! I remember that!" Tyler said. "I was still in uniform. I remember the brother being brought in. Shaun Gillespie."

The way he said it suggested Logan should know who he was.

"Made a fortune writing apps for the iPhone when he was a teenager, boss. He now owns Osmosis."

"What's Osmosis?" Logan asked.

"The nightclub."

Logan scowled at the very thought of it. "No' really my cup of tea."

"You'd love it. They do retro nights every Wednesday. For the old—"

Tyler stopped himself just a little too late, and tried valiantly to salvage the situation.

"—er music fans. Fans of older music, I mean," he said, then he flashed a smile that showed too many teeth, cleared his throat, and went back to looking at the screen. "Anyway. You think it's the same guy? Both attacks, I mean."

"Hell of a coincidence, if not," Logan said, fixing Tyler with a glare. "The suspect. Sloane. Is he still living locally?"

"Don't know, boss," the DC said.

"I wasn't expecting you to know. I was expecting you to find out," Logan told him. When this elicited no immediate response, he clapped his hands together. "Chop chop."

"Oh! Right, boss. On it!" Tyler said, wheeling himself hurriedly back to his desk.

Logan turned and looked up at Ben. "You've spoken to the guy before?"

The DI puffed out his cheeks. "Aye. Briefly. And it was a while back."

"What was your instinct?"

"My instinct? My instinct was that he was a big creepy bastard. I was surprised when he came up with the alibi. We all were," Ben said. "But he did. There was nothing we could pin on him."

"Aye, well, we'll see if he has one for last night," Logan said. He returned to the screen, closed down the image and double-clicked the first of the reports attached to the case file in HOLMES.

"If you're going to read that, let me at least get you a coffee first," Ben told him. He drew in a breath as his eyes went to the file just as it opened. "Trust me. You're going to need it."

BEN HAD NOT BEEN EXAGGERATING. Logan clicked the X in the top corner of the document and felt a palpable sense of relief when the report vanished.

"Jesus."

DI Forde was back sitting at his own desk, hidden by Logan's monitor.

"Told you. If you'd still been on the drink, I'd have suggested something stronger than the coffee."

"Tempted, after that," Logan said. "And we never caught the bastard?"

Ben stood up so Logan could see him. "Technically, it's still an open case, but doesn't look like there's been any movement on it in a good year or so."

He was ashen-faced, and looked a few years older than he had when he'd sat down. Clearly, he'd been refamiliarising himself with the case while Logan had been digging through the details for the first time.

The details of the actual attack had been bad, but not the worst Logan had ever heard. It was a sexual assault and, like most, seemed to have been all about the power trip, rather than anything resembling actual desire.

The victim had been beaten, humiliated, and degraded over the course of almost three hours, but no attempt had been made on her life. After subjecting her to all the things he'd put her through, her attacker simply let her go.

It doesn't matter.

That was the phrase that kept coming up. One of the things he said to her, over and over, as he assaulted her. Beat her. Raped her.

It doesn't matter. You don't matter. None of it matters.

Because none of this is real.

Logan rocked back and forth in his chair, chewing on his bottom lip. "I'd like to talk to her. Danni Gillespie. I think we should talk to her."

Ben looked unsure. "It's... I mean, aye. Of course," he said. "But I can't say I relish the thought of making the poor lassie relive it all again. He did a real number on her. Mentally, as well as physically."

"I'm no' exactly jumping for joy at the prospect of it either, but if it helps us catch the bastard."

"Donald Sloane is still in town, boss," Tyler said, rolling himself back from his desk so he had a direct line of sight on the DCI. "Works at the butcher's on Queensgate. He was in the paper last month. They made a big sausage."

The furrowing of Logan's brow said it all.

"It was some charity thing. He's mentioned in the online version of the article," Tyler clarified. "It's how I found him. He's not on the electoral register."

"OK. Good work. We'll talk to him, too," Logan said.

"On what pretence?" Ben asked. "He threatened to sue us after everything was dropped the last time. Came close after Danni's brother gave him the kicking, too. There's nothing to tie him to this attack. We'd need a good excuse."

Logan stood and picked up his coat. "We're three bright lads," he said, then he shot DC Neish a sideways look. "Well, two and a half, maybe. I'm sure we'll come up with something."

"I know that was meant to be a dig, boss, but it's probably the nicest thing you've ever said to me," Tyler said, grinning from ear to ear. "Thank you."

"Well, don't get used to it," Logan warned. He pulled on his coat, then motioned for Tyler to get to his feet. "And hurry up."

"What? Oh? Am I coming?" Tyler asked, springing to his feet.

"Only because Ben's running the room and there's no other bugger around," Logan said.

"Good enough for me, boss!" Tyler said, looking pleased with himself.

The door to the Incident Room opened, and DS McQuarrie stepped through.

"Change of plan," Logan said.

Tyler tutted and flopped back into his chair. "Sake," he muttered.

"Quit your whinging. You'll get your chance. Caitlyn, keep your jacket on," Logan instructed, stalking towards the door. "You're coming with me."

CHAPTER ELEVEN

THE MAN WHO ANSWERED THE DOOR DIDN'T LOOK HAPPY TO SEE them. He was in his early thirties and managed to look irritatingly handsome despite the fact he had clearly just been woken up.

"What do you want? Do you know what time it is?" he grunted.

"It's five to eleven," Caitlyn said.

"Yes. What's your point? Some of us work nights, you know?"

"Aye. That's true. We didn't think of that, right enough. Sorry if we woke you, Mr Gillespie," said Logan, demonstrating a surprising amount of restraint. "We were hoping to speak to your sister, Danni."

Shaun Gillespie looked both of them up and down in turn. "Are you cops?" he asked. "What am I saying? Look at you. You're cops, aren't you? What do you want?"

"Detective Chief Inspector Logan. This is DS McQuarrie. We're with the Major Investigations Team. Is Danni available? We have this down as her address."

Shaun had already been partially obstructing the doorway, but now he put a hand on the doorframe, fully blocking the way. "What do you want to see Danni for? You finally got your fingers out of your arses and caught the bastard?"

"We're hoping she might be able to help us with another investigation. We think there may be a connection," Logan explained.

Shaun didn't show any sign of budging.

"A woman was murdered," Logan told him.

"Stop being a dick and let them in," a female voice instructed from somewhere behind Gillespie.

Shaun didn't look happy about it, but dropped his arm and stepped back, letting the front door swing open.

A woman stood in the hallway, dressed in oversized pyjamas and Homer Simpson slippers. Her hair was cut into a boyish bob, her eyes wide and worried behind the tips of her fringe. There was a weariness to the way she stood, like a weight was pushing down on her, and Logan got the impression she'd been waiting for this day to come.

"When?" she asked.

"Last night. Near the hospital," Logan told her. "A nurse."

Danni looked down and locked eyes with Homer Simpson. She shook her head, muttered something, then drew herself back up to her full height.

"Well then," she said, her voice flat and controlled. "I suppose you'd best come in."

"You have a lovely house," said Caitlyn, as she and Logan sat on an L-shaped leather sofa positioned in front of a wood-burning stove. A large television was mounted on the wall above it, so thin and sleek it could almost have been painted on.

"It's not hers. It's mine," said Shaun. He caught the look Danni shot his way, tutted his annoyance, then slumped on through the open-plan living room and dining area. "Fine. I'll be in the kitchen."

They waited until he'd disappeared through the door at the far end of the dining area, then Danni smiled apologetically. "He's not great in the mornings."

"I know the feeling," Logan said. "Sorry. Did we get you both up?"

"What? No," said Danni, confused by the question. She glanced down at her pyjamas, then pulled her slippered feet up onto the armchair beside her. "Oh. Yeah. I don't really go out much these days."

There was a moment of slightly awkward silence at that, which Danni rushed to fill.

"What is it you think I can help you with?" she asked.

"Right. Aye. Well, as I said, a woman was murdered last night. We have reason to believe the individual who attacked her may be the same one who attacked you."

Danni nodded and raised a hand to her chest bone, her fingertips idly tracing her scars through the fabric of her pyjamas.

"You don't seem surprised," Caitlyn remarked.

"Surprised? No. I'm surprised it's taken this long, if anything," Danni said. She dropped her hand down into her lap. The other hand kneaded it, as if offering comfort. "Did he... Did he mark her?"

"He started to, yes," Logan said. "But he was interrupted."

"Was it the same?"

"It was," Logan confirmed.

Tears sprang to Danni's eyes. She looked away, out through the French doors that led to a long garden at the back of the house. "Did he... Was she..."

"There was no sexual element to the attack," Caitlyn said.

The look that flitted across Danni's face was impossible to read. Relief? Resentment? It passed too quickly for Logan to be able to identify. Whichever it was, he couldn't blame the woman.

"That's something," she said.

"I know this must be very difficult for you, Miss Gillespie. I've gone over the case files, and the statements you made at the time of the assault, so we won't take up much of your time," Logan said. "But I wanted to talk to you directly. See if there's anything you can tell us that might help us identify your attacker."

"I already told the police everything," Danni said. "There's nothing else to say."

She rubbed the heels of her hands on her thighs, like they had suddenly become unbearably itchy. "I don't want to go over it again."

"I appreciate that, Miss Gillespie. I really do," said Logan. He leaned forward on the couch. The sudden movement made Danni gasp and grab for her armchair, like the floor had started to fall away beneath her.

Logan froze, not wanting to make any other movement in case he panicked her further.

"Sir, why don't you go get us a cup of tea?" Caitlyn suggested. She looked to Danni for confirmation. "Would that be alright?"

Danni was quick to give her agreement. "Fine. Yes."

Caitlyn caught Logan's eye. A nod was exchanged between them, then the DCI got to his feet, taking his time about it so as not to further startle the woman in the pyjamas.

"What do you take in it?" Logan asked.

Caitlyn rolled her eyes and smiled in Danni's direction. "Months we've been working together now. Shows how often he makes the tea, eh? Milk, no sugar."

"And yourself, Miss Gillespie?"

"I'm fine," she replied, then she tagged a slightly reluctant, "Thanks," onto the end.

"Right. One tea coming up," Logan said.

"Thanks, sir," Caitlyn replied. She looked up at him from where she sat on the couch. "And take your time."

SHAUN GILLESPIE WAS SITTING at the breakfast bar, flicking through a copy of *Computer Shopper* magazine when Logan entered.

The kitchen, like the rest of the house, looked expensive, with smooth handleless cabinets, thick wooden worktops, and an island that would've taken up most of Logan's flat.

"What do you want?" Shaun asked, not looking up from the magazine.

"I've been sent to make the tea," Logan said.

Shaun grunted. "Girl talk then, is it?"

"Aye. Something like that."

Waving a hand, Shaun indicated the kettle. "Knock yourself out."

"Thanks. You having one yourself?" Logan asked.

Shaun tapped the edge of the magazine against a mostly-full mug of coffee. "I'm fine."

"Probably wise. Can't say it's my strong point," said Logan.

The kettle was tall, silver, and with a confusing array of buttons on the side of the handle. A light flashed orange on the side, like it was trying to tell him something. He had no idea what it was though, so he bashed on and pressed the button that looked most likely to turn it on.

Nothing happened. He leaned in, squinted at the controls, then tried the same button again. The result was exactly the same.

He was about to press it for a third time when Shaun intervened.

"It needs water," he said. Then, with a sigh he put down his magazine, got up off his stool, and nudged the DCI aside. "Here. I'll get it."

"Maybe for the best," Logan agreed. "Gadgets have never really been my strong point, either."

"It's not a gadget. It's a kettle," Shaun said, opening the top and sloshing some water into it from the tap. "Water in. Power on. It's not difficult."

"Aye. Well. When you put it like that," Logan said, watching as Shaun sat the kettle back on its base. The orange light turned green, and almost as soon as the button was pressed Logan could hear the water start to come to life. "I hear you make... games, was it? For the phone."

"Apps," Shaun corrected, appearing irritated by the mistake. He sat back at the breakfast bar and picked up his magazine. "I used to. Market got flooded. Have you arrested him yet?"

"Who?" Logan asked.

"You know who. Sloane."

"Mr Sloane was dismissed as a suspect in your sister's assault," Logan told him. "We've no reason to believe he was involved in this latest attack."

"Bollocks," Shaun barked, slamming the magazine down. "He did it. To Danni, I mean. I know he fucking did it. Creepy bastard. Everyone knows he fucking did it, and yet he gets off scot-free."

"No' quite scot-free. You did go round there with your pals and leather shite out of him, did you not?" Logan asked.

"What, and you think we shouldn't have, like?"

"I *know* you shouldn't have, Mr Gillespie. That's why you were arrested," Logan said. "That's how it works, you see? You're fortunate that Mr Sloane decided not to press charges. Although, I do wonder what brought on his sudden change of heart."

Shaun seemed like he might be about to say something, then thought better of it. "No comment."

"Fair enough. Look, I wasn't involved in the case, but from what I read, he had an alibi that proved it couldn't have been him," Logan said. "He was literally doing a show live on the radio at the time your sister was attacked."

"Aye, like he couldn't have recorded the whole show in advance?" Shaun said, sneering like this should've been obvious. "Two in the morning on Moray Firth? Not like anyone would even be listening."

"From what I understand, there were other people with him in the station at the time," Logan said. "He ran a phone-in. I can appreciate your frustration, but as alibis go, it's one of the better ones."

"It's bullshit, is what it is!" Shaun barked. His face had reddened, and a vein on the side of his neck was practically pulsing. "I don't know how he fucking did it, but he did it. It was him. I'm telling you. And if that weirdo fuck has gone and killed someone, that's on you lot. That's on you."

"I'll bear that in mind," Logan said. The kettle rolled towards the boil beside him, and he unhooked a couple of mugs from hooks on the wall. "What makes you so sure it was him?"

"Because he's a creepy bastard," Shaun said.

"There's plenty of other creepy bastards out there," Logan reasoned.

"Not like him. He was in Danni's year in school. Fucking obsessed with her, he was."

Logan set the mugs down on the worktop and looked back over his shoulder. "Were they in a relationship?"

"Fuck off! With Sloane? With *Mr Nobody*? No. She didn't give him the time of day. No one did."

"Mr Nobody? Is that what they called him?"

Shaun shook his head. "No. That'd be fair enough. That'd be *normal*. But no."

He glanced at the kitchen door, then leaned forward.

"That's what the bastard called *himself*."

"Himself?"

"Aye. 'Just call me Mr Nobody,' he'd say. 'Just act like I'm no' here. I don't even exist.'" Shaun shook his head. "Total fucking weirdo."

Snatches of Danni's statement replayed in Logan's head. The things her attacker had told her. The words he'd whispered in her ear.

It doesn't matter. None of it matters.

Because none of this is real.

"Now he gets it," Shaun said, smirking to himself as he watched the realisation dawning on the DCI's face. He picked up his magazine and flicked to a random page. "Alibi or no alibi, Donald Sloane was the one who raped my sister, and your lot did nothing about it."

The kettle reached the boil with a *click*.

"And now, he's gone and upped his game."

CHAPTER TWELVE

LOGAN CLOSED THE DOOR OF HIS CAR AND WAITED FOR CAITLYN TO get into the passenger seat beside him.

He'd been sad to see the back of the Ford Focus that had served him so well over the past couple of years, but the fact it had been comprehensively smashed to pieces by a big truck meant hanging onto it hadn't really been an option.

The blow had been softened somewhat when the car had been replaced with a Volvo XC90 seven-seater SUV. And, while the fact it was a hybrid electric model had given him some cause for concern to begin with, he'd quickly come to see the appeal.

The passenger door gave a satisfying *thunk* as Caitlyn pulled it shut. She stared ahead, not yet reaching for her seatbelt. She looked stunned. Haunted, perhaps.

"Well?" Logan asked. "Thoughts?"

Caitlyn blinked, as if coming out of a trance.

"She's, uh, I don't think she's convinced it was Donald Sloane who attacked her," the DS said. "Not as convinced as her brother is, anyway."

Logan nodded. He'd got the same impression while he'd gulped down his tea. Not a bad cuppa, if he said so himself.

As they pulled away from the house, Caitlyn recounted what Danni had discussed while Logan had been in the kitchen. Most of it, he already knew from her original victim statements.

The attacker had stepped out of an alleyway as she'd been walking home from her brother's club. He'd worn a smooth, featureless white mask, and had hit her before she could open her mouth to scream.

She'd regained consciousness during the sexual assault. He'd taken her into the shell of a shop that had been closed due to fire damage, the boarded windows hiding them from the late-night revellers passing by just outside.

Her attempts to cry for help had been thwarted by the tape across her mouth. Her hands had been bound together while she was unconscious, the trousers around her ankles keeping her from kicking out.

That feeling of helplessness had been one of the worst parts, she'd told Caitlyn. One of the many.

"What about the 'you're not real,' stuff?" Logan asked, as he nudged the car out of a junction, forcing traffic coming from the right to stop to let him out. He waved his thanks and received an angry raised finger in response.

"Charming."

"She couldn't remember what the attacker said word for word, obviously, but the gist of it was that he could do what he liked because she wasn't real. Because nothing was real," Caitlyn said. "He was... She thought he was laughing about it, but at one point she thought maybe he was crying."

Logan shot her a quizzical look. "Crying?"

"That's what she said, sir. Like he was hysterical or something, but she couldn't say for sure. Anyway, he kept telling her that she didn't matter. Told her to get over it. That none of it was actually happening."

"The hell was he saying that for?"

Caitlyn shrugged. "He said there were no rules anymore. That no one could punish him."

"Big bloody talk for a man wearing a mask," Logan grunted.

"Are we going to go and talk to Donald Sloane?" Caitlyn asked.

Logan flexed his fingers on the steering wheel, weighing this up.

"It's just... We seem to be heading in that direction," Caitlyn pointed out.

Logan glanced from the road to the DS and back again. When he'd driven away from Shaun Gillespie's house, he hadn't been consciously setting out in any particular direction, but sure enough, they were almost at Queensgate. It was slap bang in the centre of the city's main shopping area, and one of a handful of places he knew how to find without having to consult the GPS.

After a moment's thought, he swung the Volvo into a bus stop. "No.

We've no reason to talk to him yet. If it is him, we don't want to spook him. Let's wait and see if we get anything DNA-wise from Pathology first. If we can make a connection, we bring him in then. If we can't... We'll think of something."

Caitlyn nodded. "Makes sense. And in the meantime?"

Logan rubbed his chin. The growth had gone beyond stubble and into the beginnings of a beard that, a quick glance in the rear-view mirror confirmed, made him look like he had been sleeping rough for the past several days.

"You got that list, right? Everyone who was on duty at the hospital last night?"

"I did. I was going to hand it off to Hamza and Tyler to go over. Don't expect we'll get much from it."

"Right, aye," Logan agreed. That made sense. Uniform could probably handle it even, and report in anything of interest.

"Except..." Caitlyn took her notebook from her pocket and flicked through a couple of pages. "Kel Conlyn. He was the last person to see her alive. Or talk to her, anyway. Before she left. He was also there when they brought her back in. They were apparently pretty friendly. Thought he might be worth us talking to directly. Maybe she mentioned something to him."

"About how she was planning to get murdered?" Logan asked.

Caitlyn managed a grim smile. "Maybe she'd fallen out with someone, or noticed anyone acting suspicious."

Logan clicked the indicator and began forcing his way out into the traffic. "You got the address?"

"Aye, sir, it's twenty-two—"

"No point telling me," Logan said. He tapped the satnav on the dash. "Stick it in there, or I'll never bloody find it."

———

KEL CONLYN LIVED JUST a little out from the city centre, in a ground floor flat just a stone's throw from Aldi. Logan was vaguely familiar with the area, partly because of the aforementioned Aldi, and partly because one of the flats he'd had stolen out from under him by Bosco Maximuke was just around the corner.

There was no driveway for the flats, so Logan pulled the car in at the side of the road. The big Volvo stuck out like a sore thumb between an '05 plate Clio and an '07 Honda Civic with a mismatched driver's door, and he had a nagging suspicion that some bastard would come along and key it while they were in talking to Conlyn. Still, at least the repairs wouldn't be coming out of his pocket.

The hospital hadn't given much away about any of the names who'd been on the rota the night before, and DS McQuarrie hadn't yet had time to do any research, so they were going in blind.

There were half a dozen identical maisonettes along the street, each with four flats—two ground floor, two above. Each flat had its own entrance, and after Caitlyn had double-checked the address, they'd approached Conlyn's front door.

There was a metal nameplate holder fixed just above a spyhole in the door, but it was empty. Judging by the way the edges had rusted, it had been empty for quite some time.

The paint on the door would once have been a vibrant red, but a rectangle where the sun must regularly hit had faded to a salmon pink. The step was shoogly and uneven, with moss growing in a few thin cracks, and along the join where it met the bottom of the doorframe.

There was a button fixed to the wall beside the frame. It looked like it had been a recent addition, and was jarringly out of place amongst the otherwise tired exterior.

Almost immediately after Logan gave the button a press, a man's voice came from somewhere in its plastic housing.

"Yes?"

"Mr Conlyn?"

A hesitation, then: "Yes?"

"We're from the Police Scotland Major Investigations Team. If you have a few minutes, we'd like to talk to you."

There was another moment of silence, then the *clack* of a lock being turned. The door opened halfway, revealing a young man in a red silk dressing gown. There was a weariness in his eyes as he stepped aside and gave a beckoning tilt of his head.

"You'd best come in," Kel said.

"Thank you," Logan replied, then he stepped into the flat and onto a floor made of bare, unsanded boards.

"I've not long moved in," Kel explained. He gestured almost apologetically at the Magnolia-coloured walls, the paint faded and peeling in places, and peppered with drawing pinholes. "Excuse the state of the place."

"I'm in the same boat myself," Logan said. He waited for Kel to shut the door, then followed him along the narrow hallway towards an open door at the far end. "Hard to find the time to unpack everything."

"Not really a problem for me," Kel said, leading them into the living room.

At least, Logan assumed that was its purpose. Then again, it could've been anything. There was no furniture to speak of, no carpet on the floor, or curtains on the windows. It was an empty space, with a single folding camping chair and four Banana boxes stacked up in the corner.

"My parents kept most of my stuff when they kicked me out," Kel said.

He anticipated the next question before either of the detectives could ask.

"Didn't approve of my..." Kel mimed air-quotes with his fingers, "life-style choices."

"I'm sorry to hear that," Logan told him.

"Yeah, well, there's something to be said for minimalism, I suppose," Kel said. He shrugged and smiled, but there was nothing convincing about either. "Once I get a few more payslips behind me, I'll start... you know. Furniture, or whatever normal people have."

He pointed in the direction of another door that led through to a small galley kitchen. "I do have a fridge, though. Coke? Fanta?"

"You're fine, thanks," Logan told him.

Kel turned to Caitlyn. "Ma'am? I mean... Miss?" He blushed slightly. "I don't... Sorry. What do I call you both?"

"Sorry, son. Detective Chief Inspector Logan. Call me Jack. This is Detective Sergeant McQuarrie."

"Caitlyn."

"Caitlyn. Jack. Right," said Kel. He tapped himself on the side of the head, as if locking it in. "You sure I can't get either of you anything? I'd offer you tea, but I haven't got a kettle yet."

"We're grand. Thank you," Logan said.

Kel tightened the belt of his kimono-style dressing gown, then put his hands on his hips. "Well?" he asked, glancing between them both. "Did you get someone?"

"Not yet, I'm afraid. We're still working on it," Logan said. "I under-stand you and Esme were close."

"Yeah. I mean, not... *close* close, but she was good fun. We had a laugh. When I first started, she looked after me. I'd tell her about my parents, she'd tell me what a pair of bastards they were and how I was better off without them, and... Yeah. She's... *was* great."

"You spoke to her before she left last night," Caitlyn said. "Did she say anything unusual?"

"Like what?"

"Anything that seemed out of the ordinary?"

Kel thought back, his eyes darting left to right as if replaying the events of the night before in his head. "No. She said she was tired, but that's par for the course. She seemed happy, though. In fact, she was gloating about having two days off in a row."

Logan raised an eyebrow. "Gloating?"

"No, not like... She wasn't actually gloating. Joking, I mean. She wasn't like that. We were having a laugh."

"She hadn't mentioned anything that might be giving her cause for concern?" Caitlyn pressed.

"Last night?"

"Or recently?"

Another moment of silence as Kel gave this some consideration. "No. I don't think so. Chloe had Chicken Pox a few weeks back. Her daughter. Is that the sort of thing you mean?"

"Any information you can give us is useful," Caitlyn said, but she hadn't yet bothered to write anything down.

"What about people?" Logan asked, looking out of the living room window at the gardens below. There were two of them, side by side, both long and narrow, running straight back from the house. One half was neat and well-kept, the other was one sunny afternoon away from becoming a jungle.

"People? What do you mean?"

Logan turned from the window. "Had she spoken about anyone new recently? Had she fallen out with anyone?"

"Esme? Fall out with someone?" Kel said, reacting with a sort of disbelief that suggested such a thing wasn't possible. "No. Not that she told me about, anyway."

Kel's voice trailed off as he neared the end of the sentence. A frown briefly troubled his face, then he curtly shook his head, chasing it away.

"Mr Conlyn?" Logan asked. "Is there something you can tell us? Had Esme fallen out with someone recently?"

"Not fallen out, exactly, no. It was nothing. She laughed it off."

"Laughed what off?" Logan asked.

Beside him, Caitlyn instinctively reached for her notebook.

"One of the doctors. He was... not trying his hand, exactly, but he'd asked her out a few times recently. She told him she wasn't interested. He knew she was married, but..."

He caught the look that passed between the detectives.

"I'm sure it's nothing. Honestly. She laughed about it. She thought it was funny. We both did."

"Aye, I'm sure you're right, and it won't be anything," Logan agreed. "Out of interest, though, what was his name, this doctor?"

Kel looked worried, like he'd said too much.

"Just for our records," Logan urged.

"Like I say, I really don't think he'd... He's not..." Kel gave a sigh. He tightened the belt of his kimono again. "Fletcher," he said. "His name is Doctor Colin Fletcher."

CHAPTER THIRTEEN

"Colin Fletcher. Consultant at Raigmore. On duty last night around the time Esme Miller was murdered."

Caitlyn pinned a printout of a photo she'd found of the doctor online. It was from an academic website, and was a perfect head and shoulders shot. A couple of years out of date, maybe, but good enough.

"He was also the doctor who worked on the victim when she was brought in," she continued. "A colleague reports he'd been making advances towards the victim over the past few weeks. This doesn't come as a surprise, given that he tried cracking on to me earlier today."

"*You?*" ejected DC Hamza Khaled from behind his desk. He'd stumbled in the door just a few minutes before Logan and Caitlyn had returned to the office, and was still in the process of getting caught up. "He tried his hand with *you?*"

"Aye, me. What are you saying it like that for, you cheeky bastard?" Caitlyn asked him.

"Oh. No. That's not what I meant. I meant... I mean..." Hamza babbled, his panic making his Aberdonian twang that bit stronger. He shot Tyler a sideways look. "What do I mean?"

"You're on your own with this one, pal," DC Neish replied, holding his hands up to show he was having nothing to do with it.

Ben Forde cleared his throat. "I'm sure what the Detective Constable is trying to say is that making an advance on the investigating officer in the recent murder of one of your colleagues is a bit on the crass side."

Hamza clicked his fingers and pointed at the Detective Inspector. "Aye. Exactly. That's exactly what I was meaning," he said.

"Aye. Well," Caitlyn sniffed. "It's a lot on the crass side. I told him as much, but I don't think it bothered him."

"He's a sleaze, then?" asked Ben.

"And then some, sir," Caitlyn confirmed.

"So, he asks her out, she shoots him down. Pretty weak as motives go," said Tyler. "I mean, if I killed every woman who'd ever turned me down, I'd be Jack the Ripper."

Ben raised an eyebrow. "Good looking lad like you? You surprise me, son."

"Aw. Cheers, boss!"

"Must be your personality," Ben continued.

"Haha. Yeah," Tyler replied, sounding a little less thrilled.

"Or his voice, maybe," suggested Hamza. "That *meemeemeemee*. Like one of the Chipmunks shagged a Muppet."

"What's wrong with my voice? There's nothing wrong with my voice," Tyler protested. He tried it out a few times. "Hello? Hello! What's wrong with that?"

"Nothing's wrong with it. It's fine," Ben told him. "If you like that sort of thing."

At the back of the room, Logan cleared his throat. He was sitting on the rearmost desk, trying to watch DS McQuarrie's presentation as a detached observer. Much as he liked to be right in the middle of things, sometimes taking a step or two back could help bring things into focus.

"Can we get on with it, do we think?" he asked.

"Aye, let's all grow up a bit and get on with it, shall we?" Tyler agreed, smiling smugly at the others.

"We can discuss DC Neish's awful personality and voice another time," Logan concluded. "Caitlyn. Go on. What else do we have on Fletcher?"

Caitlyn referred to the notes she'd pulled together on the doctor. "Not a huge amount yet, sir. His marriage broke down a couple of years back. Divorce is still a work in progress. Two kids, both boys in their teens. They live with their mother in Elgin."

"I've just found him on a couple of dating sites," Tyler volunteered. He clicked his mouse a few times, flicking between tabs on his browser. "Looks like he's really been putting himself out there."

"Send those to print," Caitlyn said. Even before she'd finished speaking, the noisy inkjet was clanking into life.

"Done."

"That's most of what I've got at the moment, sir," Caitlyn said. "DC Khaled and I can pull together a proper profile this afternoon."

Hamza looked up from where he'd been leafing through a printout of the current case file. "Right. Aye. Just... Did I see something in here about a scalpel being used on the victim?"

"You did," Logan confirmed. "Pathology report. The letters carved into her back were done with a thin blade. A scalpel's the best bet."

"On Fletcher's desk. One of the mugs," Caitlyn began. "It said 'World's—'"

"'Best Surgeon.' Aye, I saw that."

"What's a surgeon doing working A&E?" Ben wondered.

"They're short-staffed," Caitlyn said. "Maybe there was no one else?"

Hamza looked up from the report. "I've got a 'World's Best Lover' mug at home somewhere, and that is *far* from accurate. Believe me."

He caught the bewildered look on Tyler's face.

"My point is, do we know he's actually a surgeon? Besides the fact he had it printed on a mug, I mean? You can get those mugs for anything these days, can't you?"

A few blank glances were exchanged.

"OK, that's something for us to find out," Logan said. "What is he trained in? What's his speciality?"

"We bringing him in, Jack?" asked Ben.

Logan regarded the face in the photo for a while, then shook his head. "Not yet. Let's build a better picture of him first. No point alerting him when we've got hee-haw to pin on him yet. We need to know if it was possible for him to be behind the attack. Did anyone see him on the ward before the victim was brought in? If so, how long before? She wasn't out there long, so timing would've been tight."

"And there's the gag, sir," Caitlyn reminded him.

"Shite. Aye," Logan muttered. "If he was working on her, how did he manage to go back and pick up the gag? He'd have to have attacked her, been disturbed, run back to the hospital, worked on Esme, gone *back* to the crime scene, gather up the evidence, then return to the hospital again without anyone noticing."

"Uniform was already on the scene when I arrived, sir," Caitlyn said.

"Not sure how he could've picked up the gag after returning to the hospital. I don't see how that's possible."

Logan felt his heart sink down into his stomach. It had given a flutter when the hospital porter had told them about Fletcher's romantic interest in the victim. He had fit. Scorned alpha male, based near the scene of the crime at the time of the attack. He had the means and the motive, but unless there was something wrong with the timeline of events, probably not the opportunity.

Still, it was the best lead they had.

"Stick to the plan. Caitlyn, you and Hamza keep pursuing this. Get me everything we can on Fletcher, and let's see if we can make the timeline work," Logan instructed. "But let's not put all our eggs in one basket. What else do we have?"

"Forensics report should be in this afternoon on the victim's clothes," Ben said. "Hopefully, we'll get something off them, because we've got a distinct lack of anything resembling evidence at the minute."

He gestured to the desk Logan was sitting on. "Hoon's given us a Uniform Sergeant to handle Exhibits, but I sent her away again for now, since we've got bugger all for her to do. Once the clothes come back, I'll get her to check them in."

"Uniform's been doing door-to-door around the scene, boss," said Tyler. "The houses are pretty far away, though, through the trees and over the road. Doubt we'll get anything. Appeal for witnesses going out on Moray Firth this afternoon, and we're putting a call out on social media, too. Wider Police Scotland network is going to give us a bump."

Logan gave a nod. These things were important, of course. Many's a case had been cracked by the nosy bastard at number forty-three who'd witnessed the whole thing from the kitchen window.

But it was busy-work. It was grasping. This was a relatively isolated crime scene, hidden from view. Aye, sure, someone might have heard the victim scream, but so what? What did that tell them that they didn't already know? Unless the killer had blurted out his full name and address, all the door-knocking and social media shout-outs in the world were unlikely to get them any closer to solving the case.

"How are things with the family?" Logan asked Tyler. He cut the younger detective off before he could play innocent. "Don't pretend you don't know. I've seen you texting."

Tyler glanced instinctively at his mobile on the desk, then back to the DCI. "Pretty much as you'd expect, sir. Lots of family and friends coming and going. The husband and daughter are planning to go stay with his parents. They've a big house out near Dingwall. Don't think he can face being at home right now."

"Understandable," Logan said. He stood up. "I'll go round and see him before they head off."

"Want me to come, boss?"

"No, I do not. You and your bloody hormones are the last thing I need," Logan retorted. "I want you going over the Gillespie case again."

"The rape case, boss?"

"Aye. Caitlyn will fill you in on everything she told us today."

Logan reached for his coat, then hesitated.

"Oh, and look into the brother, will you? Shaun Gillespie. Something about him got on my tits. Besides him being a mouthy bastard, I mean. There was something... I don't know. See if anything jumps out. It might be nothing."

"Will do, boss."

The phone on Logan's desk *burred* into life. It was, he thought, the first time it had ever rung, and he wasted a few moments staring at it in surprise before picking up the handset.

"DCI Logan."

There was silence from the other end. Or *near* silence, anyway.

"Hello?" Logan asked, and he heard the faint whine of an echo, as if his voice was feeding back on a speaker. "Hello? Who's this?"

The silence continued, but there was something more to it. Something different. An edge. A weight. An expectation, like the person on the other end was waiting for him to say just the right words.

A suggestion of static hissed at him down the line, soft and faint.

Or... no. Not a hiss. Not exactly.

A whisper.

The word leapt into Logan's throat and slipped out before he could stop it.

"Petrie?"

A *click*. A tone. The line went dead.

"Who was that?" asked Ben, when Logan replaced the handset.

"What?" Logan frowned, his gaze flitting between DI Forde and the phone. "Oh. I don't... I'm not sure. Hamza, try to find out, will you? See if you can get a number."

DC Khaled blew out his cheeks. "I'll see what I can do, sir, but if they withheld it then—"

"I don't need the technical details, just see what you can get," Logan said.

He stole another look at the phone, then shook his head. A bad line, that was all. A call centre trying to sell him something, no doubt. That was all.

Aye. That was all.

"Actually, you're fine. Forget it."

"You sure, sir?"

"Aye. Cold callers. Don't bother with it."

Hamza gave a nod. "Will do, sir."

"Won't do, you mean," Tyler corrected. He grinned, like he'd just made the greatest joke in the world, then shrugged when nobody else laughed. "Suit yourself."

"Right, that's me off," Logan announced. He had his coat on and was halfway to the door when he stopped again and turned. "Oh, but one more thing. Anyone needing any sausages?"

Ben looked the DCI warily up and down, like he was concerned he'd lost his mind. "Sausages?"

"Aye. Thought I might swing by the butcher's on the way back," Logan said. He pulled the collar of his coat up, bracing himself for the October chill. "I hear the one on Queensgate is worth a look."

CHAPTER FOURTEEN

HE'D DONE IT. HE'D ACTUALLY DONE IT. AFTER ALL THIS TIME, AFTER *all his observation, he'd actually done it.*

It had been harder than he'd thought at first. The sound the knife had made, the way her body had offered that momentary resistance to the blade before succumbing—those had both been... unexpected.

She'd felt real. Solid. For a moment, he'd forgotten. For a moment, he'd believed the lies. She'd gargled and gasped behind the gag, almost like she was alive. Like she was real.

And her eyes. Her eyes. Pleading, begging, accusing him, all at once. So vibrant and alive, even as death rushed towards her. He'd doubted, then. He'd wavered. Those eyes. That expression. How could something so intricate and detailed be fake? How could she not be real?

But, that was why it had worked for so long, he had reasoned. It had to be convincing. Utterly, wholly convincing. It was the only way the whole elaborate plan could work. That was how they had been able to fool all of the people, all of the time.

Almost *all.*

Each plunge of the knife had made it easier. Each thack of metal piercing flesh. Each weakening grunt and sob. Every stab had been an affirmation. A commitment to the truth. A blow struck not just against this individual lie, but against the liars themselves, wherever they were hiding.

The interruption had been annoying. He'd thought about waiting there, *about revealing himself. What did it matter if they caught him? What did anything matter now?*

But, even though he knew the truth of this world, he was still confined by its rules. What good was he in prison? Who'd listen then? One dead body wasn't enough. It wasn't clear enough, loud enough. It didn't say what needed to be said. For that, he'd need more.

Many more.

The first had been difficult to begin with, but it had become easier. The next would be easier still, and the next, and all the ones after that.

He took no pleasure in it. It was necessary, that was all.

Everyone needed to learn the cold, brutal truth of it. It was time they all had their eyes opened to their reality. A message must be sent, to the liars and the blind alike.

And he was the one who would send it.

CHAPTER FIFTEEN

LOGAN HAD JUST OPENED THE FRONT GATE OF ROWAN MILLER'S house when he heard the sharp rap of knuckles on glass.

He spent a few seconds searching the nearest windows, then clocked a white-haired woman at an upstairs window of the house next door. She made a sharp beckoning motion to Logan when he spotted her, then retreated away into the house.

"OK," he muttered to himself, closing the gate again and heading for the next one along.

The pavement outside the house was laden with flowers. Word of Esme's death had spread quickly through the local area, and neighbours had been quick to pay their respects. Logan picked his way through them, and arrived at the next door gate in time for the front door to open.

"You're with the police," the woman said. A statement, more than a question.

"Aye. That's right."

Bending forward, she glanced left and right along the street, then beckoned for him to come inside.

"There's something you should know," she said. "About..." She mouthed the next two words. "...the murder."

Logan looked back at the Millers' house. Sinead stood at a downstairs window, eyeing him curiously. He raised a couple of fingers to indicate he'd just be two minutes, then strode along the path to where the elderly neighbour was holding the door for him.

"Hello. I'm Detective Inspect—"

"Just come away in," the woman said, shooting furtive looks to the windows of the houses across the road. "Hurry, before anyone sees."

Once inside, it immediately became apparent that this was as far into the house as Logan was going to get. The old woman all but blocked the narrow hallway, holding onto a wooden railing of the staircase with one hand as if to form a barrier.

"Is everything alright, Mrs...?"

"That's not important. My name doesn't matter," she said. She was a little younger than her hair colour suggested, Logan thought, and not as old up close as she'd looked at a distance. Sixties. Maybe even the lower end.

"Well, it does. I need to know your name," Logan told her.

"Oh. Do you? Right," the woman said. "It's... Jane. Jane... Green."

"I'd prefer your real name."

Her shoulder sagged. "Fine. It's Olwyn Prosser. Happy?"

"What can I do for you, Mrs Prosser?" Logan asked.

Olwyn dropped her voice to a whisper. "You didn't hear this from me. Alright? Swear. You didn't hear it from me."

"Didn't hear what from you?" Logan pressed.

"You've got to promise. You keep my name out of it. I don't want dragged into it. I'm not having people thinking I'm a grass."

"I'll do what I can, Mrs Prosser," Logan assured her. "But I need to know what you have to tell me first."

Olwyn's shoulders sagged even further, so they were practically pointing straight down at the floral carpet. "Alright, alright. Fine."

She took a deep breath, glanced around again as if the place might be bugged, then spat it out in one big breath.

"They were arguing. The day she was murdered. Esme, I mean. Her and Rowan, they were arguing."

She clamped her mouth shut, like she was scared she'd said too much, or possibly worried about what she might blurt out next.

"There. I've said it," she announced. "Now you know."

"What were they arguing about?" Logan asked.

"Well, I don't know, do I? I wasn't listening," Olwyn snapped, although Logan found that hard to believe. He'd only just met the woman, but he was already building a pretty solid picture of her.

"You have no idea at all?"

"Well. I mean, I *may* have heard a few things," Olwyn said, cagily. "Nothing specific, but I think they were having money problems. Esme was going to be working more overtime, and Rowan—well, Rowan's been out of work for a few months now. Not right, that. Young man like that. Prime of his life. He shouldn't be out of work, should he?"

"Well—"

"Bloody shame. And it's not for want of trying, I'll give him that."

Logan smiled thinly. "Could we get back to the argument, Mrs Prosser?"

"Oh. Right. Yes. Well, he wasn't happy about her doing more overtime, and she was pointing out that they had to pay the mortgage—they bought the house a few years ago. Off the council. Just before the rule change. Got it at a bit of a song. Good investment for Chloe's future, I told them. It's where the money is, isn't it? Property."

Logan blinked slowly as he tried to follow the thread of the conversation.

"So I'm told," he said. "They were arguing about Esme doing more overtime. Right. Then what?"

"What do you mean?" Olwyn asked. "Then she was murdered. That very night." She held her hands out, palms upward, as if presenting the case to him on a plate. "Coincidence?"

"Well, I mean... Couples argue, don't they?"

"Not on the day one of them gets murdered they don't!"

Experience told Logan otherwise. He'd lost count of the number of grieving spouses, parents, or children whose final words with their loved ones had been in anger. He'd held mothers who wished, more than anything, they could take back the last thing they'd said to their child before they'd headed on a night out. He'd watched husbands break down, stricken by the lack of affection they'd shown their wives in those final days, haunted by some of the things they'd said or done.

People argued. People died. And the world kept grinding on.

"Did they argue often?" Logan asked.

"No. Very rarely. The odd tiff, but very rare. Very rare. Always seemed such a loving couple," Olwyn said. "That's what made it so strange. Them fighting, I mean. On the day that she... You know. That's not normal, is it? That's suspicious, isn't it?"

"I tend to treat everyone with a degree of suspicion, Mrs Prosser," Logan said. He smiled, showing a lot of teeth. "Even you."

The old woman's mouth dropped open.

"What? I mean... What? What are you saying?"

Logan tapped a finger to his forehead in salute, then opened the front door. "Thanks for the information. I'll be in touch," he told her, stepping down onto the path. "Oh," he said, looking back at her over his shoulder. "And don't leave town. I might be back."

The door closed behind him before he'd reached the gate. He left the garden, tiptoed through the bunches of flowers, then headed up the path of Rowan Miller's house. He saw a twitch of a curtain at one of Olwyn's upstairs windows, caught a fleeting glimpse of someone watching him, and then they were gone, swallowed by the shadows of the room behind them.

Olwyn? She'd have had to move quickly. Someone else in the house? A husband?

Before he could dwell on it, the front door of the Millers' house opened, and Constable Sinead Bell flashed him a warm smile. "Get sidetracked, sir?"

"Aye. Something like that," Logan confirmed, stepping into the house.

"Anything of interest?" Sinead asked, dropping her voice to a murmur.

"No. Just a nosy bastard, I think," Logan replied. "You know how many people live next door?"

"Not a clue. Sure Rowan will know, though. You could ask him."

Logan ran his tongue across the back of his teeth. "Maybe, aye. How's he doing?"

"He's... dealing with it, I think," Sinead said. "Chloe's over at his sister's, and he's getting sorted out to go move in with his parents for a bit."

"So DC Neish tells me. Good that you're keeping him so informed," Logan said. It was meant as a tease, but it came out sounding more confrontational than intended, and Sinead blushed at the implied accusation. "I mean that. It's a good system, you to him to the rest of us. Single point of contact. It works."

Sinead was still blushing but smiled through it. "Thanks. That's good. That it's working, I mean."

"Just as long as it keeps working," Logan said. "We don't want the lines of communication breaking down over... personal reasons."

"Oh, they won't, sir. Tyler... DC Neish and I, we're just... It's nothing. Nothing serious, I mean."

Logan grunted. He didn't seem entirely comfortable with the conversation but was managing to blunder through. "Aye, well. You've no' seen his face when he gets a message from you," he said. "Just... be professional. That's all I'm saying. To both of you. Him more than you."

"Of course, sir. Always," Sinead said.

"Right. Good."

Logan nodded, then rolled his shoulders and cricked his neck, bracing himself for the next part. There were lots of elements to the job he hated. Too many to count, in fact. But this one—what came next—was one of the parts he hated most of all.

"Right, then," he said, the words coming as a heavy sigh. "Let's go talk to Mr Miller."

CHAPTER SIXTEEN

"I think I've got something, boss."

"It's no' contagious, is it?" asked Ben Forde, not yet looking up from the report that lay flat open on his desk.

DC Neish hovered in front of the desk. It took a moment for the joke to hit home.

"Oh. Aye. Good one. It's about the brother. Shaun Gillespie. I've been looking into him."

Ben leaned back in his chair and looked up from the report. "What have you got?"

"It might be nothing. It's just, well, I was looking through Osmosis' records at Companies House. You know, his nightclub? And there was a new director brought on about a year ago."

"Right. And?"

"Valdis Petronis," Tyler announced.

Ben's nose scrunched up. "Is that no' a spell out of Harry Potter?"

"Uh, no, boss. It's a guy. He works for Bosco Maximuke. You know, the—"

"I'm well aware of who Bosco Maximuke is, son," Ben told him.

"Aye, well. Looks like 'Mr Petronis'—and I'm putting quotation marks around his name there—put in a cash injection last year and took a minority share in the club. Sixty grand. No prizes for guessing who bankrolled that," Tyler continued. "Strange thing is, they weren't struggling for money before that, and they've done nothing with it since, so I don't see why it was needed."

Ben's chair creaked as he clasped his hands behind his head and leaned back. If Gillespie was mixed up with Bosco Maximuke, then it was no wonder Logan's instincts had been nagging at him. He and Maximuke had a long and colourful history, and very little of it good. If Bosco was involved in the nightclub, then chances were the whole set-up was dodgy in some way.

"Good work," Ben said.

"Want me to keep digging, boss?"

Ben shook his head. "No. That's enough for now. The rest can wait. I want you to get on to Uniform, see if the door-to-doors have brought anything in."

He raised his voice so the others could hear.

"And any sign of that Forensics report on the clothing yet?"

"Just came in, sir," said Hamza. "Email's in the inbox, and report is up on HOLMES."

"Good. Have a scout through. See if there's anything we can use."

"Already on it, sir," Hamza replied. "Summary isn't promising, but I'll dig in."

Ben tried not to show his disappointment. "Scrutinise it. Find us something," he instructed.

"HOLMES is playing silly buggers. Think the update is slowing everything down. But, I'll see what I can find, sir."

Ben groaned. HOLMES being on the fritz was the last thing they needed right now.

"Caitlyn, anything new on our doctor friend?"

"I can give you his whole life story if you want it, sir," Caitlyn replied from her desk.

"Just the edited highlights will do."

"Well, he was a surgeon. Cardiac, down in Edinburgh. All good until three years ago, when he received a couple of disciplinaries. Three of his patients died, and NHS Lothian started asking some questions. Turned out he'd been hiding a drinking problem."

"An alkie surgeon? That's no' ideal," Ben remarked.

"No. Looks like they didn't want to make a big fuss about it, though. He went to a drying-out clinic for a few weeks, then applied for a move up here to A&E."

"That's a step down, isn't it?" Tyler asked.

"More like a vertical drop," Caitlyn replied.

"A fall from grace, you might say," said Ben.

"Anyway, his wife came with him. She's from around this way originally. But the marriage seems to have collapsed almost immediately. The dating profiles Tyler found suggest he's been actively seeking... *companionship* pretty much from the day after she moved out."

Ben scribbled a couple of notes on this, then looked up. "And can we make the timeline work? For Esme's murder, I mean."

"We've still to talk to other hospital staff. Until we know if he was seen around at the time of her murder, it's difficult to say. If he wasn't visible on the ward, then it's possible he followed Esme out of the building and attacked her as she took the shortcut across the grass, but it's that missing gag that's the problem," Caitlyn reasoned.

"Aye. The hospital called in the attack right away. Hospital's just down the road from headquarters, so Uniform would've been on the scene practically right away. There's no way he could've dealt with Esme, then gone back out and got the gag without being spotted. No way I can think of, anyway."

"Maybe he had an accomplice, boss," Tyler suggested, slumping back down into his seat.

Ben looked doubtful. "Maybe. Can't see it, though. This feels like a lone wolf thing."

"Maybe it blew away," Hamza suggested. "Or, I don't know, a bird took it."

"A bird?" Tyler scoffed. "Why would a bird swoop in and steal a big bit of gaffer tape."

"Obviously you've never lived in Aberdeen," Hamza told him. "The bastards will take anything. I had a whole bag of chips nicked out of my hands once. A whole bag!"

"Aye, but that's food, isn't it?" Tyler pointed out. "I can believe that. If you'd said it had nicked your shoes or your wallet, I'd be calling bullshit. Chips, yes. Gaffer tape? No."

"Much as it pains me to do so, I have to agree with DC Neish on this one," Ben said. "A bird isn't impossible, but it's helluva unlikely."

"Maybe, sir. But what was it Sherlock Holmes said?" Hamza countered.

"'Elementary, my dear Watson,'" said Tyler, puffing on an imaginary pipe.

"No' that, ye div," Hamza said. "It was, 'Rule out the...' Wait. No. 'Rule out the unlikely...'" He shook his head, annoyed at himself. "Hang on. It was something like..."

Hamza stared into space for a moment, trying to recall the quote.

"Forget it. I don't remember," he admitted.

Ben clicked his tongue against the roof of his mouth. "Well, that's certainly given us pause for thought," he said, drolly. "Now, everyone back to work. Let's have some progress to show by the time himself gets back, or we'll never hear the bloody end of it."

CHAPTER SEVENTEEN

There was a stillness to Rowan Miller. A quiet.

When Logan had last seen the man, he'd been an emotional wreck, all twisted up in anger and in pain. Now, though, he sat straight and upright on a wooden chair he'd turned away from the dining table that sat at one end of the living room.

It was clear from the room that a family lived here. The couch and two armchairs were angled towards a large television, beside which stood a rack of DVDs, mostly pre-school titles with bright, garish colours. A pale blue monstrosity stared out at Logan from the cover of something called *In the Night Garden*, and a soft toy version of the same creature was eyeing him up from the armchair closest to the screen.

Family photographs lined the walls. Mostly, they showed Esme and Chloe, although a very different looking Rowan appeared in a few of them. The main difference being that the version in the photograph was smiling, and didn't look like his whole world was in the process of collapsing around his ears.

"I appreciate you taking the time to talk to me, Mr Miller," Logan said. He was still standing by the door and took a moment to consider his seating options.

He decided to join Rowan at the table and took the seat directly across from where he sat. Rowan half-stood, gripping the sides of his own chair, and turned it around until he was directly facing the detective across the table.

"Anyone for tea? Coffee?" asked Sinead, hovering by the door that led through into the kitchen.

"Uh, no. No. Thanks," said Rowan.

Logan quite fancied a cup of tea, if he were being honest, but didn't want to be the only one drinking one, so declined with a wave of his hand. He turned the movement into a beckoning gesture that indicated the seat beside him, and both men waited for Sinead to sit.

"How are you coping, Mr Miller?" Logan asked.

"How do you think?" Rowan answered.

"Aye," was all Logan could really say to that. "I wanted to come round and pass on my condolences before you headed to your... sister, was it?"

"My mum and dad's," Rowan said. His voice was flat and measured, and Logan realised his stillness was not accidental. He was actively controlling himself, fighting the urge to break down and cry, or scream, or smash the place up in rage. "They've got a big place. Plenty of room for the thr—" He swallowed. "For the two of us."

"It'll do you both good. You can come back when you're ready."

Rowan's eyes darted to the pictures on the wall. Right now, Logan knew, he'd be thinking that he'd never be ready. Never be able to come back here, to move on. Right now, his only thought would be to endure. To get by. Somehow, to get by.

And he would get by.

Somehow.

He could tell him that, of course. He could try to give him the benefit of his experience. But it was the last thing the poor bastard needed to hear now. *Don't worry, pal, you'll soon get over your wife's death. Chin up, life goes on.*

Here, now, the man needed his grief. His pain. What right had Logan to try to take that away from him?

"I have to ask you a couple of questions. Standard stuff," Logan said. "But it might help us figure out who murdered Esme."

Rowan flinched at the starkness of it. The truth of it, laid bare like that.

"Fine," he croaked. "Ask away."

"Were you aware of any problems Esme was having? Maybe at work? Anyone she was having issues with?"

The question seemed to catch Mr Miller unawares. His eyes narrowed, the pupils darting between Logan and Sinead. "No. Why? You think it was someone from the hospital who did this?"

"No. Not necessarily, Mr Miller. Like I say, this is all standard stuff."

"So... what? You're just fishing around for suspects at this point? You don't have any leads to follow up?"

"We're pursuing several lines of enquiry, Mr Miller," Logan told him. "But it's important to be as thorough as we can."

That seemed to settle Rowan a little. He nodded his understanding, and offered a whispered apology.

"Right. Yes. Sorry."

"Nothing to be sorry for, Mr Miller," Logan assured him. "So, she hadn't said anything about any disagreements she'd had with anyone recently?"

"At the hospital?"

"Or elsewhere."

The wooden chair squeaked beneath Rowan's weight as he shifted himself around. "No. I don't... Not that I can remember. You should talk to her friend, Kel, though."

"Had they fallen out?" Logan asked.

Rowan's eyes widened in panic, like he'd just said something wrong. "What? No! God. No, they were friends. He's a nice kid. He's already been on the phone offering to help. Offered to drive us up to my parents, if I wasn't up for it. Nice kid."

He crossed his arms on the table and leaned on them for support. "I just meant, if anyone would know about her falling out with anyone, it'd be Kel. Esme and I, we'd barely seen each other in the last few weeks. They're short-staffed. She was doing a lot of overtime."

He put a hand over his eyes, massaging his temples with fingers and thumb. "She wasn't even meant to be on last night, but her shift got swapped. We had an argument about it. We had plans for last night. We were going to go out. Just the two of us, you know? We hadn't done that in so long. A date night."

He dropped his hand into his lap and picked at the skin around his fingernails. "But swapping meant she had two days off in a row. That hasn't happened in... Well. I don't know when. She was going to take today to rest, then we were going to head away somewhere tomorrow. The three of us were going to just pile in the car, choose a direction and—"

His voice wobbled, then betrayed him completely. He lowered his head, his shoulders heaving as big silent sobs came. Sinead reached across the table and squeezed his hand. He didn't react, didn't acknowledge it. He just sat there, too tired to fight back the tears any longer.

"I think maybe I will go get us that cup of tea," Logan suggested, easing himself up out of the chair. He caught Sinead's eye, then tilted his head in Rowan's direction.

"Coffee. Milk and one," she mouthed.

Logan headed through into the kitchen. For the size of the house, it was fairly small, barely larger than galley-style. A brushed-chrome American fridge took up most of one end, the front of it decorated with Chloe's drawings, all attached by magnets.

One of the drawings showed a smiling woman with angel wings and a halo. The word 'Mummy' was scrawled inexpertly beneath it. It was presumably a very recent addition to the gallery. Either that, or little Chloe had one hell of a gift for premonition.

Logan filled the kettle from the tap and clicked the button to switch it on. He could hear Sinead talking to Rowan through in the living room, her voice low and soothing in a way that his own rarely was. Better to leave her to it, and let Rowan get it out of his system.

There was another door that led into a utility room almost the size of the kitchen itself. From that, another door led out into what Logan guessed would be the front hall. He went for a wander while he waited for the kettle to boil.

The house was a mirror image of the one next door, he thought, based on the fact the staircase was on the opposite side. He didn't want to go poking around upstairs without permission, so he stood by the bottom step, checking out some of the framed photos that adorned the wall there.

As with the living room, most of them showed Esme and Chloe. Chloe was smiling in most of them. Esme was smiling, too, albeit far more self-consciously than her more carefree daughter.

One of the pictures showed a large group of people sitting around a table in a pub or club. They were all dressed like they'd stepped out of the 1970s, with big collars and flares all but filling the frame.

There were twenty or so people in the photograph, and it took Logan a moment to spot Esme. She was tucked away near the back of the curved booth, wearing a blonde wig with a gold hairband, and—from what little of her could be seen behind the man next to her—a silver catsuit. A vast array of glasses on the table suggested the group had been drinking quite heavily for some time.

The man sitting next to her, Logan realised, was Kel Conlyn, the porter he'd spoken to earlier. He was kitted out in a brown leather jacket, paisley patterned shirt, and a handlebar moustache that looked comically oversized for his face.

Doctor Fletcher was in the picture, too. His costume was more subdued than everyone else's, consisting of a purple shirt with frills down the front, and a sensible pair of black trousers. It was a token gesture, and judging by the way he sat slightly apart from the rest of the group, everyone knew it.

Logan half-recognised a couple of the other nurses from the hospital the night before. He got the impression that most of the people in the picture were nurses, porters, and cleaning staff, in fact, with Fletcher being the noteworthy exception. Had he invited himself along? Inflicted himself upon the party? Or had someone else suggested he join in?

There was one other face in the photograph that Logan kept returning to. Male. Twenties. He wore a long hippie wig with a garland of flowers just above the fringe. He also had a peace sign painted on one cheek. It wasn't much of a disguise, but it was enough to prove distracting and made it difficult for Logan to recognise him. He'd seen him before, though. Recently.

At the hospital? Probably, but he couldn't place him there. Still, that had to be it. Where else could he know the face from?

Taking out his phone, Logan snapped off a couple of pictures of the photo, just as the kettle came to the boil back in the kitchen.

Then, with a final glance at the wall of photos, and the many smiling faces of Esme Miller, he headed through the utility room, and got on with the important business of making the tea.

TWENTY MINUTES, and one decent-if-not-spectacular cup of tea later, Logan stood on Rowan Miller's front step, his car keys clutched in one hand.

"You don't think he had anything to do with it, do you?" Sinead asked, her voice hushed and low.

Logan shook his head. "No. Contrary to what the neighbours might say."

"That what you were in next door for?"

"Aye. She'd heard them arguing. Thought it was worth bringing to my attention," Logan said. "I suppose, if nothing else, it corroborates what he told us himself. But no. I don't think he had anything to do with it."

Sinead looked pleased at that. "That's good. I mean, not *good*, but... You know."

"Aye. Well." Logan stepped down onto the path. "You take care of yourself. Let me know if anything comes up."

"Will do, sir," Sinead said. "Oh, and sir?"

Logan stopped. PC Bell stepped out of the house and pulled the door closed behind her. She shuffled a little uneasily, like she was building up to something.

"What is it?"

"It's, um, it's Harris's birthday next week. My wee... My brother. And, he was asking me if you might be coming."

"Me?"

"I think he wants you there, sir."

"What the bloody hell does he want me at his birthday for?" Logan asked.

"I think you made a bit of an impression down in the Fort, sir," Sinead said.

"Did you point out I'm a bit tied up trying to catch a murdering rapist?"

"Funnily enough, no, sir. I neglected to mention that." Sinead gave a reassuring smile. "It's fine, I told him you'd be busy. I just, you know, didn't go into quite that level of detail."

She was disappointed. Despite the smile she was putting on, it was written all over her face.

"I just... I wanted to make it good for him. You know, after everything that happened in the last couple of years? Our mum and dad... He didn't really have much of a birthday last year, and he's not got a lot of friends here yet."

Her eyes widened and the tone of her voice became a little more urgent.

"But that wasn't me trying to guilt-trip you into it, sir!" she said. "It's not a problem. He knows you're busy."

Logan gave a noncommittal sort of grunt. "When did you say it was?"

"Tuesday, but honestly, it's fine. It's just a wee thing for him after school. Four-ish. A couple of the boys from school are coming over. And the girl from next door, much to his horror and disgust," Sinead said. "You don't have to come, though. I just promised him I'd ask."

Logan rubbed his chin and smoothed the jaggy hairs that were sprouting on his top lip. "What's the cake situation?" he asked. "I'm assuming there'll be cake."

"Oh. Yeah. It's a Groot cake, sir."

"I don't know what that is," Logan pointed out.

"From *Guardians of the Galaxy*."

"I don't know what that is, either."

"It's a film, sir."

"Ah. Right. Must've passed me by," Logan said. This did not come as a surprise to either of them. "Four-ish on Tuesday?"

"That's right, sir."

"I'll try. No promises. Depends on what's happening with..."

He looked up at the front of the house.

"Of course, sir. And thanks. He'll be over the moon. If you can make it, I mean. No pressure, obviously."

Logan retreated along the path. "Aye, well. Like I say, I'll see what... Wait." He stopped. "Is DC Neish going to be there?"

Sinead's cheeks reddened just a fraction. "That's the plan, sir."

"Shite," Logan sighed. He considered his options again, then tutted. "Ach, I'll come anyway. I can always order him no' to talk to me."

Sinead smiled. "I'm sure you can try, sir," she told him. "I'm sure you can try."

CHAPTER EIGHTEEN

LOGAN SAT IN THE VOLVO ALONG FROM THE HOUSE AND WATCHED AS another well-wisher laid another bunch of flowers on the pavement outside the garden. The woman bowed her head in silent prayer, then scurried off like she was worried someone inside would come out to speak to her.

Rowan Miller had pulled himself together when Logan brought the tea in. They'd made some small talk for a few moments, then Logan had gone back to quizzing him—albeit gently—about his wife's personal life.

She had a few good friends, mostly through work. A sister who also lived in the city, not all that far away. They weren't in touch as often as either of them would like, but made a point of meeting up a couple of times a month for lunch and a good blether.

Logan had got the impression that Rowan wasn't the sister's biggest fan, but there had been nothing about the way he'd said it that had aroused any suspicions. In-laws could just be a pain in the arse sometimes. Logan knew that better than most.

Rowan hadn't been able to identify the man in the hippie outfit in the photograph in the hall. At least, not beyond a vague recollection that he'd worked with Esme at the time. A cleaner, Rowan thought, probably long since moved on.

An itch had been forming somewhere at the back of Logan's head since he'd seen the man in the picture, and Rowan's explanation did nothing to help scratch it. If he didn't work at the hospital, then why did Logan find him familiar? Where did he know him from?

Opening his phone, the DCI brought up the picture, then emailed it to the team's shared inbox, marking it for the attention of Tyler and Hamza with a message that simply read: 'Who's the hippie? Third from the right.'

Once the email was away, he punched 'Queensgate,' into the Maps app, selected the first result, and slotted the phone into the holder on the Volvo's smooth, curved dash.

An email notification appeared at the top of the screen. Tyler.

I think it's a costume, boss.

Muttering, Logan took the phone out of the holder, tapped, 'I know it's a bloody costume. Who's the guy wearing it?' and sent the reply.

Then, with the GPS showing him the way, he fired up the engine, pulled away from the Millers' house, and headed off to buy some sausages.

"Irn Bru?" Logan asked, peering suspiciously at the orange-tinted bangers nestling in a pile behind the glass. He raised his gaze to the portly gent smiling back at him from the other side of the counter. "You're no' serious."

"I am!" the butcher laughed. "It's our own recipe. Pork and Irn Bru. The customers love them!"

Did they though, Logan wondered? Beyond the novelty value, did they *actually* love them, or did they get them home, fry them up, and then spit the bastarding things out after one bite?

"We were going to try beef and Tizer, but... no. Decided against it."

"Aye. Because that would've been mental, I suppose," Logan reasoned.

He shook his head. Irn Bru sausages. What the hell was the world coming to?

"You don't look convinced," the butcher said.

"I can't say that I am, no."

"Do you like Irn Bru?"

Logan confirmed that he was partial to the occasional can.

"Right. Do you like pork?"

"Aye. But—"

"Well, then," said the butcher, holding his hands out at his sides as if presenting a cast iron case.

"Aye, but I like curry and ice cream, too. Doesn't mean I want them on the same plate," Logan replied. He looked down at the bright orange links again, then tutted. "Right. Go on, then. I'll take a dozen," he said. "I'm sure some bugger will eat them."

"Great!" the butcher exclaimed, and from the way he said it, Logan got the impression the man was both relieved and amazed that some gullible bugger had finally bought some. "One thing I should tell you—not sure if you're interested in that sort of thing—but they're four hundred calories each."

"*Each?*" Logan spluttered.

"Aye. I'm thinking of using Diet for the next batch," the butcher said, wrapping the sausages in a bundle of waxy paper. He deposited the parcel on top of the counter and beamed a big broad smile. "Now. Anything else?"

Logan fished for his wallet. "No. That'll do. But, eh..." He glanced around the shop. Besides himself and the ruddy complexioned guy serving him, there was nobody else to be seen. "Does Donald still work here?"

"He does, aye. He's through the back, prepping for the afternoon." The butcher looked Logan up and down. "You a friend of his?"

"Not exactly, no," Logan said. He glanced at a doorway leading through to the back. There was no door, but a curtain made of hundreds of metal beads blocked the view into the room beyond. "Mind if I have a word?"

"He's got his hands full. Afternoons get busy."

Logan produced his warrant card and held it up. Squinting, the butcher beckoned for him to hand it over for a closer look. Logan watched with growing dismay as the butcher's plastic-gloved fingers left big meaty prints on the wallet.

"Right," he said, handing back a wallet that was considerably stickier than it had been a moment ago. He gave the DCI another once over with his eyes. "He in trouble? What's he done?"

"Nothing that I'm aware of," Logan said. Which was true. "I'd just like a quick word."

The butcher drew in a breath, getting ready to shout.

"In private. If you don't mind."

Whatever the man was going to shout caught somewhere at the back of his throat. He looked over at the shop's front door, then raised a hatch in the counter and beckoned for Logan to come through quickly.

"Come on, come on. Don't want customers seeing randomers piling into the back shop. Health and hygiene."

Logan considered sharing the health and hygiene concerns he now had for his warrant card but decided not to bother. Instead, he stepped through the hatch, ducked through the curtains, and came face-to-face with a man holding a cleaver.

Donald Sloane looked up from where he was doing something unspeakable to a dead pig and locked Logan with a piercing stare. He was dressed in a blood-soaked blue apron that he'd complemented nicely with a matching hairnet and gloves.

There was a white mask over the lower half of his face, spots of blood dotting the material like freckles. The sleeves of his shirt were rolled up, revealing sinewy arms with muscles standing out on them like wraps of rope.

"Donald. This fella's from the police. He wants a quick word," the butcher said, poking his head through the curtain. He eyeballed Logan, emphasised the "*quick*" part again, then retreated to the front shop.

Sloane brought the cleaver down, neatly severing one part of the pig from another. The smell in the room reminded Logan of every mortuary he'd ever been to. It wasn't exactly the same—in fact, it wasn't all that similar at all—but there was an undercurrent to it that linked both places together. Something about the scent, something primal, that connected them.

Meat. That was all they were, he supposed, in the end.

"Donald Sloane?"

Sloane raised the cleaver, brought it down again.

THACK!

"Yes?"

"I was hoping you might answer a few questions."

The cleaver came up.

The cleaver came down.

THACK!

"About?"

Sloane twirled the cleaver around in his hand, then set it down on the stainless steel worktop and pulled the paper mask down so it was below his chin. As his face was revealed, Logan's stomach tightened, ejecting an involuntary grunt of surprise.

He'd seen Sloane's mugshot on the case report, and while the lad had lost a lot of weight since then, there was no mistaking it was him.

But that wasn't the only place Logan had seen his face. How could he not have realised? How could he not have put them together?

"You're the hippie," he said aloud. "You're the hippie in Esme Miller's photo."

Sloane lunged for a heavy wooden chopping block. Grabbed it. Tossed it. Logan ducked too late, heard the *thonk* as the edge of the board clipped his head, felt the pain jar through him, rattling his teeth in their sockets.

"Bastard!" he hissed, stumbling blindly back through the curtain. He landed in the refrigerated counter, arse-deep in black pudding.

"Watch it!" protested the butcher. Across the glass, a woman and a toddler both watched the DCI in stunned silence as he hauled himself up out of the meat and went charging through the curtain, a rivulet of red running down his forehead.

Logan skidded into the back shop, fists raised, ready for anything. To his relief, nothing came flying at him. No blades came *whumming* towards his skull.

Instead, a breeze blew in through the open fire exit in the corner of the room. Another curtain of beads *chinked* and *clacked* as it wafted in and out on the wind.

"Aw, *shite*," Logan spat.

And with that, he ran.

CHAPTER NINETEEN

THE BACK DOOR OF THE BUTCHER'S OPENED ON TO A LITTLE
courtyard barely wide enough to swing a cat in. A tall gate led out to an
alleyway. It was wedged half-open by a broken brick. Logan shot a look
through the gap but saw no sign of Sloane.

Another door stood open in the wall opposite. Two stunned-looking
older women stood beside it, smoke curling from the cigarettes they held
clutched between their lips.

"Where did he go?" Logan demanded, and both women jabbed their
thumbs in the direction of the open door.

Logan barrelled in past them, his feet slapping on the cracked tile
flooring as he emerged between two of the shops in Inverness's Victorian
Market. He'd only been in the place a couple of times before and couldn't
remember the layout.

He remembered that the path he was on meandered around the covered
market's shops and cafés but had no clue which direction led to the closest
exit. A quick scan left and right brought up no trace of Sloane, but a few
heads in the thin crowd were turned along the path on his right, like they'd
just seen something interesting.

That way.

"Move. Polis. Out of the road!" Logan barked, scattering shoppers as he
set off in the direction he reckoned Sloane had gone.

"Hey, watch it!" complained a woman around a corner up ahead. Logan powered towards it, coat swishing, heart thumping, lungs demanding to know what the bloody hell he thought he was playing at.

Skidding around a corner, Logan tripped, stumbled, and kicked his way through a display of fruit that had been scattered all over the floor. An orange exploded beneath his boot. His other foot found a banana which, fortunately, turned out to be nowhere near as slippery as he'd always been led to believe.

He hurled himself past it all, barged out through the glass doors, and stopped in the middle of the pavement. He loomed there, chest heaving, eyes scanning the street around him. The traffic was mostly stationary, and a couple of dirty great buses blocked much of his view of the surrounding area.

"You alright there, pal?" asked a male voice, the tone *just* condescending enough that Logan already knew what he'd see before he turned.

He flashed his warrant card in the faces of the two uniformed officers. "DCI Logan. MIT. There's a bastard running around in a butcher's apron. Potentially armed, definitely dangerous. I want him found!"

The Uniforms hesitated, swapping uncertain glances.

"Move!"

Both officers jumped and quickly darted off in opposite directions, their high-vis vests zig-zagging through the busy streets. One of them thumbed the radio on his shoulder, calling for back-up, but Logan had a sinking feeling that it was pointless. There was no saying which direction Sloane had gone. The only hope was that he'd been picked up on CCTV, but that was out of his hands.

"You know your head's bleeding, son?"

Logan looked down to find a concerned-looking old woman peering up at him.

"I know," he said. It came out harsher than he'd intended. He tried to make up for it by smiling, but it was thin and unconvincing. "Thanks."

"Well, you look after yourself, son," the woman said, shuffling off. "We're none of us as young as we used to be."

Logan drew in a breath that made pain flare through his lungs. "Aye," he muttered. "You can say that again."

THE BUTCHER EMERGED through the bead curtains just as Logan strode back in through the front door of the shop. The side of the DCI's face was a pattern of crimson shades, and an egg-sized bump was forming right below his hairline. He also had a pound of black pudding stuck to the back of his coat, but that was lower on his list of concerns.

"What the hell was all that about?" the butcher demanded.

"I was hoping you could tell me."

"Me? He's nothing to do with me. He just works here, that's all! If he's in trouble, that's his business, not mine."

Logan grunted. "Aye. Well. You'll have his address and phone number."

"Oh. Yes. But not here. My wife handles all that stuff. She'll be at home. I'll have to give her a ring."

"You do that," Logan said.

"Right. Aye. I will. No bother," the butcher said. "I'll give her a ring now and get you the information. Oh, and..."

He slapped a neatly wrapped parcel of sausages on the counter and flashed the detective a smile.

"That'll be four pound fifty."

CHAPTER TWENTY

"I'm starting to think we should be wrapping you in cotton wool, Jack," said Ben. He dabbed at the wound on Logan's head, eliciting a sharp intake of breath. "Sorry. Brace yourself. This might sting."

"Bit late for that," Logan said through gritted teeth. "What the hell are you putting on it? Acid?"

"No, it's..." Ben looked down at the tube of cream in his hand, then held it at arm's length and squinted to try to make out the lettering. "What is that, actually? Is that the right stuff?"

"What do you mean 'is that the right stuff?'" Logan barked, snatching the tube from the DI's hand. "Maybe check it's the right stuff before you..."

He read the label, tutted, then handed it back to Ben. "Aye. It's the right stuff. Just go canny with it, eh?"

He plucked it back out of Ben's grasp again. "In fact, why are you even doing it? I'll do it myself."

Squeezing a slug of disinfectant cream onto the tip of a finger, Logan poked gingerly at the site of his wound.

"At least this one won't need stitches," Ben said, peering at the injury. "Want me to stick a plaster on it, or would you prefer to do that yourself, too?"

"Maybe if you're a bit more careful and don't just slap it on," Logan bit back. He dabbed the injury site with the back of his hand, then studied it.

Besides the creamy residue, it came away dry. "Anyway, it's fine. It's stopped bleeding."

The events of the afternoon had meant Logan had come storming back into the Incident Room like a bear with a sore head. The fact that he literally did have a sore head wasn't helping matters, either.

"So, what does this mean, then?" Ben asked, as Logan got up from the chair he'd been sitting on and stalked over to the Big Board. "Sloane's our main suspect?"

"Well, put it this way, I'm certainly keen to have a word with the bastard," Logan said. He stared at the city centre map pinned to the board, like he might see Sloane darting down some lane or side alley somewhere on it. "CCTV pick him up?"

"No, sir. Nothing," said DS McQuarrie, joining the DCI at the board. "City centre, too. Lot of cameras around, but not a sniff of him. Not sure how he pulled that off."

"Did you no' say there were buses around, boss?" Tyler volunteered from his desk. "Maybe he jumped on one of them."

Logan exhaled slowly through his nose. "Aye. Maybe." He looked back over his shoulder in the direction of DC Khaled. Hamza was hunched over his computer screen, scowling at the screen. "You got me those recordings from when he was last interviewed?"

"Not yet, sir. I can probably get you the transcripts, but HOLMES is still all over the place," Hamza replied. "Bloody update."

Logan cursed below his breath. "What about his house, did we check there?"

"He's no' there, Jack. Not that that comes as a surprise," Ben said.

"What about—"

"He left his mobile in his jacket pocket. Can't trace him through that, either," said Ben, correctly anticipating the DCI's next question. "It's just a waiting game for now. He'll turn up. We'll get him."

Logan rubbed the tips of his forefinger and thumb together, rolling up the dried antiseptic paste. "We'd better."

"What was it you said to him anyway, boss?" asked Tyler. "To set him off like that?"

"Nothing really," Logan said, his gaze still fixed on the map, and the area around the Victorian Market. "It was out of me before I knew it. I recognised him as the hippie in that photo I sent."

"From Esme Miller's house?" asked Ben. "He knew Esme Miller?"

"He did," Logan confirmed. "Used to work together at the hospital. As soon as I mentioned her name, he horsed a chopping block at me and fucked off out of there."

Ben whistled through his teeth. His eyes darted left and right as he contemplated the implications of Logan's revelation. "That's... That could be huge."

"It could. Which is why we need to find him, sharpish," the DCI said.

"We've got a heavy presence in the area, sir," Caitlyn informed him. "He has to be hiding somewhere nearby. We might still catch sight of him yet, with a bit of luck."

Logan wasn't getting his hopes up. "We've never exactly had luck to spare, have we?" he asked, then he gave a dismissive wave that made it clear he wasn't expecting an answer. "What else do we have? That Forensics report come in on the victim's clothes yet?"

"It did, but it's a bit of an anti-climax," Ben reported. "Multiple DNA samples taken from it, but apparently that's par for the course with nurses and other medical professionals. They interact with a lot of people in a day and deal with their fair share of bodily fluids.

"They're getting samples from the patients she's likely to have dealt with that day, as well as her colleagues, but it's going to be a long process. There isn't any one sample that screams 'murderer,' unfortunately, so even once they've all been identified, they're unlikely to be a big help."

This was not the news Logan had been hoping to hear.

"And no sign of the gag or the murder weapon either, I'm assuming?"

"Nothing," Ben confirmed.

From behind his monitor, Hamza let out a short sharp cry of frustration, and repeatedly hammered the space bar on his keyboard. Logan knew exactly how he felt.

"Stupid bloody thing!" Hamza spat. "Why run an update if it's only going to make things worse?"

"Still having problems?" Tyler asked.

"No, I just shouted all that for a laugh. *Yes.* Still having problems."

Logan pinched the bridge of his nose and squeezed, trying to push back against his headache. It had started as a sharp sting where the board had hit him, gradually faded into a dull background throb, but was now in the process of getting its second wind.

Turning back to the board, he studied the map for a while, then drew a circle around the Victorian Market with a fingertip. "What's the camera situation around here?"

"More than ample, sir," said Caitlyn. "The exit you took, there are four within sixty feet of the door, then one at each corner of the street."

"And none of them picked Sloane up?"

"No, sir. Like I say, Uniform is still on the scene. We might pick him up yet."

Logan sucked in his top lip and poked absent-mindedly at the cut on his head. His fingers came away sticky, pinkened by the white of the cream and the red of...

Blood.

"Wait. Hold on, hold on," said Logan, stiffening. "Shite. Gloves. He had gloves on. He'd been chopping meat. He was bloody."

Ben Forde's brow furrowed. "Aye. You said. So what?"

"Argh! Jesus Christ, what an idiot!" Logan snapped, spinning on his heels.

"Here, steady on..."

"No' you. Me. How could I have been so bloody stupid?" Logan groaned. "It's a glass door."

"And?" Ben asked.

"Glass door, blood-soaked gloves. Where was the handprint?"

Ben glanced around at the others. "Is that a rhetorical question or...?"

"There wasn't one. Because he didn't go out through the doors!" Logan announced. He jabbed a finger in Tyler's direction. "Get onto Uniform. Get them to lock the whole place down," he instructed. "The bastard's still in the building!"

CHAPTER TWENTY-ONE

CONSTABLE PENNY WILLOW OPENED THE DOOR OF THE VICTORIAN Market's fruit and veg shop, chiming the bell that was fixed to the frame above it.

The shop was dim and cramped, and lined on all sides with racks of organic produce that reeked to high heaven. It wasn't an unpleasant smell, exactly, just an overwhelming one. The fruit and vegetables all smelled fresh enough, but there was a suggestion of dampness from the fabric of the shop that added a sour note to the overall aroma of the place.

The front part of the shop was deserted, and while there was a curtained-off door leading through to what was presumably a storage area at the back, the bell hadn't drawn anyone out.

"Knock knock," PC Willow announced. "Hello? Police."

For a moment, there was nothing to indicate anyone was through there, but then the curtains were half-pulled aside and a man in his mid-fifties sidled through, smiling broadly at the uniformed officer as he dried his hands on a thin, slightly grimy-looking towel.

"Sorry. I was in the toilet," he announced.

"You leave the shop open when you go to the toilet? Bit risky, that."

"Yes. I only intended to be quick, but it took longer than expected to..." the shopkeeper began. His face took on a slightly desperate expression as he searched for an appropriate ending to the sentence. He settled on, "...get the job done," and then visibly flinched at his choice of words.

"Right," said PC Willow, not quite sure how to respond to that. She rapped her knuckles on a rock-hard Swede. "You should get more fibre in your diet."

"Ha! Yes!" he replied. "Can't beat a bit of roughage for getting the old bowels moving."

He instantly regretted that one too, judging by the way his face crumpled and he became intensely focused on finishing drying his hands.

Once done, he folded the towel and set it down on the counter, then gestured to the racks of produce lining the walls.

"Looking for anything in particular?"

"Not anything, exactly. Any*one*," PC Willow replied. "Have you seen anyone acting suspicious in the last half hour or so?"

The shopkeeper gestured to the window. "Someone knocked over the display out front. Made a right bloody mess, they did. Is that the sort of thing you mean?"

"It may be connected," PC Willow said. "Someone came through here recently after assaulting one of our officers. We believe they may be hiding on the premises."

"These premises? Here?" the shopkeeper asked, pointing to the floor.

"Not necessarily in this shop, sir, no. Somewhere in the market. We're doing a sweep at the moment, checking if anyone has seen anything."

"Right. Yes. Of course. Well, other than my display being trashed, there's not a lot I can tell you, I'm afraid."

The constable's gaze flicked to the curtain behind the shopkeeper. "You've checked through the back?"

"There's not a lot of it to check!" the man laughed. He caught the edge of the curtain. "You're welcome to have a look yourself, if you like? Just mind the mess."

PC Willow hesitated, then shook her head. "That won't be necessary. Thank you," she said. The smell in the shop was getting to her, and she didn't really want to spend any more time than necessary breathing it in. "If you see anything unusual, please just flag someone down. We'll be here for a while yet."

"Will do," said the shopkeeper.

The constable pulled open the door, sending the bell into another chiming frenzy.

"Oh, and if you do catch him, tell him he owes me for all that fruit he stomped on!"

PC Willow stopped. Turned.

"Sorry?"

The shopkeeper's smile widened just a little too far. "The... my fruit. If you catch him."

"I didn't say anything about it being a man, sir."

The bell went again as the constable let the door swing closed.

"Didn't you? Oh. I just... I must've just..."

"On second thoughts, sir, maybe I will have a look through the back."

The shopkeeper's smile remained fixed in place, but the rest of his face and his body language all conspired to tell a different story. He swallowed.

"I thought you said you didn't need to?"

"I did, sir. But I've changed my mind," said the constable, approaching the open hatch at the side of the counter. "Woman's prerogative, and all that."

"You're wasting your time. Honestly. It's a mess back there," the shopkeeper said, the words coming as a breathless sort of laugh. Sweat glistened on his brow. His cheeks, which looked to be in a permanent state of rosiness, blazed red.

He was a little taller than the officer, but seemed to be shrinking fast. His eyes flitted to the curtain, then back to PC Willow. Wide. Staring.

Pleading.

"Help me," he whispered.

Then, the curtain erupted beside them and a man in a bloodied apron exploded through it.

A hand wrapped around PC Willow's throat. Another caught her by the hair, fingers twisting until her scalp burned in pain.

"Fucking pigs!" a voice snarled in her ear. "Why won't you leave me alone?"

LOGAN PACED BACK and forth in the Incident Room, his hands folded behind his back, his tongue clicking against the roof of his mouth.

The others were all sitting at their desks, reading, or writing, or—in Hamza's case—muttering obscenities at the computer screen.

Every once in a while, one of them would glance up at the phone on DI Forde's desk, willing it to ring. It remained steadfastly silent.

"Come on. What's bloody taking so long?" Logan asked of nobody in particular. "It's no' like it's a big place. I mean, how many shops are even in there?"

Tyler looked up from the paperwork he was reading through. "Want me to find out, boss?"

"Well, obviously not. I don't actually care," Logan snapped.

"Oh," said Tyler. "Right. Sorry, boss."

Logan continued to pace. Back and forth. Back and forth. It had been forty minutes since the market had been cordoned off. If he'd known it was going to take this long, he'd have gone down there and found the bastard himself.

"Any word on... I don't know. Anything?" Logan asked.

"No updates, Jack," said Ben.

Logan tutted his annoyance. "Hamza? What's HOLMES doing?"

"Being a pain in the arse, sir," DC Khaled replied. "I've logged an issue with the help desk, but it's getting worse, if anything. Just grinding to a halt."

"Great. Well, keep on at support. If you need me to give them a bollocking, I'm more than happy to."

"It might come to that, sir," Hamza said. "I'll keep you posted."

It was Logan's turn to shoot Ben's phone a look. It was a threatening look, at that, but the bloody thing still didn't take the hint.

"Thirty-three, boss," Tyler announced.

Logan stopped pacing and stared at DC Neish. "What?"

"The number of shops in the market. I looked it up. Thirty-three. That's counting cafés and—"

"I don't give a shite," Logan told him. He made an abrupt gesture at the paperwork spread out in front of the younger detective. "Do something useful."

"Right, boss. Sorry, boss," said Tyler, turning his attention back to the paperwork.

He looked up again a moment later when the phone on Ben's desk rang.

"Well, bloody answer it, then," Logan urged, before it had even reached the second ring.

"Jesus, I'm no' spring-loaded," Ben grumbled. He reached across the desk, picked up the handset, and cradled it to his ear. "DI Forde."

Everyone watched. Waited. Held their breath.

"Uh-huh," said Ben.

"Oh," said Ben.

"Right," said Ben. "And is she...?"

His eyes darted across the faces of the rest of the team. "I see. Thanks."

The handset was barely half an inch from Ben's ear when Logan spoke.

"Well?"

Ben returned the phone to the cradle. "A female constable discovered him hiding in the greengrocers. He attacked her."

The atmosphere in the room became heavier, more oppressive.

"Bastard," Logan hissed. "And? How is she?"

"Hmm? Oh, she's fine," said Ben. A smile tugged at the corners of his mouth. "Leathered the living shite out of him. They're bringing him in now."

Logan thrust both hands in the air and looked to the ceiling, giving thanks to a god he didn't believe in. "YES!"

He spun on the spot, brought up an arm, and pointed at DS McQuarrie. "Caitlyn, get us an interview room prepped. Make sure we get our guest the most uncomfortable chair we've got. Put a pin in the seat, if you have to. Let's make it as unpleasant an experience as we can for him."

Caitlyn got up from her desk. "I like your thinking, sir. On it."

"Tyler, I want access to his house. We might not be able to tie him to Esme Miller yet, but that's two officers he's assaulted, so the bastard's hiding something. Get onto the PF, get a search warrant, and get Forensics in there to give the place a bloody good going over."

"I'll see what I can do, boss," Tyler said, reaching for his phone.

"You'll do better than that. Get it done," Logan told him. "And get the shop where he works shut down, too. I don't want anyone else in or out. They've got a lot of knives there, one of them could be the murder weapon."

Tyler nodded, his finger already stabbing at the numbers on the phone's handset.

"And Hamza?" Logan continued. He turned just in time to see DC Khaled banging his computer keyboard against the desk, then biting down on his fist.

"You get that bloody thing working, ASAP," the DCI instructed. "We can't have it slowing us down on this."

Hamza sighed. "Yes, sir. I'm working on it."

"Good lad."

Logan turned. He breathed out for what felt like the first time since he'd chased Sloane through the market. Ben met his gaze from across the Incident Room.

"You're going to have your work cut out for you, Jack. If it's anything like last time, he'll be combative."

"Aye, well," said Logan. He cracked his knuckles. "We can but hope."

CHAPTER TWENTY-TWO

It was well after six by the time everything was set up for the interview. Sloane's solicitor had been a nightmare to get hold of, and even once they had, he'd insisted on finishing his dinner before coming in.

Sloane himself had been intent on making himself as big a pain in the arse as he possibly could. With some difficulty, he'd been stripped of his clothes and given a pair of shapeless grey joggies and a t-shirt to wear. He'd refused to put them on at first, and had instead ranted and cursed and gone parading around the cell stark bollock naked.

Eventually, he'd been coaxed into getting dressed by one of the older female officers, who had made some earnest-sounding yet deeply sarcastic remarks about the size of his manhood. He hadn't quite known how to respond to that, and had begrudgingly agreed to put some clothes on as long as she agreed to stop talking and go away.

"Christ, he's a changed man," Ben remarked, watching on a monitor as Sloane prowled around inside his cell. "He was a skinny wee runt of a thing last time I saw him. Look at him now."

In some ways, Sloane was still skinny, but a runt he was not. There wasn't an ounce of fat on him, and everything else had been honed and sculpted to such an extent that he actually looked ill. He'd clearly been obsessively hitting the gym, but whereas some guys bulked out, everything about Sloane had just sort of sharpened.

He looked strong and fast, and had it not been for the female constable having the presence of mind to crack him across the knee with her baton and then drive one of her own knees into his groin, Logan dreaded to think what might have happened.

"His solicitor's here, sir," said Caitlyn, appearing in the doorway behind Logan and Ben. "We're about ready to go."

"Finally. Who is it?"

"Clive Copeland, sir. From Copeland and Fraser Legal."

Logan gave a little shake of his head, indicating he'd never heard of them.

"Either of you dealt with him before?"

"Aye," Ben confirmed. "Arsehole."

Logan appreciated the succinctness of the older detective's review, unsurprising as it was. It was rare to encounter a defence lawyer who didn't accurately fit that description.

"Who wants to go in there with me?" Logan asked.

"I have to admit, I wouldn't say no to another crack at him," Ben said. "But the fact we have history might be a problem."

Logan considered this. On-screen, two uniformed officers came to take Sloane through to the interview room.

"No. I want you in there," the DCI decided. "If he's fixated on you, he'll be paying less attention to me. Besides, Caitlyn, I want you to go round to pre-warn Danni Gillespie. Sloane didn't exactly come quietly, so it's bound to be hitting social media. I'd rather she heard from us that we've brought him in."

"Right, sir," Caitlyn said. "What about the victim's family? Are we saying anything to them at this point?"

"Not yet. Let's see what we get out of him first." He turned to look at both of them. "Everyone alright with that decision?"

"Fine by me, Jack."

"Yes, sir."

Logan nodded. "Good, then let's get to it," he said, taking a final look at Sloane as he was led out of the cell in shackles. "I want this bastard broken before the chippie shuts."

LOGAN HAD BEEN CONCERNED that getting Sloane to talk would be difficult. He needn't have been. Getting him to shut up was proving to be the problem.

He'd started ranting even before DI Forde had made the introductions for the benefit of the recording, and his solicitor had spent a few minutes trying to calm him down enough for things to proceed.

Logan hadn't needed Ben's review of Clive Copeland in the end. He'd disliked the man on sight. He had an expensive, if tight-fitting suit that suggested a high net worth and an even higher calorie intake. On the flip side, he was sorely lacking in hair. And, presumably, moral integrity, given how he'd made the money to pay for that suit.

His attempts to soothe his client were decidedly half-arsed. He sounded almost as impatient as Logan felt, evidently furious about having been called away from dinner before the dessert course had arrived.

"What the fuck's he here for?" Sloane demanded, shooting the dirtiest of looks across the table at DI Forde. "He shouldn't be here. I fucking complained about him. I fucking complained about you."

"Aye, I remember," said Ben, deflecting Sloane's anger with a well-aimed smile. "Nothing came of that, by the way. No fault found. They even apologised for wasting my time, in fact." His smile widened. "In case you were wondering."

"Fuck you," Sloane spat. He made a lunging motion, but the cuffs that fastened him to the table stopped him moving more than a few inches. Neither of the two detectives so much as blinked.

"You quite finished?" Logan asked.

Sloane sneered at him, his nostrils flaring in disgust. He looked Logan up and down, as if only now seeing him for the first time.

"How's your head, pal?" he asked, sniggering.

"Sore, actually. Feels like it took a right pounding," Logan replied. He clasped his hands in front of him and leaned in. "Which, coincidentally, is more or less word-for-word what you'll be saying about your arsehole in a few months, after we sling you in the jail."

Sloane kept his grin fixed in place, but some of the defiance faded behind his eyes. "I'm not going to jail."

"Aye, you are," Logan told him.

Sloane leaned forward as far as the cuffs would allow, mirroring Logan's own position.

"Naw, I'm fucking *not*."

Logan raised an index finger. "Hang on. Allow me to consult with my fellow officer here," he said, then he turned to Ben. "Detective Inspector Forde?"

"Yes, Detective Chief Inspector? How can I help?"

"He's going to the jail, isn't he?"

"Oh God, aye," Ben confirmed. "He's going to the jail, alright."

Logan nodded, then turned back to Sloane. "Thanks for waiting there. Aye. I just checked. You are."

Clive Copeland opened his mouth to speak. Logan jumped in before he could say a word. "Assaulting a police officer. Twice. Assault with the intent to resist arrest."

He glanced over at the solicitor. "Could we push for perverting the course of justice? What do you think? You're the expert."

"Don't forget the hostage-taking and property damage," Ben said.

"Oh, I'd hardly call it 'hostage-taking,'" Copeland protested, but the detectives both ignored him.

"Christ, aye," said Logan. "That poor shopkeeper. He'd actually slipped my mind. How is he, by the way?"

"Oh, he's shaken," said Ben. "He's badly shaken. He'll be pressing charges, alright. Criminal and civil, I'd have thought. Taking it all the way."

Logan puffed out his cheeks. "And then there's breach of the peace, after you screamed the place down when we were taking you into custody."

"Frightened the weans," Ben added.

"Frightened a *lot* of weans, aye," Logan said. He sucked air in through his teeth. "No, I'll be honest, things aren't looking good for you, Donnie. Can I call you Donnie, by the way?"

"Can you fuck."

"I'm going to go ahead and call you Donnie," Logan said, flashing a smile. "Things are no' looking good for you, Donnie. But maybe we can come to some sort of arrangement. Maybe DI Forde and I, maybe we'll go easy on all that stuff if you help us out with another matter."

"How did you know Esme Miller?" Ben asked.

Sloane squirmed in his seat. "Who?"

Logan opened a paper folder on the table and presented a printout of the photograph he'd taken at the Millers' house.

"Cut the shite, Donnie. That's you," he said, tapping the image. "And that's Esme Miller. You worked together, did you not?"

"I worked at a lot of places," Sloane grunted.

"Aye. You have that. We were looking you up," Logan said. "Why is that? All the career changes? How come you never settle in one place?"

Sloane shrugged. A petulant child. "Get bored, don't I?"

"Right. I see. Well, we phoned around and asked a few of your former employers, and that's not what they said, is it, Detective Inspector?"

"No," Ben confirmed. "That's not what they said."

"And remind me what it was they said," Logan pressed.

"They said he was an unpopular bastard," said Ben. "No' well liked at all. Bit weird, in fact."

"And wasn't there something about personal hygiene?"

"There was," Ben confirmed. "Came up a couple of times, actually. The main thrust of it was the unpopular bastard bit, though."

Logan drew Sloane a very deliberate up and down look before continuing. "But, that's by the by." He tapped the photograph. "Esme Miller. You knew her. We know you knew her, so stop pissing us about."

Sloane shot his solicitor a sideways look, but Copeland was studying the photograph and failed to pick up on it.

"I only knew her vaguely. I saw her around. That was all."

"And when did you last see her around?" Ben asked.

"Well, I don't know, do I?"

"Last night, maybe?" Logan suggested. "Say, nine-ish?"

"I knew this was going to happen. I fucking knew it!" Sloane spat, becoming agitated again. He rattled his restraints. "Soon as I heard about the writing on her. Soon as that prick messaged me to tell me, I fucking knew this was going to happen."

Logan's brow furrowed. "What prick?"

Sloane's mouth closed, his teeth snapping together with a *clack*. He breathed slowly through his nose, eyes darting between the two detectives. He'd made a mistake, said too much.

"No comment."

"Who messaged you? What did they tell you?" Logan pressed.

"No comment."

"We've got your phone, Donnie. We can find out," Logan said.

Sloane tutted. "Fine. Shaun. Alright?"

"Gillespie?" said Logan.

"No, Connery. Aye, Gillespie. He messaged me to say he knew it was me, but it fucking wasn't, alright?" Sloane said, rattling the cuffs. "It fucking wasn't!"

"Alright, calm down, son," Ben told him. "Acting up's no' going to get you anywhere."

"Don't fucking 'son' me, you crooked piece of shit," Sloane spat. "You made my life hell. All you people. You think I killed Esme, like you think I raped that stuck-up bitch. Well, I didn't, alright? I didn't do it."

"Which one didn't you do?" Logan asked. "The rape or the murder."

"Either. Both! You know what I fucking mean!"

"Then why run, Donnie? That's what I keep coming back to. Why chuck a dirty great lump of wood at me and leg it? Why hide out? Why attack one of my officers?"

"Because I knew this would fucking happen! I knew you'd find some bullshit excuse to drag me back in here."

Logan looked offended. "I was just in to buy sausages, son. Thought I'd take the opportunity to ask you a couple of quick questions. You weren't a suspect until you flew off the handle and started throwing your weight around."

Sloane said nothing, just ground his teeth together and stared straight ahead.

"As far as I was concerned, you had an alibi for the sexual assault. Far as I was concerned, it wasn't you."

"Yeah, well, it wasn't me," Sloane spat, coming alive again.

Logan's chair creaked as he leaned forward a little further. "Now, though, I've got good reason to go back over that case with a fine-tooth comb, Donnie, paying very close attention to your whereabouts on the night of the attack."

He sat back, keeping eye contact. "To think, I went in there for some sausages and came out with a new line of enquiry and a prime suspect. Talk about my lucky day."

The detectives left him stewing in that for a bit.

"Whose idea was the Irn Bru sausages, by the way?" Logan asked.

Ben did a double-take, his nose crinkling in disgust. "The what?"

"They do Irn Bru sausages now," Logan said. He still hadn't taken his eyes off Sloane. "Whose idea was that?"

"I don't know. Mine."

"Irn bloody Bru sausages?" Ben said, scowling. "We should lock him up for that alone."

Clive Copeland quickly jumped in. "You can't lock—"

"We know, Mr Copeland," Logan sighed. "Fucking up a perfectly good sausage is not currently a crime. Besides..." He returned his gaze to Sloane. "We've got more than enough to be going on with."

Logan steepled his fingers in front of him. Beside him, Ben Forde flicked to a blank page in an A4 notepad, and popped the lid off a brand new pen.

"Now, let's try this again, Mr Sloane," Logan said. "Tell me what you know about Esme Miller."

CHAPTER TWENTY-THREE

DEPENDING ON WHICH WAY YOU LOOKED AT IT, THE INTERVIEW HAD gone reasonably well.

After some more cajoling, a few thinly veiled threats, and a quiet word from his solicitor, Sloane had started to open up. He'd told them most of what they wanted to know, in the end. The problem was, it was currently difficult to verify much of it.

Sloane confirmed that he had worked at the hospital for a few months, doing general cleaning duties. He'd worked behind the scenes in the staff canteen for most of his time there, but had started out on the same ward that Esme Miller worked on. He insisted they didn't really know each other though, and even on the night out where he and Esme had both been pictured, he didn't recall speaking to her once.

Checking up on how long he'd worked at the hospital wouldn't be a problem, although it was too late to get it done tonight. A quick call in the morning would be able to confirm or deny that part of his story, at least, although it would be unlikely to shine any light on his relationship with Esme, or his lack of one.

Fortunately, Logan had an idea about that.

"Kel Conlyn," he said, after a slurp of tea.

He and Ben were the only two left in the Incident Room, and had taken up residence on either side of the DCI's desk. The world beyond the window was dark, the night having drawn all the way in over the course of the interview.

Whoever had been last to leave had turned off all the lights, and neither detective had bothered to turn them back on again. The only illumination came from an angled lamp on Logan's desk, which cast a puddle of light, pushing aside the shadows in the otherwise darkened room.

Ben took a sip of his own drink, then frowned. "Who's that now?"

"Friend of Esme's. We went round to see him earlier. He's in the photo of the night out," Logan explained. "He should be able to tell us what sort of relationship Esme and Sloane had."

"Good. That'll help," Ben said. There was a *buzz* from his pocket. He groaned. "Shite."

"Alice?" Logan asked.

"Oh, no doubt. Her sister's visiting us from Stornoway. Arrives tonight. She'll be there now."

"Well, what are you sitting around here for?" Logan asked him. He motioned to the door. "Go."

"You sure?"

"Aye, I'm sure. I'm not having Alice hold me responsible for you not being there."

God knew, the woman held enough against him as it was, from the destruction of her favourite ceramic hedgehog onwards. He didn't need something else added to what was already a fairly sizeable list.

Logan held up the Post-It note Tyler had left for him to let him know that he wouldn't hear back on the search warrant until the following morning. "Not a lot we can do tonight, anyway."

"Suppose," Ben said. He drained the rest of his tea, then set the mug on Logan's desk as he grunted up onto his feet. "I'll get that in the morning."

"It's fine. I'll get it," Logan told him. "I was going to hang on for a bit, anyway."

"Why?" Ben asked, reaching for his coat. It wasn't currently raining outside, but it was never far away.

Logan realised he had no response. Why *was* he planning on sticking around? What could he possibly do tonight, now that everywhere was shut, and everyone else had gone home?

"I won't be long," Logan said. "Just want to, you know."

Ben did know. Given the chance, he'd be sitting here with the DCI, sharing his current lack of purpose. How many nights had they done just that over the years? How many hours spent just thinking in the dark?

"Aye. Get home soon, though. Man your age needs your rest," Ben told him, heading for the door.

"You're a fine one to talk," Logan called after him. "You using your bus pass to get home, aye?"

"Thought I might cadge a lift with Meals on Wheels," Ben replied.

He stopped in the doorway, silhouetted against the light spilling in from the corridor beyond.

"You think we've got him, Jack?"

Logan rolled the response around in his mouth a few times, shaping it. Smoothing it. Sloane was a definite fit. He also had no alibi for last night. None that could be verified, at least.

And yet...

"I hope so, Ben," was all the DCI would commit to. "I really hope so."

"Aye, you and me both," Ben agreed. "But what's your gut instinct?"

"My gut instinct?" Logan exhaled. "My gut instinct doesn't matter. The evidence is leading us towards it being him. That's what matters."

Ben opened his mouth to say something, then changed his mind. "Goodnight, Jack," he said.

And with that, he slipped out into the corridor and closed the door, and the Incident Room was swallowed by the darkness once more.

THE MAIN ENTRANCE to Logan's block of flats was supposed to lock, but the condition of the door suggested it hadn't done for quite a number of years.

Logan shoved it open, plodded through the close, and was about to start up the stairs when he heard the sob. It was soft and muffled, like it was deliberately being stifled.

He found her around the other side of the stone staircase, tucked in between it and the close's back wall. She was sitting on the floor, her back jammed against the side of the steps, her face buried in her knees. The lassie from the flat on the floor below Logan's own. Damn it. What was her name again?

"Tanya?" Logan said, the name coming to him in a flash of inspiration. "You alright?"

She was a young woman, but hunched up there she looked like a child. The crack in her voice made her sound like it, too.

"Fine," she sniffed, not looking up. "Just leave me alone."

A part of Logan wanted to oblige. Quite a big part, actually. He'd much rather be putting his feet up in his flat than dealing with whatever he was about to be dealing with.

But that wasn't going to happen.

"Has something happened, Tanya? You can tell me," he said. His knees *cracked* as he dropped down onto his haunches in front of the crying woman.

He gave her a couple of moments to answer him, then pressed on with the obvious.

"Has he hurt you?"

Her voice was a squeak. A whisper. "It was my fault."

"I find that hard to believe," Logan said. "Look at me, Tanya. Let me see."

At first, it didn't look as if she'd heard him. Then, she sniffed a couple of times, pulling herself together, and slowly raised her head.

The first thing Logan saw was the blood. It had flowed freely from both nostrils, over her mouth, down her chin, and started to form rivulets on her neck. Evidently, that had been a little while ago, as it had all mostly dried into shades of dark crimson.

Her right eye had taken a clout. A hard one too, judging by the colour and size of the area around it. The eyes themselves were wide and worried. They darted anxiously across Logan's face, unable to settle on any one part.

"Jesus Christ," Logan muttered. "Listen to me, Tanya. This wasn't your fault, alright?"

"It was," she insisted, although there wasn't a lot of conviction behind it. "I could see he was angry. I shouldn't have kept on at him."

"I'm guessing he told you that," Logan said. "Listen to me, Tanya, I've seen this a lot of times before, and it's always the same story. This wasn't your fault, alright? This..." He glanced over her injuries. "...is *never* your fault."

"How... How have you seen it before?" she ventured.

Logan reached into his coat pocket and produced his warrant card. "Detective Chief Inspector Logan. Jack. I can get the bastard picked up within the next five minutes."

At the sight of the ID, Tanya's expression had become one of panic. "No. Shit. I don't want him lifted."

"He hit you, Tanya. More than once, by the looks of it. You can't go back in there," Logan insisted.

Tanya shook her head. "I don't want him lifted. I don't want to have to deal with all that. I just..."

She leaned her head back and looked up through the gap in the stairwell above. "I just want him out," she said, whispering it like she was terrified he might hear.

"I strongly suggest that I call this in, Tanya. We can get him taken away. If you give evidence, he'll do time for this. We can help make sure he never hurts you again."

Tanya didn't even waste a second considering it. She shook her head. "He'll go mental if he knows I spoke to the police. I don't want to go through all that. I just want him out."

Logan sighed. He'd seen this too many times before. He knew how it ended.

"You sure you don't want me to call it in?"

Tanya nodded. "Aye," she said. "I'm sure."

"Right. Your call. Do you have keys?" Logan asked.

"I left them in the flat."

"OK. What's his name?"

"Bud."

Logan frowned. "Bud? What's that short for?"

"Nothing. Just Bud."

Logan pulled a face that suggested he didn't approve. Then, he stood up, took off his coat, and draped it over her. "Here. Hang onto this for now. It's cold."

She watched him as he headed for the stairs and climbed the first few steps.

"What are you going to do?" she asked.

Logan stopped. "I'm going to get him out."

Tanya squeezed herself into the corner between the stairs and the wall. "I don't want him to see me."

Logan hesitated, then clicked his tongue against the roof of his mouth. "I'll see what I can do."

CHAPTER TWENTY-FOUR

THE DOOR OPENED AFTER THE FOURTH ROUND OF HAMMERING. BUD pulled it wide with a sudden yank, his scowl appearing in the space the door had previously occupied.

"What the fuck do you—" he began, then he stumbled back as Logan pushed past him into the hallway.

The place reeked of old rubbish and cannabis. An overflowing bin and a couple of loosely tied black bags met Logan as he diverted off the hallway and into the kitchen. The layout was the same as his own flat, albeit flipped around, so he had the advantage of knowing where everything was.

The stench of the rubbish was cloying in the kitchen. It got in about Logan's nostrils and reached down into his throat, almost triggering his gag reflex.

"The fuck do you think you're doing?" demanded the scrote from out in the hall.

"Bud, isn't it?" Logan asked, pulling open the door to the cupboard under the sink. There were a few cleaning products that he suspected had never been used, but not what he was after.

"I can fucking do you in for being in here," Bud snapped. "It's legal for me to do you right in."

"Is that a fact?" Logan asked him, pulling open another couple of cupboards. Pots and pans. Tinned food.

Not in those, either.

"Aye! Fucking right it is! So get out, or I'll—"

Logan spun, eyes blazing. "Or you'll what, son? Eh? Or you'll what?"

Bud's expression briefly changed to one of panic, but the sneer quickly returned. The step back he took was telling, though. Quick with his fists when he was up against a woman smaller than he was. Not so handy when a big burly bastard was staring him down.

"Aye, I thought so," Logan grunted. He turned back and was about to open another cupboard when he spotted a sausage of fabric hanging from a hook on the wall. A blue Co-op Bag For Life poked out of a hole at the bottom of it. "Aha! Here we are."

Logan took the crumpled bag from the dispenser. He straightened it out very slowly and very deliberately, maintaining eye contact with the scrote in the hall.

"I've been speaking to Tanya, Bud. She's in a real mess."

Bud shifted his weight from foot to foot. "Oh aye? And what shite has she been spilling, eh? She been talking shite about me again? Is that what she's—"

Logan put a finger to his lips. "Shh."

"Fucking *shh* me, ya old bastard!" Bud spat, finding some of his earlier venom. This pleased Logan immensely. He didn't want the man doubting himself. Much better to have him at his biggest and boldest for what was to follow, chest all puffed up, shoulders back like the cock of the walk.

"She wants you out of here, Bud. Tonight. Now."

"Oh, she does, does she? Is that so? Well she can suck—"

"*I* want you out, too. We chatted about it. Came to a wee agreement between ourselves," Logan continued.

Bud snorted and looked the detective up and down. "What? So, you're here to chuck me out, are you?"

"Hmm? Oh, no. I'm here to ask you to leave. Nicely, like," Logan said. He took a step closer.

"And what if I tell you to go an' get fucked?" Bud asked.

The plastic bag *creaked* faintly as Logan stretched its corners out, returning it to its original shape.

"*Then* I chuck you out," Logan said. He smiled. There were a lot of teeth in that smile. "So, son, what's it to be? Your choice. You going to go quietly, or am I going to have to show you the door?"

Bud's breath became faster. Shorter. More urgent. His face twisted up in rage and he launched himself into the kitchen, one hand grabbing for the detective, the other drawing back as a fist.

Logan sidestepped the attack, turned, and caught Bud by the back of the head. There was a particularly solid-sounding *crunch* as the bridge of Bud's nose was introduced to the edge of the worktop.

There then followed a moment of silence while Bud tried to work out what had just happened.

And then, the screaming started.

"Ma nobe! Ma fuckin' nobe!" he wailed, blood choking him, slurring his words. "Ye boke ma fuckin' nobe!"

It was at this point that Logan pulled the bag over Bud's head, and clamped it in place around his neck with one hand.

"Right then, Buddy, my boy. Just remember, this could've gone a lot easier for you," Logan said. Beneath the bag, Bud had stopped screaming, and was now just rasping and wheezing in ever-increasing panic.

Logan leaned in closer and lowered his voice. "Although, personally? Between you and me? I'm glad you went for option two," he said. "You're going to leave Tanya alone, alright? If I hear you've come back here, or get the vaguest inkling that you've hurt her again, it'll no' just be your head in a bag, it'll be your whole body. That clear?"

The muffled noises from inside the bag were a little too non-committal for Logan's liking.

"Is that *clear*?" he demanded, giving Bud a shake.

"Aye! Aye, I get it!"

"Good," said Logan. "Right. Out we go."

"I've got no shoes on," Bud pointed out.

Logan looked down. Sure enough, Bud stood in a pair of socks that were actually nothing of the sort. One was a dirty grey, the other navy blue with a hole at the big toe.

"Oh. Neither you do," Logan said. He shoved Bud out of the kitchen, banging him into the wall across from the door. "That's unfortunate."

Bud tried to resist as Logan huckled him along the corridor and out the door, but Logan had twenty years experience of dealing with jumped-up wee arseholes just like him and had no difficulty keeping him in line.

"Haw! Assault! This is fucking assault!" Bud wailed. Logan half-guided, half-shoved him down the stone steps leading down into the close. "I'll have you in the fucking jail for this," the scrote protested.

"Good luck with that," Logan told him, pushing him down the last couple of steps.

Tanya was peeking out from around the side of the stairs when Bud stumbled onto solid ground. He reached for the bag over his head, but Logan's hand clamped around his neck, pinning the bag in place.

"Oh no, you don't," Logan told him, manhandling him towards the door. He hauled it open with his free hand, and a swirl of cold night air blew in around both men.

"Look, I'm fucking sorry, alright?" Bud wailed. "I'm sorry."

"That's good. I'll be sure to pass that on," Logan told him. With a final shove, he sent him sprawling down the two steps that led to the block's front door.

Bud yelped in fright as, still blinded, he lost his balance and clattered onto the rough surface of the pavement.

"Ah! Fuck! Jesus!" he howled, tucking a skinned hand in under his armpit. Wrestling free of the bag, he tossed it aside and got to his feet, his eyes locked on Logan. "You can't do this. You can't just chuck me out of my own fucking—"

"Littering," Logan intoned.

That stopped Bud in his tracks. He blinked his eyes, which were already turning a shade of purple-black. Blood was smeared across his face, and dripped from the end of his chin.

"What?"

Logan pointed to the bag. "Littering," he said again. "Pick it up."

"I'm no' picking it—"

Logan stepped onto the first of the stone stairs.

"Alright. Fuck's sake. There," Bud said, snatching up the bag.

"Good." Logan pointed past him, along the street. "Now, off you go. You can phone Tanya tomorrow to arrange picking up your stuff at a time that's mutually convenient for all three of us."

Bud looked around him. Several of the streetlights were out along the road, and the place was in half-darkness. The sky was a void of black, cloud cover blocking out the moon and stars.

"Where am I meant to go?" Bud asked.

"Hmm. That is a poser," Logan said. He stroked his chin for a moment, then clicked his fingers. "Wait!" he said. He smiled. "I couldn't care less."

His smile fell away, his face becoming sombre, his eyes blazing anger. "But wherever you're going, I'd make it quick, son, before I lose my temper."

Bud bounced from sock to sock. The fingers of his free hand—the one that wasn't currently holding a Co-op Bag For Life—curled into a fist.

"You've no' heard the end of this," he warned.

Logan advanced to the next step down. Bud darted back like a startled animal, eyes wide and panicking.

"You've no' heard the fucking end of this!" he called again, then he turned and hobbled off along the street, only glancing back when the front door of the flats closed with a final, definitive *clunk.*

Tanya was standing at the foot of the stairs when Logan returned to the close. She held his coat out to him with her head down. Her eyes flitted to his for a second or two at a time, before looking away again.

"Thanks," Logan said, taking the coat.

"You know you've got a packet of sausages in your pocket?" Tanya asked.

"Aye. Want them?" Logan asked.

Tanya shook her head. "No."

"No. Can't say I'm overly enamoured with the idea of them myself," Logan said. He noticed the anxious look she shot at the door. "You'll be fine. He won't be back tonight. Keep the door locked though, and if he does come back I'll hear him."

"You knew, didn't you?" Tanya asked. "That he was..."

"An arsehole? Oh aye. Clocked that right away," Logan said.

Tanya smiled, showing the blood on her teeth. "You've got good instincts."

Logan hesitated, just for a moment. "Aye. I suppose I do," he said, then he ushered her up the stairs. "Come on. We'll get you cleaned up."

"It's... I'll be fine," Tanya said, as they made their way up the stairs together. "It just washes off."

Just washes off. Not the first time it had happened, then.

"Are you sure?" Logan asked. "I don't mind helping. I've cleaned up a few injuries in my time."

Tanya glanced at the swollen cut on Logan's forehead. "So I see."

Logan dabbed at the site of his injury. "One of the perks of the job," he said.

They stopped outside the door to Tanya's flat, which still stood open. "Right, well... Thanks," she said. "And sorry I dragged you—"

"Not your fault," Logan said, shutting the apology down. He nodded up the next flight of steps. "I'm just upstairs, alright? In fact..."

He fished in his pocket until he found a business card. "Mobile's on there."

Tanya looked at the card like it might explode in her hand, then carefully took it from him. She turned it over a couple of times, looking at the words but not necessarily reading them. "Thanks. Mr...?"

"Logan. It's on the card."

Tanya gave a dry little laugh. "Oh. Yeah. DCI Logan. Thanks."

"No bother," said Logan. He made it to the next step before stopping. "And please, call me Jack," he told her. "We're neighbours, after all."

LOGAN FLOPPED down onto the couch, his coat still hooked over his arm. He breathed out properly for what felt like the first time that day.

It hadn't been as productive a day as he'd been hoping for. Aye, they had a suspect in custody, but they had nothing concrete on him, nothing that connected him to Esme Miller's murder beyond an over-developed 'fight or flight' response and an attitude that was likely to earn him a slap in the not too distant future.

Maybe a search of Sloane's house would turn up something in the morning. Or maybe a night in the cells would soften him up a bit and make him confess to the whole thing.

"Aye," Logan mumbled into the darkness. "Maybe."

He fished in the pocket of his coat and pulled out a neatly wrapped, but slightly battered, bundle of sausages. Opening the pack, he gave them a tentative sniff. You could smell the Irn Bru, right enough. He prodded one warily, like it might spring into life at any moment and go for his throat.

"*You've got good instincts,*" he mumbled.

Then, he snorted, wrapped the paper around the bangers, and lobbed the whole thing into the waste paper basket on the other side of the room.

CHAPTER TWENTY-FIVE

"Did you see what they did?" asked Tyler. He unwrapped the bag of chips, and the smell expanded to fill the whole of the bus stop.

Big fat drops of rain *plunked* against the clear Perspex roof, and an insistent October wind swirled in through the gap at the bottom of the walls, rolling an empty Coke can back and forth across the uneven concrete base.

Sinead plucked a chip from the pile and blew on it. "No," she said. "What did they do?"

"Salt, then vinegar," Tyler said. He held up a little wooden trident. "Want a fork?"

Sinead shook her head. "No, you're fine," she said. "And what's the problem? You asked for salt and vinegar."

"Aye, but not in that order," Tyler told her. "You don't go salt then vinegar, you go vinegar then salt."

Sinead popped the chip in her mouth, spent a few seconds inhaling to try to cool it down a bit, then replied.

"Why?"

"What do you mean 'why?' Because if you go salt then vinegar, the vinegar washes the salt off, doesn't it?"

"Does it?" Sinead asked, helping herself to another chip.

"Yes! Obviously! Why wouldn't it? It's just, I don't know, physics," Tyler told her. "You go vinegar first, *then* salt. That way, the salt sticks to the vinegar."

Sinead nodded slowly, contemplating this while she chewed. "You should go back in and mansplain that to her. I'm sure she'd thank you for pointing out how she's doing it wrong."

"Good thinking," said Tyler. He took a step towards the opening in the side of the bus stop. Sinead laughed and caught him by the arm. He looked at her, wide-eyed and innocent. "What? You said I should go and tell her."

"Just shut up and give us another chip," Sinead grinned.

"You said you didn't want any!" Tyler protested, but he held the tray out to her, anyway.

"I said I didn't want my own bag. Totally eating yours, though."

"I noticed."

They stood in silence for a while, shoulder to shoulder, eating chips and gazing out at the rain. The bus stop was just a dozen or so yards from Sinead's front gate, on the other side of the street. The curtains were drawn, but there was a light on in the living room and in one of the rooms upstairs.

"Looks like your brother's in bed," Tyler ventured. "That's his room, right?"

"What gave it away?" Sinead asked.

"What can I say? I've got the detective skills," Tyler said. He gestured to the upstairs curtains with a nod. "Also, I didn't have you down as an Iron Man fan."

"Well, you'd be wrong," Sinead said.

Tyler side-eyed her. "What? That's your bedroom?"

"No, you're right about that. That's Harris's room," Sinead said. "But I *am* an Iron Man fan."

"Ah. Gotcha."

"Don't feel inferior, though," Sinead teased.

Tyler shook his head. "I wasn't."

"I mean, he is a billionaire genius superhero..."

"He didn't buy you chips, though, did he?" Tyler pointed out.

Sinead laughed. He had her there.

"True."

She helped herself to another. They were cooling down a bit now, so she didn't have to spend so long blowing on them before she could eat them.

"He didn't used to sleep with the light on," she announced, almost absentmindedly. "It's just since..."

"Your mum and dad?"

Sinead nodded, but said nothing.

"Hardly surprising, really, is it?" Tyler said. "It must've been a shock. For both of you, I mean."

Sinead continued to nod, staring straight ahead. It had been just over a year since the accident that had claimed the lives of her parents. The call had come in while she'd been down Glencoe direction with the speed gun: *Road traffic accident. Assistance required.*

She'd fired up the sirens. Rushed to the scene. She recognised the car as soon as it came into view. The make and model, anyway. Same colour, too.

Her heart had immediately plunged into the swirling morass that her stomach had become. Her legs were heavy, leaden, as she got out of the car and made her way past the line of stationary traffic.

And yet, she didn't believe it was them. Not then. Not at first.

It was only when she spotted the *Dogs Trust* sticker in the back window that the reality of it started to creep in.

And then, when she saw her dad's glasses on the ground, one lens smashed, one leg missing, the horrible, unavoidable truth of it had hit her.

She'd wanted to cry, to scream, to drop to her knees.

But she was polis. And she'd had a job to do.

"You alright?" Tyler asked.

Sinead smiled a little too brightly. "Fine. Aye. Fine."

She took another chip and bit the end off, but she'd lost the taste for them now.

"I should head in. The babysitter needs to get off."

Tyler glanced down at the still mostly full bag of chips. "Oh. Right. Aye," he said. He took a quick breath, then went for broke. "I could... I could come in with you. If you like."

He could tell right away that she wasn't keen on the idea.

"Not to... I don't mean... Just... the chips," he added, abandoning a selection of different statements, then finishing by pointing at the bag in his hand. "There's loads left."

"I'm not sure it's a good idea," Sinead told him.

It was her turn to note the change in his expression.

"I want to. I want you to," she said. "It's just Harris. He's still settling in. I'm not sure... I don't want him getting to know you and getting attached if this isn't... In case we aren't..."

She smiled weakly. "You know?"

Tyler folded the paper around the tray of chips. "I mean, he would get attached, obviously. Because I'm awesome."

Sinead laughed, then wrinkled her nose up. "At best, I think he'd tolerate you."

"*Tolerate me?*"

"Barely."

Tyler smiled. It wasn't really a smile of amusement, but one that said he understood. He didn't like it, but he understood.

"Well. We'll just have to put it to the test one day."

"One day," Sinead confirmed. "And you'll be at the birthday party. You'll get to meet him then."

"Is it weird that I'm actually nervous?" Tyler asked, then he stepped back in surprise when Sinead stepped in close and kissed him on the lips.

They stood like that for a moment, together, lips locked, the rain pummelling the Perspex above them.

And then, Sinead stepped back, blushing slightly as she pulled her jacket around herself.

"You squashed my chips," Tyler told her.

Sinead flashed him a smile. "I'll make it up to you," she said.

Then, she pulled up her hood, stepped out of the bus stop, and hurried across the road.

"Goodnight!" Tyler called after her. She waved as she threw open the front gate, and then she was up the path and inside the house.

Tyler leaned out of the bus stop just enough to be able to look in both directions along the road.

"Right, then," he said to himself. He fished a squashed chip from the bag and popped it in his mouth. "Where the hell did I park the car?"

CHAPTER TWENTY-SIX

DETECTIVE SUPERINTENDENT BOB HOON PEERED AT LOGAN AND BEN
Forde from behind his clasped hands. Logan was well aware of the trick.
Keep your fingers locked together and you were more able to resist the urge
to throttle whatever daft bastard had positioned themselves within grabbing
distance. It was an age-old technique, and Logan found himself doing the
same thing these days whenever DC Neish walked into the room.

"You're aware I've got the high heid yins breathing down my neck on
this case, gentlemen, yes?" Hoon asked. "You understand the position
I'm in?"

Ben waited for Logan to answer. When the DCI didn't, he jumped in
himself.

"We do, sir," Ben confirmed.

"Then maybe you'll explain to me why we haven't fucking charged this
Sloane character," Hoon barked. He squeezed his fingers together as he
eyeballed both detectives.

"We don't have enough to charge him yet," Ben ventured.

"Oh, I know. I know that all too fucking well, Benjamin. I looked at the
interview report once I'd finally got HOLMES to stop being a pain in the
arse, and it looks like you've got a whole lot of fuck all on him at the
moment, besides the fact he clouted this useless bastard, and gave a
Uniform a run for her money."

Ben glanced at Logan, expecting to see the DCI swallowing back his anger, but there was a slightly distant look on Logan's face, like his mind was elsewhere.

"We're working on it, sir," Ben said. "We've got Forensics going into his house this morning, and we've already seized the knives from the butcher's where he works. Pathology is going to compare them with the victim's injuries and see if we get a match. We plan on continuing the interview today. We're hopeful of a confession."

"He won't confess."

All eyes went to Logan.

"And why the fuck not?" Hoon demanded.

"Because he didn't do it."

Ben, who had been looking sideways at Logan, now turned to face him. "Eh?"

"I don't think he did it," Logan said.

"What, the rape or the murder?" Ben asked.

"Either. I don't think it was him."

Hoon and Ben both opened their mouths.

"I can't say why. I don't know, exactly. It's just... my instinct," Logan told them. "Just a hunch."

"A hunch? A fucking hunch?" Hoon scoffed. "You know what you can do with your fucking hunch?" He pointed to Ben. "Shove it up his arse and call him Quasimodo."

Ben looked taken aback, not quite sure why he'd been dragged into this.

Hoon shook his head in disbelief. "A fucking *hunch*, he fucking says."

Until he'd met Bob Hoon, Logan had thought of himself as someone for whom swearing played a large part of his daily vocabulary. Two minutes with Hoon though, had made him realise that his language was positively genteel by comparison.

He listened to a prolonged outburst of profanity while he waited for the DSup to stop ranting. Surprisingly, it didn't take too long.

All three men in the room had moved through the ranks of Police Scotland precisely because they had good instincts and knew when to trust them. A hunch could be mocked. A hunch could be derided, even. But all three of them knew from experience that a hunch should never be completely ignored.

"And does this hunch of yours happen to tell you who *did* do it?" asked Hoon, his voice gruff like he was grudging every word.

"Unfortunately, it does not, no."

"Oh. Well, surprise sur-fucking-prise," Hoon muttered.

He flexed his fingers for a few seconds, then went right back to squashing them together until the knuckles turned white.

"Well, let's not rule out Sloane yet. Keep on him. Follow through with the search. Drag him through the fucking bushes and see if you can get him to talk. Hunch or no fucking hunch. He ran for a reason. I want to fucking know what that fucking reason was. Got it?"

"Got it, sir," Ben confirmed.

Logan nodded. "Aye."

"And if it isn't him?" Ben asked.

"Then fuck me, you'd better find another fucking suspect quick smart, or a whole lot of shite is going to land on me from on high," Hoon said. He leaned closer, his eyes bulging with barely contained rage. "And gravity will not be kind to those below me, gentlemen. Is that clear? Gravity will not be fucking kind."

BEN WAITED until they were back in the Incident Room before saying anything.

"Jack. Can I get a wee word in your office?" he said.

Around the room, DS McQuarrie glanced over from the Big Board, and DCs Neish and Khaled both raised their eyes from their respective screens. When they saw Logan clocking this, they all quickly got back to what they'd been doing.

"After you," Logan said.

Inside the office, Ben closed the door. His face was creased in confusion, and Logan knew what he was going to say before he'd opened his mouth.

"I can't explain it, exactly," Logan said. "Like I said, it's just a feeling."

"A feeling? The man attacked you, Jack. And that lassie from Uniform. He has no alibi. We can connect him to the victims in both cases. He's clearly an unpleasant bastard..."

"I'm not arguing with any of that, Ben," Logan replied. He half-sat on the edge of the desk, crossed his arms, and looked down at his shoes. "Logically, he's our best bet, and we'll stay on him for now. It's just... I don't feel it. Talking to him last night... I don't feel it. My instincts are usually pretty sound, and they're telling me we're barking up the wrong tree with Sloane."

Ben sighed sharply. "I don't agree," he said. "I think your instincts are wrong on this one, Jack. I think he did it."

"I hope you're right. I really do. We've got bugger all else to go on," Logan said. He shot his old friend a smile. It was thin and weary, and barely qualified as a smile at all. "Maybe I am wrong. Maybe we'll find something in the house."

"A written confession would be nice."

"That'd be lovely, aye," Logan agreed. He stood. "Forensics in yet?"

"They were headed in about twenty minutes ago. Be a few hours, then we can go in," Ben said.

"Good. I'm going to swing round and see Kel Conlyn. Why don't you take Caitlyn in to interview Sloane? See how he responds to a woman's touch," Logan suggested. He glanced out through the office window at the Incident Room beyond. "What's Hamza working on?"

"HOLMES is back up and running this morning. He's loading everything up."

"Right. Looks like I'm taking Tyler with me to visit Conlyn, then."

Ben patted the DCI on the shoulder. "You have my condolences."

"I appreciate that," Logan said. He pulled open the door and raised his voice to a shout. "Detective Constable Neish!"

Tyler's head popped up from behind his computer monitor, looking worried. "Yes, boss?"

"Get your jacket," Logan told him. "We're making a house call."

"I MEAN, I get it, boss. I do. It makes total sense. It's early days, and everything. You know, relationship-wise. It's just, I can't help but feel like she's shutting me out, you know what I mean? Don't get me wrong—"

Logan put a finger to his lips as he and DC Neish approached Kel Conlyn's front door. "Shh," he said, with some urgency.

Tyler's eyes went to the building ahead of them. His voice dropped to a whisper.

"What is it?"

"Nothing," Logan told him. "I just wanted you to stop talking."

"Oh. Right," Tyler said. He blinked, which seemed to erase the last couple of seconds from his memory. "It's just, I like her. You know? And I think she likes me. And I *totally* get what she means about not wanting to mess her wee brother around, but—"

Logan stopped. His heels crunched on the pavement as he pulled a crisp about-turn. "What is it you want me to say, son?"

Tyler's mouth flapped open and closed. "Um, I don't know. Just, like... What do you think I should do?"

"I think you should do whatever she tells you to do," Logan said. "You're punching way above your weight with Sinead. Way above your weight. You want my advice? Keep your mouth shut, do as you're told, and try no' to make an arse of it."

He turned to move on, then stopped.

"And that goes for any woman, by the way. That's across the board advice. Mouth shut, do as you're told, thank your lucky stars, and try no' to fuck it up. Alright?"

Tyler swallowed. "Right."

"Good. Now, if you don't mind, I was about to investigate a murder. Are you going to join me, or are you going to stand here whinging about your love life?"

There was a moment's pause while Tyler cleared his throat.

"Lead the way, boss."

"Thank you," Logan said.

He led the junior officer up the path that led to Kel Conlyn's front door, waited for him to catch up, then rang the doorbell.

They waited. Tyler clicked his fingers and hummed quietly beneath his breath.

After twenty seconds or so, the DC reached for the doorbell again.

"Be patient," Logan told him. He waited for Tyler to step back into line beside him before continuing. "You can't rush some things. They take time. Aye, it's a pain in the arse, but that's just the way it is. You wait. You be patient."

Tyler looked from Logan to the bell and back again. He was about to repeat this process when the penny dropped. "Wait, you're not talking about the doorbell, are you, boss?" he asked.

Before Logan could confirm or deny that, the front door opened. Kel Conlyn appeared in the gap, bleary-eyed and half asleep. "Yes?" he asked, then recognition flitted across his face. "Sorry."

He wedged the heel of his hand into his eye socket and rubbed, then yawned. "Sorry," he said again. "Late night. Um..."

Kel pointed a finger at the older detective. "Jack?"

"Aye, that's me. This is DC Tyler Neish."

"Alright?" said Tyler.

Kel gave the DC a quick once-over, then straightened, suddenly a little more awake.

"Hi there," he said, pulling together a smile.

"We're sorry to disturb you, Mr Conlyn, but we were hoping we could ask you a few quick questions," Logan said.

A couple of faint creases formed on Kel's otherwise smooth forehead as he tore his eyes from Tyler. "Is it about Dr Fletcher? Did you talk to him?" He put a hand on his chest. "It wasn't him, was it? God, did he do it? Did he kill Esme?"

"No, it's not about Dr Fletcher," Logan said. "It's about someone else you worked with. A while back. A Donald Sloane."

Something changed in the lines of Kel's face. "Oh. Him," he said. He looked past them at the street beyond, glancing surreptitiously this way and that, like he was afraid someone might see.

Finally, he held open the front door.

"In that case, you'd best come in."

The detectives' shoes *clunked* on the bare floorboards as they stepped inside. Tyler squeezed in behind Logan, knocking over a small pile of unopened letters just by the door, scattering them.

"Shite, sorry," he said, bending to pick them up.

"It's fine," Kel said, waving a hand. "I think they must be for the last person who lived here. I keep meaning to hand them in at the post office."

Tyler finished restacking the letters, tucked them in next to the wall, then followed the other two men down the hall and into the not-yet-a-living-room. Logan had seen it before, of course, but Tyler spent a few seconds taking in the absence of... well, anything, before commenting.

"Nice place," he said. "You been watching that woman on Netflix?"

"What woman?" Kel asked.

"The tidying woman. Always on about decluttering and sparking joy, or whatever."

Kel's mouth became a lop-sided smile that suggested he had absolutely no idea what the DC was on about. "I don't have Netflix," he pointed out. "Or a telly."

Tyler looked around again, confirming this. "Right."

"Yet!" Kel said. "It's on the list. Maybe in a month or two."

"Well, you should check that show out," Tyler said. "I mean, it's all about getting rid of stuff, so I suppose you'd kind of be coming at it from the opposite direction." He shrugged. "It's good, though."

"Thanks for the hot tip," Kel said, just a little salaciously. He turned to Logan. "So, what is it you want to know about Donald?"

Logan shot Tyler a look. The DC reached into his pocket and produced a notebook.

"Anything you can tell us, Mr Conlyn," Logan said. "Anything at all."

CHAPTER TWENTY-SEVEN

Logan stood in the garden of Donald Sloane's rented house, watching the white paper suits come filing out, and waiting for the all-clear to be given for him to go in.

Technically, he could've gone in any time he liked, but if there was evidence to be found in there he didn't want to be the one to jeopardise it. Better to let the experts handle it.

Besides, he wasn't expecting them to find much, if anything, so the usual driving urge to stick his nose in wasn't there.

A cordon had been set up around the house to keep the press and the Nosy Parkers at bay. There hadn't been a big media response to the murder, which Logan was pleased about. The last thing he needed was half of Fleet Street coming up here and making the place look untidy.

Still, there was a small knot of the bastards gathered just on the other side of the cordon tape. Logan had been asked for a statement on his way past but had managed to resist giving them the two-word one that had immediately sprung to mind.

While he waited for Forensics to finish clearing the scene, he went over the conversation he and Tyler had with Kel Conlyn. It had been enlightening in some ways, but disappointing in others. Despite his misgivings about Sloane's guilt, or lack thereof, Logan had been hoping for Conlyn to drop some big bombshell.

Oh aye, he hated Esme's guts, would've been nice.

Always said he was going to kill her someday, would have been nicer still.

But no. Conlyn could offer very little about Sloane that they didn't already know, aside from one detail that had taken both detectives by surprise.

Logan had phoned it in when they'd left Conlyn's house. He'd spoken to Ben directly, in case the information could turn out to be useful.

"Sleeping together?" Ben had said, lowering his voice to a whisper like he was worried about offending someone. "Sloane and Esme?"

"No, ye div," Logan had replied. "Sloane and Conlyn. It was a fling, by all accounts, on-off. Only lasted a couple of weeks, if that. But aye. They were at it."

The line had gone silent for a few moments while Ben contemplated this. "What does that change? Does it change anything?" he'd asked.

"I'm not sure. Doesn't count him out for the rape. That's about power, it's not necessarily even a sexual thing," Logan replied. "But... I don't know. Worth bringing up with him, anyway."

Ben had agreed on that and promised to keep Logan updated of anything that came out of the interview. Sloane's solicitor had finally graced them with his presence, so Ben and DS McQuarrie were about to head in to give Sloane another grilling.

"I'll feed through on anything we find here," Logan told him, and then both men had hung up without bothering to say any goodbyes.

Logan checked his watch. Almost noon. They wouldn't be able to hold Sloane much longer without charging him. Fortunately, they had a couple of counts of assault they could hold him on, which would buy them a bit more time.

He watched the door as another guy in a paper suit emerged, carrying a cardboard box full of computer equipment. Even with the mask over his mouth and the elasticated hood pulled over his head, Logan recognised Geoff Palmer.

"Any news?" Logan asked, intercepting Palmer halfway up the path.

"Nothing obvious. If you're looking for a blood-stained dagger or a written confession then I'm afraid you're out of luck."

He gave the box a shake, juddering the contents. "Found a few computer hard drives, though. We'll go through those. We've also taken prints and swabs, but I doubt anything will come out of them."

Palmer tilted his head back in the direction of the door. "He's got a lot of swords and stuff in there, but they're all ornamental. Nothing that could've been used in the attack, from what I hear of the body."

"Great," said Logan, drawing a hand down his face. "Well, do what you can."

"Why wouldn't I?"

Logan's eyes narrowed. "Eh?"

"Why wouldn't I do what I can? What, you think I was just going to go back to the office and put my feet up? I do know how to do my job, you know."

Logan was reminded again why he disliked the man so much.

"Aye. Fine. Whatever you say, Geoff."

Palmer gave a self-satisfied little nod, like he'd just won the engagement, then continued on past Logan up the path.

Now that the Scene of Crime team had done their sweep, it was Logan's turn. Anything of any potential forensic value would've been bagged up and removed, but he squashed his hands into a pair of vinyl gloves, just in case.

A poster of a wolf greeted him as he entered the hallway. It was pinned to the wall across from the door, its silver-blue eyes fixed hungrily on anyone who dared enter its lair. On the floor below it was a black metal rack filled with DVDs. Arnold Schwarzenegger featured heavily in at least half a dozen of them, and they were all coated with a layer of dust that suggested Sloane had either lost his appetite for 80s action movies or had long-since made the switch to digital.

The door to the left of the poster led into a small, drably decorated living room. Another poster adorned the breast of a chimney, the hearth of which had been bricked up and plastered over. This one showed a blue-green dragon blasting a jet of fire from its cavernous throat. It was well done. Logan wouldn't have given it house room himself, obviously, but from a technical point of view, it was an accomplished piece of art.

There were a few bits and pieces on the other walls. A framed film cell from *Die Hard With a Vengeance*. A black and white poster of a topless Bruce Lee. A signed photograph of *Star Wars* actress, Carrie Fisher, forever preserved behind a sheet of glass.

That sort of thing.

The main attraction was saved for the wall across from the old chimney. It had been adorned with a dozen or more Samurai swords in sheaths, as well as a couple of battle axes, a claymore, and something so ludicrously spiky and multi-bladed that it could only have come from *Star Trek* or some other sci-fi nonsense.

Logan checked the blades on a few of the weapons. Just as Palmer had said, they were blunt. Far too blunt. The only way they were being used to kill someone was as a bludgeon.

The rest of the living room offered very little of interest, so Logan returned to the hall. He had just opened a door into the kitchen when his phone rang.

He fished it from his pocket and checked the screen. Ben Forde. He felt his heart skip a beat. A breakthrough, maybe? A confession?

Tapping the screen, Logan brought the phone to his ear.

"Ben. What have we—"

The phone continued to ring. Muttering, Logan pulled off one of the gloves, tapped the green phone icon, and tried again.

"Hello? Ben?"

"Jack," Ben said. Logan knew immediately that there had been a development. It was there in just that one word. Something had happened.

And nothing good.

"Aye. What's the news?"

"There's been another one," Ben told him. "There's been another murder."

CHAPTER TWENTY-EIGHT

LOGAN STOPPED AT THE EDGE OF THE CORDON AND FLASHED HIS warrant card at one of the Uniforms standing guard. With a nod, the officer stepped aside, and the DCI ducked under the tape.

"Ben. What have we got?" Logan asked, slightly breathless after the hike up the ramp of the multi-storey car park. No tent had been set up yet, but then, as far as Logan could tell there was no body to be seen.

Ben's face was grey and drawn. Logan knew then that there most definitely was a body, and could hazard a guess as to its condition.

"Call came in from a member of the public," Ben intoned.

"Where's the victim?" Logan asked, glancing around.

Ben indicated two parked cars—a big Range Rover and a smaller Kia. "Between those two," he said. "Palmer's team is on the way. They had to drop everything from Sloane's at base. Can't risk cross-contamination."

Logan nodded slowly. "You've had a look," he said. It wasn't a question.

"I did," Ben confirmed.

"And?"

"It's him, alright," Ben said. "Same M.O. 'Fake' carved right into her. Across the belly this time."

"Recent?" Logan asked.

"Recent enough that it couldn't have been Sloane," Ben said. He puffed out his cheeks. "Looks like I was wrong and your instincts were right, Jack."

"Aye. Looks like it," said Logan, although there was no victory in it. "Palmer say how long it'd be until he got here?"

"He said he'd be about twenty minutes. That was ten minutes ago, maybe."

Logan shifted his weight from foot to foot and scratched thoughtfully at his chin. "Right. We got any shoe covers? I'm going to take a look."

Ben looked sceptical. "You think that's a good idea?"

"I'm not going to touch anything," Logan assured him. "I just want a look."

That was far from the truth, in fact. The last thing he wanted to do was look.

But he was going to. He had to. And that was that.

"Here. But don't say you got them from me," Ben told him, handing over the blue slip-on covers.

Logan pulled them on, took another pair of gloves from his pocket, then nodded in the direction of the two parked cars. "You coming?"

"Once is quite enough for me, thanks," Ben told him.

Logan pulled on the gloves as he approached the cars. The smell of death started to creep in while he was still ten yards away. Clawing. Pungent. Metallic.

When he was five yards away, he knelt down and looked beneath the Range Rover. A face stared back at him through the gap, eyes wide, mouth taped, life extinguished.

Logan glanced along the underside of the car, searching for anything of interest but finding nothing. Standing, he made his way around the big four-by-four, keeping a calculated distance from it and anything else that might harbour evidence.

The victim lay on her back in a state of semi-undress. Her blouse had been torn open, one side of her bra pushed up to reveal a pale breast. There was a patina of dried blood across her stomach, the letters F A K E standing out on her skin like she'd been branded with them.

Her skirt had been pushed up. Her underwear pulled down.

Pinpricks, like little jolts of electricity, crawled across Logan's scalp. His gloves *creaked* as his fingers curled into fists.

He wanted to look away, turn away, *run* away. But he forced himself to keep looking. Forced his brain to fight the impulse to block out the horror and concentrate—*fucking concentrate*—on what had happened here.

The wounds on her stomach weren't deep, but there was a lot of blood on her clothing and pooled on the concrete floor. It flooded under the cars, mostly the smaller one on Logan's right. A set of keys lay in the pool, a Kia badge emblazoned across one of the two keyrings.

The other keyring was a square of clear plastic containing a photograph —a woman, a man, two children, all sipping milkshakes in some café somewhere. Abroad, probably. Relatively recently too, judging by the age of her in the photo. Late forties. Maybe a year or two either way.

Most of the blood seemed to have come from a neck wound. There was some arterial spray on the cars, but only low down. She'd been on the ground, then, when it had happened. Presumably, after the assault, although part of him hoped she'd been killed first, for her sake.

The tape was thick and black. Were he to pull it off, Logan guessed he'd find a rag stuffed in her mouth, too. That was a job for someone else though, and he'd rarely been more grateful of anything in his life.

He was no expert when it came to time of death, and would leave that to Shona Maguire to determine. Six to eight hours, he guessed, judging by the signs of rigor mortis on the top half of the body. That would make it... what? Between 3am and 5am? Odd time for a single woman to be returning to her car.

"What's the opening hours of this place?" Logan called back to Ben.

"Twenty-four-seven," Ben replied from closer behind him than Logan had been expecting.

He turned to find the DI standing a few feet away, but using the bonnet of the Range Rover to block his view of the victim.

"Clarissa McDade," Ben continued. "Husband reported her missing in the early hours of this morning. She was on a night out with friends. He waited up but fell asleep on the couch. When he woke up and found out she wasn't home, he called it in."

The muscles in Logan's jaws flexed as he clenched and unclenched them. "Have we told him?"

"Not yet. We're waiting to see if we can pull any ID off the body first. Car registration matches, though. The Kia's hers," Ben said. "A team from Uniform's tracking down the friends she was out with to see if they can shed any light on her movements."

Logan raised an index finger and made a little circle motion, indicating the car park around them. "Cameras?"

"Forty-nine, according to the security guard."

A glimmer of hope. A spark.

"That's something."

"Afraid not," Ben sighed.

Logan tore his eyes away from the body of Clarissa McDade. "Eh?"

"They all went down at just after midnight last night. Whole system crashed. It's been displaying gibberish all night."

"Shite!" Logan spat. "That can't be coincidence, can it?"

Ben shrugged. "That's one for the tech boys to figure out. But if it's not —if some bastard somehow brought the cameras down so he could do... this, then..." He shrugged for a second time. "I don't know what we're dealing with. It was all computer numbers, apparently."

Logan raised a questioning eyebrow. "Computer numbers?"

"Aye."

"What are computer numbers?"

Ben shifted awkwardly, like he'd been hoping the DCI wasn't going to pursue this particular line of questioning. "Oh, I don't know. One of the staff here told me. Ones and zeroes."

"You mean binary?"

"Aye. That's it," Ben confirmed. "Computer numbers."

Logan glanced around until he spotted a camera, briefly contemplated the significance of them all going down at the same time, then turned his attention back to the body.

He offered up the same silent promise he'd made to all those countless other victims he'd found himself looking down on over the years, then turned and headed back for the cordon, and the growing knot of people there.

Palmer and his team were just ducking under the tape when Logan reached it.

"I hope you weren't poking around over there, Jack," Palmer scolded. "You know the procedure."

Logan's already clenched fists became tighter. A clearing of Ben's throat behind him made him see sense before he could say or do anything stupid.

"She's all yours," Logan said.

"Oh, well, *thank you*," said Palmer, giving a little bow. "It's very kind of you to—"

"Just get it done, Geoff," Logan hissed. He stabbed a finger past Palmer's head, his hand coming so close that Palmer flinched. "Go do what you need to do so we can cover that woman up and give her some dignity. No smart-arse comments, no snidey remarks, just get on with it. Alright?"

Judging by his body language, Palmer briefly considered arguing, but the look on Logan's face was a thunderstorm waiting to break and he rapidly thought better of it.

"Feel better for that?" Ben asked, as they both watched Palmer scuttle off to join the rest of his team.

"Well, I'm not sure I could feel any worse," Logan said. "So, the only way is up, eh?"

"Fingers crossed," Ben said. He had his notebook out and was flipping to a page he'd marked with the pad's elastic strap. "Couple of things that might be of interest with regards our victim."

"Go on."

"First up, I mentioned she was on a night out."

"Right."

"I didn't say where. Osmosis. The nightclub owned by—"

"Shaun Gillespie," said Logan.

"Brother of Danni, the first victim," Ben confirmed. "A substantial stake in which was recently acquired on behalf of one Bosco Maximuke."

Logan's head snapped around. His eyes widened, then narrowed in one smooth movement. "Bosco co-owns the club?"

"Well, technically it's one of his guys who co-owns it, but it doesn't take a genius to see through that."

"No," Logan agreed. "Interesting. What else?"

"OK. Number two. Brace yourself," Ben said.

Over by the cordon tape, a couple of eager-looking members of the press were straining to see past a growing line of uniformed officers. Logan opened his mouth to bark at them to clear off, but a Uniform sergeant wasted no time in doing it for him.

"Sorry, you were saying?" Logan asked, turning his attention back to Ben.

"I was about to say that Clarissa McDade worked in HR. You know, recruitment?"

"I know what HR is," Logan said. He pulled a disappointed face. "I'll be honest, Ben, the first one was more interesting."

"That's because I've no' reached the interesting part yet," Ben told him. He closed his notepad and rocked back on his heels. "Clarissa McDade worked at the HR department..."

He lowered his voice, partly so the press didn't hear, and partly—he hated to admit—for impact.

"...at Raigmore Hospital."

CHAPTER TWENTY-NINE

THINGS PROGRESSED THE WAY THESE THINGS DID. SLOWLY. Methodically. A shroud of sorrow draped over everyone and everything.

Orders were given. Officers were dispatched. Doors were knocked. The Rose Street area was mostly commercial though, so almost all of those doors belonged to businesses which had been shut at the time of the attack.

Logan himself went down and hammered on the door of Osmosis, which was right below the car park. As expected, nobody answered, so he put in a call back to the office and gave Caitlyn the task of tracking Shaun Gillespie down and getting any CCTV footage from the club's cameras.

"Will do, sir," Caitlyn said. "Hamza wants a quick word."

There was some rustling on the other end of the line. Logan stood outside the nightclub, his phone pressed to his ear. He watched a family of four come trotting out of the big toy shop across the road, both kids eagerly clutching carrier bags to their chests like they were the most precious things in the world.

"Hi, sir, it's Hamza," his unmistakeable Aberdonian accent completely negating the need for him to identify himself.

"Aye. Hello. What's up?" Logan asked.

"It was just to let you know, HOLMES is... Well, it's fucked, sir."

"It's always fucked," Logan pointed out. "There's rarely a day when it's unfucked."

"Not like this, sir," Hamza said. "The server team think it's a DoS attack."

"A what?"

"Denial of Service, sir. Looks like someone is deliberately trying to bring it down."

Logan grunted. This wasn't a first, either. He remembered a couple of other occasions when hackers or spammers or whatever the hell they called themselves had tried something similar. He didn't really understand the details or have any interest in finding out.

"I'm sure they're working on it," Logan said. He watched the toy shop family get into their car, then turned towards the car park entrance. "Now, Hamza, if there's nothing—"

"They are working on it, sir. But, well, I was thinking. The cameras at the car park."

Logan stopped. "What about them?"

"I spoke to the security team there on the phone about twenty minutes ago. The cameras are all on a LAN—Local Area Network. It's accessible from the web, but well-protected."

The impatience in Logan's voice was obvious. "Meaning what, Hamza?"

"Meaning someone hacked the system from outside the local area network, sir. Someone who knew what they were doing."

The penny dropped.

"And what, you think it's the same person who's attacking HOLMES?"

"Maybe, sir. Aye," Hamza said. "I mean, I don't know. It just seems like a coincidence. And it might be. It's just—"

"Find out what you can," Logan told him. "Talk to the HOLMES team. See if they can tell you anything."

"I think they've got their hands full at the minute, sir, but I'll see what I can do," Hamza said. "I just thought you should know."

"Good. Thanks. Is that all?"

Hamza confirmed that it was, and after some brief goodbyes, Logan hung up. His phone rang again almost immediately.

"Ben?" Logan said, after a quick glance at the screen. "I'm on my way up."

"I wouldn't bother. There's not a lot to be doing here. I'm going to head down soon and leave them to it," Ben said. "They're going to move the body in the next half hour or so, once they've got some more photos, and done all the other bits and bobs."

Bits and bobs. Only Ben Forde could refer to the cataloguing of a murder scene as *bits and bobs.*

If he were honest, Logan couldn't help but be relieved at not having to go back up there. The car park was dark and oppressive and had done nothing to help his current state of mind. He felt helpless up there, just standing around watching while the SOC team did their thing.

Those ramps were a bloody killer, too.

"Right. I'll swing by the office, then head to the hospital," he said.

"You might want to make a detour first," Ben told him. "We've run the plates on the Range Rover that was parked next to the victim's car and got a match. Are you sitting comfortably?"

"Bosco Maximuke," Logan said. A guess, albeit an educated one. Logan had seen similar cars parked at the yard of the Russian's building company, and it was just that flash bastard's style.

"How did you know that?" asked Ben, clearly disappointed at having his thunder stolen.

"I didn't get this badge in a box of cornflakes," Logan told him. "I'll go pay him a visit."

"Want company?"

Logan counted to three in his head, making it appear as if he was considering the offer.

"No," he said, at last. "You're fine. You go back to the office and start running things from there."

He watched the toy shop family drive past him, the kids excitedly opening boxes in the back seat. He glanced up at the car park, where a mother lay who would never be going home.

"I'll deal with Bosco myself."

LOGAN WAS MET with the usual resistance when he strolled into Bosco's building yard, demanding to speak to the boss. The faces of the men who blocked his path were new, yet familiar all the same. Same shaved heads. Same angular features. Both sported neck tattoos, and both were dressed in identical black bomber jackets that didn't really fit with any 'construction worker' theme.

But then, these guys didn't work in construction. On paper, maybe. In reality, though, they helped with the business behind the business.

Various CID officers across Scotland had been investigating Bosco

Maximuke for years. Everyone knew the construction company was a front for his drug empire. There were fairly solid suspicions he was involved in people trafficking, too. The problem was, no one had ever been able to prove it.

Several raids had found nothing and had instead, led to a harassment lawsuit that the bastard had won. He was loud and brash, and revelled in his notoriety, but he was a slippery bugger too, and nothing seemed to stick to him for long.

"He not here," one of the guards said. Eastern European. No surprises there.

"Right." Logan glanced past the men to the portable office that stood at the far end of the yard, right beside a pristine JCB that looked like its bucket had never touched soil. "So, he's not in there, then?"

"He not here," the guard reiterated. The guy beside him was a little taller and heavier set, his brow furrowed into so deep a scowl he resembled an ogre of some sort. There was something vague and uncomprehending behind his eyes though, and Logan guessed he didn't speak a word of English.

"Well, when will he be back?" Logan asked.

"I do not know. I am not his wife."

The other man laughed. It was a sudden ejection, sharp and loud, like a machine-gun. "Wife!"

OK, so maybe he spoke a little English.

The first guard shot the second a disparaging look, which cut his laughter short. Both men returned to scowling at their unwelcome guest.

"Well, I'll just wait for him," Logan told them. "Maybe one of you boys could get me a cup of tea while I'm hanging about."

He smacked his lips together a couple of times. "I am parched."

"You do not wait," the first guard retorted. He sounded a little uncertain, like he wasn't sure he'd translated the sentence properly in his head.

Logan sighed, then shrugged. "Fine. Fine," he said. "You two can come down to the station instead."

The first guard side-eyed the second. He was still fully fixated on scowling though, and didn't notice.

"What?" the first asked, shifting his gaze back to the DCI.

"I need to ask Bosco some questions in regards to the rape and murder of a woman in Inverness city centre in the early hours of this morning," Logan informed the men. "If he's not around, you two can come with me, instead."

"I do not... We are not..."

"You can come quietly, or I can get a fleet of flat-footed angry bastards down here to drag you in," Logan continued. His eyes went very deliberately to both men's jackets. "They'll check you for concealed weapons, of course. Probably get immigration involved, although I'm sure that won't be a problem. I'm sure two smart lads like yourselves wouldn't be so stupid as to be in the country illegally."

He gave that a few moments to bed in, then nodded in the direction of the office. "Or, you could get out of my way, and I can go talk to Mr Maximuke."

Both men tensed when Logan reached into his inside coat pocket, their hands mirroring the movement as they instinctively thrust their hands into their own jackets.

They relaxed when he produced a phone and started dialling, but not by much.

"Hello, DI Forde?" Logan said into the handset. "I might need you to send a few officers to assist me here. One sec..."

Logan took the phone from his ear and cupped a hand over the mouthpiece. "Well, lads?" he asked, looking from one to the other. "What's it to be?"

CHAPTER THIRTY

Bosco Maximuke shook his head in mock reproach. "They told you I was out? Why would they think this? I do not know. They are new. Still to be broken in."

He wagged a finger at the detective looming in the doorway. "I tell them, 'If my policeman friend, Jack Logan, comes around here, then you let him in.' I tell them this, time and again, but..." He sighed and made a shrugging gesture. "What can you do?"

Maximuke was sitting behind his desk, hands clasped on the paunch of a belly that had been growing steadily since Logan had first met him and showed no signs of slowing down.

His taste for junk food was matched only by his taste for bad clothing. He was currently rocking an electric blue nylon tracksuit with the sleeves rolled up to the elbows. His thinning hair had been permed so recently that Logan could practically still smell the lotion. If the man were a fashion statement, that statement would be: 'Wid ye look at the fucking state o' that?'

Still, at least he'd made one cosmetic change for the better.

"You've got rid of the moustache, I see," Logan observed.

Bosco ran a finger and thumb across his top lip. "Gone, yes," he said, a note of regret colouring the edges of his Russian accent. "My wife, she not approve. My daughter, she not approve. Me? I approve, but..."

"What can you do?" Logan said, finishing the sentence for him.

Bosco slapped the edge of his desk. "Ha! Yes! What can you do when the women turn against you?"

He settled back into his chair and smiled, showing his yellowing teeth. "Now, my old friend, what can I do for you?"

Logan started to reply, but Bosco jumped in and cut him off before he could get a word out.

"By the way, it is good to see you looking so well. After accident, you not look so good. I worry. Bosco worries. Yes?" He gestured to Logan. "But now, you look good. Strong."

He leaned forward, face suddenly serious. "They ever find out who is responsible for accident?"

Logan knew full well who was responsible for his 'accident'. They both did.

"Still working on it," he said. "But when we find out, they'll be facing a murder charge."

Bosco's brow furrowed unconvincingly. "Murder? Oh! You had passenger at time, right?" He sucked air in through his teeth. "Terrible. Just terrible. Perhaps I could offer help? I have connections, yes? Business. Maybe I could help you find who is responsible. For you, my friend."

"You're fine," Logan said. "It's being dealt with."

Bosco held his hands out, palms up, fingers splayed. "The offer, it is there." His smile spread across his face again. "Now, what was it you said you wanted?"

"It's about your car," Logan said.

"Which one?" Bosco asked, his smile not shifting. "I have many cars."

"Range Rover. KT19 XOH. It's currently parked at the multi-storey on Rose Street."

"OK. And? Is ticket overdue? Is that what they sent you to tell me?" Bosco asked, practically sniggering.

"A woman was murdered. Her body was found right beside it."

The laughter died in the Russian's throat. The smile faded. "Oh. I see," he said. He contemplated this for a moment. "Any damage?"

Logan blinked. "I'm sorry?"

"It is expensive car," Bosco said. "Any damage?"

The bastard was deliberately trying to goad him. Logan wasn't rising to it.

"No. No damage," he said, adding the, "not yet," silently in his head.

"Good. This is good," Bosco said, his smile returning. "And the woman?"

"Plenty of damage there, aye," Logan told him.

"Who is she, I mean?"

"She's still to be formally identified," Logan told him. "My concern right now is why she was found right next to your car, Bosco. And not because I'm worried she might've scratched the paintwork."

He leaned forward, putting both clenched fists on the desk. A gorilla, staring down a rival. "Why was your car there?"

"I do not know this."

"What do you mean you don't know? It's your car."

"Like I said, I have many cars. My employees, they use. This one you say... Car park on Rose Street?"

Logan nodded his confirmation.

"Then all I know is it was not me driving."

"Who, then?"

Bosco gave a little shrug and a chuckle. "I do not know. It is... what is word? Pool car? Is this right? Free to use by my employees. Perk of job."

"I want to know who was using it last night. I want to know why they were parked in that spot, in that car park, and why a woman turned up dead right beside it."

"You want to know a lot of things," Bosco replied. He drummed his fingers on his belly. "I will ask around. Maybe someone will know. Maybe they won't. I ask."

"Maybe it was your man, Valdis," Logan suggested. "He's got a stake in the club downstairs, hasn't he?"

"Does he? I do not keep track," Bosco said, his face a picture of innocence.

"You must be helluva generous with the bonuses for him to be able to afford an investment like that."

Bosco ran a hand down the front of his tracksuit, smoothing the bumps on the zip. "Perhaps he has other money. I do not know. It is not my business."

Logan leaned closer still, anger creasing the lines of his face. "I want to know who was using that car," he said. "You have until four o'clock this afternoon."

Bosco continued to smile. Logan straightened, glanced around the little office, then headed for the door.

"Or?"

Logan stopped.

Logan turned.

"What?"

"I have until four this afternoon... or what?" Bosco asked. That bloody smirk was still there, pinned in place. "You cannot make threat without consequences. I have until four, you say. And so, I ask you, 'or what?'"

Logan narrowed his eyes and sucked in his bottom lip, considering the question.

"I'm sure I'll think of something," he said. He tapped his watch. "Clock's ticking, Bosco. If I were you, I'd get asking around."

CHAPTER THIRTY-ONE

LOGAN WAS JUST PULLING THE VOLVO INTO THE STATION CAR PARK when his phone rang through the car's speakers. He tapped the handbrake lever, waited for it to engage, then cut the engine.

There was a brief lull in the ringing while the phone tried to figure out what the hell had just happened, then it returned, this time chiming out from his inside pocket.

"Hamza. What's up?" Logan asked, closing the car door and setting off towards the station's front door. He glanced up at the front of the building, roughly where the Incident Room they were using was. "Aye, I'm here now. I'm on my way up. Why, what's...?"

He pushed through the front door, frowning at Hamza's garbled reply. "Slow down. I'm not... Just, hang on. I'll be up in a second."

Logan headed for the lift, returning the phone to his pocket. There was an odd atmosphere in the station's reception. A few Uniforms were gathered around the receptionist's monitor, all looking concerned. He thought about stopping to ask them what was going on, but Hamza had sounded worried. Something was wrong. Seriously wrong, judging by the way the DC had stumbled over his words.

When he reached the Incident Room, Logan's suspicions were confirmed. The rest of the team were there, including Ben, who still had his jacket on. They were gathered around Hamza's desk, all but Hamza standing with their arms folded and grave expressions fixed on their faces.

"What's happened?" Logan asked, wasting no time on pleasantries. "What's wrong now?"

"It's HOLMES," Ben said.

Logan exhaled. "Jesus. Is that all? I thought there'd been another murder or something."

The faces of the others remained stoic, and Logan knew there was something more going on than a computer error or cyber attack.

"What?" he asked. "What is it?"

Ben gestured to the screen. "It's... You'd best come and see. Hamza, can you play it again?"

"Yes, sir," Hamza said. He dragged the mouse across the screen and clicked. It seemed to take a lot more effort than it should've.

He waited until Logan had walked around the desk to join them before hovering the mouse over the *play* icon on a web video. It was embedded into the HOLMES login page, directly above the username and password boxes.

"What the hell is this?" Logan asked.

"Play it, Hamza," Ben said. He caught Logan's eye, and there was something in that look that made Logan's stomach bunch into a knot. "Just watch, Jack."

Hamza clicked the mouse button. The black rectangle of the video flashed briefly white, then a man was standing there against a dark background. Or a figure, at least—it was difficult to determine the gender thanks to the featureless white mask they wore. He or she was dressed in dark clothing, too, which made it hard to judge the build.

The voice, when it came, was male. Heavily disguised and distorted, but male. It rumbled from the computer's speakers, booming like the voice of God.

"To whomever it may concern," it began. "I am the one who attacked Danni Gillespie. I am the one who killed Esme Miller. I am the one who is about to rape and murder Clarissa McDade. By the time you see this, it will have already happened. Maybe you'll have found her. Maybe you won't. Regardless, she will already be dead."

Something seemed to dance in the dark hollows of the mask's eyes.

"She will not be the last."

"Jesus..." Logan hissed.

"You will have questions, I'm sure. Who am I? Why am I doing this? But those are the wrong questions. Those are not the questions you should be asking," the man on the screen continued. "The question you should be asking is why are *you* doing this? Why are you investigating? Why are you wasting what little time you have on something so pointless and insignificant?"

He took a step closer, his voice dropping a few decibels until it was a loud whisper. "Because those women weren't real. They were fake. Lies. All lies. Like me. Like you. Like all of this."

He gestured around at the darkness. "Fake. It's all fake. We make up these rules we're supposed to follow—that you're supposed to enforce—and for what? Why? This isn't real. This world of ours? It doesn't exist. You. Me. Those women. None of it exists."

His voice was rising again, becoming excited. "And when you realise that—when you realise that nothing is real, then nothing matters. Nothing we do matters. How can I kill someone who has never existed? How can I hurt them if they're nothing but... but... *numbers*. Code. Because that's all we are. That's all we've ever been. Not flesh and bone. Numbers and code. Digits, floating in the void."

He looked straight up, and for a moment Logan caught a glimpse of a neck. Thin, cleanly shaven he automatically noted.

"Maybe they're up there. Out there. Watching this. Maybe they're taking note. Maybe, if I do this enough, I'll attract their attention."

The mask lowered until it was facing front again. "Or maybe they'll turn us off. *Bing!* Hard reset. Game over. Reload from Last Checkpoint."

He giggled—a series of low, sinister hisses that were made to sound even worse by the audio distortion. "Or maybe they don't care. Maybe they set it all running, and just walked away. Maybe we have absentee landlords. It doesn't matter. Nothing matters."

The laughter had given a touch of lightness to his voice. It fell away then, his tone becoming sombre and serious. "Nothing ever has. We have been living in a lie. All of us. Stressing, worrying, concerning ourselves with all the petty little details they've added to keep us distracted. To keep us from seeing the truth."

He took another step closer, until the mask was almost filling the screen. The eyes remained dark, impenetrable hollows, and Logan felt like they were staring straight at him. Not at some camera somewhere, but at him in particular.

"I see the truth now. I see through the lies. And now, I'm going to help everyone open their eyes. Watch this."

The video cut to black almost immediately. Logan was about to start firing out questions and orders, but DS McQuarrie stopped him.

"There's... There's more," she said, her voice a dry croak at the back of her throat.

The black rectangle came alive with shaky movement, like the camera was now being handheld. It swept across the ground for a moment, showing a pair of black trainers, a patch of grey concrete, then a white painted line.

Finally, it settled on two cars. A Range Rover. A Kia.

From somewhere off-screen, Logan heard the sound of footsteps approaching. Heels. A woman.

"No," he mumbled. "Don't tell me..."

The camera peeked out from behind a pillar. The focus swam for a few seconds, then pulled tight on a woman in a blouse and skirt. She was approaching the Kia, her keys in her hand, a spring in her step, despite the late hour.

"Don't feel sorry for her," the distorted voice whispered. A hand came up, waving a scalpel for the benefit of the camera. "She isn't real, remember? None of what you are about to see is real. Nobody will *actually* get hurt."

Then, he crept out of his hiding place, scurried over to where Clarissa McDade was closing in on her car, and Logan and the others could do nothing but watch as the attack began.

"Stop," Logan said.

Hamza immediately clicked the mouse, like he'd been hanging on tenterhooks, waiting for the command.

Silence filled the Incident Room. On-screen, a gloved hand had caught Clarissa McDade by the hair and was yanking her head back. Only part of her face was visible, but it was twisted up in pain and fear.

Logan knew he'd have to watch the rest of it. He had no choice. But not here. Not now. He didn't have to subject the others to it any more than they already had been.

He massaged his temples with his fingertips. He had questions. Probably a lot of questions. Right now, though, none of them were forming themselves enough for him to speak them out loud.

"Is this...? This is on HOLMES?"

"Aye, sir," Hamza confirmed. "Appeared about twenty minutes ago. All over the country. It's on the login page, so non-users can access it via the internet."

"What? Shite," Logan spat. "Get it taken down then. Get them to shut down the bloody server. We can't have people watching this."

Hamza shot the others an anxious look. It was DC Neish who answered for him.

"Bit late for that, boss," he said. "Same time as it went live on HOLMES, it went up on 8Chan."

Logan's brow furrowed. "Am I supposed to know what that is?"

"It's a forum. Completely anonymous. Full of the worst kind of arsehole," Tyler explained. "It's spreading like wildfire. All over social media, Reddit... Everywhere, basically."

Logan felt something uncoiling in his stomach, like a serpent waking on the ocean floor. "People are watching that? Through choice? Fucking *sharing* it for other people to watch?"

Tyler cleared his throat. "Afraid so, boss."

"Sick bastards," Caitlyn spat.

"I want anyone sharing this arrested," Logan barked, pointing to the screen. "Get that out there now. Anyone who shares that footage is going to fucking jail, and I will personally be the one throwing them in. Get that message out. Put out a statement. Do whatever needs to be done."

"Yes, boss," Tyler said.

"And then, find a way to get it taken down. Get onto Facebook, Twitter, and whoever fucking else is helping to spread it and get it..." He shook his head, agitated. "In fact, no. I'll get Hoon on that. May as well make himself useful. We're catching this bastard. Caitlyn."

DS McQuarrie straightened her shoulders. "Sir."

"That mask. Find me a match. Where did he get it? Was it local? We need to know."

"Yes, sir," Caitlyn said. She hurried over to her desk, dropped into her chair, then spun to face her own computer screen. Logan watched her take a deep breath before she began typing out the web address for the HOLMES login screen.

"What was he on about with all that 'not real' shite?" Ben wondered.

"Simulation Theory, sir," Hamza said, in a tone that suggested he thought everyone had already figured that out.

Logan saved Ben the job of asking.

"What's Simulation Theory?"

"You know, like...?" Hamza caught the looks from the two older detectives. "You've never heard of it?"

"No, Hamza, we've never heard of it. What is it?" Logan snapped.

Hamza turned his chair all the way around to face them. "Right. Well, you know video games, sir?"

"Like Space Invaders?" Ben asked.

Hamza tilted his head from side to side. "Bit more modern than that, sir. Say, like, *The Sims*. It's a game where you control all these little people. They live in a house, have jobs, make dinner, go on dates, all that stuff."

Ben looked non-plussed. "How is that a game? Sounds like bloody drudgery."

"It's actually really popular," Hamza told him. "Anyway, all the characters in it, they have their own AI. Artificial intelligence. They get tired, can go in bad moods, fall in love, whatever. Everything we can do, really."

"What's this got to do with our guy?" Ben asked. Logan remained silent, the cogs in his brain quietly whirring as he pieced it together.

"He thinks we're in that game?" he said.

"Well, aye. Kind of. Maybe not that game specifically, sir," Hamza said. "See, the theory goes like this: If we can create a simulation, and the people in that simulation *think* their world is real, then it's statistically improbable that we're not also in a simulation of our own."

Ben blinked.

Then, he blinked again.

"You what?"

Hamza grabbed a piece of paper and a pen from his desk and began to scribble. "OK, let's say that we make some amazing computer simulation of a world. Like... *The Sims Version Fifty*."

He drew a circle on the page.

"That's it there. Now, in the game, one of the jobs your Sim can do is be a games designer. So, you have an AI character—meaning that within the confines of the game he *thinks* he's real—making games of his own. Games that he's coming up with himself, because he's artificially intelligent. With me?"

Ben and Logan exchanged glances.

"So far so good," Logan said, although Ben looked a little less confident.

"Right. Good. OK. So, let's say one of those games is a simulation like *The Sims*," Hamza said. He drew a smaller circle inside the first one. "So, now we've got a simulated world inside a simulated world. And within that new simulation, another simulation could be created, then another, then another, and on and on it goes. A chain of virtual universes, where everyone in them thinks they're real, and is unaware of the one before. They go about their business, living, working, dying, completely unaware that they're in a simulation."

"But that's not going to happen, is it?" asked Ben. "That's bloody *Star Trek* stuff."

"It's already happening, sir," Hamza said. "We're a few years off it being quite at the level we're talking about, but we're most of the way there. It's a matter of when, not if."

He pointed with his pen to the page. "So, if we assume that there will be a point in the not too distant future when this chain of simulated universes exists, then the chances of us being the Prime Universe—the original and real one—are infinitesimally small. Meaning..."

He drew a third circle, bigger than the others and surrounding them both. "This is us. And everything we see, including ourselves, is a simulation. Computer code, created by some other simulation, which was in turn created by... Well. You get the point."

Ben grunted. "Like I said, all sounds a bit *Star Trek* to me."

"There's actually growing scientific interest in the theory," Hamza said. "It's pretty interesting."

"You don't believe that shite, do you?" Ben scoffed.

Hamza considered his answer. "Doesn't really matter if we believe it or not, sir. Whether it's true or not, it doesn't change anything. Whether everything's real, or it's all inside a computer somewhere, the rules are the same. Gravity works. People get sick, fall in love."

"Get stabbed repeatedly in the back," Tyler volunteered.

Hamza gave him the finger, then continued. "Saying 'none of it is real' doesn't change the fact that, from our point of view, it *is* real. Whatever we do, we're still bound by the rules of the simulation. There are still consequences."

Logan shrugged off his coat. "Too bloody right there are consequences," he intoned. "There's us."

"What's the plan, boss?" Tyler asked.

"Same plan as always," Logan replied, his voice bordering on a snarl. "We catch this mad bastard and we put him away."

He turned away from the others, headed for the office he so rarely used, bracing himself for the video he knew he had to watch.

"And, if anyone happens to kick the living shite out of him between those two points in time, then so much the bloody better."

CHAPTER THIRTY-TWO

LOGAN SAT ALONE IN HIS OFFICE, HIS EYES FIXED ON THE MERCIFULLY blank video player that now filled half of his computer screen. His fingers were clasped together as if in prayer, knuckles white. Whiter even than his face, which had lost almost all of its colour over the course of the last fifteen minutes.

He cleared his throat, like he was about to say something. In truth, he just wanted to hear something normal. Something familiar. He wanted to be somewhere else, surrounded by friends and family, a million miles from this office and that screen and everything he had just seen. Another outlook. Another life.

Much more than that though, he wanted to find this guy. He wanted to stop him.

There was a soft, enquiring knock at the door. Logan ran a hand down his face, cleared his throat again, then sat up straight.

"In you come."

The door opened, and Ben Forde's head appeared around the frame. "You alright?"

"Fine," Logan said. "I mean... You know."

"Aye," Ben confirmed, stepping into the office and closing the door. "I know. It's rough. I mean, I haven't watched all of it. We put it off." He drew himself up to his full height. "But I will. If it'll help. I will."

Logan shook his head. "You're fine. One of the specialist teams can go over it in more..." His eyes flicked to the screen. "...detail. From what I saw, there's not a lot that can help us figure out who he is. He's edited chunks of it out. Maybe there was something in those parts, but now..."

He sighed and sat back in his chair. "Who was it who told me to come to Inverness again?" he asked. "*Nice quiet life*, they said. Can you remember who that was?"

Ben chuckled dryly. "Not a clue, Jack. But I'd have words with them, if I were you."

"Aye. I may just do that," Logan replied.

DI Forde took an exaggerated backward step towards the door, and both men shared a half-hearted smile.

"Couple of updates," Ben said, getting down to business. "Donald Sloane. We need to charge him or let him go. It's unlikely he's involved in the murder cases, but I can't stand the horrible bastard, so I thought we could get him on assaulting you and that lassie from Uniform."

"Aye, fine. Go with that," Logan said. "Anything on those hard drives they took from his place?"

"Movies. Pirated copies, we think."

"Charge him on that, too."

Ben gave a satisfied nod. "Great. We've also just had a report from the tech team about the cameras at the car park."

Logan stiffened. "Tell me it's something we can use."

A shake of Ben's head made the DCI's shoulders sag back into their original position.

"No. They've translated the code, though. You know, the computer numbers?"

"Binary."

"Aye, that. Apparently, it's a language? Did you know that?"

Logan confirmed that he was aware of that fact, albeit only vaguely.

"Well, they translated it. Turns out, it's just the same word over and over. 'Fake.' Should have guessed, really."

Logan gave a non-committal sort of grunt. He couldn't say he was particularly surprised by the information, but it was worrying, all the same. If this guy could deface HOLMES *and* get access to a secure camera network, he knew what he was doing. Logan hated the ones who knew what they were doing. Give him a drunken half-wit with a temper problem, any day.

"They're trying to find out... Oh, I don't know," Ben said. "Some technical shite. See if they can find out how he got into the system, and then try to trace him."

"I doubt they'll get anywhere," Logan said. "He'll have covered his tracks."

"For someone who says there's no consequences, he's certainly going out of his way to avoid them," Ben pointed out. "The mask, disguising his voice, and all that stuff."

"He knows full bloody well there are consequences," Logan said. "And I for one can't wait to inflict them on the bastard."

Ben nodded his agreement. "You can say that again. Oh, and the mask? Caitlyn reckons she's found a match."

"Already? That was bloody quick," Logan said, his eyebrows rising in surprise.

"Not a lot of places locally to get something like that," Ben said. "She checked the Hobbycraft website, and there's one that looks identical to the one in the video. We've sent a car over to pick one up so we can compare in person. If we do have a match, then we'll work with the shop to see if we can find out who bought one recently."

"No saying it's recent," Jack said. "Danni Gillespie's attacker was wearing one. Could well be the same mask."

Ben's glum expression suggested he'd already considered this. "Aye. Could be another dead end, but worth pursuing."

"No arguments there," Logan said. He clapped his hands together and stood up. "Right, what else? What's next? Where do we go from here?"

"Scene of Crime are finished at the car park. They're cataloguing everything and are going to send over a preliminary report later today," Ben said, flipping open his notebook. "Your doctor friend has got the body. We've got a positive ID on the victim already, and the husband doesn't want to come in and see her for himself."

Shite. The husband.

"What about the video? Has he seen that video?"

"He's aware of it, apparently, and has an idea what the contents are. If he's got any sense, he'll steer clear. A couple of folks from Victim Support are with him and the kids now, and we've got a liaison standing by. They're all in a pretty bad way, as you'd expect."

"Aye. I can imagine," said Logan, although he knew that he couldn't. Not really. Not enough.

"I went through and spoke to Hoon, while you were..." Ben gestured to the computer screen. "...busy. He'd heard about the video, obviously, and he's escalating it right up the chain. The higher-ups are going to work with the social media platforms to try to get it taken down."

"Good," said Logan.

Both men knew the truth, though. It was too late. The horse had already bolted. A million arseholes would already have downloaded that video all over the world. It was out there now, in the wild, and no matter how cooperative the social media sites might be, Clarissa McDade's degradation and dying minutes would forever be just a couple of link clicks away.

"You ever dealt with one like this, Jack?" Ben asked, his voice lowering, like he was afraid the others might overhear.

"Aye. We both have," Logan said. "He's just a nutter. We've dealt with plenty like him."

"True. But his motive..."

"The simulation shite is not his motive," Logan said. "It's his excuse. He likes the power, that's all. Funny how, if nobody's real, it's always women he goes after. No, he's not special, or different. He's the same as all the rest, and we'll catch him the same way we've caught them—solid polis work."

He checked his watch. "Right, what are we on? Jesus. OK. I'll get over to the mortuary, see what Shona's got. I want you here but send the rest of the team to the hospital. It's no coincidence that both recent victims worked there."

"The doctor, you think?" Ben said. "What was his name? Fletcher?"

"Aye, we definitely need to talk to him again. We need to find out what sort of relationship he had with Clarissa, but we need to keep an open mind. She was in HR. Had she disciplined anyone recently? Was there anyone she'd got on the wrong side of?"

"Got it," Ben said. He turned to leave, then stopped. "Oh, and you'll be pleased to know that Hoon has suggested he handle the press on this. He said, and I quote: 'I'm not having that useless big bastard knocking a journalist's teeth down their throat in front of the fucking cameras.'"

"That was a decent impression, actually," Logan said. "Well done."

"You should hear my Sean Connery," Ben said. "Itsh exshepshional."

"Nah, that was shite," Logan told him. He rapped his knuckles on the desk. "Right, we know what we're doing?"

"We do."

"Good."

Logan jabbed the power button on his computer and the screen went dark. It made an electronic whine, as if sighing with relief after everything it had just been forced to display.

"Then, let's get out there and nail this bastard."

CHAPTER THIRTY-THREE

THERE WAS NONE OF THE USUAL BANTER WHEN LOGAN TURNED UP TO speak to the pathologist. Shona's voice crackled through an intercom in the outer office, calling Logan through to what she'd once referred to as 'the business end' of the mortuary.

After helping himself to gloves and a mask, he pushed open the heavy double doors, and shuddered in the sudden blast of refrigerated air. It rolled out of air conditioning units above, as if trying to push down the rising stench of death.

Shona looked up from the body on the slab before her. There was no smile or wave, no salute of acknowledgement. There was just a sadness in her eyes, and a heaviness to the way she moved.

"You alright?" Logan asked her.

"No," she said, matter-of-factly.

Logan stopped across from her, the uncovered naked body of Clarissa McDade between them. Logan had managed to grow largely indifferent to the sight of a corpse over the years, although he could never decide if this was to his credit or to his detriment.

This one, though, he found difficult to look at. It was because of the video, he thought. He was so used to seeing victims after death, but witnessing their final, horrifying moments made it harder for him to detach himself. The body was no longer just a body. It was a person. A woman. A wife, a mother, a daughter, a friend.

And he'd had to watch her suffer. He'd had to watch the wounds he was about to discuss be inflicted upon her in leering, lingering close-up.

"She was... Not a friend. Not exactly," Shona said, her eyes downcast. "But we'd chat sometimes. In the canteen, or whatever. She was nice."

Shona puffed out her cheeks. Her voice quaked. "I fucking hate this job," she whispered. She said it so quietly that Logan didn't know if he was supposed to have heard it. He decided to pretend that he hadn't.

Shona gave herself a shake, pushed back her shoulders, then launched into what felt like a rehearsed speech.

"Cause of death, as you probably already know, was a single cut to the jugular vein. Scalpel. Same one he used to carve the letters into her stomach before he killed her. Skillfully done—small nick, but just in the right position. He knows his stuff. Medical training, I'd guess, but then again, you can find a tutorial for anything on YouTube these days."

She indicated the victim's face. "He gagged her with a rag and tape— again, I'm sure you know this. I've sent it off for analysis. You'll hear back on that before I do."

Logan glanced awkwardly down the victim's body, his eyes alighting for the briefest fraction of a second on her crotch. "What about...? From the sexual assault?"

"No obvious DNA left. I think he raped her with an implement of some kind, rather than... the usual," Shona said. Her face prickled red and she placed a hand on her stomach, like she was fighting back against a rising wave of nausea. "There's some laceration," she managed to continue. "Like it had some sharp edges."

"Like a knife?" Logan asked. The video footage had remained fixed mostly on the victim's upper body during the footage of the assault, aside from a minute or so at the start. It was one of the small mercies the footage afforded.

Shona shook her head. "No. More like... I don't know. A stick, maybe?"

"A stick?"

"With one or two little twigs coming off it. But not long. Broken down so they just stick out. It could even be some kind of sex toy."

"A lacerating sex toy?" Logan said.

"Some people are into some right weird shit," Shona pointed out.

Logan conceded this point with a nod. God knew, he'd met enough people to appreciate just how true that statement was.

"Anyway. There's a video of it all, I hear," Shona said. Her eyes met

Logan's. They were pleading, desperately hoping that he'd tell her she'd heard wrong.

"I'm afraid so," he said.

Shona's throat tightened as she stifled a sob. "Bastard," she whispered. "How could someone...? I mean, I see it all the time. We see it, I mean. But..."

She looked down at the body, or maybe through it to the floor beyond. "What makes them do these things? How can they?"

Logan heaved out a sigh. "I wish I knew," he told her. "This one says it's because we don't exist. On the video, I mean. Simulation Theory, or some bollocks. Says it's all fake, and none of it is real. Says he's going to do it again, too."

Shona looked up sharply. "And do you believe him?"

Logan wished he had another answer for her. He really did.

"Aye," he said. "I believe him."

They stood in silence for several seconds, the weight of Logan's words slowly settling in.

"Why her?" Shona eventually asked. "Why Clarissa? First Esme, now her. Is it the hospital? Is that the connection? I mean, it has to be, doesn't it?"

"We don't know yet," Logan admitted. "Ben and the others are questioning people now. I'm going to head up and join them, see if we can find some more direct connection. But aye, it looks like the hospital's a factor in it, although we're currently pursuing some other lines of—"

"Don't give me the official line, Jack," Shona replied, her voice clipped around the edges by anger. "I don't want a soundbite. Do you have any idea who did this? Honestly?"

Logan hesitated. Then, he gave a single shake of his head.

"Jesus. So... what? All the other women here, we're all in danger?"

"We've got no evidence to suggest that," Logan said.

"You've got no evidence that we aren't!" Shona spat back. "You've got no evidence, full stop!"

She appeared momentarily surprised by her outburst and looked down at the body of Clarissa McDade again. "Sorry," she said, her eyes briefly flicking back to Logan. "I didn't mean that."

"No, you're absolutely right," Logan admitted. "We don't know what he's planning next, or who might be in danger. But we're working on it. In the meantime, I can have someone from Uniform keep an eye on you, make sure you're—"

"Me? I'm not worried about me. I'm worried about everyone else. Have you got enough officers to keep an eye on everyone? There's something like eighteen-hundred women working here. Can you give them all escorts?"

"No," Jack admitted. "We can't."

"Then I don't want one," Shona told him.

"We don't know that anyone at the hospital is in danger, but we'll recommend staff travel to and from work in groups or pairs," Logan said. "Just until we know more. We've got the tech bods analysing the video and trying to trace his hack. We're hopeful they might..."

His voice trailed away into an uncomfortable silence. That wasn't the truth. He wasn't hopeful about any of it. Aye, there was always a chance they might get lucky, but his instincts told him the killer would be too smart to leave any clues that might point to who or where he was.

"You'd better get back," Shona told him, her voice losing its earlier anger. "I'll type all this up. The report, I mean, not me being hyper-critical and panicky. I'll leave that bit out."

They shared a smile, but it was small, and it was fleeting, and it barely qualified as a real smile at all.

"Thanks. And we're doing all we can," Logan said. He wanted her to know that. To believe it, and hopefully take comfort from it.

But the words sounded empty and hollow as they tumbled from his mouth. He was giving her the official line again. *We're doing all we can. We're working hard to apprehend the perpetrator of these heinous crimes. We're pulling out all the stops.*

She deserved more than that. Much more.

"I'm going to catch him, Shona," he told her, and the sincerity of it made her stand up straight and pay attention. "I promise you that."

She nodded, then the faintest suggestion of a smile tugged at the corners of her mouth. "I'd say you always keep your promises, but I'm still waiting on that lunch you owe me..."

The smile stuttered and died as quickly as it had started. "Keep this one, Jack," she urged, her eyes pleading. "Keep this one."

CHAPTER THIRTY-FOUR

THE ATMOSPHERE IN THE HOSPITAL WAS NOTICEABLY DIFFERENT TO the last time Logan had walked through the corridors. After the attack on Esme, the place had been awash with shock, anger, and sadness. Now though, there was something else in there, flavouring the mix.

Fear.

Guilt, too. Logan saw it on the faces of several of the nurses he passed. The way they looked at him, then quickly glanced away, casting their eyes down towards the floor. He could practically pick out those who had watched at least some of the video from those who hadn't.

He hoped, for their sakes, that they hadn't watched it all.

Logan had called into the Incident Room and got Ben to contact the hospital chiefs to suggest that staff pair up going to and from work.

"Safety in numbers, makes sense," Ben had agreed, before hanging up to make the call.

Logan was passing through one of the wards, trying to get his bearings, when he heard the clatter of footsteps running up behind him.

He turned in time to see Kel Conlyn running the last few steps towards him, one hand clutching his side. He winced, and gestured to his chest as he tried to get his breath back.

"Stitch," he explained, his hand massaging the side of his stomach. "Sorry."

"Take your time, Mr Conlyn," Logan said, as patiently as possible. "Was there something you wanted to tell me?"

"What? No. Sorry," Kel said. "I just... I heard about the video. People are saying that the guy who killed Esme killed that woman from HR. Is that true?"

"He's certainly claiming to have committed both attacks, yes," Logan confirmed. He looked the younger man up and down. "You haven't watched it, then?"

"No!" Kel spluttered, visibly recoiling. "Why would I watch...? Why would anyone watch something like that?"

"Beats me, son," Logan said.

The orderly shook his head, his face still screwed up in distaste. "Some people are just..." He sighed, and forced a smile that didn't amount to much. "If there's anything I can do to help, just let me know."

"Just keep your eyes peeled," Logan told him. "If you see anyone acting suspicious, report it, but don't approach. And we're suggesting anyone walking to and from work, particularly late at night, travel in pairs or groups. You can help spread the word on that."

Kel seemed to grow a couple of inches in height, like he was growing into the responsibility before Logan's eyes. "OK. I'll do that. You can count on me," he said. "I'll go start telling people now."

"Thank you," Logan said.

"Happy to help," said Kel. Then, he pulled off an almost military-grade about-turn and set off back in the direction he'd come from.

"Oh, and Mr Conlyn!" Logan called after him.

The orderly stopped and turned. "Yes?"

"I don't suppose you can point me in the direction of the HR department?"

THE DEPARTMENT WAS TECHNICALLY CLOSED by the time Logan finally found his way there, but his team had set up inside, and all the lights were blazing. Darkness had descended outside, and the office lights had turned the windows into mirrors, each one a reminder to Logan of just how rough he currently looked.

DCs Khaled and Neish were already hard at work when Logan turned up. Under normal circumstances, Logan would've expected to find Tyler spinning in one of the big office chairs, or commenting on the photo of the attractive twenty-something—someone's wife or daughter, presumably— that was sitting on one of the three desks.

But the same atmosphere that had hung heavily over the rest of the hospital had permeated this place, too, and both detectives just briefly glanced up in acknowledgement when Logan arrived, then got right back to it. Logan was glad to see that Tyler's early excitement about the prospect of working a serial case had abandoned him once he'd realised he was now doing exactly that.

There was hope for the bugger yet.

Logan took off his coat and hung it on a hook by the door. Might as well make himself comfortable. He was likely to be here for the long haul.

"Right, where are we?" he asked. "What have we got?"

DC Khaled turned in his chair to face the DCI. Tyler, who had been searching through a desk drawer paused, mid-rummage.

Hamza indicated the computer he had been tapping away at. "I'm going through her calendar and work emails, sir. Her boss gave us the login information. Caitlyn's interviewing her and some of the victim's colleagues now. A few of them were with her at the club last night, so we're hoping they might have noticed anyone acting weirdly."

Logan clicked his tongue against the back of his teeth. "Right. Good. Anything in the emails?"

"No, sir. Nothing interesting yet."

"Keep looking. Check for recent disciplinaries, too. Has she had to give anyone a bollocking in the last couple of weeks? If so, I want to know who, and what for."

Hamza turned back to the screen. "On it, sir. Oh!" He turned back again. "Caitlyn asked around about Colin Fletcher. The doctor?"

"What about him?"

"He's called in sick, sir. We sent Uniform around, but no answer at his house."

"Shite. OK. That's potentially significant. Get him found."

"We're on it, sir."

Logan directed his attention to DC Neish. "Tyler? What about you?"

"I'm looking for her notepad, boss," Tyler said. He pulled the drawer all the way out of its housing and set it on top of the desk.

"Her notepad?"

"Aye, boss. There are three people working in HR. According to the boss, they all make notes during interviews—you know, like appraisals, disciplinaries, whatever—and then type everything up later."

"I think we're already pretty familiar with that concept, Detective Constable," Logan pointed out. "What about it?"

"I can find the notepads for the other two members of the team, but not Clarissa's," Tyler said. "It's not on her desk. I've been through every drawer and cupboard apart from this one, and it's nowhere to be found."

"Could she have taken it home?" Logan asked.

"Doubt it, boss. Data protection. They're not allowed to take them out of the office."

Logan turned on the spot, looking around. The office was about a third of the size of the Incident Room back at the station, and filled with furniture that probably hadn't been updated in a decade. The desks and chairs were mismatched, suggesting they'd all been bought at different times, and a row of filing cabinets were all different heights, widths, and colours.

"You check in those cabinets?"

"Not yet, boss," Tyler admitted. "Everyone else keeps theirs in their desk drawer. Not sure why she'd file hers, but I'll go through."

Logan crossed to the first of the filing cabinets and pulled it open. The metal drawer squealed in protest, stuck an inch or two open, then finally relented when the DCI gave it a sharp tug.

The drawer was filled with dozens of suspended cardboard file holders, each one bulging with the weight of the paperwork stuffed inside. Going through this lot was going to take hours.

"I think I need coffee for this," he grunted, shunting the drawer closed again. "Tyler. You see a machine anywhere nearby?"

DC Neish stopped rummaging in the drawer and gave an almost imperceptible sigh. "Aye, boss. There's one a couple of corridors along in a waiting room. What are you after?"

"I'll get it," Logan said.

Tyler's face took on a blank expression, like he didn't know how to respond to this. "What?"

"I said I'll get it," Logan told him. "No need to stare at me like I've grown an extra bloody head, Detective Constable. I do occasionally get the tea and coffee in."

"Do you, boss?" Tyler asked, his tone one of genuine surprise. He cleared his throat. "I mean, yeah. Right. Cool."

"What do you both take?" Logan asked.

"Milk and two, boss," Tyler replied.

"I'll have a tea, if it's going," Hamza said. "Nothing in it."

"You'll have a coffee," Logan told him, striding for the door. "Trust me, we're all going to need it."

THE NEXT FEW hours passed slowly, time grinding by, minute by excruciating minute. Developments were few and far between. Breakthroughs, non-existent.

Ben called in with an update on the Range Rover at the car park. CCTV footage from earlier in the day showed Bosco's man, Valdis Petronis, arriving in it, along with Shaun Gillespie. Neither man had returned to the car in the hours leading up to the camera network being hacked, and even with the audio distortion, there was no way the killer in the video shared the same accent as Valdis. Valdis also had a neck like a bulldog that had been force-fed steroids from birth, which ruled him out physically, too.

It wasn't so easy to rule out Shaun Gillespie, and he tied into the series of attacks in a few different ways. His sister being the main one, obviously, but the latest attack had taken place in the car park above his nightclub, shortly after the victim had left said club, heading for home.

If you considered that he'd attacked Donald Sloane a few years back, and that Sloane was pictured alongside Esme Miller, then you could tie him to the second victim too, albeit tenuously.

He had computer skills, too. Some kind of teen genius, by all accounts. His app business had netted him a fortune, and while Logan was far from being an expert, he had to assume the guy had the know-how to hack the car park cameras and stick that video on HOLMES.

Logan instructed Ben to have someone keep an eye on Gillespie. They could bring him in for a chat in the morning, if nothing else jumped out at them tonight.

Colin Fletcher remained a man of mystery. He wasn't at home, and his mobile was off. Logan had instructed a couple of Uniforms to head to Elgin to have a chat with the wife, but they hadn't fed back yet.

Caitlyn's interviews hadn't turned up much. Work-wise, Clarissa had been in the office herself for most of the previous week, with one of her colleagues on holiday, and another only working part-time. Neither of them had been able to shine any light on who'd been in and out of the department over the past few days, and while they both agreed that Clarissa could be fierce in a disciplinary when she had to, everyone they knew had always spoken highly of her. If someone was carrying a grudge, they hid it well.

Logan had texted DS McQuarrie to get her to ask about the victim's notebook. Both women who shared the office had insisted it would be in the tray on her desk, and the department head had confirmed this was standard procedure.

It still hadn't turned up, even after Logan and Tyler had gone through the filing cabinets and shifted some of the most likely pieces of furniture so they could check down the back. So, it looked like someone had taken it, which opened up a whole raft of questions.

Logan sat behind a desk, sipping his fourth coffee of the night, and marvelling that it somehow managed to taste even less palatable than the previous three. There was a harsh, *ashy* taste to it, like someone had previously used the cup as an ashtray before returning it to the machine.

The moment the image popped into his head, he set the cup down, slid it a little way along the desk, and silently vowed not to drink any more of it again.

The desk had been clear when he'd set up shop at it, but now it was covered in printouts and files, none of which had proved to be all that useful. Logan had managed to build up a pretty good picture of the victim's work life and had gained some insight into her personality and who she was, but none of it was pointing anywhere yet. Nowhere useful, at least.

"This is interesting, sir," said Hamza, and Logan was on his feet at once.

DC Khaled indicated the screen as Logan joined him at the victim's desk. The DCI bent down and found himself looking at a calendar screen, with each working day broken up into varyingly sized, differently coloured blocks of time. Most days were a rainbow of activities—meetings, admin time, breaks, conference calls, and more. Clarissa had accounted for everything, scheduling her tasks with a level of discipline Logan could only dream of.

Or, more likely, have recurring nightmares about.

"What am I looking at?" Logan asked.

"It's the victim's calendar, sir," Hamza replied.

Logan tutted. "No, I know that. What's the interesting bit?"

"Oh. Right. Aye, sorry, sir," Hamza said, blushing slightly and shifting in the seat. He pointed with the end of a well-chewed pen at two solid blocks of blue on the screen, one above the other. "Three days ago. Check this out."

"Admin time," Logan said, reading the text on the top block.

"And again below," Hamza said. "Admin time twice in a row."

Logan's eyes flicked back at the previous days. The colours were always alternating, always different. Occasionally, a whole afternoon would be blocked off for something, but it would be one solid mass of colour, not two.

"I've looked back, sir, and she does admin three times a week, religiously. Always the same time, and she marks it the same colour."

He scrolled past to previous weeks. Logan saw all the blocks of light blue. They were the one constant in a sea of ever-changing hues.

"See? Always the same. Three times a week, always the same day and time, and always blocked off for two hours each time. Except three days ago," Hamza said, scrolling back to the current week. "She's got admin down twice, one after the other."

"Busy time, maybe?" Logan guessed. "If someone was off on holiday..."

"I thought of that sir, and cross-referenced with previous holiday periods. Admin time stays the same. No change," Hamza said. "Also, why not just make it one block? Why two?"

Logan wasn't ready to let go of the holiday cover idea yet. "If she was doing someone else's work, she might have split it up to differentiate."

Hamza conceded the point with a nod. "Aye, suppose so, sir," he said. "Except..."

He clicked into the top block. There was a paragraph of text in there, detailing what Clarissa had done.

"See that? List of stuff she had to do. Create a new job ad, collate applications for another job, sort out a presentation for a school careers fair..."

He backed out of the calendar event, then clicked on the one below. "And now..."

Logan read the notes in silence.

"They're the same," he said.

"Identical, sir," Hamza confirmed. "It's a copy and paste job. She copied the top event and pasted it below."

"Or someone did," Logan said.

Hamza glanced from the screen to the DCI. "My thoughts, exactly. I can't say for sure, obviously, but my guess is that someone deleted what *was* in that spot, then filled it by copying the event above. They could do it remotely if they could hack her password."

Logan shook his head. "They did it from here," he said.

Hamza looked down at the keys. The keys his fingertips had been touching for the past couple of hours. "How do you know that, sir?" he asked.

"Because they also took her notebook," Logan pointed out. "If she had a meeting with someone, she'd have made notes."

Tyler sidled over to join them. Unlike Logan, he hadn't yet given up on his latest cup of coffee, although couldn't quite bring himself to drink any more of it. He clutched it between finger and thumb, wary of squeezing the fragile plastic too firmly and sending the lukewarm contents cascading over the rim.

"So, we find out who changed the calendar and took the notebook, and we've got him?"

"It's rarely that easy, but maybe," Logan said.

"Should Hamza have been using that keyboard, then?" Tyler asked. "Should I have been rifling through the drawers? Shouldn't we get this place checked over for forensic evidence, boss?"

"Bit late for that," Logan said. "Besides, shared office, lots of coming and going—and our man is smart, he hasn't left us anything forensics-wise until now. I highly doubt anything would've come up. We've made good progress here. Now, I want—"

His phone rang, the ringtone *brrrringing* as the smartphone vibrated across the desk he'd been sitting at a few minutes before.

Picking it up, he checked the screen. *Unknown Caller*.

"DCI Logan," he said, tapping the green icon and pressing the phone to his ear.

There was silence. Not the silence of a line that hadn't yet connected, but a hollow, rasping sort of silence that suggested someone on the other end. Logan got the impression of a small room, although he couldn't even begin to explain why. Something about the colour of the silence, the way it seemed to echo off a set of closed-in walls.

"Hello?" Logan said. He heard his voice tumble off into the void. "Who is this?" he asked. "What do you want?"

A voice replied. At least, he thought so. In truth, it was so soft and faint that he might have imagined it.

"You, Jack," it whispered, and then the phone *bleeped* in his ear, and the display returned to the icons of the home screen.

"Everything alright, boss?" asked Tyler.

Logan realised he was standing motionless, staring at the phone. How long had he been like that? A few seconds, at least, maybe more.

"Hm? Oh. Aye. Aye," he said, setting the phone down on the desk. He continued to stare at it, like it might be about to do something amazing he didn't want to miss.

"Who was that?" Tyler asked.

"I don't know," Logan admitted, still not lifting his gaze from the handset on the table. The screen darkened, then went black. The spell was broken then, and Logan finally tore his eyes away. "I'll find out. But, for now, we've got a job to do. Find me who Clarissa McDade met with that afternoon, and point me in the bastard's direction."

He shot the phone another look, then picked up the coffee he had sworn to himself he wouldn't touch again.

It was going to be a long, long night.

CHAPTER THIRTY-FIVE

IT HAD BEEN A LONG, LONG DAY.

Laura Elder's muscles fired stabbing pains of complaint up her back and across her shoulders as she slipped off her navy blue NHS tunic and reached for the shirt she'd left hanging in her locker. She caught a whiff of herself as she lifted her arm to pull the shirt on, and her mind leapt to a hot bath full of soapy bubbles.

She'd texted her mum earlier, asking her to stick the immerser on. It was just about possible to get a bath without it, but she'd been dreaming of a good soaking all day, and if she didn't emerge from it a shade of lobster-red, then she was going to be disappointed.

Before then, of course, she had to get home. It was easy walking distance—ten minutes on average, less if she power-walked—but the police were recommending everyone travel in pairs or groups. Given what had happened to Esme, and now the woman from HR, it made sense, even if it did suddenly bring into focus just how much danger any one of them could be in.

She could take a taxi, she supposed. They were expensive, though, for all the distance she was going. She and Craig had been doing so well saving up for the wedding, too. She'd even stopped going to Costa, and started making her own lunch. It would be a shame to chuck it away for the sake of half a mile, even if there was a murderer on the loose.

The words struck her as she thought them, *dinging* around inside her head like a bullet ricocheting in an enclosed space.

Murderer on the loose.

Bloody hell. When you thought of it like that...

"Better safe than sorry," she sighed, as she finished buttoning up her shirt.

She had just taken out her phone and was about to call the taxi company when the door opened. A head appeared around the frame, one hand over his eyes so as not to see anything he shouldn't.

"Hey. Laura, you still here?" he asked.

"Yeah. And it's fine. I'm changed."

The man in the doorway removed his hand and smiled at her. "Better safe than sorry, I thought," he said.

Laura smiled back. "Funny, I was thinking the same thing. Was just about to phone a taxi to take me home."

"Ah, yes. Glad I caught you, then," the man replied. "I'm knocking off now, too. Want me to walk you? Police are advising—"

Laura closed her locker door, picked her coat up off the bench beside her, then shoved her phone into the pocket of her jeans. "That," she said, practically skipping towards the door, "would be brilliant!"

LOGAN WAS PACING. This was rarely a good sign.

Hamza had scoured Clarissa McDade's inbox, searching for anything that might reasonably be considered a clue. So far, he'd drawn a complete blank.

Tyler, meanwhile, was still ploughing his way through an apparently never-ending stack of paperwork. No one had any idea what he was looking for—least of all himself—but the hope was that he'd know it when he saw it.

So far, he'd seen nothing, aside from a report on a disciplinary hearing with Dr Colin Fletcher, after a nurse had accused him of using inappropriately sexual language. It had been six months ago, though, and the meeting had seemed amicable enough.

Logan was just about to ask if there had been any update on Fletcher when one came through. Uniform had found him. Or, at least, they knew where he was.

"A fucking tennis tournament?" Logan spat. "I thought he was sick?"

"Pulled a sickie, boss," Tyler said, hanging up the phone he'd taken the call on. "Been playing tennis in Aberdeen all day. Left last night, according to his ex-wife. He asked her along, but she told him to ram it up his arse."

"Did you—"

"Check? Aye. Hotel confirms he arrived just after ten last night. He's due to check out tomorrow."

Logan cursed below his breath. Another door closed.

"I think we're barking up the wrong tree with all this stuff, boss," Tyler said, opening another cardboard folder and pulling out yet another bundle of paperwork. "It feels like a dead end."

"They all feel like dead ends until you find an opening," Logan said. "That's the reality of polis work, son. Keep checking."

Tyler glanced at his watch, sighed, then turned the next page.

"I'm guessing I won't be able to get that time off tomorrow now, eh boss?" he said, his eyes scanning the neatly-spaced print.

Logan stopped pacing. "Time off? What time off?"

"Harris's birthday," Tyler said, still not looking up. Either this was the most fascinating report he'd come across so far, or he couldn't quite bring himself to meet the DCI's eye. "I'd said to Sinead that I'd come along."

"Aye," Logan said. He tutted. "I'm sorry, son, but I doubt it."

Tyler nodded. "Yeah. Fair enough, boss," he said, putting up far less of a fight than Logan had been bracing himself for. "Perks of the job, innit?"

"Afraid so."

He turned away from one DC and addressed the other. "Still nothing, Hamza?"

"Only a growing realisation that working in HR is bloody tedious, sir," DC Khaled said. "I mean, there are a lot of emails here all saying pretty much nothing. Can't find anything that could relate to any meeting she had on the day the calendar was changed."

"You check the deleted items folder?" Tyler asked.

"*Of course* I checked the deleted items folder," Hamza replied. "I'm not nine. There's nothing in there. It's been cleared out."

"What about the mail server?" Tyler asked.

Logan's head tick-tocked between both DCs, like a spectator at a tennis match.

"It's IMAP," Hamza said. "So whatever was deleted here will be deleted there, too."

"Could be back-ups, though," Tyler suggested.

"Aye, I've put a request in with the server team to see if they can dig something out, but I'm not holding out much hope. These systems are pretty ancient, and it doesn't look like they've been well set-up. I'll be very surprised if they're regularly backing up the email servers."

Logan raised his hands, interrupting. "Right, long story short. What does that mean?"

Hamza turned from the screen. "It means that someone potentially deleted any emails referencing their meeting with the victim to cover their tracks. There's a slim possibility we might be able to pull copies of the deleted emails from the server, but I doubt it, and we'd probably need to get a warrant. The HR boss's authorisation won't be enough."

"Shite. We won't get that tonight," Logan said.

"Doubt anyone from the server team would be around at this time anyway, sir," Hamza pointed out.

"They'll be around if I bloody tell them to be around," Logan snapped. He pinched the bridge of his nose and sighed. "But we won't get the warrant until tomorrow, so no point dragging them down."

The door to the office opened, and DS McQuarrie entered. She looked almost as tired as Logan felt. They all did, he realised. Time to send them home. This was getting them nowhere, anyway.

"Caitlyn. Anything?" he asked, grasping for one last lifeline.

"Nothing really, sir, no," DS McQuarrie replied. "The usual. Everyone shocked and saddened, she was always so friendly, she'll be sadly missed. That sort of thing."

Logan could only offer a disappointed grunt in reply.

"How's it going in here?" Caitlyn asked.

Logan grunted, then gestured vaguely in Hamza's direction. DC Khaled picked up on his cue and launched into a recap of what they'd found so far. This did not take long.

"So... Someone deleted references to themselves, we reckon?" Caitlyn asked, once Hamza's all-too-brief report was over. "From her email, I mean?"

"Looks like it, yeah," Hamza said.

Caitlyn ran her tongue across the front of her top teeth, her eyes narrowing.

"What?" Logan asked. "What are you thinking?"

"I don't even know if it's possible, sir," DS McQuarrie began.

"I'll try anything. What is it?" Logan pressed.

Caitlyn crossed to where Hamza was sitting. He turned to face the screen, and she rested a hand on the back of his chair. "So, she's HR. She'll have emails coming in all the time about the staff here, right?"

"She does," Hamza confirmed. "Loads of it."

"Search Esme Miller."

Hamza typed the name in the search box and clicked 'Go'. The mouse icon became a whirring egg-timer for a few seconds, then a list of emails appeared.

"Twelve results," he said. "Want me to look through them?"

Caitlyn shook her head. "No. Try Colin Fletcher."

"We've already found some stuff on him," Tyler interjected. "Here's a shocker for you, turns out he's a bit of a perv."

"Not surprising," Caitlyn said, still fixed on the screen. "Search him."

Logan joined her standing behind Hamza's chair as the DC typed in the name.

Click. Whirr.

"Nineteen results," Hamza announced.

"Right. Good," Caitlyn said.

"Why is that good?" Logan asked. "What does that tell us?"

"These search results? Nothing, sir," the DS replied. She continued before Logan could start shouting. "But, I was thinking, if we can search for what's there, can we search for what's not there?"

Hamza craned his neck to look up at her. "Eh?"

Logan was quicker to catch on. "Search for all the staff names. See if there's someone who doesn't bring up any results," he said. His eyes widened. "Christ. That could work."

"Worth a shot, sir," Caitlyn said.

"Why have I been stuck in here with this pair of clowns all night? Why weren't you here? We could've had this wrapped up hours ago," Logan said. He turned to Hamza. "Can you get us a list of all staff?"

Tyler piped up from the other desk. "I've got one here, boss," he said, kneeling down and rifling through a stack of folders that teetered beside the desk. "Somewhere. Hang on."

Logan rolled up his shirt sleeves and pointed to one of the other computers. "Can we get into her email from this?"

"Should be able to, sir. Even if her account isn't set up in Outlook, we can access the webmail to—"

"I'm no' wanting a dissertation on it, son. A simple yes or no will do."

"Yes, sir. Shouldn't be a problem," Hamza said.

"Good. Caitlyn, get set up on that one," Logan instructed, pointing to the third computer. "Tyler, find that list, then see if you can get us some laptops and a few Uniforms. We'll divide the list up and all take a section. It shouldn't take more than a few hours to work our way through—"

"Got it, sir," Hamza said.

Logan stopped midway through rolling up his second sleeve. "What?"

"I found a list and just ran an OR search in the inbox," Hamza replied. "Just copied and pasted."

Across the room, the stack of folders Tyler had been looking through toppled over and spilled across the floor. There was a *thump* and a 'Fuck' as he tried to straighten up and bumped his head on the underside of the desk.

"Oh. Right," Logan said. He rolled his sleeves down again. "And?"

"One sec, sir. Just working on the filters..."

"How long will that take?"

"Done," Hamza announced. He studied the results on-screen. "Huh. Looks like every member of staff gets mentioned at some point. Except one. No reference to him anywhere."

Logan bent at Hamza's shoulder, the glare of the monitor picking out the weathered lines of his face. "Who?"

"Some guy named... Conlyn, sir," Hamza said. "Kel Conlyn."

CHAPTER THIRTY-SIX

LAURA ELDER PULLED HER COAT AROUND HER AND SIDE-EYED TWO men standing outside The Fluke pub, cigarettes tucked at the corners of their mouths. Music blared out from within as the door was opened, and a third man—older than the others—shuffled out to join them, lighter already in hand.

She relaxed a little once she and her companion were safely past the place, and gave herself a silent ticking off. She'd walked this way... what? Two hundred times? Four hundred? She'd long-since lost count. She'd never given it a second thought, either. She'd never felt afraid, or like she was in danger.

Until tonight.

"It's really good of you to do this," she said, shooting the man beside her a grateful smile. "I should've just got a taxi."

Kel Conlyn shook his head emphatically. "The price those robbing bastards charge? I don't blame you," he said, returning the smile with interest. "It's no bother. I can get my bus from just along the road from yours, anyway. Makes no odds to me."

He glanced both ways along the street and let out a little giggle. "Can you imagine if someone does jump out on us, though? I'm not sure who'll scream the loudest."

Laura chewed a fingernail. "Shit. Good point. Maybe I should've asked Dr Fletcher for a lift home. He's always offering one."

Kel erupted into laughter. "I'll bet he is! Christ, can you imagine?" He adopted a deeper voice and gestured to his crotch. "What this? No, nurse, I always drive with my cock out, I assure you. There's nothing untoward about it whatsoever."

Laura joined in with the laughter. "Spot on."

"You'd have his fingers up you before you'd even got your seatbelt on," Kel said.

Laura pulled a shocked face, then slapped him on the arm. "Aye, in his bloody dreams. Anyway, I think he's off sick, or something. Didn't see him around."

They walked on in silence for a while, taking it in turns to shoot a quick look around them to make sure they weren't being followed by any knife-wielding maniacs, or sex-starved former surgeons. The golf course lay on either side of the road around them, the flags fluttering in the darkness beyond the reach of the streetlights.

"Did you watch it?" Laura asked. She turned to Kel, her eyes shimmering, her face alive with uncertainty, like she wasn't sure what reaction she was going to get. "The video, I mean. Of the HR woman. Did you watch it?"

"God, no," Kel said, shaking his head. "Not for me, that. I have a hard enough time getting to sleep as it is."

They went another dozen or so steps before he asked the obvious. "You?"

Laura searched his face for a moment, then nodded. The movement was quick and mouse-like. "Some of it. I didn't know what it was going to be... I didn't watch it all. It was horrible."

"I'd imagine it would be," Kel said. He shuddered at the thought of it.

"He said some weird stuff at the start. The guy, I mean," Laura continued. "Kept saying it wasn't real, that she didn't exist, so he wasn't doing anything wrong, or whatever."

She shot Kel a sideways look. "Bit mental that, isn't it?"

Kel said nothing.

"I mean, why wouldn't she exist? And not just her. He said that none of us existed. Him, too. Kept saying we weren't real."

"Maybe we aren't."

Laura snorted. "What?" She jabbed him on the arm. "You feel pretty real to me."

A flicker of annoyance darted briefly across Kel's face, then he smiled. "I mean, obviously he's mental, but if it was true—if he was right, and this was all, say, a dream, or... I don't know, a computer simulation—then would anything matter?"

"I don't follow," Laura said.

"What's not to follow? It's not difficult," Kel replied, the tone of his voice hardening. "If we were in a computer simulation—if we were characters in a game created by someone else for their entertainment—then why not kill someone? Why not just do whatever you want?"

"Well, because..."

"Because what?" Kel asked, stopping. "If it's not real, then the consequences aren't real. If it's all just a dream, then why care?"

Laura smiled again, but Kel didn't join in. She shifted uneasily from foot to foot, suddenly aware of the darkness pressing in from just beyond the glow of the streetlights.

"Well, I mean, it's still real to us, isn't it?"

Kel eyeballed her for a few long, drawn-out moments, then relaxed. "Exactly," he said, setting off again. "We get that. Even if everything's fake, the rules we've created for ourselves still apply. Kill someone, you still go to jail. Their family still grieves. But, my point is, to someone who doesn't get that part, the idea that there are no consequences to *anything* must make it pretty tempting to just go out and do—"

He stopped again, suddenly alert. Turning, he scanned the shadows of the golf course.

"What?" Laura asked.

"Shh," he urged, holding up a finger. He squinted into the gloom, eyes darting left and right, head cocked a fraction. "Did you hear that?"

Laura followed his gaze. Her voice, when it came, was a whisper. "Hear what?"

"I don't know," Kel admitted. "For a second, I thought I heard..."

He shook his head, then took Laura by the hand. "Come on," he said, hurrying her along the street. "Let's get you home."

Glancing both ways to make sure the coast was clear, he led her across the road, towards the other half of the golf course across the street.

"This is the wrong way," Laura protested, scampering along behind him.

"Don't worry," Kel said. He looked back at her, then past to the wall of darkness at their backs. "I know a short cut."

CHAPTER THIRTY-SEVEN

DCI LOGAN STORMED THROUGH THE CORRIDORS OF RAIGMORE hospital, backtracking to where he'd met Kel Conlyn earlier in the evening.

Caitlyn had remained back in the HR Department, checking shift rotas to see if she could figure out which ward he had been based in that day, while Hamza and Tyler had set off in opposite directions to try to track Conlyn down.

A nurse jumped in fright as she emerged from a side door to find Logan storming towards her. "Kel Conlyn. He's a porter. You seen him?"

"Sorry. I... I am new," she replied in a lilting Indian accent. "I do not know."

"Who's in charge?" the DCI demanded.

The nurse looked up at him, uncomprehending.

"The boss. Where's your boss?" Logan asked, lowering his voice. "Who's your boss?"

"Oh. She is this way," the nurse replied, pulling the door open and gesturing for Logan to go through. "Maybe... um... Yes. She help you?"

Logan stormed through and found himself face-to-face with a mural of *Winnie the Pooh*. Other characters had been painted onto the otherwise dull cream walls. A sign hung from the ceiling, informing those who hadn't already figured it out that this was the way to the children's ward.

The nurse led him through a brightly-painted door, and onto a corridor with a number of doors and large windows along one wall. He could see a bed through the closest window, a boy of around eight or nine sleeping soundly in it, apparently oblivious to the wires and tubes connected to various parts of his anatomy.

"Esha? Is everything alright?" asked an older nurse who sat behind a desk close to the first of the doors. She had a hawk-like appearance and gave off a distinct 'do not mess with me' vibe that Logan approved of.

The younger nurse gestured to Logan with both hands, as if presenting a gameshow prize. "This man. He looks for you."

"Does he now? And who might—"

Logan held up his warrant card. "You the charge nurse?"

She took the card from him and scrutinised it. Only once she was happy with it, did she reply.

"Yes," she said, handing the card back. She pumped a couple of squirts of disinfectant gel onto her hands and rubbed it in. "Esha, you can go for your break now. Thank you."

Esha practically bowed as she backed out of the corridor.

"What can I do for you?" the charge nurse asked.

"Kel Conlyn."

"What about him?"

"You know him, then?"

The nurse nodded. "I do. Why?"

"Where is he? Is he on this ward?"

"No," the nurse said. "But he was. Why?"

"Was?" Logan asked. "What, is he finished?"

"He's gone home, yes," the nurse confirmed. "Again, why?"

"Shite. When?" Logan demanded. "When did he leave?"

His phone rang before the nurse could answer. Snatching it from his pocket, he caught a glimpse of Caitlyn's name on-screen, then tapped the icon to answer it.

"You're not supposed to use those in here," the nurse scolded, but Logan had his back to her now, and ignored the comment completely.

"Caitlyn. What have we got?"

"We've found Conlyn, sir," Caitlyn replied. There was something about the way she said it that made Logan pause. "He's in A&E."

Logan glanced back over his shoulder at the charge nurse. "I've just been told he'd gone home."

"He had, sir. I don't mean he's on shift," Caitlyn said. "I mean he's been admitted. He's been attacked."

"Conlyn has?"

"Not just him, sir," Caitlyn said. "There was a woman with him."

Logan's breath caught somewhere in his throat. He felt his lungs burn almost at once. "And?"

"She's dead, sir," Caitlyn replied. "It's happened again."

KEL CONLYN HAD BEEN PATCHED up by the time Logan was allowed to see him. He'd taken a knife to the right shoulder, and his forearms were crisscrossed with defensive wounds. A passer-by had found him after he'd crawled out of Walker Park and onto the pavement, bleeding and semi-conscious.

Uniform had found Laura Elder twenty minutes later, hidden beneath a crop of trees in the park. Dead. Mutilated.

Fake.

Kel was sitting propped upright in bed when Logan and DC Neish entered, his gaze fixed on the window of the private room he'd been given. He had a mobile phone in one hand, but clutched it limply, like he wasn't really aware it was there.

There was a vase on the table by the bed, a bunch of tired-looking flowers drooping over the sides. They complemented Conlyn's expression perfectly.

It was only when the door closed with a *thunk* that he blinked away a blurring of tears, ran the back of a bandaged arm across his cheek, then summoned the energy to sit up straighter.

"Hello. God. Hi," he said. His voice was scarcely a whisper, lost amongst the *bleeping* and *pinging* and all the other noises of the hospital. "How is Laura? They won't tell me. Is she...?"

Logan gave a single nod. "She is. I'm sorry."

Kel's face crumpled. He sobbed for a full minute—big, silent heaves that racked his body and made Tyler visibly awkward. The DC looked around the room, then consulted the chart at the end of the bed in an effort to hide his embarrassment.

Logan, meanwhile, didn't flinch. He stood by the bed, watching Kel cry, his eye locked on the man like a targeting missile.

"Sorry. Sorry, I'm sorry," Kel said, hastily wiping his eyes again. He winced at the pain the movement brought, and Logan's gaze went to the bandage on the man's bare shoulder.

"It's fine, Mr Conlyn. We understand," Logan said. He indicated the bandage. "Is it bad?"

"Hmm? Oh, yeah. Bad enough, I think. Didn't hit anything major, though, thankfully."

"Really? That's lucky," Logan said. "Given how accurate the attacker has been thus far."

Kel smiled weakly. "Yes. Yes, I suppose so." His expression soured. "I'll be honest, though, none of it feels very lucky right now."

He bit his bottom lip so hard the skin around it turned white, then red. "Oh, God. Laura. I was supposed to be looking after her. I told her I'd get her home safe."

Tyler tried to head off another outburst of tears. "It's not your fault. There's nothing anyone could have done."

Kel sniffed, met Tyler's gaze, then managed another small smile. "Thank you. I'm not sure it's true, but... thanks."

He held a hand out. Tyler side-eyed Logan for a moment, then reached out with his own hand. Kel took it, squeezed it, then let it go again. "That means a lot," he said. "Really."

"Uh, aye. No bother," Tyler said, stepping back and vowing to keep his mouth shut from now on.

"We hate to do this so soon after what you've just been through, Mr Conlyn, but we need to ask you a few questions about the attack. Is that OK?"

Kel shuffled himself more upright in the bed, then nodded. "Of course. Anything. I want this fucker caught just as much as you do. What do you need to know?"

Logan motioned for Tyler to take a seat in the visitor chair set up by the bed. The DC took his phone from his pocket and held it up to Conlyn. "Mind if I record this?"

"Please. Anything. Whatever helps."

Tyler sat, activated the voice recorder app on his phone, then set it on the trolley table by the bed with the microphone pointed in the patient's direction.

"Talk us through what happened, Mr Conlyn," Logan intoned.

"Right. Well, he came out of nowhere, really—"

"From the start, if you don't mind," Logan interjected. "What time did you leave the hospital?"

Kel's eyelids fluttered for a moment like his brain was recalibrating, then he replied.

"Just after ten. We had both been on a bit later, and I know she doesn't live too far away—just past the park where we... Where it happened. I thought I'd offer to walk her," Kel said. "You know, after our conversation?"

"Aye. Good. So, you left the hospital together just after ten o'clock tonight. Then what?"

"We just, I don't know, walked and chatted, really," Kel said. "We passed The Fluke. You know, the pub along the road?"

Logan glanced at Tyler, and got a nod in return.

"It's pretty well-known locally," Kel said, picking up on the non-verbal communication. "There were a few people standing outside having a fag. They'll have seen us, if you want to check."

"I'm sure that won't be necessary," Logan said. "Go on."

Kel took a breath, as if bracing himself for an uphill struggle. "We kept walking. She was talking about the HR woman. What was her name?"

"Clarissa."

"Yes. Shit. Of course it was. Clarissa. She was talking about Clarissa— she'd watched some of the video that's doing the rounds, apparently. Seemed pretty cut-up about it."

"About the death or watching the video?" Logan asked.

This caught Kel off guard. He gave it due consideration before replying. "Both, I suppose. I think she felt guilty about watching it. You know, a bit ashamed? I think it was, like, a confession. Like she wanted to tell someone she'd done it, but that she regretted it."

"Understandable," Logan said. "What then?"

"Then..." Kel's brow furrowed, recalling the details. "I heard someone. Or... I don't know. I thought I heard someone, anyway. On the golf course over on our left."

He looked to DC Neish. "It's split across both sides of the road."

"I know it, aye," Tyler replied, earning himself a grateful smile from the man in the bed.

"I was sure I heard something in the dark bit over on the left."

"Something like what?" Logan pressed.

Kel's forehead was ridged with lines now, like he was wrestling against the memory, trying to pin it in place. "Movement, I think. Or... I don't know. Maybe I didn't even hear it. Maybe I just *sensed* it. I just know I had this strong feeling that someone was there. Watching us. And that we had to get the fuck out of there."

His eyes went to the polystyrene ceiling tiles as he fought to hold himself together.

"So, we did," he said, his voice barely a squeak through his narrowing throat. "We crossed the road and decided to cut across the park."

"Why the park?" Tyler asked.

"It's quicker."

"No lights, though," Tyler pointed out. "Bit risky."

The hurt registered on Kel's face like he'd been physically wounded. "Obviously, I know that now," he said, his voice going up a couple of octaves. "But we thought he was behind us somewhere. We thought it would just get us back to..."

He shook his head. Closed his eyes.

"No."

Logan glanced from Kel to Tyler and back again. "No?"

"Not 'we.' We didn't decide to go across the park," Kel admitted. He rolled his tongue around in his mouth until he could force the next two words out. "I did."

He cleared his throat. Once. Twice. His fingers flexed in and out. It looked like he was battling to keep control of his body. Battling to keep talking. Battling to keep himself from curling up into a ball and sobbing until there was nothing of him left.

"The shortcut was my idea. It was all mine," he said. His voice had become a dull monotone, like maybe if he didn't think too much about their meaning, he'd be able to say them. "It's my fault this happened. It's my fault Laura's dead."

Tyler looked up at Logan, waiting for the DCI to impart some words of comfort. When none came, he realised it was being left to him.

"You can't blame yourself, Mr Conlyn," Tyler told him. "You couldn't possibly have known."

"Thank you," Kel said, managing another of those not-quite-smiles. He placed a hand on Tyler's arm. "And call me Kel."

"Uh, OK. Cool," said Tyler. "Will do."

Logan took the reins again, and Kel removed his hand from DC Neish's arm.

"Now, I need you to think very carefully about the order of events that followed," the DCI said.

Kel immediately shook his head. "No."

Logan's eyebrows knotted so tightly together they practically became singular. "No?"

"I don't need to think carefully," Kel continued.

His gaze went to the wall directly across from his bed, eyes darting left and right like a kid at the cinema. One hand—the one that hadn't been on Tyler's arm—twisted the edge of his blanket into knots.

"I can still see it," he whispered. "I can still see it all. I can still see *him*. That mask."

He looked up at Logan, eyes brimming with tears.

"I can still see what he did."

CHAPTER THIRTY-EIGHT

BEN FORDE SIDLED UP TO LOGAN AT THE CORDON TAPE AND PRESSED A steaming hot paper cup into his hand. The DCI nodded his appreciation, then clutched the cup to his stomach, absorbing some of its heat.

"Christ, Jack, when did you last get some sleep?" Ben asked, looking his old friend up and down. He had an umbrella up to protect himself from the rain. The droplets rattled against it like a frenzied percussionist. "You look awful."

"No' that long ago," Logan said. "This morning."

Ben did a double-take. "Seriously?"

"Aye. Ye cheeky bastard. This is me on a good day, these days."

"The years have not been kind," Ben remarked.

"No," Logan agreed. "No, they have not."

They stood in silence, the rain hammering away at the umbrella, and *plinking* into Logan's cup. Had it been anyone else, Ben would have offered to squidge up a bit and share the cover, but he knew the DCI's thoughts on them. He'd rather succumb to pneumonia than be seen beneath an umbrella.

Besides, the height difference would be a nightmare. Ben would be the one to end up soaking and, quite frankly, it was his bloody brolly.

The park had so many tents in it that it had started to resemble a festival campsite. There was one out on the street, too, and the cordon had been extended right across the road, meaning traffic was having to be diverted at both ends.

Palmer's Scene of Crime team were tiptoeing around in their gradually disintegrating paper suits. Palmer himself wasn't on duty tonight, which was some small mercy. He'd invoked the European Working Hours Directive, claiming he'd done too many hours in too short a period of time, and was refusing to come back out until the following morning.

Logan didn't know whether to condemn the bastard or applaud him. If you let it, the job would swallow up your whole life. He knew that better than most.

But a girl was dead. A killer was still out there. And rest was a luxury Logan couldn't afford.

"You spoke to the fella who was with her," Ben said. It wasn't a question, exactly, more of a prompt.

Logan nodded, still watching the paper suits do their stuff. "I did. Kel Conlyn."

Ben rifled through the internal filing system in his head.

"He was the last one to see Esme Miller alive, wasn't he?"

"He was," Logan confirmed. "He was also the only one out of over two-thousand members of staff not to get a mention in Clarissa McDade's email inbox."

Ben took a moment to think this through, but didn't get very far. "Meaning?"

"Meaning, it's possible he deleted any reference of himself."

"Take a while that, wouldn't it?" Ben asked.

"No. Quicker that way than just removing anything incriminating. Search the name in the inbox, select all results, delete."

The rain pattered on Ben's brolly. Somewhere along the street, a Uniform turned away a car that had been approaching the cordon.

"Sounds like he was lucky he got stabbed," Ben said. "Or we'd have a new suspect."

"Very fortuitous, aye," Logan agreed.

"You seen the wounds?"

"Not up close, no. Stab injury to the right shoulder that missed anything vital. Slash marks on his forearms that suggest defensive wounds. I'm having Caitlyn go over it with the doctor who treated him at the moment. Tyler's staying to keep an eye on him. I think Conlyn has taken a bit of a shine to him."

"Seriously? Wow. Sounds like a wrong 'un, alright, if he's taken a liking to Tyler," Ben remarked. "We should probably haul him in now."

"Not quite yet," Logan remarked. He tore his eyes away from the SOC team, turned to Ben, and almost had an eye out on one of the brolly's spikes. "Jesus, careful with that bloody thing."

"It's no' my fault. I haven't moved."

Logan's expression said he was still very much holding the DI responsible. He made a gruff huffing sound, then glanced at his watch and winced. Later than he'd thought.

"I'm going to go check around at Conlyn's flat. Who's in the office?"

"Not sure. Hamza's away to get some sleep. There'll be CID around, though, why?"

"Find out who the landlord is. Get me a phone number. If they're local, get them to meet me there."

"Could take a while," Ben said. "If it's rented through a letting agency, it's going to be shut."

"Better get on it, then."

Logan set off walking into the rain, then stopped after a few paces. He closed his eyes and raised his head, the rain like a baptism on his face.

"In fact, on second thought, don't bother with that," Logan told him.

"Don't bother with the landlord?"

"No," Logan said. He looked back at Ben. A drop of rain hung suspended from the end of his nose for a moment, then *plinked* into a puddle at his feet. "I've got a better idea."

Logan waited until he was back at his car before taking out his phone. He tapped the Contacts app, scrolled down a few names, then hit dial. He was careful not to turn the car's engine on, in case the phone's audio suddenly came blaring out via the Bluetooth connection, broadcasting the conversation to everyone within earshot.

The phone was answered after a few rings. The voice on the other end sounded happy to hear from him. It wasn't, he knew, but it sounded it.

"Bosco," Logan said, cutting off the enthusiastic greeting. "How'd you like to get yourself in my good books?"

LOGAN FLASHED his warrant card as he approached the open front door of Kel Conlyn's flat, and a couple of neighbours stepped aside to let him through.

"That was quick," one of them—a woman in her forties—remarked. "We only called you a few minutes ago."

"I was in the area," Logan told her. He motioned to the door. "What happened?"

"Some big fella kicked it in. Just kicked it right in," the woman said. She nudged a tall, yet downtrodden-looking man beside her in the ribs with her elbow, bringing him to life.

"Just kicked it right in," the man agreed.

"We saw it, didn't we? Alan?"

"Yes," the tall man confirmed. "We saw it."

Alan's wife pointed to the block of flats directly across from Conlyn's. "We're over there. We heard a car screeching up, music blaring. I looked out, didn't I, Alan?"

"She did. She looked out," Alan said. "She just got up and looked right out."

"And there was this fella. Big. All in black. He had a balaclava on." She turned to her husband. "I'm saying, he had a balaclava on. Didn't he?"

"He did. Covering his face."

"A balaclava," the wife said. She gave Logan a meaningful nod, like he was supposed to be writing this down.

"Did he go inside?" Logan pressed.

"No! That's the funny thing. That's what I was just saying, wasn't I, Alan?"

"She was. She was just saying."

"He just kicked the door in, then ran off. Very strange behaviour, if you ask me. Very strange."

The woman shrugged and shook her head. "Anyway, we thought we should call you lot, since it doesn't seem like anyone's home. We didn't know what else to do. Did we?"

"We didn't know what else to do," Alan agreed.

"You did the right thing," Logan told them, which made them both puff up with pride. "What do you know about the person living here?"

The woman screwed her nose up, like she wasn't a fan. "Eh. Not much. Keeps himself to himself, although he can be a bit... You know?"

Logan raised his eyebrows to indicate that no, he didn't know.

"*Flamboyant*," she said, whispering it like it was some sort of slur she didn't want anyone to overhear her uttering. "I mean, not that I've anything against that sort of thing, do I, Alan?"

"She doesn't have anything against that sort of thing," Alan said, as if operating on some sort of auto-pilot.

"Each to their own, I say. None of my business. It's just, some of them can be a bit... full-on. You know? Although, I must say, we haven't really spoken much to him since he moved in last year. Like I say, keeps himself to himself mostly."

Logan nodded. "Right, well I should—Wait. Last year?"

"Yes. He moved in... Ooh, God. When?"

"Now you're asking," said Alan, scratching his head. "September, maybe?"

"Not September. We were away in September," his wife reminded him. Quite aggressively, Logan thought. "How could it have been September if we weren't here?"

"Sorry, yes. I mean, no. Sorry," Alan gushed. "It couldn't have been September, you're right. She's right."

"It was August. I remember because the kids on the other side had just gone back to school."

A year. Fourteen months.

He'd told them he'd only been in a few weeks. He'd used that to explain his lack of furniture.

"I'd better have a look," Logan said. He could hear sirens wailing in the distance now, and ushered the couple back towards their own front door. "Thanks for your help. If we need anything more, I'll let you know."

He didn't wait for them to reply. Instead, he turned to the door, already pulling on a pair of thin blue gloves.

You could say what you liked about Bosco Maximuke—and Logan often did—but the man was significantly quicker than a search warrant. Sure, he'd look for the favour to be returned at some point down the line, but Logan could deal with that then. Tonight, he'd needed a way into that flat, and Bosco—or, more accurately, one of his lapdogs—had provided it.

Creaking the door the rest of the way open, Logan stepped over the threshold and into the narrow hallway. The starkness of the place struck him, just as it had done on his first visit there. The bare walls. The exposed lightbulbs. The lack of carpets, furniture, and anything else that might make the place feel even remotely like a home.

He'd seen the hallway and living room last time, so he ventured into the other rooms. He found the kitchen first. It was similarly bare, although there was a fairly bog-standard selection of units and wall cabinets, and some dilapidated appliances that were probably included in the rent.

Logan checked the fridge and freezer. Both were empty, the power to them switched off. Most of the cupboards were empty too, although one turned up thirty or more tin cans, the labels all missing so it was impossible to identify the contents.

"The hell is all this?" Logan muttered, carefully lifting a can and turning it over in his gloved hands. The use-by date had passed recently, but there was nothing else remarkable about the tin, so he set it back down and checked the drawers.

The topmost drawer contained a selection of weathered cutlery, the metal dull, the plastic handles cracked and faded. A scattering of utensils lay in the next one down, all with the same matching plastic as the cutlery, although less worn-looking, on account of having been used less.

The drawer below that was empty, aside from four placemats showing various Highland scenes, and a pack of three dishcloths still threaded through the cardboard they'd come packaged in.

The next door along in the corridor was a bathroom. It felt less uninhabited than the other rooms Logan had seen, thanks to a single towel and a toothbrush, but there was still something cold and impersonal about it. Nobody loved this room. They used it, perhaps, but only because they had to.

There was one door left. From outside, Logan could hear the howling of the sirens getting closer. One car, he thought, although possibly two. He could also hear the murmuring of the couple who'd made the call. With a bit of luck, they'd explain to the Uniforms who he was, and that he'd already gone inside, which should hopefully deter any of them from trying to arrest him on suspicion of burglary.

The bedroom door didn't budge when Logan turned the handle. Bending, he spotted a keyhole, and tried to look through it. Either the room beyond was in absolute darkness, or there was a covering on the other side of the lock. Either way, he could see precisely hee-haw.

"Bugger it," he muttered. Coughing to cover the noise, he put a shoulder to the door. The wood was thin and weak, and the door flew open without any resistance.

A single table stood in the middle of the bedroom, and there was a blow-up mattress in the corner. It sagged pitifully, most of the air in it clearly having moved on elsewhere.

It was the table that held Logan's attention, though. Or, more precisely, the laptop computer sitting on top of it. The lid was open, the screen lit-up.

It showed the desktop, complete with a small selection of icons, and a wallpaper showing Keanu Reeves in a long black coat.

As Logan stepped into the room, two red lights started flickering on either side of the laptop's camera, then went solid. The screen flashed white, and Keanu was briefly replaced by a picture of Logan standing in the doorway.

Then, the display went black. Something inside the computer emitted a *paff* and a single flame sputtered up from the keyboard. It caught hold immediately, devouring the keys and licking up the screen before Logan could tear off his coat and throw it over the top. Some sort of accelerant. Had to be.

He slapped down on the coat, smothering and beating out the flames, but he knew it was already too late. Whatever forensic material the machine might have offered up was gone. Whatever was on the hard drive would be impossible to recover. Whatever evidence it could have provided was lost.

The fire caught hold inside the coat, quickly smouldering a hole the size of a ten pence piece through the outer material. The sudden inrush of air fuelled the flames below, forcing Logan to drop the coat as the fire tore through it.

Whatever accelerant had been used was on the table, too. Logan saw the fire go rushing down all four legs at once. The floor beneath his coat was already ablaze, and when the flames racing down the table legs met the bare wooden floorboards, they immediately ignited.

A fog of black smoke rose up from the flames, rapidly filling the top half of the room. Coughing, Logan clamped a hand over his mouth and stumbled out into the hallway, the billowing smoke chasing him through the door.

At the flat's entrance, he met two female uniformed constables coming the other way.

"Stay where you are," one of them barked, but he hurried towards them, ushering them both out.

"DCI Jack Logan, Major Investigations. Outside, now," he instructed.

Their eyes went to the cloud of black behind him, and the flames already licking floorboards of the hall. The fire seemed to leap across the threshold, whatever accelerant that was soaked into the floor of the bedroom clearly having been liberally applied in the hallway, too.

Logan emerged into the cool night air. For once, he'd have been grateful for a downpour to wash away the smoke residue and rinse his stinging eyes, but the rain had stopped on the way over, and pinpricks of light winked down on him from on high.

"Do you, eh... Do you have any ID?" asked one of the constables. The other had retreated a few steps and was talking urgently into the radio on her shoulder, calling in the fire.

"Aye," Logan said, bending double and hacking up a lungful of soot. He jabbed a thumb back over his shoulder. "It's in my coat. By all means, help yourself."

"God, Alan, look. It's on fire!"

"It is, and all. It's on fire," Alan confirmed.

Logan looked up at the two neighbours. They stood in the open doorway of their flat, peering across at the flames raging inside Conlyn's hallway.

"Is anyone upstairs?" Logan asked them, pointing to the flat above Conlyn's. The place was in darkness, but the fire was licking its way up the walls now, and anyone up there only had a few minutes to get out. "Is it currently occupied?"

"No. It's been empty for about... what, Alan? About a month?"

"About a month, I'd say, yes," Alan confirmed.

"About a month," his wife reiterated. "I was just saying that the other day, wasn't I? It's been empty a while. I was just saying that."

"You were."

"About a month."

Mercifully, Logan missed most of the exchange due to the fact he was hacking up a lung. The smoke had affected him quickly. It was lucky he'd left the front door open, or he may not have made it out at all.

"You alright, sir?" asked the closest constable, having obviously decided to take him at his word. "Maybe we should get you to the hospital."

Logan coughed again, then wiped his mouth on the sleeve of his shirt.
Shite. The hospital.

"Keys," he said, holding out a hand.

The uniformed officer briefly regarded the hand, then frowned. "Sir?"

"Keys. Mine are in my coat."

She backed away a step, glancing at her colleague for support. She was still on the call though, and only vaguely paying attention.

"I'm not sure that's... I mean, I don't know if..."

"Fine. It'll be quicker if you drive, anyway," he said, marching past her. He pointed to the other officer. "You, wait here, get everyone to a safe distance, and keep them away until the cavalry arrives. No one goes near."

"Uh..." she replied, but Logan was already past her, half-marching, half-jogging in the direction of the police car. Its lights were flashing on top, licking the front of the surrounding buildings in bright blue.

The first officer didn't seem to be moving. He beckoned to her as he pulled open the front passenger door of the patrol car. "Well, come on then, we haven't got all bloody night!"

A look passed between both officers, then a shrug. The one with the keys hurried over to the car, shot a final look at her partner, then slid into the driver's seat beside Logan.

"Where to, sir?" she asked, firing up the engine.

"Raigmore Hospital," Logan said. He clipped on his seatbelt and rapped his knuckles on the dash. "Full blues and twos."

"Right, sir," the officer replied.

And then, with lights flashing and sirens screaming, the car screeched away from the kerb, leaving a growing column of fire behind them.

CHAPTER THIRTY-NINE

DC NEISH STAGGERED OUT INTO THE HOSPITAL CORRIDOR TO FIND Logan hurtling towards him. Blood oozed down the side of Tyler's face, filling his ear and staining his shirt. He clutched a wound somewhere above his hairline and leaned on the wall to stop himself dropping to his knees.

"Shite. Tyler, what happened?" Logan asked, skidding to a stop beside the DC. He threw open the door to the room that had previously contained Kel Conlyn, and was dismayed to discover that it no longer did. "Bollocks!" he ejected. "Where did he go?"

"Dunno, boss," Tyler admitted. He winced, like speaking brought a new wave of pain. "Some alarm went off on his phone. He checked it, then he just grabbed the vase and fucking brained me with it."

His eyes were swimming as he struggled to stay conscious. "Think he knocked me out."

"The camera. He must've seen me," Logan realised, looking left and right along the corridor. A nurse appeared at the far end, and almost jumped out of her skin when Logan bellowed at her. "You. This man needs help. Look after him."

"Is it him, boss?" Tyler asked. "Is it Conlyn?"

"Certainly looks like it, son," Logan said. He waited until the nurse was almost upon them, then gave the DC a pat on the shoulder. "But don't you worry about it right now. Get yourself taken care of."

"What on Earth happened?" the nurse asked, her voice shrill when she spotted the blood trickling from Tyler's head. "What's going on?"

"He'll explain," Logan told her. "Did you see anyone running past here? Kel Conlyn. Young guy. Twenties. Skinny. He's injured."

Logan was off and running as soon as the nurse had started to shake her head. He doubled-back almost immediately, and held a hand out to Tyler. "Phone."

Tyler screwed up one eye, like he was having to concentrate to figure out what was being asked of him. "Boss?"

"Give me your phone. Mine went on fire."

"Fire?"

"Later. Phone."

"Two-seven-two-one," Tyler said, handing it over. "That's the pin."

Logan took the phone, punched in the code, then set off again, already swiping through the contacts list.

He tapped a name, and was barrelling onto a ward when the call was answered.

"Tyler. To what do I owe the displeasure?" asked DI Forde.

"Ben. It's me. Long story, no time," Logan said. He threw open the door to one of the ward rooms. Five elderly women glowered at him from beds, while a sixth snored loudly in the corner.

After a quick check behind the door, he continued the call. "We need to put the hospital on lockdown. Nobody in or out."

"What? Why?" Ben asked.

Logan closed the door and hurried to the next one along. A storage cupboard this time. Empty, besides the stacks of toilet rolls, paper towels, and disinfectant gel.

"It's Conlyn. He's behind it, and he's done a runner."

"Shite. I thought Tyler was keeping an eye on him."

"He got the jump on him. Smashed a vase across the side of his head."

"Jesus, is—"

"He'll need stitches, but he'll be fine," Logan said. "Now stop talking to me and start talking to whoever can get this place locked down."

He hung up before the DI could reply to him, spotted a young woman with a stethoscope coming out of an office, and went striding over to her.

"Kel Conlyn. He's a porter, or an orderly, or whatever they're called," he barked.

Taken aback, the doctor could only stare.

"I'm polis. DCI Logan," he said, dropping his voice a few decibels. "A patient's done a runner. He's a suspect. We need to find him now."

"I thought... A patient? Who's the orderly, then?"

"Him. They're the same. The orderly is the... Forget it. I need to—"

An alarm blared. High-pitched. Urgent. Logan turned, looking back the way he came, where the alarm seemed to be emanating from.

"Fire alarm," the doctor said. "Shit."

Logan clenched his fists. "No, no, no. *Bastard.* They can't evacuate. It's him, he's set off the bloody alarm."

"They won't evacuate if there isn't a fire," the doctor assured him. "And even then, they'll start with the section the alarm was raised."

Logan spun to face her. "Is there a way to see where it was set off?"

"Sure. Over here," the doctor said, leading him to a panel on the wall. A red light winked at him, flashing an illuminated code.

"Where is that?" Logan demanded.

"That's... I think that's... Hang on."

She consulted a laminated list on the wall beside the panel. Behind them, half a dozen nurses went bustling into the various rooms to keep the patients calm.

"Outpatients," the doctor announced.

"Where is that?"

"That way, turn right, left, then straight on," the doctor told him, her hand gestures corresponding with the instructions.

Logan had started running at 'that way' mapping out the rest of the route as the doctor shouted her instructions after him. The phone rang as he skidded around the final bend and powered along the wide corridor that led to the Outpatients department.

At this time of night, the place was in half-darkness, the clinics all closed, the staff all gone home.

The doubts crept in as Logan huffed and wheezed the final few dozen yards along the corridor. The screaming of the alarm was ear-shattering here, each squeal stabbing like an icepick into his skull.

Why set off the alarm here? Using an evacuation as cover to escape would only work if there were people to evacuate. How could you use a crowd for cover if there was no crowd to get lost in?

Logan's footsteps echoed off into the half-darkness ahead as he clattered to a stop. He turned back, chest heaving, and spat out a series of curses that were all drowned out by the sound of the alarm.

Tyler's phone buzzed in his pocket. Jamming a finger in his ear, he tapped 'answer' and pressed the phone hard against the other ear.

"Ben. Tell me you got him."

DI Forde's reply was too faint to make out.

"What? Speak up!"

"I said, 'Christ, that's loud,'" Ben shouted. "We're getting the doors locked now. Place should be secure in the next five minutes."

Logan groaned. "Forget it."

"What? I can't hear you."

"I said, 'Forget it.' It's too late," Logan said, looking back along the corridor in the direction he'd come from. "He's already gone."

THE COOL AIR *hits him as he steps outside, chilling his lungs and nipping at his injuries. They were a mistake, he realises now. A silly idea. Pointless.*

Like everything.

They were bound to figure it out eventually, but he thought he'd have more time. They'd hunt him down now. They still believed in all their little rules. They still believed it mattered. That anything mattered.

He had failed to make them see. To make them understand the utter pointlessness of it all.

It would be over soon. They'd find him. They'd stop him.

But not now.

Not yet.

Not quite.

There was still time for one more. He could still give them one final demonstration.

And this would be one they'd never forget.

CHAPTER FORTY

LOGAN STOOD IN FRONT OF THE BIG BOARD, ADDRESSING HIS TEAM, half of CID, and a dozen uniformed officers. He slapped a photograph with the back of his hand, more forcefully than was strictly necessary.

"Kel Conlyn. Twenty-two. Wanted in connection with the recent string of murders that I know we're all only too aware of. Some of you will have seen the video he made, and heard his... fucking... I don't know. Manifesto. He thinks nothing he's doing really matters. He thinks we don't exist. Well, we, ladies and gentlemen, are going to prove him very wrong on that."

Logan looked across the faces of the audience. They were crammed into the Incident Room, sitting on chairs and desks, standing where they had to. Most of them had been dragged out of their beds and brought in. Many of them had just gone off shift a couple of hours before.

Nobody had complained. Or, if they had, they'd at least had the sense not to do it within Logan's earshot.

Hamza, Ben, and Caitlyn were sitting right in the front row, DC Khaled looking marginally more refreshed than the other two. Tyler had called from the hospital to say he'd be in after they'd finished stitching his head wounds, but Logan had told him to go home and get some rest.

"No offence, boss, but that's shite," Tyler had said. "I'm the one who let him get away. I should be in there."

Logan had ordered him to go home, and not to show face until next morning. At which point, with a bit of luck, Conlyn would already be in custody. Tyler had started to grumble about it, but Logan had shouted him down and ended the call. He'd almost have felt bad about it, if he hadn't been doing it for the boy's own good.

"This man has raped, and he has murdered, and he will do it again unless we catch him," Logan continued. He let that sink in for a moment, eyes narrowed as he observed the reactions of the audience. "And so, we are going to catch him quickly and efficiently before anyone else can get hurt. We're going to find him tonight. We're going to bring him in, and we're going to put him away for the rest of his miserable life.

"He's exposed, which makes him more dangerous than ever," Logan continued. "So, we need boots on streets. We need every shed, garage, and outhouse checked. We need people going door-to-door, even if that means waking up the whole bloody city."

A hand went up a couple of rows back. One of the guys from CID, whose name Logan hadn't yet learned. He asked his question without being prompted.

"What have we got on him? Family, past addresses, friends?"

"Not a lot," said Caitlyn, picking up on the nod from Logan. "We know —at least, we *believe*—he was kicked out by his parents on account of his sexuality, but we don't know where or when that was. We're still digging, but he's done a good job of covering his tracks. It looks like he's been planning this for a while. It's looking like he created the Kel Conlyn identity for himself."

She looked down at the pad she and Hamza had been scribbling notes on for the past hour. "There was a Kelvin Conlyn who shares the same date of birth, but he died a few months later. We think he assumed that identity using copies of the birth certificate."

"So, he could be anyone? From anywhere?" asked the CID officer.

"Basically, aye," Logan confirmed. "Accent's reasonably local, though. He could be putting it on, but my instinct is not. If we get his picture out there, we might get a match."

He looked to Hamza, a questioning eyebrow raised.

"It's gone out on social media, sir," DC Khaled said. "BBC and STV are going to include it in their bulletins, but we won't get much back from those until tomorrow." He stifled a yawn. Or tried to, at least. "Middle of the night. Not exactly big audiences."

"Right. I know we're all tired. We'd all like to be in our beds, not getting ready to go out in the cold and the rain," Logan said, addressing the crowd at large. "But we all signed up to the same job, and by Christ we're going to make sure we do it."

Another hand went up. A man in uniform, this time. "You said his family kicked him out because of his sexuality."

"We believe so, aye."

"So..." The officer looked around at the others. "He's gay? But he raped those women, didn't he?"

Logan managed to keep his anger in check. "Rape's rarely about sexual desire. It's about power. You should know that, that's hardly new information. He wanted to degrade those women and make them feel worthless. That's why he did it, no' because he fucking fancied them."

He let a couple of moments slide past while he waited to see if the officer was going to argue. The way the poor guy shrank down into his seat suggested he was not.

Logan gestured in Ben's direction. "DI Forde is going to be Office Manager on this. You'll report to your own immediate supervisor, who will report in turn to him.

"You do what DI Forde tells you, when he tells you. If he says 'jump,' you don't waste his time asking how high, you just do as you're told and hope it was high enough. Normally, I'm all in favour of questioning authority, but not now. Not tonight. No second-guessing him, no questioning his orders. DI Forde is the voice of God, and anyone who fails to follow his orders will find themselves struck down pretty bloody smartish. Is that clear?"

There was a general murmuring of agreement. It sounded reasonably positive, Logan thought. Most of them had worked with Ben before, or at least seen him in action. He was a *kent face* in a way that Logan wasn't. Everyone liked Ben Forde, and they'd do their best to keep him happy.

"What about you?" asked another of the CID boys. He was an older fella, sluggish-looking from too many takeaways and nights down the pub. "If Ben's running the show, what are you doing?"

"I'll be out on the streets with you lot," Logan said. "The more of us out there, the better chance we have of finding him quickly."

A hand went up. One of the Uniforms up near the back. Logan recognised her as the one who'd given him the lift from Conlyn's flat to the hospital.

"Yes, uh...?"

"Suzy, sir. Suzy Lewis," she said. "I was just wondering... What if we don't? Catch him quickly, I mean? What if he skips town?"

A hush fell, as everyone waited for the reply. Clearly, she hadn't been the only one thinking it.

"I don't care if he skips town," Logan told her. "I don't care if he skips the bloody country. I will hunt the bastard to the ends of the Earth if I have to."

He reached for the coat Hoon had loaned him. They were both similar sizes and shapes, although the coat was a little neat across Logan's shoulders, and the puce green was not a colour he'd have chosen—not even back in his alcoholic days.

"So, let's try and save me some bus fare, and let's catch him tonight, alright?" He pulled the coat on. "Any more questions?"

Everyone glanced around at everyone else. No more hands went up.

"Good, then let's get out there," he said. "And do our jobs."

LOGAN WAS ALMOST at the front door of the station when he met DC Neish coming the other way. His head was wrapped in a pristine white bandage, although there were a couple of darker dots on the gauze about his ear where blood was starting to seep through.

The DCI didn't know whether to chin the bugger for disobeying a direct order or shake him by the hand for the very same reason. Instead, he settled for something that lay somewhere between the two.

"Christ, if it's no' Rab C Nesbitt," he said, eyes flitting to the bandage. "What are you doing here, Detective Constable? I told you to go home."

"Aye, boss."

They both stood aside, letting nine or ten Uniforms pass them, followed by a couple of officers from CID.

"And yet, here you are," Logan continued, once the stampede had passed by.

"Sorry, boss," Tyler said, shifting uncomfortably. "It just didn't feel right, me being home. I should be here. I should be helping to catch the bastard."

There would be no talking him out of it, Logan could see that. He smiled inwardly but didn't let it show on the outside. The boy was full of surprises.

"Aye, well, you can help DI Forde coordinate things from here," Logan told him. Tyler started to protest, but the DCI cut him off. "Take it or leave it, son. You're injured. I'm not having you out traipsing the streets."

Tyler looked back over his shoulder at the station door, then sighed. "Right, boss. Fair enough. There's something I want to check up on, anyway. I think he might be from Nairn. Originally, I mean."

"What makes you say that?"

"Just... when we were talking, he was asking me about the job, and I mentioned being stationed in Nairn back when I was in uniform. He seemed to know the place pretty well. I'm sure there's a connection."

"It's a start. Go check it out," Logan told him.

"Right, boss."

Tyler's gaze followed the DCI as he marched on towards the exit. "Oh, and boss?"

Logan slowed and looked back, but didn't quite stop.

"If you see him, fucking lamp him one from me, will you?"

He got a half-smile and a nod in reply.

"I'll see what I can do," Logan promised.

And with that, he was gone.

CHAPTER FORTY-ONE

THE NIGHT CRAWLED PAST, THE DARKNESS OOZING LIKE TREACLE towards a dawn that seemed reluctant to show its face.

Doors were knocked, lock-ups searched, gardens examined. Dogs were brought in, and while a couple of them seemed to get Conlyn's scent around one of the side doors of Raigmore, they lost it again by the time they reached the main road.

CCTV from the hospital had picked him up as he was leaving, and confirmed the direction the dogs' noses had led them, but cameras were few and far between beyond the boundaries, and there was nothing to suggest which way he'd gone after leaving the grounds.

The station had phoned around every taxi company in town, but nobody had picked him up. He had abandoned his phone and other belongings when he'd legged it from the hospital, which meant there was no phone on him to trace and no bank cards he might be tempted to use. For all intents and purposes, he had vanished into thin air.

"Maybe the bastard doesn't exist, after all," Logan said, his fingers flexing on the steering wheel of the Volvo. He'd been given the spare key on the strict understanding that it was the only one they had and that, if he lost it, the cost of a replacement was coming out of his wages.

They'd given him a replacement phone, too. He'd spent ten minutes trying to get the bloody thing to connect to the car's Bluetooth, before giving up.

Ben's voice came from the phone's internal speakerphone. It echoed tinnily around the vehicle's insides. "If only. It'd have saved us a lot of bloody hassle, wouldn't it?"

Logan grunted in response. He was parked along the road from Conlyn's flat. It, and the flat above, were now nothing more than charred frames and a sagging roof. Even now, wisps of smoke drifted lazily into the air, dancing and swirling against the backdrop of the rising sun.

"You spoke to the neighbours there?"

"Aye. There's been no sign of him," Logan answered. "I didn't think for a minute that he'd come back here. And if he did, he'd have seen the state of the place and done an about-turn. He's not daft."

"No," Ben agreed, somewhat glumly.

"You turned up anything there?" Logan asked. It was a silly question—Ben would have let him know of any developments as soon as they'd happened—but he felt compelled to ask it, anyway.

"I'll give you three guesses," the DI replied. "And the first two don't count."

Logan heard him exhale. It was the sound of someone trying to put a brave face on defeat.

"We'll keep looking, obviously, but I reckon he's gone," Ben said. "Out of town, I mean. For all we know, he had a car parked right around the corner with keys in the ignition. He could be in the north of bloody England by now."

"Have you—"

"Circulated the details to the airports? Aye. Ferries, too. But if Kel Conlyn is a fake name, then he could be travelling under something else. They've got his photo though, and we're hoping for a hit on social media now that people are waking up."

Logan had never put a lot of stock in social media. Or people, in fact.

"Tyler get anywhere with the Nairn thing?"

"No. He's still looking into it. We're going to get in touch with the local schools there, but there'll be nobody in until after eight."

Logan nodded, but said nothing. It was proper polis work, he knew, but it felt like they were tinkering around the edges. Knocking on doors and getting on the phone had ended the careers of countless criminals over the years, but he didn't have high hopes of it leading to a collar this time. Conlyn—or whatever his bloody name was—was too clever.

Aye, maybe he had grown up in Nairn. Maybe they'd get a real name out of it, or a family they could talk to. But would it help them find him? Logan had grave doubts about that.

He listened to Ben yawning, tried to stifle one of his own, then gave up and went with it. It had been a long day yesterday, and the night had been longer still. Logan pulled down the Volvo's sun visor, checked himself in the little mirror, then shuddered and closed it all up again.

"You'll be knackered, Ben," he said. "You should get some rest."

"I'm grand," Ben said, but a follow-up yawn betrayed him.

"Aye, you sound it. You're no good to me if you're a zombie. How's Caitlyn doing? Did she get any kip?"

"A few hours, aye. I sent her through about half three. She protested, of course, but I can be a persuasive bugger when I want to be."

"Good. Get her up and running the room. Go home, get yourself a few hours. Go see Alice."

Ben snorted. "You were making it sound quite tempting up until the very end there," he said, then he sighed. "No, you're right. You're right."

"You're no' as young as you used to be," Logan pointed out.

"Takes one to bloody know one, Jack," Ben replied. "And you could do with some kip yourself."

"Aye. We'll see," Logan said. "I'm going to take another drive by the hospital first and see if..."

His voice trailed off, unable to find an end to the sentence. Driving past the hospital wasn't going to do any good. They had footage of Conlyn leaving. There were cameras throughout the building, none of which showed him coming back in. They'd searched the building, combed the grounds, and there was still a heavy Uniform presence on-site.

Conlyn wouldn't be there. Ben was right, the bastard was probably hundreds of miles away by now. He was injured, aye, but they were superficial, and had already been treated. They'd hurt, but nothing a few over-the-counter painkillers wouldn't be enough to take the edge off.

If he had access to a car, then he was gone. Long gone. Almost certainly.

And yet, Logan couldn't shake the feeling that he wasn't.

"He's got a point to prove," said Logan.

Ben's voice crackled slightly from the phone's speaker. "Eh?"

"Sorry, thinking out loud. I'm just... I'm not sure he'll have done a runner. Out of the city, I mean. All this was to prove some point. If his point is that nothing matters, then running away and hiding so you don't go to jail sort of undermines that, doesn't it?"

"Well, we know he legged it from the hospital," Ben reminded him. "The state of DC Neish's napper is testament to that."

"Aye, true," Logan said. "But that's different. That was instinct. As soon as he knew I was in his place and had rumbled his set-up, he reacted. He didn't want to go to jail because he isn't finished. That's not the same as running away."

"So, you're saying you think he's still somewhere in the area?" Ben asked.

"I don't know," Logan admitted. He fired up the engine and the Volvo kicked into life. He flexed his fingers again, then tightened them, his big hands practically crushing the wheel. "But I certainly bloody hope so."

SOCIAL MEDIA TURNED out to be exactly as useful as Logan had anticipated, in that it wasn't helpful in the slightest. There were a few jokey answers from the usual internet arseholes, several hundred shares and retweets, but in terms of any information they could act on? Hee-haw.

The schools in Nairn were a bust, too, despite Tyler's insistence that Conlyn had known the place well. Uniform up there was knocking on some doors with a photograph of him, but nothing had come up so far.

They'd managed to get prints from the hospital, including off fragments of the vase he'd used to brain Tyler with, but they'd turned out to be another dead end. Whoever he was, he'd never had any run-ins with the law in the past.

Bills to the flat had all been in the name of Kel Conlyn. The landlord had dug out the original references Conlyn had provided when he'd taken the place on, but they'd turned out to be as fake as the rest of his identity, and none of the numbers worked, although the landlord had insisted that they had at the time.

Further investigation revealed they had been 'Voice Over IP' internet phone numbers rented through an anonymous online service. Conlyn had been out to cover his tracks from the very start, and had done a bloody good job of it.

According to his broadband provider, his internet traffic had all gone through a VPN, meaning they couldn't provide any logs of the sites he'd visited. His mobile phone was Pay As You Go, and a scan through it showed it had largely been used to phone taxis and takeaways, and not a whole lot else.

Dead ends, everywhere they turned.

The Incident Room was busier than usual when Logan returned, a couple of CID officers and some senior Uniforms having set up shop in there alongside the MIT. They all looked up as he entered, expressions heavy with expectation. A shake of his head was enough, and they all turned their attention back to the screens and documents they were working on.

"Caitlyn. Anything?" Logan asked, stopping by the desk DI Forde had been occupying when he'd left.

"Nothing, sir," the DS replied. "Sorry."

"Hardly your fault," Logan told her. He turned to where DCs Khaled and Neish were both tapping away at their keyboards. "You two got anything?"

Hamza made a non-committal noise, which was still a significant improvement on what Logan had been bracing himself for.

"Not sure, sir," Hamza said. "I've been searching through forums. There are a few dedicated to Simulation Theory. It's mostly just Matrix memes, and links to news articles on the subject. That sort of thing."

"I hope there's a 'but' coming," Logan told him.

"But, well... maybe. There's one guy, calls himself 'The Nowhere Man,' and he seems to be really into it. A lot of the language he uses in his post is similar to what we heard on the video. If we don't exist, why should we feel guilt or remorse for hurting people? Why should we follow rules? That sort of stuff."

"Hardly concrete, is it? Plenty of nutters out there," Logan pointed out.

"Aye, but if I search the same username in Google, sir, it takes me to some other forums and a Twitter account. On one of the forums, he's posted a link to the report on the Danni Gillespie attack. There's a photo of her injury—the 'FAKE' he carved into her—that I don't think we took."

"So, it's him, then?" Logan asked.

"Looks like it, sir," confirmed Hamza.

"How does that help us? Can we use it to find him?"

Hamza opened his mouth to reply, closed it while he thought this over, then winced. "Not really, sir. I mean, we might have been able to get his internet provider from the IP he posted from, and then get the address, but, well..."

"We already know his address," Logan concluded.

Hamza appeared to deflate before the DCI's eyes. "Aye. Still, there might be something I can turn up."

At the next desk, DC Neish sat up straighter. "Wait. Hold on a minute. Address," he said, mumbling the words in a broken staccato, like they were coming to him one at a time. His eyes met Logan's. "Them letters in Conlyn's flat. The ones I kicked over."

"What about them?" Logan asked.

"They all had the same name on them. He said they were for the last guy who lived there, but what if they weren't? What if they were for him?"

"Why wouldn't he open them? Why leave them in a pile in the hall?"

"Well, because..." The sentence started strongly, but quickly fell away. "I mean... Maybe he wanted to leave that identity behind or something?"

"Then why not just chuck them?" Logan asked. "Why keep them all?"

"Because he's..." The DC puffed out his cheeks. "...mental?"

It wasn't what you might call a thorough psychological analysis, but Logan couldn't really argue with it. Still, there was mental, then there was stupid, and what Tyler was suggesting fell firmly into the latter camp.

When they had so few other leads to go on, it was worth checking out, though. Everything was worth checking out at this stage, no matter how unlikely a lead it might seem.

"What was the name on the envelopes?" he asked.

Tyler's face froze. "Uh... sorry, boss?"

"The name. Who were they addressed to?"

Other than his mouth, not a muscle on the DC's face moved. "It was, eh... I think something like..." He swallowed. "Can't remember."

"For fu—"

Logan pinched the bridge of his nose, took a steadying breath, then continued.

"Get onto the landlord and see what you can find out," he suggested. "He'll be able to tell us who the previous tenants were. Maybe the name will give something a nudge in that head of yours. And get someone from Uniform round to check the house. It's possible some of the letters survived the fire, although I wouldn't hold out much hope."

"On it, boss," Tyler said, turning his attention back to the computer.

Logan took a seat and surveyed the Incident Room. DS McQuarrie was talking to a couple of Uniforms. They nodded intently, taking careful note of everything she was telling them. That was good.

What was less good was the general lack of energy in the room. After Logan's speech during the night, the place had been buzzing with excitement. They were going to catch the bastard, no one had been in any doubt.

Now that the night was over and the day was moving in on its turf, the energy had waned. Every minute that passed made it exponentially less likely that they'd find Conlyn. He could be anywhere in the country by now. With a fake passport—or a real one under his own name—he could be anywhere in Europe, in fact, and possibly even beyond.

And yet, Logan didn't think so. He was still here somewhere. Still in the city. He was going to show-face again, Logan could sense it.

It was just a matter of time.

CHAPTER FORTY-TWO

The breakthrough came just before lunchtime, and from the unlikeliest of sources, too.

"Boss, I've got it," Tyler announced, jumping up out of his seat with his notepad raised above his head. "I've got something."

All eyes were on the DC at once. Logan's legs raised him into a standing position without his brain having any say in the matter. He didn't want to get his hopes up, and yet he could feel a tingle across the skin of his arms, like electricity zipping between the hairs.

"I checked with the landlord, and aye, those letters were for the previous tenant. He told me the guy's name, and I remembered it was the same name on the envelopes," Tyler said.

Logan briefly contemplated sitting down again, but didn't. Not yet. Surely, the DC had more than that?

"Right. And?"

"And, it got me thinking. So, I got onto the Royal Mail and checked if they ever delivered letters to that address for anyone else. Any other names. They checked, and they do. Not often, but maybe once every couple of months."

Butterflies erupted into flight in Logan's stomach. "Who?"

Tyler, who had still been holding his notebook above his head like King Arthur with Excalibur, brought it down and glanced at the top page.

"David Oliver, boss."

"And did you—"

"Checked with the landlord, aye. He's never heard of him."

There was a flurry of typing from the next desk over as Hamza's fingers flew across his keyboard.

"OK, OK, let's not get too excited yet," Logan said, although he was struggling to follow his own advice. "We don't know yet if it's—"

Hamza let out a little yelp of something that may have been excitement, but could equally have been pain.

"Hamza?" Logan prompted.

"Got him!"

Hamza turned his screen so the others could see. A page from the *Press & Journal* website was open in the browser. It showed a picture of a young man wearing a university graduation cap and gown, smiling proudly as he held up a certificate. He was a couple of years younger, but there was no mistaking the man who'd been calling himself Kel Conlyn.

"Says he graduated from Glasgow Uni three years ago. MBChB in Medicine. He went in young. Some sort of child prodigy, by the looks of things."

Logan tutted. "Aye. You've to watch those bastards."

"Grew up in Nairn," Hamza continued.

"I fucking *knew it!*" Tyler cried, thrusting his hands above his head again.

"Home educated, though, so that'll be why the schools didn't recognise him."

Logan clapped his hands a few times, making sure he had the attention of everyone in the room. "Right, DC Tyler here has outdone himself and handed us a big win. We can all buy him a drink later, but for now, I want everything we can find on one—"

Logan pointed to Tyler.

"David Oliver, boss."

"—David Oliver. I want to know past addresses, friends, car registration, hobbies, shoe size, and what he had for his breakfast. You'll bring it to DS McQuarrie and DC Khaled, and they'll coordinate and decide what we're putting out to the press and social media."

He pointed to one of the CID officers at random, a redhead who looked like she knew what she was doing. "You. Sorry, forget your name."

"DS Elizabeth, sir. Hanna."

"Hanna. Right. I want you checking the airports, start local and work outwards. We need to know he hasn't left the country. Take who you need to get it done quickly."

"Right, sir," the DS replied.

"I want to see some initiative here from all of you," Logan said, addressing the audience as a whole. "DS McQuarrie can find you jobs to do if needs be, but you're here in this room because we think you can figure it out for yourself. Coordinate with each other and with your senior officers. Check everything. Leave no stone unturned. Get me everything you can on David Oliver, and let's flush the bastard out of hiding."

He clapped his hands again, signalling the speech was over. "Well? Come on. Jump to it."

The Incident Room immediately became a frenzy of activity, as officers got on phones, tapped at their keyboards, or got to their feet. The place had been whisper-quiet for the last few hours, but now it was alive with conversation, the anticipation of a collar suddenly palpable in the air.

"That was good work, son," Logan told Tyler. "I'd kiss you, if you weren't such an ugly bastard."

"I'd only have you for harassment, boss," Tyler replied. He took a breath that suggested he was going to say something more, but then just sat down.

"What is it?" Logan asked.

Tyler shook his head. "It's nothing. Don't worry about it."

"Jesus Christ, man, spit it out."

DC Neish wriggled uncomfortably in his chair. "It's just... This afternoon. It's, well, it's Sinead's wee brother's birthday."

Logan frowned and looked at the clock on the wall like it might be helpful in some way. It wasn't. "Is that today?"

"Aye, boss. But it's fine. I'll tell her I can't go."

Logan shook his head. "You've been on shift for a whole bloody day, Detective Constable," he said. "Go home. Get some rest. Clean the blood out of your ear, because—quite frankly—it's been annoying me all night. Go eat some cake and play Pass the Parcel, or whatever it is they do these days." He leaned over the desk and gave the DC a slightly awkward pat on the shoulder. "You did good, son. You did good."

Tyler blushed, just slightly. "Cheers, boss."

Logan turned to DS McQuarrie. "Caitlyn, you alright here for half an hour or so? I'll get Ben out of his bed and back in. He won't want to miss this."

"Fine, sir. Not a problem," Caitlyn said. "You off somewhere?"

"Aye. Hamza, you said he grew up in Nairn?"

"That's right, sir," Hamza confirmed.

"Good," Logan said, picking up his borrowed coat. "Then, get me that address."

CHAPTER FORTY-THREE

THE HOUSE ON NAIRN'S MILLBANK STREET WAS NOTABLE FOR A FEW reasons.

It was newer than most of the other houses along the road, and set back a little at the end of a gated driveway. It had a hedge, which was badly in need of a trim, and a scattering of weeds had started to find their way through the bricks of the drive, making the place look somewhat unloved.

The most notable features of all though, were the windows, which had been completely whited out with dried Windowlene, and the 'For Sale' sign fixed to the fence. A 'Sold' sticker had been slapped on top, which explained the sense of abandonment the whole place was giving off.

"Damn it."

The gate was in good condition, suggesting the decay was all fairly recent. It opened with barely a squeak, and Logan's eyes scanned the front of the house as he approached. Big. Detached. Expensive-looking. Conlyn —*Oliver, he corrected*—had evidently come from a comfortable background. Financially, at least.

The doors were locked, as expected. The white coating on the windows made it difficult to see inside, but from what Logan was able to tell, the place was empty. There was a smallish shed around the back. It had been locked, but someone had broken the latch, splintering the wood where the screws had been torn out. It was empty now, aside from a lingering smell of turpentine and sawdust.

The back garden was all slabs and decking, and the weeds were making more of a statement back there. They'd squeezed through the narrow gaps at the edges of the paving slabs, and were positively flourishing between the wooden boards of the decking.

The kitchen window had less of a Windowlene covering than the others, and Logan was able to get a good look inside by clambering up on an upturned terracotta pot. The appliances were all fitted, so had been left in place when the occupants had moved out. There were a few other bits and bobs scattered across the worktops—an open pack of light bulbs, some junk mail, the instruction manual for something or other—but nothing to suggest the place was still being lived in.

"Moving in?"

The voice came from the other side of a tall fence that ran along the side of the building, separating it from the garden next door. It was too high to see over, but Logan spied some movement in the gaps between the upright boards, and it quickly translated into the shape of a man. He was shorter than Logan, but then that wasn't unusual. Older, too, judging by the flashes of white hair the detective could see.

"No. DCI Logan, Police Scotland Major Investigations," he said, automatically reaching for his warrant card. He hadn't had time to arrange a replacement yet though, and he found the inside pocket empty. "Sorry, ID was destroyed in a fire during the night."

"What, fire brigade on holiday, were they?" the neighbour asked, his voice so bright and chipper it had the same effect on Logan as fingernails scraping down a blackboard. "Having a job swap, were you?"

"Something like that," Logan said. He could see the man eyeing him up through the gap, and his appearance seemed to live up to expectations.

"You look like police, right enough. Is everything alright?"

"What do you know about the owners of this house, Mr...?"

"Dawson. Do you mean the old owners, or the new one?"

"Both."

"Not a jot about the new ones, I'm afraid. Never seen them. They bought it about... what? Six months ago, I think. All very sudden. Millie and John, they just upped and left one day, by all accounts. Neighbours for eighteen years, and not so much as a goodbye. Quite hurtful, if I'm honest."

There was a touch of anger colouring his voice, like he hadn't yet forgiven them.

"They didn't mention they were selling up?"

"No. By the time the sign went up, it already had a 'Sold' sticker on it. I went around to speak to them, but it was only David, the young fella, who was there. He was carrying boxes out to a van. I asked him what was going on and he said his parents were relocating to the east coast somewhere. Said they'd get in touch once they'd settled in. But nothing. Not so much as a postcard."

Through the gap, Logan saw the older man's gaze flit to the house. "Keep expecting to see someone moving in, but nothing yet. Shame to see it sitting empty like that. Lovely house. Lovely couple."

"What about the son?" Logan asked. "Have many dealings with him?"

"Not really, no. Kept himself to himself, mostly. Very bright, though," Mr Dawson said. "Home educated. I think he had some trouble with bullying in primary school. Millie mollycoddled him a bit, and he ended up being taught at home. She quit her job, and everything."

Dawson's gaze returned to Logan. "Why? Is something wrong?"

He was going to find out soon enough. It'll be all over the telly and the internet within the hour. May as well tell him face-to-face. Or face-to-fence, at least.

"We believe David Oliver may be involved in a recent spate of sexual assaults and murders in and around Inverness," Logan said. "We need to find him as a matter of urgency."

"Good God. *David*? But, I mean... He wouldn't, would he? He's always been a bit odd, but *murder*? I can't believe that."

"We're building a strong case against him, Mr Dawson. I've got very little doubt at the moment as to his guilt, and my priority is catching him before he can hurt anyone else," Logan said. He indicated the building behind him with a thumb. "Have you seen anyone coming and going in the last few days?"

"No, not a thing. Quiet as the grave, and I'm a very light sleeper, so I'd have heard anyone coming during the night. I heard you from my kitchen," Dawson said, looking quite pleased with himself. "I was thinking of giving the estate agent a ring though, to get them to contact the buyer. There's a bit of a whiff coming from the place some days. I think the drains must be starting to back up. They'll have to get that seen to."

Logan felt his mouth puckering and his eyebrows falling into a frown. He hadn't smelled anything, but then it was cold today, and there was a bit of a wind to keep the air moving.

"Mr Dawson, I don't suppose you have a spare key for the house, do you?"

"Yes. God. Somewhere. John left me with it when I was looking in on their old dog—rest her soul—when they were away for the weekend a few years back. Told me just to hang on to it in case of emergencies. I'd have to look for it, though."

"Right. Can you go and find it and then meet me round the front?" Logan asked. "I just need to make a quick phone call."

THE ESTATE AGENT on the sign was legitimate, the phone number taking Logan straight through to the main reception. There, the authenticity of the whole thing ended. They'd never listed a property for sale on Millbank Street, much less sold one. Whoever had put the sign up, they said, it was nothing to do with them.

That had sealed it. When the neighbour turned up with the key, Logan took it, thanked him, then sent him back to his house with instructions not to come out until he'd been told otherwise.

Dawson had almost questioned the order, but the smell was more noticeable around the front, and Logan had seen the moment when the realisation had hit him. His hand had shaken when he'd passed the DCI the key, and he'd quickly turned and walked back to his own garden, without once looking back.

There was no mistaking the smell when Logan turned the key in the lock and pushed open the door. It was the same cloying, acrid stench he'd smelled so many times before. It was similar to the aromas that lingered in the mortuary, only rawer and more intense.

Matured.

It was tinted with other smells, too. Lavender, he thought, and other flowery things. His eyes went to the electrical sockets, and the air-fresheners plugged into every one. Presumably, the intention had been for them to mask the smell, but they mingled with it, amplifying it, and making it even more stomach-churningly nauseating than it would otherwise have been.

He called it into the office before he went any further. They'd need Forensics in here. He declined the offer of an ambulance. Based on the smell, they were months past that stage.

The downstairs was empty, stripped of all furniture, just like the flat that had gone up in flames. Logan *creaked* his way into four bare rooms and a small bathroom, then steeled himself as he made his way to the stairs.

The carpet had been removed, and each footfall *thunked* like a drumbeat on the exposed wooden steps. The emptiness of the place carried the sound, echoing it back to him as he made his way up to the top.

The higher he got, the thicker and more pungent the smell became, until he was forced to bury the bottom half of his face in the crook of his arm.

It wasn't until he reached the very top step that he heard the flies. Their murmuring drone guided him to the second of the four doors that led off from the upstairs landing. The pocket of Hoon's coat was completely devoid of the protective gloves Logan usually carried in his own, so he covered his hand with his sleeve and carefully pushed down the handle and let the door ease open.

The room erupted in movement, as hundreds of flies took to the air, fully exposing the corpses on the bed. They had putrefied badly, to the point that Logan couldn't quite tell where the bodies ended and the bedclothes began. The floor was carpeted with dead insects, suggesting most of the feasting had happened some time ago, and the flies that were still hanging around were scavenging what little was left.

John and Millie—because Logan had no doubt that was who he was looking at—had both been naked when they'd died, their hands wrenched in front of them, their wrists bound together. The exposed bones of their arms were linked, so that with their wrists tied they would have been unable to separate themselves.

Locked together, until the end.

Cause of death was impossible to determine from that distance, and Logan had no intention of getting any closer without protective gear. Ideally, an airtight rubber suit and a diver's helmet. Even then, the bodies were so far gone it might never be possible to figure out what had killed them.

Who had killed them was less of a mystery.

Two more victims to add to the tally. Two more lives taken by that sick bastard. His own parents, too. How many others were out there? How many would they never know about?

"No more," Logan said, announcing it like some sacred vow. He pulled the door closed and made for the stairs, the smell worming through his defences.

He made it to the front step before the urge to vomit almost became overwhelming. Had it not been for the police van screeching to a stop at the end of the driveway, he'd have thrown up right there on the driveway, and it was only through sheer stubbornness and force of will that he was able to keep the meagre contents of his stomach where they should be, and his self-respect intact.

"I wouldn't," Logan said, stopping the uniformed officer halfway up the drive. "Just keep the door closed, wait for the SOC team to get here. If you can avoid going in, I'd advise you to do that, and be bloody grateful for it."

The Uniform, who clearly didn't recognise him, started barking questions. Logan ignored them, and looked back at the house. At the whited-out window. At the flies crawling up the inside.

"No more," he muttered. "No more."

CHAPTER FORTY-FOUR

DC NEISH STOOD FROZEN TO THE SPOT, HANDS RAISED, ALMOST ALL of his weight on one leg. He didn't dare move, didn't dare blink, didn't dare breathe. He could only stand there, stock-still, or it would all be over.

Come on. Come on...

Pink's *Get the Party Started* kicked back in and Tyler continued dancing. Sinead had her back to the living room, but smirked at Tyler in the mirror as her finger hovered over the 'stop' button on her Spotify app.

Truth be told, musical statues wasn't going down all that well with Harris and the other kids, but Tyler was having the time of his life. He wasn't going to win, of course—he wasn't a monster—but he was determined to at least get to the semi-final stage. At that point, he'd throw the game, safe in the knowledge that he *could* have won it if he'd really wanted to.

The party wasn't exactly jumping. There were six kids, including Harris. They all seemed nice enough for nine and ten-year-olds, although one of them—Grant something or other—had the potential to be a right wee dick. Grant was still in the running for Musical Statues, along with Harris, the girl next door, and Tyler himself. Tyler just needed to survive one more round and—

The music stopped unexpectedly. Tyler tried to freeze, but he was midway through a *Saturday Night Fever* style fingerpoint, and he'd been caught off guard.

"Tyler," Sinead said. "You're out."

DC Neish resisted the temptation to point out that Grant was clearly moving, too, and to call for a Steward's Enquiry, and accepted the defeat with relatively good grace.

"Aye, it's a fair cop," he said, squeezing past the frozen kids until he was standing next to Sinead. "I'll be the lookout, if you like. Eyes like a hawk, me."

"All that investment in police training was money well spent, eh?" Sinead teased, as she tapped the 'play' button and Pink came blasting from the Bluetooth speaker.

He hummed along quietly as the kids shuffled awkwardly on the spot. They'd all passed the age when they could dance freely without embarrassment, and mostly now looked like they wanted the floor to open up and swallow them.

He'd helped Sinead drag the kitchen table into the living room, and she'd spent half an hour covering it in party food. Tyler snaffled a sausage roll while he watched the kids dancing. He'd already made a substantial dent in the sausages, cheese, and pickled onions on sticks, and had taken to stashing the cocktail sticks in his pocket so no one could see how many he'd eaten.

The music stopped as he was halfway through chewing.

"Grant," he said immediately, spraying pastry crumbs down his front.

"What? I wasn't moving!"

"You were," Tyler said. He swallowed the sausage roll and turned to Sinead. "He was."

"Grant, you're out," Sinead said.

"This is bullshit," Grant muttered, stomping past the other kids. He dug a sweaty hand into a bowl of Smarties, and helped himself to several dozen. "Total bullshit."

Sinead and Tyler both watched the kid go *thudding* over to the couch, where he threw himself down next to the other three who had already been eliminated, took out his phone, and started tapping away at the screen.

"And it's down to the final!" Tyler announced. "Harris 'Hot Shoe Shuffle' Bell, versus..."

Shit, shit, shit. What was her name?

"Emily 'Michael Jackson' Boardman!" Sinead finished.

They hit the music and the kids returned to dancing unenthusiastically on the spot. Now that there were just the two of them left, they turned their bodies away from each other to ensure nobody could make the mistake of thinking they were dancing together.

"Michael Jackson?" Tyler whispered.

Sinead bit her bottom lip. "I know. I panicked."

"Fortunately, they're all probably too young to have any idea who he is," Tyler said. "But if word gets back to the parents that you've been flinging 'Michael Jackson' around the place, you're going to have Social Work at your door."

Sinead grinned and gave him a playful thump on the arm. "Yeah, yeah. Shut up."

She stopped the music again. Both kids froze. Tyler's eyes narrowed, tick-tocking between them both as he really tried to ramp up the tension.

"Sorry, Jacko. You're out," he said, shooting the girl an apologetic look.

"Fix!" bellowed Grant from the sidelines. A few of the other kids giggled, and Harris looked absolutely mortified as he shuffled over to collect his prize.

"Skittles. Brilliant," he said. You could probably argue that he was trying to look enthusiastic, but his heart clearly wasn't in it.

As Harris took the bag of sweets, Grant called over to him. "Here, Bell," he said, dropping his phone in his lap and opening his hands.

Harris only hesitated for a moment, before chucking the Skittles in the bigger boy's direction. Grant caught them with a hand clap, his eyes blazing greedily. "Nice. I love these."

He ripped open the bag, spilling half a dozen of the colourful candies down the gap between the cushions. The kids on either side-eyed the sweets expectantly, but Grant was making no signs of sharing. "Can we go play Fortnite now?" he asked, masticating his way through a mouthful of Skittle-mush.

Harris looked hopefully up at Sinead. "Can we?"

"Not Fortnite, surely?" Tyler groaned. "It's full of—"

He looked around the room at the faces of the children who were all now glaring at him, waiting to see what he was going to say.

"—bugs," he said, rather than the 'bloody nine-year-olds' that had been his original intention when he'd first opened his mouth.

Harris tutted, then very pointedly looked away from the DC and back to Sinead.

"What about the other games?" Sinead asked. "We haven't done Pass the Parcel yet."

"I'm not five," Harris told her.

Sinead looked down at the carefully wrapped parcel sitting on the table. It was balanced right on the edge, the only space available after she'd set out the buffet.

"I spent ages wrapping that," she muttered, although it was more to herself than to Harris. She looked at Tyler, who offered a half-smile and a shrug in reply, then she sighed. "Fine. If that's what you want, you can go and play—"

There was a knock at the door. Heavy. Solid. Threatening, almost. The sound of traffic came rushing in from the hall as the front door was opened. Tyler and Sinead both tensed, and were halfway across the room when a hulking figure came striding into the living room. Behind them, back at the buffet table, Harris gasped.

"Right, then," said DCI Logan, rubbing his hands together. "Where's this cake?"

Harris stood in front of the other kids, holding court. Logan stood beside him, a paper plate in one hand, a fork in the other, and half a pound of chocolate cake already lining his stomach. Like Tyler, Logan was also partial to a little sausage on a stick. Like Tyler, he also now had a pocket full of cocktail sticks, and a slightly guilty conscience.

"It was amazing!" Harris said, more animated than he'd been all day. "The guy had a knife to my throat, right? Like, properly to my throat. Like, he was going to kill me. And then, *boosh!* Chief Inspector Logan comes in and just smacks him. He just totally smacks him and then goes chasing after him."

Over by the buffet, Sinead paused with a mini-Battenberg halfway to her mouth. "That's not how it happened," she told Tyler. "If there was any *booshing* being done, it was me."

"You were the principal *boosher?*" Tyler asked.

Sinead laughed. "I was *boosher* number one."

"No way," Grant sneered. "You didn't really have a knife to your throat. Did he?"

"Oh aye," Logan confirmed, chewing on another forkful of cake. "Handled it perfectly, too. Better than I could've. From where I was standing, he didn't even look worried. I actually thought he probably had it all under control himself. We almost just turned around and left him to it."

Harris drew several admiring looks from the others, not least of all from Emily.

"Did you catch him?" she asked, her eyes flitting up to Logan then quickly diverting away again, like the sight of him made her nervous. "The bad guy? Did you catch him?"

"Aye. More or less," Logan said, glossing over the details. "But I wouldn't have without Harris's help. It was thanks to him we cracked the case."

"No way," Grant snorted.

Logan stopped chewing. He took the paper napkin from his plate and dabbed at his mouth, his gaze locked firmly on the boy with the Skittles.

"Are you calling me a liar, son?" he intoned. "Is that what's happening here?"

Grant appeared to sink into the cushions. His face, which had still been red from the effort of slowly shuffling from foot-to-foot during Musical Statues, lost all its colour in one sudden flush.

"Uh, no."

"No what?"

"No... sir?" Grant squeaked.

Logan stabbed his cake with the plastic fork. "Better," he said, then he shovelled another bite into his mouth and got back to chewing.

Across the room, Tyler watched on. Harris was practically bouncing with excitement, and would look up at Logan every few seconds like he was afraid he might vanish into thin air.

"He seems to really like him," Tyler remarked.

"God, aye. He hasn't stopped going on about him since they met in Fort William," Sinead said. She caught the slightly wounded expression on Tyler's face. "He likes you, too."

Tyler shot her a sceptical look.

"I mean, he will. Once he gets to know you better."

"Right." Tyler half-turned his body towards her. "And... is that going to happen? Am I, you know, allowed to show my face round here again?"

"I don't know." Sinead smirked, her eyes darting across his features. "It's pretty horrifying. Maybe if you wore a paper bag..."

"Oy!" Tyler protested. "Bit harsh."

Sinead smiled and leaned in closer. Tyler began to lean in too, his eyes closing. But then Sinead plucked a sausage roll from the plate behind him, popped it in her mouth, and grinned.

"That was just nasty," he told her.

Sinead nodded. "Yeah. I know."

"Is this man bothering you, constable?"

They both turned to find Logan standing beside them, his plate now empty.

"Because, I can have him forcibly removed from the premises, if you like."

Sinead smiled. "Let me get back to you on that, sir," she said. "And thank you *so much* for coming."

Logan held up the plate. "Well, I realised I hadn't had breakfast or lunch, and I was in the area, so..."

Sinead looked past him to where Harris was still answering questions. "How did you get away from them?" she asked.

"Hmm? Oh, they asked me if I wanted to play Fortnite."

"And what did you say?"

"I said, 'What the fuck is Fortnite when it's at home?'" Logan replied.

Tyler and Sinead both stared at him, mouths open.

"Of course I didn't say that. Jesus Christ, what do you think I am? I said I'd maybe play another time."

The other two officers relaxed.

"I have no intention of following through on that, by the way. So we're clear. I don't know what Fortnite is, and I don't want to know. I was being nice."

"First time for everything, eh, boss?" Tyler said.

"Bold statement that, for a man who's only here out of the goodness of my bloody heart," Logan pointed out.

"Fair point, well made," Tyler conceded. He glanced at Sinead. "We didn't think you'd be able to make it."

"Any news?" Sinead asked.

Logan sighed. Never a promising start. "Car was picked up on a camera on the A9 earlier today, headed south near... what's that place? They do the adverts on the telly. All the toffs go there."

"House of Bruar?" Sinead guessed.

"Aye. Just past there," Logan said. "They found the car itself abandoned in a layby this side of the Forth bridge a couple of hours ago. The thinking is that he's in Edinburgh, so central belt has taken over the hunt for him."

"That's... good?" Sinead said. The faces on both men said otherwise. "Isn't it? We know who he is, what he looks like, and all that stuff. We're bound to get him sooner or later."

"Aye. I suppose you're right," said Logan, helping himself to a chocolate-coated marshmallow. "Still, I didn't think he'd run. Bit disappointed in him, if I'm honest. Least the bastard could've done is let us nab him ourselves."

He grabbed a handful of crisps from a bowl and cupped them in one hand. "Right, I'd better get off. Hoon wants an update, and I need to persuade DI Forde to handle the paperwork. I'll go say bye to the wee man and his pals."

Leaning in closer, he dropped his voice to a whisper. "I'd watch the lad with the Skittles, by the way. The old arsehole alarm is going off, and it's rarely wrong."

"Yeah, we're all over him, boss," Tyler said. "I'm just waiting for an excuse to crack out the handcuffs."

"Good man," Logan said. He crunched a couple of crisps. "Right, back to it, then. I'll see you both later. Enjoy the rest of the party."

He shot Sinead a warning look. "Don't let him wangle his way out of the dishes."

"No chance," Sinead said, smiling.

"Cheers for that, boss."

Logan looked between them both. For a moment, it looked like he might be about to say something, but then he just nodded. "Right. That's me," he said, then he tossed the rest of the crisps in his mouth, turned on his heels, and went to say goodbye to Harris.

Sinead and Tyler both watched him as he bent to talk to the boy, then begrudgingly accepted a round of high-fives from everyone except Grant, who just sat in the same spot, eating the Skittles and trying to look disinterested.

"He's full of surprises, isn't he?" said Sinead.

"Aye. You can say that again," Tyler agreed.

They both waved as Logan turned and shot them a final farewell look, and then he was out in the hallway, and the sound of traffic filled the room again as he opened the front door and stepped outside.

"You think he's happy?" Sinead wondered, once he was gone.

Tyler frowned. "Yeah. I think so. Aye. More or less. I mean, not 'happy' exactly. I've never seen him actually *happy*, but... Aye. He's fine, I think. Why?"

Sinead watched the door. From outside, there came the sound of a car engine starting.

"No reason," Sinead said. "Just wondering."

Harris's voice pipped up as he and the others started heading for the door. "We're going upstairs to play Fortnite!"

Sinead rolled her eyes. "Fine. If that's what you really want. On you go."

She waited until they were all clumping up the stairs before sagging and exhaling in relief. "Thank God for that. I thought they were never going to leave," she said, then she reached under the table and produced a bottle. "Wine?"

Tyler's face split into a grin. "I thought you were never going to ask."

CHAPTER FORTY-FIVE

"Now, technically, this isn't the best time of year to watch this film," Tyler explained. "*Technically*, it's a Christmas movie, but I'm so appalled that you haven't seen it that we're breaking with tradition."

Beside him on the couch, Sinead shook her head. "Of course he hasn't seen it. He's nine."

"Ten," Harris and Tyler both corrected at the same time.

"OK, well you've *been* nine," Sinead said.

"We've all been nine, Sinead," Tyler pointed out. "What's your point?"

She slapped him on the arm and swirled the final few dregs of wine around in her glass. She was curled up with her legs beneath her, Tyler on her right, Harris leaning against her on the left.

She'd eventually managed to kick the other kids out before she had to feed them, and had ordered dinner from the Chinese for the three of them, which Tyler had insisted on paying for. Pride had made her argue, but three glasses of red wine had made her somewhat more pliable and open to negotiation than usual, so she'd eventually relented.

"It doesn't look like a Christmas movie," Harris remarked. On-screen, a close-up of a young Bruce Willis eyed up the exploding Nakatomi Plaza. The film's title—'Die Hard'—was emblazoned in red at the bottom of the image.

"That's the beauty of it. But trust me," Tyler told him. "It's the *Miracle on 34th Street* of action movies."

"What's *Miracle on 34ᵗʰ Street?*" Harris asked.

Tyler leaned past Sinead, stared at Harris to make sure he wasn't on the wind-up, then shot Sinead a reproachful look. "Have you given this boy *any* film education whatsoever?"

"*Up!*" Sinead announced, a little giggly.

Tyler frowned and glanced down at the couch, in case she'd spilt something and was telling him to move. "Eh?"

"The film. *Up!* With the dog and the balloons," Sinead said. She turned to her little brother. "We watched that last week, didn't we?"

"Well, I did. You fell asleep," Harris said.

"Did I?" Sinead asked, seemingly shocked by the accusation.

"Yes. You always fall asleep."

Sinead took a sip from her glass, draining it. "Fair point. I will give you that one," she admitted. "Still, the first fifteen minutes were *amazing.*"

Tyler picked up the remote. "Right, well it's physically impossible to fall asleep during *Die Hard*, so no worries there. Everyone ready?"

"Ready," Harris confirmed.

"Go for it," said Sinead, then she immediately contradicted herself. "Wait. No. Not yet. I'll go get us more drinks first. And should we do popcorn? We have popcorn. It's in one of those microwave thingies."

She looked from one to the other. "Yes? No? Popcorn?"

"I never say no to popcorn," Tyler replied.

"Yeah, I'll have some," Harris agreed.

"Right, then!" Sinead said, unfolding her legs from beneath her. It took her a couple of attempts to get to her feet, then another few seconds to figure out where everyone's glasses were. "So, wine, wine, Irn Bru."

"And popcorn," Tyler reminded her.

"And popcorn." A troubling thought struck her. "It might be out of date, though, that's the only thing."

Tyler shot Harris a sideways look, then shrugged. "We'll take our chances. Want a hand?"

She waved the suggestion away. "It's fine. You stay here. I can figure it out."

Tyler watched her head through to the hall, swaying ever so slightly as she went. It was only when he heard her open the kitchen door that he realised Harris was looking at him.

"Alright?" Tyler asked.

Harris nodded, but said nothing.

"You're going to love it. This film, I mean. It's a classic. Just cover your ears at the sweary bits."

Harris nodded again. "Jack said it was you who worked out who's been killing them people," he said.

It took Tyler a moment to process this. "Jack? Oh, the boss? Aye. He lets you call him Jack, does he? Reckon my arse'd be out the window if I tried that." He put a hand over his mouth. "Bum'd be out the window, I mean. Sorry."

Harris half-smiled at the fake apology. "Did you?"

"Did I what?"

"Figure out who the bad guy is?"

The boy was staring at him, waiting for his response. From the kitchen, Tyler heard the *beep-beep-beep* of the microwave being programmed, then the whirring hum as it activated.

"Because Jack said you figured it out. The killer's name and stuff. He said it was you."

Tyler puffed out his cheeks. "I mean... I suppose so. Aye. I suppose it was."

Harris's eyes, which had been narrowed in suspicion, widened just a fraction. They flicked up and down, giving the DC a quick once-over.

"Cool," he said, then he faced the telly again, a satisfied smile playing on his lips.

"Thanks," Tyler said, sitting up a little straighter. "I guess it was."

They sat in a silence that wasn't entirely comfortable, but wasn't particularly awkward either, listening to the *pop-pop-popping* from the kitchen.

They hadn't said much, and yet in just those few words, Tyler had felt the atmosphere between them thawing. He wouldn't say that the boy now liked him, by any stretch of the imagination, but he at least looked like he might be prepared to tolerate the DC's existence, which was a start.

Aye, the boss was full of surprises, right enough.

The popping had all but stopped now. Tyler glanced at the hall door and picked up the remote again, his finger hovering over the 'play' button. *Die Hard* was one of his top ten favourite films of all time, and his favourite Christmas movie by far. He'd first seen it when he was around Harris's age, and if he was completely honest, it had played a big part in his decision to join the police.

It had been a few years since he'd seen it, and he wasn't sure who he was more excited for—himself, or the boy who was about to witness its brilliance for the very first time.

Assuming Sinead got her finger out.

"Popcorn nearly ready?" Tyler called through. He could still hear the microwave *whirring*, but the popping had stopped now, aside from the odd occasional *paff* as one of the more reluctant kernels finally succumbed to the heat. "Sinead?"

There was no answer from the kitchen. No movement in the hall.

"You're going to burn it again!" Harris called. "Like last time."

Tyler smiled at him and rolled his eyes, but then his attention went straight back to the door, his ears straining for any sign of movement.

"Sinead?"

"She probably went for a pee," Harris said.

"Aye. Yeah. Probably," Tyler agreed.

He settled back on the couch, trying to get comfortable. A black and white Bruce Willis stared back at him from the screen. Through in the kitchen, the microwave's droning ended with a *ping*, and a stillness fell over the house.

Tyler couldn't keep his gaze from making its way back to the door. He kept his voice as light and natural as possible as he got up from the couch. "I'll go see if she needs a hand. You wait here, OK?"

"OK," Harris said. "It's fine if it's burnt. She felt really guilty about it last time. I don't really care about the popcorn, anyway."

"I'll tell her that," Tyler said, making for the door. "I'll be right back."

The hall was empty, but that wasn't unexpected. He stopped at the bottom of the stairs and called up into the darkness. "Sinead? You up there?"

Nothing.

A swirl of cold air circulated in through the gap in the open kitchen door. Tyler nudged it the rest of the way and stepped through. The smell of burnt popcorn hung in the air. The inside of the microwave was filled with a cloud of grey-white smoke, visible even with the oven's light now out.

The back door that led out to the garden stood open. From somewhere not too far away, Tyler heard the sound of tyres crunching on gravel and the sharp, sudden *shriek* of a wheelspin. He reached the door in three big paces, was outside and onto the path in five.

The red glow of a set of tail lights vanished around the corner at the end of the road. Along the path, the back gate *clacked* as the wind blew it open and closed.

He heard movement behind him, back in the house. He ran up the path, bounded up the steps and skidded to a stop in the kitchen.

Harris stood there, looking confused. "Where is she?" he asked.

"Hey. I thought I told you to wait through there?" Tyler said. He closed the back door behind him, then started in the direction of the hall. "I need to go check the bathroom. She's probably in there."

"What's that?" Harris asked. He pointed to the fridge, and Tyler had to bite his lip to stop himself stating the obvious.

He realised immediately that the boy wasn't asking what the fridge was, and instead saw where he was pointing. Earlier, the front of the appliance had been covered in magnets—holiday mementoes, mostly, but a selection of letters and numbers, too.

Now, all but four of them were on the floor. Those that remained were all letters.

Four of them, all chillingly familiar.

F. A. K. E.

"Oh God," Tyler whispered, as the bottom fell out of his world. "Oh God, no."

CHAPTER FORTY-SIX

BEN FORDE FINISHED FASTENING THE BUTTONS ON HIS COAT, THEN placed a hand on the Incident Room's light switch. "I'm warning you. I'll lock you in, Jack," he said. "You should be getting yourself home."

Across the room, Logan glanced up from his computer and mustered up a smile of acknowledgement. "Aye. I won't be long. Just checking to see if they've caught him."

"You've been refreshing that bloody thing for the past three hours," Ben pointed out. "You're exhausted, man. Get your arse home to bed."

Logan's eyes flicked back to the screen. HOLMES was back up and running, which was something. He'd been hoping for an update on there—or preferably, a phone call—to say that David Oliver had been nabbed.

He'd been hoping it for a while now. So far, those hopes had been repeatedly dashed.

"Aye. Aye, you're right," Logan admitted. He jabbed the monitor's power button more violently than was strictly necessary and got to his feet. "We should hear something in the morning."

"Exactly. No point killing yourself."

He waited while the DCI pulled on the coat he'd borrowed from Hoon, then clicked the light switch as he approached the door.

Logan waited in the corridor while the DI locked the door, then they both wandered along it, automatically falling into step, neither man in a massive rush to leave.

"You straight home yourself?" Logan asked.

"Chance'd be a fine thing. Alice wants me to swing by Tesco for—and I quote—'a few things,'" Ben said. "A few things my backside. She's sent me a whole bloody shopping list."

He shook his head despairingly, and Logan could sense a rant coming on.

"That's the problem with the world these days," Ben began.

"What, Alice?"

"No! Well... No. Twenty-four-hour supermarkets."

"That's the problem with the world, is it?" Logan asked. "No' all the murderers and war criminals, and what have you?"

"That's the thing. Twenty-four-hour supermarkets are driving the problem. They're *creating* these bastards," Ben said. He caught the look on Logan's face. "Aye, you might laugh, but it's the sense of entitlement they're creating. Nobody can wait for things these days. It's all *now, now, now.*"

"Back in the day, if you wanted a tin of beans at three in the morning, you were shit out of luck. You had to wait. Now? No problem, swing by the twenty-four-hour supermarket, and it's right there. Instant gratification. Beans on demand!"

"You think having round the clock access to baked beans is turning people into murderers?" Logan asked. He was exhausted, hungry, and his whole body felt slightly broken, but he couldn't fight the smirk that tugged the corners of his mouth upwards.

"No' just beans, obviously."

"Spaghetti hoops?" Logan guessed.

"Everything. It's the instant gratification thing. It's turning people greedy. *Want, want, want. Now, now, now.* What was wrong with waiting, eh? What was wrong with a bit of patience?" Ben asked. "And another thing, I just know I'll go in there and there'll be at least one person wandering around in their bloody pyjamas. At *least*. I mean... If that's no' a sign of the end times, then I don't know what—"

His phone rang, and he immediately stopped talking, like he was afraid the person on the other end might somehow hear him.

"That'll be Alice," he said, dropping his voice to a half-whisper, and reaching for his phone. "For Christ's sake, don't tell her I said any of that."

He answered the phone without looking and pressed it to his ear, suddenly all smiles. "Hello, dear! I'm just on my—"

The words faltered to a stop. His expression changed. From a few feet away, Logan heard the voice on the other end. He couldn't make out the words, but the tone was unmistakeable. Urgent. Panicked. Afraid.

"Tyler, Tyler, calm down, son, calm down," Ben said. He raised his eyes to Logan, brow crinkling in concern. "Take a deep breath, and tell me what's happened."

LOGAN STOOD in Sinead's living room, looming over Tyler, who was sat in the middle of the couch, his head in his hands. He and Ben had reached the house just after a couple of squad cars. He'd dispatched the Uniforms to check the street behind the house, and to start canvassing the other buildings across the road to see if anyone had spotted the car, or seen Sinead being bundled into it. There had been no other phone calls, which suggested the abduction had gone unnoticed, but it was worth a double-check.

The word replayed itself in his head after he'd thought it. *Abduction.*

Jesus Christ.

"She was only through there for a couple of minutes, if that," Tyler said. "Like, that was it. She went through, put the popcorn on, and then that was it. She didn't stop the microwave, and she wasn't answering, so I went through to look for her, and..."

He tightened his grip on his head and rocked forward. "She was gone."

"He must've doubled back," said Ben. "Abandoned the car to throw us off, then made his way back up."

"Where's Harris?" Logan asked.

"Next door. With the neighbour. She said she'll look after him. He's in a right state, though," Tyler said.

"Aye, well, we don't need you in the same state," Logan said. His tone wasn't exactly gentle, and it drew a raised eyebrow from DI Forde. "Get it together, son. We won't find her if you're a basket case."

A flash of something like betrayal flitted across DC Neish's face, then he sniffed, nodded, and stood up. "You're right, boss," he said, his voice wobbling. "Sorry, boss."

"Better," Logan said. He glanced back over his shoulder at Ben. "Hamza and Caitlyn on their way?"

"Be here shortly. Got CID and Uniform coming from all over, too. Scene of Crime will be along at some point."

"And what then?" Tyler asked. "When they turn up, what then?"

He looked at both his superior officers in turn, eyes wide and pleading. "What are we going to do?"

Logan's hand clapped down on the younger man's shoulder. "We're going to find her, son. Even if we have to turn this whole bloody city upside-down."

CHAPTER FORTY-SEVEN

PAIN. IT JOLTED THROUGH HER, SNAPPING HER AWAKE WITH disorientating suddenness.

Her head was filled with it, consumed by it. It was a pressure, a weight, pressing sharply down, leaning on her skull and pinning it to the bed.

Bed?

Gritting her teeth, she fought back against the pain enough to lift her head off the mattress.

The room was dark, lit only by the faint orange glow of a nightlight somewhere over by the door. It didn't help that her eyes were coated with a sleepy white film. It gradually cleared as she blinked it away, and as her vision adjusted to the gloom, she saw a *My Little Pony* poster looking back at her from the wall, a purple unicorn winking like it had just let her in on a secret.

The rest of the room was similarly themed, from the toys on the shelves to the quilt beneath her on the single bed. A child's bedroom, clearly. But whose? Where was she?

And how the hell had she got here?

The pain seared through her head again, forcing her to drop it back down onto the bed. Through the brain-fog, she remembered the kitchen. The microwave. The *pop-pop-pop* of the popcorn kernels.

She'd poured another glass of wine. Her third? Fourth? And then...

And then...

A hangover? Was that what this was?

No. No, it couldn't be. She'd had hangovers. This was different. This was—

She remembered the sound in the kitchen behind her. The creaking over by the door. The soft *thup* of a footstep on lino. The brief-but-blinding agony that exploded like a bomb-blast against the back of her skull.

Some deep-seated primal instinct screamed at her, ordered her to get up, get out, get away. She rolled towards the edge of the bed, not ignoring the pain but fighting it, resisting it.

A rope cut into her wrist, jerking her to a stop. She turned, room spinning in uneven loops around her, and saw the restraints for the first time. One on each wrist, binding her to the bed frame. Her legs, too. She was spread in an X-shape, secured in place. Pinned. Helpless.

She wanted to scream, to shout, to cry out, but bit down on her lip to stop herself. What if he was out there? What if he was listening, waiting for her to wake up? What if he—

A leering white face rose up from behind the footboard at the bottom of the bed.

For a split-second, she thought it was something ghostly and supernatural, but then the truth of it hit her. It was a mask. Similar to the one Clarissa McDade's killer had worn in the video, only this time the mouth was twisted into a cruel mockery of a grin.

Eyes studied her through two oval holes in the plastic. They were deep in shadow, but she could just make out the moving reflection as he looked her up and down.

From behind the mask came a falsetto giggle, then a voice began to sing.

"*Lazy bones, sleeping in the sun...*"

He raised a hand. The blade of a scalpel *glinted* in the glow of the nightlight.

"*How you 'spect to get your day's work done?*"

Sinead almost screamed then. What harm was in it? He was already here. There was nothing left to lose.

But something kicked in, keeping her mouth shut. She had plenty left to lose—everything, in fact—and screaming was only going to panic him or make him angry. She didn't want him panicked, and she definitely didn't want him angry.

She could get through this. Somehow, she could get through this. She just had to stay calm.

"It's good that you're awake," he said, the mask shifting slightly as he spoke. "I prefer it when they're awake."

"What do you want?" Sinead asked. "What are you going to do?"

David Oliver, Kel Conlyn, or whatever the man behind the mask was currently calling himself, ducked down out of sight again. Sinead raised her head, straining to see where he'd gone. She craned her neck to the right, searching for him, then yelped in panic when she whipped her head around to the left and found him squatting beside her, the mask just a few inches from her own face.

"Anything I want," he whispered, the scalpel clutched between finger and thumb. He placed a hand on her face. His fingers were soft and smooth as they caressed her. His thumb rubbed across her cheek, wiping away a tear. "Are you scared?" he asked.

There was no point trying to pretend otherwise. "Yes," Sinead told him.

The shout was so loud it almost blew the mask off. "WRONG!" he bellowed, his fingers snaking through the hair at the side of her head and tightening. "You're not scared. You're not *anything*. Fear. Anger. Lust. Those emotions, they're not real. They're implanted."

He yanked harder on her hair, forcing her head down onto the bed. "They're fucking *digits*. That's all. Numbers and code, like the rest of you. Like the rest of everyone."

"P-please," Sinead sobbed, the pain burning through her scalp and lighting up her brain. "Stop."

"What does it matter if I stop?" Oliver asked, his voice dropping to a low murmur, the mask moving closer to her ear.

She could smell his breath wafting through the gaps. It smelled of mint and strong coffee. Combined with the sour stench of his body odour, it made her want to gag.

"Hmm? What does it matter?" he demanded. "What does anything matter? You're not real. You don't exist. What can I *possibly* do to you that's worse than that?"

"I am real," Sinead told him. "You are, too. Everyone is."

"NO!" he roared, his hand untangling from her hair and clamping onto her throat, instead. "That's a lie. You're a *fucking liar*, just like the rest of them!"

He leaned his weight on her, pushing down onto her throat. Sinead's eyes bulged as she coughed and spluttered, her body instinctively fighting for air. Her head tingled. Darkness crept in, shadows closing at the edges of her vision.

Just when she thought she was about to pass out, he eased off enough for her to gulp down a breath. She wheezed in and out, eyes streaming, chest heaving, breath coming in frantic, uneven rasps.

Oliver waited until the breathing had steadied a little, before continuing in a low, matter-of-fact voice.

"I'm going to show you what happens to fucking liars like you."

"THIS IS MY FAULT."

Logan glanced over from the driver's seat, to where DC Neish was gazing out of the Volvo's side window at the streetlights passing outside.

"It isn't."

"It is," Tyler insisted, not turning. "I told him about her. In the hospital. I was trying to see if I could get him to open up, and I told him about me and Sinead."

Logan's hands tightened on the wheel, but he said nothing.

"I actually told him her name."

"You weren't to know. We weren't sure he was a suspect at that point."

"Bollocks, boss," Tyler said, turning to look at the DCI. "We had our suspicions. I should never have told him her name."

He went back to gazing out the window. His reflection stared accusingly back at him. "This is all my fault."

"We're going to make it right, son," Logan told him. "We're going to find her."

"How? Where? We don't have any idea where he took her!" Tyler snapped. "Not a fucking clue."

"Then we figure it out," Logan barked back.

It was just the two of them in the car, the rest of the team having split up to lead searches of their own. The streets were awash with blue, officers coming in from all over the area to help with the search.

They'd run through the obvious places first, with teams checking his parents' house, the ruins of his flat, and combing the hospital from top to bottom.

Caitlyn had led a team to scope out the empty shop where he'd first taken Danni Gillespie, but it was a doughnut place now, and none of the locks had been tampered with.

Squads were checking out other empty commercial properties across the city, but the internet and years of austerity measures had taken their toll on the High Street, and there were a lot of empty shops to search through.

How much time did Sinead have? Not much, going by the bastard's past performances. Not enough for them to fine-tooth-comb the whole city, certainly. They had to be smarter than that. They had to think like he would.

"He'd have to get her somewhere quickly. If he knocked her out, he wouldn't want her waking up before he got her to where they were going. If he didn't, and had just restrained her in some way, he'd be worried about her attracting attention," Logan said.

"God. If he's hurt her..."

"Come on, Tyler, help me out here," Logan scolded. "Stop feeling so bloody sorry for yourself and help me figure this out."

Tyler sat up straighter in his seat. "Right, boss. Aye. So, he wouldn't have gone too far. Is that what you're saying?"

"That's what I'm saying," Logan said. "He'd want to take her somewhere she wouldn't be discovered. At least, not until he was ready to show off his handiwork."

Tyler swallowed like he was about to be sick.

"Sorry, son, but if we're going to get her, we need to be polis, not her friends."

The DC nodded, swallowed twice more, then managed another contribution. "He had a car, so he could've taken her anywhere. They could be miles away."

"Too risky," Logan said, pulling up at a set of traffic lights on red. "For all he might talk about there being no consequences, he goes out of his way to avoid them."

He drummed his fingers on the wheel, waiting for the lights to change. A taxi and a baker's van crossed the junction ahead of them, going about their business.

Somewhere he knew. Somewhere close. Somewhere he wouldn't be disturbed.

"Jesus!" Logan ejected, leaning forward. "I might know where he is."

He crunched the Volvo into gear and floored it through the lights, earning a *honk* from another driver who was forced to screech to a stop.

"Where?" Tyler demanded. "Where is he?"

"Somewhere he knows is empty," Logan replied. The car surged along the street as he pushed his foot all the way to the floor. "Now, hold on. And be ready for anything."

CHAPTER FORTY-EIGHT

CLACK.

Sinead watched as Oliver placed the scalpel down on the bedside table. He'd moved it deliberately so it was in her eyeline, and hummed quietly as he set out his tools, the sound muffled slightly by the mask.

He'd taken a larger knife from a rucksack and set that down first, the serrated blade pitted with rust or dried blood.

Next, he'd brought out a stick. It was a little shorter than the knife, but thicker, with eight or nine jagged points where twigs had been hacked off. She didn't know what he planned to use that for. She didn't want to.

A roll of masking tape had been next. He'd set it down with a *clunk*, then thought better of it and pulled off a strip that he'd then placed over Sinead's mouth and slapped firmly to make sure it stayed stuck.

"Do you think they're watching?" he asked, straightening the line of implements on the bedside table so they all looked neat and *just-so*. His eyes went to the ceiling, then down to the woman on the bed. His voice dropped to just above a whisper. "The coders. The creators. Do you think we've got their attention yet?"

Sinead couldn't have replied, even if she'd wanted to. She found her gaze returning to the serrated knife, then creeping sideways to the stick.

"Your boyfriend spoke very highly of you," Oliver said, his tone becoming relaxed and chatty. "He's quite a catch. You did well. If he'd been real, I'd have almost been jealous."

He reached for the knife, then hesitated.

"You know what?"

He pushed the mask up onto the top of his head and flashed Sinead a smile. "There. That's better, isn't it?"

Removing it completely, he turned the mask over in his hand. "I don't really know why I did that. What was I trying to hide? *This* mask?"

He caught his cheek between finger and thumb and pulled sharply. "Hiding one mask behind another. It makes no sense, does it?"

His eyes bulged, his brow furrowing. He crushed the plastic mask in his hand and leaned over Sinead, suddenly furious. "*Does it?*"

Sinead shook her head, tears streaming down her cheeks.

That seemed to satisfy Oliver and he leaned back, straightening. "No. Exactly. Hiding a mask behind a mask. What was I thinking?"

He looked to the ceiling again, as if in apology, then went back to humming his tune.

With his attention back on his tools, Sinead twisted her right hand. She'd been working away at the knot for the past few minutes and felt there was a chance—a slim one—that she could pull it free. It would hurt, and it would take time, but it was possible.

Please, God. Let it be possible.

"The camera," Oliver said, slapping the heel of his hand against his forehead. "I forgot the camera. People went nuts over that last video. They loved it. It really helped spread the message, you know? And that's one of the reasons we're doing this, isn't it?" he asked, like she was a willing participant in it all. "To spread the message. To let everyone know what they really are."

He placed his hand on her face again, ran it down over the purple bruising on her neck, then brushed it lightly against one of her breasts.

"You wait right there," he told her, smiling at the way she flinched at his touch. "I'll be right back."

She waited until she heard him making his way down the stairs, then tugged and wrenched at her arm. The rope tore at her wrist, each twist burning her skin and sending shockwaves of pain racing all the way up to her shoulder. She ignored them, heaving and pulling, knowing that her life almost certainly depended on it.

Downstairs, Oliver hummed quietly as he made his way through to the living room, and over to the table where he'd left the camera equipment. The GoPro hadn't been cheap, but it came with a free head mount, and the 4k footage would look incredible.

He glanced briefly at the framed family photographs on the wall, winked at a smiling Esme Miller, then started to make his way back to the stairs.

Halfway there, the front door flew open, revealing a heavy-set figure framed in the glow of a streetlight. Oliver recognised the detective at once, hurled the camera equipment at him, then flew to the stairs in a panic.

"Fuck, fuck, fuck!"

"Stay where you are!" Logan bellowed, powering across the room with DC Neish hot on his heels.

Oliver scrambled up the stairs on hands and feet, then launched himself upright at the top. He barrelled into the bedroom, hands grabbing for the larger of the two knives.

Gone. What the hell?

He looked up and jumped back in time to avoid a scything swipe of the blade. Sinead leaned on one elbow, the other arm free, the knife clutched in her trembling hand.

No, no, no!

He grabbed the scalpel, briefly entertained the notion of stabbing the living shit out of the meaningless bitch on the bed, then concluded that her knife was bigger than his.

Instead, he turned and ran back to the stairs, swishing the scalpel in front of him and driving back the detectives who had been headed in the opposite direction.

"Back off! Fucking *back off!*" he warned, slicing furiously at the air just a few inches in front of Logan's face.

The DCI put a hand behind him, stopping Tyler in his tracks.

"Where is she?" Tyler demanded. "*What have you done to her?*"

Oliver swiped with the scalpel again, coming dangerously close to Logan this time. The DCI raised an arm and heard the *sshkt* of the blade cutting through the sleeve of his borrowed coat. He retreated more quickly down the stairs, forcing Tyler back until they were both standing by the foot of the stairs, one on either side.

"It's over, David," Logan said. "Put the knife down. You're only making an arse of yourself."

"Shut the fuck up!" Oliver spat, visibly recoiling at the use of his real name. He had the surgical knife held out in front of him, his knuckles white as he gripped the handle. "You don't matter. None of this matters. You think you're so fucking important, but you're nothing."

He laughed, his shoulders shaking with silent, hysterical guffaws. "You're literally nothing at all."

"Then, there's no reason not to hand over the knife," Logan countered. "I mean, if you're right, it doesn't even exist, so why are you waving it about like that if it's not real?"

Oliver's eyes went to the blade, then back to Logan.

"You know what I think?" Logan asked. "I don't think you really believe any of that shite. Not deep down. I think you've been using it as an excuse, so you can act out whatever messed up fantasies you've got going on in that sick head of yours. If it was really about this simulation shite, why only take women? Why the sexual assaults? Why degrade and humiliate them?"

Logan's eyes narrowed. He jabbed a finger in Oliver's direction, ignoring the risk the knife posed.

"I'll tell you why, David. Because it's not about who exists and who doesn't. It's about power, same as every other rapist out there. It's about a small, pathetic wee man trying to make himself feel big and strong. That's all it is. That's all it ever is."

"Shut up! Shut up!" Oliver hissed.

A floorboard creaked beneath Tyler's feet. Oliver whipped the knife hand towards him, the blade pointed directly as his face. "Don't fucking move!" he screeched. "Last warning!"

"Oh, grow up, David, ye daft bastard," Logan spat. As diplomacy and negotiation strategy went, it wasn't exactly textbook stuff. "It's over. We've got you. This place is going to be swarming with angry polis any minute, who're all holding you responsible for getting called out of their beds two nights running. Put down the knife and I might be able to protect you from them. *Might*, mind. No promises."

Oliver gritted his teeth, the scalpel shaking in his grip. For a moment, it looked like he might be about to consider it, but then he saw Tyler's eyes flick briefly to the stairs behind him and heard the faint suggestion of a footstep.

Logan was closest, so Oliver lunged for him, slashing and swiping with the blade. The DCI raised his arms to protect himself, and the coat sleeves were sliced to ribbons. At least a couple of the swipes found skin, and Logan hissed in pain as blood bloomed through the material.

Oliver was suddenly behind him, the knife pressed against the detective's throat. Halfway down the stairs, Sinead froze, the combat knife in her hand, a rectangle of red around her mouth marking where the tape had been.

"You stupid bitch! You stupid fucking bitch! I'll kill him. I'll fucking kill him."

"DC Neish, take Constable Bell outside. Make sure she's OK," Logan instructed. If he was scared, there was nothing in his voice to indicate it.

"What? No!" Sinead said.

"No can do, boss," Tyler agreed.

Logan grimaced as the knife was pressed more firmly against his skin. Blood oozed down his neck. A trickle, for now, but a promise of much more to come.

"Do what he says. Get out," Oliver snapped. "And make sure everyone stays away, or I slit him open. He'll be dead before he hits the ground."

Tyler's jaw clenched. His gaze flicked from Oliver to the knife, then up to the DCI's face.

"You heard him. Go," Logan urged. "Both of you, get out."

Sinead passed the knife from hand to hand, sizing up her chances of making it to the murderer before he could draw the blade across Logan's throat. There was no way she could close the gap in time though. It was hopeless.

"That's an order, Detective Constable," Logan said. "Get out. Both of you. Now."

"Come on," Sinead whispered, taking Tyler by the hand. "We have to go."

Tyler stood his ground for a few moments, then let out a little groan of anguish. "We'll be right outside, boss," he promised.

Sinead opened the door, and the wailing of sirens reverberated around the room. Backup was close, but probably not close enough.

The door closed, muting the volume of the world outside.

"Right then, Davey-boy," Logan said. "What now?"

"What?" Oliver hissed.

"The plan? What's the plan, now that you've got me all to yourself?" Logan pressed. "You do have a plan, aye? What is it? You going to just vanish us into thin air, maybe? Or hack the fucking Matrix or something? You must have some sort of plan, surely? This can't be it."

"Shut up, shut up, I'm thinking," Oliver said. "You had to ruin it. You had to *fucking ruin* it. You had to interfere!"

"Is that what your parents did? Interfere?" Logan asked. "Or was there some other reason you tied them up and killed them? They must've pushed you hard, did they? You a child prodigy, and all that. I bet they never gave you a minute's peace."

"Be quiet! Fucking shut up!" Oliver snapped.

"Still, killing your own maw and da," Logan tutted. "What kind of headcase does that?"

"I said *shut up!*"

The hand holding the scalpel was shaking badly now. Logan could feel the blade digging deeper into his skin.

"Calm down, David. I'm no good to you if I'm dead," Logan pointed out. Unnoticed by the knifeman, he slowly slid a hand into a trouser pocket.

"I'm *calm*," Oliver said, the words coming out as something close to a sob. "I'm perfectly fucking calm. It's not real. Emotions aren't real. It's numbers. Just numbers. Ones and zeroes. That's all!"

"Whatever you say," Logan told him. "But if you want my advice, you'll move us away from the window before the snipers arrive."

"They won't shoot if I've got a hostage."

"Normally, aye, but none of them like me very much," Logan said. "So, better to be safe than sorry."

Oliver hesitated, then the knife relaxed just a fraction on the DCI's throat. "Right. Here's what we're going to do. We're going to go through to the kitchen, and you're going to pull the blinds shut."

"Now you're thinking straight," Logan said. "But, how about instead of that, we do this?"

He jabbed sharply backwards with his right hand, while grabbing for Oliver's knife arm with his left. A scream erupted by Logan's ear as half a dozen cocktail sticks were embedded in the thigh of the man behind him.

The knife hand jerked, but Logan yanked it away before it could slice his throat. He twisted, squeezing Oliver's bandaged forearm, then drove a punch right into the centre of the bastard's face.

Eyes blurred by tears, and choking on blood and snot, Oliver grabbed the scalpel with his free hand and lashed out with it. Logan shoved him, sending him tumbling to the floor.

He lay there on his back, coughing and wheezing, with the DCI looming over him like the spectre of Death.

"Put it down, David. It's over."

"It doesn't matter. Nothing matters. Nothing's real," Oliver whispered. He raised the knife, turning it so the blade was pointed straight at his own throat. "None of it is real!"

Logan made no move to intervene. He didn't have to.

"You don't really believe that, do you, son?"

Oliver's hand shook. Tears and snot and blood covered his face like a mask.

And then, with an animalistic roar of helplessness, despair, and a dozen other all-too-real emotions, he let his arms drop to his sides, and the scalpel fall freely from his grip.

Logan placed a foot on the knife, pinning it in place. Blood trickled down his arms and dripped from his fingertips. Hoon's coat was ruined. He'd never hear the bloody end of this.

"David Oliver," he said, not savouring the moment, exactly, but drawing some grim satisfaction from it. "You, sunshine, are nicked."

CHAPTER FORTY-NINE

The morning passed. Wounds were stitched up. Statements were given. Press announcements were made.

Some harsh words were exchanged about 'the state of that fucking coat,' but compared to the past few days, things were relatively uneventful.

It was almost noon by the time Logan was ready to go home. Ben and Caitlyn had offered to take on most of the paperwork duties, leaving Logan and Tyler free to go and get some rest.

Very few words had passed between the DCI and the DC since they'd returned to the station. Those that had been exchanged had been enough though, and most of the meaning had been there in the silences.

"You'll be sleeping the next week away, I'm assuming?" asked Ben, escorting Logan towards the Volvo. He'd been harping on at him to 'bugger off home,' for the past couple of hours, and was determined to make sure he actually left the premises.

"Something like that, aye," Logan said. Loathe as he was to admit it, he was utterly exhausted. Even the drive home seemed like some Herculean effort he wasn't convinced he had the energy for.

He clambered into the driver's seat, closed the door, and pressed the button to wind the window down. "If anything comes up—"

"Away and shite," Ben told him. "Go. Home. Rest. The world can limp by without Jack Logan for a couple of days."

Logan chuckled drily. "I suppose so."

"And you're going straight home. Right?"

Logan tapped the button to raise the glass between them. "Aye," he said. "Something like that."

THERE WAS one more thing to do. One final loose end to tie up.

He met the uniformed constable at the gate of a neat little semi-detached, explained the situation, then led him up the path and rang the doorbell.

A series of musical chimes rang out somewhere in the house. It was followed almost immediately by the barking of a small dog, then the muttering of a man as he tried to shut the animal in another room.

The door opened. Logan noted the way the man's face instantly crumpled when he saw the officers standing on the step. He knew. The game was up.

"I'm sorry," said the nurse, Bob Brews. "I'm so sorry. I don't know what came over me."

Logan just stared, saying nothing, giving the man all the rope he needed.

"When I took the tape off Esme, I just... I don't know. It felt... important. I didn't mean to keep it. Not really. It's just... It was something, I don't know. Interesting. Exciting."

He met Logan's eye for the briefest of moments, before the intensity of his stare became too much. "I shouldn't have taken it. I should've left it. I'm sorry. I'm so sorry."

Logan didn't even bother to reply. There was plenty he could've said, of course—how he'd withheld evidence, how he'd potentially jeopardised a murder investigation—but he mentioned none of it. There'd be time for that later.

Instead, he addressed the officer beside him.

"Constable, charge Mr Brews, would you?" he said, and then he turned away from the man in the doorway and strode off along the path before his anger could get the better of him.

LOGAN'S LEGS protested as he heaved himself up the stone steps of his block of flats. Never had the nickname 'the plod' been more accurate, he thought, dragging himself up onto the first landing, and turning towards the second flight of stairs.

The door to Tanya's flat opened, and Logan's nostrils flared as Bud appeared in the doorway. He leaned against the frame, a pair of grey jogging bottoms on his lower half, a variety of poorly done tattoos the only thing covering him from his waist to his neck.

He grinned, showing off his yellow teeth. "Afternoon, officer," he said. "Rough night?"

Logan took a step towards him. "I thought I told you to—"

"It's fine," said a female voice from the hallway. Tanya appeared at Bud's back, then squeezed past him and ushered him back into the flat. Logan could see him standing further along the hall, watching them, the grin still plastered on his face.

"What are you doing?" Logan asked her.

"It's fine. We sorted everything out," Tanya said. She smiled, and Logan got the impression that she almost believed the words coming out of her still-bruised mouth. "It's not going to happen again. We talked it through."

Logan wanted to argue, but what was the point? He'd seen the same thing play out over and over again. He'd be talking to a brick wall, and right at that moment, he didn't have the energy.

"Well, I hope it works out," he said, then he went back to dragging himself up the stairs.

"Uh, Mr Logan? Jack?"

Logan stopped, leaning on the metal bannister for support.

"You'll, um, you'll be around, won't you?"

Logan scraped together something close to a smile. "Aye," he told her. "I'm always around."

He waited until she had waved and closed the door, then muttered something under his breath, and fumbled for his keys.

There was a sour smell in the flat when he shambled inside, and he remembered he hadn't put the bin out in days.

It could wait. There was no way he had the energy to tackle those stairs again today.

He slumped onto the couch, and the springs *sproinged* in complaint. His head had just fallen backwards so it was resting against the top of the cushion when the phone in his pocket rang.

Logan groaned. It was a new work phone—a replacement for the one that had gone up in flames—and no one but the MIT and Bob Hoon had the number. If they were calling, then his dream of a solid seventy-two-hours of sleep would be well and truly out the window.

With some effort, he traced the ringing to the left front pocket of his trousers. *Unknown* was displayed on-screen. Hoon, then, probably. Everyone else was programmed in.

"Logan," he said, bringing the phone to his ear and letting his head fall back onto the cushion again.

His own voice echoed back at him down the line.

"Hello?" he said.

Silence.

Logan sat forward, ignoring the aching it triggered.

"Who is this?" he asked.

The reply, when it came, was a soft giggle. A *whisper*.

"Oh, Jack," it said. "You know *exactly* who I am."

And then, the line went dead. Logan stared in disbelief at the screen until it turned dark, then let the phone fall onto the couch beside him.

It was him. That voice. That damn whisper. It was *him*.

But there was nothing he could do about it. Not yet. Not right now. He hadn't slept in days and exhaustion was moving in to claim him, turning the edges of the room into a haze of darkness.

He stretched out on the couch, kicked off his shoes, and lay staring up at the ceiling.

The events of the past few days had almost killed him. People he cared about, too.

And yet, as his eyes closed and the world slipped away into darkness, a knot in his stomach told him that things were about to get much, *much* worse.

AN INTERVIEW WITH JD KIRK

Thanks for reading this first DCI Jack Logan Collection. I hope you enjoyed getting to know Jack and his team.

At the time of writing, I am stuck inside waiting for the results of my eleven-year-old daughter's COVID-19 test to come through, which means none of us are able to leave the house.

It has been a strange year.

During lockdown, I went on a 100 day fitness challenge, where I lost three stone (42 pounds) and made over 50 short videos talking about health, writing, and life in general.

I also answered questions submitted by readers of the DCI Logan series, although I couldn't by any stretch of the imagination manage to answer all of them.

And so, I thought I'd respond to a few of them here at the back of this book, to give you some insight into me, my writing process, and the grumpy man-mountain that is Detective Chief Inspector Jack Logan.

Have something you'd like to ask? You can reach me pretty much anytime via my Facebook page at facebook.com/jdkirkbooks

Thanks again for reading. If you enjoyed what you read, there are plenty more where these came from...

Best wishes,

JD Kirk

October 2020

Q. Where did the idea for A Litter of Bones come from?

A. I've got my daughter to blame for that. A few years ago, when she was maybe seven or eight, she and I took our dog out for a walk at Leanachan Forest near Spean Bridge. We walked along, blethering about everything and nothing, then--just like in A Litter of Bones--the dog went racing off into the trees, and refused to respond to our shouts.

And so--again, just like in the first book--I went into the trees, after instructing my darling child to wait right where she was. "Stay on that spot," I told her. "I'll be right back."

I found the dog rolling around in something unpleasant in the forest. When we emerged, my daughter was gone.

My heart stopped.

Every parent will be able to identify with that feeling. That moment when you realise a child is not where you expected them to be. It's one of those real punch-in-the-guts feelings that knocks the wind out of you.

I could see half a mile in each direction along the path, but there was no sign of her anywhere. She was gone, and as I stood there shouting her name, I knew--I *knew* that someone had taken her. Somehow, someone had swooped in and snatched her the moment my back was turned.

And then, I heard her giggling behind a bush. She popped up, a triumphant grin on her face, and I almost burst into tears with relief.

After a hug, a telling off, and another hug, we set off for home. As I drove back, I started to think what would've happened if my worst fears had been realised. How would I and my wife have coped? What would the police have done? How would we have gotten our daughter home?

By the time I'd made the nine-mile journey back to our house, A Litter of Bones had been born.

Q. What drew you to writing crime fiction?

A. Absolutely nothing whatsoever! I hadn't really read much crime fiction, aside from one early Rebus and some Chris Brookmyre--and even those were more his 'action adventure' stuff than straight crime writing.

I had no great plans to write a crime series, but I wanted to tell the story that started with a child going missing in Leanachan Forest. Even then, though, I put it on the back burner and rarely thought about it for a few years, until a chance meeting with bestselling crime fiction author, LJ Ross, and her husband, James.

(Incidentally, if you ever have the opportunity to meet them both, jump on it. They are two of the nicest, friendliest, kindest people you could ever hope to meet, and you will come away from the encounter determined to become a better person. It's sickening, really! I don't know how they do it.)

Anyway, I mentioned that I had an idea for a crime novel, and they both encouraged me to write it. At that point, I had been a full-time author of children's books for over ten years, and was writing a comedy sci-fi series called Space Team, so gruesome, foul-mouthed Scottish crime fiction was a bit of a departure for me.

I promised I'd start writing the book at the earliest opportunity. In truth, though, I didn't start it until two days before I was due to meet them again at London Book Fair in 2019, where I was joining LJ Ross on a panel alongside a few other authors.

Determined not to let them down (seriously, that's the effect they have) I wrote the first three chapters in a couple of days, so I could prove to them that I was working on it. They were nothing but supportive, and much of the series' success is down to their generous assistance in helping to spread the word.

I was sure that A Litter of Bones would be the only crime fiction novel I wrote, but I ended up enjoying the process so much that I decided to continue. At the time of writing this, I'm working on the ninth book, which will be released twenty months after book one was published.

Q. Humour plays a big part in the series. Was this a conscious choice?

A. Hmm. No, not really. I thought I was writing a straight, serious, quite gritty crime thriller. In many regards, it was, but humour started to creep in quite early on.

There are two reasons for that, I think. Firstly, it's down to my own personality and sense of humour. I've always been able to find something to laugh at in most situations, however grim. I've written and delivered four funeral eulogies in my time, and have gone for the laugh with every single one.

I think that's a very Scottish thing, actually, that sense of finding the joke in the direst of circumstances, and that ability to relentlessly take the piss out of ourselves. If you're not making jokes at your friends' expense as a Scottish person, are they even really your friend?

Even more than that, I think laughter is a coping mechanism for a lot of people working in the front line emergency services. There's a shared humour amongst people in those occupations that they rely on to get them through the day.

So often, they're faced with the most awful scenes and difficult situations, and without that ability to laugh it off, I think they'd all be basket-cases and unable to function. I think the humour in the DCI Logan series, which comes almost exclusively from character interactions, comes from that place of self-preservation.

Q. Did you have to do a lot of research into police procedures?

A. God, no! Haha. Absolutely not.

Actually, that's not quite true. I did quite a lot of research for the first book, but quickly concluded that I didn't need 99% of it. In real life, a murder investigation is pretty tedious. In most cases, the killer is identified very quickly--usually a member of the victim's family, or a close friend.

In the few cases each year where the killer's identity isn't quickly realised, things tend to move painfully slowly. There is a *lot* of knocking on doors, and an investigation team can be made up of scores of officers--far too many to keep track of in a story, let alone care about.

So, ultimately I concluded that what people want is an interesting mystery being solved by characters they like to read about. That's the crux of it. Very few people are buying crime fiction because they're fascinated by the intricacies of real-life police procedure, and that's why most of my research went out the window on book one.

Q. Are any of the characters based on people you know in real life?

A. Only the dead ones! That's why you never get on the wrong side of a crime fiction author. :)

Other than that, no one is specifically based on any particular individual. I think like most authors, my characters are amalgamations of all the hundreds of thousands of people I've met over the years. You build up a sort of catalogue of personality traits, ways of speaking, fashion sense, etc, and then create characters by selecting bits from that database, then throwing in a part of yourself. That's how I do it, anyway.

That said, I think with Logan there's a bit of wish-fulfilment going on. He's three or four years older than me, and while he's a big teddy bear deep down, he gets away with being pretty blunt, and saying some downright terrible things to people--although generally only when they deserve it.

I think I'd like to be a bit more like Logan in that regard. Rather than smiling politely at things people say or do, then complaining about it later, I'd like to have more of that couldn't-care-less attitude that Logan has, so I could tell a few people exactly what I thought about them without feeling guilty about it.

Q. What other genres do you write in?

A. I wrote exclusively for children for over a decade, writing for publishers like HarperCollins Children's Books, Penguin Random House, and countless others. I wrote original fiction under my own name, original fiction under pen names, licensed fiction based on TV shows, movies, and games, non-fiction... Basically, if a publisher would pay me to write it, I'd write it.

I also wrote comics, including Minecraft, Angry Birds, DC Super Hero Girls, Power Rangers, and countless others. Perhaps my proudest achievement on the comics front was writing for The Beano, a British comic that has been running for decades, which I grew up reading. I wrote loads of different strips for that, including The Bash Street Kids, which was one of my absolute favourites as a kid.

More recently, I started writing comedy science fiction for adults. You can find my Space Team series, the Dan Deadman: Space Detective spin-off series, and a superhero comedy called The Sidekicks Initiative all published under the name Barry J. Hutchison on Amazon.

Q. What's next for DCI Logan?

A. I'm not telling.

(Although, if you've just read this collection and nothing else, there are five more books available at the time of writing, and book nine is available to pre-order, so you've got plenty of reading material waiting.)

Q. If you could give one bit of advice to would-be writers, what would it be?

A. I'd say enjoy it, for the most part. If you're just starting out, there's no pressure from publishers or readers, no worries about what the market is looking for, or how to best fit into a certain genre, or whatever else we professional author types decide to fill our time worrying about.

That first book is a blessing. You can write what you want, how you want, with nobody to tell you otherwise. So, savour that. Make the most of it.

And then, once it's done, write the next one. And the next one. And the one after that. Get up early and stay up late, and write, and write, and write.

And, if the thought of that puts you off, rather than gets you excited, you might want to consider a different career...

ABOUT THE AUTHOR

JD Kirk is a pen name of multi award-winning Scottish author, Barry Hutchison, who lives in the Highlands with his wife, two children, and a particularly annoying dog.

When not writing, Barry is usually walking said dog, getting rained on, and wishing he lived somewhere sunnier.

He is the author of over 150 books, several screenplays, and an animated series for Dreamworks. Despite all this, his proudest professional achievement is writing *The Bash Street Kids* for *The Beano*.

And who can blame him?

He has no idea what the 'JD' stands for. He just liked the sound of it.

Follow JD Kirk on social media at the links below.

                    facebook.com/jdkirkbooks

                    twitter.com/jdkirkbooks

                    instagram.com/jdkirkbooks